Everything *For* *Nothing*

Valerie A. High

With God I am Everything
Without God I am Nothing

Remain in me, as I also remain in you.
No branch can bear fruit by itself: it must
remain in the vine. Neither can you bear fruit
unless you remain in me. I am the vine: you
are the branches. If you remain in me and I
in you, you will bear much fruit: apart from me
you can do nothing.

John 15:4-5 NIV

Dedication

This book is dedicated to every soul seeking to understand who they are in God. Prepare yourselves for the journey…

Lawonnis Ross,

Thank you for your support. I pray God blesses you as you read. May you find your special place in God… soon. ☺

Valerie High

Acknowledgements

First and foremost, to God my father, the GREATEST TEACHER of all time, I give you all the glory and honor! Thank you for entrusting me to write your words. I am honored that you chose me to be your *ready writer*. You alone, taught me how to write from beginning to end. You are an AWESOME teacher, and I love the ratio of one-to-one. Through this piece of work, you have shown me how you have equipped me, and invested in me. Thank you for the revelation.

To my Mom, my NUMBER ONE fan. Thank you for all the years of endless encouragement. You made me believe that I could prosper at anything I set my hands to do. I love you for stirring my potential with your words. I'm glad I made you proud. Thank you for being the wind beneath my wings.

To the man of my dreams, my husband, a most gracious THANK YOU. Daily you believed in me from the beginning. I recognized it when you spent all of your money to buy me a word processor many, many, years ago on that meager Christmas day. I loved all of the discussions about my characters, and the roads they should travel to bring forth the message of God. You always gave ear to my thoughts, my challenges, and my triumphs. Your constant encouragement helped me to take flight and keep going, until this book was completed. You are a WONDERFUL man, and I truly thank God for you.

Pastors Thomas and Carolyn Vinson, thank you for your many years of sound wisdom, and preaching the true Word of God. The works of your ministry have aided, and encouraged me to write. Thank you for giving me my very first platform in playwriting. Your encouragement to keep moving forward in God, gave me the stepping stones to launch this book. THANK YOU for the support that pushed me forward.

To my sister-in-law Sheila Hankins, thank you for sharing the letter that helped set the foundation for this book. It was a wonderful inspiration that opened doors in my mind, and stirred my creative voice — and for that I am grateful.

To my sister-in-law Sharon Williams, thank you for always seeking the *unwritten* pages. You were often my fuel when the fire was low.

A big THANK YOU to Jake Lonas, a paramedic with Puckett EMS in Austell, GA. I really appreciate you taking the time to be my "go to" guy for answers to many of my medical questions. I honored you by naming the doctor in this book, Dr. Jake Sloan (Lonas). ☺

Last but not least, I thank God for my *Road Dog* Shawniece Southall. Girl you are a godsend. Thank you for recognizing every message, nuance, and feeling in this book. Your encouraging words have catapulted me to a new level of expectation. I deeply appreciate you correcting all of my many errors, and offering me your suggestions. Your help has been priceless. Thank you for the five mile walks, trips to *The Club*, and *Swirl World*, for book discussions. May God richly bless you for your sacrifice of time. I wish I could send Brian back, just to take you to lunch.

Chapter One

It was September, and a soft Savannah wind rustled dead leaves at the kitchen door. Inert and frail as they were, Maxie felt just like those leaves. When she first woke up, it was evident that motivation would not be making its usual morning appearance. So she huddled over a cup of hot coffee, and hoped for the jolt of caffeine to take its place. Meanwhile, she contended with a weight of tiredness that went straight to her bones. It was hard to pinpoint exactly why she was so weary, especially after having a full night's rest. With no other source on which to lay the blame, Maxie toyed with the self-diagnosis of possibly being depressed. There was no progress report of anything exciting happening in her life. She was plagued with woulda, coulda, shouldas, and there was no denying the menacing presence of the twins aggravation and stagnation. She had to be depressed. So as common to those who battle depression, there is tiredness. If cooking her husband's breakfast had not been a morning routine, Maxie could have easily stayed in bed and slept the entire day away.

With the lingering aroma of fried bacon and fresh coffee hanging in the air, Maxie turned her attention to her husband Lester who sat opposite her. Fully focused on the sports section of the Savannah Morning News, he released the paper to take a bite of toast, but hardly touched the rest of his meal.

"Lester, do you want some more orange juice or coffee?"

"What?"

"Orange juice or coffee? Do you want any more?"

"Oh, no. No thank you," he replied without looking up.

"Well, I guess I'll fix myself something to eat," Maxie mumbled, and dragged her feet across the floor.

On the kitchen counter, a small radio played a soft rendition of Amazing Grace. Maxie closed her eyes and lightly smiled. That old song brought back memories of her childhood with her grandmother. When she started to hum along, a loud knock on the kitchen door startled her, and made her drop a spatula full of eggs.

"Lester, honey would you get that? I've made a little mess over here."

"Uh huh," Lester replied.

Maxie knelt to clean up the eggs, and waited to hear the voice behind the knock. On her way to the trash can, she noticed Lester hadn't moved. Shaking her head, she quickly tossed the eggs into the trash can, and opened the door without looking to see who it was. A dark complexioned woman, about 5'7 in stature, began talking as soon as she saw a face on the other side of the threshold.

"Morning all," her voice rang out as she whisked into the kitchen. "Maxie girl, what did you cook this morning? Just give me some grits and a piece of toast. You got a slice of cheese? Throw it on my grits for me. Oh, and give me some of that juice like Lester has. It looks good."

Maxie stood at the door with her hand still on the knob. "Go on and close the door girl," the woman said, positioning herself at one end of the table. "I didn't bring nobody with me."

Maxie casually pushed the door closed, and went back to preparing her own plate and the woman's requested meal.

"Hi Lester," the woman whined with a smile.

"Here again Sandra?" He said undauntedly. "You're making my kitchen table your morning pit stop, aren't you?"

Maxie placed a plate in front of Sandra and poured her a small glass of orange juice. She didn't want to make eye contact with Lester, but glanced at him long enough to see his jaw muscle flexing in agitation. Sandra waved her hand at him as if she were swatting at a menacing fly.

"Oh Lester, you know I have to come share my morning cup of gossip with Maxine. She's the only one who will listen to me."

Lester quickly folded his paper, tossed it on the table, and stood up shaking his head. "And withal they learn to be idle, wandering about from house to house; and not only idle, but tattlers also and busybodies, speaking things which they ought not. My wife doesn't need to hear your words of gossip, and I thank you to keep them to yourself." He retorted.

"Oooo, scripture so early in the morning Lester?" Sandra said as she took a bite of her toast and a spoonful of grits. "You forgot something though. That scripture applies to young women who were widows. Remember," she muffled. "I ain't never been married."

"And it's no wonder why."

Maxie knew Lester was pumped and ready to give Sandra reasons for her singleness, so she casually walked in front of him and set her plate on the table. "Lester, don't start," she said meekly without looking at him. "I'm not in the mood to hear one of your morning sermons. I heard enough at church yesterday."

"Well your friend could definitely stand to hear a little Sunday morning preaching. It might do her some good."

Maxie sat down in Lester's seat while he stood behind her anxiously rattling the contents of his pockets. "Baby get your blueprints and stuff for work," she said. "Your lunch is over there too. Go on now or you'll be late for work."

Lester slowly walked to the counter, but not without glancing at Sandra from the corner of his eyes. Sandra looked at him and smiled smugly. Retrieving his things, he walked back to Maxie and gave her a kiss on her cheek. "Pray for me today. I'll try to call you on my lunch hour."

"Be careful," she said mechanically over her shoulder.

"Bye bye Lester." Sandra cooed, with a fake smile, waving her toast at him. "You be careful out there doing all that construction work now. Wouldn't want you to get hurt or nothing like that." When Lester closed the door, Sandra howled in raucous laughter. "Oooo, that man does not like me."

"That's because you're always aggravating him Sandra."

"Oh, I know. But I don't mean any harm. I just think it's funny how upset he gets."

Maxie sipped her orange juice. "No, you think it's funny because he's a minister, and he should always show the love of Christ. That's why you taunt him so."

Sandra pointed her finger at Maxie. "You know what? I think you're right."

They both laughed softly. Sandra finished her last spoonful of grits and wiped up the rest with a small piece of toast, while Maxie picked at her food with her fork. When a long silence fell between them, it made Sandra a little uncomfortable. She hoped teasing Lester had not hurt her friend's feelings. Why should it? Teasing him had almost become an exciting ritual for the two of them. Surely Maxie wouldn't become offended by it now.

Sandra watched her twirl her fork in her food, almost trance-like. Leaning forward, she waved her hand in front of Maxie's face. "Heelloo. Can Maxie come out and play?"

"Get out of here girl," Maxie smiled, regaining focus on her plate.

Sandra sat back in her chair and breathed a small sigh of relief. "Where were you just now?"

"In a land far far away," Maxie joked, with a slight smile.

"I'm serious Maxie. You were in some deep thought just a second ago. What's going on?"

Maxie shot a glance at Sandra and then back to her uneaten food. "Listen, do you want some more orange juice?"

"Girl, I ain't Lester," Sandra said sarcastically. "You don't have to play that Stepford Wife routine with me. I know you."

Maxie put her hands under the table, and looked at some raw egg that was caked on one of her fingernails. She scratched it off and casually sipped her orange juice.

Sandra lowered her head a little to meet Maxie's eyes. "Uh huh," she said matter-of-factly.

Maxie glanced at her and shook her head with a little laugh. Sandra always felt she could read people's minds, if she was able to study their eyes. Oftentimes her interpretation of their thoughts would be right, but if she was ever wrong, she'd blame the person for not thinking in complete thoughts. To Maxie her perception was pure coincidence, but she would have fun humoring Sandra.

"Uh huh what?" Maxie asked. "You think you see something don't you?"

"Oh I do," Sandra said, sitting back in her chair, self-assured. "I do. You have a problem."

Maxie nodded her head and laughed in disbelief. "And I bet it took you all this time to figure that out."

"No. Actually, I saw it when you answered the door."

"Riiight," Maxie said skeptically. "You're incredible. So what is my problem?"

"Well, I think you'll feel better if you just confess to yourself what your problem is," Sandra said.

"So you're going to psychoanalyze me now?" Maxie took her plate to the sink and scraped the food into the garbage disposal. Now she wondered. Was there really a troubled look on her face? If so, why didn't her husband see it first?

"I'm serious. All joking aside," Sandra said as she followed her. "What's going on?"

Maxie turned on the water and then the disposal. "It's a long story Sandra and you'll be late for work. I can talk to you about it later. Honestly, it can wait." Maxie looked at her and gave her a faint smile, one that Sandra was not willing to overlook.

"But you need me now," Sandra turned off the water and the disposal. "What kind of friend would I be if I wasn't available when you needed me? I'll make time to listen. Talk to me."

Maxie smiled in appreciation. Feeling her dam of emotion break, she turned her head from Sandra quickly, unable to control the water that was welling up in her eyes. The last thing she wanted was to be overcome by her feelings before she could get her words out. Releasing a little nervous laughter, she leaned over the sink and let her head hang. Where should she begin? Her feelings had been bottled up for so long; she never really considered where she would start when it came time to release them. She never planned on sharing them with anyone.

"Maxie," Sandra whispered with urgency.

Maxie took a deep breath, and swallowed hard, desperately choking back the tears that wanted to fall.

"I'm tired Sandra," she said mildly, her voice cracking. "I am so tired."

"What's wrong?" Sandra asked with concern. "Aren't you getting enough rest at night? You've probably been running yourself ragged."

Maxie looked at Sandra and embraced herself like she didn't want to let her words go. She didn't know if Sandra could possibly sympathize with what she was about to tell her, but she needed to get it out. "I don't think I want to live the Christian lifestyle anymore. No. I know I don't want to," she nodded. "Not anymore." Maxie's eyes sought compassion and understanding from her friend. With tears rolling down her cheeks, she lowered her head and let them drop into the sink.

Sandra knew that look and opened her mouth to give comfort and support, but oddly nothing came out. So she quickly closed it. Stunned by this sudden revelation, Sandra looked at the floor with furrowed brows. This was obviously nothing she expected, and she found it a little hard to hide her surprise.

Maxie was amazed at the great relief she felt. The peace was immediate. It was done. The awkward moment had passed, leaving its aftermath to be dealt with. Now her words hung heavily in the air like a smell that could not be identified. Taking another deep breath, she glanced at Sandra.

"And you said this could wait?" Sandra asked.

"You look shocked," Maxie said plainly. "I thought you knew me."

"Oh, I…I do, but I think you got me this time honey."

Maxie laughed a little and walked to her seat. "You know, I've been doing this all of my life." She sighed, and let her head drop back just enough to see a small spider walking across the ceiling. "Ever since I can remember, I've been churchin'. I'm at church almost seven days a week. I'm practically the first one there and I'm always the last to leave. Whenever the Deaconess Union needs something, they call on good 'ole Sister Bruce. I've been faithful to the church Sandra. Faithful." Maxie turned to look at Sandra, who was still standing next to the counter with a confounded look on her face. "But I'm not happy anymore. I don't know what it's like to do anything different, and I can't help but think that I've missed out on so many things. I've never been to a party or a club. I'm in my thirties, and I don't even know what the inside of a bar looks like." The thought of life passing her by caused tears to roll down her cheeks and under her chin. Quickly she wiped them away and turned back to the spider.

Sandra was at a loss for words. She could not even compose her *'I understand how you feel'* speech, because she *didn't* understand how Maxie felt. Even so, she felt the need to offer some form of encouragement.

Repositioning herself against the counter, Sandra felt a sudden wave of uneasiness come over her. While she tried to deal with the initial blow of it all, she could not help but wonder if she had somehow contributed to Maxie's consideration of a lifestyle change. On occasional Saturday mornings, over coffee, she would give Maxie a play-by-play report of the Friday night happenings in the clubs she had been to. It was just a topic of conversation. Never anything worth giving up a lifestyle for.

Sandra looked at Maxie who was silently crying again. Quickly, she pulled a piece of paper towel from the roller, and walked back to the table. "This isn't right you know. You sound like you're giving up." Sandra sat next to her. "Here, wipe your eyes."

Maxie wiped her face in between sobs. "It's not that I'm giving up," she whined. "I just want to try something different. I need a change."

"Well, have you tried every auxiliary in your church? I heard some of them do real exciting things. Or maybe talk to one of those church mothers?"

Maxie smiled at Sandra's attempt to remedy the situation, and nodded her head no.

"So what are you saying Maxie? You want to go to a club and do some bar hopping now?"

"Maybe," Maxie whispered.

"Look at you. You're sitting here crying. Obviously you didn't think this thing through. Just talking about it brings you to tears."

"It scares me a little," Maxie confessed.

"It should! Maxie you are talking about giving up a whole lifestyle. The church is a way of life for you. It's not going to be easy to just change. What about your ministry?"

"What ministry Sandra? I have no ministry!" Maxie threw up her hands. "This is what I do all day. I am a house-wife with no life! Everything I do is either for Lester or for the church. Can't you see? I need something for me now."

Sandra sat all the way back in her chair and studied Maxie. She needed to know where Maxie was coming from with this *change* all of a sudden. Sandra knew it had to be turmoil on the inside for Maxie to come to this resolution, and she really needed to know if she had anything to do with it.

"How long have you been thinking like this?" Sandra asked.

"It's always been there Sandra. I just tried to ignore it and keep it suppressed."

Sandra rolled her eyes to the ceiling, happy to hear she had not influenced her friend. "But something made this sudden appetite for the world pop up. I mean, you must have stopped and tried to smell a rose or two somewhere along the way."

Maxie shrugged her shoulders. "Growing up with my grandmother, I was always made to go to church. There were no options. And then when I married Lester...well...I just always wanted to know what was on the other side of the fence."

"Shoot! I can tell you that," Sandra hooted. "Ain't nothing over here. Nothing but mess."

"But you're still over there. I don't see you rushing to get on this side. I just want to experience it for myself." Maxie toyed with the paper towel in her hands.

"Maxie, I'm scared for you girl. How are you going to make the transition? What are you going to do?"

"I don't know." Maxie shrugged. "I guess I'll just lay it all down."

"Just like that. Just as easy as you picked it up huh?"

Maxie looked Sandra in her eyes. "You know I didn't mean it like that Sandra."

"Well that's what you just said. You're going to put everything on freeze frame while you do your *thang*, and that's not right." Sandra knew she had a lot of nerve telling Maxie what was and was not right. She felt stupid just listening to the words pass her lips. Stupid must have been written on her face too, because Maxie was sitting there laughing softly and nodding her head.

The kitchen became silent again and for the first time, Sandra could hear the radio on the counter.

"Maxie, what about Lester?" "What are you going to tell him?"

Maxie looked at the paper towel she was wringing, and mumbled. "I'm not."

"Excuse me? Did you just say you were *not* going to tell him? Oh Maxie, you know he's going to find out! Surely you don't think you're just going to walk around here with a blasé attitude, thinking he won't know. And when he does find out, I know he'll go to blaming me for it! Oooo, I can hear him now, Maxine, I told you evil communication corrupts good manners. What fellowship hath light with darkness? You should have let that Sandra Beal alone. She's bad news! She's the one who's got you acting like this."

Maxie looked at Sandra mocking her husband and smiled. "You're crazy."

"I'm serious. Watch what I tell you. Shoot." Sandra crossed her arms like a pouting little child.

Maxie knew she was right. Lester probably would blame all of this on her. But it was only because Sandra was strong willed and sometimes outspoken. Much to Lester's adamant disapproval, Maxie guessed that was what she liked about her. Whatever Sandra wanted to do, Sandra did, and it was done resolutely. Maxie found that out a few years ago, when she met her in the atrium of Oglethorpe Mall.

Sitting alone on a bench directly in front of Russell's Men's Store, Sandra knowingly held the attention of every male shopper within her perimeter. Maxie was there to pick out a dress shirt for Lester, when a woman next to her loudly accused her boyfriend of staring at another woman. Embarrassed by the unsolicited attention he was getting from those around him, the young man softly reasoned that the woman he was looking at resembled one of his relatives. When the cashier behind the counter admonished the young man to use an original excuse next time, everyone in the store burst into wild laughter. Amidst the jeers and jesting, Maxie turned to see the cause of the sudden outburst. In observing the woman, she saw that her poise loudly declared the confidence she had in herself. She wasn't exceptionally beautiful in the manner of physical beauty. Her beauty lie in her character, and her character outwardly demanded respect.

Despite the amiable glances, all Maxie saw was a prime candidate; one to whom she could possibly persuade to dispel her wayward self, and introduce the thought of righteous living. As it turned out, Sandra was the hardest person she ever tried to witness to about Christ. She was a real challenge for her; a drive. But over time, the challenge lessened and they became friends — accepting each other's differences.

Sandra repositioned herself in her chair again and watched Maxie wring her paper towel into shreds. "Did you pray about it?" She almost whispered.

"No," Maxie answered without looking at her. "It's not a matter I choose to pray about Sandra. It's just something I've made up my mind to do."

Sandra raised her eyebrows and retreated for a moment. "Okay," she said, nodding her head.

Maxie put the shredded pieces of paper towel on the table, arranging and rearranging them like they were game pieces. "You think I'm crazy don't you?"

"No, I don't think you're crazy. I'm not sure what to think right now. This is so deep. I can tell you that I'm scared though."

Maxie slowly crossed her hands and set them in her lap, while she examined her mess on the table. "Why on earth would *you* be scared?"

"Well, you don't know what's out here and I do."

Maxie took a deep breath and looked around the kitchen. "I'm a big girl Sandra. I'll simply handle whatever comes whenever it comes."

"Okay big girl. You handle it," Sandra said matter-of-factly.

"Besides, if I get into any trouble, I know you'll be there to help me get out of it."

"Oh, you just know that do you?" Sandra said with a laugh.

"Yes I do," Maxie laughed too.

Gathering the torn pieces of paper towel, Maxie walked to the trash can. Tossing the paper in, a fleeting thought of her figuratively throwing away a lifestyle of righteous living came to mind.

"You seem to have this all mapped out. So tell me, how will this master plan unfold?" Sandra asked.

Maxie walked back to the sink and stood against the counter. Before she answered, her face lit up as if she was asked to run off a list of her secret fantasies. "Well, I'm going to start off by getting myself a job."

"A who?" Sandra chirped.

"A job girl. A job. You know, make my own money."

"Uh huh. That's what I thought you said. And where are you going to live while you work this job? 'Cause see, Mr. Bruce ain't gonna be havin' none of that up in this here camp."

Maxie bit her bottom lip and looked away thoughtfully. "You let me worry about Mr. Bruce," she smiled. "I can handle him."

"Okay," Sandra crooned, crossing her arms. "So do you know what kind of job you want?"

Maxie raised her head a little and skeptically looked down her nose at Sandra. Was she accepting her decision, or was she just trying to find another avenue to make her change her mind?

"What?" Sandra frowned. "Why are you standing there grinning at me?"

Maxie nodded her head and let the smile fade away. It didn't make a difference. The decision was made and nothing was going to change her mind. "I want a job where I can meet people. Different kinds of people. Maybe something in retail. I don't know. Maybe something clerical."

"And what kind of experience do you have?" Sandra asked in an uppity tone.

"I know the alphabet. I can file stuff."

"Okay, but where have you worked before? Tell me about your experience."

"What are you doing, conducting an interview?"

"No, but that's what they're going to ask you when you apply for a job. *Do* you have any experience?" Sandra asked firmly.

"No I don't have any experience," Maxie quipped, a little irritated.

"Well, what work history *do* you have?"

Maxie looked at the floor briefly and then back at her friend. "Sandra, what are you doing? Are you going to help me or what?"

"Believe it or not Maxie, I am helping you. If you're going to come over here, you need to know the rules and how to play. I mean look at you. You're in your thirties and you've never worked a job. That's virtually unheard of. How many businesses do you think are going to hire you? Modern technology is ridiculous right now. I mean a typical teenager has more experience at working than you do."

"And they started somewhere," Maxie retorted.

"You're in your thirties Maxie."

"How many times are you going to remind me? My age only means I'm more responsible."

"No work history. No experience. There's no record to show how responsible you may be."

"I'm not dumb Sandra. I can be taught. Besides, I don't care how much experience you have at a job, the company is still going to train you to do the job their way."

"In some cases that's true, but other jobs want experience. They don't want to waste their time and money teaching an old dog new tricks."

"Oh, so I'm an old dog now?" Maxie looked at Sandra quizzically, and the two women burst into laughter.

"You know what I mean," Sandra waved her off.

Maxie walked back to the table and sat down. "All jokes aside, what you just said is true, but I can't let that deter me."

"Okay. Well how do you feel about working in a grocery store? You can meet different kinds of people there and all of the positions are pretty easy to learn. It can be something just to get you started."

Maxie looked into the air and nodded her head slowly. "I like the idea. And there are quite a few of them right here in Midtown, so I can work close to home. I might go apply first thing in the morning."

Sandra smiled and gently slapped Maxie on her hands. "Go at it working girl. Go get yourself a job." Quickly, she glanced at her watch and jumped up out of her chair. "This working girl needs to get on her job." Sandra straightened her clothes and looked around to make sure she wasn't forgetting anything. "I'm gone girl," she said as she walked to the door with Maxie following her. "Good luck trying to talk to Lester tonight." Sandra opened the door and stood there for a moment. "Boy, I'd love to be a fly on the wall to hear that conversation." Looking at Maxie, she burst into laughter and closed the door. "Call me when it's over," she yelled.

Maxie rested her back against the door. She almost forgot about asking Lester if she could even get a job. While she thought about it, she swore she could still hear Sandra laughing in the distance.

Chapter Two

For Maxie, the morning hours went by quickly and the afternoon hours even faster. While getting dressed, and doing routine cleaning around the house, she thought of nothing else but ways to tell her husband that she wanted a job. She even practiced what she would say while she stood in front of the bathroom mirror, complete with pitiful facial expressions, if needed.

The first idea she could come up with, was to cook Lester's favorite meal for dinner and then casually bring it up in conversation as they ate. However cliché the saying was, the way to Lester's heart was definitely through his stomach. Maxie knew exactly what would do the trick, and around 4:00 p.m., she began cooking the impetuous meal — fried chicken, tossed green salad, sweet barbecue beans, a creamy baked macaroni and cheese casserole, with an extra-large cup of any flavored Kool Aid. A buttery tasting sweet potato pie would clench it. If Lester didn't fall for it, she had a back-up plan that rarely ever failed and was one that usually had him in her complete control.

After working feverishly, Maxie looked at the clock on the radio. It was 5:30 p.m., and Lester normally arrived home around 6:15. Anticipation of the evening rose and made her anxious. Rubbing her hands together, she checked everything to make sure it was just right. All was ready except for the pie, and its aroma of butter, nutmeg, and a hint of vanilla, filled the house. It was her grandmother's recipe, and a treasure in its own right.

When Maxie opened the stove to check the pie, the heat from the oven comfortably warmed her face and the front of her clothes. It also helped to release the smell of fried chicken that was now serving as her new body fragrance. That was all she needed. Here it was 5:35 p.m., and now she had to go take another shower and change her clothes. She had an impression to make, and she couldn't very well do it smelling like a big chicken.

Looking at the time remaining on the clock, Maxie tried to figure out just what could be accomplished in that short amount of time. *Lay some fresh clothes out on the bed, jump in the shower and soap down one good time, and jump back out.* She could be done in ten to fifteen minutes.

Maxie began to undress on her way to the bathroom in the master bedroom. Inside, she finished undressing and locked the door. As she lathered, her mind continued to wander back and forth between making a good impression, and what Lester's response would be. No matter what the outcome, she wasn't going to give up on the idea of making a change in her life. Change would be good. Everybody needed to do it at some point in their lives.

Finishing her shower a little sooner than planned, Maxie grabbed a towel and patted the moisture from her skin. Drying her face last, she buried it in the towel and blindly opened the door. As she began to walk through the doorway, she suddenly hesitated. Standing still, a distinct and ominous feeling quickly swept over her. Her stomach knotted and she felt the hairs on her arms rise.

There was another presence in the room.

Maxie's mind raced. How could she get away? Where would she run? Her heart pounded so hard, it resounded in her ears when she pulled the towel away from her face. A few feet away from the doorway directly in front of her, stood a large dark figure. Unable to focus immediately, a scream churned in the pit of her stomach, working its way into her throat. Even after the point of recognition, she was unable to contain it, for she opened her mouth and let out a high-pitched sound that made her and the large figure both jump.

"Lester!" She yelled, almost out of breath. "Honey don't scare me like that!"

Quickly, she wrapped the towel around herself. Her heart felt like it was beating double time, making her weak in the knees. She leaned against the doorframe with the towel gripped tightly at her chest.

"Scare you?" Lester said, practically falling back onto their bed. "Woman, you just made my curly hair stand up at attention and lay down straight!" He laughed.

Maxie bit her thumbnail and laughed nervously. "I'm sorry. The scream just slipped out. I wasn't expecting you to be home so soon."

"It's okay," Lester said softly. "I know I scared you. I'm sorry. We didn't have a lot of work today, so I thought I'd come home a little early. Come 'ere. You're shaking all over."

"What?" Maxie cooed.

Lester stretched his arms out to her and smiled. "Come 'ere. I like that towel thing you got going on right now."

Maxie reluctantly moved toward him, clenching her towel tighter as he grabbed it and pulled her closer to him.

"Dinner smells good," he smiled. Lester tried to loosen the towel from her clutch.

"I wanted to make you something special tonight," she said, maintaining her grip. Maxie knew which road Lester was traveling, and hoped to create a detour. "I have a pie in the oven I need to check on."

"I took it out when I came in," he said without diversion.

Maxie looked down into eyes full of intent, as Lester gave up the fight with the towel and now caressed her arms. The warmth of his touch against her damp skin caused her insides to react unconstrained, changing her breathing pattern. For the first time, she noticed her husband had his shirt completely unbuttoned. Not really wanting to commit, Maxie knew giving in could eventually have its benefits later on in the evening, so she loosened her grip on the towel. Slowly, she ran her free hand along both sides of Lester's face, moving up to his hair. Lester smiled, removed the towel, and gently laid her on the bed.

* * * * * * * * *

Maxie lay motionless on the bed, gazing at the ceiling. Her original plan was now thrown out of sync by Lester's spontaneous desire. What would she have to fall back on? Pulling herself up, she sat on the edge of the bed.

"What are you thinking about?" Lester asked, rubbing her back.

"How I need to get cleaned up and get your dinner on the table. Aren't you hungry?"

"Mmmmm," he moaned, motioning for her to come close to him again.

Maxie quickly stood up and walked to the bathroom smiling. "Later." She said, and closed the door behind her. Inside, she leaned against the door and tried to think of ways she could regain the ground she just lost. She jumped when Lester knocked on the door.

"Let me in so I can get cleaned up too."

"Hold on. I'll be out in a minute," she said, and turned on the water.

"You know, I came home a little early today because I wanted to take you out to eat. We need to celebrate."

Maxie turned the water off to make sure she heard Lester correctly. Quickly, she opened the door to peek at him. "Did you say celebrate? Celebrate what?" She could see him lightly bouncing the bed, looking like a mischievous child with a new secret to tell.

"I got a raise today," he beamed and winked at her.

Maxie stared for a moment, slammed the door closed, and lightly stomped her foot. She knew now, there was no way he would ever even remotely think about letting her get a job.

Lester knocked on the door again. "Did you slam the door out of excitement or what?"

"Oh, that's a real blessing honey," she called out. "I'm so happy for you."

"Yeah. Since you already cooked dinner, we can go out another time."

Maxie cleaned herself up, opened the door, and practically flew to get her clothes that were now on the floor.

"Go get washed up and we can finish talking over dinner," she said.

Lester went into the bathroom and began singing a song about the blessings of Jesus. Mumbling to herself, Maxie stumbled into her shoes frantically, like a crazed woman on a final quest to save someone. Despite what she said earlier, she had no intentions of talking about his raise over dinner. The suppertime discussion was going to be about her, and that was all there was to it.

* * * * * * * * *

Maxie sat and ate her salad quietly, while Lester talked about all his plans for his newly acquired fortune. Not really listening to him, she nodded her head occasionally, acknowledging his rhetorical questions.

"God provides our every need baby," he said, filling his mouth with a fork full of barbecue beans. "You know what I mean?"

Maxie nodded again, indifferently.

"You let me know if you want or need anything okay? I'm going to take care of my baby."

I need and want a job! She yelled within herself. Letting her fork fall into her plate, Maxie got up from the table. "Do you want some more Kool Aid Lester?"

"Just a little," he muffled, pushing his glass toward her. Maxie retrieved the pitcher and began filling his glass, while she watched him use half a slice of bread to sop up his bean juice and the cheese from his macaroni. "You want some more to eat?"

"No, I'm fine."

Maxie put the pitcher on the table and sat down. Lester wiped his mouth, and sat back in his chair with his fingers locked across his stomach, like a content king. "So, how was your day today? Sandra talk you to death?"

"No, we just sat and chatted for a while," she answered, spacing her beans out individually on the plate with her fork. "I'm glad she came by. I needed someone to talk to."

"Well, you want to talk to me now? I know I've been dominating the conversation, so you talk to me now."

"Talk to you about what?" She asked coyly.

"Well, you can start with why you fixed this particular meal?"

"I told you I just wanted to fix you something special. And see, as it turns out, I was in the spirit because this meal fits your exciting news." Maxie wanted to fall out of her chair, roll on the floor, and burst into laughter. *She* would not have even believed that corny white lie.

"Uh huh," Lester said sipping his Kool Aid. "So what do you want Maxine?"

Maxie looked at him totally surprised. Not so much because of his question, but because he called her by her full first name. That usually meant he wanted to get right to the point.

"Don't look at me like that," he smiled. "You always cook this particular meal when you want something."

"Do I?" She laughed bashfully.

"Yes you do. Now what is it?"

"Well, honey...you know our wedding anniversary is coming up soon."

Lester nodded.

"Well, I want to get a special gift for you this time." Maxie hated the way her words were coming out. They

33

sounded like she was making it all up as she went along. All of her well-calculated rhetoric left her, and now she was stammering. She couldn't even keep eye contact with him.

"Baby, all the gifts you give me are special," Lester swooned.

"But I want this one to have a special meaning for me too."

"And how is that?"

"What I want to get is something real nice, and the cost of it. ..."

"How much do you need? You know I don't want anything real expensive."

"That's just it. See, I don't want you to give me the money."

"So how will you pay for it? Do you have money saved up or something?"

"No." Maxie quickly got up and walked toward the counter. "Do you want your pie now?"

"No. I want you to sit down here and talk to me."

Maxie slowly walked back to her seat without looking at him.

"How will you pay for it if I don't give you the money?"

"Lester, I ... I want to get a job. I want to pay for my gift to you, with money I make from a job. And I want to look for one as soon as possible. Maybe even as soon as tomorrow." Maxie winced a little, like a child expecting to be chastised for doing something wrong. She sat quietly, anticipating Lester going off the deep end. Instead, a cloud of silence hung over the kitchen table. Maxie glanced at him, searching his face for a response. It was blank. He was just sitting there. *No response is a good response*, she told herself. "I won't have to do it for long. Maybe two or three months at the most, and then I promise I'll quit." In her own ears, her pleading sounded like a mother trying to get her small child to understand that she would be away from him, so she could make money.

Lester still didn't move, and Maxie couldn't be sure if he was ignoring her, or weighing out his decision. Whatever he was doing, it was making her uncomfortable.

"I'll get you a piece of pie now," she said.

When she got up, she knew he was staring at her. She could feel his eyes boring a hole in her back. What was he thinking? A million thoughts came to her mind all at the same time. She even heard her conversation with Sandra, and how she teased her about Lester not allowing her to work while she lived under his roof.

When she set the pie in front of him, Maxie watched his facial expression.

"Maxie ..."

"Lester, wait," she pleaded. "Before you decide on this, please think about how important it is to me."

"I've given thought to all of that honey. You know how I feel about you working. With this raise, there's really no need for another income, not that there ever was. Besides, you've never worked a day in your life."

Maxie narrowed her eyes and bit the inside of her lip. If she heard one more statement in reference to her past history of unemployment, she felt she would scream. Calmly, she sat down and leaned in closer to her husband.

"Lester, please," she said softly. "Two or three months."

Lester glanced at Maxie as he filled his mouth. Chewing slowly, he leaned back in his chair again and stared at her for a moment.

"Baby, if I didn't know any better, I'd say there was more to this than just a gift."

Maxie slid back into her seat and sighed heavily. Now was not the time for him to start guessing what her true motives were. She needed to be more convincing, but she didn't know how. Instead, she sat quietly. When Lester finished, he stood up and rummaged his hands in his front pockets, like he was going to give her money. With a defeated look on her face, Maxie kept her focus on his empty chair. She didn't want to look at him. She didn't want to risk appearing overthrown. When her eyes finally met his, Lester winked at her.

"Starting October, I will give you three months and only three months," he said, pointing a finger at her and raising his eyebrows in emphasis. "After that, I don't want to hear anything else about you working. And I don't want you working any nights." With that, Lester simply kissed her on her mouth, complimented the meal, and left the kitchen.

Maxie sat in confusion and disbelief. "That's it?" She whispered to herself out loud. "I tormented myself about this all day long, and that was it?"

She almost wanted to become angry at how easy it was. Where was the resistance? As incredible as it seemed, she actually felt disappointed at Lester's sudden approval. So much so, she couldn't allow the feelings of relief and excitement to switch places with disappointment and confusion. It all happened much too fast.

Maxie cleared the table and called Sandra. When she finished with all of the details of the evening, Sandra screamed in her ear, told her to pat herself on the back, and look forward to the change.

Chapter Three

L ocated across the street from Oglethorpe Mall, was a grocery store called Food King, which was set up inside of a warehouse with long aisles. There were at least twenty checkout lanes, and five Express lanes. It was always clean. When there were no lines, the cashiers would stand in front of their area and pleasantly greet the customer, offering to ring up their order promptly.

From the time she entered the store, Maxie was excited and a little nervous about applying for her first job. It would have been so much easier to apply for a position online, but Food King still embraced the old way of doing things. Instead of going straight to the Customer Service desk, it made sense for her to walk around the store to get a feel for it as a place of employment, and to calm her nerves. With it being Senior Citizen Tuesday, old people were throughout the store, complete with canes, walkers, and motorized shopping carts.

Most of the people she passed smiled at her. However, she didn't understand the reason for the overly friendly facial expressions, until she saw her reflection in a mirror slanted over the Produce area. It showed her a big goofy grin plastered on her face. Embarrassed, she quickly looked around to see if anyone else was looking at her. There was no one except for a little old white man, draped in a royal blue Food King apron, who was way past the age of retirement. He stood right next to Maxie, just below her shoulder.

"You like Collard greens? I see you smilin' at 'em. We just got these in fresh this mornin'," he said, showing them off like a prize to be won.

Maxie took a step back. "Uh...no. I was just browsing. Thank you."

"They real tender you know. Won't even have to put much bakin' soda in these."

"No, really, thank you."

Maxie forced a smile and walked away, wondering if the old man was really that friendly, or if it was just part of the job. Circling the store once more, she concluded her tour and walked toward the Customer Service desk. Behind the desk, a heavy-set black woman waddled from one end of the counter to the other. A set of keys that dangled from her wrist made Maxie instantly think of a cow. She lowered her head and smiled to herself.

"May I help you?" The girl asked without looking at her.

Maxie looked around to make sure she was the one being spoken to. "Uh...yes. Yes, I'd like to get a job application please."

"For what position?" The girl asked, continuing to search for whatever it was she was searching for.

"Uh...position?" Maxie asked, lowering her voice.

"Yeah," the girl said matter-of-factly. "What position on the board are you applying for?" The girl pointed to a large board hanging on the wall behind her. On it was a list of current job openings — cashiers, night stock, and maintenance.

"Cashier," Maxie blurted out. "I need an application for cashier."

"Do you have any cashiering experience?"

Maxie felt her eyes widen. Here was one of Sandra's questions all over again. "Well, I..."

"It doesn't matter anyway," the girl said, waving her hand. "You'll be trained on the register if you're hired."

Maxie breathed a small sigh of relief. For the first time in their brief conversation, the girl looked at her with light brown contact lens covered eyes.

"You look familiar," the girl said with a smile. "I've seen you somewhere before."

"I shop here a lot. Maybe you've seen me come into the store from time to time."

The girl shrugged her shoulders and reached under the counter to retrieve the application. "I don't know, maybe so." She tossed on the counter what seemed like a booklet to Maxie.

"I know it looks like a lot of paperwork but most of it is just a bunch of questions they want you to answer. Stuff like, have you ever been convicted of a crime, or do you take drugs, or have you ever been caught stealing from any of your other jobs. You know, a bunch of stupid junk. I don't know why they waste a person's time making them answer all of those dumb questions anyway. Ain't nobody going to tell the truth."

Maxie thumbed through the pamphlet and laughed a little to herself because she knew most of the questions would not apply to her.

"Since Mr. Martin is here this morning, he's asked me to tell all applicants to fill out all of the paperwork here, and when you're finished, he'll do your interview."

"Interview?" Maxie quipped.

"Uh huh. Soon as you're finished. Just sit right there on that bench and fill out your application."

Maxie looked at the long park bench located next to the counter. "But I'm not dressed for an interview *today*."

"Oh you look fine. You're just applying for a cashier job. Don't worry about it." The girl handed Maxie a pen. "Here you go. Just have a seat over there."

Maxie reached for the pen so slowly, it seemed like an eternity before she had it in her hand. The girl smiled at her and walked to the other end of the counter. When she sat on the bench, Maxie pondered every thought that came to mind. How should she conduct herself in the interview? What hours would she be available to work? Every question on the application posed problem after problem because she didn't readily have the answers for any of them. The biggest problem was, what was she going to say when the manager asked her why the area of *Past Work History* was blank? Doing the interview so soon, would not allow her time to put together a good explanation. Still, Maxie filled out the application as best she could, and quickly walked back to the counter.

"All done?" The girl behind the counter chimed. "You did that pretty fast. I'll take this back to Mr. Martin and he'll be right with you. Have a seat on the bench."

Maxie walked back and sat. She hated to admit it to herself, but she was a nervous wreck. Crossing and uncrossing her legs, she tried to focus her attention elsewhere. The same elderly people she saw shopping earlier were now in the checkout line. One old woman repeatedly asked the cashier what amount of change was needed to complete her purchase, all the while counting the change into the cashier's hand. Maxie took notice of how most of those behind the registers were females, varying in age. The oldest one looked to be in her fifties. *I could blend in here.* Maxie thought to herself.

"Mrs. Bruce, good morning. I'm Mr. Martin, the store manager."

Startled, Maxie took the hand that was extended to her and quickly stood up.

"You're applying for one of our cashier positions?"

"Yes, yes... I am."

"Well fine," Mr. Martin bellowed with a smile. "Come with me into my office and we will do the interview there."

Maxie returned the smile and followed. She tried to think of answers to questions he might ask, but the sight of Mr. Martin held her captive. He was huge. *He must weigh at least four hundred pounds*, she thought. He was a nice looking man, neatly dressed in black pants, a white shirt, and a tie that appeared to be choking him.

When he reached the door of his office, Mr. Martin stopped and gestured for Maxie to go in first. She did, and immediately wondered how the two of them were going to fit in there together. The room was much smaller than Maxie thought a manager's office should be. A large desk with a chair on each side, dashed any hopes of making one's self comfortable, as Mr. Martin eagerly suggested.

Maxie sat in the smaller seat she figured was for interviewees, and watched the heavy man squeeze in on the other side of the table to the larger chair. When he sat, his stomach instantly became the table on which he reviewed her application.

"Well Mrs. Bruce, I am happy you've chosen to work for Food King. I have looked over your application and everything looks good. However, and this was probably just an oversight, you forgot to list your past places of employment, and the names of your past supervisors. We like to use them as references. You can do that right here at my desk."

Maxie looked at the black pen Mr. Martin was offering to her. She slowly took it from his hand, and poised herself to continue writing on the paper that already possessed all she could give to it. After putting the pen to the paper and making a small line, she froze. Mr. Martin leaned forward a little and looked at the application, then at Maxie.

"Is there something wrong Mrs. Bruce? Is your pen out of ink? He asked while opening the drawer to his desk. "Let me get another one for you."

"No … uh … it's fine Mr. Martin. The pen works, I just haven't."

"Excuse me. I don't quite understand what you're saying."

Maxie looked away from Mr. Martin's inquiring gaze, and stared at the floor. She took a deep breath, and let it out slowly. "Mr. Martin, I didn't fill out this part of the application because I've never had a job before."

"You've never worked?"

"No I haven't."

The heavy man slid the paper from under Maxie's fingertips and examined it again. She watched quietly and wondered what he was thinking, wanting desperately to plead her case before judgment was passed down.

"You're what, thirty-four years old?"

"Yes."

"And you've never worked *any* job?"

The way he said it, made Maxie think he was having a hard time coming to grips with it. "Mr. Martin... I..."

"Oh please don't be offended. I've just never...well, you're the first *adult* I've interviewed who has never held a job before."

"Will that pose a problem?"

"Oh no. No, absolutely not. If anything, you will probably be more dedicated."

"Yes sir, I would," she beamed.

"Let me tell you about the job. It pays nine dollars per hour and..."

Mr. Martin went on and on about the position's requirements, benefits, and how Food King was an Equal Opportunity Employer. Maxie tried hard to concentrate and give him her undivided attention. No matter how attentive she tried to look, her thoughts were suddenly on Lester. Did he actually believe she was really going to find herself a job, or was he just humoring her because he knew no one would hire an inexperienced housewife?

"So, what do you think Mrs. Bruce?" Mr. Martin smiled.

Maxie smiled back, feeling goofier than ever, because she missed what he said prior to his question. "What do I think?"

"Can you handle it?"

"Handle it?" She asked, hoping he would now give her a clue so she wouldn't embarrass herself further.

"Yes," Mr. Martin laughed. "Do you think you can handle the job?"

"You're giving me the job?"

"Only if you still want it," he said.

"Yes!! Yes, I want it! I'll take it!"

"Wonderful. And I see here that you want afternoon hours. Part-time?"

"Part-time," Maxie said, nodding her head with certainty.

"Okay, well, let me get the rest of your paperwork. You can take it home, look it over and fill everything out. There will be an orientation next Wednesday at twelve o'clock. Will you be able to make that time?"

"That time will be fine," Maxie chirped.

"Okay then. I'll be right back."

Mr. Martin left Maxie alone in the quaint little room. Alone, she felt, to think over everything that transpired thus far. The quiet breakfast with Lester, the brief conversation with Sandra over the phone, the interview, and now, getting herself a *job*. She was about to embark on a whole new frontier.

"Okay Mrs. Bruce. Here is your paperwork," Mr. Martin said, when he entered the doorway. "Bring these in with you on next Wednesday. The orientation, as I've told you, will begin at twelve o'clock and should end around two, after which we will begin to familiarize you with our cash registers. That process will take another hour. Your normal shift will be from twelve o'clock in the afternoon until five. Do you have any questions?"

Maxie rose from her chair. "Should I wear any particular colors or anything?"

"No." Mr. Martin smiled. "We'll give you what you'll need when you come in for the orientation. Just wear some comfortable shoes. You'll be standing for a while."

"All right," she said. "Thank you very much."

"Thank you," Mr. Martin said, stepping aside to let her out. "And I hope you'll enjoy working at Food King."

Maxie left the office smiling in a state of euphoria. All the way to the parking lot, she had a sheepish grin on her face. This time, the only one to return her smile was the girl behind the counter with the contact lens covered eyes.

Chapter Four

Maxie sat at the kitchen table and spread out all of the papers she had to fill out and sign. It was all foreign to her and she considered it *business stuff*. She wasn't even acquainted with her own business stuff, because Lester handled it all. Maxie needed help, but she was not about to ask him to help her. She didn't need him to confirm some of her fleeting thoughts about not being ready for the working class. Instead, she filled out the parts she could, then put them in her purse for Sandra. She knew she would help her without question.

The clock on the stove read 1:15 p.m., and Maxie didn't have to start dinner for another couple of hours, so she went into the living room to lie on the couch. There, silence enveloped the room and invited her to relax. Elevating her feet, she locked her fingers across her chest and tried to imagine all of the different people she would meet at Food King.

"And how are you today?" She said out loud. "Will that be all for you? Paper or plastic?" She laughed.

It was going to be fun, and Maxie hoped the excitement of it would never wear off. Everything would have to change now. The current schedule would have to be replaced by a new agenda. She thought about everything from what clothes to wear, to quick fix meals after work. Her thinking was mid-flight when the telephone rang and made her jump.

"Hello?" She said nearly out of breath.

"What did you do, run to the phone?" Sandra asked.

"No girl, the ringer scared me to death."

"Oh. Well listen, I'm on my break. Tell me, how did it go?"

"How did what go?" Maxie asked with a smile.

"Come on girl, stop playing. I only have a few minutes before my next meeting. Did you get it or not?"

"Oh, you're talking about the job."

"Maxie!"

"Yeah, I got it." Maxie quickly held the receiver away from her ear while Sandra squealed on the other end.

"Girl, I am so happy for you. My girl went out and got herself a J O B! Her first job at that!"

"Yeah," Maxie said bashfully.

"So what will your hours be?"

"Twelve to five. You know I have to be home in time to get dinner cooked."

"I know that's right, and you better not miss a day either. Lester might have you fired, okay?"

"Hush up smart mouth," Maxie laughed.

"You're going to have to tell me all about it after I get off. What time should I call you? I don't want to interrupt that feeding process in your home. The natives get restless around that time."

"I'll feed Lester around six-fifteen or so, but I don't want you to call me. I need to come over to your place so you can help me fill out all this legal and government stuff."

"You, coming to my place? Uh huh. I see. And we don't want Lester to think we are incapable of doing it ourselves, because that would only prove we don't need to be working if we can't fill out the paperwork right?"

"You trying to read my mind over the phone Sandra? Oooo, you're moving up."

"Anyway, I might be entertaining a gentleman in my house this evening," Sandra whispered.

"That's fine. As long as he's gone by the time I get there. You get off at five right?"

"As always."

"Good. I'll see you around seven."

"Later girl," Sandra laughed.

Maxie hung up the phone, looked at the clock on the wall, and laid down again. It was just 1:30 p.m. The dinner she had planned wouldn't take long to fix, so she closed her eyes for a few minutes. As slumber crept in, she thought about Lester. There was no way he was going to let her go over to Sandra's house, so she pondered on just the right words to use on him. Maybe she wouldn't use any words on him at all. Maybe she would just go without telling him anything. Just up and go. Maxie laughed at the crazy idea. She didn't think she could ever be that bold.

"Yeah right," she said out loud. The idea was so enticing she couldn't let it go. She thought about it right up until she fell asleep.

* * * * * * * * * *

The afternoon had darkened a little, when Maxie responded to the softness of warm lips pressing against her forehead. Slowly opening her eyes, she focused on Lester standing in front of her in a ray of sunlight that made him look like a vision of God towering over her. Looking at the window through partially drawn curtains, she could see the sun setting. *Oh God,* she thought. *It's past three o'clock and I haven't even started dinner!* Maxie quickly sat up and tried to pull herself together.

"Oh honey," she pleaded, brushing down misplaced hairs with her hand. "I am so sorry. What time is it?"

"Almost six-thirty. Sweetheart, it's okay, you just fell asleep. No big deal. We can go to Mickey D's and grab a hamburger or something."

"Mickey D's Lester? You hate McDonald's." Maxie rested against the back of the couch, her voice sounding strained. "I'll fix you something to eat. Go get washed up and changed. It shouldn't be long."

Lester offered his hand to help her stand. "I'll tell you what, I'll get cleaned up and we'll go out for dinner. We can still celebrate my raise." Kissing her forehead again, he began unbuttoning his shirt as he headed toward the bedroom.

"Great," Maxie called to him. "I have something to celebrate too." Lester stopped in the middle of the doorway and took his shirt off. In silence he stood with his back to her. Everything seemed to stand still. "I got a job today. I'm going to be working at Food King."

Nothing moved.

"I remembered what you said about not working at night, so I think my shift will be from noon until four or five or so."

"That's good baby," Lester said, balling up his shirt and tossing it on the bed. "That's real good."

Maxie watched Lester disappear into the room. His last words sounded tired and hung in the air. She really didn't expect him to be ecstatic, but a *little* support would have been nice. Plopping back down on the couch, Maxie decided she wouldn't talk about her job when they went out to eat, even though he *should* be the one to share in her excitement. Eventually, he would come around. He'd have to, because that was the way it was going to be.

While Lester was in the shower, Maxie called Sandra and told her she would be late. Sandra told her if she saw a Do Not Disturb sign on the door when she got there, don't bother knocking. Maxie said she wouldn't, and promised to ring the doorbell.

* * * * * * * * * *

Few words passed between the two of them since Maxie's announcement. Lester insisted on taking his car, and solemnly held the door open while Maxie made herself comfortable in the passenger seat of the older modeled vehicle. As she put on her seatbelt, she gave the car a once over. It had been a while since she had traveled in Lester's Mercedes, but nothing in it changed much. It still had at least half an inch of powdered concrete on the floor of the driver's side, and a small dusting on the passenger's side. The back seat had become a tumultuous graveyard to rolls and tubes of architectural blue prints of buildings he worked on. Whenever she asked him about cleaning his car, he would tell her he was the only one who had to ride in it and it didn't bother him. Making mention of it again would be pointless, especially since bringing it up would only be in an effort to make conversation with him.

Maxie settled in for what she knew would be a quiet ride to the restaurant. When Lester backed out of the driveway, she looked at the front and side of the house. The paint was beginning to fade. The large oak tree in the back yard helped to spread a blanket of leaves all over the yard, and the surrounding shrubbery needed trimming. She had no idea as to when it would all be done, and wondered if Lester would use it against her, if she left it unattended while working. After all, it was *her* job to do it, or to hire someone else to get it done.

Maxie glanced at Lester in hopes of reading something warm and tender in his face, but his expression was stoic. She knew it was important to understand her husband's feelings, regarding his decision. After all, he was one of the church's most upstanding ministers, and the judgment he made about his wife working, was going against what their Pastor taught. Married women of the church were to be *chaste keepers of the home*, and all ministers' wives were expected to lead by example. Maxie wasn't bothered by what the church members might say about her, but she had to consider what they would think and say about her husband. What repercussions would he suffer when her change of lifestyle began to manifest? Whispers and chiding would be expected, but she didn't want Lester to take offense and feel the need to protect her name. That would definitely pit him against the church, and she would hate to subject him to that, because he was such a loving and God-fearing man.

Lester, a Savannah native, was the son of a prominent and strict Pentecostal preacher. He was raised in the church all of his life, and taught godly principles. His father also reared him on how to be a real man, which entailed the proper way to care for a woman. In Maxie's book, he was a cut above most men, because he was known to be a man who lived his life on purpose. Rarely, had he ever strayed from the straight and narrow. She recalled him telling her that while he was growing up, he was only enticed by the world a few times, but never really developed a hunger for what it had to offer. He was invariably focused spiritually, and Maxie was always impressed with how passionate he was about what he believed in.

From the time they were first introduced at a church picnic, Maxie was immediately attracted to Lester. She had seen him many times before in the front of the sanctuary, where he sat with the other ministers. Although she wanted to, it was unlike her to introduce herself to him like the other women did, so she admired him from afar. But on that day up close and personal, he was gorgeous and extremely polite, addressing her with a captivating dimpled smile that made her heart melt. Being somewhat shy on that initial introduction, Maxie had no problem letting Lester dominate the conversation. While he spoke primarily of his family and their ingrained way of life, she held on to his every word. She found it hard not to be mesmerized by him. She distinctly remembered having to shift her focus from him, to the picnic table they were sitting at, just so she wouldn't appear to be in awe. All the while, she was stealing images of his features and selfishly committing them to memory. Undoubtedly, Lester Bruce was the most attractive man in the church, single or married, and wanted by both categories of women.

Maxie smiled to herself, as she replayed the wagging tongues she received when he gave her his undivided attention that day. Lester told her so much about himself in that one meeting, that by the end of their single sided conversation, she was left wondering, *How could somebody so attractive, be so dedicated to someone he can't even see?*

Over time, Maxie kept her eyes on Lester. She watched as women, beautiful women, practically threw themselves at him, desperately hoping to gain the spot of being the object of his affection — tempting opportunities he chose not to take, because of his loyalty to God and to the soft-spoken woman who was swiftly stealing his heart. Maxie didn't know what Lester saw in her. She wasn't *as* beautiful as some of those women who were physically gifted, and well trained on how to flaunt it. She was rather plain, petite in stature, but filled out in all of the right places. At least that's what Lester told her. She always dressed modestly, didn't wear make-up, and she was somewhat of an introvert. He explained to her that he was drawn to her because of the type of person she was. She wasn't a "busy body" — all around the church knowing everybody's business, and she never talked anyone down. He was attracted to that. That and the fact that she had the most beautiful almond shaped brown eyes he had ever seen.

"A man could get lost in those eyes," he once told her.

Maxie wasn't convinced though. For lack of a better reason, she thought maybe there was something about her that agreed with Lester's inward part. His inner man. Maybe deep down, he was desiring to capture what had been long forbidden and ignored. Perhaps he was trapped like she was, but denying it. She even thought perchance, that he was looking for someone as inexperienced as himself, to share the joy of seizing everything the *world* had to offer.

Maxie held on to that farce, right up until the day Lester made her his wife. It wasn't until sometime later that she realized her husband was truly what he appeared to be. A man in love with his God.

Chapter Five

S eemingly timed with their entrance, a bell sounded
from a kiosk in the middle of the restaurant. Loudly,
it signaled that fresh baked dinner rolls were available. The restaurant Lester chose, The Brass Bell, was a
Sunday-after-service favorite for many churchgoers. It was
a family restaurant that served no alcoholic beverages, and
it was very reasonable. Every night they offered a choice
of buffet or ordering from the menu, and all patrons seated
themselves. It was far from Maxie's idea of being a place
to celebrate anything, but she didn't want to mention it.

The aroma of spicy fried chicken, heavily seasoned
meats, and sweet desserts, saturated the air of the restaurant. After making a salad from the bar, Maxie sat at the
empty table and scanned the area where she and Lester
chose to sit. There were no church members in the general
vicinity, but she knew it was just a matter of time before
they made their presence known once she and Lester were
spotted. She bowed her head and said a brief prayer over
her food. The restaurant wasn't very crowded, but people
were filing in steadily. Lester returned to the table with

his usual 'mile high' piled plate, full of samples of almost everything on the buffet. Normally, she would fuss at him about putting more on his plate than he could possibly eat, but she thought better of it tonight.

After his prayer, Lester took bites of each item on his plate and sat chewing quietly. He looked everywhere except for directly in front of him. Maxie waited for him to give her his full commentary on how each item tasted, and if it was worthy of being on the food bar. That was his favorite thing to do whenever they came here.

"Good?" She finally muffled.

"Fine," he said plainly.

Maxie nodded her head airily. Lightly, she tossed a few leaves to one side of her plate and croutons to the other side. "Did I do something wrong?"

"No," he answered, maintaining his focus on his plate.

"Then why are you *not* talking to me? Why are you being distant?"

Lester took a sip of his drink, and wiped his mouth before looking at her. "I'm just thinking about some things. I'm sorry if I seem distant, as you say."

"My job?" She asked softly. "Is that what you're thinking about?"

Lester forced a reassuring smile. "Sweetheart, I'm just thinking, honestly."

He looked at her for a moment longer, and then returned to his meal. Maxie wanted to know where his thoughts were. Was he thinking about her? Did he feel like he allowed her to place him in a precarious position in his ministry? Was he second-guessing his decision? Whatever the case, it was best right now to back-off of the subject and try to enjoy her meal.

It wasn't long before the noise level escalated within the restaurant. Maxie smiled, and indulged herself in small conversation with a few people from their church and other churches, as they passed their table. She was glad they stopped by, because they were reaping smiles from Lester, and they helped make the current situation and atmosphere light. The fellowship was good until a fairly older woman, who church members called *Mouth Almighty, Tongue Everlasting*, showed up at their table.

"Praise da Lawd, Minister Bruce! It sho is good ta see ya and Sister Bruce out tonight." The lady squelched with a strong southern accent, and a smile that showed a few missing teeth. "Da food sho' is good here idn't it?"

"Yes ma'am it is," Lester said with a feigned smile.

"Uh huh." The woman nearly spoke to herself, while she eyed Lester's plate.

"Dat's a mighty handsome piece of fried chicken on yo plate. I reckons ya like fried chicken all right, huh Minister Bruce?"

"Yes ma'am I do," Lester replied tolerably.

Maxie lowered her head a little, rubbed her eyes, and giggled softly. It was all she could do to keep from bursting into laughter.

"Oh Sister Bruce, I saw you at da Food King taday. Ya know I takes my Mama up dere ev'ry Tuesday sos' she can git her groceries fo' da' week, and I sez to her, I sez Mama, dere's Sister Bruce over dere sittin' on dat bench. It look like she fillin' out a application. Was ya fillin' out one Sister Bruce? My Mama sez you prolli wadn't and dat I shud mind my own bidness, but was ya?"

The woman stopped cold with her eyes set on Maxie, waiting for her to respond. Maxie wanted to inform her that her mother was right in telling her she needed to keep her nose out of other people's business, but what was more important was Lester's reaction to the question. When her eyes met his, she received a glare so hard and cold, she felt it in the pit of her stomach. It almost made her lose her train of thought.

"Uh ... well ... yes ma'am I was. I'm going to be doing a little part-time work there for a little while," she said, briefly looking at Lester as she spoke.

"Oh my," the woman went on. "Is erythin' all right? Do we needs ta lift a offerin' ta help ya'll out or anythin'? 'Cuz if we do…"

Lester was going to hit the roof. Maxie watched his jaws tighten and every muscle in his face tense up. Even if she wasn't working to help the household, she and Lester both knew the story would never be correct coming out of the mouth of this particular woman.

"No ma'am, none of that is necessary. We are doing quite well," Lester said firmly.

As the woman spoke, Lester's eyes darted around the area to see who else was listening to her, because the volume of her voice began to heighten.

"Well ya know our Pastor preaches and beliebes dat if a woman gits herself married, den she otta be a chaste keeper of da home. She ain't 'posed to work," the woman huffed.

Maxie imagined Lester letting go and telling her it was none of her business what went on in his household, and that he owed her no explanation. But naturally being the kind of man he was, he dealt with her benevolently.

"My wife has an anniversary project she is working on, and she chooses to do it without my help. There is nothing more than that," he said.

Maxie thought she saw his eyes narrow a bit. If they did, the woman wasn't paying any attention, because she just stood there looking at the two of them in disbelief.

"Uh huh," she mumbled under her breath again. "Well," she said, sighing deeply and smiling. "Mama needs me now, so I best be gettin' on back ta my table. God bless ya'll. We'll be seein' ya on tamorra' night or Sunday mornin'." The woman left without waiting for a response.

Lester watched her return to her seat, and Maxie watched him. She knew he wanted to see if she was sitting in the company of other church members, ready to spread vicious tales. As they watched the woman sit comfortably next to her mother, who was the only person at her table, they were relieved.

Maxie turned her focus back to her plate and continued eating. Lester was now stirred and at any minute, it was all going to hit the fan. Peripherally, she saw him look around, and then lean in close.

"This isn't going to work Maxine," he almost whispered.

"Oh Lester, don't start!" She snapped, in an equally low voice. "Please don't let that woman ruin the evening."

"Ruin the evening? You ruined it when you didn't have dinner done. And you probably couldn't get it done because you were out running around, trying to find a job you don't need!"

Maxie calmly placed her fork in her plate, wiped her mouth with her napkin, and sat back in her chair. She knew it was inevitable that he should say something about dinner not being prepared, but she refused to defend herself at that moment. "I'm finished."

Seemingly out of nowhere, a waitress appeared next to her and made Maxie jump a little. "Would either of you like a cup of coffee?"

"No thank you," Lester replied dryly.

"None for me either," Maxie smiled. "Thank you." The waitress topped off Maxie's glass of tea. "Can I get anything else for you?"

"Nothing for me. Lester, do you want anything?"

"No, thank you. I'm fine."

"Very good," the waitress said, and laid the ticket on Lester's side of the table. "Thank you and come again soon."

When the waitress left, Lester remained silent and continued eating. Maxie was grateful for it. With the silent truce engaged between them, she rested her chin in her hand and looked around the restaurant. Seated at the table behind Lester, was a man and a woman with a little boy in a high-chair, who captured Maxie's attention. The toddler knocked over his drink, immediately laughed, and began to play in it. His giggle was so infectious, Maxie laughed a little too. Watching the small child play, took Maxie back to a thought she tucked away years ago.

The thought of having her own child.

In seven years of marriage, the topic of having children rarely came up, nor was it a prerequisite to Lester's marriage proposal. Perhaps it was a silent agreement between the two of them, because he would not ask questions about it, and she would not bring it up. But was this to be temporal or permanent? Maxie often wanted to ask Lester if he desired a son to carry on the Bruce name, but negated the question, for fear it might give the impression that she was interested in having one right away. Even though they never really sat down and talked about it, she could see herself giving Lester the greatest gift a woman could give a man.

"Why are you staring at me and smiling?" Lester asked skeptically.

Maxie shook her head. "I wasn't. I mean…I didn't know I was."

"You were," he countered.

Maxie looked at him, while he assessed her without blinking. She hated it when he stared at her that way. His face showed no emotion, but his eyes appeared to search her spirit for any form of sinful thoughts or deeds. He didn't do it often, but when he did, it made her feel uncomfortable and totally exposed.

Maxie broke away from the unwanted attention and looked around the restaurant, gently rubbing chill bumps on her arms.

"Are you cold?" Lester asked.

"A little bit," she said without looking at him.

Lester stared at her a moment longer. Raising his leg under the table, he gently rubbed it against the outside of her leg.

"I'm sorry about the way I acted," he said softly. "It was totally uncalled for. You didn't ruin the evening and I'm sorry I said that to you. Will you forgive me?"

Maxie rested her head in her hand again. It was her turn to scrutinize. The opportunity was there, but instead she just smiled. "I forgive you. I know that lady can get under your skin sometimes. She gets under everybody's skin."

"Well, I can't blame her either. I was a little perturbed before we got here."

"No," Maxie teased and widened her eyes.

She was grateful for Lester's apology and the immediate relief it brought. She was more grateful for the door that was now open to converse with him. Settling back into her seat, Maxie locked her fingers across her chest and sat with an air of resolute confidence.

"You didn't think I could do it did you?" She asked.

"What's that?"

"Get a job. You either thought I couldn't do it, or I wouldn't do it. Which one was it?"

Lester laughed at Maxie's adamant poise and the statement it implied. "I don't know. I guess a little bit of both. Maybe I didn't take you seriously when we first discussed it. And, I…"

"And you got upset when I moved forward *with* your permission."

Lester nodded. "With my permission. Yes, I guess I did get a little upset."

"But why Lester? We agreed it would only be for a few months. I promised you nothing would go undone at home."

"Those weren't the factors Maxie." Lester quickly studied the ticket the waitress left next to him. "It's just that I didn't weigh everything out before I answered you."

Lester's use of the words *'weigh everything out'* made her nervous. Was he trying to set her up to tell her he changed his mind because his decision was premature?

While waiting for the right words to ask him exactly what he meant, Maxie felt a flood of uneasiness settle in her stomach. How could she directly disobey her husband if he *did* change his mind? She had not given it much thought before, because she had no reason to. Everything came together better than she planned, until now. If Lester told her no in the beginning, how would she have executed the whole idea?

The sudden re-evaluation made Maxie wince at how weak her scheme was. There were too many holes, and not enough concrete answers to the *what ifs*. She would definitely have to rethink it all through, but not before she found out exactly what Lester meant. "Lester, does this mean you are going to…"

"I'm *going to* get some dessert. Do you want some?" He asked, pushing his chair back away from the table.

"I want to know if..,"

"Praise the Lord," a man's voice bellowed behind Maxie. "I thought I saw you two come in. It's good to see you and your lovely wife out tonight Minister Bruce. God bless ya."

Maxie turned slightly in her chair, to see the person behind the voice. It was Earl Bayer, one of the Deacons of the church.

Lester smiled broadly as he took the hand that was extended to him. "How are you doing this evening Deacon Earl?"

"Oh I'm fine now," he said as he patted the area that slightly hung over his belt. "Got myself a few victuals, and I'm ready to head on home now. And you Sister Bruce? How are you this fine evening?"

Maxie shook his hand and feigned a smile, feeling him give her an extra squeeze. She didn't particularly care for Deacon Earl Bayer, and doubted he was going straight home. He had a reputation among the women of the church, and it was not unfounded.

Earl Bayer was a ladies' man.

He was a good looking man — in his early sixties, with salt and pepper colored hair. He was stout in stature, with an upper-body that was indicative of weightlifting habits in his youth, and he was well-endowed with charm. Maxie knew it was his deep set brown eyes that usually captivated a woman. With this package, Earl Bayer had the profound ability to lead innocent women astray and he knew it. Oftentimes, Maxie would see him cavorting and flirting before, during, and after church services. Getting invites to a Sunday dinner at the home of a single woman, was his forte. As he stood next to Maxie, she reasoned that if she was simple-minded and not married, she could easily become a casualty of this man's ventures.

Letting go of her hand, Deacon Earl moved his hand to Maxie's back, and gently rubbed the area between her shoulders while he spoke. "You two don't normally dine out on a week night do you?" Deacon Earl asked.

"No. We just thought we'd do something a little different," Lester said, glancing at Maxie as he spoke.

Maxie silently questioned herself as to whether or not Lester noticed what Deacon Earl was doing, and how uncomfortable he was making her feel. She didn't really expect Lester to say anything, but she wanted him to look as if he disapproved.

"Are you dining alone Deacon?" Lester asked astutely.

Deacon Earl stopped rubbing Maxie's back, and placed his hand in his pocket. "Oh yeah," he said matter-of-factly. "Yeah, I came here straight from work. I think I'll go home and turn in early tonight."

Maxie quickly glanced at Lester and smiled with a bit of embarrassment. It was amusing how Deacon Earl felt he needed to explain his next move to them, as if for some reason they would need to give an account for his whereabouts. Lester kept his eyes on the Deacon, looking at him much like he had looked at her moments before.

"So Sister Bruce, how's that friend of yours? Sandra is her name right?" Deacon asked. "Is she doing all right?"

"Oh, yes. She's fine. She's doing real well," Maxie said, as she sipped her tea.

"Well you tell her I asked about her."

"I sure will."

Deacon Earl pulled his car keys from his pocket and extended a hand to Lester again. "I'm going on. I'll see you all at church Sunday morning."

"Bible study is tomorrow night," Lester said. "Won't you be there?"

"No. No, I have a meeting tomorrow night so I've been excused. But I'll see you Sunday. You all have a blessed evening. It was good to see you."

"Bye." Maxie piped.

Lester's eyes followed Deacon Earl until he left the restaurant. Quietly he sat for a moment, and then nodded his head to himself. "Doesn't it make you wonder how he's able to do it?"

Maxie put a crouton into her mouth with her fingers. "Do what?"

"Get away with all the mess he gets away with, and still be a church board member. He's the perfect example of that scripture in second Peter, the second chapter and the fourteenth verse. Having eyes full of adultery, and that cannot cease from sin; beguiling unstable souls."

Maxie waved nonchalantly. "I gave up wondering about that man years ago. Everybody knows how he is. I guess they're all used to it."

"That's just like him to ask about Sandra isn't it? I mean she's right up his alley. The type of woman he likes to go after."

"He likes to go after any woman Lester. Sandra is just the kind of woman he *can't* have. He obviously likes a challenge."

"A challenge?" The slightly raised pitch in his voice indicated to Maxie that he was amply ready to tackle this new topic of conversation. Sandra.

"Lester please don't." Maxie implored, with her eyes communicating her sincerity.

Lester sighed and wiped his hands with his napkin, placating and showing her that he wiped away the thought of both Deacon Earl and Sandra.

"Weren't you going to get some dessert?" She asked.

Lester took the next crouton Maxie was about to put into her mouth, and popped it into his own. "Naw. I've lost my taste for it now. And don't think I didn't notice that little back rub you were getting either."

Maxie smiled. He was paying attention.

Lester continued to make small talk, and she was tuned in to his words until her leg brushed up against her purse on the floor. Immediately, Maxie remembered the papers she placed inside, and her meeting with Sandra. A glance at her watch revealed she was forty-five minutes late.

"So, do you want to tell me about it?" Lester asked in a soft tone.

Maxie drank the remainder of her tea and frowned a little. "Tell you about what?"

"Your new job. Do you want to tell me about it?"

Maxie quickly scanned the restaurant. "What, right here? Right now?"

Lester set his eyes on her and did not move. Maxie was pensive for a few seconds. She was pleased Lester was showing an interest in her job, but having to discuss it right then and there would only make time wax further and further into the evening. With apprehension clouding her face, she glanced at her watch again and then released herself to engage in the details.

Maxie told Lester practically everything Mr. Martin explained to her about the job. She even described the portly man to him. As she recalled the entire interview and how nervous she was, Lester smiled lightly. It was a small gesture, but enough for Maxie to see for the first time tonight, he was sharing the moment with her.

It was around 8:30 p.m., when they finally left the restaurant. If Sandra had not given up waiting on her, she might as well. Their meeting would have to take place another time. No matter what excuse she could have come up with, there was no way Lester would agree to let her go out alone after dark.

When they were first married, Maxie tried hard to be receptive to Lester being so adamant about her going out unaccompanied at night. Receptive that is, until he raised his voice at her for something she deemed petty. The incident occurred one night in late fall when she was cooking dinner and ran out of seasoning salt. It was about 6:30 p.m., and Lester had just arrived home, and hopped in the shower. Rather than wait for him to get out and redress, Maxie left a note on the bedroom mirror telling him of her whereabouts, and quickly drove to the store herself. She was gone all of twenty-five minutes. When she returned home, Lester was standing in the middle of the kitchen floor fuming. At first Maxie thought maybe she accidentally left one of the burners on under a pot, and scorched part of the dinner. But it wasn't that at all. Lester raised his voice and railed on her because she left the house alone when it was dark outside. She wanted to feel flattered that her new husband was so concerned about her leaving unattended. She loved the thought of being doted over, but when Lester went on, Maxie realized his words were actually meant to be more contentious than affectionate. That made her angry. With all that was said, it didn't matter to him that it was yet early in the evening, or that it was dusk outside when she left, or that she was 27 years old and an adult. The fact was that she was out alone at night.

The confrontation was their first and last heated argument. When they both calmed down, Lester explained the reason for his outburst and apologized. That night, Maxie learned Lester's older sister was raped, on her way to a convenience store for ice cream. She asked Lester to go with her, but he opted to stay home to watch a basketball playoff game on television. The incident happened before she ever reached the store, which was only a block away from his family's home. Lester blamed himself, and vowed he would never allow another female in his household to go out alone after dark.

"You aren't listening to me are you?" Lester asked, as he pulled into the driveway.

"What?"

"I asked you about Sister Adams. What are you going to do about her and all the rest of the sick and shut-in people you care for?"

Maxie looked at Lester and nibbled on her bottom lip. Once again, she hadn't thought that far in advance. She needed to be careful not to answer him too quickly. For the first time, she felt like maybe she needed to reconsider some things. Maybe even reconsider the whole plan. There were so many loose ends, and it seemed with every issue that arose, another end unraveled.

Unfastening her seatbelt, she quickly got out of the car, and retreated down the driveway to the mailbox. Lester watched her until she returned midway, before he walked ahead to unlock the front door.

"Well?" He asked, allowing her to pass into the house before him. "Did you even think about that?"

Without answering, Maxie turned on the table lamp. Before sitting on the couch, she risked glancing at Lester, fearing he would be standing at the door looking at her. Relieved, she saw he wasn't. Instead, Lester locked the door and continued into the bedroom — leaving his question hanging in the air. Maxie was glad she did not respond right away. The answer was definitely going to take some thought. Somehow, she felt Lester knew that, and was giving her time to figure it all out.

Heavily distracted by her thoughts, Maxie tried to turn her attention to the bundle of envelopes in her hand, but it wasn't working. Patting her knee, she wished there was something to take her mind off the question at hand. *What was she going to do about Sister Adams and the other sick and shut-in?*

Chapter Six

"You know, you need a real man in your life," Maxie said whimsically, while repeatedly turning her coffee mug around on the kitchen table.

Sandra reached into the cabinet and retrieved a small bag of imported gourmet flavored coffee. "I have French Almond Mocha. Will that do?"

Maxie shrugged. "I don't care. I'm not a big fan of flavored coffees anyway." Maxie turned her cup around one last time. With elbows on the table, she clasped her hands under her chin and rested her head.

Sandra's home was a huge, beautifully restored row house in the Historic District on Gaston Street. With refurbished homes that were over 100 years old, the entire neighborhood was a major attraction for tourists. It was so like her to want to live in the center of attention. Maxie felt Sandra purchased far more house than she needed being single, but she always insisted on having nothing less than the best. And why shouldn't she? Being the Senior Buyer at Intex Systems, Georgia's largest electronics company, she could afford whatever she wanted.

The kettle on the stove sounded its readiness, and startled Maxie. Sandra stood in front of her, and carefully dished the powdery substance into Maxie's cup.

"What was that you said about a man?" Sandra asked.

Maxie shrugged. "Nothing. I just said you need one."

Sandra quickly retrieved the tea kettle and poured the water into their cups. "I'll thank you to know that I have men in my life Mrs. Bruce."

"That's plural Sandra. I'm speaking in the singular text."

Sandra sat down and sipped her coffee, before she winked at Maxie. "But plural is more fun."

Maxie laughed and shook her head.

"Besides, I'm not ready to settle down with any one man just yet. There is no rush. Now do you want a Macadamia Biscotti? They're made by Godiva."

"No, I'm fine," Maxie said, glancing up from her cup with half a smile.

"So how did you get over here?" Sandra asked. "I'm surprised you remembered the way."

"I drove. You know, I *can* do that."

"You know what I mean. Where did you tell Lester you were going this morning? I know you didn't tell him you were coming here."

"He had to work today," Maxie smiled. "So there was no need for an explanation."

"Since when did he start working on Saturdays?" Sandra lifted her eyebrows.

"Since he got his raise. They added a couple more duties to his job description, and he may just have to work two or three Saturdays a month. So, he'll be out of the house more and...so will I."

Sandra looked at Maxie and chuckled with a sense of uneasiness. "I don't think I like that sound in your voice. Your last words sounded so mischievous. I bet Lester's new hours just gave you another game piece to your plan didn't it?"

Maxie shrugged. She hadn't really given much thought to the new convenience, but its potential spread a large grin on her face. "I think I can make it work to my advantage."

Sandra rested against the back of her chair. With her index finger over her mouth, she gazed at her friend. "You're really going to do this aren't you?"

Maxie sipped her coffee and looked at Sandra squarely. "You doubted me?"

"Well honestly I thought, or I should say I hoped, this whole idea was just a phase or something you had to go through before you..."

"Before I came to my senses?"

"Well..."

"I'm going to do this Sandra. I need to do this."

The two women were silent. Caught up in the moment, Maxie stared at the table transfixed. "It's like an appetite that needs to be satisfied, you know? I mean, it started out small and now it's bigger than I am." Maxie forwarded a glance to Sandra, in hope of viewing sympathy for her situation. "Can you understand that?"

Sandra sat motionless, and then nodded in agreement. It was clear Maxie needed *somebody* to identify with her feelings. It might as well be her. Slapping her hands together, Sandra leaned forward. "So let's get started filling out that paperwork."

"Okay," Maxie smiled.

Sandra looked on, hearing but not really listening, as Maxie went on about how complicated some of the papers were to her. The friend she loved like a sister, was entering a world she knew nothing about. Sandra would have to be there; at least in the beginning. Not just for moral support, but to guide Maxie in the right direction — if there was such a direction.

Sandra explained each form and its purpose, as they filled them out. When they finished, she encouraged Maxie to explain it all back to her, and she did perfectly.

"Okay, well, I think we're done with this." Sandra said. "If you don't mind me saying, I think it's a shame you've never held a job before now. It's like your grandmother had this preconceived notion that no matter what, you were going to be married to a good man who was going to take care of you."

"And she didn't die *until* I was married to one. I believe she prayed for that," Maxie said solemnly between sips. "My grandmother always meant well. She just hindered me a little."

"Hindered?" Sandra piped. "You mean *deprived* don't you?"

Maxie slightly lifted the corners of her mouth. "Like I said, she meant well."

Sandra smirked. She wanted to hit Maxie with a quippy rebuttal, but sat quietly instead. It was obvious the time Maxie spent with her grandmother, produced ardent memories she held dear. Sandra remembered Maxie telling her stories about her childhood and how there was a time when she hardly even knew her grandmother. Outside of the usual annual family visits in the summertime, and the occasional phone calls, she knew very little about her. Even after her mother filled her with lessons of family history, Maxie said she was too young to remember a lot of it. The only words she grasped whenever her mother spoke of *Grandma*, were Gullah-Geechee, and she only remembered those because they were funny to her. Every time her mother recited the family heritage to her and those words came up, Maxie recalled bursting into raucous laughter and falling on the floor yelling Gullah-Geechee, Gullah-Geechee. Her persistence was soon halted by a forceful swat to her rear.

Sandra learned that even though Maxie and her grandmother were as distant as the miles that separated them, the calamity of losing both of her parents in a car accident with a drunk driver, soon closed the breach and caused them to come together when Maxie was only nine. As chance would have it, Maxie was in the care of a babysitter that awful night. The babysitter reluctantly turned her over to Child Protective Services, when her parents didn't return home the next morning; accusing them of abandonment. After the social worker learned the fate of her parents, and all of the attempts to notify her next of kin proved futile, young Maxie was deemed an orphan and a ward of the state. She didn't realize until she was older, that the search for her family members never went beyond her native state of New York. They barely searched the city of Brooklyn where her family resided and where she was born. Even though both of her parents were from 'only child' families, no one even bothered asking her if she had any relatives in town or out of town. Maybe they felt she was too grief stricken to give them any credible information. Or maybe they thought she was just too young. Nevertheless, two days before she was to be transferred from a group home to a foster home, her grandmother showed up at the Child

Protective Service office with her birth certificate in hand, seeking custody of her. When her grandmother arrived at the group home, the overwhelming relief of finally seeing a familiar face moved Maxie to tears. The social worker mistook those tears to mean that she was terrified of her grandmother, and erroneously accused her of abuse, delaying the turnover of custody. Things were finally ironed out, when Maxie had a chance to answer questions that should have been asked in the beginning.

Maxie was too young back then, to understand the sacrifices her grandmother was willing to make in the winter of her life. Without a second thought, Ma Dear (a name Maxie later called her which was short for "Mother Dear") assumed the custodial position. By societal standards, she was far too old for such a role, but by her own standard of love, she embraced it.

Though her grandmother hated New York, they stayed with a distant cousin in Manhattan until the court proceedings were over. Ma Dear explained to Maxie that she would be taking her to Savannah, Georgia to live with her. Maxie hated the idea of leaving New York, but at the age of nine and with no other alternatives, she had to give in to her grandmother's reasoning.

"How did you know to come and get me Grandma? Who told you?" Maxie asked when they were waiting at the Greyhound bus station. It dawned on her that if CPS could not find any of her relatives near or far, how did her grandmother know about her and the fate of her parents?

"Nobody told me child," her grandmother said without looking at her. "I saw that you were all alone."

Maxie sat quietly for a moment, while she dangled her feet back and forth. "But where did you see me?"

Her grandmother looked at her and winked. Then she spoke in the softest tone. "I saw you in my mind, but I felt you in my heart."

Maxie slowly nodded that she understood and sat back in her seat. After only a moment, she opened her mouth to phrase yet another question, only to be silenced by her grandmother's fingers over her mouth.

"Shhh child. You will understand when you get older."

Maxie remembered watching the picturesque urban skyline of New York, change to the worn antiquated structures of Savannah. From the time she stepped off the Greyhound bus in Savannah, Georgia, she vowed she would never like the southern city. But Savannah returned more to Maxie then she cared to give it credit for. Not only did it house a fair amount of Georgia's colonial coastal history, it also offered a large window to the history of her mother's side of the family. The Saltwater Geechees.

Maxie ultimately learned that her grandmother was raised on a remote sea island called Sapelo, in Georgia, and that the Gullah-Geechees were an enslaved people brought to coastal South Carolina and Georgia, from West Africa to work the cotton and rice crops. The word Gullah possibly deriving from the country Angola in Africa, and Geechee, possibly originating from the tribal name Kissi sometimes pronounced Geegee. Still, others believe the word Geechee came from the River Ogeechee in Georgia.

Over the years the culture steadily eroded, but the attempt to keep its customs flourishing, rested in continual recitation and demonstration to the younger generations. And Ma Dear recited and demonstrated to the fullest, even speaking to Maxie oftentimes in the Gullah dialect. The unique sound of the Gullah language, which was comprised of restructured English and various African languages, seemingly rolled off the tongue of her grandmother. By the time Maxie was eleven, she could talk the talk, dance the dances, and make the special West African designed baskets of palmetto and sweet grass. Little was to be gained when it came to her knowledge of the Gullah-Geechees. She warmly embraced it, primarily because it helped to fill the void she felt concerning her mother. She needed to feel more connected to her somehow, and knowing the history of the 'Saltwater Geechees' was paramount. However, Maxie did not share all of their spiritual beliefs, and part of her reasoning was based on one instance that remained firm in her memory. That was the day her grandmother took her to church.

Maxie was always in tow whenever her grandmother went to church. Because few children her age went to this particular church, Maxie was often seeking ways to keep herself entertained, no matter how simple the activity. Sitting on a pew one Sunday morning, she spent most of the service looking up at the ceiling. Ma Dear was already kneeling and praying. Opening one eye, she got Maxie's attention by firmly patting her on the leg.

"Pray Maxine," she whispered.

"Ma Dear," Maxie whispered back. "How come they painted the ceiling a different color than the walls? How come it's blue?"

"It keeps the evil spirits away," she said matter-of-factly. "Now get on down here with me and let's pray they stay away."

In her young mind, Maxie grew fearful. She quickly snuggled next to her grandmother on the floor, frequently looking up at that ceiling. She was no longer intrigued by the color of it, but by the purpose of the color. For the following years, Maxie envisioned little demons flying outside above the church, desperately wanting to get inside, but being repelled by a blue ceiling.

It was explanations like these that made it hard for Maxie to believe her grandmother's stories of phantasm. Stories that spoke of spirits of the dead, walking through barred doors and walls of homes, to terrorize the occupants. Many of the Geechees believed when a person died, their spirit lingered behind trees to speak to the living. Some mourners would even go as far as putting glassware and clocks on gravesites, for the dead to use in their next life if they *crossed da ribber to de udder side*. Oftentimes, to make sure they stayed there, something meaningful from the deceased person's life would be put on the grave, so that their spirit would not come back to retrieve it. Maxie considered it all to be cultural fiction and tales told by the older Geechees, to keep the younger ones in line. To her surprise, despite her grandmother's commitment to the Christian faith, she would revert and hold fast to this particular part of her culture. No matter how much she was made to listen to the stories, Maxie never believed a word of it. There was no way she would ever believe in ghosts.

"...So what do you think? Would you like to go?" Sandra asked, cutting in on Maxie's thoughts.

"What?" Maxie lightly shook her head from the reverie. "I'm sorry. I didn't hear you? What did you say?"

Sandra sat with her elbows on the table, resting her head on her hands. "You know, you've been taking entirely too many mental trips lately. You sit there like you're in a trance or something."

Maxie looked down into her cup and found it near empty. She didn't even remember drinking that much of her coffee. "What did you ask me?"

"The Jazz Festival, I asked you if you wanted to go with me."

Maxie took the last swallow from her cup, and gently pushed it away. "The one they have outside at Forsyth Park every year?"

"That's the one." Sandra crooned, snapping her fingers over her head while she swayed to music only she could hear. "Three days of loud rhythmic music played by the best old and new professional jazz artists. Boney James is a featured artist this year. Girl, I love his music. Anyway, it's not happening until the end of this month, so that gives you enough time to plan. So what do you think? Feel like slippin' out?" Sandra chuckled lightly, her laughter carrying more in it than just humor. Her question sounded more like a dare than an invitation.

The Jazz Festival was nothing new to Maxie. She knew almost everything there was to know about the free event, except the performing artists. There were performances every hour on the hour, from Thursday through Saturday.

Maxie shrugged. "I don't know. I may have to work those days."

"You said the latest they would have you scheduled would be until five. The concert series doesn't start til seven. Come on girl."

Maxie studied the table a moment, before looking at Sandra. "Let me think about it."

"All right, don't think too long. I'm already doing you a favor by inviting you. You know it's not my style to be in the company of anything less than a fine hunk of male specimen, especially during a jazz concert."

Maxie smiled softly and gave Sandra a look that said *I know.*

"When do you actually start that job anyway?"

"Wednesday, for training."

"So I guess you'll be spending the next few days making those little quick fix meals to put in the freezer huh?"

"No, actually, I think I'll be spending my time tying up some loose ends. I need to visit the sick and shut-in, and Siemen's Nursing Home on Tuesday, so that leaves me with this evening and Monday to cook for the week."

"I gather going out to eat is out of the question?" Sandra asked, taking a swallow of coffee.

"Not unless it's on a Sunday. I can get away with it then. Lester figures since I cook all week, I should rest on the seventh day."

The two women laughed softly at the Biblical pun, while Sandra slid Maxie's employment papers across the table to her. "Here, put those back in your purse."

Maxie took the papers and rolled them up. When she put them in her purse, a large grin spread across her face. "Speaking of eating out, Deacon Earl asked about you this past Tuesday night."

Sandra frowned and took a long draw of her coffee. As she swallowed, her eyes roamed the table as if she were looking for the person Maxie spoke of. "Deacon Earl? Earl Bayer?" She asked incredulously.

Maxie laughed a little and shook her head. "He was at the Brass Bell and wanted you to know that he asked about you."

"Girl please!"

"You must have really made some kind of impression on him. What did you do to the man Sandra?"

Without a word, Sandra stood up to collect their dishes and set them on the counter. On her way back to the table, Maxie saw her countenance change from a frown of deep thought, to a broad grin.

"You remember that time, a while back, when I visited your church?"

"The *one* time you came?" Maxie asked acerbically, before Sandra waved her off.

"Earl was part of your church's Welcoming Committee."

Maxie grimaced. "Sandra, Deacon Earl was never a part of the church Welcoming Committee."

"Well he was on this particular day. Anyway, he asked me if he could take me out to dinner, and fill me in on the wonderful programs and activities your church had for sinners like me."

Maxie's eyes widened. "He said that?"

"Naw, I added the sinner part," Sandra smiled. "But he did ask me out."

"You never told me that."

"Well, I felt you would have been embarrassed to know one of your Deacons was trying to get his groove on with someone you invited to church."

Sandra was right. Even now, Maxie felt embarrassed. She nodded her head at Deacon Earl's audacity. Even though she and all the church members knew about his frolics, she thought he would at least have the common decency to spare the visitors. Maxie wondered how many more women were targeted before they could even become a member of the congregation. How many of them, who were not as strong willed as Sandra, actually came seeking God for help with their needs; only to be greeted by someone with a false sense of caring and a hidden agenda.

"So, did you go out with him?" Maxie asked timidly, not really wanting to know the answer.

Sandra looked at her with all sincerity and spoke with a tweak of irony. "Why do you think he asked about me?"

Maxie lowered her eyes in astonishment. The answer made her instantly regard how she defended Sandra's character that night at the restaurant, when Lester was ready to slice it up. Had she been wrong in doing so? She knew Sandra rarely went out on dates without a motive. If she went out with Deacon Earl Bayer, the motive was definitely one that was physical maintenance oriented. There was nothing else he could possibly offer her.

"I'm probably the only one he *couldn't* conquer. Naturally he would ask about me," Sandra said.

Maxie looked up quickly to see Sandra sitting with a self-righteous grin on her face.

"Now don't get me wrong, Earl Bayer is a good looking man, and I did lead him on... and on...and on," Sandra laughed. "But he's not my type."

Maxie chuckled a little too, and let out what she wanted to be a subtle sigh of relief.

"Maxine Bruce," Sandra shrieked. I heard that!"

"What?"

"You thought I slipped to an all-time low by getting it on with the Deacon!"

"Well, you made it sound like..."

"Never mind what it sounded like. You're supposed to be my girl. Believe in me at all times. Right or wrong."

"I know. Can you ever forgive me?" Maxie asked whimsically.

Sandra pointed her index finger at Maxie in the way of a reprimand. Amused, Maxie laughed again and comfortably rested her head on the back of her chair. Unintentionally, it brought the clock on the wall in to view. It was 2:45 p.m., and Maxie moaned.

"Time to go already?" Sandra asked.

Standing up, Maxie verified the time on her wristwatch. "I'm afraid so. I have a long list of things I need to get done before Wednesday, so everything will flow together when I start working."

"That's right. I guess the next time I see you, you'll be among the working class huh?"

"If the Lord says the same," Maxie voiced, before she realized what she was saying. The biblical phrase spewed out erratically, perhaps out of habit, or worse yet, out of conviction. Whatever the case, Maxie knew paraphrasing the words from the book of James, chapter 5 verse 15, undoubtedly meant, *if it was the Lord's will*. Knowing her true motives were nowhere near the path of the straight and narrow, she was instantly rapt in guilt. But just as quick as it came, Maxie dismissed the untimely assessment.

"So, you call me if you need me okay," Sandra said, as they walked to the front door. "Anything you don't under-stand, just give me a ring and I'll help you out."

"I'm hoping everything will go well, but if I do run into something confusing, I will call you."

The two women stood at the door facing each other. With nothing between them but air and silence, Sandra observed her friend wholly. With a faint smile, she shook her head.

"Phew girl. I know I've said it before, but you're *really* doing this."

Maxie smiled and nodded.

"Well, anyway, don't forget to let me know if you want to go to the Festival."

"I will. I'll probably call you on Wednesday to let you know how my first day went."

"You do that."

Hugging her friend tightly, Maxie hoped to convey her sincere gratitude to Sandra for just being there whenever she needed her. It was important to have her own connection to the *world*. Who better to fit the bill than Sandra? Willing and able.

Finally, Maxie opened the door and quickly walked down the steps to her car. "Thanks for your help," she called over her shoulder. "I'll talk to you soon."

Chapter Seven

M axie squinted against the sunlight that occasionally broke between the trees, as she drove down Gaston Avenue. Even though the sun was bright, she found it offered nothing to the crisp coolness in the air, especially after leaving the cozy warmth of Sandra's place. Heading toward Midtown down Abercorn Street, traffic was heavier than normal for a Saturday, and it made Maxie wish she had started making dinner before she left home. The chances of beating Lester there were virtually slim to none, since she didn't know what time he was getting off. Pressing her eyes closed, Maxie clenched her teeth, and firmly pushed her head against the headrest of her seat. Her anxiety mounted when she envisioned Lester sitting somewhere in the house, waiting for her to come through the door; expecting a very good explanation as to why dinner wasn't ready *this* time. Shaking her head, she sighed heavily and turned on some music. "Whatever happens, happens," she said aloud.

Soon the mellow sound of gospel singer Yolanda Adams's *Open My Heart* filled her ears. Maxie listened to the message in the lyrics, and how they beckoned her to consider a new mindset. There was even a convicting awareness that the song was right in its suggestion to seek the Lord for guidance. However, to follow that direction was not where Maxie wanted to go, so she turned the music off.

When she finally pulled into her driveway, she released the steering wheel and was immediately liberated from the tension that flowed throughout her body. Lester was not home. Even though she should have made haste to get inside the house, Maxie took a moment to look in the rearview mirror. Though it pained her to be honest with herself, she was a woman in crisis. In her own eyes, she no longer favored the woman she spent her life becoming. She was always pleasing, always soft-spoken, and quick to concur on every issue that rendered itself debatable. In a final consensus, it was warranted; things would definitely have to change.

Chapter Eight

Visiting Sister Adams at Siemen's Nursing Home was always more than a casual visit for Maxie. It was an opportunity to monitor, and make sure all things were correct and in order where Sister Adams was concerned. When she approached the nurse's station, the nurse immediately greeted Maxie with a fake smile, and a great amount of over exuberance.

"Good Morning! How may I help you?"

"Good Morning. I'm here to see Ruby Adams," Maxie replied.

"Oh okay. Great! Well, Ms. Adams will be brought right out to see you. She can't receive visitors in her room just now, because she's had a little accident. As soon as they finish cleaning her up, she will be wheeled out into the lobby to visit with you."

The petite woman reinforced her smile, and quickly moved away from Maxie to sit in front of a computer. Moving a couple of steps closer, Maxie leaned into the nurse's view.

"I'd rather visit with her in her room. I can wait until they sanitize it."

The woman looked at Maxie indifferently and forced a tainted smile. It was obvious she didn't like her authority being challenged, even if that was not what Maxie intended.

"You're new aren't you?" Maxie asked plainly, with a slight smile.

"I've been in Geriatrics for ten years," the woman answered matter-of-factly.

"But you're new to *this* facility."

"Well let's see, today is Tuesday, I've been here at Siemen's Nursing Home for about a week now."

The woman spoke with such a bite, Maxie just knew the words *if it's any of your business,* hung invisibly at the end of her response. Yet facetiously, Maxie kept her smile and extended her hand to her.

"I'm Maxie Bruce. I'm a regular around here. I didn't visit last week, which must have been when you started."

The woman hesitantly took Maxie's hand, but refused to fully clasp it. She also refused to offer her name in return. The fact that she didn't have on a name badge, was enough for Maxie to launch a complaint. Giving the nurse a firm grip, Maxie looked behind the woman and winked at a handsome young male orderly standing against the wall, observing part of their conversation.

"You here making trouble again Maxie?" He asked, giving her a beautiful dimpled grin, as he walked toward her.

"Somebody needs to bring some life into this place." Maxie released the nurse and moved to the end of the counter, where she placed her hands into the hands of the orderly. "How are you doing Brian?"

"I'm doing good, doing good. How are you? You know, I missed you last week."

"Yeah? I had a little business I needed to take care of."

"All week?" Brian asked skeptically.

"What can I say? I guess I got a little side-tracked."

"Side-tracked huh? I thought you were trying to avoid me."

Maxie frowned and smiled. "Why would I do that?"

Brian looked around quickly and lowered his voice a little. "I thought I scared you off with that question I asked. You know. The one you so conveniently never answered."

Maxie stared at him quizzically. "Brian, I don't ..."

"It was lunch Maxie. When are you going to let me take you to lunch?"

Surprised and relieved, she laughed a little. "Was that the question?"

"The fact that you don't remember, tells me you didn't take me seriously."

Maxie giggled sheepishly. The thought of a younger man requesting her company for lunch or any other engagement was flattering. Had she been about ten years younger and single, Brian would never have to ask her twice. He was extremely attractive, and terribly misplaced working at Siemen's Nursing Home.

Brian, a transplant from a nursing home in Macon, Georgia, could easily get a job modeling some designer's clothing line. Because he had thick black curly hair, which he wore in a small Afro, Maxie figured he was biracial. He appeared to be African American, with either Mexican or Indian features. Whatever the combination, she found him captivating. That alone made his proposition extremely tempting. However, Maxie sought an astute way to decline his invitation; even though deep down she really didn't want to.

Innocent as it was, Brian's request spawned a feeling in the pit of her stomach that was strange and stimulating. It awakened something in her. The feeling was so out of the norm, that she could only liken it to something sinful. A forbidden excitement. Prior to the moment, she cut down the kind of thoughts that carried those feelings. Albeit, she wanted to know what it was like to be in the company of another man.

A man other than Lester.

Brian licked his lips, and brought Maxie's attention to the dimples that always appeared with the slightest movement of his mouth. Lowering her eyes, she spoke regretfully, knowing that having lunch with him would not look right to anyone who knew her, even if it was platonic.

"Brian you know I'm married."

Brian released her hands and gently lifted her chin, bringing them eye-to-eye. "I'm only asking for lunch. Not an affair."

Maxie smiled lightly and took a deep breath. "Can I get back with you on that?"

"Only if you promise me you're not going to avoid me."

"I don't think I could ever do that. I would never avoid you."

Hearing his name being called, Brian looked over Maxie's shoulder. The same nurse Maxie had spoken with earlier, was standing at the other end of the counter interrupting their conversation.

"You're needed in Mr. Connoly's room," the nurse said.

"That man is relentless," Brian mumbled. "Every other day he lets us know how much he hates it here, because we won't let him smoke cigarettes in his room." Brian grabbed and squeezed both of Maxie's hands. "I hope to see you before you leave today. But if I don't, there's always next week right?"

Maxie started to answer, but then remembered her new job and the main purpose for her visit. She was there to explain to Sister Adams that her visiting hours would vary from time to time, and hoped she would understand. Now that her presence on next week was being questioned, she wanted to explain the same thing to Brian. Even though she knew he would be happy for her, and probably insist all the more that she have lunch with him on a celebratory note, it was best left unsaid.

"Right," Maxie said. "There's always next week."

Brian winked at her, as he released her hands and began walking down the hallway. "I'll talk to you soon," he called to her.

Maxie watched as Brian met with another orderly further down the hallway. Making long quick strides, he turned the corner and was out of sight. Standing still a moment longer, she stared down the empty hallway. If only she were ten years younger — and single.

Maxie sighed, and seated herself in the reception area, directly across from the nurse's station. Content to wait, she focused her attention on the flow of geriatric traffic. A few of the elderly residents lounged around the lobby. Some sat transfixed on a couch in front of a large colored television, while others walked around with walkers or sat motionless in wheelchairs. This place was designed to be their home, quite possibly for the remainder of their days.

Whenever Maxie visited, she made it a point to keep it short and sweet. It was depressing to see people she once observed working and functioning in the church, become incapable of caring for themselves. It was hard for her to understand it all, because the scriptures stated that long life on the earth was a reward for obedience. What good was it if the person was not in their right mind, or didn't have control of their faculties when the reward came?

"Why would God keep you around just so you could be bed-ridden and senile?" She once asked her grandmother, in reference to a great uncle.

"The Lord just will keep His promises," her grand-mother answered then. Later she said, "Who can question His ways?"

Maxie never got a concrete answer to her question, and every time she visited the elderly, that lurking question would always grip her. It was also the main reason she felt she needed to be there. The elderly needed someone to talk to. Someone who cared.

Maxie looked at the clock on the wall behind the nurse's station. Thirty minutes had passed. When she approached the counter again, the nurse she had spoken with earlier looked at her and smiled smugly.

"Oh Mrs. Bruce, you're still here."

"I've been here for quite a while now," Maxie said calmly.

"I am so sorry. I didn't see you sitting there. They called for you fifteen minutes ago. Ms. Adams has been waiting to see you."

Maxie looked down her nose at the woman and then at the chair she was just sitting in, directly across from the station. Not wanting to play the tit for tat game the nurse started, Maxie pleasantly told her thank you and walked down the east wing to Sister Adams's room. Standing in the doorway, she peeked into the room before entering. The strong smell of an unknown disinfectant, met her as she stepped inside the small foyer. The curtains that hung from the ceiling to surround the bed were drawn halfway on both sides, partially concealing the person in the bed. So Maxie tiptoed further inside, and lightly tapped on the bathroom door with her knuckles.

"Yes," a small voice squeaked from behind the curtains.

Maxie smiled to herself, walked over to the bed, and slowly pulled back the curtain.

"Well you just took your sweet time getting on in here to see me didn't you?" The old woman smiled once she laid eyes on Maxie. "I was getting ready to go on back to sleep, figuring you were out there somewhere keeping that cute young orderly company."

Maxie bent over and kissed Sister Adams on her cheek, and stroked her hair. "Sister Adams, he's ten years younger than I am."

"Uh huh. What's age got to do with it? Chile, age is just a matter of the mind. If you don't mind, age don't matter!"

Maxie burst into laughter, as she repositioned a chair next to the bed. "Listen to you! Did you forget I'm married?"

Sister Adams frowned at Maxie's words, and spoke a little slower. "That's right. You sure are. Honey you know I'm old. Don't pay me no never mind. How is your husband?"

"Lester is fine," Maxie said, offering his name as a reminder. Before she sat in the chair, Maxie pressed a button to adjust the head of Sister Adams's bed, to an upright position. The old woman arduously pulled herself up a little, to align her back with the mattress.

"Either my body is getting heavier, or my arms are getting weaker," Sister Adams huffed.

"Have you been exercising at all since I saw you last?"

"Chile, the most exercising I do, is to stroll with my walker from this wing to the west wing. It's starting to get too cool for me to go outdoors now."

Maxie propped her feet up on a small step stool next to the bed. Giving the room a quick once over, she could tell Sister Adams had not seen many visitors since her last visit. If she had, it would be signified by numerous plants and cards set up proudly on display. Sister Adams only had three. There were two bouquets of cheap withering flowers, and a small Philodendron plant with a Mylar balloon attached to it, proclaiming *We Love You.* All of which sat on a small table under the room's only window. It was customary for a visitor to bring something to liven up the room. With that not being evident, Maxie wanted to believe more people actually *had* visited, but simply came empty handed.

Sister Adams quickly rubbed the palms of her hands against her thighs, and nearly whispered. "Did you bring me that *real* chocolate I asked you for?"

"Sister Adams, you know you're not supposed to be eating anything sweet because of your diabetes," Maxie warned, refusing to whisper. "Chocolate is definitely not on your dietary list of foods to eat."

"Well it should be," Sister Adams mumbled. "Everything I eat here is either sugar-free, or low in carbohydrates. It's just a down right shame. I'm an old woman with few perks in my life. They need to give me what makes me happy sometime."

"I agree," Maxie said softly. "That's why I brought you these." In the palm of her hand, Sister Adams saw a small gold colored tin box. Gently, she took if from Maxie and unwrapped it. "They're Whitman Sampler chocolates, and there are only four pieces in the box. That should be enough to kill your craving and keep you healthy."

"Yes. Praise God," Sister Adams whispered, before she filled her mouth with one of the tiny confections. "Mmmmm."

Maxie smiled and watched as Sister Adams seemingly slipped away, shutting her out of her world of sweet euphoria. Resuming her quick inspection of the room, she was pleased with how clean it was. With her starting work, she briefly wondered who was going to take on the responsibility of seeing to Sister Adams's needs. Could she entrust someone else at the church to do it, and feel good about the person she selected? Sister Adams was special.

The widow of a deacon in the church, Sister Adams was different from the other shut-ins Maxie visited. Different because she and Maxie shared a bond, and Maxie *loved* her like she loved her own grandmother. Ironically, their relationship blossomed immediately after her grandmother died. Six months into her marriage to Lester at the time, Sister Adams felt Maxie still needed a maternal figure to guide her, and keep her versed on life's lessons, and life as a minister's wife. Maxie didn't mind the extra attention, especially after she surmised that Sister Adams really needed *her*, because she had no children of her own and was lonely. Despite the reasoning, the two grew close.

No. The decision to leave Sister Adams in the hands of someone else definitely was not going to be an easy one. Glancing at the elderly woman again, she had only hoped it would not be this hard.

Maxie looked up at the television mounted on the wall, hoping to lose her current thoughts, but there was no volume. "Sister Adams, why is your TV on mute?" Maxie asked, keeping her eyes on the television.

"So you can have my full attention."

Maxie quickly looked at Sister Adams and found her staring at her.

"You have something you want to say to me? Like maybe why you didn't come to see me last week."

"I did call you and visit with you over the phone."

"That's not the same thing. And even then, you never told me your reason for not coming."

Maxie turned her wedding ring around on her finger a few times. All of her well-rehearsed words, gathered together and retreated heavily to the pit of her stomach. What she needed from Sister Adams was her proverbial stamp of approval on the *work* issue. Why? She didn't know. It was not like her approval, or disapproval was going to be a determining factor on anything. Maxie just wanted to hear it.

"The reason I didn't come was because I was applying for, well rather, I got myself a job last week. And because I'll be working, I may not be able to come and visit with you every week like I normally do. It's only a part-time job, but in keeping up with my duties at home, I don't believe I'll have much free time on my hands."

Maxie could not bear to see Sister Adams's reaction once her words registered. Instead, she averted her gaze by looking at a couple of dust bunnies under the bed. When silence crept in and quickly filled the room, Maxie grew uncomfortable. When she finally looked at Sister Adams, she was met with the same simple gaze as before. There was no scrutinizing stare. No instant look of disappointment. Nothing.

"Are you and your husband in financial need?"

Maxie tried to choose her words carefully. "No ma'am. You see I…"

Before she could finish explaining her plans, Sister Adams held up her hand for Maxie to stop talking.

"You?" She asked, making Maxie feel like she said something wrong. "You?" Sister Adams nodded her head as if Maxie had confirmed the obvious in some prior thought she had. "Hand me my Bible over there on that table." Maxie did as she was told. "Now I'm going to read you something I know you've heard before. It may not mean anything different to you now, than it did the first time you read or heard it, but later on, these words are going to pierce your very soul. I'm reading to you from the gospel of Luke, the fourth chapter, verses eighteen and nineteen. *The Spirit of the Lord is upon me, because He hath anointed me to preach the gospel to the poor; He hath sent me to heal the broken-hearted, to preach deliverance to the captives, and recovering of sight to the blind, to set at liberty them that are bruised, to preach the acceptable year of the Lord."*

Sister Adams closed her Bible and looked at Maxie lovingly. She was right. Maxie had read and heard that scripture expounded on, but just as Sister Adams said, it meant nothing to her personally.

"Now, can you tell me that your reason for getting this *job*, is to help you accomplish this purpose?"

Sister Adams tapped lightly on her Bible, and Maxie glanced at it before she lowered her eyes again. What did she expect? Deep down, she knew Sister Adams was going to go to the Bible to use the Word of God against her. Is that what was needed? A motherly kind of reprimand? A spiritual chastening for wanting to do things her way?

"Sister Adams, that's not *my* purpose." Maxie replied softly. Her words hung in the air heavily, as a brief moment of silence fell between them again.

"What do you mean *this* is not *your* purpose?" Sister Adams frowned deeply. "Maxie, how can you form your lips to say that? You are a child of God, a born again believer, and the wife of a minister." She slapped her hand down on her Bible. "This *is* your purpose. And it's *your* time to fulfill it."

Sister Adams paused for a moment and took a deep breath, releasing it through her nose. Maxie understood it to be a breath of disappointment. Repositioning herself in her chair, she sat quietly while Sister Adams appeared to gather her thoughts.

"Maxie, the world is calling to you again with its many offerings, just as it has in times past. At those times you did what was right. You ignored it. But this time, you are choosing to answer it and your answer is wrong baby. Doing what *you* want to do is not your purpose in this life." Sister Adams smiled at her tenderly. "Maxie, you were chosen by God to carry His word in your mouth to people who need Him, just like this scripture says. There are brokenhearted people, wounded people, people who are lost, and people who feel unloved. Then there are those who are bound by their past. All of these kinds of people need to know about Jesus, and how He alone can help them and free their hearts and minds. You are one of the few He has chosen to tell them. *God* is calling you Maxie, and to fulfill divine purpose, you have to answer when you're called."

Maxie kept her head lowered as her eyes filled with tears. For the first time, she felt torn. Part of her received and embraced what was being said, because she knew the words to be true. Another part of her desperately turned it all away, recognizing it as a deterrent to keep her from fulfilling her personal desire. She wanted to say something in her own defense. She needed to explain. But when she finally looked up, Sister Adams focused her attention somewhere by the door.

"It's time for your circulation therapy Ms. Ruby," a soft voice chimed.

Maxie wiped her eyes with her hands, and turned around to see a petite white woman, dressed in green scrubs and a white doctor's coat, standing in the doorway.

"I know you have a visitor," she said, speaking both to Maxie and Sister Adams. "But it's near the end of my shift and you're my last massage today. Do you mind?"

"No, not at all." Maxie forced a smile and stood up to move near the bathroom. "I was just about to leave anyway."

"Jennifer, this is Maxie. Maxie, this is Jennifer, my personal masseuse." Sister Adams smiled after putting her special tag on the nurse. "She's new."

"What happened to...?"

"Kelly? Chile, she was too rough. Had hands like a man. Looked and massaged like one too." Sister Adams winked her eye and Maxie laughed.

The nurse stood next to the bed, and helped Sister Adams sit up straight. Slowly, they both worked to move her legs so they could dangle on the side of the bed. To Maxie, her legs looked terribly swollen and she wanted to ask questions about it but didn't.

Sister Adams glanced at Maxie, and grimaced at the nurse's firmness. "Maxie, I'm not one to tell you how to run your life, because you're grown. But if you choose to pursue what you have set in your heart to do, I only ask that you call me from time to time. Let me know how you're doing." She grimaced again. "You go on now, and remember what I said. I'm going to be all right. And don't try to send me nobody else from the church to come visit with me. If they ain't coming by now, I don't want them coming at all."

"Yes ma'am. I'll definitely call you," Maxie replied, making a silent promise to herself.

Sister Adams became preoccupied with her therapy, pointing out to the nurse the tender spots in her legs. Maxie felt a little awkward just standing there watching. It was common practice for her to give Sister Adams a kiss before she left, but this time she would have to forego it. She didn't want to get in the way. Besides, she could always kiss her the next time she came to visit...whenever that was.

"Well, I'm going to head on out now. I love you." Maxie called, moving closer to the door.

"I love you too, and I'll be praying for you."

Maxie smiled faintly, lingered for a brief moment, and left Sister Adams's room.

As she walked down the corridor, she thought about how badly she wanted to tell Sister Adams that she would be praying for her too. Albeit, God probably would not acknowledge any of her prayers now, knowing the state of mind she was in.

Chapter Nine

W hen she pulled up into her driveway, Maxie sat in her car and looked around confused. It was not so much the question as to where she was, but rather how she got there. She was home safely, true enough, but she had no recollection of the entire drive there. The trip was to be chalked up to memory, because too many thoughts flooded her mind to give any consideration to her course of travel.

Maxie sat back in the driver's seat and briefly pressed her eyes closed in frustration. Reflections on last Sunday's church service and the few moments spent with Sister Adams, clamored her brain and just wouldn't leave her alone. It wasn't enough that she allowed herself to become torn by the words of Sister Adams, but now she seemed more aware of subtle pieces of adversity. It was almost like an unwelcomed awakening. Looking in her rearview mirror, she didn't see the reflection of her neighbor's houses across the street. Instead, an instant replay of what happened to her at church on the past Sunday morning came into view.

It started out like any normal service on any given Sunday. Praise and worship had gone forth, the church choir sang three songs, and offering had been given — all before Pastor Harrison rose to preach. Near the end of his sermon, Maxie thought she heard him call for her to come and stand at the altar. The congregation was in an uproar, rejoicing loudly and giving praises to God in response to the words that were preached, so she couldn't be sure she actually heard him call her name. It became quite evident that he *did* call her, because Pastor Harrison came down out of the pulpit to stand directly in front of her, with two other ministers by his side. With perspiration rolling down his face, his eyes were determinedly focused on something beyond her physical being, making her feel transparent. She knew what was coming next, and a moment of fear washed over her. It was a prophetic word. A message from God; a declaration as to what was either happening, or going to happen in a person's life. If the messenger was a true Prophet, which Pastor Harrison was, the content of the message would be validated by actually coming to pass, or already be evident to the person receiving it. Maxie knew it also offered guidance by calling a person to live more in line with God's Word. A line she was currently straddling.

Maxie tried to appear receptive rather than rattled, and only hoped Pastor Harrison would not divulge what God was showing him. A number of people actually liked to receive prophetic words, and would use them to make preparation for whatever life was bringing their way, good or bad. Right then, Maxie was not one of the numbered. She didn't need to hear her wayward intentions proclaimed on the housetop. It wasn't for anyone else to know, and she never understood why preachers delivered their prophetic words aloud. Since it was a message from God to the receiver, she felt it should be a personal experience. It should not be a tell-all for the whole congregation to hear; especially not Lester, who was standing in the pulpit looking directly at her.

"Sister Bruce...," Pastor Harrison crooned, sounding much like Dr. Martin Luther King Jr. "The Lord would have you to know that the devil is hot on your trail. Right now, your flesh is warring feverishly against your soul because the devil has set a trap for you. Search your soul Sister Bruce. Search so that you don't become an offense to God. For your soul will get you into a place where it will make you go after the things of the world, and not the things of God. The Lord says that it is not time to be concerned about *your* will, but be concerned about His will, for many souls are required of you."

Maxie remembered tears rolling down her face, as Pastor Harrison spoke and walked away. Then, she couldn't be sure whether the words he delivered caused the tears, or whether the fear of her plan being exposed to her husband, caused them to fall. Later she realized if the tears were for Lester, they were wasted, because he never said a word to her about the whole episode; which was very unusual.

Ultimately, Maxie was left to wrestle with the indelible notion that she was to be held responsible for the salvation of others. It was the same thing Sister Adams just told her. Witnessing to someone about Jesus Christ could no longer be a choice, as she had previously thought. She couldn't randomly pick the people at her convenience. There were *specific* people assigned to her, and they were out there somewhere. The only way she was going to find out exactly who and where they were, would be to seek *God's* will for her life personally.

And that was a challenge she had absolutely no intention of pursuing.

Maxie got out of the car, and walked to the door feeling more determined than ever. Nothing would be allowed to interfere with what *she* had set into motion now. No one. No thing. Nothing.

Chapter Ten

Everything on the list was completed and checked off. Maxie lay in bed wide-awake and practically motionless since 4:20 a.m. With the ceiling as her backdrop, she mentally went over the 'To Do' list she put together the day after she was hired. Dinner meals for the week, which was number one on the list, were either partially prepared and frozen, or written out in detail in a menu form labeled *Quick Fix Meals*. Second on the list was house cleaning, and that would be done every other day (not that it ever got that dirty). Next would be laundry. She would do that twice a week instead of three times. Then, she secretly hired a boy from down the street to tend to the yard on Tuesdays as needed. All else on the list, though she considered some of them trivial, still needed more of her attention. This included visits to the various nursing homes, and homes of the sick and shut-in. She couldn't find anyone at the church willing to take her place, without going into detail as to why she needed a replacement. So Maxie made up her mind that she was simply not going to worry about it. She would visit whenever she could, and only as time allowed.

Maxie looked at the alarm clock on the nightstand, and quickly turned it off before it rang. It was 5:15 a.m., and she was more than ready to start the day. The long awaited moment had finally arrived.

It was Wednesday.

Though the room was somewhat dark, Maxie looked at a large chair where she had laid out the clothes she planned to wear. The pair of khaki pants, light blue Oxford shirt, and white leather Nike tennis shoes, was a bit more casual than what she was used to wearing, but she reminded herself that her target was extreme comfort, not impression.

Unwittingly, Maxie tuned in to Lester's breathing pattern as he lay next to her in bed. She didn't hear his usual resounding snore. Instead, his breathing was shallow and brief, indicating to her that he was not asleep. Maxie wanted to believe Lester was awake, sharing her thoughts and anxieties. Whether he was asleep or awake, she felt an overwhelming amount of love and affection for her husband right then. She didn't know if the feeling came from being excited about the day, or if she just wanted to be passionate toward him. Wherever it was coming from, it made her reach out and gently stroke the back of his head, feeling the curls of his hair wrap around her fingers. "I love you," she whispered softly.

Lester turned over to face her. "I love you too," he moaned, his voice sounding extra deep. "You nervous or excited?"

Maxie smiled broadly at the silhouette of Lester's face. She was glad to know that he *was* actually thinking about her.

"Maybe a little bit of both," she answered.

Lester yawned. "Don't worry about it. You'll do fine."

Maxie held her smile. "Why thank you for your vote of confidence Mr. Bruce. That means a lot to me."

"I'm serious. I think you'll do just fine. I know I haven't given you a lot of positive feedback lately but I'm...I'm here for you."

The words Lester chose to express his support sounded awkward and corny to Maxie, making her giggle.

"What, you don't believe me?"

"No, it's not that sweetheart." Maxie kissed his forehead. "I'm just glad you're behind me."

Silence fell between them for a moment.

"You do know that I can give you whatever you need right? You understand you don't have to do this."

Maxie placed her arm behind her head and lay quietly. She expected Lester to make a last minute attempt to get her to change her mind. She only thought he would have tried it a lot sooner than on the actual day she was to start work. Though his effort wasn't quite as intense as she anticipated, she knew that it would be out of character for him to remain silent and not give her at least one more press.

"I know," she said softly.

Lester inhaled deeply, and released it noisily. Maxie hoped he was finally retreating. Turning over on her side to face him again, she gently kissed Lester on the mouth. His lips felt extra soft and warm to her.

"What's that for?" He asked.

"I just want to say thank you. I know this whole work issue wasn't an easy pill for you to swallow in the beginning..."

"It's still bitter, even now."

"I know, but look at it as giving me something I've never had before. It's like you're giving me a level of independence. An opportunity to be my own woman."

"And that's a good thing?" Lester laughed.

Maxie instantly felt she may have said too much while trying to express her gratitude. If she said any more, it could direct Lester to a whole new line of questions.

"It's getting late and I need to get your breakfast started."

Maxie threw back the covers and sat up. In one motion, he threw them back on her and pulled her close to him. Maxie welcomed the gesture because the room was cold.

"I forgot to close that window and turn the heat on last night," she said as she snuggled next to him, pressing her back against his chest.

Lester wrapped his arms around her and pulled her closer. "You want me to turn it on?" He asked softly in her ear.

"Would you?"

"Okay."

Maxie waited for Lester to leave the bed, but he didn't budge. "Honey what are you doing? You just said you were going to turn the heat on."

"I am turning it on."

Maxie thought for a moment, and smiled before turning toward him. Lester was indeed turning the heat on, and she couldn't think of a better way to start the day.

* * * * * * * * * *

Maxie felt a heightened level of anxiety as the clock ticked away the minutes. It was only 9:45 in the morning, and she was already a fully dressed basket case. What she needed was a pep talk, and the only person to do that effectively was Sandra. However, when she tried to call her, there was no answer. Didn't Sandra remember this was the big day? Where was she? In her frustration, Maxie left those exact words on each one of Sandra's voice mails.

Pacing from room to room, she justified her actions by telling herself she was breaking in her new Nike tennis shoes. When in all actuality, she was wandering around aimlessly trying to keep herself busy. She wasn't used to having absolutely *nothing* to do in the morning. Normally, she would have the dishes to wash and the kitchen to clean after breakfast, but Lester took care of that when he took her out to IHOP for breakfast, before he went to work.

As she walked around the living room, Maxie checked her purse near the door for a third time, to make sure she had all of her paperwork. For the third time, it was all there. There was really nothing left to do but wait.

Wait and think.

All morning, Maxie was successful in keeping her psyche occupied. Lester even unknowingly contributed to her efforts, with his timely fulfillment of both his desire and hers. Now there was nothing to keep her from surrendering to the very things she spent the morning running away from — her thoughts. Since it was now inevitable, Maxie sat down and let her mind reel. Immediately, her thoughts washed over her like a tidal wave. There was so much to mull over. Questions like, was Sister Adams praying for her right then? She desperately needed somebody's prayers, but she couldn't remember if she told Sister Adams the date she would actually be starting work. What would her grandmother say to her if she were alive? Would she approve of her behavior? If no, then why not? Lester gave his consent, and that was all Ma Dear would require. Maybe she would be proud of the fact that her granddaughter wanted to be a more independent woman.

Maxie laughed. "No, Ma Dear definitely would not approve, simply because she would see straight through this whole charade."

Maxie relaxed a little and continued to acknowledge everything that came to her mind. Everything that is, except the ultimate question. Had she...?

The phone rang and Maxie jumped. Blinking her eyes quickly, she cleared herself of the reverie. "Hello?"

There was no response.

"Hello?"

Still no response.

Listening intently, Maxie heard muffled conversations and the sound of computer keyboards being used. Thinking it was a bill collector, she started to hang up the phone.

"Frazzled are we?" A voice finally said on the other end. "Maxie, are we frazzled? You leave me two messages on two different phones. ..."

"I actually left you three. You'll hear the other one when you get home. Sandra? Do you know what today is?"

"Yeah, it's Wednesday. A day when I'm the only administrative female locked behind closed doors in meetings with five of the finest, well-dressed, hard-bodied executive brothers, this side of the Mississippi River. Oh, and did I mention that I was the *only* female?"

"Yes Sandra, you did."

"Girl, my life is good." Sandra released a sigh of great satisfaction. "Now what is your problem? You scared to face the day?"

"So you did remember."

"Maxie, how could I forget? When I spoke with you on the phone Monday night, it was all you talked about."

"Okay, but you still could've called me to wish me good luck or something."

"Good luck Maxie," Sandra said plainly.

Silence fell between them again. Maxie quickly looked around the room as if someone might be listening in on their conversation. Lowering her voice, she cupped the mouthpiece of the phone. "Sandra, girl, I'm scared to death. What if I forget to give the customer back the right amount of change or something? I've spent the last two days teaching myself how to count back money. I can do it fine at home, but I just know I'm going to screw it all up when I actually have to do it. And their bread. Girl what if I get nervous and I don't pack the bags right, and I smash their bread? Not to mention the eggs. I don't even want to think about the eggs."

Maxie stopped and took a breath. She didn't know if Sandra tried to get a word in edgewise, so she waited. There was only calm on the other end. "Sandra," she said impatiently.

"I'm listening Maxie," Sandra said coolly. "Are you finished? I thought I'd just let you get all of that anxiety out. You feel better now? You feel relieved?"

Maxie took another deep breath and pressed her eyes shut for a moment. Of course she was feeling a bit anxious. After all, she was about to do something she had never done before. Unfortunately, the only people she would have around her when that pivotal moment happened, would be people she didn't even know.

"Maxie, you have waited for this moment for a long time. You can't go back now. Remember when you said the desire to be on the *other* side had grown so much, it was now bigger than you? Well, this may be the only chance you'll ever have to conquer it. You almost have to do this just to get it out of your system, so you won't have any regrets. And you *can* do this. Besides, today is only a training day right?"

"Maxie wiped her hand over her face, convinced perspiration had beaded across her forehead and nose. "I think so. I wish you could go with me," she said in a low tone.

"Do you honestly believe I would leave these five fine brothers to go with you and be your little personal pep squad? Girl, you better think again."

Maxie laughed a little.

"You'll be all right sweetie. I promise. You can do this."

Maxie was soaking up all of Sandra's words, when she heard the mouthpiece being covered, and the muffled sound of Sandra's voice and that of a man.

"Uhm, uhm, uhm," Sandra moaned.

"What?"

"This one brother. Girl I tell you, I'd hold the door open for him just so I could look at him from behind and watch him walk away. You know what I mean? The man is fine!"

"That good looking huh?"

"Words can't define him," Sandra said, sounding mesmerized. "Umph, let me get off this phone. My meeting is starting up again. Will you call me later?"

"Count on it."

"Okay, well I'll talk to you then."

"Hey Sandra?"

"Yes?"

"Thank you."

"Not a problem. You know you're my girl."

Maxie smiled. "Bye."

"Goodbye."

* * * * * * * * * *

Maxie decided she would leave the house at 11:15 a.m. Food King was only fifteen minutes away, but she wanted to be a little early so she would have time to calm herself if necessary. It would definitely be necessary. The brief conversation with Sandra was a little comforting, but Maxie didn't really get what she felt she needed — and that was confidence. Instead, what she felt was an overwhelming amount of uncertainty, and it was a feeling that was visiting her way too often. Had she been able to talk to Sandra a little longer, she may have felt more strengthened and encouraged. Even though Sandra's words didn't pump her like they normally would, two things she said definitely hit the nail on the head. One, she couldn't go back now, and two, she had to get the hunger out of her system.

Maxie picked up her purse and gave herself the once-over. When she opened the door to leave, she paused and looked back. The moment was surreal, because she was about to cross the threshold into a life she only dreamed about. The gaze over her shoulder was not to look into the physical house, but more at what she was figuratively leaving behind. In retrospect, her life was spent pleasing others with deeds and decisions that best accommodated them. Moving forward, she wanted her efforts to be more centered on herself.

While she stood in the doorway, a quick breeze rushed past her and swirled off the walls inside the house. In that wind, Maxie thought she heard whispers of admonishment, but quickly dispelled them. The wheels were in motion now, and she was making the right move toward becoming her own woman. So when she finally closed the door, the gesture was meant to be symbolic as well. In as much as she wanted her thoughts to totally switch gears and flow in the same direction, one looming thought warred against her face to face.

Was she really turning her back on God?

Chapter Eleven

Traffic was light, considering how close it was to lunch time. When Maxie turned from Abercorn St. onto Mall Blvd., there were people everywhere. The unusually warm weather, obviously played a big part in workers walking to their lunch destinations. Some were going inside the mall for lunch, while others chose to dine at one of the many fast food restaurants in the area. When she finally arrived in the parking lot of Food King, Maxie wondered if there was special parking for store employees. To be safe, she backed her car into a spot at the farthest end of the parking lot. In less than twenty minutes, she was going to be earning her very first paycheck. She wasn't nearly as nervous as she thought she would be. Her stomach felt full, but she knew it was just excitement.

After a brief wait, Maxie finally gathered her purse and prepared to go in. Only then did the thought occur to her that showing up early, might give the impression that she was overly enthused about working at Food King. Even if she was, she didn't want to appear eager, so she waited in the car a little longer.

When she finally made the trek across the parking lot and into the doors, Maxie felt important. Important because, soon the shoppers around her would be relying on her expertise of the store's inventory, to help them complete their shopping tasks. The feeling was outlandish. She would not only be *behind* a cash register, but she would now be given access to all doors marked EMPLOYEES ONLY.

Needing desperately to release a grin of satisfaction, yet not wanting to appear strange, Maxie looked at one of the cashiers she passed, smiled broadly, and continued on to the Customer Service desk. She hoped to see the girl with the contact lens covered eyes that helped her before, but there was no one behind the counter.

"Is there something I can help you with?" Maxie heard behind her. "I will be with you in just a minute."

Maxie swung herself around to match the voice with a face. There was no one close by. The only employee closest to her was ringing up a customer, and continually glancing at her. Ironically, it was the same cashier she smiled at when she entered the store.

"I'll be over in just a second." He spoke over his shoulder.

Maxie moved closer to the register. "I'm here for cashier training."

"Oh, okay. You need to go through the double doors back by Dairy. You'll see a set of stairs. Go up the stairs, turn right, and go down to the end of the hall. The training room is the last door on the right."

"Thank you," she smiled again, and turned on her heels.

Maxie walked where she was directed. When she made her entrance into the training room, all eyes were on her. The room was a lot larger than she expected. There were four eight-foot long tables placed one behind the other, each with an appropriate number of chairs, all of which were occupied. As she stood in the doorway searching, she spotted an empty chair in the back along the wall, away from the tables. Quickly, she moved toward it and took a seat.

"You must be Maxine Bruce. Right?"

Maxie looked at the person standing at the front of the room. It was the girl with the contact lens covered eyes.

"Yes, I am." She answered, feeling uncomfortable because she was obviously the last one to arrive.

"Okay, welcome. Now we'll get started. First off, my name is Regina Dawson, and I am the Lead Cashier and Customer Service Manager here at Food King. I do all of the training and if you have any problems, you bring them to me first. If a customer has a complaint about you or a problem with anything in this store, they see me. So far, are there any questions?"

Maxie was listening intently, when a young man seated at the table in front of her waved his hand to get her attention. Moving his chair over slightly, he motioned for her to come and sit next to him.

"You're going to need to use this table," he whispered with a feminine twang. She's going to hand us some extra paperwork that we need to sign."

"Thank you," Maxie said as she pulled her chair to the table. Her mind instantly shot to the words *extra paperwork*. She hoped it wasn't anything she couldn't understand.

"I worked at a Food King across town," the young man volunteered. "I mean that's how I know she's going to hand out extra paperwork."

Maxie smiled. She wanted to ask him why he was going through training again, but let it pass.

"My name is Alan by the way," he said, offering his hand.

Maxie shook it. "I'm…"

"Oh I know who you are. You're Maxine Bruce. Regina just said it."

"Oh…yeah," she stammered, feeling a little foolish.

Alan smiled and directed his attention back to Regina. Unwittingly, Maxie observed his well-manicured fingernails, and how they were longer than they should be. Not wanting to judge Alan by which gender he might identify himself with, she too directed her attention toward Regina.

"Hopefully, all of you have brought back your W-fours and all of those other wonderful papers you received when you were hired. Please pull them out, and I will collect them all right now."

As Regina worked her way between the tables, Maxie took notice of her soon-to-be co-workers. Even though her view was primarily of the back of their heads, she could see that the whole crew, which was about fifteen strong, was relatively young; at least younger than she was.

"All right, next I'm going to give each one of you an Employee Handbook. We will go over some key pages in this session, but you will be required to read the whole book at your leisure. Please sign the last page stating that you have read and understand the book, and return that page to me by this Friday. If you do not work on Friday, bring it to me at the beginning of your next shift *after* Friday. Is everybody with me?"

Everyone in the room simply nodded their heads.

"Good," Regina said, as she handed out stacks of small blue books to the first person at each table to pass down. "Now before we get started in the books, I want to introduce you to a very important piece of paper that can either be your friend or your foe." Regina smiled as she held up a piece of goldenrod colored paper. "This is our Customer Service Survey sheet. Our goal is to always please the customer. If you have an isolated incident where you have done something to please a customer, either by meeting or exceeding their expectation, they are asked to fill out one of these forms with your name on it, telling us what you've done to make their shopping experience a pleasant one. With that favorable mention, this becomes a Notice of Merit. On the other hand, if the customer has had an unpleasant experience with you and has a complaint about your services, thus an unfavorable mention, this becomes a Notice of *De*merit." Regina paused for a moment, when a hand went up in the front of the room, to which she acknowledged by nodding her head.

"Why are they both on the same colored paper?"

The same question was obviously on everybody's mind, because everyone responded at the same time.

"Well," Regina answered, smiling again. "I was getting to that. This one form is for the benefit of the customer. See, they use one color so you can't tell exactly what they are commenting on. The result that comes to you will either be on white paper, a merit, or pink paper, a demerit. In either case, I meet with the person whose name is on this form, behind closed doors, so nobody else knows your business." Again, everyone simultaneously sounded his or her approval. "That is, until you get fired. Then everybody will know your business," Regina quipped. The entire room fell silent. "That was just a little Food King humor people. Relax."

Maxie shook her head and laughed a little, along with the majority of the room.

"Okay, now that you know about this piece of paper, understand what it can get you. Seven merits in one month, will get you Employee of the Month for that following month. You will also get a twenty-five dollar Food King gift certificate, and your picture set up in the front of the store." Another hand went up. "And yes there can be more than one Employee of the Month. The hand went down. "Five *de*merits in one month will get you written up by Mr. Martin. Three write-ups get you fired. Kind of like three strikes and you're out. Any questions?" When no one answered, Regina continued. "Good. So it's obvious to see that our customers can make you or break you. And trust me, we do know that there are those select customers who are impossible to please no matter what you do for them. We do take that into consideration when we review the form. Now let's move on to the handbook."

Maxie was glad Regina was a 'let's get to it' kind of person. The time spent in the sit down portion of the training was minimal but stirring. The real anxiety kicked in, when she told them they were about to begin hands on cash register training. Before they started, Regina invited every person in the room to stand up, introduce and tell a little something about themselves. It was obvious the break in formality was welcomed, because the entire atmosphere became more relaxed with each introduction. When they all finished, Maxie was relieved to learn that her soon-to-be co-workers, weren't all as young as they appeared to be. There were actually three women who were closer to her in age.

On the sales floor, Regina explained and demonstrated the entire cash register procedure to the group. Now it was time to perform it one by one, in front of everyone. Maxie tried not to be nervous when her turn came. When it was all said and done, she did surprisingly well. She even outshined her peers when demonstrating how to process check and credit card payments. Maxie was proud of herself, and thanked God she did well — not paying attention to whom she was gracious. At the end of the session, everyone received a royal blue smock with pockets, a nametag, and their schedule for the remainder of the week.

"Tomorrow, according to your schedule, each of you will work with one of the cashiers already on the floor. You will shadow them, which means to follow their every move, for two hours. The remaining two or three hours, depending on your schedule, will be yours to showcase your wonderful newly acquired Food King talents to our customers. Are there any questions?"

"Will there be someone there with us to make sure we do everything right?" A male voice asked, at the front of the room.

"Yes you will have a babysitter," Regina replied. The room echoed with raucous laughter. Laughing herself, Regina cleared her throat and addressed the young man directly. "I'm just kidding. The person you shadow will shadow you until the end of your shift. Does anyone else have a question?"

When no one raised their hand, Regina dismissed everyone and wished them all a good afternoon, again welcoming them to Food King.

* * * * * * * * * *

In two weeks' time, though busy and extremely fast paced, Maxie never missed a beat. She prepared dinner on time, and kept all matters of the house in order — proving to herself and anyone else, that she was more than able to juggle part-time work with full-time housewife duties. Her only drawbacks were aching feet, pain in her lower back, and tight shoulders, all of which she knew would fade over time.

Every day after work, Maxie indulged herself in relaxation. Once home, she resigned to her favorite spot on the couch, kicked off her shoes, put her feet up, and listened to messages on the answering machine. Today, hardly any of the recordings were worthy of a return phone call, but she felt the need to leave them on the machine anyway. Including a message she received from Sister Adams a week ago.

"I'm just calling to see how your new job is going." Sister Adams's voice proclaimed. "I thought you would have called me by now since you can't come to visit with me. I'm still praying for you sugar. You take care of yourself now, and don't you work too hard. I hope to be hearing from you soon. God bless you baby. Bye now."

At first, Maxie was going to return her call, but decided she would pay Sister Adams a surprise visit instead. Knowing her work schedule in advance, she could plan to visit on whatever day she was off.

Maxie smiled to herself. The first visit would definitely be to see Sister Adams.

Chapter Twelve

❧

"Senior Citizen Tuesdays demand patience, civility, and an uncanny knack for keeping the old folks happy," Regina once proclaimed.

Maxie only worked it twice, but she was beginning to hate Tuesdays at Food King. It was definitely a battle of resilience, and she was glad this Tuesday was almost over. The day had been long, rough, and she was tired. Tired of answering questions repeatedly about advertised sale items; tired of her line being held up by elderly people who had cash in their hands to pay, but at the last minute decided to write a check; and tired of being told by each one of them, how to bag their groceries item by item. When it came right down to it, Maxie couldn't be sure if it was them getting on her nerves with their pickiness, or her own untimely lack of benevolence. Whatever it was, she was glad she didn't have to deal with it tomorrow. Wednesday was her day off, and she was looking forward to it. She was also looking forward to seeing Sister Adams.

Maxie had no idea she would miss visiting her elderly friend so much. She even hated not returning Sister Adams's phone call, but she knew there would be the question of when she was coming to visit, and Maxie didn't want to spoil her surprise. She planned to make it all up to her tomorrow afternoon, when she arrived with a small tin of chocolate.

As she wiped down her register area and prepared to leave, Maxie noticed Regina was on the floor making rounds. A term she learned from the other cashiers when they discussed Regina occasionally stopping by their register with a clipboard in hand, to make positive or negative comments on their individual performances. Though she appeared to be stopping at every station, she was still a good distance away, so Maxie continued to glance at her and clean, until she slowly made her way to her register area.

"Getting ready to go?" Regina asked with a big smile.

Maxie put her cleaning items away and pressed the button for her register to open. "Yep, as soon as I close out."

"So, how did it go today?"

"Fine," Maxie piped, without looking at her.

Knowing how direct and to the point Regina was, Maxie felt her approach was a bit too casual. She was sure an elderly customer had written her up, and Regina was stopping by to deal the blow, so she just continued with what she was doing.

Regina leaned her heavy body against the conveyor belt encasing, and grinned. "So what do you think about working here?"

Maxie pulled the tape from her register, and placed it in her tray. "I like it. There are some things I have to get used to, but overall, I like it."

Regina nodded and looked at Maxie skeptically. "You don't talk much, so I wasn't sure of how you felt."

Maxie smiled a little. Regina wasn't the first person to tell her that she didn't talk much.

"Well, your performance is outstanding and you already have two merits. Out of the group you trained with, you're the only one who has managed to accomplish that. Good job."

"Thank you," Maxie replied softly.

"Yeah...well listen. I'm here to ask you if you can work tomorrow. Monet phoned in sick again and I need someone to cover her shift. It's the same hours you work now..."

"I'm scheduled to be off tomorrow."

"I know tomorrow is your off day. I'm just in a bind. Tell you what, in the future, if there's any other day you want off, I'll give it to you. I'll get Monet to work your schedule then. I could really use your help Maxie."

Maxie subtly averted Regina's questioning stare, by looking at the front end of the store. A change in her schedule now, meant she would have to work five days straight before she had a day off. It also meant she would have to postpone her surprise visit to see Sister Adams.

Maxie doubted very seriously that Monet was sick. At nineteen, the girl had a sound reputation for being a slacker. She rarely did what she was supposed to, and spent most of her shift flirting with either the male employees, or the male customers, earning a not so nice name for herself. And she got away with it. To cover her, Regina must have asked every cashier on the floor if they could work her shift. And every one of them obviously said no, because they had already made plans. Maxie wanted to do the same.

"Can you help me out Maxie?"

Maxie picked up her cash tray and fixed it against her hip. "Sure Regina, I can do that. As long as in the future, you give me whatever day I request off."

"That won't be a problem. Just let me know in advance. Thanks a lot Maxie." Regina winked her eye and headed back to the Customer Service desk. Maxie followed behind her. Few words passed between the two of them until Maxie punched her timecard.

"So I'll see you tomorrow then?" Regina asked.

"I'll see you then." Maxie feigned a smile and left the store. She was glad Regina didn't come to her register to reprimand her about receiving a demerit, but she wasn't too enthused about being convinced into forfeiting her day off. At least she wouldn't have to explain to Sister Adams why she couldn't be there. It was a good idea to keep her in the dark, but Maxie needed to talk with her elderly friend at some point and time. If she didn't, it would be three weeks since she had any contact with her. That was a decision she would have to make later. Now, she had to reprogram herself and channel her thoughts to issues on the home front; like what was for dinner?

* * * * * * * * * *

With shoeless feet propped up on the arm of the couch, Maxie lay motionless while listening to the answering machine. "Okay Mrs. Bruce, time is ticking and you haven't given me a yay or nay to my question about the Festival. It started last night, and because I haven't heard from you, you know I had to go without you. Of course I wasn't alone, but that's a different story. I'll fill you in on that one later. Okay well, get in touch with me when you can. I don't know girl. Since you've been working, it's hard to catch you with a free moment. And if *I* can't catch up with you, something's wrong. Let me know if you want to go tonight. I'll holler atcha' later. Call me!"

Maxie didn't budge. None of the messages sparked an interest, except for the one from Sandra. With everything that was going on, she had forgotten about the Jazz Festival. According to how exhausted she felt, it might as well stay forgotten. Maxie had no plans of moving from the couch any time soon. Not even to fix dinner. She ordered a Papa John's pizza, with a two liter of Sprite to be delivered, and there was salad in the refrigerator. Dinner was set.

It was finally Friday, and Maxie felt like she had just completed a week of military basic training. Her whole week was regimented. She endured job performance evaluations every other day, she practically stood at attention for three or more hours every day before she got a break; and she remained cordial and professional *whenever* a customer wanted to argue about the pricing of an item. The gist of it was coming home to assume a position of a different rank.

Maxie dared to think, or say to herself that she was in over her head. All she needed was a moment of unbothered relaxation — time to gather herself, her thoughts, and refuel. Spending time at the Jazz Festival could be just the ticket. Only not tonight. Though she had it all planned out from the first time Sandra asked her about slipping out of the house, she had no intention of trying it tonight. Exhaustion had gotten the best of her, and she was submitting willingly.

"So you're punkin' out on me tonight too?" Sandra quipped on her cell phone, when Maxie called her back. "Sounds to me like that little job has gotten you beat. You're laid up on that couch with your feet up aren't you?"

Maxie laughed a little. "I'm just tired. Can a sistah be tired after a hard week at work?"

"A week? Okay, so you worked your first whole week. Initiation is over. Now it's time to go party. Come on girl!!! I'm just leaving my job. We can meet up somewhere."

Maxie sat quietly on the phone while she entertained a quick vision of a night out on the town with Sandra. It would definitely be what she needed. From Sandra's details of her evenings out, Maxie knew she could look forward to an enjoyable *let your hair down* kind of leisure, while experiencing the true night life up close and personal for the first time. She wanted to experience that side of life anyway, and who better to hang out with than her best friend? But knowing Sandra, all of that experiencing would tire her out more.

"I can't girl. Not tonight." Maxie conceded.

"Is Lester home yet?"

"No, and you should be thankful he's not. He could have very well heard that message you left on the answering machine. What were you thinking?"

"I knew you'd be home before he got there. I left it just in case I couldn't get in touch with you before the sun went down. I figured you'd get my message early enough to give you time to run out of the house *before* it got dark," Sandra giggled.

"Ha, ha, ha. That's all right. You can laugh at me now, I don't care."

"Big baby." Sandra taunted. "Well it's almost six forty, and I'm about five minutes from the park. You call me tomorrow if you want to go. Call me early, just in case I have to break a date. Oh, and Maxie?"

"Yes?"

"Your husband's in the driveway. Erase the message on the answering machine."

Maxie heard a car door slam outside, as Sandra's phone line went dead. She didn't have time to figure out how Sandra knew Lester was home, so she immediately erased the message, and pulled herself together, just before there was a knock on the door. Why Lester would knock was beyond her, but she answered the door anyway. Peeking through the curtain, Maxie saw the pizza delivery man, and Lester behind him. Opening the door, she tipped the delivery man and noticed Lester had their food.

"It's not often a girl gets her appetizer, and her main course delivered to her door at the same time." She smiled.

"Which one am I?" Lester asked, kissing her as he walked in.

Maxie licked her lips and closed the door. "Both."

Lester grinned. "I'm going to go freshen up."

Maxie took the food and began setting the table. By the time she finished, Lester was standing in the doorway.

"Come on and sit down baby," she beckoned.

Lester sat, and Maxie nearly plopped down opposite him. Holding hands, he blessed the food and gave her hand a squeeze before releasing it.

"You look tired," he said.

"Do I?" Maxie asked whimsically, without looking at him. After she took a bite of pizza and chewed a moment, Maxie shook her head and burst into laughter. "I ain't even gonna lie baby. I am exhausted!"

Lester glanced at her and continued chewing his food. Maxie could tell he was trying not to grin. Unable to keep a straight face, he too chuckled a little, and then a lot. When they both finished laughing, Lester sipped his drink. "Pretty rough week at work?"

Maxie nodded. She didn't care if Lester knew the reason for her weariness. The truth was the truth, and there was no need in trying to hide what was clearly evident on her face, and in her entire body for that matter.

"Yeah, this one was a rough one, but I don't expect to have another one like it. I'm not going to cover anybody else's shift if I can help it."

"You're saving your money though, right?" Lester asked with a twinge of skepticism.

Maxie looked at him questioningly and narrowed her eyes. *Why this question out of the blue?*

"I mean for the special anniversary gift you want to buy," he added.

"Yeah Lester. I'm saving my money."

"That's good." Lester set his pizza crust back in the box and pulled out another slice. "Do you want another piece?"

Maxie nodded no. She was barely finishing her pizza, and losing interest in it fast. Although it was only 7:00 p.m., she was ready to crawl into bed and call it a night; certain that she could sleep through until the morning. She didn't want to think about the reason for the sly innuendo Lester just made about her working. It was a tired subject, and she wasn't going to waste any more energy on it.

"How is Sister Adams doing? She's been in my spirit this week," Lester said.

"She's fine," Maxie lied. She didn't know if the old woman had a cold, or was blessed with enough strength to move out of the nursing home, because she still had not so much as returned her phone call. "I'm going to see her tomorrow." Maxie couldn't tell Lester that it was going to be a surprise visit. That would let him know she wasn't keeping up with every duty like she promised.

"I want to go with you tomorrow," Lester said nonchalantly.

Maxie abruptly stopped chewing, and rested her fork in her salad bowl. Trying not to show the surprise on her face, she lowered her head to wipe her mouth with her napkin. Lester *never* went to the nursing homes. He would visit the sick and shut-in people in their homes, but he never went to the nursing homes. For him to say that he wanted to go with her, Maxie felt he was doing a checkup on her.

"Did you hear me?" Lester looked at her straight on.

Maxie looked at him, but was careful not to show any signs of alarm. "Yeah baby. I think it would be good for both of us to go to the nursing home. Sister Adams hasn't seen you in a while. That would be a nice surprise for her."

"And it would be good to see her again too." Lester filled his fork with salad, and started to put it into his mouth. "But I have to work."

Maxie howled with joy on the inside, but tried to show genuine disappointment at the same time. "But didn't you just work last Saturday, and the Saturday before that? I thought you only had to do two a month."

"Yeah that was the plan, but we're two weeks behind on this project, so I may have to work next Saturday as well."

"Well baby, I'll just let Sister Adams know your intentions, and that you send your love instead." Maxie knew she was pouring it on thick.

"Maybe I'll have you take her something special from me," Lester said.

"The only thing she wants special is a small gold tin of chocolates, and I already have that in my purse. She'll be fine knowing you were thinking about her."

Lester wiped his mouth with his napkin, sighed heavily, and stood up. "All right. I'm finished. I'm going to watch a little television, read my Bible, and then call it a night. What about you?"

"I think I'm just going to call it a night."

"Do you want me to help you clean up in here?"

Maxie looked at Lester for a moment, before she answered. Though the question was an unusual one for *him*, she thought it was sweet of him to consider how she felt and to offer his help. "No baby," she smiled. "I got this in here. But thank you anyway. You go ahead in the living room and relax. I won't be long."

Lester winked his eye at her, and left the kitchen.

Maxie kept the smile on her face as she cleaned. Seeing this side of her husband fascinated her. Housework was not Lester's forte. For him to offer to help clean the kitchen, proved one sure thing to Maxie; if she ever had to work to help pull the income load, Lester would definitely be there to help her pull the housework load, and that meant a lot to her. While she swept the floor, Maxie grabbed hold to the rationale, that if she *hadn't* been working a job, she never would have seen that legitimate display of unveiled sensitivity from her husband.

When she finally finished and turned the light off, Maxie wanted nothing more than to walk into her bedroom, fall across the bed, and fall fast asleep with no problem. Tomorrow was going to be a busy day, and she needed to be totally rejuvenated in order to face it.

"Goodnight sweetheart," Maxie said, as she stood over Lester, and softly kissed him on his forehead.

"Goodnight baby, I'll be in soon."

Without hesitation, Maxie did exactly as she said she wanted to do. She went to bed and called it a night.

Chapter Thirteen

Lester had awakened, fixed his own breakfast, and left the house without waking Maxie. Smelling the residual aroma of bacon and coffee, she opened her eyes to his empty side of the bed. With a quick glance at the clock on the nightstand, Maxie wondered why it did not ring, especially after she made sure it was set before she went to bed. Leaning closer to the clock, she saw the alarm time was set, but the alarm was turned off. It was 7:30 a.m. Maxie plopped her head back down on her pillow. How could she have slept through an alarm that obviously woke Lester and made *him* turn it off? It never happened before. She had never slept that deeply.

Feeling a chill in the room, because once again she left the window slightly opened, Maxie reached for her robe on the bed post, swung her feet over the edge of the bed, and went on a quick search for Lester. What she found was an empty house, and a plate of breakfast wrapped in Saran Wrap, on top of the stove just for her. The gesture was a sweet one, but Maxie could not help questioning why Lester did not wake her up, to fix his breakfast. Was he trying to prove the point he had been making all along, that she couldn't possibly work and keep up with the home life and the church life at the same time? She recalled him telling her something would definitely go lacking, and it was just a matter of time before that *something* became obvious. Had he purposely left the proof on the stove? Contrary to how she was thinking, it was easier and more acceptable for her to believe that Lester simply let her rest because she was dead tired.

Without wasting any more time, Maxie walked back into the bedroom to get ready to take a shower. She would have showered the night before, but she was totally incapable of dragging herself into the bathroom. Once her head hit the pillow, and her body was stretched out, she couldn't remember performing the simple task of closing her eyes and drifting asleep. It was more like she was snatched into it, yet not against her will — and she rested well because of it.

In front of the bathroom mirror, Maxie examined her face while she disrobed. She had to make sure tiredness was fully purged from her body, and that no remnant was left under her eyes. Satisfied with her reflection, she considered the bath salts, beads, and aromatherapy candles that sat unopened on the shelf. The thought of a good soak was inviting, and it would definitely be an extreme luxury, but it was one she could not afford to take today. There was too much for her to do, and the plan was to get as early a start as possible. If everything could be conquered in the early morning hours, she could have the afternoon to herself.

And she wanted that desperately.

Until now, no real thought was given to the little time she had for herself since she started working. Even though she didn't want to admit it, much less think about it, she had to be honest about feeling overwhelmed. She needed some *me time* to regroup. The slow change of lifestyle, the constant echoing of words of admonishment, all came together and wrestled with her daily. Spiritual regression had become a mental battleground.

Every morning, Maxie literally had to remind herself that she *willingly* chose to abandon her spiritual life. Therefore, there was no need to continue with the daily routines she did because of virtue. A lot of the things she did every morning, had come to be just that. Routine. The praying every morning before she started her day; the prayer over her food; even the daily prayer she said for her husband while he was at work. It all had become routine. Though she went through the motions, Maxie hadn't felt the sincerity in the words of her prayers for quite some time. Yet deep down, she could not fully identify why she felt intensely obligated to continue doing these things. Therein was the battle. Was it really out of habit, or was it truly a strong intrinsic desire to intimately commune with God?

* * * * * * * * * *

Emily Brewster was the last homebound person Maxie had to visit, and she was very excited to see Maxie. From the time she came in the door, Emily happily filled her in on everything that happened to her since their last visit, and Maxie listened to her attentively the entire time. At the end of the hour long stay, Emily decided she wanted to hear about everything Maxie experienced in the last few weeks. Maxie detected the cute ploy to keep her there, and promised to tell all on the next visit.

When she finally left Emily's, Maxie headed towards Siemen's Nursing Home. Visiting hours didn't start for another fifteen minutes, and she was glad. It would take her about that long to get there. She knew Sister Adams would be ecstatic to see her, and frankly, the feeling was mutual. The last time she had even heard Sister Adams's voice, was the message she left on the answering machine. She hadn't heard from her again since then, but thought maybe Sister Adams made a couple more attempts to contact her during the week, because the nursing home's phone number appeared on Caller ID. Strangely, there was no message left either time.

When she pulled into the parking lot and got out of her car, Maxie looked over the well-manicured lawn and noticed something was missing. A large oak tree that stood to the left of the parking lot, which provided a huge amount of shade for the residents, had been cut down. There was nothing but a large mound of dirt and ground up wood chips in its place. It was odd to not see the tree standing there. It was old enough to be a landmark in its own right.

Having been away for three weeks, Maxie wondered if there were other drastic changes of which she wasn't aware of. With that question lingering on the inside, she felt totally out of touch with the goings on at the nursing home. Immediately, she opened the door to see what else had changed. Everything was the same. The only thing that seemed strange to her, was the fact that there were not a lot of visitors in the facility for a Saturday morning. The clock on the wall quickly reminded her, that at 10:00 a.m., it was still early.

While she walked across the lobby to the nurse's station, Maxie ran her fingertips along the outside pocket of her purse to feel its contents. It was still there. The little gold tin of chocolate was tucked away and ready for giving. Maxie smiled as she approached the nurse's station. The woman behind the computer wasn't the same woman she encountered before. This one looked up from the computer screen and smiled at her warmly.

"Hi, how may I help you?"

Before Maxie could answer, her attention was drawn to an older woman down the east wing hallway, who was walking and sobbing uncontrollably into a wad of paper towel. As she was being consoled in the arms of a nurse, Maxie thought she recognized the woman as Rose, a resident neighbor across the hall from Sister Adams, and a sufferer of dementia. While the two headed toward the nurse's station, Maxie hazarded a questioning glance at the friendly nurse.

The nurse shrugged her shoulders. "She's been like that for the last two days now. She keeps telling us that somebody in her family died."

Maxie kept a steady watch on Rose and the nurse. When they were close enough to her, Maxie's eyes met Rose's, and the woman wailed eccentrically, reaching out to her. Maxie jumped a little, startled by the response. She knew dementia could impair the recognition of familiar people and even cause severe confusion, but a response like that caught Maxie totally off guard. It even surprised the woman behind the counter.

"Maybe you look like somebody she knows," the nurse offered.

Maxie quickly looked at the nurse and smiled weakly before she looked down the west wing at Rose. "Maybe I do," she mumbled.

"Well," the nurse continued, sounding relieved. "Tell me again how I may help you?"

Maxie opened her mouth to speak, only to shut it at the sight of the rude nurse she encountered on her last visit. Maxie was sure she could feel the hairs on her neck rise, because she just knew that this woman would be bent on rubbing her the wrong way today.

"Mrs. Bruce." The rude nurse practically hissed as she slithered behind the counter next to the friendly one. "Why are you…? Didn't you…?"

Maxie observed how the woman was seemingly over-anxious to divulge some meaningful information to her, but was stopped cold at the pressure of a hand being placed on her left shoulder. Glancing peripherally, the nurse closed her mouth and slightly moved aside.

"Hey Maxie," a smiling gorgeous face said to her. "How are you?"

Maxie instantly forgot about the rude nurse and returned the smile. "Hello Brian. I'm doing well. Kind of early for the drama this morning isn't it?" Maxie tilted her head slightly to give reference to Rose.

"Yeah, well you know. There's never a dull moment here." Brian came around the counter. "Ladies, I'm going to take a break right now." Grabbing one of Maxie's hands, he gently pulled her away. "Mrs. Bruce is going to be with me for a while."

Maxie looked at the two women. The friendly nurse now looked at her dolefully, while the rude one simply stared blankly.

"Please don't tell Ms. Adams that I'm here to see her," Maxie said to the both of them. "I want it to be a surprise." The friendly nurse slowly feigned a smile, and acknowledged Maxie's request with a slight nod. The other nurse didn't move. Thank you both," she said, directing her statement to the rude one.

Brian clasped Maxie's hand behind his back as they walked. "Come have a cup of coffee with me Maxie," he said without looking at her.

She smiled. "Wow, you must have really missed me, if you're willing to settle for a quick cup of coffee instead of a long lunch. And you're even taking me to the employee cafeteria. You must think I'm a cheap date."

Maxie waited for the usual response she always got from Brian, whenever she said something quippy, or particularly funny to him. And as always, the rejoinder was the appearance of a big dimple in his cheeks.

When they entered the cafeteria, Brian asked her what kind of coffee she wanted, and motioned for her to have a seat anywhere while he got their drinks. Maxie looked around the quaint area for an out of the way table, preferably in a corner. There was no problem finding one, because there was only one other staff member in the cafeteria, and she was leaving. The area was filled with café style tables and chairs, but along the walls were intimate booths with seating for two. There were fewer vending machines than she thought, and there was a food steam table with a cafeteria attendant. It was really more than she expected for a nursing home.

Maxie sat in one of the booths and waited for Brian. When he returned, he set her cup on a napkin and sat across from her. Maxie smiled and looked him over. She was convinced this man could never have a bad looking day.

"So how have you been?" He asked without looking at her. "You didn't tell me you had a new job."

Maxie watched Brian slowly open and pour a small container of flavored cream into his coffee. While he stirred, she wondered why he was being so evasive with the eye contact. She took notice of it from the time they left the nurse's station. Because he mentioned her job, she considered that maybe Brian was a little upset with her for not telling him about it. But why would he be? Did he feel that she just callously shucked her duties of friendship where Sister Adams was concerned?

"Sister Adams told you huh?" Maxie asked.

"Yeah," Brian said, focusing on something very distant behind her.

Maxie couldn't remember a time when she had seen him so solemn and serious.

"She really missed you. A lot," he continued.

Maxie heard the tense in Brian's words, but refused to let them sink in. "Yeah, well I'm here now," she said, becoming a little agitated. As an air of unrest and guilt tried to settle over her head, Maxie wanted, and needed the conversation to shift to a more even ground. She didn't want to be the proverbial bad guy anymore, and she didn't want Brian to look down on her for temporarily walking away from what should have been foremost. "So how has Rose been doing? Are her symptoms of dementia getting worse? She didn't look too good to me."

"She lost someone very close to her a couple of days ago."

Maxie took a quick sip of her drink. "Yeah, that's what the nurse at the counter was telling me. She said Rose was telling everybody that someone in her family died. Did you know the person? Had they visited here before?"

Brian fidgeted with his hands a little, looked into his coffee cup, and then directly at Maxie. In his eyes, Maxie saw so much pain it scared her. It was so intense, she tried to look away but couldn't.

"Maxie ..."

"No Brian!" Maxie said angrily, reaching for her purse next to her.

"I tried to call you twice this week to tell you," he pleaded.

Maxie fumbled with her purse and tried to stand up, but her knees had suddenly become so weak, they wouldn't let her. "I have to go see Sister Adams now," she said with a voice of determination. "I'm going to surprise her today." Again she tried to stand up, but her vision was blurred as her eyes filled with tears. Breathing in short heaves, she shook uncontrollably. Reaching into her purse, she pulled out the gold tin of chocolate and held it out to Brian like a small child presenting something precious and dear. "See, I have to give her these ..." Her words slurred. "I have to give her these ... these chocolates. I brought them just for her."

Brian looked at Maxie with tears in his eyes, and grabbed her by the wrist. "She's gone baby," he whispered. "She's gone."

Maxie looked at Brian skeptically, as if he had spoken forbidden words. *This isn't happening.* Her mind reeled. *Oh God, please don't let this be happening. Not this way.* Everything around her suddenly became surreal. Finally, after fighting her own disbelief and the uncontrollable actions of her body, Maxie covered her mouth and sobbed loudly, as she helplessly cowered in her seat.

"Oh God! Brian what have I done? What have I done?"

Chapter Fourteen

The time was far spent before Maxie had any regard for it. She had spent most of it on the floor of the cafeteria, in the arms of Brian as he futilely tried to comfort her. Though she didn't know how or when she ended up on the floor, she could only believe her uncompromising legs were the culprits. While Brian softly rocked her and spoke words of encouragement, Maxie sat trancelike with the back of her head against his shoulder, hearing his words but not listening. The only thing she could think about was how she failed someone she loved, while seeking her own selfish fleshly desires. Though most of the things Brian said were often tuned out, she did hear him say that Sister Adams passed peacefully Thursday evening around 7:15 p.m., of congestive heart failure.

"Thursday," Maxie mumbled almost inaudibly, and still trancelike. "She died Thursday. I was supposed to see her Wednesday. I could've seen her Wednesday... if I wasn't working. If I was doing what I was really supposed to be doing, I could've seen her on Wednesday. Wednesday before she died."

Brian wiped tears away from Maxie's face, and spoke softly to her. "Stop it Maxie. Don't do this to yourself. It's not fair. Ms. Ruby wouldn't want you to do this."

"I was supposed to have that day off. But if I never had the job to begin with, I could've been here with her."

"Maxie..."

"You know what?" She rambled on. "I didn't even get to give her a goodbye kiss the last time I saw her. I figured I'd see her again, and I could give it to her then."

"Maxie, you couldn't have known when..."

"No." Maxie said sharply. "She would have told me. She knew. She had to have known her time was coming. And if I had been around, she would have told me."

Brian pressed his lips together firmly. It was obvious there was nothing more he could say to Maxie, to help soothe her pain. She was shutting him out. So in complete silence he continued to hold her, until she suddenly pulled herself away from him to stand up.

"I have to go," she said, glancing at her watch and straightening her clothes. With a wadded piece of paper towel in her hand, she searched for a trash can. When she returned, Brian stood up and looked at her.

"What about the family and the funeral arrangements?" She asked softly.

"Don't you remember? I told you her family is flying in today and tomorrow to handle everything. I assume the services will be held at her home church. Your church. So you'll know what's going on."

Maxie lowered her head and turned her wedding ring around on her finger. "Yeah, you did tell me that." Glancing around the room quickly, she looked at Brian again and smiled faintly, desperately choking back a wealth of emotion. "I'll probably see you at the funeral, but in case I don't see you again after that, I want you to know that you've been a true friend to me and Sister Adams. I really appreciate everything you've done."

Brian gave Maxie a dimpled smile, and opened his arms to her. "Come 'ere."

Maxie embraced him tightly and let her tears fall. "Thank you Brian," she whispered in his ear. "Thank you for being there for me." Maxie didn't want to tell him that she was going to miss him. She couldn't handle the finality those words contained, so she just held on to him.

"You take care of yourself Maxine Bruce. I'll see you again. You still owe me a lunch date right?"

Maxie giggled a little, and loosened her embrace to pull herself away from him. "That's right, I do." Situating her purse on her shoulder, she and Brian once again entered a moment of complete silence.

"You gonna be okay going home by yourself?" Brian asked sincerely. "I mean you've just …."

"Oh yeah," Maxie piped. "I'll be fine."

"I'm going to call you at home later, to make sure you arrived safely."

Maxie smiled, nodded her head, and took Brian in one more time. This time, she also leaned in and kissed him on his cheek. Turning slowly, she began to walk away. "I'll see you Brian," she solemnly called over her shoulder. He watched her as she stopped just shy of the doorway, and turned toward him. "Hey, did she say anything … or leave anything for me?"

Brian slightly nodded his head no. Before she turned to walk away, Maxie's eyes fell on the little gold tin of chocolate she left on the table. "Throw that away for me will you?"

Brian looked at the table, and then at Maxie. "I will."

Maxie turned, waved at him over her shoulder, and left Siemen's Nursing Home.

* * * * * * * * *

For over an hour, Maxie drove around aimlessly thinking about Sister Adams, and the loneliness she probably felt when family should have been near. She had never known, or felt failure to the extent she was feeling it right now. It gripped her, and weighed heavily both mentally and physically. She couldn't even do what came natural to a person in her shoes, which would be to place blame. There was no one to place blame on. Who could she possibly censure for her own neglect? No, the only thing Maxie wanted to do was run. Run as far away from the situation as she could get. She needed a place where she could concisely remove all thoughts, all memories, and absolutely all admonitions. She didn't want to think anymore, and she didn't want to talk to anyone else. She simply wanted a place where she could disappear.

And home was not that place.

So Maxie headed for the Jazz Festival.

* * * * * * * * *

Everything around her was fitting for the way things had transpired in the past several hours. Fitting, because it all felt like it wasn't *really* happening. Sister Adams hadn't *really* died and left her full of guilt and pain, and she wasn't *really* sitting in a booth in Mickey's Bar and Lounge, feeling the full-fledged sound of the live band reverberating in her chest, while casually sipping on a glass of Merlot.

"You're really not my idea of an exciting date," Sandra said as she poured herself another glass of wine.

Maxie sat quietly, ignoring the overt comment while she tried to absorb the ambiance of the nightclub.

"So what do you think?" Sandra asked, eyeing Maxie's glass.

"About what?"

"Everything. How's the wine you've barely touched? What do you think about the nightclub scene? Did you like the music at the Jazz Festival? Say something girl. You've hardly spoken to me since we met at the park."

"Well ..." Maxie began coolly. "The inside of this night-club looks pretty much the way I pictured the inside of a club to look. It's not as loud as I thought it would be, and it's a little darker than I expected, but it's pretty much the same as I envisioned it. Uhmm, the Festival ... all of the acts were very good, and the featured sax player was nice."

"And the wine?" Sandra asked, looking at Maxie skeptically while raising an eyebrow.

"I've had wine before, Sandra."

"Uh uh. This ain't communion wine or cooking sherry honey."

Maxie smiled, and casually waved her off. "It tastes like black cherries and plums mixed up with some other fruits or something. I don't know. It tastes all right."

Sandra had a mouthful of wine and nearly choked, trying not to laugh at Maxie's description of the Merlot. "I don't believe I've ever heard it quite described that way."

Maxie smiled a little, and scanned the lounge again. She watched as some people danced happily, while others sat in small groups laughing, and acting like they were having the time of their lives. Maxie longed to feel just a small piece of that excitement, but contrary to the electric momentum that flowed throughout the club, she felt nothing.

Nothing except out of place.

Lowering her eyes, she slowly let her smile fade away, as her thoughts pulled her in closer. True enough, she needed a diversion from all of the pain she harbored, but being in a setting where she felt uncomfortable, was definitely not the escape she hoped for. Now that she had experienced it, she didn't understand why people sought nightclubs as a means of temporary refuge away from their problems. It was clearly doing nothing for her. The club scene was overrated.

"This is stupid," she whispered to herself.

"Why is that?" Sandra asked.

Maxie quickly looked up into Sandra's tender face of concern.

"Maxie, what's going on?"

Maxie glanced at the wine bottle. "Sandra, I don't belong here. This is doing nothing for me. I shouldn't even be here."

"What do you want it to do for you Maxie? You haven't given it a chance. You haven't even finished half your glass of wine. You're all tensed up, and have been since we met earlier this afternoon. You know what? You should've danced with that cute guy who made a special trip across the room just to ask you. It would've loosened you up."

Maxie looked at her hands and began turning her wedding ring around on her finger.

"Maxie, what happened today?"

"I got a wake-up call this morning."

"A wake up call? I'm not following you."

"Let's just say that me, trying to do my own thing was a stupid idea. I can't just walk away. There's too much involved."

Sandra was quiet for a moment before she scratched her head, and looked at Maxie quizzically. "Okay. And you came to this conclusion what, after three weeks of working? You've made up your mind based on that?"

Maxie picked up her wine glass, took a small sip, frowned, and pushed the glass across the table to Sandra.

"Maxie…?"

"Sister Adams died this week Sandra," Maxie blurted. "And she died without me being there." Maxie rolled her eyes upward, and swallowed hard. She didn't want to burst into tears right there in the nightclub. Before she knew it, she got caught up in the moment and the tears began to roll down her cheeks anyway.

"Oh, hey," Sandra said, quickly reaching for a cocktail napkin. "Here, wipe your face." Maxie took the napkin and gently wiped under her eyes. "Oh sweetheart, I am so sorry. I had no idea. That was the old lady you looked after in that nursing home right?" Maxie nodded. "Sweetie, you can't blame yourself? Nobody knows when death is coming."

Maxie put her hands in her lap and looked at them. "I should have been there with her, instead of working that day. She probably needed me then, and I …" Maxie lowered her voice. "I wasn't even available to her. She called me on the phone, and I chose not to return her call."

"Why didn't you call her back?" Sandra almost whispered.

"Because I was planning a surprise visit. She hadn't seen or heard from me since I started working, so I planned to surprise her today. Instead, I was the one who got ..." Maxie's voice trailed off.

Sandra took a deep breath and sat quietly for another moment before she spoke. "But like I said Maxie, nobody knows when ...."

"Anyway, I've decided that I'm not going through with all that stuff I said I wanted to do."

Sandra jerked her head back. "Why? Why now? Because of guilt?"

Maxie stared at Sandra hard, only to receive a hard questioning stare back.

"Listen to me Maxie." Sandra leaned in.

"No Sandra, don't. Don't even waste your time. My mind is made up."

"Would you just listen to me a minute?"

Maxie conceded, and sat back further in her seat with her arms crossed.

"Now I know you're hurting, because Sister Adams meant a lot to you. But you can't let this pain change every-thing. I know you. You will never be able to forgive your-self. You're practically asking to carry around two heavy pieces of luggage. One with Sister Adams's name on it, and the other one labeled, *Maxie's Desire to Be Her Own Woman*. And inside that particular suitcase will be the ques-tions you ask, *when* you ask, what your life *could have* been like outside the proverbial box. Now do you really want to walk around with all of that? Needlessly? Yes she died, and you weren't there. And yes it hurts. But you can't hold on to it Maxie. Grieve, let it go, and keep on strokin'."

Though Sandra's words sounded hard and cold to her, Maxie knew she was right. She also knew the latter part was much easier said than done. "Okay, now that you've said *your* piece, hear mine," Maxie said, keeping her arms folded. "I understand what you're saying, and it's all well and good. But I'm going back to what I know. It was crazy for me to think that I could do something so ... so ... stupid!" Maxie fanned her hand toward the lounge area. "This is not me. This could never be me. It all seemed enticing in the beginning, but that moment's gone now. There's nothing to this. It's just like you said. There's nothing out here."

"I hardly think three weeks is enough time to give a fair assessment. And forget about what I said in the beginning. I didn't understand back then, how much you desired to be a part of this. You need to experience it."

"Correction," Maxie piped. "Past tense. I *needed* to then. I don't anymore. It's done now."

Frustrated, Sandra wiped over her face with her hand, and let it rest on her mouth while she stared at Maxie.

"And now," Maxie looked at her watch. "I need to get home to my husband, and explain to him where his wife has been all day and half the night. It's ten thirty."

"The night's still young," Sandra mumbled under her hand.

"And I have had enough," Maxie said, forcing a smile. "How much do I owe you for the bottle of wine?"

"Nothing. I got this."

Maxie gathered her purse. "Thank you for meeting me this afternoon. I really needed you."

"I know you did," Sandra grinned.

"I have to get out of here now, so I can drive home real slow and think about what I'm going to tell Lester."

"I know that's going to be ugly," Sandra said. "But before you go Maxie, tell me one thing. Has the real hunger you were telling me about, vanished? Just like that, it's gone?"

Maxie looked at the patrons of the lounge, with all of their giddiness and free-will hedonistic attitudes.

"No Sandra," she said softly. "It's not gone. I just need to redirect it."

"You used the word *need*. What about want? Do you *want* to redirect it?"

Maxie smiled lightly, and stood up. "I gotta go," she winked. "Call me okay."

Sandra nodded, and casually took a sip of her wine.

"Thanks again for everything," Maxie said. "Talk to ya soon." Maxie headed for the exit door, committing everything she saw to memory, because she had no plans of ever being in a nightclub again. When she got to the small foyer area of the lounge, she looked back at Sandra's table, only to see three men standing there. Undoubtedly, asking her to dance.

* * * * * * * * * *

The decision to retrace her footsteps back to familiar ground was not an easy one to make, and may have been made hastily, but Maxie was glad she hadn't ventured out beyond the point of no return. All she had to do was perform a rewind on all of the things she had put into play, and send it back out in a different way — with a different purpose. At least that's what she kept telling herself during the ride home. She also told herself that first and foremost, she needed to ask God for forgiveness. Without asking for it, a simple rewind would not be enough, so she prayed the rest of the way home.

Pulling up into her driveway, Maxie's headlights shone brightly on a figure coming out of the kitchen door, and walking briskly to her car.

"Thank God! Maxie, are you all right? Baby I was worried sick about you," Lester said.

"I'm fine," Maxie said, as he helped her from the car.

"I think I called everybody I knew, looking for you. Come here."

Lester held his wife close to him as if he had found a precious jewel he once lost.

"I guess you heard about Sister Adams," she said, resting against his chest.

"Yes I did. I figured you went somewhere to be alone. Come on. Let's go inside." Lester held Maxie's hand and led her into the house, where they sat side by side in the corner of the couch. Lovingly, he lightly stroked the side of her face, and ran his fingers into her hair. "I was so worried about you. Brian from Siemen's called here about five times. He caught me as soon as I got home, and told me about Sister Adams passing."

"Oh, yeah," Maxie nearly whispered, staring at the floor. "I believe I gave him the impression that I was coming straight home." Maxie sat quietly for a moment, waiting for Lester to ask her where she was. She knew the question was on the tip of his tongue, but now she suddenly wanted to volunteer the information. She chose all of her words carefully with the intent of delivering them in such a manner, there would be no more questions for him to ask.

"Baby, I want you to know where I've been all night," she began, looking him in the eye.

Lester stared at Maxie with the same amorous look on his face that he had when they first sat down. Slowly, he took his index finger and placed it over her lips. "I don't need to know where you were tonight. That's not important. What's important to me is that you're here now, and you're fine. I know what Sister Adams meant to you, and I understand that we all deal with death differently. There's no need for you to explain to me how you dealt with it."

Maxie forced a faint smile and lowered her head. Though his words came as a surprise to her, she was grateful he didn't want to hear her explanation. With the guilt she already harbored, she couldn't imagine it being compounded with her husband's disappointment in knowing her whereabouts.

Lester softly kissed Maxie's forehead, and pulled her closer to him. Cuddled in the corner of the couch, Maxie rested in her husband's arms with her head on his chest. It was the safest she had felt all day.

Chapter Fifteen

S unday morning rolled in on the winds of an unpre-
dicted rainstorm. Beads of rain, sounding more like
hail stones than drops, beat against the window with
torrential force. In bed, Maxie considered the irony of the
storm and her own emotional squall, because the agony of
yesterday was still ever present — and just as painful. What
she wanted to do was turn over, pull the covers over her
head, and go back to sleep. The day could go on without
her. It probably would have, had the phone not rang. Maxie
leaned over to the nightstand and picked up the receiver
quickly, in an effort to stop the ringing before it awakened Lester, but he was already awake and heading for the
bathroom.

"Hello," Maxie said with a scratchy voice.

"You didn't even get to experience a hangover did you?
You sound terrible though," Sandra piped.

"Awww," Maxie moaned and plopped her head back
down on her pillow. "I think what I'm feeling is far worse
than any hangover."

"Still hurting huh?"

"Like it all happened this morning."

"Maybe you'll feel better after you go to church. I just called to make sure you made it home okay."

"Your call is a little late isn't it?"

"Well, I didn't think I should've called you last night, just in case you hadn't told Lester where you were. Did you tell him?"

Maxie watched Lester come out of the bathroom.

"Maxie?" Sandra said.

When he walked around to his side of the bed, Maxie watched him grab his robe, and come around to her side.

"Maxie, did you tell him?" Sandra asked again.

As he came closer to her, Maxie removed the phone from her ear and met Lester's lips with her own; tasting the residue of toothpaste on his mouth.

"I love you," he said softly. "Come on in the kitchen and I'll fix you breakfast."

Maxie smiled, "Let's do breakfast together. I'll be there in just a minute."

Lester winked his eye and walked out of the room.

"Hello? Hello?" Sandra called. "Maxie!"

Maxie put the phone back to her ear. "No Sandra, I didn't tell him. I didn't have to."

"What are you doing? Why did it take you so long to answer me? Hold up. Did you just say you *didn't* have to tell him?"

"That's what I said. I'll tell you about it later. Now I have to go because we're getting ready to cook breakfast together."

"You're what?"

"Bye bye Sandra." Maxie hung up the phone. Laughing to herself, she grabbed her robe, refreshed herself in the bathroom, and met her husband in the kitchen. Lester amused her as he attempted to move around the kitchen like it was his area of expertise. A few times, when he would search for an item, Maxie had to appear to stumble on it, so as not to make him feel like he was lost and out of his league; though it was obvious that he was.

Maxie graciously welcomed the subtle changes Lester had been displaying lately. She was pleasingly surprised at how the changes weren't just happening in episodes, but rather continual. Things like helping her clean the kitchen after dinner, or washing his own work clothes, or occasionally making the bed while she cooked breakfast during the week, were a few of the niceties she was enjoying. And she wanted to enjoy them without question. She wasn't about to raise a voice of suspicion to any of his peculiar acts of kindness. However, she was inclined to believe that her own desire to make changes in her life, sparked an interest for him to make adjustments too. Whatever the reason, she was happy for it.

* * * * * * * * * *

Maxie and Lester were forty-five minutes late for church. Even after arriving late, the service was long and drawn out. People sat in their pews yawning, and leaning forward with their head in their hands, while others actually slept, using the side arm of the pew as a pillow. Maxie blamed it on the weather conditions. Outside, the gray overcast sky seemed to draw strength from almost everyone. She intended on staying home, but at the last minute, Lester answered a phone call from one of Sister Adams's family members, and promised that Maxie would meet with them immediately after church.

That was the last thing she wanted to do.

Being directly involved with the funeral arrangements of someone close to her, had proven to be very trying emotionally. She gained that first-hand experience with the death of her grandmother. Still grieving over Sister Adams herself, Maxie knew she was going to be used as a pillar of strength to support the bereaved family. Just how much support she would be, was a question to be answered. But she wanted to use the opportunity to get herself on the right track. Her grandmother once told her that a funeral was a wonderful time to win souls to Christ. Nearly everyone attending would be emotional and giving more thought to their own mortality, so it was the prime time to offer them the *right* place for eternal life. At the risk of sounding like an insurance agent selling a burial plot, Maxie knew that was what she would have to do. She'd have to sell Jesus. Witnessing had to be a favorable act that would put her back into good graces with God, or at least be a step in the right direction.

Maxie listened as the week's announcements were read, and the information about Sister Adams's untimely death. Her memorial service would be on Monday, and the funeral was scheduled for Tuesday afternoon. A low moan echoed in a wave from the front of the sanctuary, to the back.

"Yes, we mourn the loss of our fair Sister Adams," the reader moaned, sounding as if he were delivering a eulogy instead of an announcement. "The Lord needed another rose in His beautiful garden of precious flowers, and saw fit to take our dear Sister Adams from us down here, to be with Him up there. She will be sadly missed."

In her mind, Maxie went back and forth between hearing the reader and replaying Sister Adams's last words to her, about the church people visiting with her.

"And don't try to send me nobody else from the church to come visit with me. If they ain't coming by now, I don't want them coming at all."

Now, she was being spoken of as if everyone in the church knew her and shared in the latter part of her life.

"Incredible," Maxie mumbled.

For the remainder of the service, she fought sleep. Just before it was finally over, Maxie received word that she would not have to meet with the family of Sister Adams after all, to which she was relieved. She was an emotional wreck. When the benediction was said, Maxie was more than ready to go. Instead of waiting for Lester, she walked quickly through the vestibule, pining for a quick exit into the parking lot. She knew she would begin crying at the drop of a dime if anyone spoke with her directly about Sister Adams, and she wanted to avoid that. Lester would just have to meet her in the car.

Maxie hoped the sight of her scurrying would deter anyone from stopping her for small talk, but it didn't work. Many of the congregants stopped her anyway, to share their condolences and ask her to express their sorrow to Sister Adams's family. Some walked by and simply patted her on her back. Others obliged her with a weak smile and a face of concern. Contrary to how she thought she would react, Maxie felt she handled it all pretty well. That is until she opened the passenger side of her car to get in, and heard her name being called.

"Sister Bruce. Oh Sister Bruce."

Maxie looked up to see three elderly women waving their arms frantically to get her attention, as they paraded across the church parking lot. Not pleased at all by what she was seeing, Maxie took a deep breath, closed the car door, and pushed a broad smile onto her face.

Blanche Grammerson, Emma Teal, and Joyce Rodgers, were three of the nosiest, discord sewing, hypocritical women in the entire church, and they stood as three pillars. Nearly every word they spoke, no matter how inflammatory, was believed beyond the shadow of a doubt. Where these three were concerned, a person was always guilty until proven innocent, and they made sure *everyone* saw it their way.

Maxie was not a fan of the trio, ever since they voted Sister Adams out of the office of President of the Union a few years back. They subtly coaxed members into believing that Sister Adams was incapable of exhibiting leadership qualities, because she missed a few so called emergency meetings that were scheduled by the Board (on which these three women sat). It mattered to no one that Sister Adams's only knowledge of the meetings came just minutes before they were set to begin.

"Sister Bruce, praise the Lord. How are you doing this afternoon?" Blanche asked, taking Maxie's hand to force a handshake.

"I'm fine ladies. How are you all?"

"We're blessed," Emma and Joyce said in unison.

Blanche released Maxie's hand and continued. "Sister Bruce, as the leaders of the Deaconess Union, we all just want you to know that we are very pleased with the care you have given to our dear sister in her time of need. She often spoke very highly of you."

"Why thank you. Sister Adams was very special to me. You said she often spoke highly of me? You visited with her?" Maxie knew her question would undoubtedly make these women squirm, so she leaned against the car door and crossed her arms to watch, keeping her feigned smile.

"Well actually," Emma Teal started. "Despite the many times we attempted to visit with her in that nursing home, we were physically unable to be there because of all that we do here at the church. So we ...."

"Oh, so one of you called her," Maxie interrupted. "That was sweet. She must've forgotten to mention that to me." Maxie watched the women become agitated.

"Sister Bruce," Joyce Rodgers expressed with an air of piousness. "Our duties here at the church leave us little time for telephone conversations. However, one of the members here phoned the nursing home from time to time in our stead, to make sure all of Ruby's needs were being met. Workers at the facility there, reported ...."

Reported? Maxie screamed within herself. *Reported? Have these women been checking up on my visits with Sister Adams?* Maxie's smile faded.

"... that she was very well taken care of and that she often spoke of you quite favorably."

Blanche smiled, scrunched her nose, and nodded her head. "We just wanted you to know that you did a good job,"

"Yes, thank you Sister Bruce. And may God bless you for everything," Emma said.

In the same fashion that they walked across the parking lot to her, the three of them turned on their heels and began to walk away. Abruptly, Emma Teal stopped, and briskly walked back to her.

"Oh, by the way, in reference to the three weeks you *weren't* there, we understand the reason why. You be blessed." She turned and walked away.

Maxie was totally appalled. She didn't know what to think or say. Obviously there was nothing left to say. She had been spied on for almost a year and a half. Somehow, she suddenly felt violated, with no possible recourse. All she could do was watch these three, in all of their wicked grandeur, as they walked back into the church. Affably, they spoke with Lester in passing, as he was coming out of the door. When he reached the car, Lester looked at Maxie quizzically.

"What's wrong? Why are you standing out here? Don't you have your key?"

Maxie quickly looked around her as if Lester's words just slapped her out of a state of being mesmerized. "Uh, yes. Yes, I have it."

"Well come on and get in," he smiled, and slid into the driver's seat.

When Lester started the car, Maxie got in and sat quietly, looking straight ahead.

"Are you all right?" He asked, leaning forward to get her attention. "You look as if you're about to cry."

Maxie pressed her lips together firmly, and looked down at her lap. "I'm fine," she said lowly. "Can we just go?"

Lester looked at her a moment longer, and then drove out of the church parking lot.

Chapter Sixteen

Maxie couldn't bring herself to attend the memorial service for Sister Adams on Monday night, and Lester didn't question her decision to stay home. Her reason for not going was not because death was something she feared, but because it would be hard to look on the face of someone she let down — with no time left to change anything. Even at the funeral, she didn't go up to view the body. For her, death always offered those remaining, a cup of unsettling finality. It also rendered the survivors totally helpless. A helplessness that was the foundation of the frustration and anger, that was felt by all who loved or cared for the deceased.

Maxie drank from that cup. Only hers was spiced with guilt.

On the day of the funeral, it was protocol for all of the minister's wives to lend their support wherever needed. So clad in a white dress with white gloves, Maxie stood in the vestibule feigning yet another soft smile, while she passed out programs with Sister Adams's smiling face on the cover. All that was required of the minister's wives was to sooth, pet, and offer words of encouragement to the family. All Maxie really wanted to do was to sit in the furthest corner away from everyone, and silently pray for the opportunity to fix everything that had gone wrong.

When the funeral service ended, Maxie and the other wives stood in a military perfect line outside the sanctuary doors, ready to direct the family to the limousines. Slowly, the mahogany colored casket was pushed down the aisle toward the vestibule.

And that was all Maxie saw.

She didn't lift her eyes again until the casket passed. After it was put inside the hearse, and there was no one else to escort, Maxie helped to bring out the flowers and the wreaths. When she finally returned to the sanctuary, she stood and waited for Lester, who was standing in the pulpit speaking with another minister.

"Aren't you riding out to the cemetery with the other wives?" He asked when he came down.

"No. I want to ride with you."

"But you know you're supposed to..."

"Lester, please," Maxie frowned, not wanting to give an explanation.

Lester looked at her for a quick moment. "Well, let's go."

* * * * * * * * *

When they arrived at Broadview Cemetery, Maxie got out slowly. Tossing her gloves on the seat, she closed the door and stood next to the car. The day was unusually warm, and the sun's rays peeked through the many trees that were planted throughout the graveyard. Maxie looked around and took in the picturesque view.

"It's so beautiful here," she whispered.

All of the trees were massive in size, and each one offered its own kaleidoscope of autumn colors on leaves that dangled freely. Maxie smiled at the wind that caused a small mound of leaves on the ground to disburse, and seemingly run toward her feet as if they were in a race to greet her.

"You ready?" Lester asked, holding out his hand to her.

Maxie walked around the car, and fitted her hand in his. Feeling Lester give her a little squeeze, let her know that he was totally aware of how she was feeling, and that he was right there for her.

Because Lester had to park the car at the tail end of the processional, they were a distance from the gravesite. When they finally reached the green canopy that marked Sister Adams's final resting place, Maxie and Lester stood behind the crowd. After a few minutes, Maxie noticed the other wives who were still on duty. With tissue boxes in hand, and standing at attention, at least three of them looked at her and cut their eyes. She didn't care. Right now *she* needed support, and there was nothing any of them could offer her. Glancing at her husband, she faintly smiled and set her focus on the Funeral Director.

"I read to you now from the second book of Corinthians, the fifth chapter, verses one, six, eight, and nine. For we know that if our earthly house of this tabernacle were dissolved, we have a building of God, a house not made with hands, eternal in the heavens. Therefore we are always confident, knowing that whilst we are at home in the body, we are absent from the Lord. We are confident I say, and willing rather to be absent from the body, and to be present with the Lord. Wherefore we labor that, whether present or absent, we may be accepted of Him. For I am now ready to be offered, and the time of my departure is at hand. I have fought a good fight, I have finished my course, I have kept the faith; henceforth there is laid up for me a crown of righteousness, which the Lord, the righteous judge, shall give me at that day: and not to me only, but unto all them also that love His appearing."

Lester squeezed Maxie's hand again. She had forgotten she was still holding his hand.

"Are you okay?" He leaned over and whispered in her ear. "You're shaking."

Maxie lowered her head and watched tears drop from her eyes. Apparently, she was crying too. She maintained her composure right up until the Funeral Director said *I have finished my course.* Then her body began to act on its own. Lester motioned for one of the wives to bring Maxie a Kleenex. Only then did she hear her own sobs mixed in unison with the sobs of those around her.

"Come 'ere baby," Lester said, pulling her closer to him. Maxie buried her face in his chest and cried uncontrollably.

"I know," he whispered to her as he stroked her hair. "I know."

Maxie wished he did know. She wanted to tell him how she probably would never have closure where Sister Adams was concerned, and how in the previous three weeks, she opened doors in her life that she never should have opened.

But for now, she just cried.

For the duration of the ceremony, Maxie stayed in Lester's arms, finding comfort in his embrace as the Funeral Director continued.

"Don't grieve for me, for now I'm free. I'm following the path God laid for me. I took His hand when I heard him call. I turned my back and left it all. My life's been full. I've savored much. Good friends, good times, a loved one's touch. Lift up your hearts and share with me. God wanted me now; He set me free."

At the end of his speech, the Funeral Director released three white Homing Pigeons from their cage, to accent his words. After he shared brief words of consolation with the family, he thanked all of those who attended and expressed the family's gratitude. It wasn't long before everyone left the gravesite. Everyone except Maxie and Lester.

"Are you...?" Lester began.

"I want to be alone with her for a minute," Maxie said softly.

"You sure?"

"Yeah. I'll be fine."

"Well, I'll go get the car and move it closer."

Maxie smiled briefly and watched Lester walk away from her. Remaining in the same spot, she looked at the casket a moment before she walked toward it. Although she knew there was nothing in the casket but an earthly shell, Maxie felt it was necessary and soothing for her to express her own final words. Firmly, she gripped a wad of tissues in her hand, as she stood in the area between the first row of chairs and the casket.

"Hey," she said, a little louder than she wanted to. Quickly, she looked around to see if anyone heard her, momentarily forgetting that she was the only one there.

"Hey," she said again in a lower tone. "I think you're really going to like this place. It's really beautiful here." Maxie scanned the area. "There are a lot of trees here. I remember how you liked to sit underneath the big tree at Siemen's whenever the weather was nice." Maxie glanced at the wad of tissue, and then at the casket. "Oh God," she whimpered. "I am so sorry Sister Adams. I am so sorry I wasn't there for you when you needed me the most. If I had listened then to what you were trying to tell me about being in my place and doing God's will, I could have been there with you, and you wouldn't have died...alone. No one should have to die alone," she whispered. "And I pray that you've forgiven me." Maxie heard Lester pull up and turn the car off, but he didn't get out. "Don't you worry about me, okay?" She continued. "I'm going to do fine. I remember everything you told me. And I think you'll be happy to know I'm not going through with doing my own thing anymore. I'm going to be more dedicated to the plan God has for me. I understand my purpose, so I'm going to do fine. You'll be proud of me." Maxie glanced at the car through blurred eyes, and then back at the casket. "God knows, I sure am going to miss you." Giving in to the silence, Maxie just stood there for a moment. "I have to go now Sister Adams. I love you. And give my love to my parents and my grandmother too okay?" Maxie picked up a clump of dirt from the ground, and removed a single red rose from one of the many wreaths. With tears streaming down her face, she crushed the clump of dirt over the casket and laid the single rose on top of it. "I'll see you soon." With all that was said and done, Maxie kissed her fingertips, touched the casket, and walked away.

Chapter Seventeen

I t was a good idea for Maxie to ask for time off. Since Regina promised her a favor, she was able to redeem it to get Monday off. For Tuesday, she took bereavement leave, and Wednesday was her normal day off. When she returned to work, Maxie had enough time to seriously decide as to whether or not she was going to continue working. The job she so desperately wanted in the beginning, had now become a crooked area in her road to recovery. After careful consideration, Maxie decided she would have to maintain her work schedule — her decision being based solely upon necessity. Simply put, she had to fulfill what she said was her purpose for getting a job in the first place. Buying Lester an anniversary gift with her own money.

And that would have to be her focus.

With the worst part behind her, and a change of view ahead, Maxie planned to return to what now seemed incredibly more important to her than it ever was before; her walk with God. Only this time, it needed to be different. It *had* to be different. She didn't want to return to doing things the old way. She didn't want to fit into the ancient mold of living the Christian life, only when it was convenient (which was usually when others were watching). That is not what she was taught in her youth. Though she had previously followed others after that manner, now was the time to stop and go another way. She had a new determination, so her walk would have to be new too.

It didn't take Maxie long to switch gears and begin to make progress. Two weeks after Sister Adams's funeral, she found herself witnessing in the jails on Sunday evenings, going door to door with the church's Outreach Team on some Saturday mornings, and even planting seeds of encouragement into the customers who came through her line at work. She knew her heart was really into what she was doing, when she was able to persuade her homosexual co-worker Alan, to give his life to Christ.

"So you convinced the little gay boy to accept Christ as his personal Savior. That's good, because he needs Jesus," Sandra conveyed over the phone. Her call was perfectly timed, just as Maxie arrived home from work.

"You need Him too," Maxie said, holding the phone between her ear and shoulder.

"I know I do girl. Just not right now though."

"Sandra, when are you...?"

"Uh uh Maxie. I said not right now though."

"Whatever. Anyway, I was just filling you in on what's been happening on my end, since I haven't heard from you in about three days." Maxie unbuttoned and removed her shirt, before stretching herself out on the couch.

"You haven't bothered calling me either."

"Girl, I have been so busy, it's unbelievable."

"Just as well. I was out of town on a business trip. So how are you doing? You holding up okay?"

"Yeah, I'm fine. You know me. I got that bounce back ability."

"Bounce back ability huh?" Sandra echoed, with a slight air of skepticism. "So gone are the days of old?"

"Yeah, I guess. Whatever that means."

"You know exactly what it means."

"If you're asking me am I ever going out with you to a club again, the answer is no. So, yes, gone is *that* day of old."

"I'm telling you girl, you're doing yourself a great injustice by not fully gaining the true experience. Why don't you tag along with me tonight? I'll take you some place where you can have yourself a really good time. That one night we went out really shouldn't count anyway, because you were hurting. Your mind was elsewhere. It's Friday night, come on and try it again."

"Sandra?" Maxie said. "Give it up. That's not me. I don't have the desire to live that life anymore."

"Maxie!" Sandra yelled into the phone. "Who are you kidding? It's me remember? I know you, and you were feeling this thing full throttle. It doesn't just fade away. That monster is going to stay hungry until you feed it Maxine Bruce. You opened the door and teased it, and just as it was about to escape, you shut the door and tried to lock it up again. You can't lock up desire Maxie. It makes itself known. Let's take your job for instance. Keeping it is proof that you're still secretly yearning for the other side of the fence. Remember the *real* reason you wanted to get a job?" Sandra waited for Maxie to respond, but she said nothing. "I'll give you a hint. It was desire making itself known."

Maxie kept her silence. Sandra's words were toxic, and normally would have hit her in the tender zones. But those areas were covered now, and the poison didn't penetrate. Or so she thought.

"You're right Sandra. It is a monster. And nobody knows better than I do how it works. One thing you failed to recognize is that I'm stronger now than I was before. I can fight the monster, because I have help on the inside. And I intend to beat it, every single time. Now you're supposed to be my girl, and you're talking to me like the devil. Who are you?" Maxie joked.

"Oh! You ain't right! You ain't right! You know I'm here for you. I just want you to make up your mind. You're making me dizzy. Now I have to go get myself a drink so I can get my bearings again."

"Get off my phone Sandra," Maxie laughed.

"I'm gone girl. I'm here for you when you want to get your groove on again."

"I'll talk with you later."

"Bye."

Maxie hung up the phone. When she did, it was her intention to never think about the subject of that conversation again, but something Sandra said catapulted her into deep thought and made her question herself. Had she used Lester's anniversary gift as an excuse again? Maybe she unconsciously used that motive as a ploy. Was the real reason she chose to continue working at Food King, a desperate attempt to hold on to that past secret desire? If it was, Sandra was right.

To channel herself in line with what she wanted to accomplish, Maxie knew there could be no self-made obstacles. No more excuses. And no more excuses meant one thing. She would have to quit her job at Food King immediately.

* * * * * * * * * *

"I'm sure that's not the sale price young lady," the old woman said harshly. "Would you please check the sale paper? I just know your register is ringing up the wrong price."

Maxie looked at the diminutive old woman, and genuinely smiled.

"I'm sorry ma'am. This item was on sale last week. That sale ended yesterday. Our sale prices run from Friday to Friday."

"No, no. I just got the sale paper in my mailbox yesterday, and that can of peaches is in it for eighty-nine cents, not a dollar thirty-nine."

Maxie leaned in a little, and scoped the line that was rapidly forming behind the old woman. Right at that instant, she hated the fact that yet again, she was covering a shift for Monet. Only this time, Monet asked Maxie herself, and she agreed, forgetting how hectic Saturday mornings could be.

Maxie reached underneath her register, and handed the old lady the weekly ad paper. "Here you go ma'am. Would you please show me the page you saw these canned peaches on? I could be wrong."

The old woman thumbed through the paper frantically, mumbling to herself, while Maxie glanced down the line again. All she could see was a never ending line of full grocery baskets, and the many faces of disgruntled customers.

"I don't understand," the woman squeaked. "Are you sure this is the new ad paper? This doesn't look like the one I have."

"Yes ma'am. The date is right there on the first page."

"Oh dear. I am so sorry. Oh my goodness."

After the woman paid her, Maxie quickly helped the courtesy clerk bag her groceries, to help move the line along.

"Thank you for being so patient with me," the woman whined. "You're a very good cashier."

Maxie smiled, said thank you, and proceeded with the next customer.

"Hi, how are you today? Sorry about the delay." She said routinely. "Did you find everything you needed?" Maxie hated asking that semi-rhetorical question. If the customer ever said no, it wasn't like she was going to leave her register to go help them find the items they lacked.

She couldn't wait for two o'clock to roll around, and only hoped the person replacing her would be on time. She had been there since nine o'clock. It was only twelve-thirty and it seemed like everyone in Savannah decided to get their weekly shopping done early, and then file into her line for checkout. There was barely enough time for her to clean her conveyor belt of leaking milk and dripping meat containers.

"Excuse me ma'am," a man's voice said directly behind her.

"Uh huh," Maxie answered. Without turning around, she hoped the cordial sound in her voice was enough to make whoever was questioning her, ask their question anyway, even if she didn't turn around to address them directly. She wanted to keep her momentum going.

"Can you tell me where the batteries are located?"

Maxie briefly looked over her shoulder, only not in the direction of the customer, but in the direction of the aisles. "They're at the end of aisle three," she said, quickly pointing to the right of her.

"Thank you," Maxie heard. Then the man's voice went away.

The line that formed for checkout at her register was relentless, and continued steadily for the next hour. When it did finally die down a little, it was close to the time Maxie was scheduled to get off. Regina was on the floor making rounds and heading her way.

"Maxie," Regina called from the end of the conveyor belt. "Go ahead and turn your light off. It will probably take you the next twenty minutes to ring up the rest of the customers in your line, and get cleaned up."

Maxie quickly flipped the little switch at the bottom of her number marker, before Regina walked away. There were two customers left, and she wanted to offer the last customer the suggestion of using the Express Lane, but that line was longer.

"I bet you're ready to go home aren't you?" The woman in front of her asked.

Maxie glanced at her long enough to see her throw her blonde hair out of the way so she could write a check.

"Oh yeah. It's been a long and busy day."

"Wow," the woman let her voice drag. "What time did you get here?"

Maxie didn't feel like having idle chatter with the lady, but since she was next to the last customer, she obliged.

"Since nine this morning."

"Wow. Nonstop?"

"Nonstop." Maxie smiled. "There's no rest for the weary."

"I guess," the blonde nodded.

Maxie finished with the transaction, thanked the woman, and invited her to come again. By the time she got to the last shopper, her professionalism died. She still greeted in her usual manner, but she was not the least bit interested in making eye contact. So she reached for the items that were on the conveyor belt, and began scanning them.

"I couldn't find the batteries you said were on aisle three. I guess you just wanted to send me to the wrong place huh? Do you send the customers on wild goose chases often?"

Maxie listened attentively to the tone in which she was being spoken to, only because she needed to decipher whether this customer was actually angry, or jokingly teasing her. The last thing she wanted, this close to her shift ending, was a confrontational customer. She had worked the entire five hours, with only the slightest bit of conflict. She wasn't about to have it now. Pushing her ever faithful grin into position, Maxie focused on scanning the grocery items. She didn't want to risk looking into the face of an angry shopper, and have the rest of her day ruined.

"I'm sorry about that," she said. "They should've been in that aisle on the same shelf with the lightbulbs."

"They were there, just on the endcap of that aisle. It took me a while to find them."

"And I guess it didn't help matters when you had to get into this long line."

"I didn't mind the wait. It was worth it just to see that smile."

With those kind words, Maxie finally looked at the face that went with the voice, and was immediately captivated. The man who stood before her was about 5'11", and truly chiseled. Even though he wore a light jacket, she could see he was built like a professional football player. His coffee-with-cream colored skin, highlighted his brown eyes and dark smooth eyebrows. His hair was closely cropped, and his hairline was trimmed precisely to his shadow thin side-burns. Maxie wasn't captivated by his good looks alone, but it was his lips that kept her enthralled. Underneath a smooth mustache, they were full, but not overly so, and incredibly appealing. When he licked his lips, it came to her how she was staring at this man. When she looked him in his eyes, he was clearly assessing her too — sweeping her from head to torso.

"So do you look at all the customers like that …?" He leaned over a little to look at her nametag. "... Maxie?"

Maxie blushed and laughed a little, as she scanned the last few items. "No. No I don't."

"So I should feel special then."

She laughed again, more at his candidness. "Sure, you can feel special if you want to."

"I want to," he nodded.

Maxie hit the total key. "That'll be twenty-seven twenty-nine."

With his eyes on her, he pulled two twenty-dollar bills from his pocket. When he handed Maxie the money, she felt him deliberately touch her fingers.

"So what's a beautiful woman like you doing, working in a grocery store?"

"Thank you for the compliment. I won't be working here too much longer."

"Oh, so you're quitting soon?"

"Within the next couple of weeks," she said, handing him back his change. Maxie suddenly realized what she was doing, and couldn't understand for the life of her, why she was telling this stranger her business.

"So I guess if I want to see your beautiful face again, I'll have to make quite a few trips here in the next two weeks huh?"

Maxie was speechless. She had never been hit on at the speed this man was moving.

"Well ... Maxie. My name is Marc."

"It's nice to meet you Marc," she said, this time trying not to stare. While Marc was busy gazing at her, Maxie's eyes followed a courtesy clerk that was rapidly approaching her lane.

"Sir, may I take this to your car for you?" The clerk asked.

"No thank you," Marc replied, without moving his eyes from Maxie.

She wished the clerk would move faster, because Marc was beginning to make her feel uncomfortable with his appraising eyes.

"Here you go sir. Are you sure you won't need any help?" The clerk asked again.

Marc finally acknowledged the courtesy clerk with a broad grin. "No. I think I can handle these few bags."

Both Maxie and the courtesy clerk watched as he moved to the end of the conveyor belt, and grabbed all seven of his bags with one hand.

"Well Maxie, thank you for your assistance. You've been very helpful, and you've made my shopping experience a memorable one," he smiled.

"Thank you and come again," she said sincerely.

"Count on it," he winked.

Maxie watched him walk away, observing his stride and how he walked with such confidence. When she finally began to clean up her area, she thought about her last customer. She was glad he wasn't upset with her about having to search for the batteries, even though she sent him in the right direction. Not only was he not upset, but he told her she made his shopping experience a memorable one. Maxie knew that statement could be either bad or good. She opted for the latter.

It would have been nice if Marc backed up his statement by completing a Customer Service Survey sheet at the front desk. Storewide, Maxie was running neck and neck with Monet on receiving the most merits. They both had six, and Maxie took pride in knowing she had gotten hers because of excellent customer service. Monet on the other hand, flirted her way to the top. But Maxie decided the monthly race really should not matter to her anymore, since she wouldn't be contending much longer. Even though she had not formally submitted her two weeks' notice, she knew quitting was a done deal.

Smiling to herself, Maxie entertained a question she felt Regina might ask her upon receiving the notice.

So what would it take for you to stay here at Food King with us?

Well, Maxie would begin. *If you could get me more customers like Mr. Marc there, I just might be persuaded to stick around a little longer.* With that thought, Maxie's smile grew into a grin.

"I know you're glad to be off, but you don't have to make it so obvious."

Maxie spun around. "Hey, Alan. Are you my replacement?"

"Uh uh. I'm just standing here holding this cash tray. I figured I could use it as an accessory to go with this tired blue smock, and this tired little nametag. What do you think?" Alan turned around in a small circle, holding up his free hand like a female runway model.

"I think you're crazy, and you need some help," Maxie laughed, and opened her register to pull her cash tray out.

"Pray for me girl."

Maxie took all of her belongings and let Alan replace her. Though his last statement was meant to be comical, Maxie took it at face value. The result of a change in life-style was something that would appear gradually over time, but in Alan's case, Maxie wished it would hurry up. She knew he had given his life to Christ, but she wanted other people to know it too. Right now, Alan's spiritual commitment in the eyes of others was only a verbal expression. He still walked the same and much to Maxie's disapproval, spoke with the same feminine resonance. She understood she was expecting a great deal more than what she should expect in such a short amount of time, but she wanted it nonetheless.

"I'm always going to pray for you Alan," she said with a smile.

Alan looked at her squarely, and returned the smile. "Will you go on and get out of here already, before you make me start crying and praising God up in here?"

Maxie laughed, and walked toward the Customer Service desk. "I'll see you Monday," she called over her shoulder.

When she approached the desk, Regina stood at the little entranceway, holding her hands out.

"Here, I'll take that," she said, reaching for Maxie's cash tray. "I'll count it down for you. You can go ahead and punch out."

Maxie handed over the tray with a look of surprise. Regina never counted down *anyone's* cash tray. If a cashier had to leave due to an emergency, she was quick to remind them that number one on their job description was, *count down your own cash tray*. Suspiciously, Maxie eyed Regina, before she walked to the time clock to punch out.

"I want to thank you for taking over Monet's shift again," Regina said, with her back to Maxie. "I tell you, that girl is treading on thin ice around here. I don't think any of her co-workers care for her much. And I'm sure it's because she rubs most of them the wrong way."

"So why do you and Mr. Martin put up with her?"

"Well," Regina paused. "I don't know how long Mr. Martin is going to put up with her, but I'm fed up. I want to fire her...but I can't."

Maxie walked to the counter and stood next to Regina, with a quizzical look. "Oh?"

"Yeah," Regina muttered lowly. "She's my sister's daughter."

"Your sister's daugh... Oh, so she's your niece."

"Uhm hmm," Regina said, frowning as if the words *your niece* had a foul stench to them.

That would explain a lot, Maxie said within herself.

"And Mr. Martin has this crazy little schoolboy crush on my sister. So ...." Regina shrugged her shoulders. "My hands are kind of tied."

Maxie stood quietly, careful not to interrupt Regina's *never before seen* display of genuine human emotion.

Regina glanced at Maxie. "I guess you're wondering why I'm telling you all of this aren't you?" Maxie raised both of her eyebrows and simply smiled. Regina laughed a little. "I feel like you're an easy person to talk to Maxine

Bruce. I mean you come in here, you do your job, socialize only as you need to, you get along with everybody, you don't get involved in gossip, and then you go home. You're pretty easy going. I like that about you Maxie. You're good people."

Maxie was bewildered. Never in a million lifetimes would she have expected to be observed so meticulously, by someone who appeared to only take notice of work performance.

"I just wanted to let you know that it's good to have someone with your character working here. It's appreciated."

Maxie blushed. Grinning softly, she lowered her head. "Thank you Regina. That was really nice to hear. It's good to be appreciated."

"You do a good job. Which is more than I can say for a lot of the workers here, including my niece. Thanks again for covering for her."

"Not a problem." Maxie looked down at her watch. It was 2:30 p.m. "Well, I have to get on home. You have a good weekend Regina."

"You too Maxie."

Chapter Eighteen

L ester looked out of the kitchen window, and immediately moved himself out of view when Maxie pulled
into the driveway. She was surprised to see his car,
but it was Saturday and she knew his schedule could be
very flexible. Maxie thought she saw Lester peeking out
of the kitchen window. If he did, she didn't question the
reason, because another question popped in as soon as she
got out of the car. Like where was that incredibly delicious
aroma coming from?

Having missed the time she could have eaten something
at work, and refusing to stop anywhere on her way home,
Maxie was starving. The smell she was experiencing now,
only deepened her hunger. Tilting her head upward, she
let her nose discover which direction the appetizing scent
was coming from, and what food it identified. In the whiff
were scents of onions, spices, and a hint of fresh garlic. The
further she walked up the driveway to the house, the more
the smell intensified. When she arrived at the threshold of
the kitchen door, Lester opened it before she could insert
her key. Pulling the door open wide, he emancipated every

aroma that filled the kitchen, and Maxie walked into it like walking through a wall.

"Welcome home my queen," Lester said, dressed in a short apron and a smile from ear to ear. Leaning in quickly, he kissed Maxie after she stepped through the doorway. "I hope you're hungry."

Maxie looked at Lester in surprise, and searched the kitchen from where she stood. "Mmmm, something smells good! Who's cooking in here?"

"What do you mean who's cooking in here? I'm cooking in here," Lester piped, as he closed the door.

Maxie looked at him and frowned, trying to conceal a broad grin that was becoming increasingly hard to control. "You're cooking?"

"Yes. I'm cooking. I felt like you deserved a break today, and instead of going to McDonald's," he winked. "I thought I'd cook dinner for us." Lester walked to the stove. "I know it's early for dinner, but I wanted to have enough time for unexpected mistakes." After a brief moment, he looked at Maxie still standing by the door, and laughed. "Are you going to stay awhile?"

"Stay? Yeah. Oh ... yeah. I'm just ...."

"Surprised? Yeah, I figured you would be. You know I *can* cook."

"I know you can baby. You just...."

"I just don't."

"Right. It smells delicious."

Maxie made her way to the stove and examined the contents of every pot. There was steamed cabbage, scalloped potatoes in a creamy white garlic herb sauce, a broccoli, cauliflower, and carrot medley steamed in butter, and fresh baked dinner rolls. Underneath the top of an iron kettle, Maxie saw smooth brown gravy gently bubbling.

"What's in the gravy?" She asked.

"It's smothered pork chops." Lester beamed.

"Oh baby," Maxie swooned. "This is so sweet. And I am so hungry."

"Well go get cleaned up and change your clothes. By the time you get finished, everything will be on the table."

"You better move fast," Maxie warned. "Because I'm not going to waste any time."

"Go. I'll be ready."

Maxie looked at the dinner again, and then back at Lester. "Okay," she cautioned, and left the kitchen. When she returned, everything was prepared and on the table just like he said. Lester sat down opposite Maxie, and prayed over the food. When he finished, she immediately sampled everything but her smothered pork chop. Lester watched her amused.

"How is it?" He asked.

Maxie lifted her index finger as she chewed. "Let me taste this pork chop." She started to cut into the chop with a steak knife, but noticed she didn't need it. The meat was tender enough to cut with her fork. After she put it into her mouth and savored the flavor a moment, Maxie looked at Lester and nodded her head negatively. "Baby, you cooked this by yourself?"

"I did."

"Well I'm upset."

"Why?"

"Because you've been holding out on me all this time. I didn't know you could cook like this. Why haven't you done it before now?"

"I've never had a reason to. I mean, you're a good cook and there's no reason for both of us *good cooks* to be in the kitchen, so ...."

"This is delicious sweetheart. Thank you."

"You're welcome."

Lester watched Maxie enjoy her meal a moment longer, before he joined her. Besides a little idle chatter, silence fell between them for the better part of their meal. When they were finished, Maxie told Lester to sit still, while she cleared the dirty dishes from the table. After completing the task, she stood over her husband and gently rubbed his head.

"You out did yourself this time Mr. Bruce. That was very nice."

"Thank you Mrs. Bruce. I'm glad you enjoyed it. I thought it was very good too. Now I'm stuffed."

"Really? But I have something else to go with your meal."

"What could possibly be good enough to complement my feast?" He joked.

Maxie bent over and kissed Lester passionately. "Something you forgot." Casually, she walked to the doorway leading to the living room and stopped. Facing him, she unbuttoned the top two buttons of her blouse, and looked at him alluringly. "Dessert," she said, and walked away toward the bedroom.

Lester sat still for an instant, before he made one swift movement to get out of his seat, take off his apron, and follow her. "Oh yeah," he called to her. "That's a good complement."

Chapter Nineteen

Maxie traced the rim of her coffee cup with her finger, while she listened to the low hum of conversations around her. It was just enough to keep her from drifting into a daydream while she sat in Starbucks, waiting for Sandra to order. The heavy aroma that saturated the café, encouraged her to try a specialty coffee, but she decided to go with a small cup of House Blend.

"You sure you don't want a muffin or something to liven up that boring cup of java you got there?" Sandra asked, when she sat down opposite Maxie with her large cup.

"I'm fine," Maxie replied. "What did you end up getting? It took so long, I thought you had to wait for the coffee beans to be imported."

Sandra blew into her cup gently. "It takes time to make Arabian Mocha Sanani, girl. You can't just rush it. Got to get the intensity just right."

"An exotic drink no doubt. You have a thing for flavored coffees don't you?"

"You know there's flavor in everything I do." Sandra smiled, and looked around the shop. "Saturday afternoon at Starbucks is a little crowded isn't it?"

"Yes. We could have done this at my house. I don't know why you couldn't have met me there."

"Uh uh. This is better. So tell me, how have you been? It's been a while since I've seen you."

"You talk to me on the phone often, and I'm fine."

"Yeah, but it's good to *see* you Maxie. I know everything is fine when I can physically see you."

Maxie smiled. "Don't try to read me Sandra. All is well."

Sandra smiled, and took another sip. "So what's up with all that crazy stuff you were telling me about Lester? You said he was making some changes."

"Yeah, nothing negative. It's just taking a little getting used to on my part. It's little things here and there. I told you about the dinner he cooked for me last Saturday didn't I?

"Yeah, and that was bizarre. Who knew old boy could cook?"

"I knew he could cook. Just not like that. I really enjoyed it."

"Aw you were just hungry," Sandra joked.

That too, but it was something more than that. I really enjoyed *him*. There's something different about our relationship. It's almost like we have this new chemistry between us now. I don't know. He seems more in tune with my concerns. I can't explain it."

"Well, it could be one of two things. One is, maybe he appreciates you now."

"He's always appreciated me."

"No, I mean for real. Men gain a certain sense of security when their wives are at home. Their confidence grows when they know they have their women at home on lock-down. There's no threat of her looking at anybody else, and no one is looking at her. Except for maybe the mailman. And I've seen your mailman, so Lester ain't got nothing to worry about there."

The two women laughed.

"But since you've become gainfully employed, he may be feeling a little threatened. You're out among people more. Maybe he thinks you might be looking for that compassionate man, who *already* knows how to be concerned, and in tune with how a woman feels. So, if Lester *shows* you his appreciation, and he loves on you a little bit more, you won't have a reason to look elsewhere."

"Now that's silly. Lester knows he has my heart. I'm not looking for anyone else." Maxie drank from her cup. "You said it could be one of two things. What's the other one?"

Sandra took a long swallow before she spoke. "Well, the other thing is that ... he's having an affair."

Maxie looked at Sandra bewildered, and then burst into laughter. "You obviously forgot who we are talking about. How could you say that about Lester? You know that's a mold he could never fit."

"I don't know girl. He is a man. And what you're describing to me sounds like evidence. I read in a magazine that men who are cheaters, usually exhibit an overwhelming amount of clinginess. They tend to overcompensate. They all of a sudden want to start spending more time with you, trying to show you more love. And they're only doing it to cover up their guilt, and to make sure their women don't become suspicious."

"Sandra stop it. You know Lester is nothing like that."

"I know," Sandra smiled. "I'm just messing around with you."

Silence fell between the two, as they both gave attention to their drinks, and the people around the coffee shop. After a moment, Sandra turned her lips up in a sinister way and looked at Maxie.

"So what about you Maxie?"

"What about me what?"

"What about you? Could you ever cheat on Lester?"

"Cheat on him with what?" Maxie asked incredulously.

"Okay, now you want to play stupid with me. Another man! Could you ever cheat on your husband with another man?"

"All right. Now I know you've lost your mind. What's with these questions Sandra? Is your brain stuck on infidelity?"

"Oh I don't know," Sandra said coyly. "I was just thinking about that guy you said hit on you last week, and I was wondering what you would do if he pursued you. Would you succumb? Or could you fight it? You know he's coming back right? You do know that you're going to see him again."

Maxie felt herself becoming upset. "What difference does it make Sandra? I work in a grocery store. I probably will see him again. And many other men like him. What's your point?"

"My point is, and don't be angry with me, you're getting ready to go through a test. And it's going to be a test like nothing you've ever faced before. The strength of your marriage is about to be tried baby girl, and the door it's coming through is that job of yours."

Maxie narrowed her eyes, and smiled. "You trying to get prophetic on me?"

"I'm serious Maxie."

"Yeah well, it's going to be pretty hard for any *test* or anything else to come through my job, because I'm closing that door."

"You're quitting?"

"I thought I told you that. I'm getting ready to put in my notice."

"No, you didn't tell me. But it doesn't matter. It's all going to happen before you quit."

"You're sitting here telling me that I may be enticed to have an affair, and that it's all going to transpire within two weeks time."

"Do you believe me?" Sandra asked.

Maxie searched Sandra's eyes, and saw no hint of humor. "Tell me something. How is it that you can live the life that you live, and yet be compelled to warn me about someone you *feel*, might be a temptation for me? Just out of the blue. Is God speaking to *you* now? Wouldn't I be the one more likely to hear from Him?"

Sandra raised both of her eyebrows, and gently nodded her head. "That hurt Maxie."

"I'm sorry Sandra but ...."

"So what you're saying is, because I'm a quote unquote *sinner*, I can't come to you and warn you about something I see coming your way?"

"Sandra, you know I value your opinion on certain issues, but this one is a matter of the heart. My heart. So no, you can't. You can't call this one. Now can we just drop this? I don't want to talk about it anymore."

"Just promise me one thing. Promise me that when this happens, you'll let me help you through it."

Maxie nodded. "*If* it should happen, I promise you will be the first one to know about it. Okay? And I'm sorry about what I just said. I had no right pointing out the differences in our backgrounds. And to do it now, out of anger, simply wasn't fair."

Sandra smiled. "It's cool. I understood what you meant."

Maxie hated how she made herself superior to Sandra. She looked at her ring, and began turning it around on her finger. Sandra reached across the table, and grabbed her hand.

"I said it's okay. You felt I was out of line, and you corrected it. No harm done. Okay?"

Maxie forced a smile. "Yeah, but you know I would never ...."

"I know. Now are you going to spend the rest of this Saturday apologizing, or are we going shopping like we planned?"

Maxie took a deep breath, shook her head, and grinned. "Let's go shopping."

* * * * * * * * *

She was nineteen, and walked around with an air of total narcissism. To watch her make trips from her register to the Customer Service desk, would appear to anyone as if she were strolling down a model's runway. Fully endowed, her choice of tight fashioned garb, allowed her to openly advertise what would be a private asset on anyone else. With Monet however, few things were private. Maxie

recalled how her second day on the job, was her first run in
with the asinine young woman.

"You're one of the new girls aren't you?" Monet asked,
as she bounced herself over to Maxie's register.

"Yes." Maxie answered, trying hard not to look at how
tight the girl's work vest hugged her upper body.

"I'm Monet," she said, profiling. She clearly expected
everyone in the store to stop and clap at the sound of
her name.

"Nice to meet you Monet. I'm Maxie."

Monet looked her up and down, as if she were sizing
her up, before she nodded her approval.

"If you ever forget my name, just think about the artist."

"Excuse me?" Maxie frowned.

"You know. The artist with the same name as mine.
Monet. He was just like me," she said, patting her ample
bosom. "He was an Impressionist, and I'm one too. I'm all
about making a good impression," she said, profiling again.

I'm sure you are, Maxie thought to herself. She wanted
to tell the silly girl that the word she chose to describe herself, had a different meaning when it came to Monet the
artist, but she declined. It wasn't worth it. From that day
on, Maxie tried to keep her dealings with Monet, to a bare
minimum. Watching her in action from across the store,
was enough for Maxie to form a concrete opinion about the
young lady. And her opinion was justified. Monet Benson
was in a category all by herself.

Maxie hated the fact that she had to work with Monet
today. As usual, business was slow on Mondays. It was
a common practice for cashiers with empty lines to go
visit with other cashiers, but Maxie wasn't in the mood for
random conversations. She didn't feel like speaking with

anyone outside of the normal customer, who would just come and go. It was easier to put on a facade of pleasantness for just a few minutes, than to keep it for longer than she wanted to. To help pass the time, Maxie thoroughly cleaned her register area, and stood in her aisle straightening the magazine racks. As she worked, article titles from the magazines like *Why Your Spouse Cheats*, and *Is Your Love Really Enough*, reached out to her and jogged her memory of the accounts from the weekend.

For almost two days, Maxie refused to mull over her displeasing conversation with Sandra. Then, and even now, she didn't need to give her attention to something so irrelevant and petty. The mere thought of allowing anyone to ruin her marriage, was definitely not worth her consideration.

"Hello Maxie," a voice said behind her, crashing in on her thoughts.

Normally, she would have quickly turned around and cordially acknowledge the person who was speaking to her, but since the voice was that of a man, the deep resonance of it instantly brought Sandra's words to mind. *You know he's coming back right? You do know that you're going to see him again.* Everything within her froze, making it virtually impossible for her to turn around.

"Maxie?" He said again.

Maxie closed her eyes and took a deep breath, to calm the nerves in her stomach that wanted to rage. How should she handle herself if that customer named Marc, was standing behind her right now? She wished she had at least given a *little* thought to the answer of that question, prior to this moment. Opening her eyes again, Maxie slowly turned around. In front of her was a smiling face she had grown accustomed to seeing, but had lost touch with. The dimples were a welcomed sight.

"Brian!" She almost screamed. "How are you?"

Maxie threw her arms around Brian's neck, giving him a hug. As she embraced him, she caught a glimpse of Monet traipsing by, and looking at her with a goofy grin on her face. Maxie beamed from ear to ear, as she looked Brian over.

"It is so good to see you," she said. "How have you been?"

"It's good to see you too lady. I'm fine," Brian said, returning her smile.

"What are you doing here? You're a little far away from the nursing home aren't you?"

"Naw, not too far. I had to buy a few extra first aid supplies," he said, motioning toward the items already on the conveyor belt. "Our supply truck had mechanical problems, on the highway coming from Alabama. So I thought I'd buy some of the stuff from here, and come on out to see if you were working today. I miss seeing you Maxie."

Maxie watched a woman with a full cart, begin to approach her lane for checkout. Without a word, she looked at Maxie and then at Brian, and proceeded to push her cart to another aisle.

"I miss seeing you too. I wanted to come visit, but you know ... too many memories there. Did you get to go to the funeral? I didn't see you."

"I was there. You could have called me," Brian said. "I know you haven't forgotten the number."

"No. No I haven't forgotten it. I just didn't think it would be ...."

"Appropriate. I know." Brian slightly shook his head. "You're some kind of woman Maxine Bruce."

Maxie smiled.

"Well, I didn't just come by to pick up these supplies. I actually came by because I wanted to see you, to tell you goodbye."

Maxie frowned a little, yet tried to keep her smile. "Goodbye? Where are you going?"

"I'm transferring back to Macon. There was a position open at the old nursing home I used to work in, so I applied for the job. You're looking at the next patient care supervisor. I'm going to be one of the head men in charge."

Maxie looked at Brian, and felt something heavy in her chest gently drop to the pit of her stomach, taking the sincerity of her smile with it. "Well, congratulations Brian. I know they picked the best man for the job. I never thought you should have been at Siemen's anyway."

"If I hadn't been at Siemen's, I wouldn't have had the pleasure of meeting you."

Maxie looked at the floor for a moment. She couldn't believe how emotional she was becoming at Brian's words. She actually felt a lump in her throat. "Wow," she said lowly. "So when do you leave?"

"I was supposed to be there for training this morning. But I told them I had to take care of some unfinished business here. So they're expecting me first thing Wednesday morning."

"So I guess the answer to my question is tomorrow. You'll be leaving tomorrow."

"Yeah."

Maxie felt a lot of emotional energy where she stood, and she couldn't quite tell if it was coming from her, or from Brian. "So this is how you get out of taking me to lunch huh? You move to another city?"

Brian burst into laughter, making Maxie laugh too.

"We can go to lunch right now if you want, or I'll drive one hundred and sixty five miles back here, just to take you whenever you're ready."

"I honestly believe you would drive all the way back here for that. Come on and let me ring up your stuff."

Maxie moved behind her register and scanned Brian's items. She didn't want the momentum of their conversation to die down, but she couldn't help thinking about not seeing him again. It wasn't an issue that she never contacted him after Sister Adams died. She was comfortable knowing that if she ever wanted to meet with him, or needed to talk to him, all she had to do was call and he would be there for her. Now he would be too far away.

"So may I have the pleasure of dining with you this afternoon? Or are you going to turn me down again this one final time?" He asked.

Maxie bagged Brian's supplies. When she finished, she set the bag on the belt and looked at him squarely. "If I had an hour lunch today, I would accept your offer."

Brian playfully grabbed at his chest. "And she shoots me down again."

Maxie smiled, and briefly stared at him. "Whenever you're in town again, I promise you we'll do lunch. It'll give us a chance to catch up on things."

"I'm holding you to that promise Maxine Bruce."

Silence fell between them briefly, as they both stood staring at each other. "I'm really going to miss you," Maxie said softly.

"I'm going to miss you too. Would it be okay to call you from time to time, just to keep in touch?"

"You'd better," Maxie said.

Brian opened his arms to her, and Maxie stepped in to embrace him. "Goodbye sweetie," she almost whispered.

"Goodbye Maxie. You take good care of yourself, you hear me?"

"Always," she said, and kissed his cheek.

Before releasing her, Brian kissed her cheek also. "I have to get back. There's still a lot of stuff I need to get finished and packed."

Maxie handed him his bag. "Be careful on the highway."

"We'll do. I'll see you later."

Maxie waved slightly, and watched Brian leave. Only a few seconds passed, before she felt something slither up next to her.

"Girl, baby boy is fine!" Monet drawled. "Is he your boyfriend? If he is, you need to tell me where you met him. If he isn't, you need to tell me how *I* can meet him."

"He's a friend," Maxie said dryly, as she walked back behind her register, with Monet in tow.

"Okay, next question. How can I meet him?"

"No need Monet. He's moving out of town."

"Aw, too bad," she said, looking at the exit doors. "Somebody that fine, needs to be the father of *all* my future children."

Appalled at her statement, Maxie opened her mouth to give Monet a few choice words, but stopped just short of delivering them, when she heard a light tapping sound at the end of the conveyor belt. It was Regina with her clipboard.

"Maxie, go ahead and turn off your light. Take your break. Monet, get back to your register please. This is not a social hour."

Monet scrunched her nose at Regina, and walked back to her register. Maxie turned off her light, and headed to the break room. She wished Regina had come around earlier. Her fifteen-minute break could have been spent with Brian. But it was just as well. There was nothing else to say.

When she got to the break room, it was empty and Maxie was glad. She just wanted to sit down, browse through one of the many magazines on the tables, and relax in total solitude. Within five minutes, Maxie accomplished that desire. In a corner with her feet up on a chair, she became engrossed in a magazine.

"So you roll like that Maxie Bruce? You got it like that?"

Maxie jumped a little at the sound of the voice, but after she recognized it, she refused to look up. "What are you talking about Monet?" She asked plainly.

"That guy. I ain't seen nothing that fine in a while. You know a lot of men who look like that?"

Maxie glanced up long enough to see Monet in the doorway, with her arms stretched out. "I'm not understanding your question. Anyway, does Regina know you're up here?" Maxie asked. Trying hard to sound uninterested in the tête-à-tête the girl was trying to make.

Monet waved off Maxie's question, and headed to her table. "So is he like a boyfriend or ex-boyfriend of yours?"

"He's not an ex-boyfriend, and I'm married Monet."

"Okay. And? What does that mean? You don't play around?"

Maxie pulled herself away from her magazine, and gave Monet the hardest stare she could muster.

"Humpf," Monet snorted. "You *don't* play around. You're a good girl huh?"

"Whatever that means," Maxie mumbled, and returned to her magazine. She was ready for this conversation to be over. The thought of wasting her break time talking to Monet, infuriated her. Rudeness meant nothing to this girl. Maxie was going to have to use another approach to get rid of her, and she had a sure method that was certain to make an uninterested person, voluntarily leave a conversation.

"What church do you go to Monet?" Maxie asked casually.

"I work on Sundays."

"There's always Sunday night services."

"I go when I can. Well let me get back downstairs, before Regina comes hunting for me."

Maxie watched Monet leave, and smiled slyly. "Pitiful how that never fails," she said to herself, and continued reading.

It was 3:45 p.m. when Maxie returned to the floor. The afternoon dragged on slowly, leaving her another hour and fifteen minutes before the end of her shift. She took her time walking down the aisle to her register. She was in no hurry to get back to work, nor were her thoughts there. Instead, she promised herself that when she got home, she would entertain thoughts of the soon approaching holidays, Lester's anniversary gift, and what day she should give her two week notice.

Close to the end of the aisle, Maxie straightened a few bottles of ketchup. When she turned to walk across the floor to her register, a feeling of fear came over her that was so great, it made her freeze in terror.

Something was wrong. Very wrong.

Looking around concerned, Maxie found no reason for her fright. There was nothing visible around her that put her in any danger, only customers walking to and fro. Yet she felt surrounded, as if she were about to be ambushed at any moment. The entire atmosphere was filled with an ominous energy, and it made Maxie very uncomfortable. She was paranoid about the wave of anxiety she walked into. Paranoid, because of how it immediately took her captive.

Maxie recalled having these same threatening feelings a few times as a teenager, and describing the sensations to her grandmother. "Maxie, what you're feeling is a warning. We can't control the things that are going to happen to us baby. So sometimes, God gives us a special way of knowing when something bad is about to happen. Whether it is for us, or for someone else, it allows us time to pray and make preparations as best we can for whatever comes. Don't ever ignore it. Be watchful. The Lord is trying to tell you something." Maxie couldn't remember the outcome of the *warnings* she had back then, but she never forgot her grandmother's words.

Since there was nothing around her that warranted what she was feeling, Maxie instantly thought of Lester; and became even more fearful. Had something bad happened to Lester? Was there an accident on his construction site? She couldn't be sure if he put down her job's telephone number on his list of Emergency Contacts. The thought of anything bad ever happening to him made her shudder. She wanted an answer to what she was being pressed with, and she wanted it now.

Instead of going back to her register, Maxie continued straight to the Customer Service desk to use the phone. She knew she risked being written up for using the telephone while she was supposed to be working, but this was an emergency, and Regina would simply have to understand that. As she dialed Lester's work number, Maxie prayed softly that everything was all right.

"Thank you for calling Onyx Construction and Supply, this is Solange. How may I help you?"

"Yes Solange, I would like to speak with Mr. Lester Bruce please."

"Mr. Bruce is out of the ...."

"This is his wife."

"Hold on Mrs. Bruce. He just walked in the door."

"Thank you."

Maxie listened intently, as she heard the receptionist whisper to someone in the background.

"Hello Maxie?" Lester said quickly. "Baby what's wrong? Are you okay?"

Maxie closed her eyes and smiled. The deep sound of Lester's voice warmed her, and caused everything inside of her to calm down. "Hi sweetie," she almost whispered, opening her eyes to search for Regina. "I was just thinking about you and ...."

"Honey is something wrong? You hardly ever call me at work unless something is wrong. Are you all right?"

"I'm fine Lester. I just wanted to hear your voice. Make sure you were okay."

"Why wouldn't I be okay honey?"

"I don't know. I just had this weird feeling come over me, and I thought maybe you were in danger or something. I got worried, so I called to make sure you were okay."

Maxie heard Lester chuckle a little. "I'm in no danger baby. I promise you I'm fine, and when I come home in a few hours, you'll be able to see for yourself. Okay? I'm glad you're thinking about me though. Keep a prayer in your heart for me all right?"

"Always," Maxie smiled.

"I'll see you when I get home. I love you."

"I love you too," Maxie said. She listened to Lester hang up the phone, before she did the same.

"Emergency?" A voice next to her asked.

"Yes, it was," Maxie answered quickly. A little startled, she looked into Regina's inquiring face. Maxie didn't know where Regina came from, or how much of the conversation she heard, but as close as she was standing, she may have heard the discussion on both her end and Lester's. "I had to speak with my husband. I'll work a few minutes over to make up the time."

"That won't be necessary," Regina smiled, and walked away.

Maxie furrowed her eyebrows, and slightly lifted the corners of her mouth into a soft grin. She didn't expect the meek response from Regina, but she gladly welcomed it.

Speaking with Lester, settled Maxie for a moment. As soon as she was back behind her register, the entire episode happened again. In spite of it, Maxie turned on her lane marker light, and watched as three patrons immediately pushed their buggies her way.

Chapter Twenty

The evening rush hour was on. As usual, there were soccer moms, working moms, and *Mom's Taxi* driving moms, all making that last minute dash into the store to buy dinner, and hurry home to prepare it. It was against his better judgment to stop in the store at this time, but he too had to pick up a few items for dinner before going home. He actually hoped to beat the rush of hurried mothers, but instead, found himself standing in the checkout lane amongst them. Not wanting to lose his place, he searched for a shorter line from where he stood. They were all about the same length, five or six people deep, and moving at the same speed. Slowly. Even the lines in the Express Lanes were long. The thought to simply put his items down and walk out of the store, was becoming more appealing to him by the minute, except he was craving the tender piece of filet mignon he had in his basket. Just as he was about to search the other side of the store, a lane marker light came on at the far end. He thought, rather hoped he was the only one to see it, but as three shopping baskets shifted in that direction, his hopes were dashed. Frustrated, he rubbed his eyes, loosened his necktie, and followed the short convoy of buggies. He thought about making a little noise in his throat, to get the attention of the patrons with the three full shopping carts. Hopefully, they would see the few items he was holding, and allow him to go before them. However, when he looked toward the front of the line, he no longer wanted to rush through it. What he saw captured his interest, and made him want to stand where he was; just so he could stare and take it all in. He even let other customers with full shopping carts go ahead of him.

She was incredible.

The most beautiful woman he had seen in a long time, and he wanted to tell her that when he met her the first time. Her beauty was real and simple. Nothing fake to enhance it. No make-up to heighten it, just raw and simple.

"Is that all you have?" A young woman getting in front of him asked, as she leaned into his view. "Are you sure you want me to get in front of you? I'm not in that big of a hurry. And you don't have that much."

Raising his hand, he wanted to assure the woman and silence her, so she wouldn't bring attention to him and his few groceries. "I'm fine, thank you. I'm actually waiting on someone," he said.

"Are you sure? I don't mind. Really I don't."

"Yes, I'm sure. But thank you again."

"Well … okay."

He was glad he could discourage her, because she was interfering with the only thing he wanted in his view. The cashier whose name was Maxie.

Maxie smiled and tried to coax a little boy to be quiet, as he sat in the shopping cart screaming and kicking his little legs. "Oh. What's the matter sweetheart?" Maxie asked, while she waited for his mother to finish writing her check.

"Candeeee," the boy cried. "Me candeee," he pointed to the candy on the end cap.

"I said no Robert. That's not your candy," his mother said without looking up. The boy screamed louder, and his mother remained unmoved by his dramatics.

"Aw. Don't cry." Maxie pleaded with a pretend frown. "You're cuter when you don't cry."

"No!!" The child screamed angrily.

"You do that one more time Robert, and you're going to get yourself a time-out," his mother cautioned, as she handed Maxie her check.

Maxie glanced at the child as he angrily wrapped his arms around himself, and lowered his head with a frown. While the register finished processing the check, she looked at the mother who wearily shook her head.

"He's my full-time job," she said.

"I don't doubt it," Maxie smiled, giving the mother her receipt. "You have a nice evening."

"When he goes to sleep, my nice evening will begin," she smiled back.

Maxie greeted the next patron, and quickly began scanning. Occasionally, she looked at the store entrance, and watched the steady stream of evening traffic begin to file in. She was so glad she was close to getting off. Today seemed longer than any other day she had worked. She was tired, her feet were beginning to hurt, and her mental state had reached a peak of anxiousness she had never known. Maxie knew once she got home, she could totally relax in Lester's arms. That was where she needed to be.

Home.

It was decided. As soon as she punched out, she would give her two week notice to Regina. After almost six weeks of trying something new and different, she was finished. It was to be the end of doing her own thing. A door she would gladly close, and should have closed a long time ago.

Maxie wondered what Regina's response would be when she handed her the notice. She would expect Regina to try to talk her out of it. She would probably tell her what an excellent worker she was, and how close she had come to being Food King's Employee of the Month. Whatever accolades Regina was going to use, Maxie would be more than ready for them.

Out of routine, Maxie finished scanning her next few customer's items, taken their money, given back their change, and told them to have a nice evening; all the while thinking about quitting and what she would do in her free time. She would have continued on with the next customer in line, but she stopped to look at the time on her watch. It was 4:40 p.m. When she looked to see how many people were in her line, Maxie locked eyes with a familiar pair of eyes, staring right back at her.

It was *him.*

In that instant, she lost her entire train of thought. Her stomach roiled, and her hands began to shake and become sweaty. She actually forgot what to do next. The woman in front of her stared and smiled cordially, as if to say *Okay cashier lady. You can get started at any minute now.*

Maxie closed her eyes for a brief moment to get her focus back. *What is your problem girl?* She asked herself. *That man is a customer just like every other customer that comes into this store. Get a grip!* Opening her eyes, she tried to function normally.

"Are you all right dear?" The woman in front of her asked. "You look like you've seen something that scared you to death."

Lady, you have no idea. Maxie wanted to say. "Oh, yes ma'am. I'm fine. Thank you for asking."

She tried to act as normal as possible, but it was hard with echoes of Sandra's words bombarding her psyche again. *You know he's coming back right? You do know that you're going to see him again.* Maxie took a deep breath to help get herself in complete control. It wasn't like he was at the end of her line, giving her time to regroup. He was the *next* customer in line, and she was sure he was watching her every move.

Maxie took the woman's money, put it in the drawer, closed the drawer, and handed her the receipt without saying anything. After the lady took the piece of paper, she looked at it, smiled, and remained standing in front of the register. When a few seconds passed and the woman was still standing there, Maxie looked on the conveyor belt to see if there was some item she possibly overlooked during her scanning. All was clear.

"Is there something wrong?" Maxie finally asked.

"Yes there is," the woman said with a hint of humor. "You didn't give me back my change."

Maxie thought about it for a quick second, before embarrassment flushed her face. "Oh my goodness. I am so sorry. I've never done that before."

"That's okay sweetheart. There's a first time for everything."

Maxie hit the button to open her drawer, and quickly glanced at *him*. Undoubtedly, he was watching the whole thing. When she looked, he pretended to focus his attention on a People magazine in front of him, with an ever so slight smile on his face.

Maxie handed the lady her change and apologized again, while *he* pushed his items forward on the conveyor belt. After the woman left, Maxie turned her lane marker sign off. He was her last customer. Surprisingly, the nervousness she felt a few moments earlier had faded.

"So that was funny to you huh... Marc? That is your name right?" Maxie asked as she scanned, trying not to exhibit a girlish grin.

"Oh yeah," Marc blurted. "That was pretty good. You're beautiful, you send your customers on wild goose chases, and then you keep their money. I think that's called stealing, by the way. And don't pretend like you've forgotten my name."

Maxie stopped scanning, took a step back, and laughed at Marc's cockiness. He laughed with her. Though she tried not to notice, Marc looked *very* good. Just like the time before, his hair was impeccably kept, and his facial hair neatly trimmed. He wore a soft purple Hugo Boss dress shirt, which was neatly tucked into single pleated black trousers, which Maxie recognized as being part of the Armani collection. Marc was definitely a dresser. She couldn't identify the cologne he was wearing, but its invigorating fragrance played around with her nose. As she watched him loosen his silk tie a little more, Maxie assumed he had just gotten off from work. She couldn't help but to wonder what kind of work this man did, to afford him the luxury of wearing top-notch designer clothing from top to bottom. Even though she couldn't see them, she figured he had on Logo Loafer shoes by Prada, with the emblem on them. Mr. Marc, whatever his last name was, looked like he just jumped off the cover of GQ magazine. Every inch of his athletically built body, fit his clothes nicely.

Suddenly, Maxie felt awkward and under dressed, and quickly began scanning the rest of his items.

"What's the matter?" Marc asked. "You don't like what you see?"

"Excuse me?"

"You were staring at me again. And then you stopped. Didn't you like what you were looking at?"

Maxie was embarrassed. She had no idea she was so obvious. "Marc," she began smoothly. "If you weren't looking at *me*, you never would have seen me looking at you."

"Ah, but you didn't answer my question. You see, I can tell you that I like what I see. Can you say the same?"

There he was being forward again.

"I have no problem saying what I like," Maxie responded matter-of-factly.

Marc raised his head a little, and clasped his hands down in front of him, as if he were posing for a picture. Undauntedly, he gave Maxie a look that said *I dare you*.

She knew he was enjoying this impromptu game they were playing, so she continued on. "I think you ... the clothes you're wearing are very nice," she giggled. Marc released his stance and laughed. "That'll be fifteen nine-ty-two for your groceries," Maxie said, grinning from ear to ear.

"Okay, okay. You got me. I'll let that one go." Marc handed Maxie a twenty-dollar bill from his shirt pocket. "And don't forget my change."

When Maxie handed him back his change, and he accepted it into his left hand, she noticed the absence of a wedding ring.

"No, I'm not married. Never been married."

Quickly she looked up into his face, surprised at how he guessed her thoughts.

"But I see that you are," he continued. "How long?"

"Almost eight years," she said as she bagged his groceries. Instantly, Maxie felt she was letting herself get carried away in conversation with this stranger — again. Yet she didn't know why. There was something about this man that made him easy for her to talk to.

"So, I gather you're happy. I mean, if it's been almost eight years and you're …."

"I'm very happy," Maxie interrupted, and handed him his bags. She didn't want her response to sound like she was adding finality to their conversation, but she had to give him a clear understanding as to where she stood.

"Well, you're a very beautiful woman Maxie." He took the bags from her hand. "And your husband is a very lucky man."

Maxie lowered her eyes, and looked at the conveyor belt for a moment. She wondered if she could be so bold as to return the compliment, by telling him how good he looked to her. Facing him squarely, Maxie smiled and spoke softly. "Thank you."

Marc nodded. "So, how much longer do I have to look at you?"

Maxie was taken aback by his question, and frowned a little in confusion.

"The last time I was in here, you told me you were quitting. How much time do I have left? I'd really like to see you again."

This time she was floored. Marc's words hit her hard and totally off guard. At the same time, something in the lower part of her stomach jumped and gave her the weirdest sensation. She hadn't felt anything that strange since she first met Lester. She didn't know what to say. She didn't know if Marc was asking to see her outside of work, or if he could visit with her from time-to-time, while she worked. Maybe she took his question out of context. Maybe she was reading more into it than was actually there. How could she really know? Asking for clarification, might send the wrong signal that she was interested in seeing *him* again. Maxie honestly didn't know how to answer.

Marc knew he was stepping out on a limb making a statement so direct, but he had to throw caution to the wind. He needed to know exactly what he was up against. Was Maxie the kind of woman who could stand to be honestly appreciated by a man who may have had no ulterior motive, except to express himself? Or would she be offended, believing he had disrespected her marital status, and shoot him down mid-flight?

"I ... uh ..." Maxie stammered.

Out of nowhere, a hand was extended to Marc, with a fake sexy sounding voice behind it. "Hi, how are you? My name is Monet."

The moment between Maxie and Marc died instantly, and dropped heavily between them.

Marc looked at the hand and reluctantly shook it, as he glanced back and forth between Maxie and Monet. Maxie looked at the floor a bit upset.

"Hello," he said.

"And your name is?" Monet went on.

"Monet, is there something you need?" Maxie asked with a hint of sharpness. She could not believe the unmitigated gall of this girl.

Before she focused on Maxie, Monet gave Marc a full once over with a smile so broad, and a gaze so literal with intent, Marc would have to be an idiot not to recognize it.

"Well Maxie," Monet said, barely taking her eyes off of Marc. "I just thought I'd come over here to see if you needed any help. I thought you must be tied up, because it's almost five-fifteen and you're still on the clock."

Maxie looked at her watch and panicked. "Oh my goodness."

"Yes," Monet added cynically. "I guess dinner is going to be a little late for hubby tonight huh?"

Maxie gave Monet a hard look, and tightened her jaw without saying a word.

"Hey look," Marc said directly to Maxie. "I'll take my chances. Maybe I'll see you again ..." he looked at Monet and then back at Maxie. "....the next time I come into the store." Marc turned himself away from Monet and winked at Maxie. "You take care of yourself."

"You too. And have a good evening," Maxie said.

When Marc walked away, Maxie didn't risk watching him. Not with Monet standing there. Instead, she ran across the floor to punch out. Luckily, Regina was not there.

"Goodbye, come back and visit us soon." She heard Monet screech to Marc.

When Maxie returned to her register, Monet was gone. Like a thief, she stole the moment and left the scene of the crime. Maxie knew she would hear lewd comments from

Monet later. Right now, that didn't matter. The only thing that was important, was getting her register closed down and getting home as soon as possible.

* * * * * * * * * *

As she drove home, Maxie was fascinated with the ironic events of the day. If she wanted to, she could say she experienced both evil and good at the same time. But which was which? Was the doomed feeling she had earlier, a real warning? If so, it did caution her to become more aware of her surroundings, and to look for a way of escape if needed. Maybe that was the good. On the other hand, was it a pure coincidence how she was overcome with the eerie feeling, just before seeing Marc in her line? Was he the evil?

Maxie felt silly pondering on something that had no solid foundation. She didn't know if Marc was the reason for the dark cloud that seemed to follow her for part of the afternoon. Although she was able to have a full-fledged conversation with him, she was totally aware of the ill-omened air that was ever present. In all actuality, what she felt could have resonated from anyone or anything. It was unfair for her to offhandedly assume that Marc was the culprit. Besides, what could possibly be wrong with a man who looked that good?

Maxie knew Sandra would be the one to answer that question, but she had no intentions of telling Sandra anything about her brief conversation with Marc. There was really nothing to tell. He came into the store, purchased a few items, they shared words, and then he left. At least that was how she wanted to view it. She didn't want to hear Sandra dissect Marc's motives, or listen to her say *I told you so*, because he came into the store again just like she said he would. No. This time, Maxie was going to withhold information from her friend. They would both be better off if Sandra knew nothing.

Chapter Twenty-One

Maxie remembered how good she felt in Lester's arms yesterday. When he finally got home, she didn't wait for him to come into the house. She met him in the driveway, and threw her arms around him as if he was a long lost soldier returning home from the war. Everything felt right. She was safe, he was safe, and they were together. It was a wonderful ending to an otherwise hectic day. Now here she was again at Food King, parking her car and herself in a place that seemed not so inviting anymore, and a little less exciting. Maxie knew that for the next five hours, she was going to have to make the most of it.

When she walked through the automatic doors, she was met with a few smiling faces of co-workers standing behind their registers. She returned their smile and continued on to Customer Service to punch in. When she approached the counter, Maxie witnessed a heated discussion between Monet and Regina.

"That's not going to happen. There's no one to take over for you," Regina said casually, while writing on her clipboard.

"But it's just for this weekend," Monet pleaded. "Come on Regina. I'll make sure you have enough coverage. I can find somebody. You won't even miss me."

Regina looked up from her clipboard and acknowledged Maxie with a slight nod, before she focused on Monet. "Monet, my decision is final, and this conversation is over. Now take your cash tray, and open up on register twelve."

"But Auntie ..." Monet whined.

Regina narrowed her eyes and spoke through clenched teeth. "Don't even try it."

With that, Monet snatched her cash tray and moneybag, and hurriedly walked past Maxie without a word. Not wanting to appear as if she were eavesdropping, Maxie kept her distance at the end of the counter.

"So how is the weather outside Maxie? I'm sure it's cooler out there than it is in here right now," Regina sighed.

Maxie lightly smiled, as she gathered the things she needed to begin her shift. She didn't want to know the topic of Regina and Monet's conversation, although she had a pretty good idea of what it was. She only hoped Monet wouldn't come to her with the same proposal she tried on Regina.

"You have a choice today Maxie," Regina said. "You can take one of the fast lanes, or you can work the bottom."

Maxie hated working the fast lanes. The pressure to perform continually at a high rate of speed for five hours, was the last thing she wanted to do. "I'll take the bottom."

By taking the bottom, she would work at the last register, closest to the Produce section, which was commonly known as *the bottom of the line*. Maxie hoped she had just set herself up for an easy workday. Customers ready for checkout, would normally go to the registers that were closest to whatever aisle they emerged from. The bottom register wasn't close to any of the aisles, which made it the least sought after. That was exactly what she wanted today. To be the least sought after.

Maxie performed in her usual manner, until it was time for her to take a break. Instead of going to the Employee Break Room, where some of her co-workers were probably hanging out, she chose to sit in the store's café. It was quaint, quiet, and hardly any Food King employees took their break time there. She ordered a small French fry, and a small Coke, before retreating to the furthest corner of the café, where she was practically out of sight.

When she finished eating, Maxie rested her head on the back of her chair, and stared at the ceiling. If she could trust herself to wake up in the next five minutes, she would have used her remaining time to take a quick nap, but this method of relaxation would have to do.

"I have looked all over this store for you Maxie. I think you're trying to hide from me."

Maxie lowered her head, more at the mentioning of her name, than the recognition of the voice that was speaking to her. It was Monet, with another big goofy grin on her face.

"I'm not hiding from anyone," Maxie said plainly. "I'm on my break, and this is where I've chosen to take it. Now are you in need of something? Because whatever it is, it will have to wait for another five minutes."

"No," Monet said, as she took a seat opposite Maxie. "It's nothing I can't ask you right now. I don't mind that you're on your break. So listen, do you have any plans for this weekend?"

"As a matter-of-fact, I do," Maxie said, straightening herself in her chair. "I sure do." Maxie watched her response register on Monet's face. She knew the girl wanted to ask her to cover her shift again. To deny her that opportunity, was a wonderfully simple payback, for the snide remark she made yesterday about dinner being late for Lester.

"Oh are you tipping out on a date with that guy who was in here yesterday?" Monet waved her hand. "Girl I can't blame you. That man was fine. He was just about as good looking as the one who came to see you yesterday afternoon."

Maxie casually picked up her cup, and shook a piece of ice into her mouth, as she looked at Monet. She knew exactly how she wanted to answer this girl, but if someone was watching, they might have a hard time believing she was a Christian woman, if they witnessed the *way* she wanted to answer.

Monet was playing a childish game of tit-for-tat, and Maxie was too old for childish games. She was aware of Monet watching the arrival of every good-looking man who came into the store, and Maxie believed that was her sole purpose for working at Food King — to meet men. But now she was straying away from her purpose, rerouting herself, and trying to make Maxie's life her destination.

"You know what Monet? Between yesterday and today, you've spent a lot of time concerning yourself with the matters of my life. What's wrong? You a little bored with your own?" Maxie hinted a smile, at how she delivered her words with just enough bite to make Monet rear her head back and blink rapidly.

"You are trippin'!" Monet howled, and rolled her head around on her neck for emphasis. "Nothing you have can compare to how I got it. I got it going on."

Maxie looked at Monet and frowned. Pretending to be concerned, she let her words flow with an even tone. "Are you sure? Maybe you're searching for something. I know. A little excitement perhaps. And my life just happens to appeal to you."

Monet shook her head and stood up abruptly. "Okay Maxie, look. Like I said, you're trippin'. I'm not here to play games. I was just sent to look for you. Regina wants to see you in her office."

Maxie nodded her head slowly. "Thank you for the message Monet."

Monet looked at Maxie with a vile gaze. Sucking her teeth loudly, she rolled her eyes and walked away. Maxie didn't budge. She hated the fact that once again, a portion of her break time was spent on Monet. The girl was becoming a nuisance. Though she had a pretty good idea of how the other workers felt about Monet, Maxie was tired of getting the repeated first hand experiences that were causing her to form the same concrete opinion as everyone else. She was supposed to look at people differently. Focus on the positive, not the negative. See the good in everyone. Always give the benefit of the doubt. *Yada, Yada, Yada.* Whatever the cliché, Monet was going to have to remain the one exception to the rule.

When she arrived at Regina's office, Maxie stood in front of the closed door and barely knocked two times. She had no idea what Regina wanted, but she decided whatever it was about, she wasn't going to concern herself with it. Yesterday, she forgot to put her notice in before she left, but today could serve the same purpose, especially if she was about to be written up for something erroneous.

"Come on in Maxie," Regina said.

Maxie opened the door, and stuck her head in just enough to see Regina sitting behind her desk viewing papers. "Monet said you wanted to see me."

"Yeah, come on in," Regina motioned with a quick wave. "Have a seat."

Maxie did as she was told. She had never been in Regina's office before, and by judging what she saw, she wasn't missing anything. Regina's office was just as small, if not smaller than Mr. Martin's.

"Did you finish with your break? I told Monet to wait until you were finished."

"Thank you," Maxie replied.

"Well, let's get down to why I called you in here. There's a little problem with your time card, and I need your help with it. Now I know you had a little extended break yesterday, and I excused that. But in looking at your time card, I see you worked past your scheduled time by almost fifteen minutes. Can you give me a reason for that?"

Maxie paid close attention to the tone in which Regina spoke. She wanted to find out if she was upset with her, or if her question was purely mechanical.

"Close to the end of my shift yesterday, I got involved in a conversation with one of our customers. Before I knew it, the time slipped by," Maxie said plainly.

Regina absently nodded her head as she looked at Maxie's time card, and then back at Maxie. "It must have been some kind of a conversation huh?"

Maxie smiled lightly. She wasn't volunteering any information.

"Okay, well that answers that question. I'll have to fix your card. Now on to the next question."

Regina shuffled the papers around on her desk, until she came to one that Maxie noticed as a Customer Service Survey sheet. She couldn't see her name on it, but she could see that whoever filled it out, had a lot to say in the area marked COMMENTS.

"Maxie, have you received a demerit since you started working here?"

Maxie nodded no. Feeling her jaws tighten, she alternated her focus between Regina and the goldenrod piece of paper she was viewing as she spoke.

"Well, this is going to be a first for you, and it's definitely going to impact your placement in the running for the store-wide Employee of the Month contest. Now seeing how this survey was turned in on yesterday evening, which was the last day of October, it obviously gets tallied in with October's results." Regina picked up another piece of paper and traveled its length from top to bottom, with her index finger. "And looking on this graph, I see you and Monet were in close running, six and six. But this survey will obviously change that."

Pressing her lips together firmly, Maxie was becoming annoyed with the way Regina was meandering around. She was ready for it all to be over. She wanted to inform Regina that she would be leaving Food King in two weeks, and she could really care less about the bogus comments of some disgruntled customer.

Regina held up the survey sheet, and looked Maxie in her eyes. "Maxie, I want you to know that no matter what this paper says, since you first came on board with us here at

Food King, I have observed you to be an excellent worker. And because of this, I have to inform you that ...."

"Don't worry about it Regina," Maxie interrupted. "I don't mind."

Regina frowned. "You don't mind what?"

"It's not a problem that I've received my first demerit. I did my best, so I don't mind the outcome of the contest, and I'm really not too concerned about it anyway."

"Well Maxie, I think you should be concerned."

"And why is that?" Maxie asked, with a little attitude.

"You're November's Employee of the Month."

Maxie was silent for a moment. "I'm what? But you just said...." she started, totally confused. "But you just said I had a demerit."

"I never said you had a demerit. I *asked you* if you ever received one," Regina said calmly.

"But when you said ...."

"When I said this would be a first for you, I was correct. Isn't this the first time you've been Employee of the Month?" Regina smiled.

"Yes," Maxie replied sheepishly.

"Well, congratulations Maxie. You earned it. And forgive me for seizing the opportunity to tease you a little bit. I couldn't help it. You're so serious all of the time."

Maxie smiled.

"You had very nice comments from the customers who took the time to write them. Especially this last one."

"May I read it?" Maxie asked.

Regina handed her the paper. Maxie read silently, and tried hard to suppress her facial expressions.

Maxie is an exceptional employee and a great asset to the Food King staff. I witnessed her demeanor in the face of

adversity with an unhappy customer, and it was very profes-
sional. She greeted me with a genuine smile that brightened
my day, and she was very helpful to me. Other cashiers could
learn a great deal of hospitality on how to properly greet and
serve the customer, if they observed this woman's incredible
technique. I wish your store had more workers like her.

After she finished, she handed the paper back to Regina.
"That was very nice."

"Any idea as to who wrote it?" Regina asked.

"Not really."

"Well anyway, congratulations again. Your gift certificate
will be with your check on Friday, and we'll put your picture
up in the front of the store."

Maxie rose from her seat and stood in front of Regina.
"Thank you again, and sorry about my time card."

"Just don't let it happen again," Regina winked. "Next
time, I'll have to dock you."

Though she knew Regina meant it, Maxie laughed a little
to herself and made steps toward the door.

"Hey Maxie?"

"Yes?"

"Keep up the good work. You might be a Shift Leader
before you know it."

Maxie feigned a smile, and left Regina's office. When she
closed the door, her smile quickly faded as she leaned against
the wall. "Employee of the Month," she whispered regretfully. "Employee of the Month and a possible Shift Leader
position. Just great. How can I possibly quit a job where I'm
Employee of the Month?" Maxie looked at Regina's door,
and walked away.

Chapter Twenty-Two

Maxie shuddered as she looked out of her living room window early Wednesday morning. The weather that opened the month of November, offered a miserable prelude of what the winter season had in store for Savannah. It was rainy, and it was cold. Because it was her day off, Maxie initially planned to visit with the sick and shut-in, but quickly changed her mind after getting a foretaste of what she would have to deal with on the outside. The day gave every indication that it was going to be a sleepy kind of day, and she felt like being nothing more than lazy in it.

With the outdoors being less than inviting, Maxie naturally assumed no construction work could be done, and anticipated sitting in front of a cozy fire with Lester. There nestled in his arms, would be the perfect place and moment to tell him about her personal victory on the job, since she refused to bring it up the night before. Although she wanted to tell him, Maxie quelled the desire to announce her incredible accomplishment. To go from being a woman who never worked a job, to being Employee of the Month and quite possibly a Shift Leader in little over six weeks' time, was an admirable feat and she was proud of herself. But she had to admit, she was a little apprehensive about what Lester would say. She didn't doubt he would be happy for her, but that was probably as far as it would go. Maxie felt her husband might find no real reason for hoopla, if she was going to quit working at the time they both agreed upon anyway. Whatever congratulatory words he'd use, she expected they would soon be followed by a quick reminder of how long she had left to work. Those were words she need not hear, so she purposely kept it quiet until the right moment arrived. However, it appeared the right moment was not going to arrive.

Contrary to what the weather dictated outside, Lester stood behind her at the window, and told her he still had to go in to work. With disappointment on her face, Maxie quickly turned around to face him. Before she had a chance to say anything, Lester wrapped his arms around her waist and pulled her to him.

"Believe me baby," he said when he kissed her forehead. "I want nothing more than to be at home with you, holding you in my arms, and wasting the day away in front of a roaring fire. But daddy can't make a living if he's sitting at home." Lester quickly pecked Maxie on her mouth and released her to put on his coat and gather blueprint tubes under his arm.

"Lester, it's just one day," Maxie whined, following after him. "Besides, it's so messy outside. What can possibly be done today?"

"I'm sorry sweetheart. I have two meetings back to back, and I don't believe they're going to be cancelled due to a little bad weather. But I promise you as soon as they are

226

over, I'll be right home." Lester quickly walked through the kitchen, stopped at the door, and turned to her. "Are you praying for me?"

Maxie gave a weak smile.

"That's my girl," he winked. "Don't start the fire without me." Quickly Lester opened the door, and closed it behind him. Soon after, she heard him yell. "I love you."

"I love you too," she said in a low tone. Maxie stood in the middle of the kitchen, until she heard Lester back out of the driveway. Slowly, she walked back into the living room and sprawled herself out on the couch face down. What to do now? She could call Sandra at work, and invite her to offer a congratulatory word. Maxie knew Sandra would be ecstatic about what she had achieved. But it wouldn't be right for Sandra to know about it, before Lester. Maybe another special moment would present itself, and she would have the opportunity to share it with him again. She hoped it would, because she was dying to tell somebody.

With little effort, Maxie reached for the TV remote, and turned the television on, putting it on mute. She didn't really want to spend the rest of the morning watching television, but she didn't want boredom to settle in either. Since all of her household chores were completed with Lester's help, there was little else for her to do. While different thoughts danced around in her mind, Maxie's eyes settled on a commercial presented by a neighboring grocery store that was a rival to Food King. Instantly, her thoughts went to Regina, and what she said in their brief meeting. *Keep up the good work. You might be a Shift Leader before you know it.*

The suggestion that she was capable of performing that kind of a duty was nice, especially coming from Regina, but Maxie had some doubts. She knew that not just anybody could hold that position. So why was she a candidate with potential? It didn't add up. Alan, who came from another store in hopes of obtaining some kind of managerial position, had more experience than she did. Everybody who was working there before she started, had more experience. So what could be the reason?

Maxie told herself she was reading too much into the issue. But instead of stopping and letting go, she took it a step further. Thinking on the spiritual side, she had to ask herself what if it was a trick? If she was offered the chance to be a leader, and she accepted, could the whole thing really be a setup? Was it a plan of the devil, to get her all caught up in working, only to have her once again neglecting her godly service? No. Suffering through that the first time, was a lesson learned. She was way too smart to allow that to happen to her again. Besides, her job was to no longer be an issue nor an avenue, no matter what the perks. But what if she changed her mind about quitting? What if she decided to work until the actual deadline that was previously set? Nobody close to her knew she planned to quit except for Sandra. If she did change her mind, that would give her almost two months of working on Lester-approved time. She would have the chance to experience the entire moment of being Employee of the Month. If the opportunity of gaining the Shift Leader position should arise, she'd have some time to experience that too. More importantly, Maxie would have that ultimate time.

The time to experience Marc.

There on the couch alone, Maxie felt assured that now was the time to let her mind wander into the place she dared not go before. Even though a part of her wanted to steer clear of entering in, the better part of her wanted to know the answer to that one burning question. Why was Marc so intriguing? What was it about him that caused her fear, and at the same time, ignited something inside her those two times she saw him? Was it some kind of admiration? How could it be? She knew nothing about the man, except the confidence he had in himself. She only knew that by observing the way he carried himself when he walked, and because of his direct comments toward her. So what was it about him that piqued her curiosity? The answer was like searching for a missing piece to a puzzle. A very intricate piece. Within herself, it was safe for her to say that something inside her agreed with some part of Marc's character. She just didn't know what that *something* was. She wanted to find out, and the only way to do that was to have him come to her on mutual ground. A ground they could share without commitments. That ground was Food King.

* * * * * * * * * *

Marc relaxed in his executive chair, and gently swiveled from side to side. With his head pressed against the back of it, he looked at the tiles in the ceiling. Because he was at work, his mind should have been on work related issues. But ever since yesterday afternoon, he gave clear passage to the only thoughts that held his interest.

Those were thoughts of Maxie.

Monday morning was a stressful beginning to the work week, so by that afternoon; he was more than ready to go home and wind down. Marc didn't know why he subjected himself to stand in a long line at Food King, but he was glad he did. It felt good to see Maxie again. Watching her lose her concentration when she saw him in her checkout lane was priceless. When she accidentally kept her customer's change and admitted it never happened before, he knew then, he was able to unnerve her.

The visual recount made Marc smile and shake his head. Gently he tapped a pen against his lips and creased his eyebrows. He couldn't quite put his finger on it, but he knew there was something different and special about Maxie. There was no question about it. She possessed something way beyond her beauty, and it made her very attractive.

Marc prided himself on being an excellent judge of character when it came to women. He could almost always tell what kind of person a woman was, with the smallest of conversation. He honed that skill because his job kept him in the company of many women — beautiful women. But of late, none of them had that special *something* he detected in Maxie. Marc knew if he planned to find out what that indescribable thing was, it was going to be a challenge. But was it a challenge worth facing? Maxie told him she was married. With or without intention, those words were a warning that said either *DANGER! Proceed with Caution*, or *NO TRESPASSING*. Since she made sure he heard her say she was *very happily* married, the warning was probably the latter.

"Psst. Hey good lookin'. Can I take you to lunch today?"

Marc quickly looked toward the door, where a head with a flowing stream of blonde hair, and a smiling white face was peeking. "What's going on Jaunee?" He smiled back. "Come on in."

The woman immediately walked into the office, and salaciously sat herself in a chair at the front of his desk. Marc observed her poise briefly, and then gave his attention to a few papers and a tablet on his desk.

"So what do you say? Is it a date? If we leave now, we can take an extra hour," Jaunee said.

"I don't think so. I need to finish transcribing these appraisals. Besides, in case you haven't noticed, Old Man Winter is checking in a little early this year."

"Marc, you have to eat. Who cares about the weather? Let's change the pace a little. Let's go to Spanky's," Jaunee said, leaning in closer.

"I'm not in the mood for pizza. If I go out, I'll probably pick up a sub sandwich later from the store."

"The grocery store?" Jaunee asked incredulously. "You're going to pass up a lunch date with me, to eat a store bought sub sandwich? You're beginning to scare me. I asked you out to dinner the other night, you told me you were going home to cook. I ask you out for lunch today, you tell me you're going to get a grocery store sub sandwich. Marc?"

"A little out of character huh?" He frowned.

"To say the least."

Marc looked at the papers on his desk and stood up. "I guess an early break wouldn't hurt."

"Great," Jaunee jumped up and smiled. "Just let me save the designs I was drawing on my computer. I'll get my jacket, and meet you in the lobby." Quickly she walked to the door.

"I guess since you're buying, I'm driving right?" Marc asked.

Jaunee glanced over her shoulder and gave Marc a broad grin, before she walked out of his office.

"That's what I thought," he said into the air.

Marc placed his papers into his briefcase. He felt a little relieved Jaunee interrupted him when she did. He wasn't being very productive; sitting and thinking about a woman who could possibly care less about him. It would do him good to get out of the office for a while. He needed to change his train of thought, and Jaunee was just the person to do it.

Though their relationship was understood by both to be platonic, Jaunee never let up on her efforts to take it to another level. From word go, she sought more from Marc than a friendly relationship. It all became obvious not long after she was hired on as a designer at Whitley Jewelers. With gifts of candlelight dinners, vintage Dom Perignon wine, and tickets with paid airfare to Broadway plays being left on his desk, Jaunee made her intentions very concrete. To quell her gestures, Marc privately told her he was flattered and appreciated the gifts, but he was not interested in having a relationship with her, or anyone else for that matter. He went on to explain that he was still recovering from ending a relationship with a woman he loved very much, and that the reason for the break-up was because they didn't share the same level of commitment. He even tried to allude to the fact that he may have been the one with the lesser level of commitment, but Jaunee didn't care about all of that. She felt she was supposed to be the one to heal his pain, and if he would not allow her the access she desired, then she would be content to just be a part of his life.

That was almost two years ago.

Though his feelings remained the same, Jaunee continued trying to worm her way into that special place, making Marc uncomfortable at times with her unsolicited attention. It was almost smothering. At other times, he enjoyed having her around as a listening ear, for whatever he wanted to talk about.

Marc retrieved his black trench coat from a coat tree in his office, and closed the door behind him. "Beatrice," he said, as he stopped at the desk in front of his office. A woman in her sixties sat slightly hunched, with glasses on her nose and an operator's earpiece in her ear. Engrossed in a magazine, she was totally oblivious to Marc's presence. "Bea," he said again, speaking a little louder. The woman jumped a little, pushed her glasses up, and quickly looked up at him.

"Yes Mr. Thomas. Oh, please forgive me. I got a little carried away with this story I'm reading. I didn't hear you call for me from your office."

"Don't worry, I didn't call you. I'm going to take an early lunch. I will probably be back in a couple of hours. Take messages for all phone calls that aren't urgent. The urgent ones ...."

"I know," Beatrice chirped. "You want me to forward them to your cell phone."

Marc smiled and nodded, as he turned to walk away.

"Have a nice lunch with Ms. Jaunee," she teased.

Marc stopped, and started to turn around to question Beatrice's taunting statement, but changed his mind. He didn't feel like humoring her little innuendo with a response. Though loveable and harmless, he knew how nosey Beatrice was, and how she loved to involve herself in the lives of anyone who was in the upper hierarchy of the business. Instead, he continued to walk to the elevator. Curious as to whether Beatrice was watching him, Marc quickly glanced over his shoulder at her. Just as he thought, her eyes were dead set on him. Not only was she watching him, she was watching with a huge grin and a bashful look on her face. Marc immediately stepped into the elevator. He didn't want to do it, but when the doors were closing, he looked at Beatrice again. Like a picture frozen in time, she sat with the same look on her face. Amused, Marc let her see him laugh a little before the doors closed between them.

* * * * * * * * *

The ride to Spanky's was less than twenty minutes, and Jaunee talked the entire ride. Marc couldn't tell if she was talking about something exciting, or excited about the mere fact that she was once again exclusively in his company. Between his *uh-huh* acknowledgments, and slight head nods, Marc was with Jaunee in body only. His mind carried him elsewhere. Once inside the restaurant, they were seated near a window, placed their order, and served their drinks. Jaunee had a glass of water with a wedge of lemon, and Marc had a sweet tea.

Jaunee swirled her lemon around with her straw, while glancing at Marc. She watched him loosen his tie, take a sip from his drink, and casually look out the window as if he were the only one at the table. Jaunee smiled softly. "You know, when I ask someone out for a lunch date, it's usually so we both can enjoy each other's company."

Marc continued to look out of the window a moment longer, before he realized Jaunee was speaking to him. "I'm sorry Jaunee. I have a little too much on my brain. What did you say? I promise, you have my undivided attention."

"I didn't say anything." Jaunee said. "I just wanted you to come back to me."

Marc smiled.

Jaunee continued to swirl her lemon around slowly. "So. Who is she?"

Marc's smile faded, and was immediately replaced with a look of confusion. "Who?"

"The woman you're thinking about. Who is she?"

"Why on earth would you believe I'm thinking about a woman?" He frowned.

"Marc, I've known you for what, a couple of years now? I know whenever you get that far away look in your eyes, there is someone special you're thinking about. You had that same look in your office, just before I asked you to lunch." Jaunee stopped stirring and looked at Marc squarely. "Can I know who she is?"

Marc averted Jaunee by looking out the window again, and then behind her at the waiter who was bringing their food. Silence fell between them while they were being served. As soon as the waiter left, Jaunee sat motionless and watched Marc unroll his utensils from their napkin.

"You don't want to answer me do you?" She asked.

Marc continued preparing to eat, without looking up. "There is no woman Jaunee," he said casually. If he lifted his eyes to meet hers, she would instantly see he was lying. He didn't feel like being flooded with a bevy of questions, or countering any unnecessary fits of jealous rage. So he thought it best not to meet what he knew to be an inquiring gaze. Marc wanted lunch to be simple. No controversy. No drama. Just simple.

"Okay," Jaunee said as she unwrapped her utensils. "I just wanted to know if there was any competition I needed to size up."

Marc smiled absently, more at his current thoughts than at Jaunee's unfounded statement. For him, Maxie was in a class all her own. He already placed her there. It was inconceivable for Jaunee to think she could remotely be "sized up" with that caliber of woman. The thought of her even considering it, almost made him laugh.

"So have you decided about London yet? Are you going to go, or are you going to let someone else go for you?" Jaunee asked.

"No. I haven't decided yet."

"Marc, somebody is scheduled to be there at the Central Selling Organization in two weeks."

"I know, I know," Marc said, a little agitated. "I don't want to go, but I know they're expecting me to make the buy."

"I'd gladly go to the CSO for you," Jaunee smiled.

"Me? Trust you with almost a million dollars in diamonds? I'd never see you again," Marc laughed.

"Then take me with you," Jaunee said sincerely.

Marc continued to laugh, until he saw Jaunee was serious.

"It could be a business and a pleasure trip. At least it would be for me anyway. What do you say Marc? Let me go to London with you."

Marc chewed his food and said nothing, occasionally glancing at his plate and Jaunee.

"Marc?"

"Is that what this is all about? You wanted to take me to lunch to proposition me?"

"This is hardly the proposition I had in mind. But in light of making this trip with you, your stomach is the way to your heart right?"

Marc took a bite of his food, and sipped his tea. "Jaunee, I don't … I don't think that's a good idea. You know I don't want …"

236

"I know, Marc. I know what you *don't want*," Jaunee retorted.

Marc sat silently, and watched her for a moment. "Jaunee ...."

Jaunee feigned a smile. "Hey, I tried you know. Eat your food before it gets cold."

Chapter Twenty-Three

Maxie walked into the store Thursday afternoon and immediately noticed a giant poster-sized picture of herself, on a stand near the front entrance of the store. Underneath the image were the words EMPLOYEE OF THE MONTH. The portrait that was used looked very good even to Maxie, particularly since she didn't consider herself a very photogenic person. She tried hard to subdue the pride she immediately felt swelling up inside of her. In spite of all her efforts, by the time she reached the Customer Service desk, Maxie gained a smile on her face that stretched from ear to ear. She was surprised to see her picture up so soon, and thought Regina told her it would be set up on Friday. As she walked past the desk, Maxie saw Regina standing with her back turned.

"Hey Regina. I thought you said you …."

Regina held up her hand for Maxie to stop because she was on the phone. "Yes, I understand that sir, but it's not fair to the rest of the cashiers if this is allowed to continue."

Maxie looked at Regina's face and saw a great deal of anger in it. Sensitive to the moment, she backed up a little, punched her timecard, and followed the normal routine for beginning her shift. She tried hard not to listen to the conversation on the phone, but the near growls in Regina's response to the person on the other end, made it impossible for her not to hear.

"Mr. Martin, I don't have anyone who can do that, and I assure you this particular employee and myself, have discussed this week's schedule at length. There is no way I can ..."

Not wanting to hear any more of the conversation, Maxie desperately wanted to get to her register, but she didn't know which one Regina had her assigned to. Instead of waiting for her to finish her phone call, Maxie casually walked next to Regina, tilted her head and looked at the clipboard she held in her hand.

"Don't go anywhere," Regina whispered as she moved the phone away from her mouth. "I need to talk to you."

Maxie nodded her head, and returned to the place where she was standing. She refused to let her mind wander as to what Regina could possibly want with her, so she just waited patiently.

"Yes sir. I'll see what I can do," Regina said, and hung up the phone.

Maxie watched her as she took a deep breath, rubbed her eyes, and exhaled slowly. "So, how are you today Maxie?" Regina asked without looking at her, her voice sounding tired.

"I'm fine."

"I wish I could say the same."

"Rough day already?"

"Don't ask," Regina said, as she moved closer. "What were you saying to me while I was on the phone?"

"It wasn't that important. I just wanted to know why you put my picture up today instead of tomorrow. I thought you said Friday."

"Oh yeah, I did. But I figured you earned every shining moment of fame I could give you, so I put it up today. Nice picture huh?"

Maxie grinned. "Yeah it is. It looks pretty good."

"So ... how would you like to spend some time here at the store, showcasing your award winning talents? Let's say ... tomorrow for about eight hours?"

Maxie looked at Regina squarely. "Monet got the weekend off again didn't she?"

"She went over my head, straight to Mr. Martin. I may not be able to do anything here to get back at her. But outside of the job, she's mine."

Maxie nodded her head negatively. "And no one else can cover her?"

"I didn't ask anyone else. I just got off the phone with Mr. Martin. He just told me about Monet, so I really haven't had the chance to ask the other cashiers."

Maxie was silent for a moment. "I'll tell you what. If you don't get any of the other cashiers to commit, I'll consider it. Okay?"

"Deal," Regina smiled. "And since you are Employee of the Month, I'll let you choose your register. You can have number seven, Express Lane, or the bottom."

"Maxie smiled broadly. "I'll take the Express Lane today."

"You sure?"

Maxie nodded.

"Okay," Regina said. "She's all yours."

Maxie gathered her things, and walked to the top end of the store. She didn't want to tell Regina that the choice she made to work the Express Lane, was based solely on making the time go by faster. She wanted the workday to end just as it had begun — with a quickness. She had a good reason. She wanted to be home with Lester. He reminded her the night before, that once again, he would be attending the yearly convention of Faith Keepers, with the men of their congregation. So she wanted to be home to help him pack, and to see him off.

Every November, the brotherhood meeting of Faith Keepers took him away from her for two days. This year, they would be in Dothan, Alabama, fellowshipping with other Christian men from all over the southeastern region. Maxie was surprised she had forgotten all about it, especially since the days he would be gone, were as soon as the upcoming Friday and Saturday.

After seven years of marriage, and seven yearly occasions of separation, Maxie could honestly say she was not accustomed to being apart from her husband — not even for two days. She hated those yearly trips. Why couldn't the Faith Keepers rededicate themselves to God right in Savannah, Georgia? Wouldn't He hear their prayers at home? Maxie once asked Lester that question. Only to be told that they were merely following examples of men in the Bible. His response offered nothing to counter how she felt.

Obviously with nothing to do on the weekend now, Maxie decided she had no real reason for not covering Monet's shift. No reason outside of simply not wanting to. But she figured, working a straight shift on Friday would turn out to be a wonderful time-killer.

* * * * * * * * * *

The purpose of working the Express Lane was accomplished. With the accolades of well-wishers, and the sounds of her register scanner beeping in her ears, Maxie happily ended her shift. She could see that being Employee of the Month was both a blessing and a curse. On one hand, she loved the verbal pats on the back in tribute to her hard work. On the other hand, her new label caused her to be even more conscientious of her overall performance; which in turn, made her work even harder to continually showcase what got her the honor in the first place. She wasn't going to do that tomorrow. Friday was going to be a very laid back day. If she was to have her choice of registers again tomorrow, she was definitely going to choose the bottom.

Maxie closed out her register, cleaned her area, and headed to the Customer Service desk.

"Well, needless to say, no one wanted to cover the shift." Regina said, holding out her hands for Maxie's cash drawer. "So would it be possible for you to come in tomorrow morning at nine?"

Maxie handed her the money, and considered Lester's early departure on Friday. "Yeah. I can be here at nine."

"Thank you Maxie. I promise I'll make your shift as easy as I can. I'll even give you an extra fifteen minutes for your lunch time tomorrow."

Maxie punched her card and headed for the exit doors. "I'm sure I'm going to need it. You have a good evening Regina."

"You too Maxie."

On her way out, Maxie glanced at her picture again. It made her feel good to know her image was going to be stationed up front, for the entire month of November. It also made her change her thoughts about turning in her notice to quit. She wasn't going to stop working at Food King. Definitely not now. Besides, Lester gave his approval for her to work for three months, and that is exactly what she intended to do.

Chapter Twenty-Four

M arc sat behind his desk and pensively tapped his mechanical pencil on his lips; his focus fixed on a tablet in front of him. Even though it was a part of Beatrice's job description to write out his travel itinerary, Marc always chose to do it himself. Once again, he planned his trip to London down to the second. It was his fourth time there in the past eleven months, so he had his travel agenda down to a science. The only obstacle he could possibly face would be a flight delay, and he hadn't encountered one of those yet.

His trips abroad were always planned to be strictly business, and handled in the quickest way possible. Although his job flew him to beautiful countries all over the world, and many people viewed it as glamorous, there were many days he thought just the opposite. Purchasing diamonds and other precious gems from international sellers was a profession he used to enjoy, but the novelty of it wore off sooner than he wanted it to. For the last two years, in spite of the exciting places he'd visited, Marc rarely experienced many of them. He often chose to keep himself isolated in his hotel suite.

But it wasn't always that way.

There were times when he welcomed the luxuries his job afforded him. In destinations around the globe, there were tasty exotic foods, evening strolls through garden-filled plazas bordered by sidewalk cafés, fine wines, and beautiful sunsets.

And there was Shari.

Marc tore the papers from the tablet, and straightened them between his hands. He hadn't allowed himself to go into deep thought about Shari for the past year, and he wasn't about to do it now.

"Beatrice," Marc spoke into his intercom. "Would you step into my office please?"

Marc released the intercom button before he got a response. It was only a couple of seconds before there was a knock on his door.

"Yes, Mr. Thomas."

"I'm going to be a sight holder again in London next week, so would you take this itinerary and type it up for me please? Fax or email a copy to the Diamond Trading Company there, give a copy to Jaunee, and as always, put a copy in your computer under my file. Make my reservations for my hotel and car rental, according to what I have on the itinerary. And ah ... let me see ... can you think of anything I may have left out?"

Beatrice took the papers, and frowned with a look of confusion. "Well Mr. Thomas, you made mention that I should give a copy of this to Ms. Jaunee, and she told me she may be joining you on your trip. So will she still need a copy?"

Marc stood up and pulled his suit coat together. Looking at his watch, he casually walked toward Beatrice with a reassuring smile. "Jaunee *will not* be joining me. I don't care what she said to you." Beatrice smiled weakly as Marc patted her on the back, and gestured for her to walk through the door before him. "I don't have any lunch appointments today do I?"

Beatrice sat behind her desk and nodded. "No sir, not today."

"Good. It's a nice day today. I think I'll go out and enjoy it. I'll probably get some lunch while I'm out. Hold all of my calls all right? I don't want to be disturbed."

"You're going to lunch alone?" Beatrice frowned again.

Marc winked his eye, kept his smile, and headed toward the door marked STAIRS.

* * * * * * * * * *

Lester had only been gone a few hours, and Maxie was already missing him. On her lunch break, she quietly sat in a booth in the Food King Café, gazing out of the window, as she recalled their last conversation.

"I promise you I will be fine," she told Lester as he prepared to leave. When they hugged each other, she whispered in his ear. "I'll be home before sundown, and I'll make sure every window and door is locked tight."

"I know I sound a bit overprotective," Lester said, holding Maxie away from him. "But I just want the security of knowing you'll be safe while I'm away. And you working that job until the evening does not offer me that security."

"Lester, I get off at five."

"And it starts getting dark at five-thirty."

"Baby, it will be no different than the way it is now. I get off at five, I come home, you get off at six, sometimes six-thirty ...."

"And I won't be coming home. Not for two days. You know I thought about getting you a cell phone. It would be perfect for an occasion like this. I hate the thought of not being able to speak to you for who knows how many hours."

"You can always call me at work," Maxie purred, as she came closer to him and rested her head on his chest.

"I may just do that." Lester wrapped his arms around his wife, giving her another tender squeeze. Gently, he lifted her chin just enough for their eyes to meet. "But in the event I don't call you at work, I know you'll answer the phone when I call here at twenty minutes after five this evening."

Maxie remembered gazing up at her husband with a glint in her eyes, and a hint of humor subtly tugging at the corners of her mouth. She hadn't heard him make any comments about her being out alone after dark for quite some time. But she knew he was genuinely concerned about it now, especially when he implied earlier, that she should consider spending the weekend with Sandra.

"Hmmm?" Lester raised his eyebrows in emphasis.

"Yes Lester. I'll be home by five twenty."

Now, as she looked out of the window, she couldn't remember ever missing him so much. Shaking her head lightly, Maxie tried to dismiss the thought and took a bite of her hamburger. Right now she needed to relax herself from head to toe. Though it wasn't her first time working a full day, she couldn't recall feeling quite as fatigued as she was right now; and she still had about four more hours to go. Even the effort of picking up her burger, and bringing it to her mouth seemed to zap her strength. Working one day for eight hours was enough for her. She couldn't imagine having to do it every day for a week.

Slowly, Maxie swirled the ice around in her cup and took a long draw of her Coke. More than anything, she wanted to rest her feet, so she quickly propped them up on the opposite booth seat. With her back facing incoming traffic, Maxie waited for an order of French fries to be freshly cooked and brought to her table. The café cashier automatically recognized her as a store employee, even without her smock on, so Maxie hoped she wouldn't have a problem identifying her in the growing crowd of people who were quickly filling the area. She considered switching her seat and sitting on the other side of the table for the cashier's benefit, but thought better of it. Her purpose was, if possible, to hide in plain sight of any co-workers. She couldn't afford to waste her remaining energy, engaging in uninterestingly dry conversations.

Maxie looked at her watch. It was twelve fifteen and she had an hour left on her lunch break. Regina kept her promise to give her fifteen extra minutes as a bonus for covering Monet's shift, and Maxie felt she deserved every minute of it. She was beginning to get a little irritated about waiting for hot fries, but no sooner had the thought crossed her mind, an outstretched hand offered them to her on a small plate. Maxie reached for the plate without looking into the face of the cashier.

"Thank you," she muffled.

"It's the least I could do for the Employee of the Month."

The response startled Maxie. It wasn't the voice of the café cashier like she expected, but it was definitely one she recognized instantly. When she looked into the face of the male imposter, the only words that came out of her mouth were "how?" and "why?"

"Oh you're wondering how and why I had your order." Marc said. "I was standing behind you when you placed it. I told the cashier we were together, and that I would save her the trip by bringing them to you myself. I had to wait for them to make this sandwich anyway. Do you mind if I join you? You should really go ahead and set that plate on the table."

Maxie was speechless. Slowly she set the plate on the table and removed her feet from the bench, so she could sit up straight. She watched incredulously as Marc sat opposite her, as if the removing of her feet was an answer of *yes* to the question of intrusion.

"So. How are you Maxie?"

Maxie wiped her mouth with her napkin. "I'm fine Marc. Dare I ask how you are?"

Marc smiled broadly, and leaned in a little. "I'm great. I can't complain. I'm having lunch with the Employee of the Month. So I guess all of the wonderful comments I put on that survey sheet, pushed you along huh?"

Maxie smiled softly. "I figured it was you. There was one survey where the nice comments were abundant."

"Hey, everything I wrote was true. You do your job well. Go ahead and eat your lunch. Don't let me stop you. Your fries are going to get cold."

Maxie smiled again, and squirted a large mound of ketchup on the side of her plate. It was almost a wasted gesture. She knew she was going to have to force herself to eat, because with all that was going on in her stomach right now, there was no way she could eat anything. As hungry as she was, the sight of Marc sitting at the table with her, made the hunger disappear.

Maxie dipped a fry into the ketchup, and watched Marc take a small bite of his sandwich. When he looked at her again, he wiped his mouth, smiled, and continued to chew. To see him up close put Maxie in awe. *He was gorgeous.* His eyes were actually a shade lighter than what she remembered. But everything else she observed about him was the same. Marc looked handsome in his brown suit and black turtleneck. The two colors brought radiance to his facial features.

"That picture they have of you in the front of the store looks real good. It was nice to see your face as soon as I walked in here."

"Thank you," Maxie mumbled.

"So how long is your lunch break?"

Maxie looked at her watch. "I have about fifty minutes."

"Great. That gives us time to sit and talk. Unless you have something else you have to do."

"No, I don't."

"Do you mind if we sit and chat? I'd really like to get to know you. I guess I should have asked you that in the beginning."

"No ... No, it's fine."

Marc took a deep breath, and released it noisily with a smile. "You looked a little nervous a few minutes ago when you first saw me. I'm glad you didn't shoot me down. I wasn't sure you'd allow me to impose."

Maxie smiled shyly. His presence was hardly an imposition. She didn't even question herself, as to how it was that he should be there right at that moment. A great part of her was happy to see him standing there. Because she felt that way, it was her own overwhelming ambivalence that made her nervous. Nervous because, instead of making a better judgment call on dining with another man, curiosity was quickly getting the best of her. There were things she wanted to know about Marc, so the desire to get better acquainted was mutual. Without a second thought, Maxie decided there was no place she'd rather be at that particular moment. In that frame of time, she was glad to be covering Monet's shift.

Marc was glad he went with his instincts on coming to Food King for lunch, instead of going to a fast food restaurant closer to his job. He hoped he would see Maxie, and his hopes panned out far greater than expected. He was finally able to spend some time with her.

From the moment he first laid eyes on Maxie, he couldn't get her out of his mind. Many times after that, he came into the store hoping to catch a glimpse of her at work. To his dismay, his fake shopping sprees left him wanting, because Maxie was either off, or had not yet arrived. He didn't want to inquire about her. That would look unseemly. He even ran into Monet a couple of times, but he made no mention of Maxie, and doubted Monet even remembered who he was.

Maxie grabbed the peppershaker and lightly sprinkled her fries, occasionally glancing at Marc. She couldn't identify what it was she was feeling, but she knew there was an obvious change in the atmosphere, and it had her dumbfounded. What was it about him that almost held her captive? Whatever it was, it wasn't physical. It went so far beyond his good looks, it was hypnotically enticing. Almost intoxicating.

And she liked it.

The mere thought of being enticed, and the feelings that went along with it, caused a massive surge of energy to flare throughout her entire body, leaving her tingling all over. Maxie conceded that she had to converse with Marc, in order to gain knowledge of what it was he possessed. How else was she to know why she was so drawn to him?

"On your Customer Service Survey sheet, you wrote down how you wished Food King had more employees like me," Maxie said. "What makes me so different from everyone else who works here?"

Marc smiled, and wiped his mouth with his napkin. Maxie's somewhat subtle approach to understand why he finds her intriguing, amused him. "So what you're really asking me is why you? Why do I want to know you?" Maxie gave him a look that confirmed his question. "Oh I don't know. You captured my interest."

"Me capturing your interest, has nothing to do with my performance."

"Sure it does. I witnessed your persona as you dealt with the customers, and how you paid attention to their needs, and … I saw your genuine concern … and … I … I liked what I saw and …" Marc looked at Maxie and how her facial expression seemed to make light of his reply. She sat with crossed arms, a slight smile, and a glint of disbelief in her eyes that caused him to laugh. "You aren't buying any of this are you?"

Maxie kept her smile, and released her crossed arms to reach for a French fry. "I'm just listening," she said, as she put the fry into her mouth.

Marc stared at her, and nodded lightly. "To be brutally honest with you, I want to get to know you, because I'm very attracted to you, and I don't know why."

Maxie looked at him with a raised eyebrow, and a questioning look.

"Now don't get me wrong. As I told you before, you're a beautiful woman and that's reason enough to be attracted to you. But there's something mysterious about you that's different from other wom ... from the others, and that mystifies me. Can you understand what I'm saying?"

Maxie pressed her lips together firmly, and nodded her head. It was interesting how they shared the same inquisitive feeling. The energy between them was definitely mystical and mysterious, and Marc clearly decided to peruse the unknown.

"So you think I'm different from other wom ... from the others."

Marc laughed a little. "Oh I see you caught that huh?"

"Yeah I did."

"Look, don't believe that I only want to get to know you just because I think you're a challenge. I don't play games like that. You seem like a nice lady and I ... like to be around nice people."

Maxie tried hard not to giggle at Marc's corny words. "So the fact that I'm married doesn't create a problem for you?"

"Should it?" He asked in all sincerity. "Does it create one for you? I mean, I figure you want to know about me as well. And if things go the way I would like them to, we could possibly be spending some time together, on occasion, chatting like this in order to get better acquainted."

Maxie took her straw, and swirled it around in her cup. Without looking at him, she spoke softly. "I don't think that would be a very good idea Marc. We have time right now to get better acquainted with each other. I don't see any reason why we would have to go beyond this moment."

Marc stared at Maxie. Raising his head a little, he rested against the back of the booth in total resignation. Did he just read her wrong? When he alluded to the fact that she wanted to know about him as well, she didn't deny it. Was she purposely sending mixed signals? He didn't know what to say. He couldn't remember ever being turned down so succinctly. On any other occasion, words like Maxie's would warrant an instant comeback, in the form that would deliver a smooth line of rhetoric, totally appealing to the listener, thus rendering him whatever he sought after. But Maxie didn't deserve that kind of a comeback. She was proving herself to be a woman of integrity, and that was to be respected. It was also a characteristic that only added fuel to the fire for him.

Maxie glanced at Marc, long enough to read the disappointment in his face. She knew she grazed his ego. It was obvious he was not expecting the response she had just given him. Frankly, she was surprised by it herself. She *wanted* to spend time with Marc. Since their second encounter, she entertained fleeting thoughts of being in his company, and though the door of opportunity stood wide-open, trepidation was keeping her from walking through it.

"So why don't you tell me about yourself," Maxie said after looking at her watch.

Marc pushed the rest of his sandwich aside and locked his fingers. Maxie thought he was being funny; positioning himself as if he were being interviewed.

"What is it you want to know?"

"Well, for starters ...," Maxie began casually.

"Let's start with my thoughts," Marc piped.

"Okay," Maxie replied, a little thrown off.

"For starters, I think you're afraid of me."

"Excuse me?"

"Yeah. You're afraid of me. Better yet, I think it scares you when you think of yourself *with* me."

"I don't even know you," Maxie said, a bit miffed.

"So *get* to know me. I know you want to."

"Now wait a minute ...."

Marc held up his hand. "No, no. Let me finish. You're afraid of the fact that you are just as attracted to me, as I am to you. You want to spend time with me, but you feel you would be compromising your marriage if you did. And that's cool with me. I respect that. It says a lot about you. But I don't believe the two of us being in each other's company would pose a threat. I'm not looking to have that kind of a relationship. You're scared because you feel something might develop between us. You're unsure of *yourself* because, maybe you'll *like* me just a little too much. Maybe you'll like the things we do when we're together. Maybe you'll enjoy *yourself* just a little too much. Then before you know it, you've allowed yourself to go beyond the place you intended to go. And that frightens you ... now doesn't it?"

Maxie sat quietly, and looked at her plate of half eaten food. *Cocky rascal.* She didn't want to agree or disagree with him. She didn't even want to admit to herself that most of what he said was true. As a matter-of-fact, she almost felt violated with how boldly he just searched her soul, reached in, pulled out some of the secrets of her heart, and set them on the table for intense scrutiny.

To him however, the revelation meant nothing. He knew he hit the nail on the head. It was all over her face. If he wanted to, he could have kept going. But what would be the purpose? He revealed enough.

"Now to tell you about myself," he continued. "My name is Marc Thomas. I work for Whitley Jewelers on Bay Street near the Historic District, where I'm a gemologist. I often travel all over the world to buy diamonds and other precious gems, and I make an insane amount of money. I live on Skidaway Island in a gated community called The Landings …."

"That's where they have mansion homes isn't it?" Maxie interrupted, springing back to life.

"You've been there?" Marc smiled.

"No. I tried to take a little tour through there one time. I was turned away at the gate, because I didn't have an invitation from one of the residents, nor did I want to pay the fee they charged to casual onlookers."

"Well if you really want to tour the area again sometime, I'll see to it that you get in. Maybe you'll let me be your tour guide." Maxie said nothing, and Marc shook his head and laughed a little. "Anyway, I'm thirty-five years old, never been married, no kids, and … currently, I'm not romantically linked with anyone."

"I find that hard to believe," Maxie said.

"Which part? The no wife or no kids?"

"No girlfriend. Surely you have interested parties."

"I never said there weren't interested parties. There are. But *I'm* not interested."

Maxie nodded her head. As much as she wanted to ask him questions on that subject, she decided against it.

"So you're a gemologist. That would explain your modish taste in clothing."

"What? This old thing?" Marc said, as he pulled his suit coat open. "It's just something I had in the back of my closet."

Maxie laughed.

"I love to hear you laugh," he said sincerely.

Maxie looked at him directly, before a wave of shyness washed over her and made her lower her eyes.

"You have beautiful eyes too," he continued. "I bet you get a lot of compliments on them."

"Thank you. I hear that from my husband often." She shot him again. This time when she looked up to see the damage, Marc was observing the people in the café. After a brief moment of silence, he looked at her.

"Why do you do that?" He asked.

"I'm sorry. Why do I do what?"

"Withdraw yourself when you feel uncomfortable with a compliment."

"Is that what you think I'm doing?"

Marc reached across the table, and gently grabbed her hand with a smile. "You don't have to be cautious of me Maxie."

Maxie shuddered on the inside at the gentle firmness of Marc's grip. Slowly, she pulled her hand away and hugged herself. It was another wasted gesture; because there was no way she could control the feeling his touch left with her. Being mystified and enticed at the same time, was already not a good combination. To make matters worse, her emotions were rapidly dealing her a large hand of fear. The kind of fear Marc just told her about.

It was fear of herself.

It was true. She didn't know what to expect of herself in any situation that found her giving time to another man. She had no gauge to measure by, because she had no knowledge of that area. So why couldn't that be something positive? She didn't have to be *in* a situation to know she had God-given restraints. What law said it was impossible for her to maintain her Christian composure, when in the company of a man, other than her husband, for great lengths of time? It wasn't like she was taking fire into her bosom. Maybe she *could* exhibit complete control with Marc.

Marc resumed his position. "So tell me about Maxie now."

Maxie looked at her watch again. It was twelve forty-five. "My name is Maxine Bruce. Everybody calls me Maxie for short. I'm thirty-four years old. I've been married for almost eight years. I don't have any kids, and I work in this grocery store." Maxie shrugged her shoulders. "Exciting stuff huh?"

"That's it?"

"Pretty much."

"Okay, well tell me something about your husband. He must be some special kind of guy, to have a woman like you who's so dedicated to him."

Maxie smiled a cunning smile. There was no way in the world she was going to tell Marc that her husband was an ordained minister. She also decided not to tell him that her level of integrity and *dedication*, as he had called it, was due to her commitment to God, and not just because she loved her husband. She didn't understand why she wanted to be so discreet about those things, but it was all best left unsaid for the moment.

"My husband's name is Lester. He's a construction foreman and ... he's very special to me. He's my heart."

Maxie made her statement with raised eyebrows, a shrug, and a firm look.

Marc gently shook his head in affirmation. Though her words seemed to make a simple conclusive declaration, he couldn't be sure if it was just a statement, or another way of letting him know where she stood; just like she did before. One thing being certain, her eyes unmistakably told him, *tread lightly here*.

Marc balled up his napkin, and sat it next to the remainder of his sandwich. "Our time is just about over isn't it?"

Maxie didn't want to look at her watch again. She knew the time was slipping away quickly. Instead she just stared at him. Returning her gaze, Marc assumed either she was thinking about something, or absorbing the moment to remember; because she thought it best that they not meet like this again. He wanted to ask her where her thoughts were, in an effort to keep the conversation going, but changed his mind. Instead, Marc looked at the food they had on the table.

Finally, Maxie looked at the time before she rested her hands on the table, and turned her wedding ring around on her finger. "You're a gemologist right?" She asked without looking at him.

"Yes I am."

"So do you design rings and other pieces of jewelry?"

"Sometimes," Marc answered, with a hint of suspicion in his voice.

"I guess you're pretty reputable huh? Whitley Jewelers is a very renowned jewelry company."

"Yes, I guess you can say that."

Maxie glanced at her watch. She had seven minutes to say goodbye, punch the time clock, and get back on the floor.

Marc perceived her movement to signify that they were at the end of their conversation. He pulled his jacket together, and stood up to gather his plate and napkin. He hated the thought of this being the only time he could spend with Maxie, but he had to respect her decision.

"Well Maxie, I hope you're comfortable with what we know about each other. Thank you for allowing me to have lunch with you. I ...."

"Marc, there's a gift I need to get for my husband for our wedding anniversary." Maxie focused on her ring, as she continued turning it. "I figure since you work at a jewelry store, and you can design things, maybe you can assist me in getting something uniquely special for him. You know, maybe a design like no one else has." Finally, she looked at him squarely.

Marc raised his head a little, and looked down his nose at Maxie. Everything she didn't say to him was in her eyes, and again he read them perfectly. After taking a deep breath and exhaling, he lifted one corner of his mouth into a sly smile and sat down again.

That's not a problem. I could design something for you."

"What do I need to do?"

"Well, do you have a piece of jewelry in mind? A tie or money clip? A watch, ring, or a bracelet?"

"I don't know. You're the professional," she smiled.

"Okay, we'll decide on something together. That means we'll have to meet from time, to time to discuss the different designs."

"I understand that," Maxie said softly, and looked at her ring again.

"And I may call you to let you know what I've come up with."

"Wouldn't that be a bit risky? You calling my house? I mean, what if my husband should answer the phone. That would make him assume the gift I plan to give him is some kind of jewelry."

"That's right," he grinned. "We definitely don't want that to happen. So I'll tell you what," Marc reached inside of his suit coat, and pulled out a card and a pen. "Let me give you my business card. It has the phone numbers where I can be reached. I want you to call the cell phone number on there. And so I know that it's you calling, and not one of my other clients, I'll give you your own special number. Let's use three twos." Marc wrote the numbers on the back, and handed the card to Maxie. "Instead of leaving me a voicemail, leave a call back number of three twos. That will let me know it's safe for me to call you … to discuss my designs."

Maxie examined the card. It was interesting how quick Marc's plan unfolded. It all flowed like it was second nature to him — practically rehearsed. Before she could think about it anymore, she remembered that her time was up. Quickly she shoved Marc's card into her smock, stood up, and attempted to gather her items from the table.

"Don't worry about this," Marc said. "I'll take it to the trash for you. I know you have to get back on the floor."

Maxie glanced at her watch, and smiled nervously. "Yeah, I have about two minutes to get there. So I guess I'll be … calling you right?"

Marc smiled, and nodded his head. "Whenever you're ready."

"Okay. Well, I enjoyed having lunch with you Marc. It was nice."

"I enjoyed it too. I hope we'll have an opportunity to do it again Maxie."

Maxie put her hands in the pockets of her smock. With her right hand, she gently caressed the raised lettering on Marc's business card. "You have a good day," she said, and walked away.

Chapter Twenty-Five

I t was hard for Maxie to keep her mind on her work for the rest of the afternoon. The duties she normally performed, were being executed by a woman on autopilot — never missing a step. Even though she watched Marc leave the store shortly after she was back behind her register, she continued to see his face on every male customer who entered the doors. When it came time for her to clean up her area at the end of her shift, Maxie did so in haste. She was more than ready to go home. There were things she needed to mull over, decisions that needed to be weighed, and a deep self-interrogation would obviously be in order.

"Was it that bad?" Regina asked when Maxie stood behind a co-worker, waiting to punch the time clock.

"I'm sorry." Maxie looked over her shoulder. "What did you say?'

"I asked you about your shift. Was it that bad? You're rushing to get out of here like there's a fire in the back of the store."

Maxie punched her card and put it away, before she walked near Regina. "No, it was fine. I'm just rushing to get home because I don't want to miss my husband's phone call. He's out of town."

"Oh. Well don't let me be the reason you miss it. I can't believe you don't have a cell phone. Necessity is the mother of invention you know."

"I'm learning that," she smiled.

"Thanks again for covering for you-know-who. I hope that little extra fifteen minutes for lunch did you some good."

"It was ... it was good," Maxie nodded. "Thank you."

"Well you go home and rest now. And you better not miss that call."

"Gotcha." Maxie agreed. "Have a good weekend."

In a matter of minutes, Maxie was driving out of the parking lot. The clock on her dash told her she had plenty of time to make it home before Lester called, but before she could turn on Abercorn Street, her car's gas light came on. "Not now," Maxie muttered through gritted teeth. She was fortunate enough to be stopped at a red light with a BP gas station just ahead of her. After urging the light to change, she pulled into the gas station and got out of the car with lightning speed. She was glad there was no one in front of her, forcing her to wait. That was all she needed right now. In one fluid motion, Maxie made her credit card purchase, chose the grade of gas she wanted, and shoved the nozzle into her tank. It wasn't until she squeezed the handle, did she notice someone standing right next to her. Frightened by their sudden presence and close proximity, Maxie jumped a little and quickly turned her head to face the person. "Ooo!" She said.

"I'm sorry. Did I scare you?" Marc asked, reaching out his hands to calm her.

Maxie closed her eyes and took a deep breath. Her heart was pounding in her chest. "Lord Marc," she managed between pants of breath. "You almost scared me to death! What are you doing, stalking me?" Maxie forced a smile to her lips, still shaken.

Marc put his hands into his front pockets, and looked at her earnestly. "I hope you don't think that's what I'm doing. When I got back to work, I remembered something important that I forgot to tell you. Since I don't have your home number, I called to see what time you were scheduled to be off. I hoped to meet with you before you left Food King, but just as I was pulling into a parking space at the store, I saw you getting into your car. You seemed a bit eager to leave, so I figured I'd just follow and try to catch up to you. Lucky for me, you stopped for gas. Otherwise, at the rate of speed you were going, I don't think I would have caught up to you. Not even in my car." Marc grinned, and lightly gestured toward an area where two cars were parked. One was an old blue Buick Skylark, and the other a shiny silver Mercedes S600. Maxie squinted against the waning sunlight, as she looked at the cars and then back at Marc.

"Let me guess. The Buick Skylark is yours."

"Yes," he said with a straight face. "Good guess."

Maxie looked at the cars again, and then back at Marc. "You're kidding right? I was only kidding."

"Why?" He shrugged. "Nothing's wrong with it. I happen to like old cars."

The gas handle popped to signal Maxie's car was full. After retrieving her receipt, she gave Marc a look that said *stop pulling my leg*.

Marc returned her gaze with the same look that echoed his last words. Finally, after a moment of exchanging nonverbal responses, Marc burst into laughter. "No, that's not my car."

"I knew it," she grinned broadly.

"The Mercedes is mine. Do you like it?"

Maxie looked again. "It's you. It's definitely you."

"Come on over and check it out real quick," Marc gestured with his head.

"I can't. I have to ...."

"I promise it will only take a minute. Come on."

Before she could say anymore, Marc headed toward his car. Maxie took a deep breath, exhaled, and took her keys out of the ignition before she followed him. Marc opened the door on the driver's side, and stood behind it like a chauffeur holding the door open for a movie star.

"Go ahead. Sit in it and look around."

Maxie did so with little ambivalence. The inside of Marc's car was so luxurious, she was afraid to touch anything for fear of leaving a visible fingerprint somewhere. The atmosphere of the cabin was filled with the *new car* smell, and the bell that signaled the door was open with the key in the ignition, sounded melodic. The interior was made up of beautifully crafted grained wood, and soft gray colored leather.

"Wow, this is beautiful. Where are the normal air conditioner and radio knobs?" She asked, allowing her eyes to continue their tour.

"See that screen in front of you? It's all right there. That's called a Comand System. It handles the adjusting of my radio, CD player, air conditioning, all that. Because it has hands free communication, I can make and receive phone calls without taking my hand off the steering wheel. Let me take you for a spin."

Maxie quickly snapped out of her awe-stricken state and stood up, remembering Lester's phone call. "Oh no," she frowned.

"What's wrong?"

"I can't ... I mean, my husband is expecting me to be home at a certain time." Maxie made sure she phrased her words just right. She wasn't going to lie to Marc, but she needed him to believe her husband was waiting for her. After all, Lester *was* expecting her to be home at the time he called. Centering her thoughts, she gave Marc her undivided attention. "What did you need to tell me?"

"Oh, yeah. I wanted you to know that I'm going to be out of town all of next week. I'm flying to London. I'll still be able to get your call, but I may not be able to return it until later that evening."

Maxie nodded her head and looked at her car just in time to see someone pulling in behind it. "Okay, I'll keep that in mind, *if* I call you. I'm keeping someone from getting gas, and I really have to get home. Thank you for giving me the tour of your luxurious car. It's very nice." Maxie started her trek back to her car, and then turned around to wave at Marc. "Have a good trip," she yelled.

Marc waved back and watched Maxie get into her car and drive away. He had to smile at how complex she was turning out to be. One moment, she showed him a woman who would be willing to let her hair down and be fancy free, joking and laughing. The next moment she was a woman with inhibitions, bound by her own integrity. It was plain to him that somebody needed to show Maxie Bruce the other side of life, and he planned to make himself the man for the job.

As she drove away from the gas station, Maxie looked in her rearview mirror. Marc was still where she left him. Only now he was leaning against his car, watching her drive away. She hoped he wasn't offended with her abrupt exit. She did offer an excuse. However, there was no valid excuse she could give to Lester. The sun was down, she was off from work, and she wasn't at home when she told him she would be. For Lester, there would be no explanation. No other explanation but the truth. She had to stop for gas.

Chapter Twenty-Six

M axie thought about her lunch with Marc consistently from the time she got home Friday,
until well into Saturday afternoon. It was hard
for her to think of anything else. She couldn't believe how
much that man permeated her psyche, and yet she still
knew so little about him. He had a good job, his house was
located in a guarded area on a very exclusive side of town,
and he had a very nice car. Then there were the obvious
things like his good looks, extreme self-confidence, and
experience. Mr. Marc Thomas definitely had experience.
The experience of the world.

"So we all agree then? If so, this meeting can be
adjourned." Emma Teal said, interrupting Maxie's thoughts.
Occasionally, she peered over the top of her glasses at
everyone, waiting for a response. All were silent.

"Well now, let's go over everybody's assignments one
more time," Deacon Earl piped in. "We all need to be sure
of what it is we're supposed to be doing. Ain't nothing
worse than mass confusion during the holidays."

Even though she didn't want to change her thought pattern, Maxie sat quietly in her seat and watched as Emma Teal exhaled a breath of aggravation at Deacon Earl's request. A little irritated herself, she gently tapped her pen on the small steno tablet she doodling on, rather than taking notes. She was ready to go home.

Since the Deacon and Deaconess Union meeting started, they reviewed the minutes from the last meeting, moved past the current financial report, and were now bringing finality to the discussion of new business. The meeting at the church was already at the top of her list of *Least Favorite Things to Do,* especially on a Saturday afternoon. Now, Deacon Earl just extended the boring gathering for an undetermined amount of time; making the task at hand sound as if it had a history for going awry. In actuality, those routinely involved knew it went off every year without a hitch.

The occasion for the meeting, was hardly the reason for Maxie's annoyance. Assisting the elderly and helping those less fortunate, were part of her duties as a Christian, especially during the holidays. It was the surrounding group, and their disdainful attitudes that made her wish she was somewhere else. Maxie hated the air of the company she was in. The average age of everyone in the group was over fifty-five, and because of their age, no one wanted to be subject to anyone. They all acted as if they were chiefs with no Indians, and that made the atmosphere contentious. The friction in the room was thick enough to be cut with a knife. Not to mention the black cloud of dissimulation that hovered above them all. It was so heavy, Maxie was sure she could hear whispers of the backbiting thoughts of those around her. It was these very things that made her plan a year ago, to opt out of the so-called *festive meeting*. And she would have, if she was not responsible for getting a small truckload of turkeys donated to the church by Food King. It was only right that she be there to oversee their distribution.

"Now you say Brother and Sister Renfrow will be responsible for gathering the information on all of the elderly folks, who will be in need of a Thanksgiving basket. Who did you say would be making the list of the families in need of a basket?"

"That would be Brother and Sister Brown. The same ones who have been compiling the list for the last fifteen years," Emma Teal said, with a hint of sarcasm in her voice. "Maybe you should get a pen and a piece of paper Earl, so you can write all of this down like everyone else is doing."

Maxie repositioned herself in her chair. Emma Teal dropped Deacon Earl's title like a woman with no shame, or regard for his delegated authority. It wasn't necessary to disrespect a man in front of his peers, but it was a part of Emma's character to do just that, especially where Deacon Earl Bayer was concerned. Maxie could not pinpoint the real root of Emma's repugnance toward the Deacon, but she had a pretty good idea of where some of it came from. With all of Deacon Earl's flirtatiously womanizing ways, not once had any member of The Ominous Three become the object of his affection. So obviously, in retaliation, whenever the opportunity arose, Emma always jumped at the chance to show her utter dislike for Deacon Earl Bayer. For Emma, it was pure sport to do it during a Union meeting, because there was an audience. Luckily for Deacon Earl, most of the other Deacons were on the Brotherhood trip.

Emma had the floor because the Deaconess Union was the department chosen by the Pastor, to head up the

Thanksgiving assignment. Otherwise, everyone in the room carried out equal administrative duties of the church, in one variation or another, so the ground was level. But every now and then, Emma Teal would find a platform to set herself above the rest; exalting and abasing whenever she felt it was necessary, — with absolutely no regard at all, for anyone's feelings of hurt or embarrassment.

"So once again, are we all clear on our assignments for Thanksgiving?" Emma squawked. Everyone in the room sounded their approval with a low moan, while Maxie said nothing at all.

"Well, does anyone make a motion for …?"

"I make a motion for this meeting to be adjourned," Maxie piped quickly.

"Very well then," Emma said, as she looked over the top of her glasses at Maxie. "We thank Sister Bruce for helping to provide us with the blessing of abundance in the food donation from The Food King."

Maxie smiled to herself at Emma's mispronunciation of the grocery store's name. "You're welcome," she said softly.

"I second the motion," Blanche Grammerson tooted.

A low grumble of voices immediately rose as everyone began to gather their personal belongings.

"This meeting is adjourned," Emma almost yelled.

In preparing herself to leave, Maxie attempted to flip the cover of her steno tablet over, when she noticed two words that were written repeatedly on the sheet she planned to take notes on. Clearly, all over the paper in many artistic forms, were the words *Marc Thomas*. Quickly, she closed the tablet, grabbed her purse, and left the meeting without speaking to anyone. Once she was in the car and moving,

Maxie tore the paper from her steno tablet, balled it up tightly, and tossed it out of her window.

In a matter of minutes, she was home and sitting on the couch in front of the television. She had to watch something. Hear something. Anything. Anything at all, to keep her from thinking about that piece of paper. But her mind would not let it go. "God," she closed her eyes and whispered frantically. "Why did I do that? Doodling like that is something a young girl does when she has a crush on a guy, not something a grown woman would do. Definitely not a grown woman who is *married*!"

Maxie jumped when the telephone rang.

"Hello," she huffed.

"Maxie?"

"Yes. Who is this?"

"Honey, it's me. Your missing husband. You don't recognize my voice?"

"Hi baby," she said, relaxing her shoulders, her voice, and her thoughts. Hearing Lester was calming and soothing to the storm of anxiety that was building within her. "I wasn't expecting your call so soon. Are you on your way home?"

"Not yet. We have two more seminars to attend. Is everything okay?"

"Everything's fine. I just miss you so much."

"You do?" Lester teased. "So absence has made your heart grow fonder?"

Maxie could tell he was smiling. Cuddling the phone, she lay back on the couch. "Uhm hmm. I'm always fond of you. Will you be leaving there soon?"

"Not until about two in the morning. I should be there by the time you wake up tomorrow."

Maxie closed her eyes and moaned her dissatisfaction.

"Honey, are you sure everything's okay?" Lester asked. "I don't remember you ever missing me quite this much during the other times I've taken this trip. I guess I should feel special then, huh?"

Lester's words zapped Maxie's memory like a lightning bolt. Before she knew it, Marc's face appeared before her. *"I should feel special then,"* were the exact words Marc said to her at the store, during their first encounter.

Maxie quickly opened her eyes, took a deep breath, and exhaled. What was going on? For most of the day, she felt as if she were under the influence of some hallucinogenic drug, with no control over her own faculties. She would see Marc, think Marc, and hear Marc. For the life of her, Maxie didn't understand how a brief conversation over lunch, could have such a lasting effect.

"You are special baby," she answered dimly.

"So, how was the meeting?"

"It was fine. Same ol' same ol'. Nothing ever changes with that crew. Same people doing the same thing, from the same agenda, year after year."

"I know sweetheart. But don't be discouraged by them. I want you to continue doing *your* duty as unto the Lord. *You* remain faithful. God's going to bless you. Okay?"

"I know." Maxie answered lowly.

"Good. So what are your plans for the rest of the afternoon? It's a little after three there isn't it?"

"Uhm hmm. I was thinking about doing some window shopping for that anniversary gift I want to get you," Maxie smiled.

"Oh yeah? And just what kind of stores will you be window shopping?"

"Oh, I don't know. Could be at a cheap department store. Could be at a specialty shop. It might even be at a jewelry store. More than likely though, it will be a pet shop."

Lester burst into laughter. "Woman, you better not try to pawn no animal off on me, talking about it's a gift!"

Maxie laughed too. "I think my feelings are hurt, just knowing you would not appreciate my living gift of love."

"Hey, there are other gifts of love I would appreciate more. You want me to name one?"

"Uh uh. "You're too far away to be talking like that."

Lester sighed. "Yeah, I know. Hold on a minute baby."

"Okay." Maxie listened as her husband cupped his hand over the phone to speak with someone. In the background, though a bit muffled, she heard the voice of a woman.

"No, we didn't order room service," she heard Lester say in a low, almost whispery tone. "Thank you," he said a little louder, before speaking into the phone again.

"So who is your roommate this year?" Maxie inquired.

"He's a visitor. He's actually a guest of Deacon Earl's."

"You mean to tell me that Deacon Earl invited someone to a conference, and then he didn't even go himself?"

"Poor example isn't he?"

"I'll say."

"I figured I'd take the young brother under my wing. His name is John."

"Well John is in good company. He couldn't be with a better man." Maxie smiled.

"Why thank you Mrs. Bruce. That's very sweet of you to say that."

Maxie tried to hold the phone closer, and speak with every ounce of passion she was feeling. "I love you Lester."

"Will you stop already?" Lester whined. "You're making me *not* want to be here right now. And that's not a good thing, because I have to leave for a seminar in just a few minutes."

"So come home to me now," she moaned.

"Baby ..." Lester started, before a man's voice was heard in the background. "They're waiting for me downstairs, so we can all travel over to the conference center at the same time. Now, you got me wanting to keep this little suggestive phone chatter going."

"This meeting can convene when you get home. We can pick up right where we're leaving off."

"You promise?"

"I do." Maxie replied.

"Then it's a date. We'll have a closed door meeting tomorrow morning."

"I look forward to discussing these matters with you at length, Mr. Bruce."

"However long it takes Mrs. Bruce, I promise you'll have my undivided attention. And I'll address every issue you have."

Maxie heard a knock at Lester's door, and listened to him sigh heavily.

"I have to go sweetheart. If the Lord says the same, I'll see you in the morning. Be careful, and let's not run low on gas again okay?"

Maxie smiled. "Goodbye baby."

"Bye."

Lester hung up the phone, but Maxie held on and cradled the receiver to her ear as if it were a lifeline. To perform a task as simple as hanging up the phone, seemingly created an imagery of something more final — and it had an eerie feeling attached to it. She didn't want to hang up for fear of somehow being permanently disconnected from her husband. She knew the thought was silly, and she didn't want to entertain it, but it was there nonetheless, right out of the blue. In essence, for the first time, Maxie wondered if anything or anyone *could* come between the two of them. She couldn't imagine it ever happening, but she had to consider the possibility. Would either one of them allow a situation to arise that would compromise their relationship? Their marriage? Could one of them become so displaced, that they would forget the true meaning of their vows of commitment to each other, made before God? Maxie couldn't fathom the thought of either one of them giving in to fleshly desires, for even one moment.

"If you'd like to make a call, please hang up, and dial again. If you need help, hang up, and then dial the operator," the recording said, before it was followed by loud rapid beeps. Slowly, she set the receiver in its cradle and resumed her position on the couch. After lying there motionless for a few minutes, toiling with implausible possibilities, Maxie knew she needed to set up some kind of a hedge — a boundary of protection, as a precautionary measure. Much like the blue ceiling she remembered at her grandmother's church. There was only one recourse for what she needed, and she knew exactly what to do. Maxie got down on her knees, closed her eyes, and prayed. "Father God, in the name of Jesus, I come to you in the humblest manner I know how. Thanking you for this day that you have made. I will rejoice and be glad in it. Lord, I ask you to forgive me for all of my sins of omission, and commission. Create in me a clean heart, and renew a right spirit within me. Help me to be the godly woman you would have me to be. God, continue to use me for the up building of your kingdom, and Lord, bless our marriage. Encourage and strengthen us for what may lie ahead. Your word says that we, the children of light, shall not be ignorant of the enemy's devices; devices that will aid him in his efforts to steal, kill, and to destroy us. God, bind the adversary and the evil devices he plans to use to come against our marriage. Let us see the enemy coming afar off, and give us your strength to fight the battle. Without you Lord, we are nothing. We need your hand to guide us. Help us to be watchful in every area. ..."

Maxie prayed for more than an hour. Before she finished, she asked God to show her what might be their adversary, living or inanimate. What device would the devil use? She wanted to know in advance with whom, or what, would be their fight, if there were to be a fight at all.

When she ended her prayer, Maxie got off her knees and sat on the couch. Opening her eyes, she let the tears flow down her face. After questioning God about the adversary, Maxie realized she may have gotten her answer sooner than she expected. For what God may have just revealed, she knew that *she* was the one who would have to put on strength. In front of her, slightly balled up on the edge of the coffee table, was the work smock she placed there the night before. Sticking out of the smock pocket almost fully, was the business card with the name *Marc Thomas*.

Chapter Twenty-Seven

M arc smiled cordially at the flight attendant's persistent effort to make him feel comfortable.

"We're very sorry about the long layover here at the Dallas Fort-Worth airport, Mr. Thomas," she said. "The fog in London is very dense, and there are many flight delays in and out of the Heathrow Airport."

"I understand," Marc said. "Some things just can't be avoided."

As the flight attendant went on apologizing, Marc watched her busy herself fluffing a pillow he didn't want, pouring him half a glass of complimentary wine he didn't ask for, and replacing the Conde Nast Traveler magazine with Ebony, Jet, and GQ.

"Is there anything else I can get for you?" The flight attendant piped, while handing him a landing card to be filled out for Passport Control and Customs.

Marc looked at the card that requested his name, address, passport number, and the address of the hotel where he would be staying. Casually, he slid the card into a side pocket of his laptop case. Though the presentation of the card was a necessary routine for foreign travelers landing in London, he felt that as often as he had been there, a flash of his passport should be enough.

"No," Marc said pensively. "You've supplied me with everything. Thank you."

The flight attendant stood a moment longer, fully observing him from head to toe, before she nodded her head. "Okay ... well, I'll be close by if you need me."

Marc thought he detected a slightly seductive allusion in her voice, but dismissed it and smiled at how much she acted like a giddy, overzealous schoolgirl.

"Thank you again," he said. When he was finally left alone, Marc examined the rest of the First Class area. With the exception of two other passengers seated on the opposite side of the cabin, the secluded area was empty. For that reason, he was glad. He still had a lot of preparing to do before his meetings, and a near empty area to work in, was exactly what he hoped for.

Marc waited for the seatbelt sign over his head, to go off. While the pilot thanked everyone for flying British Airways, Marc set up his laptop and pulled out numerous file folders. The flight was to be five hours long, and for him, that was more than enough time to complete what he had before him.

Prior to settling in, Marc checked his phone for e-mails, voicemails, and text messages. All were business related, except for the voicemail from Jaunee, wishing him a pleasant trip and hoping to see him soon. Her usual. Though the messages were pretty much what he expected, he hoped to be surprised by a call or a message from Maxie. He tried to fight it and keep his mind on his work, but Marc couldn't help but to think about her. The question that lingered in his mind, wasn't *would she call?* But rather, *why hasn't she called?* The little time they spent together conversing and sharing things about themselves, only proved to be an appetizer for him. Now he wanted the full course. What was to keep him from having it? Weren't they on the same wavelength when they discussed how they would meet from time to time?

Feeling his angst rise with each question, Marc took a deep breath, exhaled, and swallowed all of the wine the flight attendant poured into his glass. He even used the pillow to rest his head against the seat. He needed to calm himself and give her time. But because anticipation had never been a friend to him, Marc didn't want to wait. He had never been made to wait, and now hated the fact that he put the ball in Maxie's court, when he chose not to take down her home phone number. Now he had no choice. Over the next seven days, there was no way he could see her, and if she didn't call, there was no way he could even hear her voice.

Marc casually looked at his phone again. He could get in touch with Maxie if he really wanted to. Calling her job and getting information about her work schedule for the week, was an option. He could even look her up on the internet.

Marc briefly closed his eyes to center his thoughts. He was thinking like someone who was obsessed. He was going to have to wait for Maxie to call him, and that was all there was to it. So why was he feeling so anxious? It was almost as if she unwittingly had some kind of a hold on him. That in itself was strange, because Maxie never flirted or teased him; yet he felt overwhelmingly seduced. Marc couldn't recall ever feeling so eager about wanting to spend time with any one woman, least of all one who was married.

When he finished mulling over his thoughts, Marc decided that once Maxie contacted him, there would be no time wasted. Her call would be a direct invitation to have his curiosity quenched, and he was going to set up meetings with her every chance he got.

For now, she had the ball.

For now, he would just have to wait.

＊ ＊ ＊ ＊ ＊ ＊ ＊ ＊ ＊

For the better part of his days in London, Marc was busy with gem manufacturers, third party salesmen, merchandise evaluations, and diamond purchases. Checking the color, cut, clarity, and carat weight of each diamond he bought, was rapidly becoming a tedious job. He was more than ready to head back to the states. Every morning and afternoon was filled with bids, small cases of cut goods, and hob knobbing with stone purchasers from all around the world. He was used to the hustle and bustle of the daily routine, and somewhat welcomed it, because it kept his thoughts on business.

But his nights ....

There was little to occupy his nights, and they were just as long as the days. The only difference — he had a lot more time for roaming thoughts. Thoughts that led to flared assumptions, because at one o'clock Wednesday afternoon London time, Maxie had yet to call. Marc considered the five-hour difference from London to the United States, and thought since it was early morning in Savannah, Maxie still had the whole day to call him. But when she hadn't called by nine o'clock that evening, his time, Marc could only assume she changed her mind about everything.

All morning Thursday, while in meetings, he checked his cell phone for unknown numbers with a Georgia area code on it, or the special three-digit number he gave to her. It was all to no avail. He even placed a call to Beatrice, his secretary, to see if there were any messages left for him back at Whitley Jewelers. Perhaps Maxie may have tried to call him there.

There was nothing.

By lunchtime, because of the obvious, Marc forced himself to come to grips with the fact that maybe Maxie Bruce wasn't quite as interested in knowing him, as he was in knowing her. Even though the thought of a woman being *uninterested* in him was far-fetched and inconceivable, he had to consider it.

At the end of the day, instead of winding down in his hotel room, and settling in with room service, Marc decided to take a walk through Hyde Park. Rebellious to the autumn season, the weather was warmer than usual, and the golden glow of autumn on the trees in the park, beckoned him to come. The fresh air was needed, and he wanted to do something different. His frequent trips to London, allowed him to visit all of the popular tourist sights. A couple of his favorites were the London Eye, where he observed London from 400 feet in the air in a glass module, and the Tower of London where he witnessed the beauty of the Star of Africa; the world's largest diamond. As spectacular and inviting as these sights were, neither was worthy of another visit — at least not today. A casual stroll through the park would do him good.

After purchasing a sandwich at a nearby eatery, Marc continued his trek to the Serpentine Bridge. In the middle of the bridge, he leaned over and watched the Serpentine Lake flow beneath him. As he stood gazing, he observed that the park had few visitors. Even the traffic going over the bridge was minimal. Further down-stream, children and adults took advantage of the Indian summer, by riding on the lake in paddleboats.

"Excuse me. You wouldn't happen to have the time would you?" A voice said, with a strong British accent.

Marc turned slightly to face a skinny young man with mused red hair, freckles, and a skateboard under his arm. When he raised his hand to look at his watch, his cell phone rang.

"Uh ... yeah, it's four-thirty."

"Thank you." The boy waved, and rolled away.

Marc immediately pulled out his cell phone, and looked at the number. The area code was from somewhere other than Georgia, so he considered not answering it and letting the call roll into his voicemail. It would take six rings before the call would be forwarded into his mailbox, but on the fifth ring, he changed his mind and answered it.

"This is Marc Thomas," he said with an air of professionalism.

"Hello Marc Thomas. How is it in London? You know, I've always wanted to travel there."

Marc quickly pulled the phone away from his ear, to look at the Caller ID again. He had no idea who was on the other end. Normally, whenever he received a business call, he would say his name, and the caller would identify himself or herself immediately. Since this person did neither, his only clue was that it was a woman. Without any other helpful hints, Marc remembered he recently had a call from the same area code, and that call came from Wyoming. Putting the phone back to his ear, he tried to recognize the voice of the woman on the other end.

"You're calling from Wyoming. I don't recall having any clients in Wyoming. You must be new. How may I help you?"

"I am a new client, but I'm not calling you from Wyoming. It must be this long distance calling card I'm using. I'm calling you from Georgia."

Marc visibly relaxed against the bridge wall. Smiling broadly, he whispered to himself, "Maxie."

"So Mr. Thomas, you didn't answer my question. How is it in London? I have it down on my list as one of the places I'd love to visit."

"It's beautiful. Maybe the next time I come here, I can make it a business and a pleasure trip, and you can come with me." Marc listened for a response to his proposition. When there was no answer, he thought maybe the call was disconnected. "Maxie?"

"I heard you," she replied softly.

Since no more was said, Marc continued the conversation. "You took your time calling me. I figured you were having second thoughts."

"There was a lot I needed to think about. Some things I hadn't considered."

"Well since you're calling me now, is it safe for me to say that all is well in moving forward?" Maxie was silent again, and Marc felt she was either struggling between giving him an outright answer of *yes*, or mustering up a polite way to put an end to what had yet to begin. As he listened intently for her to say something, he remembered he promised himself that once she called, he was going to set up a meeting with her immediately. "Maxie, I want to see you. I want to meet with you on Monday, early afternoon, around two. Would that be possible?"

Still, there was no response.

"Maxie?"

"I believe that can be arranged," she relented, with the same soft voice.

"Maybe we can have a late lunch, and discuss some of the designs I have available."

Maxie sighed into the phone gently. "I have to get to work now. I'm supposed to be on the floor in a few minutes."

"Is that where you're calling me from?" Marc asked.

"Yes. I left home a little early so I'd have enough time to talk to you."

Marc laughed a little at Maxie's idea of *talking*. "Why didn't you call me from your home?"

"I couldn't," she simply stated.

Marc understood, and realized at the same time, that he still had no home phone number to contact her whenever he wanted to. "So how will I know if you are able to definitely make this meeting happen?" He asked.

"I'll call you Monday morning with the details. How many designs do you have anyway? I need to know how to plan my time."

"Just plan to spend a couple of hours with me."

"So you're saying we'll be together from two to four?"

"Exactly."

Maxie was silent for a moment. "I'll see what I can do. I really have to go now."

"Maxie wait."

"Yes?"

"I'm glad you called. I'm really looking forward to seeing you again."

Another moment of silence fell, before Maxie finally said, "Enjoy the rest of your trip Marc," and hung up the phone.

Marc put his cell phone back into his suit pocket, and smiled reflectively. She called. She actually called. For those few moments of conversation, he had absolutely no regard of his surroundings. When he finally looked around, the sun was waning, and there were fewer people in the park than before. But at that moment, Marc felt like every diplomat in Parliament had just honored him right where he stood. On this trip to London, he felt he captured something far greater than his purchases of diamonds, rubies, and sapphires. To Marc Thomas, Maxie Bruce could quite possibly be the gem of a lifetime.

Chapter Twenty-Eight

~~~

Since her brief conversation with Marc, Maxie couldn't believe how quickly the rest of the week passed. She busied herself with everything she could put her hands to do, trying not to think about meeting with him. Although she agreed to it, the decision was an impulsive one.

Despite the fact that she enjoyed hearing his voice on the phone, Maxie somewhat regretted making what she thought could be a life changing phone call. When she first began dialing Marc's phone number, she paused midway through to ask herself if she really wanted to do it. Ambivalence made her hang up the phone quickly, after she decided it really wasn't a good idea to speak with him, before she had a chance to weigh everything out for the hundredth time. She had to consider what might have been a God-given revelation about Marc.

Instead of heeding her own admonition, she dialed the phone number again, this time with the hope of getting his voice mail. She told herself it was a logical decision, because he was probably in meetings most of the day, and ringing cell phones in a business meeting was unacceptable. She didn't anticipate him actually answering, but when he did, she started the conversation with a bogus statement about wanting to travel to London someday (for which she repented immediately). Moreover, she didn't know what to say when he invited her along on his next excursion. She wished she had that same loss of words when he said he wanted to meet with her. Marc Thomas was proving himself to be a man who was quick and to the point. If she ever had to describe him in one word, that word would be *aggressive*.

* * * * * * * * * *

"So now *you're* asking to switch shifts with Monet?" Regina asked, when Maxie phoned her at the store Sunday evening. "That's a first."

"I have an important afternoon appointment to keep," Maxie said in a low voice. Sitting on her bed, she kept a close eye on Lester in the living room while he watched a football game.

"Well, I don't believe that will be a problem," Regina said. "Like I told you, she works from nine until one on Monday, and she's aware that she owes you for the times you've covered her butt. I'll call her tonight and let her know that she'll be switching shifts with you tomorrow."

"Thanks Regina," Maxie smiled.

"Not a problem. I'll see you at nine tomorrow morning."

"Great."

Maxie hung up the phone gently, and continued looking at her husband. Slowly, her smile faded. It wasn't enough that the plans she was making from the beginning, made her feel a little off center and guile. But now, as she watched

Lester, she saw him in a light that showed him to be oblivious and totally innocent; and it caused a sharp pain to pierce her heart, because the thought of betrayal came to mind.

But why?

Granted, she switched her working hours to the morning without him knowing about it, but it wasn't like she did it with any malicious intent. She had a meeting with a jeweler named Marc, and it was business. He was going to help her to surprise Lester with a meaningful anniversary gift, and she in turn was going to teach him about the salvation of the Lord.

Plain and simple.

After mulling over what she believed God was trying to show her about Marc, Maxie figured she could make the most of what might be a bad situation. If Marc was to be the tool the devil planned to use to come against her marriage, she knew he wouldn't be doing it willingly. Obviously, he was ignorant of the devil's devices, and he lacked the knowledge of his manipulating power. Marc needed someone to help him to get an understanding. Someone to teach him about God's saving graces. After all, he did have a soul that needed to be saved, and it was becoming increasingly evident to her that *she* was to be that *someone*.

So why was she feeling so guilty? No lies had been told. There was no deception.

Or was there?

If so, who was the one being deceived?

* * * * * * * * * *

At five forty-five in the morning, Maxie awoke to the sound of a gentle wind, whistling around the crevices of their bedroom window. Even though the sound was menacing, she kept her eyes closed because she wasn't ready to get up yet. Her sleep had been a deep one, and she didn't want to let it go. She didn't even know what day it was, and at that moment, she could have cared less. But when the atmosphere in the room became charged with a momentum only she could feel, Maxie knew it had to be Monday. Only then did her thoughts go to Marc, and the day that was ahead.

While she tended to Lester by helping him to get ready for work, Maxie thought about the call she had to make to Marc, with the details of where they would meet. At first, she thought about waiting until she got to work and calling him from there, because she couldn't be sure she wanted him to know her home phone number. However the more she thought about it, the more sense it made for him to have the number, especially if he needed to meet with her to view his new designs. So as soon as Lester backed his car out of the driveway on his way to work, Maxie made the call. Once again, she hoped to get Marc's voicemail, only because the time was so early. Once again he answered the call, surprising her by picking up on the first ring.

They agreed to meet at the Shrimp Factory, a seafood restaurant on River Street, at two-thirty. For Maxie, it was a restaurant on the other side of town that she had never been in; for Marc, it was near his job, and a place he frequented often. When all was said and done, Maxie quickly got herself ready for work, putting on a dressier ensemble than normal, because she had no intentions of returning home to change her clothes. She wanted to look nice, but careful not to overdo it.

As she observed herself in the dresser mirror, Maxie saw the message light on the telephone, blinking in the reflection. Turning to make sure she was viewing correctly, she mumbled to herself how she could have missed hearing the phone ring. Quickly, she sat on the bed and retrieved the call.

"You have two messages," the answering machine piped. "Message number one. Monday, seven fifty-five a.m."

"Maxie! Dang girl! I hate playing phone tag with you. You need to get yourself a cell phone! In case you haven't recognized my voice by now, this is your girl Sandra. Remember me? I haven't heard from you in about a week or so. Anywho, listen up. I called to tell you two things. First of all, don't try to return this call. I'm on my way to the airport to fly out to Detroit for a huge corporate meeting. Something about a merger with Sony Electronics, so you won't be able to reach me. I'll be there for a couple of weeks, so I'll try to reach you. Second, I had this wild dream about you last night girl, and it kind of disturbed me. In this dream, you were this little girl at the zoo with these three older women, and you all were having a really good time, especially you because you were the center of their attention. All of a sudden, one of the women left. But before she did, she told you not to feed or play with the animals in the cages. You cried when she left, and you told her that you wouldn't play with the animals. With the next two women, you looked like you were getting older, and then the second one left, and she told you the same thing the first woman told you. You cried again, and said that you wouldn't play with, or feed the animals in the cages. Now with the third woman, you looked like you were all grown up, and she was leaving you too. And she said ...."

"End of message," the recording on the phone said. "Message number two. Monday. Seven fifty-seven a.m."

"Okay, you also need an answering machine with longer time limits on it. Back to what I was saying. The third woman was leaving you alone in the zoo, and she told you the same thing the other two women said. But this time, you looked over your shoulder at this one particular cage, and you told this woman that one of the animals was really hungry, and that you just wanted to feed it a little bit of food. She still warned you like the other two women did. Now when she left, you cried a lot, and you just sat down on one of the park benches, looking at this cage that had a funny looking bear in it. No, it wasn't a bear, it was one of those Tasmanian devils, but this one was abnormal in size, and it kept smiling at you. Then out of nowhere, you had this brown paper bag of food, and you started throwing a little bit of food into this cage. Now because this animal liked what you were throwing to it, you kept getting closer and closer to his cage. All of a sudden, next thing I know, the animal is out of the cage and you're running down this pathway with it following you right on your heels. The thing that bothered me Maxie, was the look on your face. You looked terrified in that dream girl. Man, I wish I could see you and talk to you about this. I'll keep trying to get in touch with you when I can. Take care of yourself Maxie. Bye."

Maxie played the messages two more times before she erased them both. With her thoughts primarily channeled on one thing, it simply slipped her mind that she hadn't talked to Sandra in over a week. On one hand, she was glad her friend didn't have the time to talk to her about the dream. A discussion now would only give Sandra cause to find out what's been happening in her life recently, and Maxie didn't want to explain a thing. On the other hand, she hated missing her call. She would have liked to at least touch base with her briefly.

Although there was excitement and genuine concern in Sandra's voice, the events of the dream were no surprise to Maxie. She had a good idea about its meaning, because she knew about the animal in the cage and its appetite. What she couldn't understand, was the look of terror Sandra said she saw on her face. Why would she be terrorized by something she had complete control over? And how could the animal be loosed in her life and chasing her, if she never *really* opened its cage to begin with?

* * * * * * * * *

When she walked into work, Maxie thought for sure that one of her co-workers would make a comment about her coming to work dressed up, but no one said a word. At least not with their mouths. It was all said with their eyes, as they sized her up when she walked past their registers.

"Look at you," Regina smiled broadly when Maxie punched her timecard, and retrieved her cash tray. "I know you're still Employee of the Month and all, but you don't necessarily have to dress the part."

Maxie quickly glanced at Regina, as she put her smock on. Unconsciously, she put both of her hands in the pockets. When she felt Marc's business card in one of the pockets, she discreetly pulled it out just enough to see it, and then put it back.

"Remember, I told you I had an appointment to keep this afternoon," Maxie said.

"Yeah, I remember. But I hope you ain't going to a doctor's office, or sitting in a dentist's chair dressed like that. You're sure to mess up your hair."

Maxie lowered her sight a little, and placed a small strand of hair behind her ear. After a moment, Regina eyed her skeptically.

"You wouldn't be going on an ...."

"No I'm not going on an interview," Maxie nodded and laughed a little.

"Well that's good," Regina sighed. "You clean up nicely Maxie. Shoot, you almost make me regret putting you on the schedule for today."

"Well we both know you need me this morning, so where am I working?"

Regina pretended to look all around the store from where she stood. "Shoot, with you looking so good and all, let me see which end of this store needs beautifying, and I'll stick you there."

Regina and Maxie looked at each other and burst into laughter.

"Why don't you just put me on one of the Express Lanes? It will make my shift go by faster."

"Sounds like a plan. Take number three."

Maxie gathered her things, and began walking to her register near the store's entrance.

"Hey Maxie," Regina called. "If the traffic is slow in here today, I'll let you go a little early."

Maxie simply smiled, and waved with her free hand. Once behind her register, she moved swiftly to receive her first customer. With a smile, she greeted the gentleman, but doubted he even heard her, because he was deep in a conversation on his cell phone. As his credit card purchase processed, Maxie inadvertently listened in on the man's one-sided crass discussion.

"There is no way I can meet with them today," he said firmly. "I'll have to shift them to tomorrow. I forgot I have two meetings this morning, and with three this afternoon, there's just no way I can do it. Now you tell them if they can't wait until tomorrow, that's just too bad. Their business isn't that vital to us anyway."

Maxie bagged the man's groceries. Listening to his dilemma, forced her to consider a possible one of her own. If her meeting time with Marc had changed, due to some business related circumstances beyond his control, how would she know? How could Marc get in touch with her? He had no idea she rearranged her work schedule, just so she could meet with him. What if he phoned her at home, and his number showed up on the Caller ID? If Lester's gift was supposed to be a surprise, it would definitely be blown if Whitley Jewelers showed up on the home phone. Or worse yet, what if he left a message about the change in their meeting time on her answering machine, and Lester decided to come home for lunch?

In that instant, Maxie became paranoid, and thought about the inconvenience of not having a cell phone. In the meantime, she needed to get in touch with Marc to see if anything had changed, and to let him know she would not be home all morning, so he shouldn't call her there. With no one in her line, Maxie flipped the switch on her aisle marker sign so it would blink on and off, signaling to a floor manager that she needed assistance.

"Bathroom or money?" Regina asked when she approached Maxie's lane.

"Telephone. I need to make sure my appointment time hasn't changed. If it has, I wouldn't know because I didn't give my work number as an alternate contact number. It'll only take me about five minutes."

"Go ahead and turn your light off."

"Thanks," Maxie smiled, and quickly walked to the service desk.

When she got to the phone, she pulled out the business card and dialed Marc's cell number. When a woman answered, surprise and trepidation leaped on Maxie simultaneously.

"Hello?" The woman said.

Maxie was silent. She had no idea of what to say. Obviously, she misdialed.

"I'm … I'm sorry. I believe I dialed the wrong number."

"Are you trying to reach Marc Thomas?" The woman asked, with a friendly voice.

"Um, yes I am."

"Well you dialed the right number. I'm one of his co-workers. I only answered his phone, because he just stepped out of the office for a moment. If this is business related, I'd be more than happy to take a message for him."

Maxie was silent again. She didn't want to leave a message. Why would a co-worker answer someone else's personal phone anyway? Her whole purpose for calling Marc's cell phone in the first place was to either speak with him directly, or leave a message on his voicemail. Now, she couldn't be sure he would even get her message.

"Okay. Well, I'd like to leave a number to where I can be reached in the event our meeting time changes." For a few seconds, Maxie heard absolutely nothing on the other end. "Hello?"

"Oh, I'm sorry. I was writing down what you were saying. Let me make sure I have this correct. You have a meeting with Mr. Thomas, and you want to know if anything has changed."

"That's right. Are you ready for the number?"

"Oh, yes. Go ahead."

Maxie gave the woman her name, and the phone number to Food King. She was about to hang up the phone when the woman continued.

"Now I'm sure Mr. Thomas remembers your scheduled meeting time, but in the event that it slips his mind, or becomes overlooked because of his other meetings, would you mind telling me the time so I can write it on this message as a reminder to him?"

Maxie paused. At first she thought the woman was being nosey, but after brief consideration, she felt maybe the woman was simply being very efficient. "It's at two-thirty. To whom am I speaking? I'd like to know who I'm leaving this message with."

"Oh, my name is Jaunee. And don't worry, I'll make sure Marc gets your message. You have a good day."

Before Maxie could tell her thank you, the line went dead. Maxie looked at the receiver for a moment. She had no idea who that *Jaunee* person was, but if Marc didn't get her message, she would be sure to tell him about her.

* * * * * * * * * *

Jaunee put Marc's cell phone back on his desk, the same way she found it. Unbeknownst to her, Marc stood in the doorway watching.

"What were you just doing with my phone?" He asked, as he walked in and stood behind his desk.

"Oh!" Jaunee jumped. "Oh my goodness! You just about scared me to death." Jaunee put her hand on her chest, and laughed nervously. "Why I was ... you were ... phew! You had a call when you stepped out, and I figured ... well ... it must have been something important if someone was calling you on your cell phone. So ...."

"So you answered my phone," Marc said casually, as he thumbed through a file of papers in his hands. "Well did you take a message? Who was it?" While he gave his full attention to the papers, Marc waited for Jaunee to answer. When she said nothing, he set the file down on his desk, and looked at her squarely. "Jaunee, who was it?"

"It was some woman named Maxie," Jaunee huffed, with a slight twist of her neck. "She wanted to leave you a phone number where she could be reached, in case you changed your meeting time with her at two-thirty."

"Where is the number?"

Jaunee handed him the little Post It note she virtually scribbled on. "Is she the reason why we couldn't go to lunch this afternoon? I really want to hear about your trip to London?"

Marc looked over the note. "Jaunee, you know it's always business before pleasure with me. Besides, there was nothing different about this trip, than all of the other ones."

Sensing her disappointment and a slight change in the atmosphere, Marc glanced at her long enough to see a solemn look on her face. With a wink and a smile, Marc caused her whole demeanor to change, producing a veritable smile from Jaunee.

"Is she the one you're showing my designs to?"

"Yes she is," Marc replied, turning his attention to the file again.

"Hmmm," Jaunee said airily. "She sounds pretty."

"It's business Jaunee," he said casually without looking at her. "Strictly business."

Jaunee slowly moved toward the doorway and stopped. "So maybe we can get together tomorrow?"

"It's possible."

"Well look, I have a few unfinished ring designs left on my computer, so ... I need to go and get those completed. I'm glad you had a nice trip, and I'm glad you're back." Jaunee smiled awkwardly, and stood in Marc's doorway as if she were expecting him to say something that would keep her from leaving. When he didn't reply, and still had not looked at her, she took a deep breath and released it as if she had been defeated. "See you later."

"Okay. I'll see you." Just as Jaunee made her first step to walk away, Marc called out, "Oh Jaunee."

"Yeah," she said, turning around so quickly, it made her hair bounce.

"Don't ever answer my cell phone again."

Jaunee forced a smile, and walked away.

Chapter Twenty-Nine

Marc arrived at the Shrimp Factory almost thirty minutes early. Even though he purposely scheduled lunch with Maxie during an off-peak time at the restaurant, he knew Savannah tourists had a tendency to straggle into the popular eatery and linger, which prompted his early advent, and a phone call to reserve the perfect table. Wanting to see Maxie as soon as she arrived, Marc temporarily sat near a window that gave him a full view outside the restaurant. He didn't know anything about her history of promptness, so he couldn't be sure she would be on time. But whatever time she arrived, he would be waiting.

Maxie parked her car in the lot above the Drayton ramp to River Street. She wanted to park closer to the restaurant, but the few spaces off the ramp were full. Quickly she put her coat on, and walked briskly against the wind that was par for the area. When she finally entered The Shrimp Factory, she just knew her hair was all over her head, and did her best to straighten it with her hand. Looking around for the man she would be spending the next two hours with,

Maxie saw a selection of both booth and table seating. The booths had high backs on them, so she wondered how she was going to find Marc if he was already there waiting for her.

"Hello. Welcome to The Shrimp Factory. Seating for one this afternoon?"

Out of nowhere, Maxie was face to face with a lanky male host smiling at her. She didn't know if she was supposed to give her name for reserved seating, wait for Marc, or search throughout the restaurant for his whereabouts. She fully expected him to arrive there first, and greet her at the door. Just as she was about to tell the host she was waiting for someone else, Maxie saw Marc coming toward her from the other side of the restaurant. Immediately, the strange exciting feeling filled her stomach again. A bit more casual than she expected, Marc was dressed in a cream-colored turtleneck sweater and black slacks. Nonetheless, the very sight of him was something to behold.

Marc watched Maxie through the window the moment she came into view. He couldn't believe how beautiful she looked. Even with her hair slightly blown across her face, she was stunning. With her coat opened, he could see Maxie arrayed herself in all black, and it was a color that distinctly complemented her beauty. When he came to greet her, Marc wanted to take both of Maxie's hands into his, and gently place a kiss on one of her cheeks. But not wanting to overstep his boundaries, he simply smiled at her.

"Hi. It's good to see you. I'm glad you could make it," he said.

"Hi," she smiled back. "Sorry I'm late. I couldn't find a good parking space off the ramp."

"You're only a few minutes late," Marc said, ushering her to their table. "I hope you don't mind sitting here in The Ballastone. It's the most secluded area of the restaurant, and I thought it would be great for this meeting."

Maxie quickly looked around the quaint area, before Marc stepped behind her to help remove her coat. The gesture yielded him the soft fragrance of her perfume, and the opportunity to appreciate all that was before him. *Black is definitely your color,* he thought.

"This room is usually reserved for large groups, but today it's been reserved for a party of two," Marc smiled.

Maxie sat in the chair he offered. She was honored that he reserved an entire area just for their lunch meeting. When he sat down opposite her, she noted how everything about the man was the same, except for a small little something she missed before, but was now catching her eye. In Marc's left ear hung a small gold hoop earring. The sight of it made Maxie smile. She probably wouldn't have noticed it, except a glimmer of light from the candle on the table caused it to sparkle.

"What?" Marc asked, furrowing his eyebrows slightly, with half a smile.

"I like your earring."

"Oh yeah?" He grinned. "Thank you. I've been told that it makes me look sexy."

Maxie nodded her head gently. She dare not tell him she agreed. Before she could say another word, a petite waitress stood next to their table with menus in hand.

"Hi. How are you today?" The waitress piped.

"We're fine." Marc said, before Maxie could answer.

"Great! Well my name is Amber, and I'll be your waitress. Here are your menus. Will you be having drinks from the bar?"

Marc looked at Maxie, and raised his eyebrows inquisitively.

"Uhm, I'll have a sweet tea with lemon please," she replied.

Marc smiled at Maxie's restraint. He didn't know if she drank alcoholic beverages or not, and since it was obvious that he wasn't going to find out through self-disclosure, he definitely wasn't going to ask her about it, or risk offending her by ordering one for himself.

"I'll have the same."

"Great." The waitress replied. "If you're new to Savannah, I'd love to make some meal suggestions."

Maxie looked at Marc this time, with a questioning gaze.

"Thank you, but I don't believe that will be necessary. We're both natives," he said.

"Oh, okay," the waitress practically bounced in place. "Well, I'll just go and get your drinks."

"Thank you," Marc said.

"So you're a native of Savannah?" Maxie asked, as soon as the waitress left.

"No. New York. I've just lived here long enough to be a native."

"Me too," Maxie smiled. "I came here when I was nine. From Brooklyn I might add."

"Oh yeah? I'm from New York City. I've been in Savannah for quite a few years now." Marc stopped talking when the waitress returned, and set their drinks on the table.

"Do you need more time to look over the menu?" She asked.

"Give us about five more minutes," Marc replied.

"Okay. That's not a problem. I'll be back."

When she left, Marc leaned in and whispered, "I think we'd better decide on what we're going to order."

Maxie smiled, and opened her menu. She already decided she was going to order some kind of a salad; she just needed the name of one. When she found the salad that fit what she had a taste for, she closed her menu and set it aside to wait for Marc to finish. Maxie wanted to stare at him in silence. When she raised her eyes to look at him, Marc was staring at *her.*

"You've already made your decision?" She asked.

"I made my decision a long time ago," he said in such a manner, he hoped Maxie understood his connotation. "Remember I told you I eat here often. The menu hasn't changed."

"Oh."

There was no way she was going to feed into Marc's answer to her question. Instead, she looked around for the waitress. In perfect timing, she came around the corner and took their order. When she left, Maxie propped her elbow on the table, and rested her head in her hand.

"I gather your business trip was a pleasant one," she said.

"London is always pleasant. It's a beautiful place. There's nothing like the London Bridge lit up at night."

Maxie smiled lightly. "Mmmm."

"I hated not being able to see you," Marc said. "You know, you had me a little worried while I was over there. I didn't think you were going to call me."

Maxie looked at her glass, and stirred the ice around with her straw. She recalled how she felt when she made that phone call to Marc. "Why would you be worried? I told you I would call, and I ...."

"No, at the gas station, you used the words *if I call you.*"

Maxie kept her eyes on her glass, and gently smiled.

"See, I pay attention," Marc grinned. "I have to admit, I thought you weren't as interested in knowing me, as I am in knowing you. I felt like maybe I read you wrong."

Maxie looked at Marc, and let her smile fade. "I'm very interested in knowing you Mr. Thomas," she said sincerely. "I'm intrigued by you."

When the words passed through her lips, Maxie couldn't describe the sudden feeling of passion that enveloped her right then. She couldn't believe what she just said, or that she even said it. She was revealing her innermost thoughts straight and to the point, without restraint. It all just flowed out like she was no longer in control, but fully aware of what was going on. Just like the time before, the feeling was nearly intoxicating.

"I'm glad to hear that," Marc said nonchalantly. "I think you'll find I possess everything you've wanted, but never had."

Maxie could only smile, and sip her tea. Marc's words were delivered with either an extreme amount of self-confidence, or a crafty sense of knowing what she secretly desired. "So where do we go from here?" She asked sincerely.

"I don't know. What do you feel you've been missing?"

Instantly, Maxie's gaze locked with Marc's like a deer in headlights. She was taken aback by his words. She didn't know what to say. *What do you feel you've been missing?* Resounded in her ears. *What do you feel you've been missing?* No one ever asked her that question before. Sure, she may have thought about it, but to have someone *ask* her — another man — she didn't know what to say. When she regained her focus, Marc was still staring at her. Only now, he was smiling.

"Hard question to answer isn't it?" He asked. Maxie nodded. "Yeah, I knew it would be. I'll tell you what. Why don't we just change the subject for a little while?"

"Good idea."

"So did you quit working at Food King while I was gone? When we first met, you said you were quitting."

"I did say that didn't I? No, unfortunately that hasn't happened yet. I feel a little guilty walking out on a job that's just made me Employee of the Month."

"Good. I'm glad you haven't quit. With you at Food King, I can see you anytime I want to."

"There's not a lot of visiting time when I'm working."

Marc leaned forward. "I'm not talking about visiting with you while you're at work. What I'm saying is, whenever we want to meet … to look over designs, you'll always have an alibi. Your husband will think you're at work, but you'll be spending time with me."

"And how is that going to happen? I'm supposed to say what to my manager?"

"Maybe some days, you can just call in to work sick, or conveniently have car problems."

Maxie furrowed her brow, and looked at Marc intently. "You're suggesting I lie?"

"Maxie, have you ever had one of those days where you just didn't feel up to working?" Maxie nodded yes. "Then that's what you say when you call in. I'm not *feeling* up to working today. Even though you never really said you were sick, whoever's on the other end will assume you are.

And as far as your husband is concerned, does he ever call you while you're at work?" Maxie nodded no. "Then you don't have to say anything at all to him. You just keep on rolling along as you normally do. He won't know anything different."

Maxie and Marc silenced themselves, when the waitress returned with their food. Marc watched Maxie closely, as she tried to mull over everything he said to her. With a disconcerting look on her face, Maxie eyed her plate as if it was something foreign and tasteless. When the waitress left, she looked at Marc solemnly.

"Marc, I can't lie to my husband."

Marc casually peppered his meal, and spoke without looking at her. "If no words pass between you Maxie, where is the lie?

"It's ... it's deception. That's the lie."

"And how will you have deceived him? Simply because you didn't make mention that you're *not* going to work on a particular day?" Marc reached across the table, and grabbed her hand. "Maxie, you're a beautiful woman of integrity. I'd never compromise that. Now eat your lunch," he winked.

When Marc released her hand, Maxie looked at her plate again. She felt like she had been slapped and propelled out of a whirlwind, where she struggled with moral and immoral values. It was unbelievable. From the moment she got out of her car to meet with a man she barely knew, to the candidly verbal revelation of her secret thoughts, right down to the discussion of premeditated deception, time moved rapidly. It was all surreal and very overwhelming.

"Marc, would you excuse me for a moment? I'm going to the ladies room."

Marc looked at Maxie with concern, and stood up. "Is everything okay?"

Maxie forced a smile, and stood up. "Yes. I'm fine. I'll be right back."

"Okay, well it's right around the corner."

"Thank you."

When she opened the door to the women's restroom, Maxie looked around quickly for the presence of other women. It was empty. From the door, she caught her reflection in the long mirror over the sinks, and walked to it almost entranced. Examining herself, she realized she should have stopped in there when she first arrived. Her hair was a little mused. Smiling to herself, she attempted to set the misplaced locks in order without using a comb. To Marc, she must have looked like she had just gotten off of some wild amusement park ride. A little embarrassed, Maxie smiled softly at the thought, but it soon faded when she looked at herself in the mirror more closely. In all actuality, she just *boarded* a ride.

Willingly.

Although she anticipated the tugging feelings of ambivalence and trepidation, she didn't expect everything to move along as fast as it was going. Marc was wasting no time in conveying his intentions of being with her, and she was trying to match him stroke for stroke. Continuing her stare in the mirror, Maxie looked into her own eyes. "You can get off if you want to," she whispered. After a brief moment, she washed her hands and gently shook her head. She wasn't going to get off the ride. She didn't want to. Not yet. Even though everything was moving quickly, and she felt like she was losing control, the thrill of it all was extremely fascinating.

When she left the restroom, Maxie purposely ignored looking in the mirror again.

Back in The Ballastone room, Marc kept his face of concern. "Are you okay? Did I say something that offended you, or made you upset?"

"No," Maxie replied calmly. I just needed to take a little restroom break."

Marc nodded his head, and watched Maxie pick at her salad. "So what do you think about what I said earlier?"

"About how we will meet from time to time?"

"Yes."

Maxie took a fork full of leaves, and placed them into her mouth. Slowly, she chewed with her focus fixed on her plate. Marc wondered what she was thinking. He knew there was a lot to consider, but he was confident she would see it all his way.

After wiping her mouth with her napkin, and taking a long draw of tea, Maxie looked at Marc pensively. "Well, since you pointed out the fact that I won't be directly lying to anyone, I don't see a problem with it."

Marc smiled. "That's great. There's nothing I'd rather do than to spend time with you."

"As for that other question, about what I feel I've been missing ...."

"Yes."

"I'll get back to you on that."

Marc laughed lightly, and Maxie smiled.

For the next thirty minutes or so, Maxie and Marc made idle conversation while they ate their lunch. Talk of hometown memories, and family history was exchanged with casualness. Just as he was the first time she met him, Marc Thomas was very easy to talk to, and Maxie was truly enjoying his company. Even when their conversation turned formal, and he showed her the jewelry designs he brought for her to view, she still felt pleasure.

"I really like the ring," Maxie said, as she pointed to the computer-generated picture of a man's starburst diamond ring.

"In yellow gold, or white gold?" Marc asked. "We can do it in platinum too."

"Ooo, won't platinum be expensive?"

"For you, I'll cut a deal," Marc smiled.

Maxie gently bit the outside of her bottom lip, and smiled coyly. "Why thank you Mr. Thomas. I like the way you do business. Platinum it is."

"Good choice. You'll find platinum helps to capture more of the brilliance of the diamond."

"So how long will it take for you to make it?"

"This design? Oh, I don't know. A couple of weeks."

"That's all. Is that a rush job, or can you take your time with it?"

Marc looked at Maxie, and knew instantly what she was asking of him. Before he could answer, once again, the waitress stood at their table.

"So can I get you folks one of our delicious desserts this afternoon? We have a great Key Lime pie."

"No," they both said in unison, and laughed a little.

"Okay, well great. Here's your ticket, and you can pay whenever you're ready."

"Thank you," Marc said, sliding the little black folder next to him.

After the waitress was out of earshot, he continued. "Are you requesting that I spend quality time on this piece?"

"I'm asking you to handle with care. Can you promise me that?"

"Maxie, I would never handle a precious gem carelessly. I would handle it as if it were my very own."

Maxie smiled and nodded; satisfied with Marc's response.

Marc was pleased with the way their meeting was going. He could tell Maxie was more relaxed with him, but he still wanted to tread lightly. To him, Maxie was like a magnificently rare and delicate flower. One not often found, but when it was, the beholder wanted to stay and observe its beauty.

"What's wrong?" Maxie asked, slightly frowning. "Why are you staring at me like that?"

"Oh nothing," Marc smiled.

Maxie continued to look at him skeptically.

"Tell me something," he said. "Why don't you have a cell phone?"

"How do you know that I don't?"

"Because if you did, I would've had your phone number by now."

"I don't have one because I've never needed one. I'm usually at home, so I can be reached there. And even if I did have one, you don't know that I would have given you my number."

Marc grinned, and nodded his head with affirmation. "Yes I do."

Maxie laughed. "You're cocky. You know that? You were cocky the first time I met you, and you're still cocky."

Marc laughed too. "Not cocky. Just confident. Confident and convinced."

When their laughter died down, a brief moment of awkward silence fell between them. Strictly out of habit, Maxie glanced at her watch. It was 3:50 p.m. She hated the routine gesture, because it often brought some form of finality to whatever she was enjoying. Unbeknownst to her, Marc noted the subtle movement, and the slight smirk of disappointment that twisted her mouth. Slowly, he reached across the table to caress Maxie's hand.

"Do you want to leave me already?" He asked.

Maxie looked at Marc's hand on hers, and marveled at the sensation that shot through her body from that point of contact. "No," she whispered with a slight nod.

"Then stay with me," he said, lowering his voice to equal hers.

Maxie looked into Marc's pleading eyes without saying a word. She was surprised at her own desire to be with him. "I can't," she sighed. "I have to be home by five-thirty. You forget my husband does know my work schedule."

"Give me just a few more minutes. I promise I won't make you late."

Maxie smiled at Marc. "Don't you have to get back to work or something?"

Marc removed his hand. "Hey, this is a business meeting. I can take as long as I need to seal this deal."

Maxie hesitated for a moment. "Okay, I'll stay for a few more minutes. But after that, I really have to go."

"I know you do. It's just that I'm really enjoying your company, and I don't want you to leave me just yet. I want to know more about you Maxie. I want to know the things you like to do in your spare time. Where you like to go, what kind of people you keep in your inner circle. I want to know everything. Like your husband for instance, tell me about your husband."

Maxie thought twice before she answered. For her to reveal anything else about Lester, would be like inviting Jesus into the midst of their conversation, and she wasn't ready to do that yet. "I've already told you about my husband. Remember?"

"Yeah, but why do I feel like you're hiding something from me? I mean when I asked you about him that day on your lunch break, your answer was short and sweet."

"Then that's the way I'd like to keep it."

"But from what I've heard you say about him, you're leaving me with this mental picture of a man whose presence hovers over you, reminding you of what he thinks your duties are supposed to be as his wife. You have to be home in time to greet him with dinner prepared, and on the table by the time he gets home. That whole idea seems a little archaic to me, and I just wanted to understand where the brother is coming from."

"So you don't understand the meaning of *submission?*"

Marc sat back a little more in his seat, and looked at Maxie skeptically. "Submission? The only time I've ever heard that word, was in a church I visited with my grandmother back in the day."

Maxie quickly lowered her eyes, and then looked at her watch again. "Why don't we use the rest of this time talking about you. Now you answer some of *my* questions. Why isn't there a woman in your life?"

Before he spoke, Marc took a swallow of his drink, with his eyes fastened on Maxie. "Whatever gave you the impression that I don't have a woman in my life?"

Almost immediately, Maxie felt something heavy drop into the pit of her stomach. Marc's words came across the table and landed cold and calloused. Embarrassment punched her so hard, she felt like she lost her wind. "Well, when we first met, you said you weren't married and ..."

"And that I wasn't *romantically* linked with anyone. I didn't say there wasn't a woman in my life. You can have someone of interest in your life, and not be romantically involved with them."

Maxie briefly considered his statement, and silently agreed with him. After all, she had chosen to let him become a part of her life, with no intentions of romance. So a platonic relationship was plausible. However, no consideration was given to the fact that there might be a woman, a jealous woman, who might see them together in what could be viewed as an intimate setting, and misconstrue everything.

Marc watched Maxie's countenance change ever so slightly, when she focused her attention on her glass. It was a little amusing for him to watch how the impact of his words changed the amiable atmosphere they were in, and he tried hard not to raise the corners of his mouth into a grin.

"I really have to be going," Maxie said, with another glance at her watch.

Marc pulled out his wallet, and fished out thirty dollars. Without saying anything, he laid it in the folder and stood up to help Maxie with her coat. "I'll walk you to your car."

Maxie welcomed the chivalrous gesture again, and smiled. "Okay."

Outside the restaurant, the overcast sky was immediately noticeable, and the wind had died down significantly. The cold air had a bit more bite to it than earlier, but Maxie didn't want to rush to get out of it. She simply buttoned her coat, before beginning their stroll down River Street.

"So much for the hopes of an Indian summer huh?" Marc said as he looked at the sky.

"I believe it's all gone." Maxie glanced upward. "I've always hated wintertime in Georgia."

"Really? Coming from New York, I would think you'd feel just the opposite. I mean how many times does it snow in Savannah?"

"I don't remember too much about Brooklyn, so I really can't compare it to here. I just know Georgia cold always chills me to the bone."

"So what do you do in the wintertime? You hibernate right? You're one of those babes who goes on lock down until the sun comes shining through."

Maxie laughed. "No, I'm still out and about. I have to admit, I do keep my activities to a minimum."

"Aw see!" Marc teased. "I knew you were like that. If you did more things outside in the wintertime, maybe you'd change your mind about it."

"It would still be cold Marc. Nothing would change that."

"Yeah but you'd have a new appreciation for it."

"Oh, I appreciate it just fine. While it's doing its thing outside, I'm inside sitting in front of my fireplace, keeping myself warm. Besides, what could you possibly do outside in freezing temperatures?"

"You ever been ice skating?" Marc asked, as they turned the corner to walk up the ramp.

"No," she lightly giggled.

"We should go sometime. I think you'd really enjoy it."

"And now you want me to believe that you ice skate?"

"All the time at the Civic Center."

Maxie giggled again, and unlocked her car door. "Incredible."

"Hey, don't knock it until you've tried it."

"I don't believe that's ever going to happen Marc." Maxie got into her car, and rolled down the window. "I don't skate. Not on blades, not on wheels. I even have an anti-locking brake system on my car, so my tires don't *skate* on thin ice while I'm driving."

Marc looked at Maxie for a quick second, before they both burst into laughter.

"That was pretty good," Marc said. "Corny, but pretty good." Stepping closer to Maxie's car door, he stooped down to her level. "So what do you do for entertainment? You still haven't told me."

"Well, you know one thing I definitely have no interest in doing."

Marc nodded, and was silent for a moment. "Maxie, I want to see you again. Soon. We can do whatever it is you want to do, or go wherever you want to go. You name it."

Maxie lowered her eyes, before she met his gaze. "Walking is nice. Maybe next time we can walk somewhere and just talk."

Marc smiled. "Then it's a date. You call me when you want to get together."

"You have my home number, you can call me."

Marc stood up straight, and put his hands into his pockets. "No, I think it's best if I keep the ball in your court. That way, you make all of the decisions on how you want to move."

Maxie nodded her approval, and started her car. "Thank you for lunch Marc. It was very nice."

"You're more than welcome. I enjoyed your company. Now don't go screeching down the street, rushing to get home. You drive safely."

Maxie put her car into reverse, and slowly began to pull away. "Always."

"Hey Maxie," Marc called.

Maxie quickly stopped, and looked at him inquisitively.

"It's my grandmother."

"Your what?" She frowned.

"It's my grandmother. She's the woman in my life. I'd love for you to meet her."

Maxie stared at him for a moment, and then smiled broadly. "I'd like that. I'll talk to you soon."

"I'm looking forward to it."

Marc smiled, gave a single nod of approval, and watched Maxie merge into rush hour traffic.

Chapter Thirty

M arc had not heard a word from Maxie in almost
a week. No phone call. No messages. Nothing.
He desperately wanted to call her at home to
find out why, but remembered he told her she would be the
one to make the calls, and determine the speed of their relationship. Nonetheless, it was turmoil for him to not see her,
or talk to her. Even preplanned attempts to catch up with her
at work yielded him nothing, because Maxie wasn't there.

For the few times he arrived at Food King pretending
to shop, Marc looked for Maxie in every checkout lane.
Hoping maybe she was on break each time, he waited
around for fifteen to twenty minutes, browsing the magazine shelves half focused, and flipping through the pages
impatiently. When she didn't show, he could only assume
she was either off work, or she worked an earlier shift. He
didn't really want to inquire about her, but deemed it necessary when he thought about how agonizing it was to wait
to hear from her when he was in London. He didn't want a
repeat of that whole episode again, so on his next visit, he
approached the Customer Service counter at Food King,

with the intention of looking oblivious. Behind the counter were two women, one whom he recognized as Monet. The other woman he had seen before, but did not know her name.

"Excuse me," he said to the woman whose nametag read *Regina*. "Would it be possible for me to write a personal check for cash here? I don't have my bank card with me, and I'm not making any purchases."

Regina looked at him for a brief moment before she answered. "Sure. I'll need your driver's license, and you can only write it for up to fifty dollars."

"That's fine. I only need thirty-five."

While he wrote out his check, Marc occasionally glanced at Regina who was focused on her clipboard. To him, now was as good a time as any, to ask about Maxie.

"Hey, whatever happened to that girl who's the Employee of the Month? I haven't seen her around here in about a week.

"Who Maxie?" Regina responded.

"Is that her name? The girl in the picture down there by the doors?"

"Yeah that's Maxie. She's been sick. I guess it's some kind of virus. I don't know when she's going to be back," Regina said.

Marc stopped writing, and looked up to see Monet leaning against the wall with her arms crossed, staring at him suspiciously.

"Really?" He continued, shifting his focus back to Regina. "For your sakes I hope it isn't anything contagious." Marc handed Regina his check. "Those viruses can really take you down. Does anyone know how she's doing?"

Monet slowly walked closer to the counter, with her eyes fastened on Marc.

"The last time I talked to her ..." Regina started.

"She's fine," Monet interjected with a wicked smile on her face. "As a matter-of-fact, she said she would be back to work tomorrow."

Regina looked at Monet quickly. "Tomorrow is Wednesday. That's her day off. When did you talk to her, and why would she come in on her day off?"

Monet shifted her eyes between Regina and Marc. "She called yesterday afternoon while you were making rounds Regina. She asked me if she could work my hours tomorrow to make up for lost time. I told her that was cool with me."

Regina handed Marc his money, and lowered her voice to speak directly to Monet.

"And you were going to tell me this when?" Regina huffed.

"I was just getting ready to tell you when this gentleman asked about her."

"Well that's a good thing," Marc interrupted, as he put the money into his wallet. "I'm sure you'll be glad when she comes back. She's a good worker. Please let her know that one of the customers asked about her."

"You can let her know yourself," Monet said. "She'll be here around noon."

Marc didn't like the way Monet was eyeing him. The look on her face asked *don't I know you from somewhere?* He was sure she recognized him from that previous conversation with Maxie. He also felt she was playing along, yet making fun of his attempt to present himself as a plain concerned customer.

"Would you like to leave your name?" Monet asked coyly. "I'm sure she'll want to know the name of the customer who asked about her."

"Leave him alone Monet," Regina said through clenched teeth, hoping Marc did not hear her. Smiling quickly, Regina addressed him. "I'll make sure she gets your message sir. It's a nice gesture that you inquired about her, and I'll see to it that she knows."

Marc shook his head lightly and looked at both Monet and Regina. "Thank you ladies. You both have a good afternoon."

As he left the store, Marc looked at Maxie's picture under the title Employee of the Month. Seeing her smiling face heightened a desire in him that he didn't understand, and it took him to the point of sheer frustration.

He needed to see her.

Was she really sick? Why didn't she consider how he desperately needed to hear her voice? Was there anything wrong?

Something had to give.

Marc decided he could no longer wait for Maxie to make the next move. He had her number. He was going to call.

* * * * * * * * *

Maxie clutched a steaming mug of hot chocolate, as she peered languorously out of her living room window. With her head against the window frame, she held back the curtain to a view of an overcast sky and a persistent mist of rain. With all she was feeling, there was little regard for the weather. All she could think about was Marc Thomas. Every chamber in her mind was filled with thoughts of him, and she felt helpless in trying to reflect on anything else.

That day at the restaurant, Maxie knew she crossed the line the moment she told Marc he intrigued her. The excitement that gripped her caused her to spew because she felt so good, and she couldn't think of any other way to explain to him how much he was affecting her.

And she wanted him to know it.

When she drove away from River Street, Maxie knew she wanted to spend more time with Marc. Everything about him brought her pleasure. The way he talked, the confidence he conveyed in his walk, she enjoyed it all. What she liked most was how important he made her feel the few times she was around him; as if only what she had to say and what she thought mattered. It felt good to have that feeling again. Lester used to make her feel that way, but she figured the commonness of their marriage caused that aspect to settle. With Marc everything was fresh, everything was exciting, and everything was new. What Maxie saw in him was the ultimate freedom to do whatever he wanted. She was sure he could decide to do things out of the norm, and ride with spontaneity to do it all on a whim; without fear of condemnation, watchful judging eyes, or any threat of being rebuked. That was exciting to her.

She couldn't find that in Lester.

When she looked at her husband outside of his love for her, there was his ministry. With his ministry, there were limitations that were extreme and binding in every viewpoint. These parameters made her feel weighted and severely slighted. Even though comparison was not her aim, she found herself weighing her husband's actions against another man's intentions, and highlighting the areas of her life that lacked all she thought Marc Thomas could offer her.

For days after her lunch with Marc, Maxie repeated the assessment, causing her to fight an emotional battle within herself that was so intense, it rendered her exposed, exhausted, and physically worn; and it was showing. In spite of her efforts to conceal the effects of her personal war, a few members at Wednesday night's Bible study asked her how she was feeling. One member went as far as to say, "You look like you're carrying the weight of the world on your shoulders." She couldn't contest how she looked to those who observed her, nor did she try to justify her appearance with viable reasoning. Her only response was, "Pray my strength in the Lord."

Maxie listened to the clock ticking on the wall, before she eventually released the curtain to lie on the couch. Melding with the silence, she looked at the ceiling and wondered what Marc was doing. What was he thinking, since he hadn't heard from her since that day at lunch? She hoped he would have called by now, but remembered she was the one who would be initiating every move. Maxie assumed Marc had already looked for her at Food King. On one hand, she hoped he left the store feeling disappointed with not seeing her. On the other hand, she thought maybe she should have told him she used the ruse he suggested, and called out for a few days. Maxie was surprised the ploy actually worked, and glad it did, because she wanted to think things over one final time.

As she laid mulling over everything and trying to put it all into perspective, Maxie drifted into a light slumber when the telephone rang loudly. Startled, she quickly picked up the phone without looking at the Caller ID.

"Hello?" She quested weakly.

"It's so nice of you to think about me."

Maxie paused to recognize the voice. "And you're just so sure that my thoughts were of you."

"It's only natural that you should be thinking of me. You haven't seen me in a while."

"Haven't heard from you by phone either Sandra. Now tell me, why is that?" Maxie asked with a bit of sarcasm.

Sandra spoke casually. "Oh I don't know. I started to call you earlier, but I was feeling you really didn't need to hear from me while you're in the valley of decision."

Maxie took the phone away from her ear, and looked at it with a frown. *God, how does she know these things?* Putting the phone back to her ear, she decided not to comment on Sandra's statement, or the fact that she really did give her a thought just before going to sleep.

"So I gather you're back home? When did you get in?"

"About three days ago. I hate working abroad. There's just something about living out of a suitcase that aggravates me."

"I'm sure traveling from place to place and all the sight-seeing you did, more than made up for it. I'm glad you had a safe trip. Did Intex merge with Sony?"

"Yeah they did. We are now a subsidiary of Sony Electronics. Which means I get to spend even more of somebody else's money."

The two women giggled lightly, and let a moment of silence settle between them.

"So." Sandra said finally. "Did you make the right decision?"

Maxie remained quiet. Her first instinct was to act totally oblivious to the question, but she thought better of it, figuring Sandra would probably see right through it anyway. With all things considered, there was no way in the world she was going to open the door and let Sandra in to examine all of her intentions. Instead, she quickly chose to challenge Sandra at her own game.

"You know what? Since you are so good at this little sport of fortune telling that you like to play, why don't *you* tell *me* if I've made the right decision."

"Did you listen to the message I left on your answering machine right before I went out of town?" Sandra asked.

"Yes I heard it, but I really didn't commit it all to memory. Why?"

"Did you at least understand what I was talking about?"

"I understood what you were describing, if that's what you're asking."

"So you understood about you and the beast in the cage?"

Now Maxie felt herself becoming angry. "Sandra, you and I have talked about this thing before. And I told you then that I...."

"You just asked me to tell you if you made the right decision."

"Sandra, I was joking!" Maxie almost yelled. "I was just joking!"

"Maybe. But let me say this. I'm not the one to say if you've made the right decision Maxie. Time is going to tell you that answer baby girl. Time will tell."

"Okay great!" Maxie huffed. "Let's just let time tell. Right now, time is telling me that I need to get started on dinner. So I'll have to talk to you later."

Before another word passed between the two of them, Maxie angrily slammed the phone down on its base. Jumping up quickly, she frantically walked into the kitchen, where she paced back and forth. Every thought in her mind raced at ninety miles an hour. The nerve of Sandra calling, and waking her up from her sleep to discuss absolute nonsense! Who did she think she was anyway? Why couldn't they just have a casual conversation about her trip, and leave well enough alone?

When the phone rang again three minutes later, Maxie knew it was Sandra. Bypassing the kitchen phone, she marched back into the living room to answer the call without looking at the Caller ID. She jumped at the chance to shoot first, as soon as she picked up the receiver.

"I told you I have to cook dinner. So why are you calling me now? Are there some other great words of knowledge you feel you need to tell me?" Maxie quipped.

"Ummm. Only that I miss seeing you."

The voice wasn't Sandra's. It was Marc's, and the resonance of it caressed her warmly. Maxie immediately felt everything in her cool down and gather into the pit of her stomach.

"I miss seeing you, and I just wanted to make sure you were okay," he said. "Those are the only great words of knowledge I have."

Maxie sat down on the couch, closed her eyes for a moment, and ran her hand over her hair as if to straighten out ruffled feathers. "Oh Marc," she almost whispered. "I am so sorry. I was just...."

"That's okay. You don't have to explain. It's nice to hear that you have a little bite to you. I just wish I could see you right now. I bet you're even more beautiful when you're angry."

Maxie smiled.

"Like I said, I miss seeing you. Are you feeling all right? I got a little worried when I didn't see you at the store, so I asked about you."

Maxie rested against the back of the couch, and figuratively wrapped herself in the warmth of Marc's voice. Enjoyment took the place of the tension that filled the room, and she wanted very much to relax in it. "You asked about me?"

"Don't worry. I did it tactfully. I led them to believe I was just a casual customer, asking the whereabouts of their Employee of the Month, since she was missing in action. I doubt either one of them suspected anything unusual."

"Either one of them? Whom did you speak with?"

"A heavy set woman. But that other young girl, remember the one who interrupted our conversation that time? She stared at me like she couldn't place where she had seen me before."

"Monet," Maxie said softly.

"Anyway they both told me you called in sick, but you're expected to return tomorrow. I didn't want to wait that long."

"I thought you said I would be the one to make all of the phone calls," Maxie said.

"You were taking so long, I thought I was going to have to wait for you like I did in London. You know I couldn't take that again. I had to make this call. Since I couldn't see you, I had to at least hear your voice."

"What if I hadn't answered the phone?" Maxie smiled coyly.

"Then I would have had to settle for hearing your voice on your answering machine."

"You might have been a little upset if it was my husband's voice you heard on the machine instead of mine huh? And what if *he* was the one who answered the phone?"

"I would've been disappointed if I heard your husband's voice either way. I admit, it was a bit risky making this call, but that's a chance I was prepared to take."

Maxie looked at the Caller ID and saw Marc's phone registered UNKNOWN NAME, UNKNOWN NUMBER. "I see that."

"So how are you feeling? You sound fine."

"I am now." Maxie brought her knees up close to her chest, and held herself in a ball. "I used that little suggestion of yours to get some time off."

"Obviously it worked. But there was one thing you did wrong."

"Really? I thought I did it pretty well. It got me what I wanted."

"Uhm hmm. But it didn't get me what *I* wanted. You're supposed to be spending your time with me when you make those calls. Remember? You're not here with me Maxie. Something is very wrong with this picture."

Maxie laughed. "Where are you calling me from?"

"I'm a very lonely man, sitting here at work, looking at the wall behind my desk, desperately desiring the company of a beautiful woman."

"Ah but remember, you told me your line of work keeps you in the company of beautiful women all of the time."

"This is true. But they don't have what you have. They don't entice me."

"Wow, that's a pretty strong word Mr. Thomas."

"I know it is. But it's the only word that describes what you do to me. It's like you persuade me to be a better person. Not that I'm a bad guy, mind you. But your persona, who you are, just seems to demand so much more from me."

Maxie started to pause and consider Marc's profound revelation, but quickly changed her mind. "Mmmm," she simply stated. "So who am I?"

"Your constant presence is what's needed for me to find that out," Marc replied. "So how will you make that happen?"

Maxie sighed heavily into the phone, and giggled a little. "Wow. I don't know. You know I used a good amount of time off from work already."

"Mmm hum."

"So I probably won't be able to use the 'I'm not feeling up to working', excuse for quite a while."

"Mmm hum."

"And I probably won't have any lunch hours this week, since I'll be working my regular schedule."

"Okay."

"But if you really want to be with me ...."

"I really want to be with you," Marc quickly interrupted.

"Then maybe I can make that happen on Saturday. I'm off on Saturday."

"Saturday is good for me. How shall we meet? Place? Time?"

"Some place secluded," Maxie said. "Let's meet mid-morning, somewhere around eleven, at Oglethorpe Mall. I'll park my car there, and we can ride together in your car."

Maxie heard Marc laugh a little, and it made her frown. "What's wrong?"

"What you just described to me, sounds like a much-thought-over plan for a secret rendezvous. You sound like a pro. You sure you haven't done this before?"

"No," Maxie whined.

"I bet you know exactly where you want to go too, don't you?"

"Tybee Island."

"You want to go to the beach?"

"It's only about thirty minutes or so from the mall. It's a good place to walk and talk, and ...."

"And it's secluded," he continued.

"Exactly."

"Maxie, do you know why it's secluded this time of the year?"

"Yes, and I plan to wear a coat. What about you?"

Marc laughed again. "Okay so you *do* have this all planned out, and it sounds great to me, but Saturday is three days away. What am I supposed to do in the meantime? I want to see you."

Maxie smiled. "Come to the store tomorrow. I clock in at twelve."

"No chance of seeing you before you start work?"

"Slim to none."

"Well hey, I guess a man has to settle for what he can get then huh? I'll see you tomorrow Maxie."

"I'm looking forward to it Marc. Bye."

"Goodbye."

Maxie hung up the phone and stared at it for a moment. She hadn't realized how much she missed seeing Marc, until she heard his voice. It was amazing how the sound of it soothed her. "What is it about you man?" She whispered into the air. "How are you doing this to me?"

Maxie was glad Marc agreed to meet her on Saturday. With all of the preliminaries, and self-assessments concluded and set aside, her sole intention now was to find out more about Marc Thomas. Their walk on the beach could be a long one or a short one, but they would have a three-mile stretch of sand to decide upon. Whatever the case, she knew she would have time to ask him every question that came to mind, including what kind of women he had been involved with. Nothing would be more precise, than him divulging information on the kind of women he had dated, more importantly, loved.

Chapter Thirty-One

Marc made it a point to see Maxie every chance he could. Arriving around early afternoon, he bought items he had absolutely no use for. Although he loved being greeted by her smiling face, he hated the fact that his visits were timed and rushed by someone behind him in her checkout lane. It was made worse when a customer requested her assistance in finding an item they needed, and she had to oblige. At the risk of being selfish, every brief meeting with Maxie left him longing for the arrival of Saturday morning, and the pleasure it would finally bring him. Then, he would have her to himself without any interruptions.

When Friday arrived, it brought a level of excitement to both Marc and Maxie. Now whenever their conversation was interrupted, neither of them was bothered by it. Instead, the simple statement, "We can talk about that tomorrow," took away the frustration and replaced it with great anticipation of their time together.

After fifteen minutes of light chit chat, Marc looked at his watch. "I guess I'd better get out of here now, or I'll be late for my two o'clock appointment."

Maxie casually glanced at him, while she scanned a customer's items. "Another appointment with a beautiful woman?"

"I don't know if I can really say that she's beautiful," Marc replied.

"Why is that?"

"I'm not at liberty to really do that. I do believe however, that her husband finds her beautiful since he's been married to her for thirty-eight years."

"Oh. So she's an older woman."

"An older woman with a black wart right on the tip of her nose, and a face only her husband could love."

Maxie and her customer both burst into loud laughter. It was so loud, a few of the customers and cashiers in the surrounding area, turned to look at them inquisitively. Maxie glanced around at the different faces, and closed her mouth to hold back her giggle. When she looked at Marc again, he winked at her and smiled.

"I think you'd better go to your appointment," Maxie said. "Before you end up missing it."

"Aaah, it's not that important. What I'm really looking forward to, is the appointment I have tomorrow."

"Really," Maxie said astutely, as she turned toward him to bag her customer's groceries.

"Oh yeah," he continued. "Now *that* meeting will be with a beautiful woman. I just hope she'll be able to show up, and show up on time."

Maxie tuned in fully to the smooth way Marc was speaking to her. Without losing her focus on him, she continued to bag the groceries. "I don't believe she'll have any problem with showing up, or being on time. As a matter-of-fact, I bet she's quite eager to see you … I mean, eager to see the wonderful jewelry designs made just for her."

Marc looked at the floor, coughed a little, and laughed at Maxie's subtle reminder of the ruse they were using to meet. When his eyes met hers again, she raised her eyebrows in a questioning manner.

"Thank you for reminding me," he said, feigning seriousness. "That's the whole purpose of the meeting."

Marc stepped to the side, as a courtesy clerk came to assist Maxie with the bagging.

"So what's the name of the store in the mall?" Marc asked, hoping Maxie would pick up on what he was requesting.

"Russell's Men's Store."

Marc repeated the words to himself softly, and looked at his watch again. "Well I'd better get going. It was nice talking to you again Maxie. You take care of yourself, and keep up the good work," he winked. "I'll see you soon."

Maxie smiled at Marc's comical attempt to make those around them believe he was just another customer participating in idle chatter, and nothing more. When he walked away, Maxie watched the confident stride that impressed her from day one. For her, Saturday couldn't come soon enough.

* * * * * * * * * *

"I think I want to take you out for breakfast this morning," Lester said when he rolled over in the bed, and put his arm around Maxie. "We can spend some quality time together today. What do you think about that?"

335

Lester nuzzled Maxie's neck and ear, as she lay motionless under the covers. Slowly, she opened her eyes just enough to see the numbers on the clock beside the bed. It read 6:00 a.m., and she wondered why the little red dot that signified the alarm was set, was now missing.

"Not again," she moaned into her pillow. Opening her eyes fully, revealed nothing but silhouettes of everything in their bedroom. "I know I set that stupid alarm," she huffed.

"I turned it off," Lester said casually in her ear.

"Baby, you let me oversleep," Maxie moaned without moving.

"You didn't hear what I said did you?"

Maxie felt the warmness of Lester's breath against the back of her ear as he spoke.

"I said I want to take you out for breakfast this morning. I turned the alarm off so you could get a little extra sleep. There's no need for you to get up early, because I'm off today. We're going to spend some quality time together. So after breakfast, what do you want to do? I think we should catch up on some Christmas shopping. I don't want to get my sisters gift cards like I did last year. I want to put a little more effort into. ..."

Maxie lay still, as she listened to her husband ramble on and on about how he thought the day should be spent. Though she had not moved, she was sure if she was on her back, and there was more light in the room, every beat of her heart could be seen moving the bedspread up and down. What did he mean he was off today? His new job title now required him to work Saturdays. Was it every Saturday, or just some Saturdays? She couldn't remember. Whatever the case, she didn't want him at home *this* Saturday.

Maxie turned over to lie flat on her back. "Lester why didn't you tell me last night that you were off today?"

"That would have spoiled my little surprise now wouldn't it?"

"Well," Maxie started. She had no idea of what to say. How could she tell him she had other plans for the day? How on earth could *any* married woman, tell her husband she would be spending her day walking down Savannah Beach with another man? "Baby, if you had told me, I could have arranged ...."

"Maxie don't tell me you have to work that job today," Lester said in a deep warning tone.

Maxie was prepared to say she could try to arrange her schedule to fit in Lester's outing, but she visualized his last statement as a line handed to her to save herself. Without much more consideration, like a woman who was drowning, she took the lead and swam with it. Quickly she propped herself up on one elbow, and placed her other hand on Lester's chest, as he lay back facing the ceiling.

"Baby I'm sorry. If I had some idea of what you were planning, I would have never told Monet I would cover her shift today." Maxie's heart raced, and the pace of it changed her breathing to the point where she almost sounded winded. "If I didn't think it would count against me, I'd call in to see if someone could replace me. But it's such short notice, and since I'm not sick or anything ... I mean I can tell them that if you want."

Maxie tried to regulate her breathing pattern, which was now running neck and neck with her heart rate. In a matter of a few seconds, she managed to accomplish something she had never done in almost eight years of marriage.

She lied to her husband.

For the first time, her spiritual conscience immediately wrestled with the feeling of knowing a direct untruth crossed her lips. The relaxed attitude that accompanied the lie, hurt Maxie to the core. It just slipped out of her mouth casually and totally unrehearsed; and right now, it dealt a painful repercussion. Maxie couldn't fathom the thought of Lester knowing what she just did. He would be devastated. For him, it might as well be considered a heinous act, because she just lied to the priest of her home. *God forgive me*, she prayed inwardly.

Lester sighed heavily. Even though she couldn't see his face, Maxie knew he was pouting.

"No. I'd never have you to tell a lie Maxie. And I'm surprised you would even think I'd consider it as an option."

Maxie was silent. Frankly, she was surprised too. With all that was happening with her, was her integrity changing also? "I'm sorry Lester," she said before falling back on her pillow. "I don't know what I was thinking. I just didn't want you to be so disappointed."

"It's fine," he said plainly. "At least you don't have to work all day. We can do something when you get home. What time will that be?"

Maxie drew in a large amount of air, and exhaled slowly with a hum that made it sound as if she were trying to recall something. In all actuality, she knew if she gave Lester a definite time as to when she'd be home, she would be putting an exact ending time on her meeting with Marc, and she didn't want to do that.

"I can't remember if Monet asked me to cover her four hour shift or her eight hour shift. I know both of them start at ten, but I'll have to check on the ending time, and call you when I find out."

"That won't be necessary," Lester sighed. "Either way, I'll be here when you get home. We'll just do something soon afterward. We can still go out for breakfast. But I want you to know this job ...."

"Lester don't," Maxie contended. "I already know how you feel about my job. Now I only have about a month and a half left before I quit. Do you think maybe you can hide your obvious sense of disapproval for the time being? Please?" Maxie waited for her husband to respond, but heard nothing. After a brief moment, he took a deep breath and noisily released it into the air with a slight hissing sound.

"I'm going to take a shower," he mumbled.

Maxie watched the silhouette of Lester's frame, as he walked into the bathroom and shut the door. After a few minutes alone in the dark, she considered her lie and justified it by telling herself she had Lester's best interest at heart. She had to lie for the sake of keeping his anniversary gift a secret. After all, that's what it was all about.

Chapter Thirty-Two

From the moment he drove into the parking lot of Oglethorpe Mall, Marc was eager for his meeting with Maxie to begin. Saturday morning delivered an overcast sky, and a gentle breeze that kept the temperature in the low fifties. But it was a day of sunshine, with a high in the eighties for him. He was finally going to have a full conversation with Maxie, with no interruptions or time restrictions. It was the moment he patiently waited for.

Slowly, Marc drove around the parking lot searching for Maxie's car. At 10:30 a.m., he knew he was a bit early for canvassing, but since Maxie told him she would meet him *around* 11:00 a.m., he thought it best to get an early start. He hoped she would be early too.

After the fourth time around yielded him nothing, Marc parked his car at the farthest end of the parking lot, in a position where he was sure to see Maxie whenever she arrived. What Marc didn't know was that Maxie was already there. Her early arrival was due in part to anxiety, but mainly because she had to make it look like she was on her way to work.

With the doors opening to mall walkers at 9:00 a.m., and shoppers at 10:00 a.m., Maxie found herself window shopping outside of dimly lit stores with lowered gates. Other than the usual elderly mall walkers, who zipped by her at remarkable speeds, Maxie saw only a handful of customers who were sharing her view of various store advertising. With Christmas lights blinking on fake trees, and mannequins dressed up as elves or Santa Claus, Maxie smiled at the thought of shopping 'til she dropped. From one window to the next, she casually strolled with no regard for the name of the stores she observed. It wasn't until she noticed a bevy of wonderful and familiar gift ideas, did she look up to read the name of the store she stood in front of. It was *Things Remembered.*

Maxie recalled the times she shopped the quaint little store for many of Lester's anniversary gifts. *Things Remembered* always had the right item, the right price, and no matter what it was, she could have it personalized with her own loving sentiment. Lester told her the gifts were either just what he wanted, or in their practicality, just what he needed. With that in mind, she wondered what he would think of the gift she was getting him for this anniversary. True enough, the gift would be very extravagant and out of the ordinary for her, but what she hadn't really thought about was what memories would be tied to it for her. When she presented her husband with the keepsake reminder of the love they shared, would she remember how she went about obtaining it? Maxie stood in front of the store totally transfixed on that thought. For years to come Lester would wear that ring, and think of it as nothing more than a celebration of their matrimonial covenant. But for her, in all of that time, what would be the *things remembered*?

* * * * * * * * * *

Marc looked at his watch again. It was 11:15 a.m., and still no sign of Maxie. Even though he knew another forty minutes was still within the parameter of the time she stated, he was growing impatient. Tapping his fingers lightly on the steering wheel, and patting his foot on the car floor, did little to ease the restlessness that crept on him. So Marc got out of his car to stretch. The only movement in the parking lot was a woman pushing a small child in a stroller, and a young couple walking hand in hand into the mall's main entrance. When he opened his door to get back in, he looked toward Russell's Men's Store. A few feet away from the store's entrance, Maxie stood waiting. Quickly Marc jumped back into his car, coasted up to her, and rolled down his window.

"Excuse me ma'am. You look like you need a ride, and I'd like to say I would be simply delighted to take you anywhere you need to go."

Maxie bent down a little to look into the car, and gave Marc a soft smile. When he stepped out and walked around to her, she was almost riveted. Marc Thomas looked even more handsome than before. All the other times he was up close and personal, could not compare with how he looked to her now. There was something different about him. He was neatly dressed in a gray Polo sweater that hugged every bulge in his upper body, and it was complemented by how well he wore his dark blue Levi jeans. Feeling a little awkward about staring, Maxie quickly lowered her sight, only to capture Marc's unblemished white Nike tennis shoes.

Marc smiled, and observed Maxie for a moment before he opened her door and said, "Hello beautiful." He didn't think it was possible for her to be any more gorgeous than she was, but the radiance he saw this morning proved him to be wrong. In her blue denim stretch pants, black cashmere sweater, and black Sperry Top-Sider shoes, Maxie was ravishing.

"Good morning Mr. Thomas," she smiled back.

Maxie seated herself in the car and Marc shut the door quickly. When he finally got behind the wheel, he immediately took notice of the alluring scent of perfume that filled the cabin of his car.

"You smell nice," he stated, glancing at her as he started to drive.

"Thank you," Maxie said softly.

Falling victim to a slight sense of paranoia, Maxie looked out of the passenger side window for anyone familiar who may have seen her get into Marc's car. She had no idea what she would have done if she spotted someone she knew, but she scanned the area nonetheless. Maxie was grateful to see Marc's car windows were tinted enough to offer her a little security on the inside, but it did little for anyone who may have actually seen her get *into* the car.

"Didn't you drive here?" Marc asked. "I didn't see your car parked in the lot. Nor did I see you drive up. I've been waiting for you since about ten-thirty."

Maxie looked at him and smiled. "You've been here that long? I'm sorry. I parked on the other side of the mall. I was inside window shopping. I got here around a quarter til."

"A quarter til eleven?"

"No, ten," Maxie said casually.

Marc quickly glanced at her. "You've been here since nine forty-five? The mall doesn't open until ten."

"Nine o'clock for mall walkers."

Marc smiled. "Well, unless you're a mall walker, I guess we just wasted about an hour of time together."

Maxie looked at her watch. "It's eleven twenty, and we have until almost five. I think we'll be okay."

Marc glanced at her again. He wished he had the time right now to just stare at her, and take in all of her beauty. But he told himself he would have to be patient. That time was right around the corner.

"I'm hungry," Marc said. "What about you?"

"I could eat a little something," Maxie replied, as she looked out of the window.

"Great. Before we go to the beach, I want to take you to eat somewhere that's uniquely special. It's right on the way."

Maxie looked at Marc skeptically. "What do you mean when you say *uniquely* special? I don't do exotic foods well."

Marc grinned. "I promise it won't be anything you haven't had before. Trust me on this."

Maxie looked out of her window again, and spoke with an air of caution. "Okay Mr. Thomas. It better be good."

Marc laughed, and headed for Highway 80. As he drove, he reached in between the seats and handed Maxie a file folder. "Business before pleasure," he winked. "I picked out these ring designs for you to view. This way we can both agree this meeting is a legitimate one, and you won't have to feel like a married woman sneaking around on a tryst."

Maxie rifled through the pictures. "The master of justification. And what gives you the impression that I feel like I'm sneaking around?"

"I saw how you scanned the parking lot at the mall when you first got in the car. Looking for anyone in particular?" He asked, looking at her squarely.

Maxie laughed lightly, and returned his gaze. "No."

"Good, because I don't think I could stand being with you, and you're feeling uncomfortable the whole time we're together."

Maxie assessed Marc fully before she smiled, and spoke. "I believe I'll be okay."

"That's what I want to hear," he smiled, and gently stroked her cheek.

Maxie wasn't surprised at how Marc touched her. What caught her a little off guard, was how she leaned in to capture the warmth of his hand against her face.

And she didn't regret it.

She was firm on her decision, with preliminaries and self-assessments being set aside. How else was she going to learn about this man, if she didn't at least take down some of the fences?

Chapter Thirty-Three

While they traveled, Maxie and Marc tried to keep the conversation going between them, even if most of it was random small talk. When there were episodes of silence, with the exception of the radio's soft jazz music, Maxie looked out of her window at the landscape. It had been a while since she had seen marshland. It all looked like broken sticks standing up in thick slimy mud. Besides the autumn changing palm trees that occasionally lined the road, she wished the view was more scenic.

When Marc finally parked the car, it was along the curb in a very nice residential area on Talahi Island. Maxie marveled at the immaculate scenery. As far as she could see, every lawn was cut to the same length, and it reminded her of the well-kept grass on a golf course. In spite of the season, it was all still green.

When Marc got out of the car, Maxie looked at the house they were parked in front of. It was a ranch style home that was a little more than moderate in size, and very nice.

Marc opened her door with a big smile.

"This is a restaurant?" She asked, with a look of confusion.

"The best kitchen this side of Savannah."

Maxie exited the car, only to stand at the end of the sidewalk that led up to the house. Looking around suspiciously, she observed what looked like a garden near the side of the house, neatly surrounded by a white picket fence. Marc closed the car door and stood next to Maxie. Gently, he put his hand on the small of her back, to guide her.

"Shall we?" He asked.

Maxie looked at him with the same confused look as before, but yielded to his lead.

"Marc, whose house is this?" She whispered.

Marc only smiled and kept walking. When they reached the front door, he opened the screen door and pulled out a set of keys. When he opened the door, Marc looked at Maxie and winked, motioning with his head for her to go in. Maxie stood her ground as a sudden wave of fear washed over her.

"It's okay," he said assuredly. "I know the person who lives here."

"I hope you do, or somebody's going to be upset about you having a key to their house," she whispered again.

Marc laughed, and opened the door wider for Maxie to go in. With caution she stepped inside, and peered around. Instantly, the smell of fried chicken, potpourri, and cinnamon, enticed her nose. The clash of aromas floated in the air on top of what Maxie knew to be a faint smell associated with the homes of elderly people. From where she stood, she observed the somewhat spacious room and how it was neatly kept. The living room and dining room were combined, but the space was large enough to give the illusion of being separate areas. To the left of her, on the center wall, Maxie eyed a quaint little fireplace with a mantle that was filled with pictures of obvious loved ones. There were various sized glass figurines, and at each end of the mantle, two small bouquets of fake roses in the most beautiful antique vases she had ever seen. Almost mesmerized by what she saw on the mantle, Maxie moved across the floor to get a closer view of the pictures. There were men and women together in many of the pictures, but the majority of them were either of a grown woman with a little boy, or the little boy by himself. There were no other children in any of the pictures. Maxie continued to look at what seemed to be a chronological display of the child from about age two to almost manhood. When she got to the last picture, she recognized the person and quickly turned to Marc, who was still standing near the door smiling at her.

"Oh my ... this is your grandmother's house!" She said incredulously.

Marc simply beamed. "Mama!" He called out, with his eyes still on Maxie. "Mama. I'm here."

"Marcky? Is that you baby?"

Maxie heard a woman's voice screech from somewhere in the house.

"I'll be right in there in just a moment," the woman said.

Maxie looked in the direction of the voice, but saw nothing. Feeling a little apprehensive, she moved back to stand by the door.

"Come on and have a seat," Marc said. "She spends a lot of time in her garden and her greenhouse, so she's probably freshening up." Marc motioned with his hand to a couch next to them, and Maxie quickly sat down. "You might be a little more comfortable if you shed that extra layer of skin you have there," he said, holding out his hand.

"What?" Maxie asked with a look of confusion.

"Your coat. You do plan to stick around for a little while right?"

Maxie laughed nervously. "Oh yeah."

When she stood up, she automatically turned her back to Marc, who helped to remove her coat. Observing her fully, he didn't care what angle Maxie was standing in, she was always going to be beautiful to him. Before she turned back around, Marc smiled slightly and nodded his approval.

"Go ahead and make yourself comfortable. I'm going to hang this up and check on my grandmother. Would you like something to drink?" He asked as he walked toward a small coat closet.

"No, I'm fine," Maxie replied. Unconsciously, she wrapped her arms around herself.

Marc hung up her coat, and turned to observe Maxie's impulsive movement. "Maxie, relax. She's just a little old lady who's cooking us lunch."

"Who are you calling an old lady?" Asked a small woman who entered the dining room area. "I may not be quite spry, but I ain't old yet," she said as Marc walked to her and planted a kiss on her cheek.

Marc was tall next to his grandmother. Together they both faced Maxie, and the sight of them instantly made her think of their many poses captured in the photos on the mantle. Maxie looked at the diminutive woman and smiled. She was beautiful. Whatever age she claimed as a grandmother, she obviously defied nature on accepting the wrinkles that came with it. Had her hair, which was totally silver and wrapped in a French Twist, not given a hint to her years of life's experiences, the older woman could have fooled anyone into believing she was much younger. Her fair complexion was flawless. As she stood next to Marc, Maxie could see where he inherited his good looks.

"Now who is this we have here?" The woman asked, looking at Maxie.

"Mama, this is my friend Maxie."

Maxie stood up quickly, and stepped across the floor to greet the woman. With an extended hand, she smiled nervously. "Hi, how are you? It's nice to meet you."

The woman took Maxie's hand and held it for a moment, as she assessed her from head to toe. Before she released her, she looked at Maxie's wedding ring and then at Marc. Marc hoped Maxie wasn't paying attention to the questioning stare his grandmother was giving him, but now Maxie was looking at him in the same way.

"Well it's nice to meet you too," the woman finally said, repelling the tension that tried to enter the room. "My name is Stella. Stella Anderson. Marcky has told me so much about you."

Maxie looked at Marc. "Oh, you did … Marcky?"

Marc put his arm around his grandmother and gave her a little squeeze. "My grandmother knows you're one of my clients. Don't let her tease you. She's notorious for that," he laughed.

"Oh you never let an old woman have her fun," she chided, playfully elbowing Marc in his side. "I'm going on back into this kitchen to finish up lunch. Maxie, I hope you're hungry," Stella called over her shoulder, as she headed for the kitchen. "Did my grandson offer you anything to drink?"

"Yes ma'am he did," Maxie said as she looked at Marc. "I'm fine. Thank you. Lunch smells delicious."

"I'll be done in just a few minutes. Ya'll sit on down and relax."

"Mama, do you need any help?" Marc asked.

"Now you know I don't. Sit on down."

Marc smiled and made an attempt to move toward a chair, but Maxie stayed still with her eyes set on him. When he noticed she wasn't moving with him, he stopped and looked at her. "What's wrong?"

"You had this planned all along didn't you?

Marc grinned.

"So why didn't you tell her I was married?"

"Why? What difference would it make? I told you, she knows you're a client of mine."

"I just don't want her to suspect anything. She looked at you a little funny after she saw this ring on my finger. So I think the two of us together, has to appear pretty unusual to her. After all, how many *clients* do you bring to your grandmother's house for lunch on a Saturday afternoon Marc?" Maxie walked back to the couch and sat.

Marc followed behind her with a sinister grin on his face. "Wouldn't you like to know?" He teased before he sat on the couch.

Maxie took note of the space he put between them. "Your grandmother's a very beautiful woman," she said, admiring the pictures again. "Whose mother is she, your dad's or your mom's?"

"My dad's. Remember, I told you I don't know too much about my mother."

"That's right," Maxie nodded slightly. "I forgot you told me that. I can't believe your mother just abandoned you. That seems so wrong."

Marc sat casually with his elbow propped on the arm of the couch, resting his head on his fingertips as he spoke. "I don't know if I'd use the word abandoned. She just sort of dropped me off in my grandmother's arms when I was two, and never came back. My dad was away at college in Tennessee at the time, and we all lived in New York City. Mama agreed to keep me until he graduated. After he did, he married his college sweetheart, and they decided to make the Volunteer state their home."

"Didn't he at least want you with him?" Maxie asked solemnly.

"Oh yeah," Marc chirped with a broad grin. "But by that time, Mama was so in love with me, she couldn't bear the thought of sending me down the road to be with my dad. Instead, we moved here to Georgia to be a little closer to him, and they agreed it would be better that I just stay here, but visit with him from time to time. Mama was getting older, and I was like a companion to her, someone to keep her company. Like an old dog." Marc looked at Maxie and burst into laughter. The fact that he could make light of his mottled past, made her laugh with him.

"I hardly believe you're like an old dog to her," Maxie said. "She looks at you with pride. I'm sure she appreciates having you around, especially now. You seemed to have grown up into a nice respectable man from what I can tell." Maxie looked at Marc sincerely, as a soft smile crept across her lips. "You came out all right Marcky."

Marc stared at Maxie a moment, and acknowledged her compliment with a slight nod of his head. "Don't get used to calling me that. That's reserved for my Mama."

"That's right," the old woman said, as she placed a platter full of fried chicken on the table.

Maxie had no idea as to when she entered the room, or how much of their conversation Stella Anderson heard.

"That's my pet name for my grandson. Been calling him that since he was two. But if our conversations are about serious matters, then that's when I call him Marc. Now ya'll come on so we can eat. I'm going to get the collard greens and cornbread. Marcky honey, you get the iced tea out of the refrigerator for me. Maxie, you go on and freshen up in the bathroom down the hall there, and then come on and have a seat. We'll be set in just a few minutes."

Without a word, Maxie and Marc both did as they were told. When Maxie returned from the bathroom, she watched the small procession of food being brought to the table by the spry old woman. "Are you sure you don't need any help Ms. Anderson?"

"Naw baby. This is all there is."

Maxie looked at the small feast that was spread on the table. There was fried chicken, fried and baked fish, collard greens, cornbread, baked macaroni and cheese, boiled potato slices with onions, and black-eyed peas.

"All of the vegetables came from my garden," Stella beamed.

While Maxie eyed all of the food, Marc returned to the dining room carrying a serving tray with glasses of iced tea, and a crystal pitcher full of the brown beverage. Before he set the tray on the table, he walked behind Maxie's chair, and bent over to whisper into her ear.

"Looks like Thanksgiving doesn't it?"

Maxie could only nod.

"Oh Marcky," Stella said, as she sat down at the end of the table. "You know how I do it whenever we have company."

"I know Mama, but this is just supposed to be lunch for three people," Marc said as he placed everyone's drink before them.

Stella waved her hand, as if she were swatting a fly. "Oh go on."

Marc sat down across from Maxie and laughed a little. Within minutes, the food was blessed by Stella, and each platter made its way around the table. After the gentle piling of the plates was finished, all three of them indulged themselves in food and casual conversation.

"Does everything taste all right?" Stella asked. "I don't use much salt when I'm cooking so ...."

"It's all delicious," Maxie said. "It reminds me of my own grandmother's cooking."

"Well thank you. Does your grandmother live in Georgia?"

Maxie wiped her mouth with her napkin. "No ma'am. Uh, I mean yes ma'am. She did live here. She died a while back."

"Oh, I'm sorry to hear that," Stella said. "I'm sure she was quite special to you."

"Yes ma'am, she was."

"So do you have any other family here?"

"Yes ma'am. Most of my mother's side of the family lives here. She was an only child, so the family I do have are either great uncles or aunts, and distant cousins."

"Oh, I see. And what about your husband? Is his family from Georgia?"

Maxie shot a questioning glance at Marc, only to see him eating his food as if no one else existed in the room except him. "Yes ma'am, they are." Maxie quickly turned her attention back to her plate, and put a forkful of greens into her mouth in an attempt to deter Stella's line of questioning. She couldn't help but to wonder what the old woman was hoping to gain from her inquiries. She also wondered why Marc was being so quiet.

"Now you work in a grocery store, is that right?" Stella continued.

Maxie put her fork down gently, and placed both of her hands in her lap under the table. It was obvious she was going to be ambushed with a barrage of questions. Why? She didn't know. But she could only assume Ms. Stella Anderson was putting forth an effort to make sure she knew everything about her grandson's friends, and their possible intentions.

"I do, part-time." Maxie now felt it necessary to force a slight smile to her face, in order to hide her heightening annoyance.

"Uhm hmm." Stella said airily. "Now what kind of work does your husband do?"

Maxie glanced at Marc again, only to capture him doing the exact same thing he was doing the last time she looked at him. In that instant, she wanted to kick him under the table, so he could see the questioning expression that was plastered on her face. Most of all, she wanted him to chime in and come rescue her from the fifth degree.

"My husband is a contractor for a construction company," Maxie said simply.

355

"And you've been married for ...."

"Eight years in January," Maxie interrupted abruptly.

"And that's where I come in the picture," Marc said finally. As he casually wiped his hands and mouth, Marc looked at Maxie, smiled a half smile, and winked his eye at her. She in turn, narrowed her eyes at him and returned to eating her lunch. "Remember Mama, I told you Maxie asked me to design a special ring for her husband, to celebrate their eighth wedding anniversary."

Stella frowned as she tried to recollect. "Now I do remember you telling me something to that effect." After a moment, Stella looked at Maxie. "Sweetheart I'm sorry if I made you feel uncomfortable with all of my questions. Marcky did tell me about you, and I just forgot some things. Please forgive me baby. Charge it to my head and not my heart. I blame age for that." Stella laughed lightly and sipped her tea.

"That's fine," Maxie said.

"Maybe you can make it up to Maxie with that delicious apple pie you have sitting on the stove in there," Marc said with a smile.

Stella looked at Maxie's plate. "Oh, are you ready for dessert honey? It doesn't look like ...."

"I'll get it for you Mama, if you want." Marc said quickly.

"No, no. I'll get it," Stella said as she stood up, and looked at Marc. "Do you want your piece now too?"

"Sure, but I can get it for us," he answered.

"No now you just go on and eat. It's only going to take me a few minutes. I might as well get pie for all of us."

Marc watched his grandmother walk into the kitchen, before his eyes met Maxie's.

"Can you tell me what that was all about?" She whispered.

"It was nothing. She was just trying to get to know you. She does that to everyone she meets for the first time."

Maxie looked at him for a brief moment longer, before she continued to eat her lunch.

"Now you owe me one," Marc said casually, as he too returned to eating.

"What?"

"I saved you. So now you owe me."

"What are you talking about?"

"My grandmother would have been so far up your family tree, you would have been sitting over there in that chair squirming. But I saved you."

Maxie smiled and nodded her head. "She was getting pretty close. So what do I owe you?"

Marc looked at Maxie squarely. "Answer a question for me."

Maxie wiped her mouth with her napkin, and sipped her tea. "Okay. What's your question?"

"Why do you always get so tense whenever you have to discuss your husband?"

Maxie instantly felt hesitant about answering Marc's question. She didn't know what to say. She had no idea she was displaying tension whenever she had to talk about Lester. Just as she opened her mouth to say so, Marc's grandmother entered the room again. Maxie smiled, as the woman handed her a small plate with a large piece of apple pie on it. Marc moved his focus from Maxie long enough to take his pie from his grandmother, but he immediately returned it to her, fully expecting her to answer him.

"This pie looks delicious," Maxie piped, giving her attention to Stella and ignoring Marc's stare.

"Well I didn't grow the apples myself, but I did make it from scratch this morning. When Marcky called me earlier in the week, and told me he would be bringing somebody over for lunch, I figured I'd have to make him his favorite pie."

"Really? Maxie said skeptically. "He told you *earlier* in the week that he was bringing me over here."

Stella took a bite out of her chicken, and slowly chewed as she nodded her head. "Uhm hmm. He said there was something special about you, and that he wanted me to meet you."

Maxie nodded her head, and looked at Marc who sat relaxed in his chair, staring at her the whole time. Though their eyes were set on each other, Maxie directed her response to Stella.

"Really?"

"Oh yeah," Stella continued. "Marcky knows not to bring just anybody in his mama's house. When he told me he was bringing you, I trusted him because I know he's a good judge of character."

"So I guess I'm okay huh?" Maxie smiled and looked at Stella.

"Girl you're fine," Stella waved, and cackled. "I knew it the moment I laid eyes on you." Silence filled the room for a quick moment, before Stella spoke again. "Would you like some more to eat? Some more tea or anything?"

"Oh no. Thank you so much." Maxie pleaded. "This was all very nice. I'm just going to finish it all off with this pie."

"Well you just help yourself," Stella said as she wiped her mouth with her napkin, and stood. "I'm just going to clean up in the kitchen a bit. If you want to take some of this food home with you ...."

"No, I'm fine. Really," Maxie conceded.

"Well I'll tell you what. Why don't you and Marc finish your dessert and tea in the living room, while I straighten up in here? Marcky, Mama's going to wrap up some of this food for you to take on home with you. I know your eating habits, and you probably haven't had a home cooked meal all week."

"I can do that Mama. I'm coming in there to help you clean up anyway," Marc said, as he stood also.

"Do you mind if I help too?" Maxie chimed.

"Now I won't have that," Stella protested. "You go on in there and rest yourself. Marcky, let Maxie look at the photo album while she waits for us to get finished."

Maxie followed Marc into the living room with her pie in hand. Without an exchange of words, he led her back to the couch, and picked up a large blue photo album from a table in the room.

"Before I give you this album," Marc started. "I want you to know that I will not be answering any questions about what you view in here, and I want you to keep all giggles to a minimum, and the volume of them mute. Deal?"

"Maxie looked at Marc and grinned. "Sure Marcky. I don't have a problem with that."

Marc returned her grin with a slight raise of his eyebrows, in a manner of caution. Instead of giving her the album, he set it on the coffee table in front of her. "Finish your pie first," he said, and turned to join his grandmother.

Maxie watched as Marc walked away from her, and disappeared into the kitchen. It wasn't long before she heard muffled voices and brief stints of laughter. It was obvious to her, that the relationship Marc had with his grandmother, was much like the one she had with her own grandmother. They were close, and they were friends.

Maxie eagerly wanted to view what she could of Marc's past, so she hurriedly cut into her pie with her fork and put the piece into her mouth. Immediately, she savored the buttery flavor that coated her tongue. "Mmmm," she said softly. It was delicious. While she chewed, Maxie looked around the room again, trying to imagine what it must have been like for Marc growing up with his *Mama*.

Stella Anderson was both a mother and a father to him, and that could not have been a very easy pill for Marc to swallow, especially during his teen age years. But in line with what she told him earlier, and all that she knew of him, he turned out all right.

Just as she finished her last bite, Marc peeked his head out of the kitchen. "Are you finished?" He asked.

"Yes I am. Thank you." Maxie held up her plate and cup for him to take.

"Pretty good wasn't it?" He asked as he walked toward her.

"It was delicious. Tell her I'd like to have that recipe so I can make one of my own sometime."

Marc chuckled, and took Maxie's dish. "Naw, that's not going to happen. That old lady wins contests with that pie. She won't even tell *me* how she makes it, and I'm her own flesh and blood. But I'll tell her how much you liked it. Go ahead and look at the photo album to kill time. When I finish helping her in here, we'll go to the beach."

Having lost all regard for the time, Maxie looked at her watch to see it was 1:15 p.m. "Oh, okay."

Marc picked up the album, and handed it to her. "Remember, no questions about this."

"No questions," Maxie smiled, and took the photo album from him.

"I'll be back in a few."

Once again, Maxie watched him walk back into the kitchen. This time she settled back on the couch and opened the small door to the past of Marc Thomas.

Chapter Thirty-Four

M arc put the dishes into the sink for his grandmother to wash. Leaning his back against the
counter next to her, he flung a dishtowel onto
his shoulder.

"Maxie said to tell you your apple pie was delicious,
and she wants your recipe for it. I let her know you'll be
carrying that secret to your grave." Marc laughed, but his
grandmother merely smiled. "So what do you think of her
mama?" He asked sincerely. "She's special isn't she?"

"Oh, she's a sweet girl Marcky," Stella answered nonchalantly, as she washed a pot.

Marc understood his grandmother well enough to know
there was more to be said, than the simple little answer she
just gave him. He was a little surprised at her attempt to go
around the issue, rather than giving it to him straight forward like she normally would.

"I know she's a sweet girl mama. But could you see that
special *something* I told you about?"

"Yes. I did," Stella replied again without looking at him.

"So what is it?" Marc quested eagerly. "I know that girl possesses something. And I knew you would be the one to see it and identify it for me. That's why I brought her over here. So tell me Mama, what is it?"

Marc's grandmother took a deep breath, stopped what she was doing, and wiped her hands on her apron. With all sincerity, she looked at her grandson squarely.

"Marc, I want to know what your intentions are with this woman. This *married* woman."

Marc looked into his grandmother's eyes, and instantly felt like he was a child again, being chastised for doing something wrong. In an equal amount of time, he recovered. "What?" He asked incredulously, lowering his voice. "Mama, I have no intentions at all. I just want to know why I'm drawn to get to know her. She's not like any other woman I've met ...."

"No, I'm sure she's not Marcky, and there's a reason why. What you see or feel where Maxie is concerned, is something you *need* in your own life, but right now you don't desire to seek it out. Baby, you have a void inside of you that longs to be filled. And it's that very thing that attracts you to Maxie. She, herself, has nothing to do with it. You're not attracted to the *person* Marcky. You're attracted to what she has."

"Wait a minute Mama, now you're confusing me."

"Do you remember when you were growing up, how I kept you in church?"

"How can I forget it? You didn't leave me much choice in the matter."

"And do you remember when I used to tell you that God has a plan for your life?"

"Mama, you said God has a plan for everybody's life, whether they were good or bad. What does this have to do with Maxie?"

"Marcky, that girl has a call on her life. God has a wonderful work for her to do, and He has anointed her to walk in that calling right now. What you feel when you're around her is the presence of God, and your soul desires Him. She's a sanctified vessel. That means she's ...."

"Set aside for the Master's use," Marc said thoughtfully. "I do remember you telling me that much when I was growing up."

"Does she ever talk to you about her husband?"

"No, I was hoping to get her to do that when we leave here. We're going to take a walk along the beach."

"Listen to me. Her husband is a minister Marc. Just as sure as your grandmother is standing here before you right now, I guarantee you, her husband is a minister."

Marc lowered his eyes, and looked at the floor. If what his grandmother just said was true, it could explain why Maxie always avoided talking about her husband.

"You can't be a hindrance to her Marc. Remember, waters from stolen canteens are always sweeter. Don't let the devil use you to complicate things for her."

"Mama, I'd never ...."

"I know *you* wouldn't sweetheart, not on purpose you wouldn't. But if you're not careful, your feelings will get involved, and it will all go bad quickly."

Marc nodded his head slowly. "What was it again that you said about me, about why I'm so drawn to her?"

Stella Anderson smiled and gently grabbed Marc's face, to kiss his cheek. Afterward, she held his face in her hands. "God's working on you baby. He's working on you. Now what Maxie has to do with all of this, I'm not quite sure. But I'll be praying for an understanding. All right?"

Marc smiled, and gave his grandmother a hug. "You know I love you Mama."

"I know baby," Stella said. "I know. Now ya'll go on and get out of here."

Marc stepped back and looked at his grandmother. "God tells you an awful lot doesn't He?"

"Only what I need to know. Now go on, I'll get the rest of this stuff. I have nothing but time."

Marc took the dishtowel off his shoulder, and handed it to his smiling grandmother. When he retrieved Maxie's coat, he walked back into the living room area with Stella in tow. "Are you ready to go?" He asked, standing before Maxie.

"Are you sure I can't ask you *any* questions about what I've seen in here?" Maxie smiled, as she patted the photo album before setting it on the table.

"Oh honey, you can save those questions for the next time you come to visit," Stella cackled. "It'll give us something to talk about. I love talking about my baby growing up."

Maxie stepped into her coat, as Marc held it open for her. "And I'm sure I'd love to hear it," Maxie said when she faced Marc. This time, it was her turn to wink.

Marc looked at Maxie with a little smirk on his face, and walked to the door where he held it open for her. Without moving, she looked at Stella and smiled.

"Ms. Anderson ...."

"Oh call me Ms. Stella," she waved off.

"Okay, Ms. Stella. Thank you so much for the wonderful lunch. Everything was delicious."

Stella reached out and hugged Maxie around her neck. "Oh sugar, you are more than welcome. You come and see me again now."

While she was embracing Stella, Maxie looked at Marc who was standing at the door with an ever so slight smile on his face. "I'll do my best." Maxie said, before they released each other.

Stella followed Maxie to the door. Out on the porch, Marc turned to his grandmother and kissed her cheek.

"My, it's turning out to be a beautiful day. It's not as cool as it was earlier," Stella said. Not as cloudy either. Maxie, I don't reckon you'll be needing that coat today. Marcky, now you drive carefully. And don't forget about all of this food I have wrapped up for you."

"I'll be careful Mama," he said amiably. "Keep the food in the fridge for me, and I'll be back either tonight or tomorrow to pick it up."

"All right. Goodbye Maxie. It was nice meeting you."

"Good bye, and thank you again," Maxie answered.

Marc opened the door for Maxie. When he closed it, he looked back at his grandmother still standing in the doorway, and mouthed *thank you*. Stella Anderson smiled, blew her grandson a kiss, and closed the door.

"It was nice meeting your grandmother. She's so sweet," Maxie said as they pulled away from the curb.

"In spite of her probing into your business, I could tell she really liked you."

"Really? How do you know?" Maxie asked eagerly.

"She gave you an open invitation to visit again."

"When did she do that?"

"When she said you two could discuss the photo album another time."

Maxie looked out of her window pensively. "Yes she did say that didn't she? So I guess me being married wasn't a big issue with her then," Maxie stated, clearly seeking a response. When she heard nothing, she turned to Marc.

"Marc?"

Keeping his focus on the road, Marc responded casually. "She asked me what my intentions were, knowing you're a married woman."

"And you said ...?"

Marc glanced at Maxie. "I told her I had no intentions at all, and that I'm just getting to know you."

Maxie looked out of her window again. She wanted to tell Marc his response must have offered his grandmother little security in knowing nothing would ever happen between them, and she wished he'd just told Stella that. She was sure the old woman's next question was, *why do you want to know her?*

Maxie continued looking out of the window, and slightly nodded her head. She didn't want to ponder on questioning thoughts that were once again barraging her, especially not the thought that this whole meeting with Marc was crazy, because it wasn't. Now, it was purpose. Marc Thomas had to be one of the people Sister Adams spoke of, in their last conversation. It was all plain to her. Just as God commissioned Ezekiel in chapter 3 to be a spiritual watchman for the house of Israel, she too was commissioned. Her initial meeting with Marc was supposed to happen, because he was to be the first of many souls she would be responsible for.

Maxie glanced at Marc quickly, and then looked straight ahead. *I just wish he wasn't so good looking*. She smiled to herself. Talking to Marc was never a problem. He was always receptive to any topic of conversation she introduced, and he approached almost all of them open-mindedly. Her only concern was how to look into his gorgeous face, and explain to him that he needed to turn his life over to someone he didn't know, in order to save his soul, or lose his life to the adversary.

When Marc turned left off of Highway 80, Maxie instantly became more aware of her surroundings. She knew of different ways to get to the beach, but the way Marc was traveling was foreign to her. The houses on the street were both large and small, and they all seemed crowded in together on one strip of avenue. There were no sidewalks, but the area was lined with pathways of sand.

Marc continued through a short series of turns through the residential area, with the last turn leading him to a clearing that seemed to appear out of nowhere. When he parked, Maxie tried to take in all that was around them. To her right was a building with a sign in its yard that read FORT SCREVEN, and to her left was the tallest lighthouse she had ever seen.

Marc turned off the car and looked at her with a big smile. "Don't tell me you've never been to the Tybee Island Museum and Light Station."

Maxie leaned forward in her seat, to peer upward through the windshield. Keeping her eyes on the top of the tower, she spoke airily. "Okay, I won't tell you."

Marc laughed and quickly got out to open her door. "Come on and get a better view of everything."

Totally fascinated, Maxie obliged and put on her sunglasses. "What is this building?"

"This was Fort Screven." Marc said. "It was built back in eighteen eighty-five. Men trained and stood guard here, through the Spanish American War of eighteen ninety-eight. They also used it for World Wars one and two." Marc looked around the area. "Yeah ... they closed it in nineteen forty-seven though. That's why you see all of these different businesses here. Only a small part of the Fort is actually being preserved. That's it over there with the canon in the yard. They made it a museum." When he turned back to face her, Maxie was smiling at him. "What?"

"You sound like a tour guide. Either you're a history buff, or you've been here a few times."

"Naw. Neither. As a teenager, I kept hearing about how historic Savannah was to the state of Georgia. It seemed only right for me to know some of the history of the place I was calling home. So in my junior year of high school, I took a class on Georgia history. It was incredible. So many significant things happened here. Even as far back as The War of Eighteen Twelve."

"So I guess you know something about the Gullah-Geechees too huh?"

"Oh yeah. Now there's a very interesting culture of people."

Maxie nodded her head. She couldn't be sure if his response was an expression of skepticism, or great fascination. Either way, they really didn't have the time for him to elaborate.

"So where will you be taking me?" Maxie asked.

"Remember, the choice was yours. But I hardly believe either one of us would feel like talking if we're climbing one hundred and fifty-four feet, step-by-step in that lighthouse over there," Marc grinned.

Maxie put her sunglasses on, and looked up at the towering building. "I agree with you on that. So lead me to the beach."

"Do you want to get your coat? Even though it's warmed up quite a bit since this morning, it can get real windy out there along the water."

Maxie pulled a black knit cap from her purse. "No, with this sweater and cap, I should be fine."

"Okay. Put your purse in the trunk, and let me get my sunshades, then we'll be on our way."

Maxie set her purse in the trunk, and admired the area again. When Marc was ready, she turned to see he covered his eyes with a pair of Prada Aviator sun glasses. It was a style usually worn by men who wanted to send the message that they were urbane, and totally in tune with the times. Once again, the man found a way to captivate her. Her focal point finally broke when she heard the car horn beep twice, signaling the car was locked and the alarm set.

"Shall we?" Marc directed with his hand.

"You know the area Mr. Tour Guide. I'm following you."

Unconsciously, Marc reached for Maxie's hand, but then withdrew it before she really noticed. "Let's go this way."

Maxie followed Marc along a pathway that went in between Fort Screven, and a little hole in the wall restaurant. When they hit the sand, Marc slowed his pace enough to walk with Maxie side by side. As they approached a small wooden bridge, Maxie noticed a quaint little pavilion with built in seats, and briefly considered sitting there and talking. Marc obviously had the same thought, because he looked at her and slightly nodded his head in that direction. Smiling gently, Maxie nodded no. When they came to the end of the bridge, a sand path led them straight to the glistening waters of the beach.

"Which way do you want to walk? To the left, or to the right?" Marc asked.

Maxie looked both ways, and saw swings in wooden casing on both sides of them. To the left was only sand and weeds. To the right were large vacant houses that lined the beach. Some were older looking, while the others were new homes under construction. Maxie quickly surmised that if their conversation ever got to the point where it stalled, she could always strike up another one on how large and beautiful the houses were.

"Let's go to the right," she said.

"Okay."

This time Marc held out his hand to help her walk through the small sand dunes, until they got to the leveled area of the beach. Maxie grasped his hand, and instantly felt awkward holding it for that short moment. When she released it, she looked around to see if anyone noticed them, but the gesture was wasted because there was no one else on the beach. It was just like she wanted it. Secluded. But for how long? With the weather extremely warmer than usual, Maxie knew people walking their dogs, or flying their kites would soon accompany the two of them.

"I'm glad the weather turned out to be nice," Marc said. "I was a little worried about it this morning. But I was sure the company I was keeping would make all the difference for me."

Maxie smiled.

"So what are we going to talk about?" He asked, placing both hands in his pockets as he walked.

"Oh, you want me to start?"

"Well, walking the beach was your idea. You obviously have a lot you want to talk about, because this beach is about three miles long."

Maxie nodded her head, and put both of her hands into the back pockets of her jeans. "Okay. Well, tell me about growing up with your grandmother."

Marc looked at Maxie and smiled. "That's not what you want to know."

"Sure it is. I want to know how it was growing up without your parents."

"Pretty much the same way it was for you," Marc answered.

Maxie nodded. "Okay ... well ...."

Marc laughed. "Why are you having such a hard time with this? Just ask me what you want to know."

"Well you could help me out here. You *could* volunteer some information."

"Okay. Let me think. Uhm, how about that time when we were at the Shrimp Factory. You asked me why I didn't have a woman in my life. Do you want to start there?"

Bingo!! Maxie thought. "That's fine," she said casually. "We can start there."

Marc looked at Maxie with a smirk on his mouth, as if to say *I'd figured you'd say that*. Maxie read his expression and giggled lightly.

"All right Mrs. Bruce. But after I finish telling all, you have to do exactly the same with whatever questions I have. No holds barred. Fair enough?"

"That's fair."

"Okay. Simply stated. I don't have a special woman in my life right now, because I haven't found one I want to spend my time with."

Maxie walked looking straight ahead, but listening attentively. When Marc said nothing more, she looked at him. "That's it?"

"Yes."

"Oh come on Marc. Am I supposed to believe there was never anyone special? You're a very handsome man. You can't lead me to believe that there was not a woman who captured your heart at one time or another."

Marc took a deep breath, and exhaled heavily. "Okay, there was one."

"See, I knew it," Maxie grinned. "Tell me about her."

"Why? I hate drumming up the past."

"It will tell me more about you."

Marc stopped walking, causing Maxie to do the same. "What about me do you want to know? I can answer whatever questions you have."

"Okay. Here's the question. Who was the one woman who captured the heart of Marc Thomas?"

Marc nodded negatively, and started walking again. Looking out over the water, he struggled with bringing up a subject he effectively kept suppressed for almost two years. "Her name was Shari," he said.

"That's a pretty name," Maxie said softly.

Marc looked at her, and then glanced at the sea foam that came close to his shoes. "She was a beautiful woman. Anyway, we met when I moved back to New York. I was finishing my studies at the Gemological Institute of America in New York City, and she was a pre-med student at NYU. She wanted to be a pediatrician."

"Wow," Maxie interjected softly.

Marc smiled. "We met at a club in Jersey and hit it off instantly. We talked almost the whole night. I knew then that she had the right combination of brains and beauty. And she was so grounded. She knew what she wanted in life, and didn't have a problem going after it. I admired that about her. Shari was totally her own woman. We dated exclusively for about a year. After that, we moved in together for more than a year and a half; against my grandmother's wishes I might add, and we were pretty involved. At least that's what I thought. I was sure she was going to be the woman I would settle down with. I mean, I would have done anything for Shari. I was just that in love with her."

"So what happened?"

Marc looked at Maxie for what seemed like a long moment before he answered. "I didn't fit into her plans. She didn't love me."

"Excuse me?" Maxie said, with a deep frown.

"She didn't love me." Marc laughed a little. "Let me phrase that exactly. She wasn't *in love* with me. You know there is a difference between the two."

"I know."

"When I started alluding to the fact that I wanted to get married, because I felt she was my soul mate, she politely told me she didn't feel the same way about me. Her exact words were, 'Marc, I want my career to come first. To get married now, would only interfere with what I'm trying to accomplish'." Marc stopped talking, and they both walked in silence for a short moment. The only sound between them, was the soft splashing of the waves on the sand.

"So she hurt you."

"Yes. Yes she did. Needless to say, I ended our relationship after that. No need to continue pursuing something I couldn't have."

"And there was no one after that?"

"Nope. I think I got a little gun shy after that one."

"That's understandable," Maxie said, with a voice full of concern. "I'm sorry that relationship didn't work out for you."

Marc picked up a small rock, and threw it into the water. "Yeah, me too. At least she was honest with me. I appreciated that."

"So let me get this right. You like a woman who has her own mind. That's easy enough. There are plenty of women out there who have their own mind Marc."

"I'm sure there are Maxie. I'm just not ready to get involved in another relationship right now."

Maxie nodded her head gently, and released the conversation. Playfully, Marc bumped into her arm. "Now it's my turn," he grinned.

Maxie grimaced, and groaned her discontent.

"I want to know ... I want to know who you are for real," Marc said pensively. "I see you often, and you're this beautiful woman who captivates me every time I lay my eyes on you. Even when I picked you up at the mall. Woman you floor me!"

Maxie laughed, and quickly walked away from Marc.

"Hold up," he said, catching up to her. "Now you have to tell me what this is all about. You have me going crazy here. I even had to ask my grandmother what it is about you that reaches out to me."

Maxie stopped walking, and took on a more serious look. "Marc, you asked your grandmother questions about me? What did she say? More importantly, what did she think?"

Marc stood in front of her, and spoke nonchalantly. "Maxie, I ask my grandmother questions about a lot of things I don't understand. What do you mean what did she say and think? I told you, she thinks you're great."

Maxie sighed, and looked around aimlessly as they continued walking. "Marc, I don't know what it is that you see in me. I don't see myself as being any more different than any other woman."

"Tell me about your lifestyle. What do you do when you're not working?"

"Pretty much nothing. I don't go out to clubs, I don't go to parties, I don't drink, I don't smoke, I just go to ...."

Maxie didn't want to say another word, and she couldn't understand why. For no apparent reason, she felt incredibly inhibited about her lifestyle. She felt like it should be kept a secret. The logic that swept over her right then was so juvenile; it made her nod her head no. She never entertained the thought that if Marc knew her lifestyle, he would no longer want to be friends with her. But here it was.

Marc gently bumped into Maxie again. "Hey. You just go where?"

Maxie looked at Marc for a moment, and then looked away. Focusing her sight on an empty lifeguard chair tower a short distance away from them, she continued. "I just go to church."

Marc grinned. "You looked like that was the hardest thing in the world to say. Why did you struggle with saying that? Everybody goes to church at some point in their life. Some just go more than others."

"I'm the latter," Maxie said, forcing a smile.

"So you mean like ... the church is your way of life."

"Uhm hmm. It has been for almost all of my life."

"And what about your husband? He goes with you?"

Maxie paused again; revealing to Marc that she was an avid churchgoer was hard enough. To talk about Lester, that was an even bigger hurdle. "Yes, he goes with me."

"So the church is his way of life too isn't it?"

Maxie nodded yes.

Marc looked out over the water, at a flock of seagulls hovering over one particular spot. He couldn't believe the ambivalence he was feeling, about the next question that sat on the tip of his tongue. On one hand, he wanted to know if his grandmother was right about Maxie's husband being a minister. On the other hand, he didn't want to ask her, for fear of her possibly lying to him. He couldn't be sure that she *would* lie, but hadn't she purposely avoided every opportunity to discuss her husband before?

Marc took a slight detour to the edge of the shore-line, and picked up a large conch seashell that was slightly embedded in the sand. Maxie stood and watched.

"Do you believe you can really hear the ocean in these?" He asked, as he walked back to her. Maxie smiled. "Here, listen." Marc handed her the spirally shell, and watched her put it close to her ear.

"I hear nothing but a hollow sound," she said.

"Let me try it." Marc removed his sunglasses, and rested them on his head. When he put the shell close to his ear, he looked at Maxie squarely. Even though her sunglasses were a little dark, he could see her eyes perfectly. "Uhm hmm," he said in a low tone. "I definitely hear something."

Maxie smirked her lips.

"Do you want to know what I hear?" He asked.

Maxie said nothing, but allowed a slight smile to form across her lips in reply.

"I hear that your husband is a minister." Marc took the shell from his ear, and tossed it on the ground.

Instantly Maxie's smile faded, and she felt an immediate heaviness in the pit of her stomach. Not wanting to look at him anymore, she lowered her head, only to have Marc raise her chin gently with his fingertips.

"That's nothing to be ashamed of Maxie."

"I'm not ashamed. I just thought ... I just thought if you knew my lifestyle and the fact that I'm married to a minister, then you wouldn't want to be friends anymore. I know it sounds stupid, but I didn't want to lose you ... your friendship. So that's why I didn't jump at the opportunities to share that part of my life with you."

"I think I'd be a pretty shallow person, if I allowed your lifestyle to prevent us from being friends. Is that how you view me? As shallow?"

"Well," Maxie joked.

"Now come on."

Maxie smiled again. "No that's not how I view you. That's not how I view you at all."

"Well good." Marc pulled down his glasses, as they began walking again. "Now that we've each shared a dark secret and everything is out on the table, tell me what kind of person your husband is."

"Before I do, tell me how you knew he was a minister."

Marc laughed. "Uh uh. I answered all of your questions remember?"

"Marc, that's not fair. You just sprung this on me, and I want to know how you knew."

Marc glanced at her, and looked straight ahead. "If I tell you, you can't ask me any more questions about it. Okay?"

"Okay."

Marc paused. "My grandmother told me."

Maxie quickly moved in front of him and walked backwards, facing him. "Marc, how?"

"Uh uh," he laughed. "No more questions. I mean it."

Maxie turned around, closed her mouth, and pressed her lips together firmly, making Marc laugh even more.

"Now tell me about your husband."

"There's really not much to tell. A mutual friend of ours introduced us at a church function, when there was really no introduction needed."

"Why not?"

"Lester was known and wanted by every woman in the church. Young, old, married, and single."

"A hot commodity huh?"

"To say the least." Maxie grinned.

"But he wanted the one woman who could pull on his heart strings. The one woman who was like no other woman in the church." Marc's voice escalated. "The one woman who had the ability to captivate strong men. ..."

Maxie punched Marc in his arm. "Would you stop already?" She laughed. "Anyway, I was attracted to who he was, so I agreed to be his wife."

"What do you mean you were attracted to *who* he was?"

"You know how some people act one way at church, and then a different way outside of church?" Marc nodded yes. "Well Lester was never like that. What you see is what you get with him. He was then, and probably always will be, a man true to his faith."

"So he's firm in every aspect of what he believes."

Maxie looked at Marc directly. "Yes, he is."

"And he knows nothing about this meeting does he?"

"No." Maxie replied in a voice so low, Marc almost didn't hear her.

"So I guess you compromised your integrity, in order to be with me today."

Maxie gently kicked an empty Coke can that was in her pathway. "I may have compromised a lot more than that," she said solemnly. "I lied to my husband so we could have this time together."

Marc mouthed the word *wow* and looked at the ground. "Maxie, now that I know more about you, I never would have encouraged you to ...."

"I know," she said without looking at him. "The choice was mine. I even tried to rationalize it by telling myself it was all for the gorgeous anniversary gift I'm giving him."

"But that didn't work."

Maxie nodded her head no. "I've never lied to him before."

Marc witnessed the sudden onset of anguish and remorse on Maxie's face, and then he looked out over the ocean. Feeling somewhat aggravated, he shoved his hands into his pockets. He hated to think he was the reason for what she did and what she was feeling, but there was nothing he could do.

For what seemed like a long moment, the two of them walked without a word. Maxie was grateful for the sound of the waves, which seemed much louder than before. For the first time, she noticed there were a few other people on the beach, and wondered how long they had been there, and why she hadn't noticed them before. Almost intuitively, she looked at her watch. It was 3:25 p.m.

"It's getting late," she said. "I think we should turn and walk back now."

Marc looked at his watch, and agreed. Quickly they shifted, and walked the other way.

"This was great," Marc said. "I'm sorry you did what you felt you had to do, to be here today. But I've enjoyed every minute of being with you."

Maxie blushed, and looked at the sand.

"Maxie, I don't want this to end. I want to spend more time with you. Maybe if we're more spontaneous with our meetings, you won't have to give any explanation as to where you're going. No more lies to your husband. It can all be spur of the moment. Let me take you places you've never been before."

Maxie listened to the keenness in Marc's voice, and felt the twinge of enticement in her stomach. "How could we ever be spontaneous? I won't be able to talk to you when I'm at work, and you know you can't call me at home too often."

Marc took his left hand out of his pocket, and extended it to Maxie. "I want you to have this. I bought it just for you."

Maxie looked in the palm of his hand, and saw the smallest cell phone she had ever seen. "Oh my. You bought this for me?" She grinned.

"I want to be able to talk to you on a whim. If I'm feeling lonely, and I need a friend, all I have to do is call you. Everything on it is ready to go, and I'll be taking care of the bill. I've set your phone to vibrate softly, so no one will know you have it on, or that you even have a phone for that matter. I've also programmed all of my numbers into it. You can call me anywhere I am, even if I'm overseas. I'll show you on the way home how to send me a text message or video message, unless you already know how to do that."

Maxie kept grinning and observing her phone, like a little child getting to hold a brand new toy for the first time. "I've seen other people do it on their phones, so I'm sure I can figure it out, but you can show me too," she said, glancing at him. "Marc this is so nice. What's my phone number?"

"You won't be needing it," he said, looking straight ahead. "I'll be the only one calling you."

Maxie opened her mouth to reply, but considered what Marc said, and changed her mind.

"There's a way to lock your phone, so if it's ever found by someone, they won't be able to access your list of my numbers or anything else. We'll set that up on the way back too."

"You talk about *me* having things planned out." Maxie said. "You've been holding on to this all day."

"Actually, I bought it for you as soon as I got back from London. I held on to it until I was sure you were on board with this little arrangement of ours."

Maxie nodded her head, clutched the phone in her hand, and looked at Marc sincerely. "I'm here for you whenever you need me."

Marc observed Maxie and the intensity of her words. They were so literal; he considered them to be a sound promise, bringing a soft smile to his lips. "I believe that."

"This was nice for me too," Maxie said, looking around. "The weather is nice, we had a nice lunch. I got to meet your grandmother. Even the company and conversation was good."

"You doubted it would be?" Mark chuckled.

"No. Doubt never entered my mind."

"Good, because I want us to have more days like this. Maybe even longer days."

"Marc, I don't. ..."

"We'll work up to it." Marc looked at Maxie with a grin on his face. "Right now, my only concern is to get my Cinderella home before the stroke of midnight."

Chapter Thirty-Five

"This is the day, this is the day, that the Lord has made, that the Lord has made. I will rejoice, I will rejoice, and be glad in it, and be glad in it ..." the church choir sang ardently. Maxie sat on her pew and then stood, as the choir director prompted the entire congregation. Every movement Maxie made, was made out of habit. She clapped her hands, and even sang the song with everyone else, but her thought process was far away from the Sunday morning church service. Every thought she could conceive, dwelt in the reverie of yesterday's jaunt with Marc. It was hard for her to remember the last time she ever felt so stimulated. Not only was she left with that indelible feeling, but she also had an unfailing vision of it all, because everything was right yesterday. So right, she didn't want it to end.

When Marc dropped her off near her car at the mall, he left the motor running. Maxie could see the expression on his face echoed what she felt the instant they left the beach.

"You know there's a song that fits this moment." Marc said, just as she opened the car door to get out."

"Time in a Bottle?" She asked, forcing a smile.

"Yeah, that's the one. How did you know which one I was talking about?"

"I guess I'm feeling the same sentiment you're feeling." Reluctantly, she turned and got out of the car.

"Maxie?"

"Yes," she answered, bending a little to see him.

"I love being with you, and I want to be with you again soon. I don't know where we'll go, or what we'll do. I just know that I want it to be soon."

Marc held out his hand to her. Without forethought, she clasped it tightly.

"Promise me that," he said softly.

"I promise."

"Soon."

Slowly she released Marc's hand, but felt a gentle firmness as he held on to her. "Goodbye Marc."

Maxie closed the door, and immediately got into her car. She didn't want to look at Marc again, because the sight of him clouded her thoughts, and she needed to mentally prepare herself for spending the rest of the evening with her husband. In-lieu of watching Marc drive away, she busied herself by removing her hat and fluffing her hair in the mirror.

When she arrived home at 5:25 p.m., and walked through the kitchen entrance, Lester was sitting on the couch in the living room, with a less than favorable expression on his face. When she greeted him, and he slightly motioned for her to come to him, Maxie knew the essence of the day was about to be ruined.

"What's wrong?" She asked as she walked to him, noticing the TV was not on.

Lester pensively looked at the floor, then at her. "Why didn't you just tell me Maxie?" He asked in a low tone.

Maxie set her work smock on the table, and stood in the middle of the floor. "Why didn't I tell you what?"

"I went to Food King a little while ago. I was hoping to surprise you. When I didn't see you there, I went to ask someone at the Customer Service counter if you were still in the store."

Panic set in.

Immediately, Maxie began to feel as if she were hyperventilating. Her heart went into overdrive so quickly, the pounding of it in her chest reverberated in her ears. She needed desperately to sit down, but she doubted if the now quivering muscles in her upper thighs would even carry her to the couch.

"Anyway, they were so busy, I didn't want to wait around. As I was leaving the store, that's when I noticed it."

Maxie slowly moved to the couch, and sat down close to her husband, who had his focus on the floor again.

"I don't know how I missed it when I first walked in, because there it was right in the middle of the floor," Lester said.

Maxie's mouth was so dry, her voice was reduced to almost a whisper. "Honey, what are you talking about?"

"Your picture," he said, looking at her. "Maxie, why didn't you tell me that you were Employee of the Month at Food King?"

Maxie swallowed hard. Relief washed over her like a tsunami tidal wave. Trying hard not to heave a heavy sigh, she smiled softly. "I don't ... I don't know. I guess I felt you wouldn't be interested in something like that. I mean, you weren't very fond of me getting the job in the first place, so…" Maxie shrugged her shoulders. "I don't know."

Lester looked at his wife earnestly. "Baby, I never want you to think that I wouldn't be interested in something that's as meaningful as this. This is something you've achieved. This was a great accomplishment. What kind of man would I be if I didn't want to share that with you?"

Maxie searched Lester's eyes, and saw both joy and pain. "I'm sorry," she whispered. "I wasn't fair."

Lester held her face in his hand, and gently kissed her forehead. "I'm proud of you," he said, before kissing her cheek. "So very …" he kissed her nose. "…very," he kissed her other cheek. "…very proud of you." Lester kissed Maxie so passionately then, that as she thought about it now right there in church, it sent chills down her spine. What happened after that, made her put her stamp of approval on that entire day.

After the choir sang their last song, Maxie looked up into the pulpit where the ministers were seated, and immediately locked eyes with Lester. Ever so discreetly, she puckered her lips at him, as if she were giving him a kiss. Lester acknowledged her flirtatious gesture with a slight nod, and a wink of his eye. Maxie smiled modestly, and glanced around quickly to see if anyone noticed their game of silent banter.

"Can we all say Amen for the choir this afternoon?" Pastor Harrison chimed. "Now can we all say Amen for the choir? Didn't they just bless our souls? Praise God!" The entire congregation responded loudly, as if Pastor Harrison had already begun preaching. "We thank God for that song. And just like the choir sang in the beginning, this is the day that the Lord hath made. And we should all rejoice and be glad in it. For the Lord woke each and every one of us this morning, giving us another chance to do His will by fulfilling our purpose in this life. For He that hath begun a good work in you, shall perform it until the day of Jesus Christ. Can I get an Amen?"

Maxie responded with the rest of the congregation, but remained seated, unlike some of those around her. Instead, she immediately began to think about Pastor Harrison's statement, on fulfilling one's purpose. She was proud of the fact that she could count herself among those, who were working toward fulfilling the plan of God in their lives. She identified one of the many souls God had given to her hand, and she was actively working toward having him accept Jesus Christ as his personal Savior. She was now a willing vessel, available for the Master's use.

Maxie gently ran her hand over the leather cover of the Bible in her lap, and considered how silly she was to try to walk away from God and His plan, especially when there was no better place for her to go. Just as she had come to that realization herself, she knew she was going to have to persuade Marc with that exact same argument. She just needed the right words, and the right timing to do so.

Maxie looked at Lester again. He was totally tuned in to the Pastor's words. She wished she could share with him how God was using her. She greatly underestimated his response to her being Employee of the Month, so there was a good chance he would be elated to know that she was diligently working in the Lord's vineyard. However, to divulge that much information would mean she would have to reveal the lie she told him yesterday, and she wasn't quite ready for that. Besides, she didn't believe for one second that Lester would support the idea of her spending that much time with another man, even if the purpose was to win his soul to Christ.

When the service was over, Maxie stood and waited for Lester while he performed his usual tête-à-tête with other ministers who stood around in the pulpit. Different church members greeted her and said, *God bless you*, as they were on their way out. When she looked around the near empty sanctuary, Maxie saw The Ominous Three looking at her, as they chatted against a wall that was distant to where she was standing. Inwardly she groaned, because she knew it was just a matter of time before they accosted her about the delivery of Thanksgiving baskets to the elderly. Even when the announcement was made over the pulpit that more people were needed to make deliveries, Maxie knew someone from the committee would seek her out.

In an effort to remove herself from plain sight, Maxie slid down into a folding chair that was next to the pew she was standing beside. Her first instinct was to go to the bathroom and hide out, but she didn't move with the idea. Regretfully, she wished she had, because now the three women were marching their way across the sanctuary with their faces set on *mission*.

"Oh Sister Bruce," Blanche Grammerson's voice rang through the air. "May we have a short chat with you?"

Maxie didn't want to stand. She didn't even want to acknowledge that she heard anyone call her name, but with the church practically empty, how could she deny it? Before she looked in the direction of the quick moving women, Maxie looked up at Lester who turned his focus to the women, at the calling of her name. Looking at his wife, he saw a face that asked, *how much longer are you going to be?* And *please help me now.* Lester nodded that he understood, and held up his forefinger for her to wait until he finished. Maxie groaned again, and forced a smile to her face as she stood up to greet the women.

"Good afternoon ladies."

"Praise the Lord Sister Bruce," Joyce Rodgers said, giving Maxie a hug.

Maxie conceded, as the other women followed suit.

"I'm sure you heard the announcement today, concerning the need for more volunteers to deliver our Thanksgiving baskets to the elderly," Emma Teal said.

"Yes I did," Maxie replied. "I was sorry to hear that Brother Renfrow has taken ill, and won't be able to run his route this year. I know how much he always looked forward to doing that."

Emma went on at a full rate of speed. "Yes it is such a shame for that poor man. God bless his soul. Anyway, what we think you need to do is to deliver. ..."

Blanche Grammerson looked at Emma Teal with a quick hard glance, and interrupted her by raising her voice a little. "What we are *asking* ..." she glanced at Emma again. "...is if you would possibly be available to help us to do the deliveries on this coming Wednesday. You know Thanksgiving is Thursday."

"Yes I know," Maxie said, briefly looking at the floor as if she were thinking. "So I gather no one responded to the announcement."

"There were a few," Joyce Rodgers chimed in. "But not enough. We have quite a few more elderly people in need this holiday, than we did last year. We're also extending the project to include needy families."

Maxie looked at the faces of the three women, and considered the answer to the question she was about to ask. "I believe I can give you a few hours on Wednesday. Which one of you ladies will I be making deliveries with?"

Once again the women were predictable in their body language. Emma Teal put her hand to her chest, Blanche Grammerson looked the other way, and Joyce Rodgers smiled and scowled as if Maxie had asked the most ridiculous question.

"Oh we aren't *making* the deliveries ourselves," Joyce said. "We're overseeing everything here."

"All three of you?"

"Why yes of course," Emma said. "That's what we do."

Maxie nodded her head lightly, and looked up into the pulpit to see Lester coming down the steps.

"All right ladies. I can do them alone. I was going to do my weekly visit with the sick and shut-in on that day. I'll just change my schedule. That won't be a problem."

"If you think you'll need assistance, Deacon Earl Bayer will be helping out also," Blanche said.

"No, I believe she can handle it alone," Lester piped in. Nestling up to his wife, he put his arm around her waist.

"Good afternoon Minister Bruce," all three women said in unison.

"Hello ladies. Well, if you're all finished here, I'd like to take this beautiful woman home with me."

Maxie looked up at her husband and smiled.

"Oh that's so sweet," Blanche cooed.

"Yes we're finished," Joyce said. "Thank you Sister Bruce for your time, and we'll expect to see you on Wednesday."

Maxie forced another fake smile, and simply nodded her head as the women left with a final God bless you.

Maxie looked at Lester again, and nodded her head negatively. "Will you ever be there in time to save me?"

Lester chuckled, and kissed her on her forehead. "Let's go woman."

Chapter Thirty-Six

M arc sat motionlessly in front of a big screen television in his living room, trying desperately to give his attention to every NFL football game that he could. He had virtually watched the clock on the wall tick away the morning hours, only to have the late-afternoon hours take their place and find him in the exact same position — reclined in a leather chair, dressed in a pair of old cut-off sweatpants, and a nameless white football jersey.

The effort he put in to being a spectator was wasted, because he really wasn't watching the television at all. Every time he tried to get into the game, his mind wandered back to the day before.

The day spent with Maxie.

Everything went right Saturday. Though he tried not to have expectations on how the day would ultimately turn out, the time spent with Maxie was all he expected it would be, and more. She openly shared with him the things that anyone else might deem as personal, and she answered every question he posed to her, with little or no hesitation.

In return, at the risk of appearing vulnerable, he was able to share with her the piece of himself that he planned to always keep hidden.

In spite of whether she wanted to reveal it or not, Marc was grateful for Maxie's honesty when he inquired about her husband. Even on the way home, as he asked more questions about Lester, Maxie continued to oblige. The fact that she opened up and made herself transparent, said more to him than almost anything else she could have said. He appreciated that kind of genuineness, and noted how rare a woman Maxie was. He also noted how different he felt whenever she was around him. It was a little hard for him to pinpoint one word that summed up all of the feelings that surfaced whenever he saw Maxie, so he didn't waste his time trying to come up with one. He just knew that the very sight of her seemingly brought out a greater side of him. He felt encouraged to do better, and strive to be better. That fact alone, in conjunction with what his grandmother said, was cause enough for him to consider *why* Maxie Bruce was rapidly becoming a part of his life.

Marc stood up, and walked to the French doors that overlooked his massive patio. Leaning against the door jamb, he put his hands in his pockets and looked out the window. The day that started out as brilliantly sunny, was now waning and he had done nothing constructive in it. There were appraisals to transcribe, clients to contact, and designs to finish, but all he could do was think about *her*. In an effort to get a little bit of clarity to what was quickly becoming mass confusion, Marc replayed his grandmother's words over and over again, in his head.

What you see or feel where Maxie is concerned, is something you need in your own life, but right now you don't desire to seek it out. Baby, you have a void inside you that longs to be filled. And it's that very thing that attracts you to Maxie. She, herself, has nothing to do with it. You're not attracted to the person Marcky. You're attracted to what she has.

Marc caught a glimpse of his own reflection in the panes. For the first time, he considered his grandmother's words and opened his mind to questions he never really entertained. *Could God really use him? Was there a plan for his life?* If he understood his grandmother correctly, it was the God in Maxie that was drawing him. But what kind of sense did that make? Why would God be reaching out to him at this point in his life? He had nothing to offer God. He really didn't even know that much about Him. Even though his grandmother was quite diligent in making sure he grew up with some kind of spiritual knowledge, he couldn't really say he ever developed a relationship with God. So why would he be *attracted* to Him?

Marc shook his head, looked at the floor, and rubbed the back of his neck. The more he thought about it all, the less sense it made. To further construe everything, he had to wonder what Maxie was getting out of all of this. He knew she was attracted to him. He could see it in her eyes. Even though neither one of them was looking to have a relationship beyond platonic, they were both very much attracted to each other. So was there something about him that was drawing her?

Just as Marc was about to hone in on possible answers to that question, his telephone rang. Quickly, he moved into the kitchen, and pulled the cordless phone from the wall.

"Hello?"

"Well I guess since I saw you yesterday, you won't be coming by to have Sunday dinner with this old woman huh?"

Marc smiled. "Mama, I was just thinking about you."

"Not enough to call obviously. What are you doing over there? I hope you're not working. Even the Lord rested on the Sabbath day Marcky."

"Actually, I'm doing absolutely nothing. Which is not good, because I do have a lot of work to finish."

"Oh pishaw," Stella said. "Why don't you come on over here and help me eat some of this apple pie you left here with me on yesterday."

"You're in need of some company too?"

"Who me?" Stella started. "You know by now I ... well, yes I do."

Stella and Marc both laughed.

"Me too. I'll be over in about an hour. I want to talk to you about something you said anyway. We can have a nice conversation."

"Well good. You have your key right?"

"Yes ma'am."

"Well come on. Stop by the store on your way, and pick up some of that vanilla ice cream I like, and we can turn this pie into ala mode."

Marc smiled again. "I'll be there in about an hour," he said, and hung up the phone. Visiting with his grandmother was exactly what he needed, to help him quell what was going on inside of him. She could definitely shed some light on the *God* issue. He only hoped she could help him to understand where Maxie fit into all of it.

* * * * * * * * * *

"So your old mama was right about Maxie huh?" Stella asked, as she cut into her ice cream and apple pie. Slowly, she placed the dessert into her mouth, and kept her eyes on Marc, who sat cater-corner from her in the dining room.

Marc stared at his bowl and played around with his ice cream. "I can't recall too many times when you were ever wrong mama," he said with a slight smile.

Stella nodded her head. "You enjoyed yourself on the beach yesterday too didn't you?"

Marc raised his eyebrows, nodded yes, but still did not look at his grandmother.

"So what is it that has you so down in the mouth?" Stella pushed her bowl aside, giving her full attention to her grandson.

"I don't know mama. I guess I'm just confused about a few things."

"Things that have to do with Maxie?"

"Well, yeah in part."

Stella nodded knowingly, and kept her focus.

"You remember what you said to me in the kitchen yesterday, about me being drawn to whatever it is that Maxie possesses?"

"Yes."

"Well I don't understand that. I mean Maxie is a beautiful woman, and I believe I am attracted to her as an individual like any normal man …."

"Marcky, you were the one who said there was something special about that woman, when you first told me about her. Remember our phone conversation?" Marc nodded. "You said you felt something strange whenever she was around you. All I did was listen. And then when you brought her here, I merely confirmed what you felt and told you what it was. Now you can accept it, or leave it."

Marc rubbed his hand over his head, in a gesture of frustration. "Yeah mama, but it makes no sense. All day long I've been thinking about her, and what you said. If my fascination with Maxie is only because of that ... that...."

"Anointing," Stella said calmly.

"Anointing. Then what is it that she sees in me?"

Stella observed how aggravated her grandson was becoming, and gently smiled. "You mean besides your good looks and boyish charm?" Marc gave her a *give me a break* expression. "Well it's true," Stella piped. "You get your good looks from me you know. Your biological mama was ugly."

Marc tried to keep a straight face, but as soon as his eyes met his grandmother's, they both burst into laughter. He was grateful for the small explosion, because the air around him was beginning to thicken with tension.

"To be honest baby, I don't know what or even *if* Maxie is supposed to gain anything from you. If she doesn't have an ulterior motive for spending time with you, then I'd venture to say maybe she knows God is working on you right now, and she is in your life just to help you along the path."

Marc sat pensively for a moment, and then looked at Stella. "So do you think I should ask her about it, see what she knows?"

"In time. But answer these questions for me. How do you feel? Do you feel God pulling on you?"

Marc looked at his bowl again. "Mama, I am so confused right now, I don't know what I feel. I mean I enjoy being with Maxie so much, I almost crave the atmosphere around her. It's like everything in it is so right, even though I know she's married. So if His presence is there like that, I don't know. Maybe I do feel Him pulling on me. And if He is, then I don't understand why. I have nothing to offer Him. I don't know the scriptures, and I haven't been to church in I don't know when. I don't even think I want that special relationship with Him that you used to talk about when I was growing up, simply because I know it requires change. I don't think I'm ready to change anything about my life right now." Marc quickly stood up, shoved his hands into his front pockets, and walked into the living room. With his back to his grandmother, he stood next to the fireplace and looked at the pictures on the mantle.

Stella remained seated, with an ever so soft smile on her face. After a brief moment she returned to her dessert, eating a few spoonfuls before she pushed it away again.

"Marcky. When your mother dropped you off practically at my doorstep, did you have anything to give me?" Marc nodded no, but did not turn around. "You had nothing, and you barely even knew me. But after spending time with me, you came to love this old woman, and we have a pretty good relationship I believe." Stella walked to Marc, and stood close to him. "It's the same way with the Lord baby. Spend some time with Him. Get to know Him a little bit, and see how you feel after that. Just take one step."

Marc looked down at his grandmother and laughed a little, before nodding his head. "One step at a time?"

"That's how you learned to walk," Stella smiled.

Marc gave her a hug. "We'll see mama. We'll see."

Chapter Thirty-Seven

With Thanksgiving two days away, and Christmas not far behind, Maxie knew for the next month or so, Food King was going to be swamped from open to close. Since she anticipated an increase of hours in her work schedule because of it, she was glad she volunteered her time at the church now, while she was still somewhat available. Between working, keeping up with things at home, and plans to be with Marc on a whim, Maxie's time was limited. But no matter what she laid out on the table before her, she refused to let it be said that she wasn't available for the *work of the Lord*.

"We're so glad you were able to come out and help us to make these Thanksgiving baskets this year Sister Bruce," Blanche Grammerson said.

Maxie tied a ribbon at the top of the last basket she put together and smiled, more to herself than to Blanche. It never ceased to amaze her how The Ominous Three always claimed some form of *active* participation in whatever the church did for the community, or its members. If there was a dinner to be fixed at the church, they were the ones who claimed to do *all* of the cooking. If there was a sick church member in the hospital, they were the ones who claimed to make the initial visit. If there were kudos to be received from the Pastor for a job well done, no matter how many people actually performed the duties, those three always placed themselves at the forefront of the receiving line. Prim, primed, and ready.

Maxie looked around the Fellowship Hall before she looked at Blanche. There were fifteen other people who were with her, counting, stuffing, wrapping, and tying baskets. They were practically in an assembly line format; each with a four-foot table in front of them.

"I'm sure that your schedule is quite tight these days," Blanche went on. "I mean with everything you have to do in working that job and all. However were you able to get away for two days? It was such a wonderful surprise to see that you could avail yourself to us this fine Tuesday afternoon."

When Maxie finally looked at Blanche, it took everything within her to keep her temperament cordial. She wasn't going to let Blanche's snide remarks get the best of her. Not today. She came to help out in preparing the baskets she would be delivering tomorrow, and that was exactly what she was going to do. She didn't have to explain anything. It was none of Blanche's business that she had already been to work, because she made prior arrangements to work at Food King from nine to one.

"I believe this is the last basket I need," Maxie said amiably. "Would you check your list to make sure our numbers match?"

Blanche blinked her eyes rapidly, before she looked at the stapled list in her hand. "Yes of course I can."

While she waited for Blanche to count the names, Maxie felt a vibrating sensation in the front pocket of her jeans. Just as Blanche opened her mouth to give Maxie the answer, Maxie held up her forefinger.

"Would you excuse me for a moment? I need to run out to my car real quick."

Before Blanche could answer, Maxie briskly walked through the Fellowship Hall doors, to the parking lot. Once inside her car, she pulled out the phone, and read the text message. *I miss you and NEED to see you. Call me.* Maxie smiled softly, and surveyed the area. If anyone witnessed her quick sprint across the parking lot, they were probably wondering if she had some kind of an emergency, and might be making their way to her car. Relieved no one was following her, Maxie proceeded to dial Marc's cell phone number. While she waited for him to pick up, she glanced at her watch. It was 3:30 p.m.

Maxie hadn't talked to Marc since their walk on the beach last Saturday. For the past couple of days, their only form of communication was through text messages that said *Hello, how are you? Thinking about you,* and *Hope you're having a great day.*

"It took you long enough to respond to my text and call me," Marc said gently, instead of saying hello. "I was wondering if you knew how to use your new phone."

The sound of his voice on the phone always did something to Maxie. She couldn't explain exactly what it was, but she liked it. "You haven't allowed me the opportunity to really use it, considering the fact that we haven't spoken to each other in almost three days," Maxie replied genially. "Besides, I think I did pretty well. If I were at work right now, you may not have gotten this call until after five." Maxie listened for Marc's response, and heard nothing.

Marc could tell she was smiling, so he closed his eyes to picture it. He wanted to tell Maxie all he had been feeling since they were together last. The confusion, the frustration ....

"Marc?" Maxie almost whispered. The sudden empty sound on the other end of the phone, made her feel uneasy. "Marc, what's wrong?"

"Nothing."

"Don't do that. Don't tell me nothing's wrong, when things aren't all right with you. Is something wrong with your grandmother?"

Marc listened to the sincerity in Maxie's voice, and felt a part of him relax in it. "No. No, I ... I just want to ... I really need to see you."

Maxie looked at her watch again. "Right now?"

"Would it be possible?"

"Yes, of course it would. I'm at the church right now. I'm almost finished with what I was doing. Where do you want to meet?"

"Maxie, I don't want to interrupt ...."

"Marc where?"

Marc paused a moment. "How far are you from River Street?"

"Not far at all. Maybe about fifteen minutes at most."

"Meet me at Spanky's. Do you remember which ramp gets you closest to it?"

"Of course. Lincoln Street."

"So I'll see you in what, an hour?"

"No, I'll be there in thirty minutes. Is that good?"

"Perfect," Marc said. "I'll be waiting for you."

Without either of them saying goodbye, Maxie flipped her phone closed, and put it back into her pocket. Immediately she got out of her car, and sprinted back to the doors of the Fellowship Hall. Just as she was about to grab a hold of the door's handle, someone on the other side pushed it open.

"Well aren't you a sight for these sore eyes. Come on in here and bring some beauty to this room of ashes."

Maxie smiled, and stepped inside. "Thank you Deacon Earl. How are you?"

"Oh I'm fine now. Just like yourself," Deacon Earl said with a sinister grin, quickly sizing Maxie up with his eyes.

Maxie ignored his compliment, and impious assessment. "Were you just leaving? Please don't let me stop you. I need to put my baskets into boxes for tomorrow's deliveries." Maxie walked away from Deacon Earl quickly, hoping her abruptness would deter any conversation he planned on having. Unfortunately, it didn't work, because he was following right behind her.

"Well actually, I came here for the same purpose. I signed on to help do the deliveries myself this year. Lots of women ..." Maxie glanced at him. "I mean families are in need of assistance this year. So it just seemed proper that I should help out."

Maxie quickly placed her baskets into large empty boxes, and pushed them under the table. "I don't mean to be rude Deacon Earl, but I'm kind of in a rush to leave." Maxie put on her jacket. "Would you please tell Sister Blanche that I'll be back sometime tomorrow morning to get these boxes? Thank you so much." Before Deacon Earl could say another word, Maxie turned on her heels and headed for the doors.

"Well that won't be necessary," Deacon Earl called to her. "You and I are supposed to be making our deliveries together tomorrow. That is, according to the sheet they just showed me. I can go ahead and just put these boxes in my truck tonight."

Maxie stopped dead in her tracks, but did not immediately turn around. Glancing at her watch again, it clearly told her she needed to leave now, if she were to arrive at Spanky's when she said she would. Turning around quickly, she addressed Deacon Earl head on.

"Deacon, I don't know who told you that, but there has obviously been some kind of a mistake. My husband made arrangements for me to deliver alone, at his special request. I'm sure you understand. But should I need any assistance, you'll be the first one I ask. Have a good evening."

Without another word spoken, Maxie left the Hall.

* * * * * * * * * *

Marc leaned against a light post across the street from Spanky's. Even though the weather was less than favorable with its gray sky, the temperature was moderate enough for him to wait outside for Maxie. Keeping the restaurant doors in his view, he watched the huge cargo vessels move in and out of the Savannah Port Authority. He didn't know exactly why he wanted to meet her outside, and for lack of a better reason, it just felt more secluded to him in spite of an occasional passing tourist.

Pacing a little back and forth, Marc tried to quell his anxiety. The view of the ships against the backdrop of the Talmadge Bridge, made him consider taking a trip far away somewhere — a small attempt to run away from what was troubling him. He knew the thought was a silly one, especially when he remembered an old adage his grandmother used to tell him whenever he threatened to run away.

"Remember baby," Stella said. "Wherever you go, you take yourself with you, and that includes all of your problems."

Marc couldn't understand how a decision he always deemed as trivial, could come to be almost crucial now. Just a couple of weeks ago, he was footloose and fancy free of any cares concerning the final destination of his soul. It was the furthest thing from his mind. Now he was weighted and puzzled with this out-of-the-blue decision of where he planned to spend eternity, and what sacrifices would come along with his choice.

But why? Why all of this now? Because of Maxie?

He was so confused, he couldn't even be sure she was the reason. Granted, she came into his life with a phenomenal package of invisible enticement, which she obviously had no idea she was carrying. But why did she appeal to *him*? And why was the pull so strong? Weren't there others out there just like him? Undoubtedly they had crossed her path. Were the results the same?

Marc gently kicked a small rock that was in front of his foot. It grieved him the way he just summarized Maxie's intentions, casting her in a light that made her look as if she were a manipulating woman of ill-intent. When in all due honesty, he had no idea of what her intentions were. But he purposed in his heart to find out, and to find out soon.

* * * * * * * * * *

Maxie finally arrived at Spanky's. Just as she put her hand on the door to go inside, she heard her name being called. As she turned to look behind her, she heard her name again.

"Maxie, I'm over here." Directly across the street, she saw Marc standing in a black trench coat.

"Hi, I thought you said you wanted to meet here at the restaurant," she said, as she walked across the street. "You changed your mind?"

When she was closer to him, Maxie observed a look on Marc's face that she was not accustomed to seeing. It was somber and full of worry, and he tried to force a smile in an effort to greet her anyway.

"Hi yourself. I wanted to meet you over here first," Marc said plainly, with both of his hands in his coat pockets.

Maxie stood directly in front of him with a deep look of concern. Searching his eyes, she watched him avert her gaze by looking at the ground and then back at her, letting his smile relax and fade, only to force it up again.

"What's wrong?" Maxie asked softly.

Marc looked at her. Relieved at her concern for what was troubling him, he suddenly felt overwhelmed. "Maxie, can I just hold you right now?"

Wanting to fix whatever was wrong, and to heal whatever pain Marc was feeling, Maxie immediately stepped forward without another thought, and allowed him to fully embrace her. Instantly, she felt something between them that quite possibly should have never been. As Marc held on to her, she noticed she was holding on to him as well. With her arms inside of his coat, and her head resting just above his chest, she felt the exact firmness she imagined the very first time she met him.

Maxie felt Marc sigh heavily. "Please tell me what's wrong," she whispered.

Marc squeezed Maxie a little, before he released her and took a step back. "I'm sorry. I just needed a hug from a friend. I'm all right. I promise." When Maxie looked at him skeptically, he smiled and kissed her on her forehead. "Don't worry. I'm fine." Marc took another step away from her, and put his hands back into his coat pockets.

"So you're not going to tell me what this is all about? You've scared me Marc. I think I deserve an explanation."

"You're everything I need. Do you know that?" Marc said sincerely. "You're the kind of friend everyone needs."

"That's not an answer."

Marc looked across the street, and with his hands still in his pockets, he motioned toward Spanky's. "Do you have enough time to join me for pizza?"

"You aren't going to tell me are you?"

Marc stared at her briefly before he spoke. "I will. Soon. I promise. Now can you join a friend for pizza?"

Maxie gazed at him pensively, before she looked at her watch. It was 4:30 p.m. "All right," she said in a tone of resignation. "But I'm buying."

Chapter Thirty-Eight

Although it was 6:30 p.m., and they both knew she needed to get home, neither Marc nor Maxie wanted to leave the company of the other. After feeling a heavy cloud of conviction, Marc knew it was time to walk Maxie to her car. The realization of just how much time had actually passed, came when they both left the restaurant and looked into the dark evening sky.

After Maxie settled into her car and rolled her window down, Marc stood in the direct flow of light from a street lamp above them. "I hope your husband won't be too angry with you. What are you going to say to him if he questions you?"

"You mean *when* he questions me don't you?" Maxie smiled. "I'll just tell him I had to minister to someone in need. A friend."

"Is that going to work? I mean, will that be enough?"

Maxie laughed a little. "He's not a tyrant Marc. He may blow a little bit of steam, but I can handle it."

Marc nodded. "I just don't want to put you in a position where you feel you have to lie to him again, because of me."

Maxie stared at him for a brief moment. "I don't believe that will happen again."

Marc smiled slightly. "Good. I don't want anything to keep us from seeing each other."

At that instant, Maxie wanted to tell Marc she would never allow anything to come between them, but she thought better of it and said nothing.

"So will I get to see you before Thanksgiving?" Marc asked.

"*Before* Thanksgiving? That would be tomorrow."

"Mmm humm. You're not working are you?"

"Not at Food King. But I am doing some work at the church. I'll be delivering Thanksgiving baskets to some elderly and needy families for the better part of the day. What did you have in mind?"

Marc looked at the passing headlights of the traffic, which was still quite heavy. Focusing on Maxie again, he smiled mischievously. "So you're doing this alone tomorrow?"

"The deliveries? Yes, I'll be doing them alone. Why?"

"Would you like some company?"

"Who? You?" Maxie asked, with a quick laugh.

"What? I've served the community before. I used to be a bell ringer for the Salvation Army at Christmastime when I was younger."

Maxie laughed even harder.

Marc looked at the traffic again. "Okay, now she's laughing at me."

Maxie put her hand over her mouth, and tried to stop the laughter. "I'm sorry. I'm not laughing at you."

"Well you're not laughing *with* me. So what's so funny?"

"I don't know. I was just picturing you of all people, in a Santa Claus hat, ringing a bell for money." Maxie burst into laughter again.

"Hey, there was nothing wrong with a young brother developing a sense of community."

"Is that what you called it?"

Marc pressed his lips together to keep from laughing with Maxie. "Do you want company tomorrow or not?"

Maxie regained her composure, but Marc could see she was trying hard to stifle her amusement.

"Yes Mr. Thomas. I would love the pleasure of having your company on tomorrow. But I have to tell you that it might be a little mundane. I mean, you may not find it very appealing."

"Just being in your company will be appealing enough for me," Marc said sincerely. "Besides, I think I'll enjoy seeing the *servant* side of you. So do I meet you at your church?"

Maxie laughed a little. "Uh ... no. Meet me at the shopping center on the corner of Abercorn and Montgomery around ten-thirty. We can go in my car."

Marc nodded his head lightly, and focused on the traffic again. Putting his hands in his coat pockets, he set his sight back on Maxie. From the moment she agreed to meet him at Spanky's, his mind harbored an asinine thought that kept resurfacing. It beckoned him to entertain it, but because of better judgment, he didn't. But right now he couldn't help it. At the risk of being selfish, and for the first time since they'd met, Marc wished Maxie was not married. She was rapidly showing herself to be the kind of person anyone would want to have around, and he wanted to spend more time with her. He didn't want that time to be taxed with any of the other commitments she had, including her commitment to her husband.

Maxie noticed the intense look on Marc's face, and considered asking him where his thoughts were. Instead, she looked at the clock on her dash, and saw that she was over an hour and a half late getting home. Looking back at Marc, she opened her mouth to speak, only to have him interrupt her.

"I know you have to get home. I'm just not ready for you to leave me yet."

Maxie smiled coyly. "You'll see me again tomorrow."

Marc assessed Maxie for a moment. "I will won't I?"

Maxie started her car and turned on her headlights. The simple gestures jolted her thought pattern to Lester, causing a slight twinge of paranoia to creep upon her. "I really have to go," she said. "Ten-thirty tomorrow?"

Marc moved closer to the car, and extended his hand to Maxie. Because it wasn't extended in the position of a handshake, Maxie knew he purposed it to be a point of contact, so she grasped it without hesitation. Squeezing her hand gently, Marc looked at her as if it pained him to only hold her hand.

"Thank you for coming to me when I needed you Maxie. That meant a lot to me."

"That's what friends are for Marc. Right there when you need them."

Marc squeezed her hand a little tighter, before he let go. "Goodnight."

"See you tomorrow," Maxie winked, and rolled up her window.

Marc put his hands back into his coat pockets, and watched as Maxie pulled off into traffic. In spite of how he felt earlier, and the turbulence that roiled inside, the evening brought him an angel of peace, and he was grateful for it.

He couldn't wait until tomorrow.

* * * * * * * * * *

On the way home, Maxie thought more about Marc, and the reason for meeting him, than she did the antagonistic encounter she might face with Lester, for getting home late. Because she had never seen Marc with a solemn look on his face, it worried her as to what might be the reason for his discontent. Even during their conversation over pizza at Spanky's, she was unable to get him to commit a few words to what was actually bothering him, and why he arranged their meeting with a tone of urgency. It meant nothing for her to drop everything she was doing, to be there when he needed her. Like she told him, that's what friends do. Besides that, it was her Christian duty to offer assistance to the hurting soul, and to avail herself to those who were broken hearted, and heavy laden — of which Marc was a definite casualty. She just wanted the opportunity to fix whatever was wrong. More than anything, Maxie could not stand to see the look of anguish in place of Marc's normal smiling face. She was definitely going to have to remedy the situation if it continued. Tonight, she allowed him to have distinct ownership of his dilemma. Tomorrow, she intended to make him share it.

When she pulled up into the driveway next to Lester's car, Maxie fully expected to be charged and drilled before she got out of her car. Instead, she was greeted by total silence, except for the sound of a barking dog somewhere down the street. All of the lights in the house were off, and the only light she could identify was the ever-changing glow of the television set in the living room. Because she saw it done in a movie once, Maxie touched the hood of Lester's car to see if it was still warm. When she didn't get the result she was hoping for, she groaned inwardly. The cold hood told her that Lester had not gone anywhere for some time, and that he may have been sitting at home alone since 6:00 p.m., or 6:30. If that was the case, he had been sitting in her absence for an hour and a half, because it was now almost 7:30.

When she put her key into the door lock, Maxie took a deep breath to calm the anxiety that tried to grip her. Because she thought only of Marc on her way home, she didn't really have anything prefabricated for Lester. She had no other recourse except for the truth as to why she was not home when he arrived, and why there was no dinner prepared and on the table. Besides, she didn't want to lie to Lester again, and she told Marc she wouldn't.

Once the kitchen door was opened, Maxie started to turn on the light, but changed her mind because the television in the living room was casting enough light for her to find the entryway. When she set her purse and keys on the kitchen table, Maxie wondered why Lester had not come in to acknowledge her arrival. She didn't really expect him to have a genial attitude considering her tardiness, but she did want to see that he was at least concerned about her getting home safely. Being able to drive up into the driveway at night, with no welcoming committee was odd enough. But to walk into the house with jingling keys in hand, and the gentle click of a closing door, signaling her arrival, and still no welcoming response? That was totally unexpected.

Maxie continued toward the living room. At the threshold of the doorway, she saw Lester sitting on the couch. Her eyes met his, but because of the continual flickering of the television's light, she couldn't read the expression on his face. He was obviously relaxed, because his feet were stretched out in front of him, and he was leaning against the armrest with his arms folded across his chest.

"Why are you sitting in the dark?" Maxie asked, as she walked opposite him to turn on the table lamp. When the light immersed the area, Maxie continued to stand and look at her husband. Without answering her, Lester turned his focus back to the television.

Before she sat on the couch, Maxie took a deep breath and exhaled it slowly. Lester was obviously upset with her, but she wasn't going to allow him to give her the silent treatment.

"Lester. ..."

"Did the meeting at the church last a little longer than planned?" He asked dryly, without looking at her.

Maxie stared at him incredibly. He was actually asking her a question he already knew the answer to. If she didn't know him better, she would believe he was essentially expecting her to lie to him.

"I don't know if it did or not Lester. I ...."

"I know, because you left early," he chided, still focused on the television.

Maxie simply nodded her head.

"May I ask what was so important to you, that you had to leave before everyone else at the church was finished?" He asked.

"Are you checking up on me?" Maxie furrowed her brows so deeply; her eyes almost looked like slits. She knew the expression on her face alone, being the one in the wrong, was enough to send Lester over the edge.

Straightening himself and sitting forward, he looked at Maxie with a hard stare.

"I called the church to see where my *wife* was, since she wasn't at home when I got here. I knew you were supposed to be there, because you volunteered to help with the baskets. But when I called there at six-fifteen, Blanche told me you left hours ago, in some mad rush. What was the rush Maxie? What was it that could keep you from having dinner ready, and cause you to walk through the door two hours later than you should have? Did you even finish your work at the church?"

Maxie allowed her facial expression to relax, as she searched Lester's eyes before she spoke. The tension that now filled the room, grew exponentially in his face. She couldn't remember him ever being so angry with her.

"Yes, I finished," she said softly, and let silence fall between them.

"I'm listening Maxie," Lester finally quipped. "You've only answered one of my questions."

"I'm sorry I'm late Lester. I. ..."

"I didn't ask for an apology. I asked for an explanation."

Maxie started to turn her ring around on her finger, but immediately stopped, in order to concentrate on the words that would help her explain herself truthfully.

Truthfully?

Where did that thought come from? How is it that lying all of a sudden became an option? Maxie asked herself. Without taking that question any further, she gathered her words and tried to let them flow.

"First of all, let me start by saying I didn't leave the Hall in a mad rush. I got a message that someone needed to be ministered to, so I. ..."

"*You* got a message?" Lester piped skeptically. "*You* were requested to go and minister to somebody? Why did they call for you? Why didn't they call on one of the other real ministers? One who was already there in the Fellowship Hall and available? Blanche didn't say anything about you getting a message."

With regard for the possible threat of having to explain *how* she got the message, Maxie remained silent. Instead, she considered the tone in Lester's voice and his deliberate choice of words, as he insinuated what she knew he felt from the very beginning — *she had no ministry.*

In the simplest way possible, her husband struck her down with the meanest, most callous words he had ever said to her; and for the first time since they were married, Lester's rhetoric loudly proclaimed that she had no business ministering to anyone at any time. If an ordained minister was available, he should be the one to address the problem at hand. If one was not available, then one should be sought out. Whether she could effectively handle the problem or not, was not the issue. Her place was to be silent. She heard it all before, just not from the lips of her husband.

Until now.

It was so plain. Her ministry was to him, and him only. Lester's expectations of her as his wife were no secret. He expected Maxie to govern herself according to the Word of God, and that's what she did in honoring him, and trying to be obedient to his every word. But was that to *totally* define who she was? Was honoring him her only purpose?

Lester continued to rant, while Maxie looked at the floor. For some odd reason, she didn't want Lester to see the impact of his statement in her eyes, which were brimming with water. Swallowing hard, Maxie felt belittled, confused, and almost angry. How could the evening go from something so positive, to something so incredibly negative? One moment, she's being told that everyone needs somebody like her in their life. The next moment, it's implied that she's not qualified to minister into the life of anyone, in any capacity. Maxie went from feeling important, to feeling almost totally insignificant.

"Did you even think to call me to let me know you were alright?" Lester went on. "You didn't call, you didn't leave a message with anyone at the church, and you didn't even so much as leave a note for me here at the house, explaining where you were."

"I'm sorry. Time just slipped away from me," Maxie croaked.

"Maxie this is so unlike you. Who was the person you had to talk to?"

Maxie nodded her head negatively, and wiped her eyes with the heels of her hands. Slowly, she stood up feeling fatigued and battle weary. The harshness of Lester's tongue-lashing seemingly took away all of her strength.

"What difference does it make Lester?" She shrugged. "If you're hungry, I can fix you something to eat." Without waiting for his response, Maxie began to make a slow trek into the kitchen.

"Maxine, it's not as easy as that!" Lester yelled and stood up. "You're in the wrong here, and you owe me an explanation!"

Maxie stopped dead in her tracks, and whirled herself around quickly. "What do you want me to say Lester?" She yelled back. "I know I was wrong! And I said I was sorry! But you don't want to hear that! So what do you want me to say huh? What do you want me to say? Forgive me Lord, I was out of order! I shouldn't have tried to minister to anyone! I should have been in the house before it got dark, and I should have had dinner ready! Forgive me! I never should have tried to be a help to someone in need, because it's not my place! Is that what you want to hear? Is that what you need to hear me say?" Maxie felt the tears coming back to her eyes. Only this time they were burning, so she let them fall freely as she looked at Lester.

Taken aback by her fuming response, Lester stood still and observed his wife. Nodding his head slowly, he looked around the living room until he saw his coat hanging on the door to their bedroom. Quickly, he retrieved it and walked past Maxie, into the kitchen.

"I'm going to get something to eat," he said, in a low cold tone.

Without looking at her, Lester walked out of the house and slammed the door behind him, causing Maxie to jump. Standing still for a moment, she thought about all that just transpired. Leaning her back against the wall, Maxie slowly slid down to the floor and cried uncontrollably.

* * * * * * * * *

Lester returned home an hour later with an apology, a hug, and a kiss, to mollify each of them. It was only right that their argument concluded with Ephesians 4:26, but at 11:45 p.m., Maxie lay in bed wide-awake because her spirit was still troubled. As she listened to Lester's light snore, she wondered how he could sleep so soundly, after using words that basically stripped her down to nothing. Everything he said to her could have erased the words of her grandmother and Sister Adams, concerning the will of God for her life, but Maxie used their words and the scriptures she remembered, to cover her like a Band-Aid. Scriptures like Acts 2:18, and Joel 2:28, supported what she knew about women who ministered. She also knew it wasn't for just a certain time in the past that women operated in some form of ministry. It was happening right now, in the present.

Maxie turned away from Lester, and sighed heavily. Surely being a minister himself, a devout man of God, he had to know those same scriptures. More than anything, he had to either know, or come to realize that she was more than just a submissive wife. She did have a purpose, and God was using her *in* that purpose.

With all she pondered, Maxie surmised the only way Lester was going to see that she had a ministry, was through some kind of proof other than the scriptures. That proof was going to be the salvation of Marc Thomas.

Chapter Thirty-Nine

On the eve of Thanksgiving Day, Maxie waited for Marc in the shopping center as planned. Parking in a spot visible to both Abercorn and Montgomery Street traffic, she sat in her car and sipped on a cappuccino. In spite of the shining sun, the morning was a bit colder than Maxie expected. It would be okay if she was able to stay nestled in the warmth of her car, but she had nine Thanksgiving baskets that had to be delivered. So that was nine occasions to brave the cold, and the very thought made her shudder.

Maxie took a swallow of her drink, and surveyed the area around her. It was 10:45 a.m., and still no sign of Marc. With her back seat and trunk full of Thanksgiving baskets, she had to consider that the later it got, the later she would be out going door to door. Just as she was about to start her car and slowly canvas the parking lot, she heard the gentle hum of her cell phone vibrating in her purse. Quickly she retrieved it and flipped it open. *Good morning beautiful* was the text message. Smiling, Maxie began to type her reply when another message came through. *Been waiting long?* And then another one, *I'm looking forward to being with you today.* Before another message came through, Maxie dialed Marc's cell phone number.

"Hello?" Marc answered.

"Good morning. I haven't had the displeasure of experiencing your tardiness before now," Maxie said.

"Really?" Marc responded coolly. "You still haven't experienced it. I'm just waiting for you to finish your coffee."

Maxie opened her mouth to reply, but stopped to think about what Marc just said, and to listen to the sound of passing cars in the background. Looking out each side window, Maxie spoke with a hint of skepticism in her voice.

"What do you mean you're waiting for me to finish my coffee? How do you know I'm drinking coffee?"

"You've been drinking it for ahhh … the last fifteen minutes or so."

"Marc how … where are you?"

"I'm right behind you," he said with a little laugh.

Maxie looked in the rearview mirror. Standing dead center, was Marc with a big smile. Maxie returned his smile, thinking how much happier he looked to her than when she saw him yesterday. Without hesitation, he walked to the passenger side and opened the door.

"You've been standing out there for fifteen minutes? Marc it's cold out there."

"I was sitting in my car. I've only been out here for about five minutes. Even so, seeing that face of yours warmed my insides," Marc grinned as he got in.

Maxie looked at him with a *give me a break* grimace on her face, and started her car.

"Too corny for this time of morning huh?" He asked.

"Mmmm," she responded.

"Yeah," Marc whispered to himself, and put on his seatbelt.

Maxie put her car in reverse, and turned around in her seat to guide it backwards. With her hand behind the passenger seat, she was daringly close to Marc's handsome face. So close in fact, she could smell the residue of a breath mint he had in his mouth earlier. With Marc so near to her, Maxie lost track of what she was doing, and barely pushed the accelerator to complete the backward motion. Out of nowhere, a twinge of desire gripped the pit of her stomach and rose to her brain, causing her to focus on Marc's lips.

"Good morning to you too," he smiled, and gently kissed her on her cheek. "Doesn't the Bible say to greet one another with a kiss?"

Maxie looked at him with surprise, and then amusement. "You're so cocky. Do you know that?"

"Yeah, but you can greet me like that on the next time."

Maxie nodded her head in disbelief, and continued driving out of the parking lot. It was imperative for her at that moment, to not give consideration to the desire that tried to hold her captive just moments ago.

"So how was your night?" She asked. "I was worried about you."

Marc looked out of his window, and then at Maxie. "The question is, how was your night?"

Maxie's eyes met his briefly, but she said nothing. Nodding his head assuredly, Marc looked away. "He was angry with you wasn't he?"

"Yes," she answered lowly.

"Are you okay?"

"He said some things that were hurtful. But I'm a big girl. I'll get over it." Maxie looked at him and smiled.

Barely lifting his mouth into half a smile, Marc nodded and looked away. "Do you believe that all of this is worth it Maxie?"

"All of what?"

"The lying, the sneaking, the pain."

"Do I believe our friendship is worth it?"

"Yeah," Marc said, finally looking at her.

Maxie thought about their friendship for a moment, before she answered. Although some negative things had transpired since they'd met, Maxie knew it was all one-sided. All of the negative characteristics were stemming from her, and she believed it was all because of what she was trying to accomplish. Naturally, she should expect to have some form of adversity. She was working toward a greater good. So any impairment that happened along the way, would simply be chalked up as collateral damage — or better yet, a sacrifice.

"You're hesitating," Marc said.

"No, I'm not hesitating. I believe in what we have Marc. So I guess I'd have to say yes. I think it's worth it."

"Why? What are you getting out of it? I mean, what do you expect to get?" Marc was glad he opened the door to the question that was troubling him. Now he would know if Maxie had something to do with any part of his dilemma.

"Honestly?" Maxie asked.

"Of course."

"Well, first of all, I'm not getting anything out of it, other than I enjoy your company, and I like how I feel when I'm with you."

Marc and Maxie looked at each other and smiled.

424

"Is that all?" He asked.

"Marc, what's going on? Where are you going with all of these questions? Is there something specific you want me to say?"

"Just checking you out," he answered, looking out of his window again.

"I thought you already did that all those times you were coming into the store," she teased.

"True, but that was for me. I knew I wanted your friend-ship, but you were a little more apprehensive in the beginning. Downright cold. So I want to know what you see in me. What made you warm up to me?"

Maxie parked her car in front of a house, and took off her seatbelt.

"What are you doing?" Marc asked.

"This is my first delivery."

Marc looked out of his window at a small white run-down house, with an equally worn down chain link fence. Inside the fence, toys were strewn everywhere, on a sparsely patched lawn. Maxie got out of the car and opened the door to her back seat. After acquainting himself with the side of town they were on, Marc got out of the car also.

"Is it okay for me to help you with these?" He asked.

"Okay?"

"Yeah, is it okay?"

Maxie looked at Marc quizzically.

"I don't want you to have to explain who I am," Marc said.

"You should've thought about that yesterday when you asked to come," Maxie laughed.

Marc stood still, and watched as Maxie quickly walked to the rear of the car, and disappeared behind her open trunk. After a moment, she peeked at him.

"So are you going to admire the scenery here, or do you want to carry this turkey?"

Marc laughed, and came to Maxie's aid. Allowing her to lead the way, he followed closely, carrying the box of goods. Maxie's arrival was expected, because just as she was about to knock on the door, it opened quickly. A short, heavy set, dark woman stood in the doorway with her sight set directly on Marc. While Maxie greeted the woman with a hug, and a kiss on the cheek, Marc set the box on the floor just inside the door as was suggested. When the woman kept looking at him with an inquiring gaze, Maxie finally introduced him by name, and as a community volunteer who was assisting the church with the holiday deliveries. Maxie made sure the visit was short and sweet. She knew if they stayed one moment longer, the woman would begin to change the topics of their idle chatter, and make Marc the subject, wanting to know everything about him.

"Well God bless you," Maxie said. "And you have a wonderful Thanksgiving."

Once they were back inside the car, Marc released a little laughter. "You're something else, you know that?"

Maxie put her seatbelt on, started the car, and pulled away from the curb. "Why? What did I do?"

"I'm a community volunteer now?"

"Well I had to say something that sounded legitimate. What else was I going to say? That you're a friend of mine who just wanted to spend some time with me?"

"That's the truth."

"I didn't lie to the woman Marc."

"Ah, but you did deceive."

"Would you stop already? You are a volunteer who lives and works in a community, and since you're helping me to do a work for my church, you are assisting the church."

Marc put both of his hands up in surrender. "Whatever you say pretty lady," he grinned.

After they shared a quick laugh, the two were silent for a moment.

"So are you going to answer the question I posed to you earlier?" Marc asked.

"What made me change my mind about you?"

"Yes."

"Honestly?"

"Yes."

"Well ... to be *honest* ..." Maxie glanced at Marc. "I thought it would be interesting to have a man as a friend."

"Interesting or challenging?"

Maxie glanced at him again. "I guess a little bit of both."

"I say that the scale leans heavily on the side of challenging."

"You would," Maxie mumbled.

"I'm glad you accepted the challenge," Marc said, with sincerity. "I don't know what I would have done if you decided otherwise. Other than Shari, I'm not well versed when it comes to rejection." Marc looked out the window again. "I guess it's safe to say that I really haven't had a whole lot of experience in that area."

Maxie glanced at Marc quickly, and tried to study his face for a hint of humor. "See what I mean?" She laughed. "You are so cocky. Now you're telling me that other than your ex-girlfriend, no other women have rejected you."

"Is that what I'm saying?" Marc asked with a pretentious look on his face, before he too burst into laughter.

"Naw, I'm just kidding around with you. You know I'm nothing like that."

"I don't know," Maxie drawled.

"Oh come on."

Maxie continued laughing, as she parked her car in front of another house. Just as before, she and Marc did the delivery together. For the remaining names on Maxie's list, Marc assumed the position of helper, as if the job was cut out for him; even introducing himself with his name, and the title Maxie had given him.

When they finished with the last house and were walking away, Maxie looked up and stopped immediately at the sight of an old gold Cadillac parked in the street, parallel to her car. She recognized the vehicle instantly, and equally as fast, her heart dropped and her stomach knotted when the owner opened the car door and stood up.

Marc stopped with Maxie, and saw her facial expression change to a look of dread. Following the direction of her eyes, he saw the car that was parked so close to hers, there was no way she could get in on the driver's side.

"Well fancy meeting you here," Deacon Earl called out, with a bit more twang than Maxie wanted to hear. "There must have been some kind of a mix up with our lists. You had the Pettigrew family on your list too?"

"Why yes ..." Maxie stammered. After the seconds of initial shock passed, she walked toward her car again with Marc in tow. "Don't tell me you have a basket for them too, Deacon Earl." Maxie looked at Marc, as she put emphasis on the name, hoping he would understand how official this sudden encounter was.

Marc already decided that he was going to let Maxie handle everything. He just looked at Deacon Earl and smiled, waiting for Maxie to introduce him. Deacon Earl continued to stand with one foot inside of his car, and the other on the street. Quickly he pulled his list off the seat and began to examine it, all the while glancing at Marc.

"Yeah, I do believe the heads of that Union have messed up this time, Sister Bruce."

Maxie picked up quickly on how Deacon Earl was watching Marc. When they reached her car, she started her formal introduction. "Deacon Earl Bayer, allow me to introduce a friend ... an acquaintance of mine. This is Mr. Marc Thomas. He's volunteering his services to the church today, and came along to help me with my deliveries."

Marc extended his hand on cue, as Deacon Earl quickly tossed his paper on the seat to grasp it. "How are you?" Marc asked.

Deacon Earl shook Marc's hand, but kept a skeptical look on his face. "I'm right fine this afternoon. Thank you for asking." Deacon Earl gave Marc the once over, as he released his hand. "Did you say a volunteer Sister Bruce? Don't see too many of those anymore."

Maxie hated the way Deacon Earl was darting his eyes suspiciously back and forth, between them. How dare he question her. "Actually, Mr. Thomas has a history of committing himself to volunteer work. He's been doing it since he was a young man," Maxie stated.

"Oh, I see. Well we're glad to have you on board Mr. Thomas. I'm sure Sister Bruce greatly appreciates your help."

Sensing a slight air of sarcasm, Marc caught Maxie's attention, "I'll wait for you in the car." Casually he extended his hand again. "It was nice meeting you Deacon."

Deacon Earl took his hand and quickly released it. "Same here."

Maxie watched Marc walk to the passenger's side of the car. Before he got in, he shot Maxie a glance with raised eyebrows.

"So this is why you didn't want to deliver your baskets with me," Deacon Earl motioned with his head, and a sinister smile.

Maxie glanced at how close the Deacon's car was to hers. She wanted so badly to slap his face at his blatant innuendo, and drive away. "Deacon Earl, I have a lot of things to do this afternoon, so if you wouldn't mind moving your car, I'll be able to get into mine and get on with the rest of my day."

Deacon Earl maintained his position, and assessed Maxie slowly from head to toe. Nodding his head pensively, he assessed her one more time before he practically hissed his words. "You be careful there Sister Bruce," he said in a low voice. "You don't want your good intentions to be evil spoken of. Having a handsome man like that in your company ... alone ... well it just doesn't look too good. I'd really hate to see you get all caught up in the game." Deacon Earl gave Maxie a fateful smile.

Maxie closed her eyes for a brief moment. Though it was cold outside, she suddenly felt warmth from the inside out. "What game would that be Deacon?"

"Oh you know. The one where you give people something to talk about. Something to accuse you of. Everybody gossips. And then you're left having to defend yourself. Defending your actions ..." Deacon Earl glanced at Marc. "... as innocent as they may be."

"I'm sure you would know a great deal about that," Maxie said, looking at him directly.

Deacon Earl held his smile. "Well, you have yourself a real nice Thanksgiving now. And tell *your husband,* I said hello." Deacon Earl winked at Maxie as he got back into his car, and drove away.

Maxie wanted to spew more words at him, but instead, pressed her lips together tightly. Remaining still, she looked at the ground and tried to regain her composure before getting back into her car. Deacon Earl was the last person she wanted to see while she was with Marc. Though she didn't really want to consider it, the sudden encounter with the Deacon made her question herself. What was she thinking when she agreed to have Marc accompany her? Why didn't she at least consider the fact that Lester would somehow hear about her *good looking* escort?

Maxie felt the sudden chill of the brisk wind, and shivered against it. When she got back into her car, she knew Marc's eyes were on her, but she refused to look at him. "Are you hungry?" She asked, as she started the car and pulled away from the curb. "That was the last house on the list. What do you have a taste for?"

Marc knew Maxie hoped her conversation with Deacon Earl was not heard. If he did hear it, she'd want him to ignore everything that was said, but he couldn't. Before he could answer her questions or say any other words to her, Maxie turned on her music and started humming.

Marc casually turned the volume down and stared at her. "Maxie. ..."

"Marc, don't," she said with her hand up. "Please don't."

"I don't want you hurt, or talked about. This isn't worth it."

Maxie abruptly pulled her car next to the curb, and turned off the ignition. Looking at Marc firmly, she unleashed her feelings. "What do you mean it's not worth it Marc? Are you saying that our friendship isn't worth a little aggravation sometimes? Do you think I care about what that man said to me? I don't."

"But what about Lester, Maxie? You think this won't get back to him? When I said it's not worth it, I'm talking about you being hurt unnecessarily."

"Marc, do you enjoy being with me?"

"I love being with you. It's just that …."

"And I love being with you. Being with you is not just a challenge. There's a freedom I feel inside of me when I'm with you. I don't have to do anything to be pleasing to you, because that pressure is not there. I don't have to choose my words carefully because anything I have to say, I can say it without being judged. I feel like you hang on to my every word Marc. I enjoy talking to you, and I love to hear your voice whenever we talk on the phone. I love the warmth of your smile, and I can't even explain how I feel every time I see you. Even your cockiness amuses me." Maxie laughed a little, and then became serious again. "Don't say you want to take all of that away from me, just because you heard a few threatening words from a man who couldn't walk the straight and narrow if that was all there was in front of him. What he said means nothing to me. I value what we have more. I don't care about the repercussions."

Marc gently stroked Maxie's cheek. "I didn't know you felt that way," he said in a low tone.

Maxie leaned into his touch, and grinned. "For what other reasons would I put up with you?"

"And here I was, thinking it was all about my good looks."

Maxie laughed. "Your good looks are what got you in the door."

"Oh! See?" Marc laughed.

Maxie started her car again. "Let's go get something to eat Mr. Thomas. I'm starved."

Chapter Forty

~⨍~

Maxie was glad Thanksgiving had come and gone. At the last minute, Lester decided the two of them should entertain his three sisters and their families for the holiday, so she had a lot of work to do. She cooked the majority of the meal, and all of the desserts at the request of her husband, to which she received rave reviews, but the end of the evening could not come soon enough. Even though she had a great relationship with her sisters-in-law and their families, she longed for the time when they would all go home. Feeling guilty about his late request, Lester helped around the house in an effort to make things easier for her, but it was her thoughts of Marc that kept tedium at bay.

Maxie couldn't help but to think about everything that transpired Wednesday, including what Marc thought about it all. When they sat down to lunch at Chili's restaurant in Midtown that day, she refused to let the whole *Deacon Earl* ordeal, be the topic of their conversation. So she didn't get a chance to hear if Marc had any further views on the matter. The only communication she had with him since

434

the incident was Thanksgiving morning, when he sent her a text message telling her to enjoy her holiday, and that he would be thinking of her. Maxie in return, texted back the same sentiment.

Now, mid Friday morning, as she sat alone in her kitchen sipping a hot flavored tea, she considered calling Marc to let him know she had taken the day off, and if he was available, she'd like to spend it with him. Maybe he could take her to shoot pool, or show her how to ice skate like he promised.

Smiling to herself, Maxie replayed all of the words she expressed to Marc, on how she felt about their time together. It felt so good to be able to tell him how comfortable she was with him. She found a true friend in Marc, and his sweet demeanor only enhanced what she felt about him.

Maxie finished her tea, and put her cup into the sink. Just as she was beginning her trek into the living room, a loud rap on the kitchen door startled her. She tried to identify the silhouette through the curtain panel, but the morning sunlight didn't cast a defining shadow. All she could figure was that the person was of medium height. When the knock came again, Maxie moved to the door quickly and peeked through the curtain. Closing the curtain, she waited a moment before she opened the door. It was Sandra.

"I was told this was the place I needed to come to, if I wanted a delicious piece of leftover sweet potato pie," Sandra said. "Do you mind if I come in?"

"Your voice sounds familiar, but I can't say I recognize the face, because I haven't seen it for a few weeks now," Maxie replied.

"Well, if you open the door some more, I can come in and we can get reacquainted."

Maxie allowed Sandra to come in, and then closed the door. While Sandra hung her coat on the back of a kitchen chair, Maxie retrieved a piece of pie from the refrigerator.

"The pie is cold. Do you want me to warm it in the microwave?"

"Sounds good," Sandra said, as she sat at the table. "How was your holiday feast?"

"It was good. We entertained Lester's sisters this year."

"You cooked?"

"My house, my kitchen. How was your Thanksgiving?" Maxie removed the pie from the microwave, and set it in front of Sandra, before she sat opposite her.

"Quiet. I ordered a take-out dinner. How's the job going? You're still there right?"

"Yeah. It's great. I don't know if I told you, but they might be looking at making me a Shift Leader."

"Get out of here," Sandra drawled.

Maxie nodded and beamed.

"And Lester? How is he?"

Maxie looked at the floor briefly. "He's good."

Sandra nodded, smiled, and started eating.

"So how have you been Sandra?" Maxie asked sincerely. "The last time we spoke ...."

"You mean the last time you chewed me out, right?"

Maxie looked at the table and sighed. "Yeah. I'm sorry about that. Please forgive me."

"It's cool. I didn't take it to heart."

"So why haven't I heard from you before now?"

"I don't know. Did you try calling me? Maybe you left a message. If you did, I must've missed it."

Maxie looked at Sandra with a smirk.

"I figured as much," Sandra said. "That doesn't matter either. I've been meaning to touch base with you a few times, but I've been working like a Hebrew slave since we merged with Sony. I had to press pause. I haven't even had time for a little romantic rendezvous. Now you know that's something!"

The two women laughed.

"How did you know I was home? Normally I would be at work, but I asked for the day off.

Sandra quickly glanced at her, and continued eating.

"Okay," Maxie drawled knowingly. "Do you want something to drink? Coffee? Milk?"

"Ice water will be fine."

Maxie retrieved the water, and sat down again.

"So tell me what's been going on in your life lately," Sandra said. "Since I haven't seen you or talked to you in the past few weeks, I feel like I've missed out on so much."

Maxie looked at Sandra skeptically. "I find that hard to believe. Remember, you know everything about me."

Sandra glanced at Maxie again, and indulged herself in sweet potato pie and silence.

Maxie was glad to see her friend after her lengthy absence. She didn't really notice how much time actually passed since the two of them had spoken, but it was just as well. There was no new topic she wanted to discuss anyway.

When she finished, Sandra walked to the kitchen sink and set her dishes down. Instead of returning to her seat, she leaned against the counter and crossed her arms. Maxie kept her back to her and pretended not to see peripherally.

"So how's everything going at the church? Are Fric, Frac, and Jack, still messing with you?"

Maxie laughed a little. "You mean The Ominous Three? Girl, their life would not be complete if they didn't have somebody else's life to dig into. I'm glad to say it's not mine this time."

Sandra nodded assuredly. "That's a little odd for them isn't it? I mean, seeing how there is so much going on in *your* life right now."

Maxie slightly tilted her head toward the ceiling, and heaved a sigh. *I knew it*, she mouthed to herself. From the time she peeked through the kitchen window, and saw Sandra standing at the door, she knew there was no way this was going to be a casual visit. Without turning around to face her, Maxie faked a little laugh. "What are you talking about Sandra?"

"So now you don't know what I'm talking about?"

"Did you come over here to pick up where we left off on the phone?" Maxie quipped, with her head half turned toward Sandra. "Because if you did, I'm putting a stop to it right now."

Sandra casually walked back to her chair and sat down. Leaning forward, she looked at Maxie squarely, but Maxie looked at the floor. "How long has it been Maxie? Did it happen when I said it would happen?"

Maxie refused to acknowledge Sandra, and kept her eyes downcast.

"God!" Sandra exclaimed, as she thrust herself against the back of her chair. "You're already in it aren't you?"

Maxie glared and raised her voice. "In what Sandra? What are you accusing me of?"

"That guy from the store. You're spending time with him aren't you?"

"What difference does it make? Marc and I are friends."

"Friends," Sandra said, wryly.

"Yes friends. As if you need to know, he's a designer and a gemologist for Whitley Jewelers, and he's helping me to put together a nice anniversary gift for Lester."

Sandra spoke with a strong hint of skepticism. "You know a lot about him don't you? So that's the ruse you two are using? Custom designed jewelry?"

"Sandra, I don't appreciate the way you're talking to me."

"And you'd appreciate it even less, if I weren't real with you Maxie. I told you this was going to happen. I tried to warn you, and you promised me that you would tell me when it did."

"Nothing is happening. I promised you if I had an *affair,* then I'd let you help me get through it. Hello? I am not having an affair, so there's nothing for you to help me through."

"Okay, then tell me this. How long have you two been spending time together? I mean, you *are* spending time together right?"

Maxie shrugged her shoulders. "Yeah, we get together to talk every now and then. Sometimes we get something to eat. That's what friends do. It's no big deal. And to answer your first question, we've been getting to know each other for about a month and a half now. So you see, you're getting all worked up over nothing Sandra."

Sandra took a deep breath, exhaled, and nodded her head gently. "You purposely didn't tell me about all of this. May I ask why?"

Maxie shrugged her shoulders again, and nodded her head. "It's not an issue for you to be concerned with. This is a portion of my ministry, and ...."

"Your ministry? Don't tell me you're using that one too."

Maxie narrowed her eyes. "Sandra, if I didn't love you so much, I'd tell you that right now, you need to leave."

"And Maxie, I wouldn't be sitting here saying all of this to you, if I didn't love *you* so much. Why can't you see what's happening? This is like the worst kind of trick. This game you're playing is dangerous!"

"Game? Sandra this is no game. I'm trying to save a soul."

"And lose yours in the process?"

Maxie huffed angrily. "Don't you talk to me about ...."

"Don't talk to you about what? Lost souls? Why? Because you think I am one? That's right isn't it? That's what you think. Where do you get off being so self-righteous Maxie?"

Maxie glared at Sandra, and then lowered her eyes.

"Let me hit you with this," Sandra said, with bite. "Remember how we met? You came to minister to me. You thought I was a wayward soul, needing your divine guidance to get my life on the right track. You remember that?"

Maxie remained still.

"Where am I now Maxie?" Sandra snapped. "Have I turned my life around yet? Does it even look like I'm headed in that direction? Maybe, just maybe you didn't have what it took back then, to convince me to give my life to Christ. And if you didn't have it then, for me, what makes you think that you have it now, for *Marc*?"

Maxie felt her heartbeat racing. In that moment, she couldn't identify what she was feeling. There was angst, confusion, pain, and betrayal, dancing on the inside of her. The more she thought about Sandra's words, the more pain was magnified.

Slowly, Maxie looked at Sandra with sad eyes, brimming with water. Another person had questioned her ministry — another person who was close to her. When their eyes met, Maxie saw anguish in Sandra's face. Frustrated, Sandra stood up and walked to a corner of the kitchen, obviously not wanting to look at Maxie at that moment.

"God," Sandra spewed, as she looked at the wall. "Maxie, I don't want to hurt you like this. I just don't want you to be fooled. I told you there was nothing on this side of the fence. I told you that."

"I am not on your side of the fence," Maxie said through sniffles.

Sandra took a paper towel from its roller on the counter, and went back to sit down. When she handed it to Maxie, she was reminded of the time Maxie said she wanted to change her walk with Christ.

"Whether you believe it or not, you're straddling that fence much more than you know."

"How do you …?" Maxie started.

"Do you remember the dream I told you? The one where I said you were feeding the Tasmanian devil at the zoo?" Maxie acknowledged with a gentle nod. "And all of those times I could tell you what was going to happen, before it actually happened, or identify your insecurities right at the moment you were feeling them, whether I was with you or not? Do you remember all of that?" Maxie met Sandra's eyes, and nodded again. "Maxie those weren't coincidences. Just like me coming over here to talk to you today. It's not a coincidence. You took the day off, because we were *supposed* to have this conversation."

Maxie squinted her eyes, and stared at Sandra quizzically. "What?"

Sandra looked up at the ceiling, took a deep breath, and exhaled. "I thought I'd never have to bring this up, because I've tried to deny it for most of my adult life, but it seems like it just won't leave me alone. The things I see, the things I know beforetime, there's a reason behind it. Maxie, there's nothing you can tell me about the church that I don't already know, because I was born in it. It was a huge part of my life until I graduated from high school. I lived a Christian lifestyle. My dad was the Senior Pastor of the church I attended."

Maxie closed her eyes for a moment to focus her thoughts. "You grew up in the church? When we first met, you told me you didn't know about God."

When we first met, I was in a pit of denial. I told you that I didn't have a *relationship* with God. I didn't want God's will for my life anymore. When I saw how church people acted no different than the common sinner, I wondered, what's the use in trying to be or do anything different? So I gave up, and did my own thing. But my gift never left me."

Maxie shook her head negatively. "And your gift is ...?"

"Prophecy."

"Prophecy?" Maxie whispered.

Sandra nodded. "Before I left the church I used to see visions, at night I'd dream dreams, and they'd all come true. For the most part, before I met you, all of that had subsided. It was still there, just not as much. And then after we met, well, it all started coming back to me like it never left."

"But how is that? I mean you party, you drink, you do *other* things."

"I know. When I was growing up, my daddy always expounded on Romans eleven and twenty nine, for the

442

sinner who once knew the way of salvation. It says, for the gifts and calling of ...."

"God are without repentance," Maxie chimed in.

"So I guess that's why I still have it."

"That's an awesome responsibility Sandra."

"Tell me about it. Why do you think I'm running from it? I couldn't even mention it to *you*."

Maxie nodded her head, and both women were silent for a moment.

"Maxie, I'm leaving for Tokyo Sunday morning, and I won't be back until the end of January. I'm being groomed for one of the positions of Acquisitions Manager, and I'm scared to leave you with all of this going on right now. That's why I'm here. I'm scared for you Maxie. Whatever it is, you have to end this thing with Marc."

At Sandra's last words, Maxie felt the impact of a door closing within her, shutting Sandra out. Little did she know, Sandra felt it also.

"At least promise me you'll move in that direction quickly," Sandra continued.

Maxie smiled a little. "Two months huh? Well congratulations. I'm glad you're moving up in the company, but I can't say the same about you going away from me. Who will I talk to?"

"You can call me anytime you want," Sandra said sincerely. "I'll make sure that I receive all of your calls, even if I'm in a meeting. I just won't be able to run to your aid. Tokyo is a little far."

Maxie reached out and embraced Sandra. "What am I going to do without you? Just when I'm feeling closer to you, you tell me that you're leaving."

"I know. This is hard for me too. Why don't we just hang out for the rest of the day? I'll finish packing tomorrow. We can shop the After Thanksgiving Day sales, and you can pick out your early Christmas gift."

Maxie pushed away from Sandra. "You're going to be in Japan, so I want something from Japan for Christmas. So we can go shop for *your* early Christmas gift."

"Sounds like a plan," Sandra smiled. "Are you ready to go? We can take my car."

"Let me grab my purse."

When Maxie left the kitchen, Sandra put on her jacket and exhaled as if she had been holding her breath the entire time. In all sincerity, what she was holding back were her tears. Tears for a friend in need. She had not cried for anyone in a long time. Nor was there the need to pray for someone else. But with all that was said and done, the only thing that was going to carry Maxie through would be prayer. Somebody was going to have to do it. And for the first time in a long time, that somebody would be her.

Chapter Forty-One

Instead of going to church on Sunday morning, Maxie asked Sandra to cancel the limousine service, and allow her the pleasure of taking her to the airport. Sandra happily agreed, and Maxie was grateful for the extra moments they would have together. After conversing for a couple of hours at a pub outside the terminal, Sandra convinced Maxie to make a few ridiculous promises. Before they knew it, the time had come for them to part ways. Because of heightened security measures at Savannah /Hilton Head International Airport, Sandra and Maxie had to say their goodbyes at the security check point entrance. Feeling very awkward in that moment, Maxie frantically fiddled around inside of her purse.

"What are you searching for Maxie? Somebody walking by might think you're giving that purse a shake down."

Maxie laughed nervously, and gave up the hunt. "Girl I don't know what I'm looking for."

Sandra studied her friend, only to observe Maxie unconsciously turning her ring around on her finger.

"You sad and nervous?" Sandra asked.

Maxie pressed her lips together tightly, and swallowed hard. "Yeah," she croaked.

"Aw man," Sandra almost whispered, as she looked around. "Don't do this, or you're going to make me cry too."

"I don't want you to go," Maxie said softly. As tears rolled down her cheeks, she let out a little nervous laughter again. "I meant it when I said I don't know what I'm going to do without you. I feel like everyone who has ever really meant anything to me, has either passed on, or moved on somewhere else. I think I'm starting to take it personal." Maxie tried to smile again, only to have it fade away quickly.

Sandra blinked hard, and tried to look everywhere except for at Maxie. "Hey, you know I'll be back in a couple of months, and I'm just a phone call away."

"My luck, you'll meet some good-looking Japanese man, and want to get married and stay overseas."

Both of the women laughed heartily.

"Girl, you know that ain't happening. I'll take an American brother any day, thank you."

Sandra looked at Maxie, who tried hard to hold her smile. Everything in Maxie's face read pain, in spite of her trying to hide it. Feeling the heat in her own face, Sandra looked at her watch, and then at a clock on the wall, before she shrugged. "My flight ...."

Maxie nodded, and swallowed hard again.

"Come 'ere," Sandra said, holding her arms out to Maxie. "I gotta go."

Maxie and Sandra embraced each other tightly, each giving words of encouragement, along with kisses on the cheek. When they finally separated, Maxie grinned at Sandra.

"I've never seen you cry before."

"I've never had an occasion like this one," Sandra said, wiping away her tears with her hand.

Maxie nodded. "You know I love you."

"I know. And I love you too."

Sandra put her carry-on bag on her shoulder, and leaned in to quickly embrace Maxie again. "Kiss Lester for me, okay?"

Maxie laughed a little. "I'll do that."

"You take care of yourself Maxie." Sandra began to walk away backwards. "And think about what I said okay?"

Maxie gave a slight smile, and mouthed, *I will*, as she waved slowly.

"I'll call you when I'm settled in. Remember they're nine hours ahead of us," Sandra called out.

Maxie nodded again, and watched as Sandra turned around to go through the security check lane. When she finished the scan, Sandra didn't turn around to wave. Instead, she continued to walk forward.

"Goodbye girl." Maxie whispered.

Almost in response, and without turning around, Sandra raised her hand, formed a fist, and then put up two fingers. Maxie smiled, and nodded. She interpreted Sandra's sign language to say *stay strong, it's only going to be for two months.*

* * * * * * * * * *

Maxie returned to work Monday, with a cloud of heaviness hanging overhead. Off and on for the entire weekend, she thought about what Sandra revealed to her. She even shared a little of their conversation with Lester. The only response he gave was, "You just never know about some people."

It was a struggle for Maxie to think about not having her best friend around to bounce things off of, from time to time. Their relationship changed in so many ways since Sandra's revelation, and now she felt robbed of the opportunity to glean from her. In the beginning, she thought she was the one who had to share the information about the love of Christ. When in all actuality, Sandra could have given her just as much, if not more, foundational truths. To Maxie, it was a shame that Sandra kept all of that to herself. It was like holding the key to the door of everything they had in common.

As the hours passed, Maxie continued the motions of greeting and scanning, almost mechanically. Her mind was so far away from what she was doing, she barely felt the vibration of her cell phone in the pocket of her smock. Reaching into her pocket, but without taking it out, Maxie quickly looked at her phone and saw a text envelope. In the past three days, she had one brief conversation with Marc, and that was on Sunday during her drive back from the airport. Marc relayed the message that his grandmother had invited her over for pie and ice cream anytime she wanted to come, and that he missed seeing her beautiful smiling face. Maxie told him she would call him right back, but she never did.

"Maxie, are you okay?" Regina tapped her clipboard on the end of the conveyor belt. "You look a little out of it today. Do you want to take your break now?"

"Just to go to the restroom," Maxie replied.

"Go ahead and go. I'll run your register until you get back."

"Thank you."

Maxie moved quickly to the rear of the store, and stood in the storage area to check her phone. *Can I see you sometime today?* Read the text message from Marc.

Maxie stared at the words, and immediately wanted to answer his message, but she decided against it. Instead, she closed her phone, leaned against a pallet of canned vegetables, and exhaled a breath she felt she had been holding for days. It didn't take long for her mind to conjure up the highlighted events of last week. In every idle moment she'd had since then, the events banded together and stole a place in her thought pattern; positioning themselves at the forefront. It all played out like a constant rerun of an old movie. From Lester questioning her ministry, to Deacon Earl's somewhat intimidating and untimely approach in front of the Pettigrew house (she now wondered how much Sister Pettigrew saw), to Sandra's staggering revelation — the vision was incredible.

Maxie closed her eyes, and gently rubbed the area below her brows. For the first time, she felt like her venture was aimless. She didn't expect these kinds of stumbling blocks.

And it played again.

Her best friend wasn't really who she thought she was. By her husband's report, she *really* didn't have a ministry. And by the time Deacon Earl finished scandalizing her name and her efforts. ...

Maxie took a deep breath and exhaled. She needed a spiritual hiatus, and a physical refuge, in order to regroup. Looking at the text message again, she knew if there was nothing else she was sure of, she was sure that being with Marc would give flight to those thoughts and shadows that wanted to linger. He appreciated the woman she was, without expectations.

I would love to see you today, was the message she returned. Maxie told Marc to meet her across the street at Oglethorpe Mall around 4:30 p.m., which was soon after she got off from work. Marc immediately responded that he was looking forward to their meeting, and he would be waiting for her at the east end of the parking lot.

Maxie closed her phone, and put it back into her smock pocket. Taking another deep breath, she exhaled, exited the storage room, and walked down the aisle to her register. She couldn't explain what came over her, but a new kind of determination seemed to envelope her tighter and tighter, with every step she took. By the time she returned to her register, the cloud that hung over her all morning had been replaced.

* * * * * * * * *

Maxie grinned as she briskly walked across the parking lot to Marc's car. "Hey you," she said, when she opened the car door to get in.

"Hey yourself," Marc smiled back. "Long time no see."

When they embraced each other, Marc instantly felt the coolness of the evening on her cheek, and drew in the delicate scent of perfume she had dabbed behind her ear at some point in the day. Softly he kissed her cheek, knowing she would accept it on the premise of a Christian greeting.

Maxie immediately noticed the warmth of Marc's lips on her face. Keeping her smile, the gentle tickle of his facial hairs against her cheek, made her grin even more. Before she released him, Maxie inhaled his Prada cologne.

"Mmmm, you smell good this evening," Maxie said.

"You *look* good," Marc smiled.

"In this old thing?" Maxie pulled at her smock. "I forgot to take it off."

"That's because you were excited about seeing me. I understand."

"So cocky," she grinned. "Anyway, it's already late, so you know I can't stay long. You wanted to see me because …?"

"I haven't seen you for three days, and that's a problem for me."

"A problem."

"Yes." Marc paused. "Maxie, I can't go on like this."

Maxie pondered Marc's words, and wondered when the shift in the atmosphere happened. Her smile faded, and a clouded look of concern took its place.

Marc looked away, and stared straight ahead. "I know this might be hard for you, but seeing you just every now and then isn't working for me."

Maxie sat quietly. Feeling an instant heaviness in the pit of her stomach, she knew she couldn't fathom experiencing another major disappointment right now. "What are you saying?"

Marc looked at her directly, taking in her slightly parted lips. Gently, he touched her on her chin and removed his hand. "I want to see more of you."

Relieved, Maxie smiled softly. "You can come into the store any time you want."

"You don't work every day. And even if you did, that's not what I'm talking about."

"What? Are you saying you want to see me *every day*? Exclusively?"

"Exclusively? That's not possible."

"I'm glad you understand that," she said with a bit of humor.

"I understand your commitments. I'm just asking for a little more of your time. You told me the day before Thanksgiving, that you enjoy being with me. I never got to express to you totally how *I* feel."

"Well, you agreed with everything I said."

"Yes I did. But me being in agreement doesn't really account for how I feel."

Maxie smiled lightly. "Okay. I'm listening."

"Even though we're closer now than we were before, I still feel there's something very special about you. And now that I know more about the kind of person you are, I'm even more fascinated. You're not like any other woman I've ever met Maxie. And I've told you that before. There's a quality in you that I've never experienced. Shari didn't even have what you have." Maxie raised an eyebrow, and Marc laughed a little. "Let me rephrase that. I'll just say that you're very special to me. And when a person comes in contact with something that's so special, they like to keep it in a special place."

"And your special place is …?"

"Near me."

"Which means?"

"Like I said, I want us to spend more time together."

Maxie acknowledged Marc's words with a slight nod, as she looked straight ahead. "So our relationship is taking a turn?" She asked.

"Just a slight one."

Maxie stared pensively, and nodded again.

Sensing her ambivalence, Marc spoke up. "Maxie don't be scared. You'll be compromising nothing. You just heard me say that I understand your commitments."

"Yes. ..."

"You think you'll get in over your head don't you?" Maxie looked at him with eyes filled with uncertainty. Touching her chin again, Marc spoke with assurance. "Nothing will ever happen that you don't want to happen. Do you hear me?"

Maxie wanted to question Marc. What if she should ever actually *want* something to happen? Instead she nodded, and gave him a soft smile, at which time, Marc took his hand away.

"So? He asked. "What do you think? Is there any room in your world for me?"

Maxie quickly revisited the conclusion of the thoughts she had, when she was in the store's storage room. "I'd love to accommodate you Marc. I believe we'll have a lot of fun together."

"Some days you might feel like you're sneaking around."

"It can't be any worse than the way it is now," Maxie conceded.

"Well, we do still have the designing of your husband's anniversary gift. If you want, we can beef up that project. As a matter-of-fact, I'd like for you to come into the jewelry store to view what we have on computer."

"Come into the store? Don't you have a laptop? I don't think it's a good idea for me to come to your job."

"Are you a customer?"

"Well ... yes. Sort of."

"Then you can come into the store to view the designs, just like my regular customers do."

"No curbside service huh?" Maxie asked, furrowing her brows.

"Whitley Jewelers is a first class company."

Maxie took a deep breath, and exhaled it slowly. "I guess I can do that."

"Great. What day do you want to come? I'll need to tell our designers."

"I don't know. Wednesday I guess. I'm off Wed ..."

"Wednesdays. I know. What about tomorrow? I want to see you tomorrow."

"Marc, give me tomorrow to work out how we're going to do this, okay. I can't afford to miss one step." Maxie looked at her watch. "Like right now. I have to go." Maxie opened the door.

"Keep your phone close to you. I'll call you tomorrow."

"Okay."

Just as she was about to get out of the car, Maxie stopped and leaned back in toward him. Softly, she kissed him on the cheek and smiled, waiting for him to look at her surprised. When he only grinned, Maxie nodded her head. "I meant to greet you when I first got into the car." Maxie got out, closed the door, and headed for her car the same way she had come. Briskly.

Marc watched her with a look of great satisfaction on his face. Maxie Bruce was more than what he wanted, and everything he never had.

Chapter Forty-Two

S ince his last discussion about God with his grandmother, Marc decided he wasn't ready to turn his life over to someone he couldn't see, didn't know, and trusted even less. He determined that everything linked to God would have to be done either in faith, or because of faith — all of which he had none.

"Faith is the substance of things hoped for, and the evidence of things not seen," Stella Anderson once quoted to him from the book of Hebrews. Unbeknownst to Stella, her words helped Marc to make up his mind on the whole matter. He decided a few days after their conversation, that he was finished agonizing over the thought of how, after accepting Christ as his *personal Savior* as his grandmother put it, he would maneuver his life to totally depend on God for all of the things he hoped for, with the evidence of his hopes coming from nothing he did on his own. What real man could do that? He was used to making his own way. He'd done it for most of his life, and he had been successful thus far. What would be the reason for him to change now?

Marc worked through lunch Tuesday, and without any breaks Wednesday morning. He talked Maxie into viewing a few ring designs at the store, and he wanted to take her to lunch soon after. He wanted nothing business related to interfere with their time together, so Wednesday afternoon was all theirs. He could not get Maxie to commit to a time when she would be coming to Whitley Jewelers, but she did promise it would be somewhere around noon. Satisfied with her decision, Marc made preparations with the store's seven jewelry designers, to have their pictures readily accessible on their computers when she arrived. He wanted this to be the last day for her to make a decision on the style of ring she wanted for Lester.

With Maxie arriving at any moment, Marc prepared his office as if he were expecting a million dollar buyer to come through the doors. On his desk was a small tray of imported cheeses, imported crackers, and an array of fresh fruit. The only thing lacking was an expensive bottle of wine that would usually accent this kind of presentation, but Marc knew with Maxie it would be a wasted gesture. Instead, he had a bottle of chilled sparkling apple cider. On a small table covered by a black velvet cloth, just to the side of his desk, Marc aligned various pieces of men's jewelry with different metal encasings and different gems, to help Maxie decide. All of this preparation was a normal routine for special customers of his, and his calculated movements were viewed as the norm by every employee in the store — everyone that is except for Jaunee.

Even though the other gemologists at Whitley Jewelers prepared for their customers the same way, Jaunee saw there was something different about the way Marc was handling this presentation. From the time he stopped at her desk to inform her of his *nameless* visiting customer, and the designs he wanted her to have available, it was obvious that this person was not one of the ordinary buyers. With this in mind, she intended to keep her eyes on Marc's actions and reactions while this customer, whom she was sure was a woman, was in the store.

When Maxie finally arrived, she was dressed for the occasion and the weather. After exiting the elevator, she canvassed the area with her eyes. Taking off her black wool trench coat, she revealed a slightly below the knee, charcoal colored sweater dress that gently hugged her in all of the right places. Fixing the cowl neck of her dress, she draped her coat over her arm, and walked to the Receptionist's desk.

"Hello, I'm here to meet with Mr. Thomas." Maxie said to the magazine reading Beatrice.

"Oh, yes ... why of course," Beatrice said, a little startled. "You must be Mrs. Bruce. Mr. Thomas is expecting you. However, he has stepped away for just a moment, but asked me to make sure you are made comfortable in his office."

Maxie smiled as the woman untangled herself from the cord of her earpiece, and opened the door to Marc's office.

"Let me hang your coat for you. And please help yourself to the fruit and cheeses. It's all been imported. Well the fruit wasn't, but the cheese and crackers were." Beatrice grinned and nodded.

Maxie handed over her coat and kept smiling, because Beatrice's rhythmic head movement reminded her of a bobble head doll. When she finished hanging her coat on the coat tree, Beatrice simply stood in front of her as if there was more Maxie required of her.

"Thank you," Maxie said. "I'll be fine."

"Okay. Okay, well ... great. Uhm, if you need anything, I'll be right outside here," Beatrice pointed as she attempted to make her exit. "I'll leave the door open."

"And your name is?"

"Oh. I am so sorry. I'm Beatrice. You can just call me Beatrice."

"Okay. Thank you Beatrice."

Beatrice pointed again. "I'm right outside the door here."

Maxie nodded.

"Okay ... good. It was a pleasure meeting you." Beatrice left the office before Maxie could respond.

Laughing lightly to herself, Maxie looked at the colorful tray of food, and wondered if imported cheeses tasted much different than the cheeses made in America. She didn't immediately want to find out, because the last thing she wanted was to greet Marc with the smell of cheese on her breath. Instead she looked around at Marc's lightly decorated office. He obviously had a thing for the color of mahogany, because all of his furniture was made from that color of wood. Continuing to peruse the office, Maxie noticed the table of beautiful jewelry. But what immediately caught her attention, were all of the certificates of recognition and certificates of completion that covered the wall next to Marc's desk. Impressed by their number, Maxie moved closer to read each one.

"I guess they make me look kind of smart don't they? It's either that, or a lot of people lied about my abilities," Marc said.

Maxie jumped a little at the sound of his voice, and quickly turned around to face him. Marc stood in the middle of the floor, dressed in a double-breasted suit and tie. Looking fine as usual.

"So what do you think? Am I smart, or do they just make me look good?"

Maxie wanted to answer the question about him looking good, but left it alone. "How long have you been standing there?" She asked.

"Long enough to admire the sights. And I must say that I love what I see."

Maxie smiled.

"So do I get a greeting? I mean you're all the way over there, and I'm right here," Marc said.

"You want me to hug you here?" Maxie whispered.

"No. I want you to hug me *and* greet me with a kiss over here. You know, like the Bible ...."

"Don't you think you're taking the biblical greeting thing a little far?"

"I think you're stalling, and we don't have that kind of time to waste. Now come over here and ...."

Maxie immediately walked over to Marc, wrapped her arms around him, and softly kissed him on his cheek, at which point he did the same. "Good afternoon Mr. Thomas," she grinned.

"Hello Maxie," he said in a low tone. "I'm glad you could make it."

"Well you made it sound like I didn't have any more time left to make my decision, so I don't believe I had too much choice in the matter."

Marc gestured to the fruit tray. "So did you try the fromage?"

"The what?"

"Fromage. That's French for cheese. These were imported from France."

Maxie nodded pensively. "No I didn't try any of them."

Marc picked up a piece of cheese that was orange-brown in color, and offered it to her. "Try this one, it's called Mimolette. They also call it Boule de Lille."

Maxie opened her mouth, and allowed Marc to feed her the cheese. As she chewed slowly, she smiled a little. "It has a nutty taste to it."

"Yeah. The taste changes as the cheese ages. It's still a good cheese though."

"I guess you've tasted a lot of different gourmet foods haven't you?"

"Oh yeah. I don't eat a hamburger everywhere I go. And my grandmother doesn't like to fly, so I had to develop a little sense of taste on my own."

"That's good," Maxie said. "Judging by those plaques and certificates on the wall there, you seem to be a very accomplished man. I like your office by the way."

"Thank you. It's subtle at best."

"Which is totally unlike you," Maxie grinned.

"Aw see, there you go."

Marc and Maxie shared a laugh, before a light tapping on Marc's opened door interrupted them. It was Jaunee.

"Oh, I hate to bother you Marc, but I'm on my way to lunch, and I know you were expecting … Oh is this the customer we're all waiting for?" Jaunee asked, with a smile so fake it could be detected a mile away.

Maxie looked at Marc with a hint of surprise on her face, when she heard that other employees were expecting her arrival.

Marc knew Jaunee planned to interrupt him the minute she was aware of his customer's arrival, and she probably had Beatrice to alert her as soon as Maxie got off the elevator. Knowing how cunning she could be, Marc didn't doubt for one second that Jaunee was probably perched somewhere, watching him like a hawk while he entertained Maxie.

With her hand extended, Jaunee entered the office uninvited. "Hello, my name is Jaunee. You must be Mrs. Bruce."

Marc nodded his head lightly at Jaunee's gall. He knew in that instant she had talked to Beatrice, because no one else knew Maxie's name.

Maxie took Jaunee's hand, and glanced at Marc. "Hello. It's nice to meet you."

"Jaunee is one of our designers," Marc said casually. "The set of pictures I showed you that Saturday were hers."

"Oh. Those were very nice," Maxie said. "You're very talented."

Jaunee released Maxie's hand. "Well thank you. I try to give Mr. Thomas the best that I have. Sometimes he doesn't accept it, but I put it all out on the table anyway."

Marc loudly cleared his throat, and Jaunee ignored him. He knew she was beginning to play a game.

"So how long have you been a friend of Marc's? Or should I say a customer of Whitley Jewelers?"

Maxie looked at Marc inquisitively. "It's been what? Since I spoke to you when you were in London right? Or maybe it was that time we spent together when you got back."

Marc smiled, and nodded his head. Maxie was playing a little game of her own.

"I guess the answer to both of your questions would be about a couple of months," Maxie said, looking at Jaunee cordially with a smile.

Marc watched Jaunee's face become flushed, as she stared at Maxie. "You said you were getting ready to go to lunch?" He asked.

"What?" Jaunee asked, keeping her eyes fastened on Maxie one moment longer, before she looked at him.

"Lunch. You said you were on your way to lunch. Will I be able to view your designs on your computer? No passwords or anything?"

"Uhm ... yes. I am going to lunch. You should have no problem pulling up my pictures. I keep them in the Shared Folder. Well Mrs. Bruce, it was certainly nice to finally meet you face to face. I hope you enjoy your shopping experience at Whitley Jewelers, and I hope to see you again," Jaunee tooted.

Maxie smiled again. But this time her smile was a facade, because she was mulling over the words *finally meet you face to face*. When Jaunee left Marc's office, Maxie finally realized she was the woman who answered Marc's cell phone, the time she called about their first meeting for lunch. If she didn't know it then, she definitely knew it now. That woman had a thing for Marc.

"I'm sorry about that ..." Marc started.

"Oh by the way Marc," Jaunee interrupted. "Please don't forget about the Christmas party at the boss's house. Remember, you promised we'd go together as a couple this year. And I'm really looking forward to our date."

"Jaunee, that's almost three weeks away," Marc said, a little annoyed.

"I know," she whined. "I was just thinking about it, so I thought I'd remind you."

"I haven't forgotten. I'll see you after lunch."

Jaunee left without another word, but Maxie could have sworn she sneered at her.

"She's a real piece of work isn't she? I do believe she feels threatened by me, especially after that last display."

Marc looked at the fruit tray. "Yeah. She likes to play games like that sometimes."

"So you know she has a thing for you."

Marc put a grape into his mouth. "Yes, but she knows I'm not interested. And I've made that clear on more than one occasion."

"Hnmm. So she's relentless too."

"Somewhat. But it doesn't matter."

"Do you think it's wise to promise her a date? I mean that's sending a mixed signal isn't it?"

Marc looked at Maxie squarely, and grinned. "What do you care?"

"I ... don't. I mean ... I'm just saying."

"You know, it sounded to me like you were trying to make her believe that you and I have something going on together. I mean, the way you were playing tit for tat with her. Who was sending mixed signals then?"

Maxie laughed a little. "That's ridiculous. I admit I got a little defensive, but that was because she was coming down on me, like I was standing between her and something she wanted. That's the only reason why I responded the way I did."

Marc put another grape into his mouth and stared at Maxie, before he chuckled and walked to the jewelry display table. "Well come on over here Mrs. Bruce, and let's get this process started."

Chapter Forty-Three

M axie toured Whitley Jewelers, met the people Marc worked with on a daily basis, and viewed all of their designs for men's rings. When she found nothing that came close to the starburst styled ring Marc had shown her before, he suggested she use that same design and add her own flavor to it, using a computer program called Ring Builder. Maxie loved the idea of being able to add her own sense of flair to Lester's ring, because it made it seem more personalized. With Ring Builder, she was able to pick out every facet of the ring, from the carat, cut, and grade of the diamond, to the clarity, color, and price. When she was finished, Maxie created what she thought to be a one of a kind men's platinum diamond ring. She took pride in knowing she would be giving her husband a gift that reflected a little bit of herself in every angle.

Over the next two weeks, Maxie and Marc spent as much time together as they possibly could. There were moments after she got off work, minutes or hours before she was scheduled to punch in, and Saturdays when Lester worked. No matter what length of time was available to them, they made every minute count. They spent time in arcades playing air hockey, video games, and shooting pool. They also met for quick lunches on River Street, and light conversations in the corners of the Carnegie Library. Maxie's favorite excursion was ice-skating at the Civic Center, where Marc had taken her twice. Even though she had never skated a day in her life, she didn't have to worry about how wobbly she was, or falling down. Marc held on to her every move, and made sure she was properly fitted into the double blade beginner's skates. Holding her hands and sometimes her waist, Marc gracefully led her around the ice rink, laughing whenever she released little squeals of delight and anxiety. In spite of her shins feeling like they were on fire, she couldn't remember a time when she had so much fun. She felt like a child who had escaped through a window, from a locked bedroom.

Maxie always knew life could be so much more plea-surable, if she could just release herself to enjoy the sim-plicity of what it had to offer. She also knew everything she was experiencing was greatly enhanced, because she had Marc Thomas to share it with. Anything she wanted to do, any place she wanted to go, Marc was there to make it happen for her. No cautious decision-making. No premedi-tated movements. No judgment calls. Everything was done in uninhibited spontaneity.

And she loved it.

Maxie grew to love it so much, she allowed her ulti-mate strategy of discussing God's plan of salvation, to be diverted. Though she promised herself the diversion would only be for a short time, she justified it on the premise that she needed to continue escaping the monotonous routine of living just for the church. Knowing Marc Thomas caused that cycle to be capriciously broken, and she didn't want that to change. If she encouraged Marc to accept Christ as his personal Savior, which she felt she would have no problem doing, everything she was currently experiencing would abruptly come to a halt, undoubtedly because of his newly acquired convictions. She couldn't settle with that reasoning. Having Marc Thomas in her life at this point, was like finding a treasure chest filled with everything just for her. For now, Maxie had to suspend time. Not indefinitely. Just momentarily.

At least until she felt fulfilled.

Chapter Forty-Four

M axie heard the phone ringing repeatedly, before she could finally stumble inside her front door. With her purse and a bundle of department store bags in hand, she let everything fall to the floor to lock the door, and answer the phone.

"Hello?" She huffed.

"Konichiwa girl!" Said the voice practically screaming on the other end.

Maxie frowned as she held the phone between her cheek and shoulder, to take off her coat. Her first instinct was to ask who was calling, but since the person was obviously speaking in a foreign language, they must have called by mistake.

"I'm sorry, I think you have the wrong number."

"Maxie?"

Maxie took her hat off, and looked at the Caller ID. It read OUT OF AREA.

"Yes," she answered, with an even deeper frown.

"Maxie it's me girl. Sandra."

Maxie smiled broadly, and plopped down in the corner of the couch. "Hey Sandra. How are you? I didn't know who this was. What was that you just called me when I answered the phone?"

"I said Koh-Nee-chee-wah," Sandra laughed. "That's hello in Japanese."

Maxie laughed too. "Oh, well … Konichiwa to you too. What's going on with you? I haven't heard from you since you first got there. Now you're calling me trying to speak the language."

"Girl please. I'm only learning what I need to know to communicate for business purposes only. With the way they work here, I might be fluent in the Japanese language by the time I get back to Savannah. When it comes to working, I think they might have the Latinos beat." She and Maxie laughed. "So how is it down south? What have you been up to? You sounded like you were out of breath when you answered the phone."

"No. I was just getting in from doing some Christmas shopping, when I heard the phone ringing. I'm glad I caught it. I would hate to have missed your call."

"Did you work today?"

"I went in for a few hours this morning. I want the extra money for my shopping expenditures this Christmas. Have you done any Christmas shopping there yet? I imagine it's beautiful over there this time of year."

"Yeah, it's real beautiful for a culture that doesn't believe in Christianity. If I wanted to find a church around here, I probably couldn't because less than one percent of the Japanese people are Christians. Christmas isn't even a national holiday here. If Christmas day falls on a weekday, everybody still goes to work or school. They celebrate the day, but it's just a commercial event to them. It's just another reason to drink Saki. Girl, they even have Christmas parties, but they mix it with something called Bounenkai season, which means 'forget the year'. And I mean they're doing a lot of forgetting. I have never seen so many drunken Japanese people in my life. You can see them all on the streets at night. It's like a cultural thing."

"Wow," Maxie said. "But you did go shopping right?"

Sandra laughed a little. "If you're asking me did I send your Christmas gift in the mail, the answer is yes. Now one of the items I sent you is called a Kumade Rake. If you want to know what it's good for, you'll have to look it up on the internet. I know what it symbolizes, but I bought it for you because I thought it was beautiful, and you would like it."

"Thank you. And the other item?"

"I ain't tellin'."

Maxie laughed. "I guess I'll see it when it gets here. Hey, what day is it there? Saturday night or Sunday morning?"

"It's Saturday night, about a quarter to twelve. It's a quarter to three your time right? We're nine hours ahead of you."

Maxie looked at her watch. "Yeah. Why are you up so late?"

"I wanted to talk to you. Since I haven't called you in a while, I thought I'd touch base with you. See what's going on. How is Lester?"

"He's doing well. I think he has some big plans for our anniversary next month. He hasn't said too much about it, but I know he's up to something."

"That's good. And what about you? What plans do you have for your anniversary?"

Maxie closed her eyes, and gently shook her head. Reading between the lines, she knew Sandra was alluding to her relationship with Marc.

"Sandra don't."

"Nothing's changed has it?" Sandra asked, with disappointment in her voice. Maxie was silent, and Sandra sighed heavily. "Maxie ..."

"Sandra, it's not what you think. I ... I can't even explain it to you. But it's not what you think."

Sandra spoke softly. "I know exactly what it is. You don't have to explain it to me Maxie. I see it. I saw it way before I left, and I told you that."

Maxie silently looked up at the ceiling.

"I didn't call to fuss at you, or argue with you. I'm praying for you. I just wanted to see how you were doing."

"I'm fine," Maxie almost whispered. Clearing her throat, she repeated, "I'm fine."

"Okay well ...."

"Hey, are you still coming home next month?"

"January? Yeah. I thought I'd be here until the end of the month. But now it looks like I'll be home around the first week or so. I've purposed it in my heart to go to this festival here called Tamaseseri. I was told it's where half-naked grown men are scrambling for two balls for some kind of prosperity, all while they're being splashed with cold water. I can't leave until I've seen that. Grown men in nothing but a loin cloth? Girl, I think I'm going to take pictures."

Maxie and Sandra burst into laughter. "I'm sure you will," Maxie said.

The two women continued to laugh, and then a brief stint of silence made the moment awkward.

"Well I better get off this phone and get some sleep," Sandra said. "I need to get started early tomorrow."

"You work on Sundays too?"

"Uh uh. I plan to have a full day tomorrow. These people have a festival for everything around here. So I'll go to one or two of those, do some shopping. Stop and have lunch with a co-worker. Do some more shopping. Come back here, take a nap, get up and ...."

"Do some more shopping," they both said together, and laughed.

"I hope that co-worker you're having lunch with is a female."

"Now other than spending time with you, when have you ever known me to waste my social time having lunch with a woman? Girl please."

Maxie smiled.

"You take care of yourself Maxie. I'll try to call you again soon okay? You have my phone numbers here right?"

"Yes."

"Good. You call me when you need me. Tell Lester I said hello okay? And I'll talk to you soon."

"I love you Sandra."

"I love you too Maxie. Bye."

Maxie heard the dial tone before she said goodbye. When she finally hung up the phone, she was left with a lot to think about. But she refused to acknowledge those things that might seem adverse. It was nice to hear from Sandra, and the brief conversation was good, but the instant Sandra started talking about Christmas in Japan, most of Maxie's thoughts ran away to rest on Marc. She couldn't help but to think about the fact that today was the first Saturday in over a month, she and Marc would not be spending time together.

It wasn't because they didn't want to get together, or that priorities prevented them from doing so. Maxie would have found that easier to accept. But it was because of Marc's holiday commitment to Jaunee, that he would not be seeing her today. Not only would she not be seeing him, she obviously would not be hearing from him either. So far, Marc had not answered the voice or text messages she left him. He hadn't even so much as sent her a text message that said *Hello*.

Maxie questioned herself, as to why Marc felt obligated to keep a promise to someone he wasn't the least bit interested in romantically. But she guessed that was a side of the single life she didn't know about — the ability to date the opposite sex, but yet remain uninterested and unattached. After all, isn't that the same kind of understanding she has with him? So why did she feel a twinge of emotion when Sandra mentioned the words *Christmas parties*?

Maxie sat still on the couch fixed in deep thought. She didn't want to go where her mind was leading her, but she relented anyway.

And there they were.

Marc and Jaunee coupled together at the office Christmas party, smiling and laughing at each other. Marc was casually dressed in a red and black Jacquard crewneck sweater with black slacks, and Jaunee wore the most seductive red dress she owned, making sure that Marc stayed in her presence, by wrapping her arm around his for the entire time. She even whispered sweet salacious promises in Marc's ear, describing what she'd do if he'd accept her invitation to a night cap at her place after the party.

What do you care?

Were the words Maxie recalled Marc saying to her when she was in his office, asking him if it was wise to promise Jaunee a date, knowing how she felt about him. *What do you care?* She heard again. This time his face was before her. Maxie blinked her eyes quickly, and stood up to retrieve her purse and the bags she left by the door. "I *don't* care," she said aloud with an angry bite.

"You don't care about what?"

The words scared Maxie, and caused her to jump and quickly turn toward the kitchen doorway, where Lester stood. "Oh! Hi baby. How long have you been home?"

"About two minutes. Didn't you hear me when I asked you what you were sitting there thinking about?"

"No," Maxie said airily, as she continued to pick up her bags. "No, I didn't."

Lester walked closer to her. "So what were you thinking about that made you look so angry, and yell out that you don't care?"

Maxie had no idea that what she saw in her mind's eye, reflected an immediate and unexpected show of emotion on her face. She had no idea why she was angry, and now was not the time to be concerned with it. Smoothly, she changed her entire train of thought, to the man who was standing in front of her.

"I don't know sweetheart. It could have been anything. I have so much on my mind. I just finished up my Christmas shopping. I hope I didn't forget anyone."

Lester laughed and placed his hands on her waist, pulling her closer to him. "Well if you did forget somebody, you just loudly proclaimed that *you don't care*." Lester kissed Maxie's mouth, and spoke with a tainted Spanish accent. "You want I should help you with your bags madam?"

"No thank you sir," Maxie said, pushing him away and hiding her bags behind her back. "I got this."

Lester put both of his hands up in the air in submission. When Maxie walked away from him into their bedroom and closed the door, he sat down on the couch. "Hurry up in there," he called over his shoulder. "I want us to do something special tonight, so I want to hurry and get cleaned up."

Maxie quickly tossed her purse on the bed, shoved the shopping bags into a spot in the walk-in closet, and came back to her purse. "Okay," she yelled through the closed door. "Just give me a minute."

Frantically, she searched through her purse for the little cosmetic bag she kept sanitary napkins in, and pulled out her cell phone. When she flipped the phone open, Maxie's eyes became slits, and her lips pursed firmly together. There was still no envelope stating that she had a text message, or any other kind of message from Marc. Sitting slowly on the edge of the bed, she kept her eyes transfixed on her phone. It was nearing 3:30 in the afternoon, which to Maxie was too early in the day to have a Christmas party. So what was Marc doing? Turning off all outside communication with any and everybody, just like he did almost every time he was with her? Jaunee didn't deserve that.

She didn't deserve that.

Maxie didn't want to believe Marc was sending her the indelible message, that she was no better than all of the other women he spent his time with. If she did believe it, then that would cause her to grab a hold to the first accusing thought that came to mind. One that screamed to her, that with Marc, all women were the same. They were all the same, and they were all treated the same way. No one was more special or more preferred than the others, and they all deserved his undivided attention.

Maxie's breathing became labored, as she bounced gently on the edge of the bed. She didn't see any of this coming. When she spoke with Marc briefly over the phone yesterday afternoon, he made no mention that she would not be hearing from him today. She even replayed that conversation over and over again in her mind, just to be sure.

"Honey are you wrapping the gifts or what?" Lester asked.

Maxie could tell he was standing directly on the other side of the door. Quickly she put her phone into its special place in her purse, and zipped the entire bag shut before she opened the door.

"Sorry I took so long," she said, a little winded.

With her hand on the doorknob, Maxie opened it wide, allowing Lester to walk into the room. With slow calculated steps, he entered with half a smile and a look of skepticism on his face.

"Don't even think about searching for them," Maxie grinned. "None of them are for you anyway."

Lester let his smile fade, but wholly accessed his wife with eyes full of intent. The somewhat subtle implication made Maxie laugh a little.

"None of that either," she said plainly. "You have a shower to take, and a date to keep. So move along."

Lester moved closer to her. "How about I take my shower *with* my date?"

Maxie matched Lester's gaze with an alluring one of her own. "I don't believe the outcome would be conducive to what you have planned for the evening."

"I beg to differ," Lester said in a low tone, and moved closer, practically pressing Maxie against the door. "They're my plans. Let me predict the outcome. As a matter-of-fact, I believe it would greatly enhance the evening."

Lester moved in, and kissed Maxie passionately. She in turn, responded to him immediately with a hunger that surpassed his desire. Pulling himself away from her a little, Lester looked at his wife with half a smile.

"I see that you agree with my approach."

"Mmm," Maxie said, before kissing him softly. "Let's just say that you've inspired me to follow your lead."

"Really?" Lester said, as he pulled her away from the door. "Let's see what else I can inspire you to do."

Chapter Forty-Five

I t was more than a week before Christmas, and the merriment of the season was evident in the smile of every Food King customer Maxie greeted in her line. Ever since she arrived at noon, there were wishes of Merry Christmas, Season's Greetings, and Happy Holidays. Maxie returned their smiles and their greetings, but contrary to what she faked on the outside, on the inside she was full of frustration.

From the time she woke up, it was clear that Monday arrived with all of the weighted baggage from the weekend, and she wondered what would transpire before its departure. There were many avenues that could charter the course the day would take, but if it followed along the path based solely on Maxie's feelings, the route would be a rocky one.

From Saturday on, Maxie had yet to hear from Marc. It was almost like he simply dropped off the face of the earth, leaving her with feelings that ranged from scared to angry. She didn't know if he was sick, hurt, bleeding to death somewhere, or simply not wanting to be a part of her life any more. It was the not knowing that was making her crazy and frustrated.

All weekend long, she thought of ways that would help her quell the anxiety that held her bound, but they all produced a dead end. She didn't know Marc's address, so she couldn't drive by his house. She couldn't remember exactly where his grandmother lived on Talahi Island, so she couldn't go there. All she knew was the location of Whitley Jewelers, but she remembered Marc told her they would close early so everyone could attend the Christmas party.

But today was Monday.

The store would be open for business as usual, so if she did not receive a text message or phone call from Marc by the end of her shift, she would definitely be taking a drive to that side of town. It was purposed in her heart Sunday afternoon, to go to him using the ruse that she was there to check on her ring order. If he was available, then and only then, would she let him know how inconsiderate she thought he was.

Maxie glanced at her watch. It was 12:30 p.m., and she grimaced at the thought of only being there for thirty minutes. Even though she chose to work the Express Lane with the hope of making her shift go by faster, it wasn't working. The traffic was minimal. Most of the customers coming into the store now, were coming in for lunch and briskly heading toward the Café.

Maxie looked at the magazine rack she recently straightened, and the candy shelves near her register that she already aligned and realigned. With nothing else to do, she pulled out a bottle of all-purpose cleaner, and a paper towel from under her register. Just as she was about to spray down her area, she felt the vibration and heard the pulsing hum of her cell phone in her smock pocket. In one fluid motion, she put down all that was in her hands and discreetly retrieved her phone. Maxie felt her heart race when she saw that there was a text message from Marc. As anxious as she was to receive it, her movements displayed just the opposite when she slowly flipped the phone open. She took a deep breath, exhaled, and read the text.

Hello beautiful.

After she read the two simple words, Maxie felt a great lifting inside and smiled softly to herself, before she remembered that she was supposed to be annoyed with Marc.

Thinking about you, read the next text, with two more following in succession.

Miss you so much.

Can we get together for a moment?

Maxie quickly closed her phone, and shoved it into her pocket when she heard the intentional sound of someone clearing their throat, obviously to get her attention. Without looking at the person she said, "I'm sorry," and smiled as she began scanning the few items on the belt. "That was a little emergency."

Maxie kept her smile and glanced into the face of the elderly gentleman who stood in front of her, only to get a scowl in return. But that didn't affect her. After she took his money, she continued to smile as she bagged his groceries, and wished him a good afternoon. When another customer came through her checkout lane, she felt the vibration of her phone again. Quickly, she began scanning without acknowledging the patron with the normal rhetorical greeting. While she waited for the customer to process the total, Maxie flipped her phone open in her smock pocket, and peered at the lighted image.

Come see me at my job when u get off. No one will be here after 4. I'll be waiting.

The sound of Maxie's heartbeat was reverberating in her ears, and she had no idea as to why she was so anxious. Granted, she hadn't heard from Marc in a couple of days, but did finally hearing from him really warrant the response of anxiety? If it did, something was wrong. Maxie quickly assessed her range of emotion, to see if there was any probability of her feeling anything unusual for Marc, and just as quickly, she dismissed the very thought.

She willed the rest of the afternoon to move along speedily, and it did. Though she was normally scheduled to work until five o'clock, she quickly made arrangements with Regina, to have Alan move from his register to hers, because she wasn't feeling up to finishing out the rest of her shift. She hated to be deceptive, but it was for a good cause. She needed time to get to the Historic District to meet Marc. If she didn't leave at four o'clock, that would mean she would arrive home late to cook dinner, and she couldn't fathom going through another argument with Lester about her tardiness.

Before she knew it, the four o'clock hour rushed in along with the routine arrival of last minute dinner preparers. When she punched her time card, and was on her way out of the store, Maxie put on a face that would make anyone believe that she was in physical pain. Her charade even provoked an "I'll pray for you", statement from Alan when she passed him at the register. Simply nodding, she wrapped herself with her scarf and wool trench coat, and creased her brow to produce a look of genuine anguish. Albeit, she dropped the act the moment her feet hit the parking lot.

Maxie made the drive to Whitley Jewelers in record time. Instead of parking her car on the street in front of the building like she did before, she drove into the side lot marked EMPLOYEE PARKING ONLY. Even though the sign threatened violators would be towed, Maxie doubted her car could be identified as a trespasser's car, rather than that of an employee. Looking around, it was clear she had her choice of parking spaces, because only three cars were in the lot. One of which she knew to be Marc's. Briefly, she considered who the other cars might belong to, especially since Marc told her everyone was supposed to be gone by four o'clock. Parking next to his car, Maxie quickly got out and made the short trek to the front of the jewelry store. As she passed the large security barred window, Maxie could see the store was dimly lit, and all of the display counters were covered with black cloths. When she got close to the entrance and reached for the door, someone from the inside opened it. The sudden gesture made Maxie jump a little. Standing in the doorway was a big burly security guard, who looked down at her.

"Mrs. Bruce?" He bellowed.

"Yes, I … uh …" Maxie stammered, totally thrown off by the guard's massive size, and baritone voice.

"Come in. Mr. Thomas told me to expect you. He's waiting for you upstairs in his office."

Maxie stepped inside the doorway, and stood still while the security guard locked the door. When he finished, he turned around and looked at her with an element of surprise, because she was still standing there.

"Is there something else you need?" He asked.

Maxie looked around as if she were lost. "Oh, no I … I … Thank you. Thank you." Briskly she walked to the elevator. When she got in, and the doors closed, Maxie felt a sudden rush of ambivalence and something else she couldn't identify in the air around her. It reminded her of that threatening feeling she felt a couple of months back, in Food King. "Oh God," she whispered to herself. "I shouldn't be here right now."

But still she pushed the elevator button that would take her to where Marc was waiting. Maxie felt fear grab a hold of her, but before she could panic, the doors of the elevator opened and the paranoia seemingly disappeared. Taking a measured step forward, she stood still as the doors closed behind her. In front of her across the room, Marc stood leaning against the doorway of his office. Maxie tried hard to understand the amorous signals her mind was receiving from the pit of her stomach, but it all made no sense to her. What she thought she was feeling, was an emotion that was totally forbidden. Therefore it didn't make any sense. It couldn't make sense. So she erased it, by replacing it with the annoyance that caused her to be there in the first place.

"There's my girl," Marc grinned. "I can't tell you how much I missed you. Come on over here."

Maxie put on her attitude and walked across the foyer, as Marc moved further inside of his office.

"How are you?" He asked. Gently pulling her to him, he leaned in to kiss her cheek. Without a word, Maxie moved her face so his lips would not touch her. Puzzled by her response, Marc stepped back and looked at her with a little frown. He assumed she was as glad to see him, as he was to see her. Obviously he was wrong.

Maxie stood her ground, and stared at him. All of her emotions were in a ball of confusion now, while her thought pattern was on a totally different avenue. There were thoughts of Lester, the church, Sandra, — everyone she held in high regard, or who had ever given her sound advice. But why? Why were they all there?

Maxie shook her head, removed her coat, and looked at the floor to help her regain the moment. Casually folding her coat across her arm, she left her scarf around her neck. Looking at him directly, she spoke with enough bite to get her point across.

"You just said you can't tell me how much you missed me. I can understand that. With no phone calls, no returned text messages, I couldn't tell either. I guess you must have really enjoyed yourself at that Christmas party. Did time get away from you? Since I didn't hear from you, I figured it was either that or the fun lasted all weekend."

Marc looked at Maxie a moment before he nodded his head knowingly, and walked to the front of his desk. Sitting on the corner of it with one leg off the floor, Marc clasped his hands down in front of him and looked at Maxie quizzically. "Are you mad at me?"

Maxie said nothing, but allowed her pursed lips, and the slight cocking of her head to speak for her.

Marc observed Maxie and her stance. To view this side of her amused him. But he dare not show it with laughter. Instead, he slightly turned up the corners of his mouth. "You are mad at me. But is it really because I didn't respond to your messages, or because I took Jaunee to the Christmas party?"

Instantaneously and with the simplest form of rhetoric, Marc was tapping in to parts of her that she refused to believe existed. Maxie felt as if her true feelings were slowly being uncovered. The unveiling seemed somewhat second nature to Marc, because his body language told her that he was confident in his discovery. In an effort to throw him off, Maxie stepped closer to him, and added more attitude.

"You think I'm jealous? I could care less about who you took to the party, or spent your weekend with. That's your business. My concern is that if we're to remain friends, and we don't see each other, you give me the common courtesy of a phone call or something to let me know you're alright. I deserve that much. I shouldn't have to spend my entire weekend looking at my silent phone, wondering if something happened to you, or if you suddenly decided to end our friendship."

Marc noted the seriousness in Maxie's tone, and let his smile fade. "I'd never end what we have. And you're right Maxie. You're absolutely right, and I'm sorry." Marc shrugged his shoulders. "What else can I say?"

Maxie put her coat on the desk and studied Marc for a moment. She could see in his eyes that his apology was sincere. She only wished she had another reason to be upset with him. Her aggravation had been stirred the entire weekend and she was wielding the upper hand, so to grant forgiveness so soon would make it all pointless.

"I'm sorry," Marc said again with resignation.

Maxie nodded her head gently. After releasing a soft sigh, she reduced her confrontational heat and stepped closer to him, experiencing the soft scent of his cologne. "Why didn't you at least call me Marc? Even a text message takes little effort."

"I know," he nodded. "But you would never tell me directly, what you just told me a few minutes ago."

Maxie frowned. "What are you talking about?"

Marc grabbed both ends of the scarf Maxie had around her neck, and toyed with it. "Let me put it this way. You confirmed something for me."

Maxie kept her frown, and it made Marc smile.

"Tell me something," he said. "How did you feel when you couldn't get in touch with me, and the last thing I told you was that I would be at my boss's house for the office party, with someone who had an extreme interest in me?"

Maxie lowered her eyes. "I don't ...."

Marc lifted her chin so they were eye to eye. "Be honest and tell me."

Maxie stared into his eyes, and spoke slowly as if she were mesmerized. "It made me crazy."

Marc pulled her closer to him with her scarf, leaving little space between the two of them. "And so ... it made you jealous?" He whispered.

Maxie let her focus drop to Marc's mouth, and then into his eyes again. "Yes."

Without another word, Marc leaned in and lightly brushed his mouth against hers. The movement was an inquisitive one. He wanted to know if she would be receptive.

She was.

Feeling the warmth of his lips and the heat from his mouth on hers, was a tease that ignited every nerve in her body.

Everything changed.

Her heart raced. Her breathing became labored, and her appetite for him increased. She wanted more than the light brushing of Marc's lips. She wanted to taste him. Closing her eyes, Maxie abandoned every rational and discriminating thought that came to bring her to her senses. She was too far-gone.

Sensing no resistance, Marc wrapped his arms around her waist and at the small of her back, pulled her even closer. At first he tenderly pecked her with small kisses to invite a return. When she yielded, Marc pressed his mouth against hers fully. Before she could think twice about it, his tongue quickly found hers and the touch caused Maxie to jump weakly. The response was expected, but Marc hoped it was due to feeling instead of surprise.

All through her body, Maxie felt the heat of desire. Marc was holding her, and kissing her with a possessiveness she had never known. Even if she wanted to resist him, there was nothing she could do. The kiss was like a drug, slowly removing all of her defenses and making her weak. She had secretly waited for this moment. It was the first step to the release of all of her inhibitions and suppressed longings.

Just as she was on the brink of giving in totally to what was happening, Maxie felt something deep inside her soul being pulled from her. The sensation was so profound; it caused her to break away from Marc immediately. With confusion clouding her face, Maxie searched his eyes for a brief moment.

"God," she whispered, removing his hands and walking away from him.

With her back to him, Maxie stood in front of the wall that was covered with plaques. Slowly she nodded her head negatively, and looked at the floor.

Marc sat motionless and said nothing. He knew he over-stepped his bounds, but at that moment he didn't care. Everything he did that led up to that very second was worth it. He knew not communicating with Maxie for a few days would send her over the edge, and cause her emotions to rise at full boil. Just as he supposed, she did what was expected; she relented.

"Maxie ...."

Maxie put her hand up to stop him.

"Maxie come here," Marc pleaded softly.

"No," she said faintly.

"Please."

"No. No, this is crazy. This isn't right."

Marc looked at the ceiling and sighed. "Maxie, it was just a kiss."

"It was wrong."

"What was wrong about it?"

Maxie shook her head and said nothing.

"Tell me what was so wrong about it Maxie. I know you wanted it just as much as I did."

Maxie refused to respond. Instead, she wrapped her arms around herself. When she finally turned around, Marc saw tears streaming down her face.

"You're right. I did. I did want it. I've wanted it for quite some time." Maxie paused as her tears continued to flow, and then she whispered, "But I didn't *want* to fall in love with you."

Chapter Forty-Six

Maxie's words caused dead silence to settle in the room like an unwelcomed guest. As she stood there looking at Marc somberly, she rubbed her arms as if a brisk wind had suddenly enveloped her. With the heel of her hand, she attempted to wipe away the tears that continued to fall. The moment was so surreal. She had no intentions of ever acknowledging openly, her feelings for Marc. She even lied to herself about the possibility, of ever being in love with someone other than her husband. But here she was, with her feelings out on the table again. She didn't know what to do, or what to say.

Even though he could read that her eyes pleaded with him to say something, the only thing Marc could offer her was a gentle smile. After remaining seated through the awe of her revelation, he walked to her and gently caressed her arms. Relieved, Maxie rested the front of her face against the center of his chest, where she again inhaled the fragrance of his cologne. Marc wrapped his arms around her, and rested his chin on the top of her head.

"So what are we going to do about this?" He asked.

Maxie slightly shrugged her shoulders, but stayed in the same position.

"Don't you want to know how I feel?" He grinned.

When Maxie didn't answer, Marc lifted her chin to where her eyes met his. Kissing her forehead, he wiped away her tears with his thumbs and looked at her. "Maxine Bruce, I was in love with you from the first time I saw you. I just had to wait until you could tell me you felt the same way."

Maxie put her head against his chest. Wrapping her arms around him, she closed her eyes and whispered. "I'm scared."

Marc thought about his grandmother's words of warning, about interfering with Maxie. "I know," he whispered back. "I know."

Maxie opened her eyes, and mentally retraced her steps to the visual warning she received when she first arrived. She was now certain that the glimpse of all of those faces, appeared just to warn her about going over the edge. But none was more vivid than the face of her husband Lester. When she saw him in her mind's eye, the vision caused her to quickly close her eyes again, in an effort to hold back her tears. The attempt was futile, because warm streams of water seeped from under her eyelids.

Maxie was perplexed.

One part of her was devastated with what she allowed herself to get into, while the other part was elated that she was finally liberated and acquainted with the side of herself she always wanted to know. The door was now fully open, and she had really crossed over the threshold.

But what was she to expect?

She was always on the outside looking in, to a world she knew nothing about. What curiosity showed her was something exciting, something new, and that stirred her to gain the emotional position she was currently in. But it didn't show her how to be in love with two men effectively, if that were at all possible. It didn't show her how much the very thought of hurting either one of them, would cause her more pain than she could ever fathom, and it didn't show her a way to get out of it all.

Marc continued to hold Maxie close in silence. Feeling her shudder from time to time, he was certain it was an involuntary reaction to the moment, and not caused by the sheer fear of what she shared. The novelty of what they were entering into was not only going to be an experience for her, but something they would both share equally, because he had never been involved with a married woman.

Taking a deep breath and exhaling slowly, Marc considered how there was never a time where he felt like the odd man out. But the object of his affection had him standing in an adverse situation; one where everyone would undoubtedly view him as the proverbial *bad guy,* simply because he loved a woman who was not his own.

"This is wrong on so many levels," Maxie said finally. "You know we can't do this."

Marc gently pushed her away enough to see her face, without releasing her. "And what have we been doing these past months? Maxie nothing has changed. All we did was verbalize the love we feel for each other. That doesn't mean we have to stop seeing each other. Everything else can still be the same."

Maxie stepped back. Breaking free of his hold, she moved away from him. "But it's not the same now Marc. I know you see that."

"Maxie, I know what just happened here scares you, but don't react impulsively."

"Impulsively? Marc how am I supposed to react? I've just put my marriage on the line here. Everything is on the line. Who I say I am. My position in the church. My integrity. You told me you'd never compromise my integrity."

Marc stood directly in front of her. "Did I compromise it? You want to blame me? Maxie all I did was say that I love you. How am I compromising your integrity? Part of the definition of that word means honesty. And isn't that what we've just been to each other? Honest? Honest about the way we feel? How can you say your integrity is on the line?"

Marc moved closer to her. Maxie tried to consider his words, but being in such close proximity of him and looking into his eyes, made her thoughts more confused. So she closed her eyes to focus herself, unknowingly signaling to Marc that her guard was down. Before she knew it, she felt the gentle touch of his hand on her face and the warmth of his mouth on hers again, as he sought her tongue once more. Maxie felt everything in her begin to melt. The little bit of a standard she tried to raise a moment ago, was faltering to the fervor of this temptation. It felt like a war was raging within her. A battle of the wills, and her will was losing. With turmoil on the inside, Maxie felt as if she were two different people. One part of her was engaging in an act that brought immediate satisfaction, while the other part was trapped, and could only express its discontent through the release of tears.

Marc tasted Maxie's tears between his lips and hers. Without moving away from her, he stopped what they were doing, and pressed his cheek against hers so his mouth was close to her ear.

"Maxie ... don't do this," he whispered. "Please don't do this. Don't cry."

Maxie kept her eyes closed and tried hard to fight back the tears. "I don't know what to do," she whispered back.

Marc looked at her squarely. "Look at me. I told you. Don't do anything. Leave everything the way it is. Trust me on this. It will be fine. Just leave it alone."

Maxie stared at Marc and said nothing.

"It's getting late," he said. "You need to get home. I don't want your husband to be angry with you again. I wish I could drive you. Let me at least follow you there. I want to make sure you get there all right."

"No. I'll be fine. I can call you or text you when I get home."

Marc gazed longingly into Maxie's eyes, before a slight smile crossed his face. "I love you Maxie. And I'm glad I can say that to you now."

Maxie forced half a smile and moved away from him. "I love you too." When she retrieved her coat and put it on, Marc noted the air of ambivalence that surrounded her.

"Tomorrow ..." he started.

"No," she quickly interrupted without looking at him. "I need to be ... just let me call you. I'll send you a text when I get home, and I'll call you sometime tomorrow. Okay?"

"Okay," Marc answered with uncertainty in his voice. "Okay. Well ... I'm leaving too, so I'll walk you down to your car."

Maxie simply nodded, and continued buttoning her coat while she watched Marc gather his things.

In the elevator, Marc noticed how the moment somehow turned awkward, and that Maxie didn't even acknowledge he was in the elevator with her. Instead, she silently watched the floor numbers as they counted down to the first floor.

Before they left the building, Maxie stood close to the door while Marc had a few words with the night security guard. Looking at her watch told her she was doing okay with the time, but she would probably have to speed a little to make it home by 5:45 p.m. Seeing how dusk had settled in, Maxie's thoughts went to Lester. Though the notion was a crazy one, she immediately wondered if her indiscretion would become evident on her face when she saw her husband. It was obvious she would have to mask it in her demeanor, but there was nothing she could do about how she looked on the outside. How would she ever answer him if he questioned her out of suspicion?

Maxie shook her head at the idea. She didn't want to think about it now.

"What's wrong?" Marc asked.

For the first time since they had left his office, Maxie looked at him and smiled softly. "Nothing. I was just thinking about something."

"Are you okay?"

"Um hum," Maxie continued to smile. "I'm fine."

"Yes you are," Marc joked lightly. "Let's get you home."

Their walk to the parking lot was a silent one, only interrupted by an occasional horn blowing, and cars that zoomed by in rush hour traffic. Once Maxie was inside of her car, she rolled down her window.

"I want to know you're okay when you get home," Marc said. "Not just that you arrived safely. I want to know how you're feeling. I mean about everything that's happened tonight. It's easy for me to say what I said, and I don't regret it because there's no one else in my life. But you ... you have so much...."

"Marc, I understand what you're saying. And I don't regret what I expressed to you either. I've been feeling that way about you for quite some time now. I'm just surprised I actually said it. It was like an admission to myself, as much as it was an admission to you. Besides, spending as much time together as we've been spending, it was bound to come out at some time or another," she smiled. "Don't worry about me tonight. I'll be alright." Maxie winked. "Remember, I'm a big girl."

Marc gently touched the side of her face with his hand, and Maxie grabbed a hold of it to kiss his palm.

"Come 'ere," she said. "I have to go."

Marc leaned inside the car window, and softly kissed her mouth. "Be safe."

"Always." Maxie started her car, rolled up her window and mouthed, *I love you*, before she pulled away.

Marc smiled and watched her drive away from the parking lot.

Chapter Forty-Seven

"So have you given Food King your two weeks' notice?" Lester asked, as he casually sat at the kitchen table with a hot cup of coffee in one hand, and the morning newspaper in the other. Maxie stood at the counter and placed two pieces of buttered toast on a small plate, before grabbing a glass of orange juice and joining him.

"I have time," she said, before biting into her toast.

Lester put his paper on the table to eye Maxie, who continued to eat as if she were the only one in the kitchen. "It's a week before Christmas. The end of the month follows soon after." He said.

"Today is Tuesday. Technically, it's one week and two days until Christmas if you count today. I have time," she said dryly without looking at him.

Lester set his coffee mug on the table. "What's with the attitude?"

Maxie took another bite of her toast and a long swallow of juice, before she answered in the same tone. "I don't have an attitude."

"You're acting like you're having some kind of a problem this morning."

"Maybe it's because you're acting like I'm a child who doesn't know what day, what week, or what month it is." Maxie glared at him. "I'm well aware of what needs to be done Lester. I don't need you to remind me of how to take care of my business."

Lester studied Maxie with a questioning frown on his face. "What's gotten into you Maxie? You had an attitude for no reason last night when I came in from work. You barely even talked to me, and now you've awakened with the same attitude. Are you angry with me about something I did? Something I said? I know it's not because of what I just asked you about Food King, because like I said before, you've been carrying this thing since last night. Now I want to get to the bottom of it before I leave for work this morning. So what is it?"

Maxie turned her focus back to her glass of orange juice, which she finished off in a few quick sips. While Lester waited for her reply, she shot glances at him. She didn't know how to answer his question, because she had no idea as to why she felt so antagonistic toward him. In all honesty, he did nothing to warrant the behavior he was receiving, so she couldn't justify it. It just came upon her like a fog last night when he arrived home soon after she did, and it stayed with her. His attitude was the same as it always was whenever he came home from work; he was happy to see her at the end of the day. But she didn't feel the same way she normally did. She felt angry with him. She felt angry with him then, and at 7:15 in the morning, nothing had changed.

Maxie looked at her toast and nodded her head before she softened, and looked at Lester. "I don't know what's wrong with me. I guess I'm having PMS."

"You've never acted like this before."

"I know," she sighed. "And I'm sorry. They say this kind of stuff gets worse with age."

Maxie shrugged, as Lester gently nodded his head and stared at her. Sensing that he was searching her inwardly, she quickly got up and gathered the dishes before walking to the counter. "You can go to work now. I'm fine."

"Come back over here," Lester said.

Maxie pressed her eyes closed, and balled her hands into fists in frustration. He was rapidly getting on her nerves, and at that moment she just wanted him to leave. "Aren't you running late for work?" She piped. "I said I was fine. Let's just drop this please."

"Maxine."

Maxie sucked in a good amount of air, and released her aggravation noisily before she returned to her chair. With her hands on the table, and her fingers locked together, she gazed at Lester directly with a callous look plastered on her face.

Lester leaned in. "Now look, I don't know what spirit is oppressing you, depressing you, or trying to possess you, but you need to get rid of it. I'm not coming home to this crazy attitude this evening. So wherever you picked it up, you need to take it back. Am I understood?"

With her eyes still on him, Maxie raised her head a little and breathed in deeply, bridling the anger she felt on the inside. Even though he was right, she still felt he was speaking to her in a tone that would be used to reprimand a child; but she said nothing.

"I didn't hear you," Lester egged on.

"Yes," Maxie said.

Lester looked at her a little longer before he stood, kissed her on her lips, told her to have a good day, and left the kitchen. A few minutes passed until he actually left for work, but Maxie didn't budge. She sat at the kitchen table with her head relaxed on the back of the chair, looking up at the ceiling.

When Lester finally left and shut the door behind him, she closed her eyes and willed everything to stop, and start all over again. He was right. Her attitude was lousy, and she swore she could taste it in her mouth. All she wanted to do right then was to think about something pleasant, and the only something pleasant that came to mind was Marc.

Maxie reminisced about last night, over and over again. Every time she did, she felt the same undulating sensation in her loins. It was pure pleasure. The smell of him, the firmness of his arms around her, the warmth of his mouth on hers; it was all a consuming pleasure. Even on her way home last night, she could think of nothing more than Marc and the new level their relationship had catapulted to. Even though in the beginning, she struggled with her own personal inhibitions, by the end of last night, she no longer felt that way. The struggle was over. What happened happened, and it happened because she wanted it to. For once, Maxie felt in control of herself. The rule of subjectivity would not be present in her relationship with Marc, and she looked forward to it. She smiled at the thought of discovering herself in this new light. She was going to learn about her true and uninhibited capabilities, and she was going to enjoy doing it. More importantly, she now had somebody she loved to share it with.

Chapter Forty-Eight

M arc tried hard to concentrate on the paperwork in front of him. A sleepless night and a psyche full of Maxie, was not the best combination for all of the tasks he expected to conquer today.

"Beatrice," Marc spoke into his intercom. "I'm going to need you to hold all of my calls this morning. I have a ton of orders that need to be transcribed by noon, so unless it's one of our international customers, take a message please."

"Yes sir Mr. Thomas. Does that go for the co-workers too?"

Marc frowned. "Excuse me?"

"Well sir, Ms. Jaunee just phoned to see if you were in your office. She said she needed to come and speak with you. Should I let her know that you are very busy?"

"Beatrice, did she say what it was regarding?"

"No sir. I'm sorry she didn't. If you'd like, I can call her to find out."

Marc looked at his watch and sighed heavily. "That won't be necessary. It's nine-thirty right now. If she comes within the next thirty minutes, she's fine. Any time after that, I don't want to be bothered."

"Yes sir. I will let her know."

"No! Don't call her and tell her anything. Just wait, and keep your eyes on the clock." Taking his finger off of the intercom, he said the rest of the words to himself. "Maybe she'll forget about it."

Marc took the stack of papers, and began to separate them into little piles across his desk. The high dollar totals on the top sheet of each pile, reminded him that he needed to keep himself focused on his job. Diligently, he attempted to work through the papers. Each pile required his undivided attention, because they were the accounts of Whitley Jewelers' highest paying clients. But with even that in view, he knew it was going to be hard not to think about *her*.

Marc recalled how he spent the night sipping on half a bottle of Mike's Hard Lemonade, while watching a television on mute, and listening to R&B ballads on the radio. With verses of different love songs leading him to many avenues of thought, he considered how what happened in his office earlier that night, could have been a turning point in his life — even if it was just a kiss.

In spite of the feelings they had for each other, Marc knew there was a down side. Maxie had a lot of baggage. All night it troubled him to think about the fact that no matter how much he wanted to, he would never be able to help her carry it. There were going to be personal issues on both sides, and sooner than later, they would have to be addressed if their relationship was going to progress. What troubled him even more than that, was the question he asked himself about his own emotional abilities. With everything in view, could he really love Maxie like a woman who had no strings attached?

"Mr. Thomas, you have a call on line two," Beatrice said through the intercom.

Marc looked at his watch and became a little aggravated, as he put his phone on the speaker function. "Beatrice, are you watching the clock?"

"Yes sir, I am."

"So you know that it's now after ten o'clock."

"Yes sir I do. But I also know that it's your grandmother on line two."

Marc quickly took his phone off speaker, but not before he told Beatrice thank you. Placing the phone between his head and his shoulder, he continued to work and talk at the same time.

"Mama what's wrong?" He asked quickly.

"Well good morning to you too. Why does something have to be wrong when an old woman makes a call to her grandson?"

"Maybe because you never call me at work unless something is wrong."

"Well, I don't know if something is wrong, but you were in my spirit very heavy this morning, so I decided to call you. Now you tell *me* what's wrong?"

Marc stopped what he was doing, and sat idle. He wasn't accustomed to lying to his grandmother, and he wasn't about to start now. "Other than being a little tired mama, I'm fine. There's nothing wrong with me."

"Uhm hmm. And Maxie? How is she?"

"As far as I know, she's fine. I haven't talked to her."

"Uh huh. You haven't talked to her since when? Marcky, God don't trouble my spirit for nothing. Now maybe you're spending too much time with that married woman."

"Mama, I don't even know the last time we've spent more than an hour together. It's been a while."

"Maybe it's not the hours that God is looking at. Maybe it's the intent of your heart."

Marc laughed a little, and stacked one of the piles on his desk between his fingers. "Mama, why does any of this trouble in your spirit have to be about Maxie? Why couldn't it be about another woman I spent my time with this past weekend?"

"Is she married?"

Marc set the papers down again. "Okay Mama, you've expressed your point about married women. I have it. Now don't you worry about me all day. Do you hear me? I don't want you making yourself sick over me for nothing."

"Your soul is hardly nothing baby."

"I know Mama. I know. Listen, I'm a little backed up with work this morning, so I'll call and check on you when I go to lunch okay?"

"All right baby. Mama loves you Marcky."

"I know Mama. I love you too. I'll call you in a little while." Marc hung up the phone, and exhaustedly relaxed himself against the back of his chair. It was either tiredness or tension that was building up between his eyes, so he closed them and began massaging the area. In spite of the fact that he didn't want to think about any of the conversation he just had with his grandmother, her words would not release him. Just that quick, all of the conversations he had with his grandmother concerning Maxie, flooded his mind and bathed him in words of warning.

"Incredible," he whispered.

"Mr. Thomas?" Beatrice piped into the intercom again. "I tried to …."

Before she could finish, Marc's door swung open, and Jaunee sauntered in with Beatrice stumbling behind her.

"Good morning Marc."

"Mr. Thomas, I am so sorry. I tried to tell her ...."

Marc put up his hand. "It's fine Beatrice. Don't worry about it."

"Yes sir."

On her way out, Beatrice angrily looked at Jaunee, who obviously cared less about her attempt to stop her from entering Marc's office. Even now she didn't acknowledge Beatrice being there. Her eyes were dead set on Marc.

"Close the door Bea," Marc said without much movement. When Beatrice closed the door, Marc sighed noisily. "Good morning Jaunee. What can I do for you? "Will you be needing a seat?"

"No. Thank you. This won't take long. You look tired. Did you have a rough night last night?"

Marc rubbed the area between his eyes again, and loosened his tie. "I stayed and worked a little after everyone left last night. As you can see by the piles of paper on my desk, I have a lot of work to catch up on."

"Hmmm." Jaunee said nonchalantly. "Well, since I didn't get a chance to speak with you yesterday, I wanted to tell you how much I really enjoyed being with you at the company Christmas party. I felt special being on your arm Saturday night. I ... I needed that."

Marc smiled lightly. "I enjoyed being with you as well Jaunee. You looked very nice, and I felt privileged to have you accompany me."

"Thank you," she blushed. "I don't know whether you heard any of it or not, but there were a lot of compliments from our co-workers on how good we looked together."

503

Marc rubbed between his eyes again. He knew exactly where Jaunee was going, and the calculating tone in her voice instantly put him on the defensive. "No, I didn't hear a thing. But you know. ..."

Jaunee moved to the wall with the plaques and pretended to put her focus there, as she interrupted Marc. "You know, I wanted to take you out to dinner last night, to show my gratitude."

"Jaunee, there was no need for that."

Jaunee continued as if she did not hear one word Marc said. "I assumed you planned to work late last night. So I thought I'd hang around here until dinner time, when I figured maybe you were hungry."

Marc leaned forward a little in his chair, put his elbows on his desk, and locked his fingers together. "So that *was* your car that I saw in the parking lot when I left last night."

Jaunee turned around and moved closer to his desk. "Yes. And do you want to know what *I* saw last night, when I came up the stairs to your office to ask you to dinner?"

Marc looked at his papers and then at Jaunee, as she put both of her hands on his desk, and leaned forward.

"Don't you want to know what I saw Marc? I saw that maybe you've developed a *new* kind of appetite, and that I was just wasting my time, because an appetite like that can only be satisfied by one kind of a woman. A *married* woman." Jaunee stood up straight and let silence briefly claim the moment. "She is married right Marc?"

Marc loosened his tie a little more, before he stood up and put both of his hands into his pants pockets. "Jaunee, that's none of your business, and you're overstepping your bounds."

"Am I Marc? I guess you would know right? I mean since you have experience when it comes to overstepping bounds. Now don't you?"

Marc moved from behind his desk, and walked toward the door. "All right, now it's time for you to leave." At the door, he grabbed the handle to open it, but stopped when Jaunee stood directly in front of him.

"I'll leave, but I want you to answer one question for me. With all that you see standing before you right now — single, smart, beautiful, and willing. Why didn't you just choose me?"

Marc briefly considered Jaunee's question, and the answer that sat on the tip of his tongue. He didn't want to hurt her feelings, but she was trespassing on dangerous ground, and he had to let her know it.

"You just called it Jaunee," he said somewhat smugly. "Don't you remember what you just said? You don't satisfy my appetite." To punctuate his words, Marc opened the door and glared at Jaunee as she walked out. Noting how flushed her face was, Beatrice looked at Marc, then at Jaunee as she passed the Receptionist's desk. When Beatrice looked back at Marc again, he smiled at her and winked his eye, producing a smile on Beatrice's face that was a mile wide.

Marc closed his door, and walked back to his desk. Before he sat down, he hit the intercom button. "Beatrice?"

"Yes sir?"

"No more visits from anyone please."

"I'll make sure of it Mr. Thomas."

When he finally sat down in his chair, Marc looked at his watch. It wasn't even eleven- thirty, and already his morning had been more eventful than any other workday he could remember. Turning back to his papers, he began to stack them back into one pile, but in a collated manner. When he finished, he reached for his briefcase and placed the pile inside. With one fluid motion, Marc closed his case and hit the intercom button.

"Beatrice, forward all of my important calls to my cell, and take messages for all of the other calls. I'm going to be working from home for the rest of the day."

"Is everything all right Mr. Thomas? Are you not feeling well?"

Marc continued to move around the office, preparing himself to leave. "No, I'm fine. And thank you for asking. I just believe I'll be able to get more work done from home."

"All right Mr. Thomas."

"If I think of anything else, I'll give you further directions on my way out."

"Yes sir."

Within minutes, Marc was out of his office and in the employee parking lot. Though the attempts were made, he was determined that nothing was going to ruin his day.

Chapter Forty-Nine

When she got off work at one o'clock, Maxie stopped at the BP gas station on Abercorn Street for gas and something sweet to eat. She didn't anticipate recalling the time Marc had scared her there and showed her his car, but the memory was welcomed nonetheless. It warmed her against the cold Savannah wind. Every moment of the day thus far, her thoughts were on Marc. She didn't know why she told him she would call him today, instead of being with him. That was crazy. There was no other place she'd rather be than with him, and since she switched shifts with one of her co-workers again, she had almost four hours available to do so.

When she got back to her car, Maxie stayed in the BP parking lot and called Marc. It concerned her when his cell phone rang so many times, without the voicemail coming on. But when he finally answered, groggy as it was, his voice made her smile.

"Were you sleeping?" She asked, and listened to Marc stretch before he answered her.

"Initially, I was sitting here thinking about you. I must have dozed off a little. Wow, I guess I needed that."

"I don't think your boss is going to be too thrilled to know you're sleeping on the job."

Marc stretched again, and laughed a little. "I'm the boss today baby. And I'm not at work. I'm at home."

"At home? Are you okay?"

"Uhm hmm. I'm just working from home today. There was so much activity going on at the office, I couldn't concentrate. So I brought it home with me."

Maxie felt the outside temperature slowly creep into her car, so she started her engine and turned on the heat.

"Where are you and what are you doing?" Marc asked.

"At the BP on the corner of Abercorn and Mall Boulevard, talking to you."

"Are you on your way to work?"

"No, I just got off."

"So you switched shifts again. What are you going to do with all of that free time you now have?"

"Well, I was hoping to spend it with you, but it sounds like you're too busy for me."

"Never in this life would I ever be that busy."

Maxie could tell Marc was smiling, and his words made her smile too. "Sooo ... You want to meet me somewhere?"

"Yes I do. You said you're on the corner of Abercorn and Mall Boulevard?"

"Yes."

"Okay. I want you to go the other way, like you're headed back to your job except keep going. Take Mall Boulevard to Waters Street. Tell you what, get out a pen and paper. I know you don't use the GPS on your phone, so I'm going to give you the directions to where I want you to go."

Maxie searched through her purse for pen and paper, and wrote down the directions. When she finished and looked at the list of streets she was to travel, she frowned. "Marc where is this? It looks like you have me meeting you somewhere on Skidaway Island."

"Uhm hmm. And the place where I'm going to meet you is called The Landings."

Maxie continued to frown, as she silently repeated *The Landings* to herself. When she realized where she was going, her eyes widened. "Marc you have me meeting you at your house?"

Marc laughed at the surprise in Maxie's voice. "Yeah. It's far away and it's secluded. Nobody will know you out here but me." Maxie was silent, and he figured she might be considering a change of venue. So before she could suggest it, he interjected softly. "Come be with me Maxie. I have a nice fire going here. If you haven't already had lunch, I can fix us something to eat and we can dine fireside. It'll be nice. Just the two of us."

Maxie smiled at the thought, and looked at the clock in her dash. "Okay. Okay I'll be there in …."

"It'll take you about thirty minutes from there. And don't worry about the guard at the gate when you get here. Just tell him who you are, and that you're coming to see me. He'll have your name."

Maxie grinned at the idea of finally seeing the luxury homes at The Landings. "Okay, now if I get lost …."

"Call me. I'm not going anywhere."

Marc and Maxie ended their conversation, as Maxie pulled out of the parking lot. Because of how far Skidaway Island was from her, she wanted to speed across town. The sooner she could get there, the more time she'd have to spend with Marc. As it was now, the trip there and the trip back home would consume a good portion of her time.

While she traveled on the final street that led her to Skidaway Island, Maxie scanned the scene. Most of the area was covered in small bodies of water. With the exception of a mobile home park that was about two miles from The Landings, the area was otherwise desolate. When Maxie finally approached the gate, the attendant asked her for a pass. She did as Marc told her, and the attendant smiled broadly as he welcomed her to the community. Moving forward, Maxie was in awe of every house around her. The view was so incredible, she instantly wondered what kind of job each homeowner had, that would surrender to them the kind of income needed to purchase such grandeur. It wasn't easy for her to take in the beauty of every home, and navigate the necessary turns to get to Marc's house, but she tried. All the while, gaping and gawking her way to her destination.

When she finally arrived at the home that matched the address Marc had given her, Maxie was awestruck. The French influenced two story house was elegant at best. With light sage colored stucco exterior, highlighted by dark charcoal roofing tiles, and large windows trimmed with black panels, the building was enormous in size. Could this really be Marc's house? There must have been at least four or more bedrooms in it, which was far too much room for one person. The large lawn was closely cut and covered in fescue, which was taking its time turning brown. Small manicured bushes with little Christmas light bulbs peeking out, neatly lined the front of the house and served as the centerpiece in the semi-circular driveway. Somewhat hesitantly, she traveled half the length of the driveway and parked her car almost directly in front of the door. Before she got out, she quickly scanned the driveways of the other homes, searching for other cars that were parked in the front. All she saw in the front of a few houses were reindeer, waving Santa Clauses, and giant iron angels. The view alone made Maxie wonder if the community had some special vehicle parking ordinance. Maybe she was supposed to park on the side of the house where Marc's car must be. Once she decided to move, Maxie started her car, but before she put her foot on the accelerator, she heard her name being called. When she looked out the passenger window at the house, Marc was standing in the doorway, waving his hand at her. Quickly she rolled down her window.

"Are you leaving me so soon?" He asked. "You just got here."

Maxie noticed how handsome Marc looked in his untucked, half buttoned, white dress shirt. "Don't I need to park somewhere else? Nobody in the neighborhood is parked in the front of their homes."

Marc nodded his head slightly and smiled. "You're fine girl. Come on inside. It's cold out here."

Maxie quickly turned off her car, and sprinted to the door. Before she entered fully, Marc stopped her at the threshold, by blocking her with his arm.

"Hey you," he said, looking up at the top of the door. "Guess where you're standing?"

Maxie looked up at the fresh piece of mistletoe dangling above her head, and smiled. "Either you put that there because you knew I was coming, or you have plans to ambush every female who walks through this door."

Marc brought himself closer to Maxie. "You're the only woman who's come through this door in quite some time."

Without any hesitation, or regard for anyone but herself, Maxie wrapped both of her arms around Marc's waist, and received the same act of passion he gave her the night before. When they finally stopped, Maxie grinned broadly.

"So does that get me admission into this mansion of yours, or are we just going to stand here in your doorway where everyone can see us?"

Marc smiled, and pushed the door open for Maxie to enter. When she stepped into the foyer, she was announced by the resounding noise her shoes made against the hardwood floor. Quickly she gave Marc a questioning look, as he took her coat and hung it up. He assured her that all was well, because the entire living area and dining room, was covered with durable Brazilian mahogany flooring. She didn't need to take her shoes off unless she wanted to.

Maxie continued to move around in awe and silence, with Marc following a few paces behind her. From what she could see, every square foot of the spacious home was custom designed with Marc's astute taste. Outside of the beautiful Christmas decorations catching her eye, there were vibrant colored paintings by Alix Baptiste, columns and arches, marble and granite, hardwood and tile, all over the place. Maxie moved around the main level of the house, like a woman who was helplessly driven by an insatiable curiosity to see how the more fortunate ones lived.

Marc leaned against the island in the kitchen and smiled. "Do you want the tour of the rest of the house?"

Maxie looked at him as if she were surprised he was even in the room. Closing her mouth out of embarrassment, she nodded her head sheepishly. "If it looks as luxurious as it is down here, than yes. Yes I do."

With Marc leading the way and describing parts of the house to her, the two of them walked back into the living room. Maxie didn't understand how she missed it before, but the fireplace was lit and all aglow. Soft jazz music was playing surround sound throughout the entire house. Marc told her the house was *smart wired* for sound. As she looked around, she could see why he chose to work from home today. The atmosphere positively induced calmness.

On the tour, Marc showed Maxie three of four spacious bedrooms, and two of the bathrooms that were equipped with oversized jetted tubs, walk-in marble tiled showers, and double vanities. It was all beautiful. When she followed him back downstairs, she couldn't help but to notice there was one room he did not show her, and she refused to ask him about it because the door was closed.

"Your house is really beautiful baby," Maxie said, as she perused the kitchen.

While he placed their sandwiches and chips on plates, Marc glanced at her with half a grin. He wanted to say something about the term of endearment she just casually used, but changed his mind. "Is turkey on wheat okay with you?"

"That's fine," Maxie said, running her fingers along the granite countertop. "Did you decorate all of this yourself?"

"If you're asking me did I have a woman help me with the décor, I have to say yes." He handed Maxie her plate and a glass of iced tea, before they both sat down at the kitchen table.

"My grandmother helped me. I wanted her to come here to live with me, but she wouldn't have it. You know how some older folks can be about their independence. She claimed she would be cramping my style, if I ever wanted to entertain." Marc bit into his sandwich.

"Meaning a woman."

"Mmm humm," he nodded.

Maxie quietly began eating her sandwich. Marc knew she wanted to ask him the question of how many women, if any, had he entertained in his home, so he opted to change the thought and break her silence.

"It was pretty interesting how this little rendezvous worked out, don't you think?"

"What do you mean?" She asked.

"Well, I didn't plan on working from home today. And judging from the way you were last night in my office, I don't believe you planned to even see me today."

Maxie nodded. "I didn't. I thought I needed to take some time to reassess things. But there was no need."

"Okay," Marc nodded. I have to say, jealousy was your color last night. It looked good on you."

Maxie scrunched her nose, and stuck her tongue out at him. "You probably set the whole date up just to see if I'd get jealous."

"I guess you'll never know now will you?"

Maxie gently kicked Marc under the table, and the two laughed briefly before they were silent again. Taking a bite of her sandwich, she watched Marc pick over his potato chips.

"So ... Did Jaunee try to put any moves on you, or ask you back to her place after the party?"

Marc put a chip in his mouth, and chewed slowly. With a glint of humor in his eyes, he looked at Maxie. "There were some innuendos she hoped I picked up on, but naturally I ignored them."

Maxie continued eating. She figured Jaunee made some kind of advance toward getting her clutches into Marc. The opportunity would have been ideal for any woman. The party was a wonderful entrance to the weekend. The night was probably still young. There was undoubtedly plenty of liquor, and she was an attractive single woman. What else could a man to want? Had the shoe been on the other foot, Maxie felt she probably would have tried the same thing.

"It bothered me last night when you said you were scared. Do you still feel that way?" Marc asked, breaking into her thoughts.

"Not of you. I was scared of my feelings for you. Marc, I've never been here before. To be honest, everything happened so fast. I don't even know how I got here. Like I said last night, I never wanted to fall in love with you. It just ...."

"Maxie, you don't have to explain it to me. I know what you're talking about. I've never been here either." Marc reached across the table, and held Maxie's hand. "It's a strange place, but I love where I am. And I love the woman who is here with me."

Maxie lowered her eyes and tried to smile, before she looked at him sincerely. "But Marc, where do we go from here? How can we ever expect to have a true and meaningful relationship? I'm not just in love with you. I'm in love with my husband, and I don't believe that's ever going to change."

"We'll just let it take its course. Who knows what will happen over time, right? I mean, you never expected this." Marc shrugged his shoulders. "Like I said last night, we'll leave everything the way it is. That's what's working right now."

Maxie gently squeezed Marc's hand, before she released it. "I'm not sure how much longer that's going to work. Remember when we spent time at the library, and I told you about the time limit my husband gave me to work?" Marc nodded. "Well, this morning he asked me if I had put in my two weeks' notice."

"Okay, so what's the problem?"

"If I'm not working at Food King, how are we going to be together? That's the excuse I use for where I'm spending my time when I'm away from home. That's my alibi."

Marc looked at her pensively, and chewed in silence. "You could use the time you spend visiting the elderly. When you quit working, you'll have more time available to visit the nursing homes. So, you'll just split that time with me. No lies will ever have to be told. Actually, it will probably work out better for us that way."

Maxie smiled at the idea, and nodded her head. "And you said you've *never* been here before?"

Marc laughed a little. "No. I just believe things have a way of working themselves out, when two people in love want to be together."

Maxie nodded her head at his reasoning, and continued eating her lunch.

After chatting a good while longer, Marc took their plates and put them into the dishwasher. While he busied himself in the kitchen, Maxie offered to help but was denied. Instead, she went into the living room and stood by the fireplace. She loved the warmth of a good fire, and the large plush black rug lying in front of the fireplace, beckoned her to sit. When she did, she noticed there were two very large matching pillows within the area. Pulling one close to her, and taking off her shoes, Maxie looked into the fire and became mesmerized. Everything in the moment was right, and she just wanted time to stop and stand still for her to enjoy it.

"Have you ever had wine before?" Marc asked. He wanted to make a joking comment about communion wine, but thought better of it.

Maxie quickly looked up to see him holding two wine glasses filled halfway, with a liquid that looked almost as clear as water. "I gather that's what's in the glasses."

"I can get you something else to drink if you don't want it. There's hardly any alcohol in it. I'm not trying to get you drunk," he smiled.

Maxie took the wine glass and sipped from it, while Marc stretched out on the rug, and propped himself up on one elbow. "I love it when it's cold outside, and I can waste the time away sitting in front of a nice fire." Marc said. "I don't get to do it nearly as often as I'd like."

"Your job?"

"Yeah. Sometimes it takes me away too long."

Maxie sipped her drink, and looked into the fire before she spoke. "So are there any excursions in the near future?"

Marc finished his wine and smiled. "Why? Do you desire to take a trip with me?"

Maxie didn't answer right away. Instead she took his empty glass, and set it on the marble ledge of the fireplace with hers. She couldn't help but to giggle a little at the idea of just picking up and leaving the country with Marc, on a whim.

"No. It sounds great, but I don't think that would go over too well with my husband."

Marc nodded in agreement. "So why are you asking?"

"I don't know. I guess I don't want you to go away from me, for any length of time just yet."

"You would miss me?"

"Terribly."

"Come here," Marc said.

Placing his fingertips under Maxie's chin, he guided her toward him. When she leaned in and her mouth met his, Maxie noticed immediately that the intensity of what they were doing had changed. It wasn't the same as before. Either she was more sensitive to the moment, or the fire was generating more heat, or the wine and the heat together were doing something to her; she didn't know. All she knew, was that every nerve in her body sparked with a heated passion like never before. With the warmth of Marc's hand on her face, and the heat of his mouth on her neck and ear, she found it impossible to control her breathing. She even closed her eyes to focus, and quell the swirly sensation she felt in the lower part of her stomach, but it was futile. She was lost. Her own thoughts defied her, and showed her a position that gave Marc everything she wanted him to have — gaining the intimate satisfaction her own body was screaming for.

Maxie wasn't the only one to feel the change. Marc knew he was taking more liberties with Maxie than he should have, but he couldn't help it. It was like all of his moral characteristics were snatched away; they simply didn't exist. It had been a long time since he felt close to a woman, and the heightened level of desire that he was experiencing now, surpassed all of the feelings he'd ever felt for *any* woman at any time. It was more heat than he could stand, and he needed to be as close to her as he possibly could.

"Maxie, let me make love to you," he whispered in her ear. His voice was desperate, and the warmth of his breath caressed her ear.

Maxie kept her eyes closed, and drifted wherever the flow this intense current was taking her. In it she felt passion, and a peculiar sense of liberation. She wanted nothing more than to meld with Marc, and receive all that he had to offer her physically. But deep down inside, she felt a gentle tugging. Slowly she pushed away from Marc, and gazed into his eyes.

"I ..." she started.

Marc lowered his head. "I know."

"I love you, and I want you Marc. But I'm just not ready to go that far," she pleaded.

Marc laid his head in Maxie's lap exhausted. Embracing her legs, he tried not to think about what might have been. "I understand."

Maxie stroked his head, while silence briefly settled between them. "I'm sorry," she whispered regretfully. Focused on the flames in the fireplace, it amazed her how she was just at the pinnacle of desire, only to crash and burn miserably at the bottom. The denial of the moment was hard on her. She could only imagine what Marc was feeling.

"What time is it?" He asked without moving.

Maxie looked at her watch. "Three forty-five."

Marc sucked in a large amount of air, and exhaled as he stood up. Holding out his hand, he offered her help to stand. When she accepted, and stood before him, Maxie observed the solid look of disappointment on his face.

Marc tried hard to suppress what he was feeling inside. But Maxie's look of concern, told him he wasn't doing a very good job of it. Without a word, he picked up their glasses and walked into the kitchen, to put them in the dishwasher. Maxie followed and watched. When he closed the dishwasher, she gently wrapped her arms around him from behind, and rested her head on his back.

"Marc please don't think for one moment that I don't want you. I do."

Marc remained still, and then turned around to face her. "All I'm asking is for you to join me, in showing you what I feel for you. I know you have standards you choose to live by, and live up to. And that's fine. But baby, you're here with me right now. So you can relax all of that. I'm the only one you have to deal with. I don't see you the way the church people see you. And I'm not measuring you by anyone else. I'm not going to judge you. I'm not going to whisper and tell lies about you. And I'm not going to condemn you. I just want you to think on me. Not anything or anyone else. Okay? Can you do that for me?"

When Maxie didn't answer, Marc kissed her and felt a strong sense of resistance, even though she kissed him back.

"No one will ever know what happens in my house," he said, and kissed her again, before he whispered in her ear. "We've never been here before Maxie. Come explore this place with me."

Maxie felt temptation rush in with a fire she didn't know it had. The lower part of her stomach churned with excitement and passion together, and she felt herself becoming heated again.

"I ... we ... we can't," she muttered. "I can't do this."

Maxie's words meant nothing to Marc, because he could feel her resistance failing. As he kissed her lower neck, and nibbled on her ear lobe, he whispered, "I'm the only one you have to think about. Let me show you how much I love you."

Immediately after him, Maxie heard a very faint voice quote the last part of I Corinthians 10:13, "*but will with the temptation, also make a way to escape, that ye may be able to bear it.*"

"There's nobody here but me," Marc whispered over the verse. "Just me and you."

Maxie looked at the kitchen cabinets above Marc's head, but she couldn't see them. She couldn't see anything. Where was the way to escape? All she could see was the plan of giving in to her desires, and satisfying the whirlwind of lust that was raging on the inside.

Marc stopped what he was doing, and looked into Maxie's eyes. "Tell me that you want to go home right now, and I won't try to stop you."

Maxie stared at him fully focused with her body tingling. In his eyes, she could see how much Marc wanted her — and what she saw, mirrored exactly how she felt.

Marc felt more of her resistance falter, so he continued with what was working, and kissed her eagerly before he captured her sight again. "Do you want to go?"

Her stare was likened to that of a deer in headlights. Maxie knew at that moment, her answer to Marc's question was not going to be what it should be. "No," she said breathlessly.

Marc stared at her a moment, before he wrapped his arms around her and held her. Maxie closed her eyes, and held on to him as if her life depended on it. Gently Marc stroked her back, and kissed her with a hungry fervor, before moving to other sensitive parts of her body.

"This is just about us," he said.

Maxie couldn't understand it, but when her chest was pressed against Marc's, she thought she felt both of their hearts racing in the same rhythm. Not only was her heart racing, but so was everything else. She was losing every attempt to get a hold of the situation, simply because she couldn't think straight. With every touch of Marc's hands, Maxie felt the nerves in her body respond to him like static electricity. At the same time, she experienced guilt, exhilaration, fear, wantonness, and confusion. In a position she should have feared, Maxie felt oddly safe. As her desire began to fully take over, faces flashed in her mind like lightning, and all of them were the same faces she had seen before.

Only this time they were fading.

Before she knew it, her blouse was completely unbuttoned, and she was standing with Marc at the top of the stairs, in front of the closed door that she saw earlier. Maxie looked at him, and concentrated solely on the words he recited, holding her spellbound. *This is just about us*. When the door was opened, she couldn't think prudently one second beyond what was happening at that moment. She didn't want to. All she knew was that Marc wanted her, and she wanted him too.

Chapter Fifty

A torrential rainstorm started the same time Maxie left Marc's house, and the downpour was nearly relentless in its intensity for three days. After a loud clap of thunder, and the release of a blood curdling scream from the pit of her stomach, Maxie immediately sat upright in her bed in total darkness, shaking in a cold sweat. Wiping the beads of perspiration from her forehead and breathing heavily, she felt her heart pounding against her chest, as it mingled rhythmically with the beat of the thunderstorm that raged outside.

"Maxie," Lester said with a strained voice. "Baby what's wrong? That same dream with your grandmother in it?"

Maxie nodded yes without looking at her husband, and continued to take deep breaths to calm herself.

Lester propped himself up on one elbow, and gently stroked her back. "Isn't that the third time this week?"

Maxie looked at Lester's silhouette, just before a flash of lightning partially lit their room, and showed her his look of concern. "Yes," she managed to whisper.

Lester sighed heavily.

Maxie looked at the window, as flashes of light burst beyond the curtain that hung over it. As she listened to the thunderstorm continue its furious assault, she cringed at the sound of the rolling thunder, and howling wind gusts that terrorized their bedroom window. She couldn't remember a time when a storm like this scared her so much — its character being almost wrath like. It might not have bothered her so much if the storm just passed over, but it had been there for three days; and the identical timing of its arrival, with her departure from Marc's, was too much of a coincidence for her.

In spite of the thought being fleeting and almost ridiculous, Maxie came to the conclusion that through the storm, God might be unleashing his anger toward her for all of her indiscretions. If that were the case, she was getting off lightly.

"Come 'ere," Lester said, gently pulling her to him, and wrapping his arms around her. Holding her close, he spoke softly in her ear. "I know that dreams can sometimes be prophetic in their purpose. And because this one is reoccurring, and has someone you believe is your mother, Sister Adams, and your grandmother in it, I don't doubt there is some kind of message to it. But I want you to calm down and try to go back to sleep. It's a little after six, and since this is Saturday, I don't have to go to work until later. So right now I'm just going to hold you. Close your eyes, relax, and try not to think about it okay? We'll discuss it later."

Maxie nodded her head, and nestled herself against her husband's bare chest, hoping to find solace in his arms and his words. The warmth of his kiss on her ear, and the soothing tone in which he spoke was calming, but she couldn't close her eyes. She wished that closing her eyes and not thinking about the images that haunted her, was all that was needed to make them go away. She knew better.

As she lay in the darkness, Maxie mentally took the journey back to where she stumbled. That entire evening was surreal. As she watched what her memory was showing her, the observation was that of a woman she had come to know. A woman who was consumed by her own lust.

A part of her.

The heat of passion and the lustful hunger, flared and consumed nearly all within her that was righteous. That night she was driven. Her lust guided her mentally, and physically to the places *it* wanted her to go. Places she otherwise never would have gone. As wrong as it was that evening, a great part of her enjoyed relinquishing itself to that desirous will.

That night, when the passion and the momentum waned, fear lifted the fog that she and Marc were in, allowing her to clearly focus. In total silence, she laid in Marc's king-size bed with her back to him, feeling his fingertips gently riding the length of her bare arm as she held herself.

"Don't think about it Maxie," Marc said softly. "It wasn't supposed to happen."

Maxie remembered feeling the warmth of his lips on her naked back, as if he were punctuating his statement. Regretfully, she willed everything in that moment to just disappear, but in facing reality, she closed her eyes and prayed. *Oh God. What am I doing here? What have I done? Lester ...* When she opened her eyes again, she gazed at the nightstand. What she saw brought tears to her eyes. On it was a lamp, a Bible, and an empty condom package ...

Lester snored lightly, but it was noisy enough to pull Maxie away from the difficult memory. Gently she rubbed the soft patch of hair on his chest, causing him to stir and tighten her in his embrace. "Go back to sleep," he whispered.

Maxie sighed. How could she go back to sleep? How had she been able to sleep for the past three nights, knowing the burden that weighed heavily on her? Since that evening, she no longer possessed the feelings of comfort, safety, or peace, that once accompanied her Christian walk, and she knew why. The course of her life shifted. Integrity, restraint, and steadfastness, were now replaced with lies, indulgence, and compromise.

Maxie wrestled with the thought of how her grandmother spent her latter years, instilling the former values into her, with the hope that one day she would grow to be a woman of virtue. Confident that her granddaughter was the righteous reflection of her laborious efforts, she believed her grandmother was able to die peaceably. *Oh but you would turn over in your grave now.* Maxie said inwardly, as she pressed her eyes closed in anguish.

Lightning flashes lit up the room again, only to be accompanied by a resounding rumble of thunder that echoed off of the trees, and gave the impression of something moving violently underground.

"I'm sorry," Maxie whispered, her voice echoing the distress of her heart. "God, I am so sorry."

* * * * * * * * * *

It was 10:00 a.m. when Maxie kissed Lester, and saw him off to work. After doing some light cleaning around the house, she made up their bed and sat on the edge of it. Gently smoothing out the wrinkles next to her, she recalled the earlier hours with her husband, and how during breakfast, Lester kept his word. Giving her his undivided attention, Maxie's reoccurring dream was the only topic of conversation.

Maxie remembered feeling a small sense of fear as she explained to him how her grandmother, Sister Adams, and the woman she felt was her mother, were in the Food King grocery store. Each woman was in a different aisle, at different times, and she was always positioned behind the register looking at them.

"So what do you think all of this means?" Lester asked. "They didn't say anything to you? What did their faces look like this time? Was there anything different about them? Were they smiling? Angry?"

Maxie sipped her orange juice. "No. It was just a relentless stare, without any expression on their faces. They didn't even look where they were going. They just walked with their eyes dead set on me, except for the one I believe was my mother. Every time I've seen her, her face is always distorted. And their steps ... They were so calculated. It was eerie. They looked so real Lester. That is until they faded away."

"You could actually see them fade this time? They didn't just walk down the aisle to where you couldn't see them from your register anymore?"

"No. They faded."

"Like ghosts."

"Yes, like ghosts."

Lester sighed, and was silent. Sipping his coffee, he watched his wife twist her wedding ring around on her finger, before her eyes met his. "Did it scare you this time?"

Maxie shrugged. "I don't know. I don't know."

"Didn't you tell me a while back, that your grandmother used to believe in ghosts?"

Maxie laughed a little, "Yeah, she did."

"Yes, but there was a reason *why* she believed in them." Lester frowned as he appeared to search for the answer. "What was it?"

"Actually, there were two reasons. Either they were haunting a person, or they were speaking out to them to warn them about something that wasn't good. It's like a myth in the Gullah Geechee culture."

"So?"

"Well, in the dream they don't say anything to me, so there's no warning, and I don't feel like I'm being haunted."

"Well, I for one don't believe in ghosts, but I do know that God can use people in our dreams whether they're close to us or not, dead or alive. A lot of times they can be used to give us warnings of some kind of danger. Now think about it. Are you doing, or have you done something that would cause that kind of warning?"

Maxie remembered her heart dropping heavily, and looking at her husband with eyes that were so pleading, it made him frown with concern. But before he had a chance to question her on it, she opened her mouth and lied.

"No, I'm not doing, nor have I done anything that would need a warning." Once again, having to lie to her husband pierced her to her soul.

Maxie replayed the lie twice in her mind as she bounced lightly on the bed, and it caused warm streams of tears to run down her face. She knew why all three of those women were in her dreams. It *was* a warning. They came to warn her about being with Marc.

"God," she whispered. "How did I get here?"

Maxie thought about the dream Sandra shared just before she left for Japan, and how she was warned even then about the animal in the cage and its release. But why wasn't the warning more explicit? Why didn't she know that the animal wasn't just *the world,* but a man who could offer her the world? And why had a hunger for the world, turned into a full blown love affair? She never knew, or expected it would come to this. Even Sandra's words about her marriage being tested, washed in like a tidal wave, making her feel queasy.

The more she thought about everything she did that led her up to that point, and the casualness in which it was all done, the more nauseous she became. In a matter of minutes, Maxie was in her bathroom bent over the toilet, violently releasing her breakfast, her tears, and more. When she finished, she sat on the floor in the corner between the toilet and the wall, and cried profusely. She knew something was going to have to be done to fix her life back. She just didn't know what that *something* was.

Chapter Fifty-One

The wee hours of Sunday morning, found Maxie wrapped in her housecoat and sitting at the kitchen table alone, with a hot cup of chamomile tea. She hoped the soothing properties of the tea would help to calm her, but it was doing nothing to quell the thoughts that were running rampant in her mind. Every mental picture she saw, had a trail of questions to which she didn't have the answers.

For the first time in months, Maxie felt alone and trapped. Alone, because there was absolutely no one she could go to and explain her situation. Trapped, because in spite of all the doors she had opened, there were none that would lead her to where she needed to be spiritually. Somehow, she would have to retrace her steps and go back to the place where she felt safe, and covered by God. But how could she do that? She had no idea how to get back to that place. Even if she did, how could she unload and forget about the contents of her heart? For over half an hour, Maxie mulled over that question alone.

Feeling a sudden chill, she pulled the top of her house-coat a little tighter. The steam from her cup of tea was gone, but she continued to dip the teabag anyway. When she looked at the clock on the stove, it read 4:45 a.m. Just like she had done for the past five mornings, Maxie wondered what Marc was doing. She also wondered where his thoughts were, since she had made no contact with him in nearly five days. Even though he sent her numerous text messages and left heartfelt voicemails on her cell phone, pleading with her to call him, she didn't respond.

Maxie knew she had to put forth her best effort in separating herself from Marc, cold turkey.

But it was killing her.

She could only liken the sickening feeling to that of someone suffering from a horrible addiction, and being harshly denied the very thing that gave them pleasure. The pain was staggering. From the depth of her soul, Maxie longed for Marc. The scent of his cologne, the feel of his muscular firmness when he held her, the warmth of his lips upon hers, and the resonating sound of his gentle voice against her ear — she longed for him. Since Wednesday morning, she successfully fought hard against the desire to see Marc. But by Friday, it took everything within her not to pick up the phone and ask him to meet her somewhere, just like she had done so many times before, to satisfy the craving she felt.

But she didn't yield.

Continuing on with the slow detox, Maxie put in her two weeks' notice. Then she went a little farther, and made a change to her work schedule for Thursday and Friday, just so she wouldn't have to face Marc, in case he came into the store during her normal work hours. Food King was the only communal ground they shared, so she knew he would come there to find her.

With regret clouding her eyes and causing them to brim with water, Maxie peered into her cup of tea and saw more than the brown liquid that filled it. Figuratively, she considered her own spiritual cup of all that God had appointed to her life, and it made her wonder. Was there really a test of her integrity in that cup, or did she allow herself to get so far off the path, that she *wandered* into the place where her integrity was tested? There was no mystery in finding out all that was actually in that spiritual cup. Just like a bowl of vegetable beef soup, the heavy ingredients sat on the bottom, and needed to be stirred to reveal the actual contents. Maxie knew how to stir her cup. In order to see most of what was being required of her, she knew it entailed diligence in fasting, praying, and studying the Word of God. But in the past few months she willfully refused to do any of that, because she knew God's plans and her plans, did not agree.

But now it was time out for *her* plans.

The warnings were repetitive, and she had seen and heard of enough calamities from her grandmother's circle of friends, to know that the warnings were nothing to play with. Everything in her current lifestyle needed to change. Things needed to go back to being normal, and that meant everything needed to turn. But how could she make that turn with Marc in full view? He still had a soul that needed to be saved, and she was certain he was one of the many souls God assigned to her hands. How was she to accomplish that task, now that she allowed her credibility to be tainted in the worst way?

Maxie pressed her eyes closed, and covered them with her hand. Everything in her life right now was like a massive ball of tangled thread, and any efforts to detangle it were almost futile. It was easy to entertain the thoughts of how to make the crooked places straight, but she had to be honest with herself. There was no way she could leave Marc alone. She needed help.

* * * * * * * * *

Marc tossed his cell phone down on the couch next to him, and tightened his jaws. He didn't want to let anger get the best of him, but Maxie was giving him reasons to be annoyed, and he didn't understand why. After months of being in each other's company, and recently sharing intimate moments together, her sudden and impetuous actions were not only out of character, but confusing to him as well. She did not return any of his phone calls or text messages, even after he left a threatening message to call her home number if she didn't answer. He was beginning to understand exactly how Maxie felt the weekend he chose not to return her calls. But the reasoning for *why* he did what he did was justifiable, and it only took him a weekend.

From Thursday through Saturday afternoon, during his lunch periods and after work, Marc visited Food King in hope of catching her during her shift, but to no avail. He was reassured by someone at the Customer Service desk that Maxie had not quit her job, but that person refused to give him any more information as to *when* she would actually *be* at work. With all of this being said and done, Marc could only come to one conclusion.

Something was wrong.

Knowing Maxie loved him, and hearing her express how she felt about him on many occasions, didn't equate with not hearing anything from her for almost five days.

When he didn't receive his usual *good morning* text message from her on Wednesday, he should have been concerned. From the day he gave her the cell phone, she often sent him special messages of encouragement, or sentiments to let him know she was thinking about him. The last message he received was Tuesday evening after she left him, letting him know she made it home safely through the storm.

Marc looked at his muted television, and saw one of Savannah's renowned ministers preaching like a mad man. The body language was interesting, but not enough for him to listen in. However, seeing the preacher made Marc consider thoughts about Maxie he didn't want to entertain. Did her husband find out about their relationship? Was she being forbidden to see him or talk to him? Marc couldn't bear the thought of Maxie ever having to defend their relationship. He also couldn't bear to think of her being hurt again by the chastening words of her husband, all because of him. The mere idea made the pit of his stomach roil.

Marc quickly turned the television off, and sat in silence. There was no way he could go another day without hearing from Maxie. He had to see her, and he had to know the reason behind her sudden withdrawal. If she wouldn't or couldn't respond to his efforts by way of the norm, he would have to meet her where he knew she would not deny him, and where his presence would be accepted by everyone.

Chapter Fifty-Two

While the morning scripture was being read, Maxie stood at the end of her row and held her Bible as if she were presenting gold to a king. Looking at the colorfully highlighted scripture verses, she lightly smiled at how they made her look studious.

"And may the Lord add a blessing to the reading, and the hearing of His Word. You may all be seated."

Maxie sat down and closed her Bible. Contrary to the momentum she hoped and needed to feel in the service, she felt a stall and a weight hanging in the atmosphere. The praise singers didn't usher in the spirit of the Lord like they were appointed to do, and most of them looked like she felt — heavy in spirit. With the morning service already deemed to be dry and boring to her once again, Maxie began to wonder about Marc. How was she going to separate herself from him romantically, and still be able to lead him to give his life to Christ? Shaking her head lightly, the thought was as preposterous as the deed. How could she even think to approach Marc with an agenda like that?

When the choir finished their rendition of *Grateful* by Hezekiah Walker, Maxie tuned in for the announcements that were next. With it being so close to Christmas, she needed to hear about all of the auxiliary meetings and out-reach plans. While she wrote down the information that was being given, the service conductor continued on to the acknowledgment of visitors. As they stood, the congregation clapped and Maxie did the same, without looking up from the paper she was writing on. Even when each visitor was asked to introduce themselves, she continued to write. It wasn't until she heard a voice that she recognized, did her head whip around to see the face that came with it. When her brain finished processing and registering the face in her psyche, and the actual location of *where* she was observing the person clicked in, pandemonium gripped her insides like a fitted leather glove.

It was Marc.

Her first reaction was to look in the pulpit at her husband to see if he noticed anything. But all she saw was Lester looking upon Marc with pride, because he was a man who had chosen their church as his place to worship this Sunday. He was totally oblivious as to *who* that particular man really was, and Lester's ignorance hurt Maxie to the core. Lowering her head a little, she closed her eyes, and pressed the bridge of her nose with her hand for a quick moment. To anyone who noticed her, she would appear to be in deep thought, or alleviating a sudden bout of sinus pressure. When in reality, she was really trying to calm herself and get her breathing back under control. The sight of Marc standing diagonally adjacent from her, made her heart beat so loudly, she just knew the woman sitting next to her could hear it.

"Girl that man is fine," Maxie heard one of the women in front of her whisper, as she peered over her shoulder to look at Marc. "I wonder if he's married."

"Even if he isn't," the woman next to her replied. "You are."

"Girl, since when did that make a difference?"

Maxie felt like she was going to be sick. The surprise at seeing Marc, mixed and swirled with the love she had for him, and a fear that almost paralyzed her. She wanted to go to the restroom, but doubted her legs had enough strength to carry her there.

"Sister Bruce, are you all right?" An usher whispered in her ear.

"Yes, I'm fine," Maxie whispered back without looking up.

"Do you need a napkin or maybe a fan?"

"No, thank you."

"Okay, well just let me know."

Maxie nodded. Knowing the usher's concern had probably drawn attention directly to her, she lifted her head and once again looked in the pulpit at Lester. This time he was gazing at her with a look that asked *what's going on?* Forcing a smile, she winked her eye at him and watched relief change his countenance.

She had to go to the restroom, and she had to go now. With every ounce of strength within her, Maxie stood up, gathered her purse, and immediately headed for the sanctuary doors, without once looking in Marc's direction. As she entered the restroom, two little girls who were leaving practically ran into her. Maxie didn't acknowledge them or anyone else, but headed straight for an empty stall where once again her breakfast was released, only not as violently as before. *Get yourself together girl,* she thought, as she fought against the heaves. Not until recently, had she ever been under so much stress that it would cause her to be nauseous, to the point of actually vomiting.

When she was finished, Maxie rinsed her mouth, washed her face with cool water, and patted it dry with a paper towel, before she looked around for witnesses. The restroom was empty.

"What were you thinking to come here?" She said aloud, as she paced the floor. "Why on earth *would you* come here? How did you even know where to find me?" Maxie audibly voiced every question that came to mind, until someone came into the restroom; at which point she pretended to wash her hands and fix her hair.

For at least fifteen minutes, she continued going back and forth with herself, and a mental picture of Marc. In that time frame, Maxie decided that when the service was over, she would attend the visitor's reception with the Welcoming Committee, in order to question Marc. She was certain he would go there, with the hope that she would come to him, and act like she was meeting him for the first time. She already factored in that he would be surrounded by many women of the church, primarily those who were hungry to know his marital status. With that understanding, being discreet was going to be a challenge. Even The Ominous Three would undoubtedly try to get his attention, but that wasn't going to deter her.

Maxie took a deep breath, straightened her clothes in the mirror, and returned to her seat.

* * * * * * * * * *

The remainder of the service seemed to drag on the heels of eternity. Maxie did her best to keep her mind in the service, but it was hard to do when the man who held her heart was staring at her every time she glanced at him. *God, why does he have to look so good?* She questioned. Throughout the church service, she wanted to signal for him to meet her outside in the hallway, but thoughts of Lester and the insinuating words that he might hear from those passing by, kept her planted in her seat.

When the benediction was given and closed with an Amen, Maxie turned in Marc's direction just in time to see him being escorted by Emma Teal to the visitor's reception. Before he walked out of the doors that led to the vestibule, Marc looked at her, and lightly gestured with his head for her to follow them. Without any acknowledgment, Maxie looked around the sanctuary at the remaining crowd, and the slow procession to the hallway. Her exit was hindered because of congestion, so getting to the reception immediately was not possible.

Maxie quelled her anxiety a little, and knelt down to pick up her purse and Bible from underneath the seat in front of her. When she stood up, Lester was directly in front of her.

"Lester!" Maxie gasped softly. "What ...?"

"I have a quick meeting with the Pastor and the Brotherhood Committee. You want to hang around here, or head on home? I can have one of the brothers give me a ride to the house."

Maxie glanced at the waning processional, and looked back at her husband. "I'll hang around for a few minutes.

We're supposed to go to that new restaurant down on River Street remember?"

"Yeah, Brother Askew and Brother Johnson said they might join us. Do you want to wait with their wives?"

"No, I'll be fine. I need to find out some more information about how the Outreach Team wants to do the Toys for Tots program. Go ahead. I'll be around the church somewhere."

Lester smiled, pulled Maxie to him, and kissed her on her forehead. "I love you woman. You know that right?"

Maxie smiled back. "I know you do. And I love you too."

When Lester started to walk away from her, Maxie instantly thought about how many times those words passed between lovers and *others*.

"Hey," Lester stopped and said. "What was wrong with you earlier? Before you winked at me, you looked as if you had seen a ghost. You all right?"

Maxie nodded, "I'm fine baby. Now would you go to your meeting, so it can be over already? You know they're not going to start unless you're there."

Lester smiled again, and walked away.

Quickly, Maxie looked at her watch and tracked the minutes that Marc had been in the reception. If she went in there now, the crowd of well-wishers and onlookers would have moved on. Cradling her belongings, she left the sanctuary, and made a bee line for the Fellowship Hall. When she arrived, she stood in the doorway and peered in. There were more people claiming to be on the committee than she had ever seen before, and most of them were women. Collectively, they stood around Marc as if he were delivering a presidential address. Without drawing attention to herself, Maxie walked in and remained close to the wall.

When she came into Marc's view, he glanced at her long enough to discreetly smile at her, and then continued to give all of the women his attention. The scene made Maxie chuckle inside. It was like Marc was in his element with all of those women, and she felt somewhat jealous. She didn't want to appear as if she were waiting, so Maxie started random conversations with different church members who were a little resistant to leave. All the while, she kept watch on Marc's crowd, as it slowly began to diminish. When the last woman left, and The Ominous Three found another life to harp on, Maxie moved in slowly. With half a smile on his face, and a cup of juice at his lips, Marc watched her walk toward him.

"Truly, you are the most beautiful woman in this church," he said in a low tone, without moving his cup from his mouth.

"Truly, you are the craziest man I know," she said, in an equally low tone. Scanning the room, Maxie saw that there were three other visitors, still talking with a few committee members.

"Marc what are you doing here?"

Removing the cup from his mouth, Marc kept his tone low. "Wow. Is that the normal greeting a visitor gets when he comes to this church? I'd hate to see the response I'd get if I had chosen to give my life to Christ."

"You know what I meant. And that's not funny. What are you doing here? Better yet, with all of the churches in this city, how did you know this was my church?"

"Love always finds a way baby. Didn't your grandmother ever tell you that?"

Maxie looked at the floor, laughed a little, and then looked at Marc again. "Why are you …?"

"Why are you avoiding me?" Marc said with a gentle measure of sternness in his voice.

Maxie gazed into his eyes, and noticed the humor was gone. For what she'd swear was an eternity, a moment of silence fell between them. She didn't know what to say. She couldn't even look at him anymore, so she looked at the floor again. "Marc ... I ... It's so complicated."

"Maxie look at me."

Feeling the weight of guilt and shame on the back of her neck, Maxie raised her head slowly, to capture Marc's gaze again.

"Are you still in love with me?"

She looked around.

"I'm over here," Marc said. "You do still love me don't you?"

"Yes," she said after gaining her focus. "Yes I love you."

"I'm sorry. I hear nothing complicated there. My feelings are the same for you, so nothing's changed. What are you trying to do? Walk away from me? Why Maxie? Are you being forbidden to see me? Does your husband know about us?"

Maxie pressed her eyes closed for a brief moment, and nodded. "No, no. It's nothing like that."

"So what are you trying to do to us? Why did I even have to come here to see you? Track you down. You wouldn't return my messages ... my texts. I know you changed your schedule at work." Marc sighed heavily and shrugged. "What? You want this to be over?"

Maxie's head was swimming. Once again she looked around the room, but this time it was to get her bearings. However, that which she intended, only made matters worse when she saw Deacon Earl Bayer across the room.

With a pungent smile on his face, he sat watching Maxie's entire exchange with Marc.

"Oh God ..." she whispered. "This is too much."

"What? Our relationship is too much for you now?"

Maxie instantly felt overwhelmed. With downcast eyes, the floor began to blur behind her tears. Her secret life had literally crept into the church, and was standing right in front of her. "Marc, don't do this here," she pleaded.

Marc whispered strongly, "Where then Maxie? You won't talk to me on the phone. You choose not to talk to me, and I don't even know why! One minute you're telling me how much you love me and the next minute you're. ..."

"There you are," Lester said as he entered the room, and walked toward her. "I started not to check in here. Good thing I did."

Lester's quick movements toward her, coupled with the heaviness of the moment, caught Maxie totally off guard with no time to recover. With tears still in her eyes, she looked at her husband as he approached her.

"Are you ready? Baby what's wrong?" He asked, without even acknowledging the fact that someone was standing directly in front of her.

Maxie forced a smile, and began wiping away her tears with her fingertips, before Lester took her face in his hands, and cleared the rest away with his thumbs.

"I'm fine," she said, laughing a little. "You know how emotional I can get, when I hear other people's testimonies about what God has done for them. This brother was just sharing something with me."

Lester looked at Marc with a furrowed brow, before a slight smile crossed his face. "Oh yeah, you were the only brother in the crowd of visitors today. How are you?" Lester extended his hand. "I'm Lester Bruce."

Marc glanced at Maxie quickly, before he shook Lester's hand. "Marc Thomas."

"Mar … Mr. Thomas, Lester is my husband," Maxie said. Keeping her eyes on Lester, she smiled at him, and tried to show happiness and contentment in him being there.

Lester looked at her, and wrapped one arm around her waist, as he kissed her forehead. "That's right," he said without taking his eyes off of her. "And I love being that. You a married man Mr. Thomas?"

Maxie looked at Marc and saw that his jaws were tightening, as he briefly focused on the floor. She knew instantly what he was feeling, and it cut her like a knife.

"No," he replied, looking at Lester and then at Maxie. "I can't say that I've met a woman worthy of that kind of commitment."

Again, tears flooded Maxie's eyes. Marc's words accomplished the damage he sent them out to do.

"Well, I'd like to say that God broke the mold when He made my wife, but I think that comment would be a little biased," Lester chuckled.

Without a word, Marc took a sip of his drink with Maxie in his focus. She did not even look at him.

"Well I hope you enjoyed the service," Lester continued. "We're having a special Christmas Eve service this Wednesday night. If you're available, I'd like for you to come on back and visit with us then."

Marc finished his drink, and held his empty cup. "Thank you for the invitation, but I'm due to be out of the country next week on a business trip."

With a soft look of question and surprise, Maxie's eyes locked with Marc's briefly, but intensely. As of the beginning of last week when she was with him, he told her nothing about going out of the country, even after they discussed how often his ventures were abroad. Obviously he felt it was something she didn't need to know, and even now as he made the statement, there was a look of indifference on his face. Perhaps if she had stayed in touch with him, she would have known this important piece of information.

"Maybe I'll stop through another time," Marc said to Lester.

Lester extended his hand again, and Marc grasped it quickly. "Not a problem brother. We're always here."

Maxie opened her mouth to concur with Lester, and just as she did, another voice boomed over hers.

"My God. Is this another brother in the house?"

Lester grinned. "Deacon Earl Bayer, this is Mr. Marc Thomas. He's a visitor that I'm trying to coax into coming back, and joining us for our special service on Wednesday night."

Maxie felt the temperature in the room begin to rise, making her feel a bit uncomfortable.

"Mr. Thomas," Deacon Earl said, as if he were throwing Marc's name into the air and catching it. "Well God bless you. I'm happy you decided to worship here with us today. We love it when new brothers come into the house of God. Don't you agree Sister Bruce?"

Maxie looked at the sinister grin on Deacon Earl's face, and to her own surprise she matched it with a look that said *I dare you*. "Yes we sure do Deacon Earl. As a matter of fact," Maxie said as she looked directly at Marc. "I was just getting ready to tell Mr. Thomas that outside of my husband, this church lacks *real* and *quality* men, and that his presence here would be a great addition to the ministry, should he ever think of returning and joining." Maxie smiled. Not so much at Marc, but at her own witty comeback to the meddling Earl Bayer. But just as she delivered her gentle blow to his ego, she knew to expect a comeback of equal or greater proportions.

"So Mr. Thomas, haven't I met you somewhere before?" Deacon Earl quested.

Before Marc could even think to open his mouth to answer the question that might incriminate him, Maxie interjected. "Lester honey, aren't the Askews and Johnsons waiting for us?" Quickly, she locked her arms around one of his.

"Oh you know what?" Lester glanced at his watch. "I forgot all about them. We better get going. I told them we'd all go over to the restaurant together. Hey Marc, why don't you join us? Every single man needs a good meal. If we were going home, I'd invite you over to our house for a delicious meal cooked by my wife. But restaurant food will have to do today. Would you like to join us?"

Deacon Earl coughed deeply as if he choked on something, and Maxie squirmed a little at Lester's innocent invitation. Chuckling lightly with his eyes on Maxie, Marc calmly replied. "Thank you Mr. Bruce. But I've made other plans. Again, maybe we can set a date another time."

"Honey," Maxie pleaded.

"I know sweetheart," Lester said. "Well Marc, it was nice to meet you, and I do hope you'll be coming back to visit with us soon."

"Thank you," Marc said. "And thank you too Mrs. Bruce, for making me feel so welcomed here."

Maxie forced a smile under Lester's watchful eye. "God bless you," was all she could say, and grasped Lester's arm even tighter.

"All right Deacon Earl, you have yourself a blessed evening, and we'll see you at the Christmas Eve service," Lester continued.

"Yes ... same to you all. I'll see you then," Deacon Earl said. "I think I'm going to be heading on out myself." Without further acknowledgment to Marc, Deacon Earl walked back to the area he came from, and exited through a side door.

When Maxie and Lester began their trek through the doorway, Maxie vowed to herself that there was no way she was going to turn around to look at Marc. The entire discussion from start to finish, presented enough drama in it to last her a lifetime, and she just wanted to leave. Besides, she knew she could not stomach the look in his eyes, as he watched her walk away from him — on the arm of her husband.

Chapter Fifty-Three

Maxie took a fifteen minute break, and sipped on a Cherry Coke in the café of Food King. Just coming in to work was challenging, because she came in feeling perplexed and weighted. The fact that it was Senior Citizen Tuesday, and two days before Christmas, didn't make it any better. Since Sunday evening and all of Monday, her heart and spirit waged a war within her mind. *He didn't deserve what I did to him,* she kept telling herself. The comment was made in reference to the last time she saw Marc, but she found that with all she had done, it applied to Lester as well.

Maxie's world was unraveling at a scary pace, and trying to redirect her life was like fighting against what she already knew was a hopeless battle. The control she claimed would be so easy to keep — had long been lost. Marc Thomas had *fully* captured her heart, and she was nearly certain she didn't want to continue the efforts of trying to recover it. She acknowledged that fact to herself Sunday, when she walked away from Marc on Lester's arm.

She tried to refute it, but the feeling of love for him was too overwhelming.

Maxie wanted to be with Marc.

That was the reason why she cried, when she stood before him Sunday. She felt trapped in two different worlds; wanting full access to the one that benefitted her heart, but knowing the other held her ultimate destiny. Trying to choose on the side of destiny, prompted her to compliment herself for at least making attempts to turn the other way.

For almost five days, she had gone without seeing Marc, and it was helpful for what she was trying to do. "But there you were," Maxie whispered to herself and sighed, as she slowly twirled the ice around in her cup. Seeing Marc at her church cast a new light on everything, and it made her consider his words from a while back. Maybe they could continue spending time together. Nothing had to change. Their relationship could remain the same, and they didn't have to do anything different to accommodate the way they felt about each other. Everything was already in place.

Or was it?

Quickly she considered the way she left Marc Sunday afternoon, and the fact that neither one of them had so much as made an effort to contact the other since then. Rubbing the outside pocket of her smock, Maxie felt the compact flip phone inside. Had Marc already left the country? Where was he going this time?

Maxie looked at her watch. Surveying her surroundings, she pulled out the phone and pressed the number one for speed dial. After four long rings, and the beginning words of Marc's voice mail, she closed the phone and held it in her hand. *Would you really leave the country without telling me goodbye?* She didn't want to add the fact that it was close to Christmas. The mere thought of him actually leaving now, without saying anything, hurt her deeply. But could she really fault him? After all, hadn't she inflicted the same amount of pain on him, and simply walked away?

* * * * * * * * *

Marc was grateful he was able to get a flight to India, on such short notice. Because of the Christmas holiday rush and a last minute decision, he spent most of the morning on the phone with his travel agent, and other gemologists around the city. They were all gathering for a meeting, and a tour of the newest GIA laboratory in Mumbai. He was also grateful that his plane was scheduled to leave later on in the evening, because for the first time in his corporate career, he was not prepared for departure.

Marc had not totally made up his mind about the three day overseas venture, until after he saw Maxie with her husband Sunday. He didn't really know what he expected to see, or how he expected her to act. All he knew was that seeing her with Lester, struck a nerve in him that he forgot existed. Until that moment, he hadn't considered that Maxie could *never* be completely his. He knew she was married, but for the moments she was with him, she *was* his. Seeing her hanging on the arm of another man — her husband — doused him with a cup of reality that penetrated him to the core. With all that Maxie had been to him recently, the realization of having to share her love, was more than he cared to accept right now.

He wanted to get away.

Against the wishes of his grandmother, Marc hastily accepted an invite from one of his colleagues, to leave the country. Even though he offered Stella the opportunity to travel with him as a Christmas present to her, the elderly woman didn't budge one inch toward the thought of joining him, just as her somber comments of having to spend Christmas alone, didn't move him to stay.

With last minute phone calls to the voice mails of Beatrice and Jaunee, explaining his whereabouts for the next few days, Marc finished packing, and set his suitcases near the door to the garage. Just as he was about to retrieve his laptop bag from his bedroom, both his home phone, and the doorbell sounded off simultaneously. He wasn't expecting any company, and opted to answer the phone first. Then he quickly remembered his conversation with his neighbor's daughter, about the arrival of his Sally Foster fundraiser order.

"Hold on Candace. I'm coming," he yelled over the ringing telephone, and rushed to the door. When he opened it, what he saw made him stand still and stare.

"You're replacing me already? Who is Candace?" Maxie asked, forcing a slight smile.

With no expression on his face, Marc said nothing, and kept his stance with his hand on the doorknob.

"I guess this mistletoe up here doesn't work when you're mad at me huh?"

Again he said nothing, nor did he move.

"Baby let me in so I can explain."

Standing and staring expressionless for a moment longer, Marc pushed the door open wider, and walked toward the living room without looking back to see if Maxie walked in or not. Casually, he stopped and stood in front of the fireplace with his back to her. With clenched teeth, he pressed his eyes closed, and took a deep breath. He wanted to be angry with her. He *needed* to be angry with her, just so he could continue with his plans of leaving the country. But in all honesty, the sight of Maxie on the other side of his door, softened his heart and lifted him. Her radiance immediately reached out to him, and he wanted to reach back, but he couldn't be that easy.

"What?" Maxie asked, as she removed and hung her coat. "You can't look at me now?"

Marc took another deep breath before he spoke, and refused to turn around. Judging from the sound of her voice, he figured she was standing a few paces within the living room.

"Maxie why are you here?" He asked dryly.

"Marc, we need to talk."

"Really now? And you came to that conclusion when?"

"I know that I ..."

Marc turned around quickly. "I have a plane to catch, and you're about five days too late with an explanation."

Maxie lowered her head, and raised it slowly with somber eyes that pleadingly met his. Marc was crushed, but kept his composure.

"I accept your anger," she said. "You have every right to be upset with me. After we'd spent that afternoon together here ... I ... it wasn't ... well you just didn't deserve the way I treated you afterward. And I'm sorry."

Marc tried hard to appear cold, and unmoved. "Are you finished?"

"Marc don't do this ... please. I was confused. I thought separating from you would help me to get everything back into the right perspective. I didn't know what else to do. I had to try to balance the things in my life. God. My husband. Who I am to other people. *You*. My ministry. Right now, I don't even know if I have a ministry." Maxie paused, shrugged her shoulders, and barely spoke audibly. "I didn't know what else to do."

Marc looked at his watch, and heaved a sigh in an effort to show his indifference. But when he saw the steady stream of tears running down Maxie's face, his heart got the best of him. Walking to her, he wrapped his arms around her, and held her close; something he wanted to do when he first saw her standing outside of his door.

"Didn't I tell you that you don't have to do anything?" Marc said in a low tone. "Just leave things the way they are." Maxie quickly wrapped her arms around him. He could tell she was letting her tears flow more freely, because as she rested her head against his shoulder, he felt her catching her breath in between sobs. "Shh," he whispered. "Stop crying."

"I hurt you," Maxie whispered back. "I never wanted to hurt you Marc. I just didn't know ...."

"I know you didn't. And it's fine now. See, look at me." Marc lifted Maxie's chin so she could look at him squarely. When their eyes met, he studied her briefly before giving in to the passion that was permeating the moment. Gently he kissed her, as if he were reacquainting himself with something that once belonged to him. When he finished, Marc wiped away Maxie's tears with his thumbs, and held her face. "Even with tears streaming down your cheeks, you're beautiful. Do you know that?"

Maxie smiled weakly.

Marc held her close again, and briefly looked at his watch with a glance that was two-fold. One reminded him he had less than three hours before his flight was scheduled to leave, and the drive to the airport could be over an hour with traffic. The other told him Maxie arrived at his front door, at a time when her husband expected her home.

"Oh Maxie," he moaned. You came here straight from work didn't you?"

Maxie nodded her head just enough for Marc to feel the movement. "I had to take the risk," she said lowly. "I wasn't even sure you would be here. I just knew I had to come, because I couldn't bear the thought of you leaving the country, with things the way they are between us. We need to talk." Maxie pushed herself away from him a little, and looked at the luggage near the garage door. "What time does your flight leave?"

"I was actually on my way out the door when you rang the bell. I only have a little more than a couple of hours to get to the airport."

Maxie pushed further away from him, and sighed heavily. "Marc, why are you leaving two days before Christmas?"

Marc simply looked at her. Maxie turned and walked a few paces away from him. Pensively, she stood with her back to him, and put her hand to her forehead before she laughed a little.

"You're trying to get away from me."

"Maxie ..."

"I can't believe this. What I did, hurt you to the point where you need time away from me?"

"Maxie, I just ..." Marc walked behind her, gently grabbed her arms, and leaned in close. "I couldn't stand to see you with him that way."

"Marc he's my husband."

"I know that, and I understand it, and I don't care. The fact that he is your husband, doesn't make it any easier for

me to see you interact with him. And then you made everything harder, when you decided you didn't want to talk to
me for nearly five days. I just need to get away for a little
while to clear my head."

Maxie turned to face him. "So you admit this is getting
harder for you too?"

Marc narrowed his eyes and gave her a questioning
look. "Maxie, I'm not always going to have to see you with
your husband. But it's apparent you have an issue with this.
What's really going on? Is that what you want to talk about?
Is this relationship getting hard for you?"

"Baby I just need you to understand where I am."

"Where are you Maxie? I thought that you were here
with me."

Maxie walked away, and stood with her back to him
again. "My mind is everywhere Marc. I am so confused."
Silent for a moment, she turned to him with tears streaming
down her face again. "You and I share something that is so
special. I don't always have that with Lester. You understand the side of me that I'm still coming to know, and you
open me up to ideas and thoughts I never would have considered. I love who I am when I'm with you. Everything
feels so good. So right." Laughing a little, she negatively
nodded her head. "I am so in love with you ... I am so in
love with you, that it's hard for me to be honest with myself
at times. That's my dilemma. I know what we're doing is
wrong. We both know it's wrong."

"Maxie ...."

"No. Let me finish. I know it's wrong." She shrugged.
"But I can't let you go. I don't want to. Marc, I *want* to be
with you. I want nothing more than to be with you all of the
time, and that scares me right now."

"Maxie why are you scared? You don't have to be afraid of me. I love you. I would never knowingly hurt you."

"I know you wouldn't. It's not that. There's so much ... so much that you *don't* know about me. Who I am and what I've come from, the purpose of my life, and where I need to be in my walk with God. It all pulls on me. I'm the wife of a minister, and I minister to the sick and shut-in. I'm committed to other duties at my church. ..."

"Maxie stop. You're rambling. What's going on? What are you trying to tell me?"

Maxie took a deep breath, and released it in a manner that equaled her frustration. Shaking her head negatively, she shrugged her shoulders and said nothing.

"Why are you fighting?" Marc asked, as Maxie walked to the sofa and sat. "Talk to me Maxie."

Without a word, she bowed her head, and held it with one hand.

"Maxie?"

"Marc, do you understand me when I say there is a divine calling on my life? A divine purpose I need to fulfill?"

"Yes I do," Marc replied, as he sat next to her.

"Then you must understand what I'm feeling inside of me. I'm trying to walk and operate in two totally different worlds. I'm leading a double life, and it's causing a fight within me. It feels like turmoil right now."

"Maxie the turmoil you're feeling, comes from the fact that you are trying to answer this call when you're not ready. You're simply not ready. You just said that you love what we have together. Our relationship has a lot of meaning to the both of us right now." Marc paused and gently turned her face toward him. "Hey, I'm in here with you, baby. Why don't you just let what we have, run its course? Nothing compares with what's between us now, right?" Maxie nodded no. "So aren't we entitled to this? You've been more than faithful to your church, and to God. And I'm sure He is pleased with you thus far. Why can't you be faithful to yourself for a just a little while? Be true to you. You've spent a lot of time caring and seeing to the needs of others, but when was the last time you tended to your own needs? Maxie don't get me wrong on this, I know that fulfilling your purpose is important. One day I'll find out what my purpose is, and it will be just as important to me. But I don't believe that it's going to be a fight. When a person has a made up mind, they can accomplish anything. Your mind isn't made up, so I don't believe you should answer the call right now. Baby be honest. Wouldn't it be more of a disservice to God if your heart isn't in what you're trying to do for Him?"

"Yes ... I know that," she whispered.

Marc kissed her forehead, both of her cheeks, and then her mouth, as he whispered, "Then don't think about this anymore. Just stay with me Maxie. Your heart is so open to me now. Let me take you places you've never been before."

Maxie closed her eyes, and relaxed in the warmth of Marc's kisses and his words. Recognizing the ambiance as one she had been in before, she let herself slip away as Marc gently laid her back on the sofa.

Chapter Fifty-Four

Maxie sat on the floor near the Christmas tree, and gently removed the silver bow from the small gift box Lester had given her. When she opened it, a flight boarding pass fell from its sleeve. In silence, she picked it up and read all of the information on it, before a broad grin spread across her face.

"Lester? You're taking me to Paris, France for a week?" She asked in amazement, as she continued to examine the paper.

"Yeah. I want us to do something special, since next month marks our eighth year of marriage," Lester said proudly, as he sat next to her on the floor. "Our itinerary is in there too. I'm planning on it being like a second honeymoon."

Maxie gently nodded, without taking her eyes off of the paper.

Lester watched her for a moment and grinned. "So? What do you think? I wanted to surprise you with it on our anniversary. But I thought since it's Christmas, today would be just as good, and you'd have enough time to prepare for the trip."

"Baby I … I'm surprised. I think this is the best Christmas and anniversary present you've ever given to me," Maxie beamed, when she finally looked at him. "We're actually going to Paris." Maxie hugged Lester tightly. "Oh, thank you baby. This is so nice."

"Not only that. But we're staying at the Crowne Plaza Hotel Paris-Champs Elysees."

"Really? I think I read about that place. It used to be a private mansion right?"

"Um hum. It's a beautiful place."

"And a very expensive place. Lester isn't it like over three hundred dollars a night to stay there?"

Lester smiled.

"Oh my goodness! Baby?" She pleaded.

"Nope. It's already paid for, and we're going. Our anniversary falls on a Sunday, so we're leaving out that Thursday afternoon, and we'll arrive at Charles De Gaulle airport early Friday morning. The flight will be long, but I'm planning on us resting for a couple of days, and ordering a lot of room service."

Maxie glanced at her husband, and smiled. "So this is what you've been up to. The little secret you've been planning." Lester kept his smile, as Maxie kissed his lips. "I can't believe you did this. Thank you again baby. I'm so excited."

Maxie placed the ticket back in its box and stood up, while Lester searched through the gifts under the tree.

"Anything in particular you're looking for?" Maxie teased.

"Yeah. I gave you your anniversary gift. Now I'm looking for mine."

Maxie laughed. "Don't even try it Lester. Today is the twenty-fifth of December, not the twenty-fifth of January. You're just going to have to wait."

Lester stood up in front of her. "Well it better be something pretty spectacular," he said, pulling her closer to him.

Maxie wrapped her arms around his neck. "It's not nearly as spectacular as your gift to me, but I think you're going to like it."

"You do huh?"

"Umm hum," Maxie purred, brushing her lips against his. "Merry Christmas baby."

"Merry Christmas Maxie."

Chapter Fifty-Five

Saturday morning, Maxie peered out of the living room window at a thick blanket of snow that unexpectedly fell overnight. In spite of its calming effect, and how beautifully the snow glistened in the sun's rays, Maxie felt herself growing anxious. Snow in Savannah was rare. Even though she welcomed the chilly reminder of wintertime in Brooklyn, she felt the timing of it could not have been any worse. Marc was due home today, and now his flight from India would ultimately be delayed.

Maxie sighed heavily, as she recalled her last conversation with him the night he left for India. She also recalled the promise she made to honor his urgent request to meet with him, as soon as he returned home. Now with the weather being the way it was, and Marc's arrival time possibly being much later than originally planned, she doubted very seriously that she would be able to keep her promise.

"I made us some hot chocolate." Lester said. "Come over here and sit by the fire with me."

Maxie continued to look out of the window. "Did you know it snowed last night?"

"Uhm hmm. I was surprised by it when I stepped out to get the paper earlier. I think the weather man was surprised by it too. He forecasted rain. It's beautiful isn't it?"

"Yes it is," Maxie replied, sounding almost mesmerized. "And very cold."

"That's why I made us some cocoa. I put extra marshmallows in yours. Now come over here and cuddle with me by this fire."

Maxie turned to see Lester standing and holding a mug in each hand. "Lester it's ten o'clock in the morning. Isn't it a little early for cuddle time?"

"Woman this is the first Saturday in months, where both of us are off work at the same time. The entire city is shut down because of this weather, and I plan to enjoy it. So it's cuddle time whenever I say it's cuddle time today. Now come on over here."

Maxie laughed lightly, and walked to Lester. "It's been a while since we've had hot chocolate." Maxie took her mug and lightly blew into it. "I'm surprised you remembered how much I like extra marshmallows in mine."

Lester smiled, and sat on the blanket he laid in front of the fireplace. "It's been a while since we've done a lot of things we used to do. But all of that's going to change now. That's one good reason why I'm glad you put in your notice at that store. I want some things back to the way they used to be."

Maxie quietly sat down next to Lester, and rested in the crook of his arm, as he leaned his back against the couch. She didn't want to think on her husband's last statement, but the words *back to the way they used to be,* rang loudly in her ears.

As the fire spread from the starter log, Maxie looked around. The moment had the characteristics of everything romantic, but she found it somewhat hard to grasp. Something felt out of place. It wasn't until Lester stroked her hair, and gently touched the side of her face with his fingertips, did she begin to feel an inkling of being in sync with him.

"This is what I miss," Lester said in a low tone, and tucked a tendril of hair behind Maxie's ear. "I miss you. I miss us."

Maxie glanced at him, before she laughed uneasily. "What do you mean you miss us Lester? Baby nothing's changed with us."

Lester nodded. "No, something *has* changed. I don't know exactly what it is, but it's something. You seem preoccupied or distracted. Almost like you're pulling away from me."

Totally surprised by his statement, Maxie was at a loss for words. Immediately she searched the area with her eyes, before looking at him again. "Me? Lester are you serious?" Maxie watched half a smile come to Lester's face, and fade quickly.

Gently, he blew into his cup before taking a few sips. "I'm just telling you how I feel, and what I've observed."

Maxie was silent, and briefly stared at the blanket. *Lester noticed a difference in her.* When she honestly considered where her focus was, and how much her thoughts were consumed by all things Marc, a sudden twinge of anxiety roiled in her stomach. Her wayward thoughts found a way to become evident in her demeanor, and that meant only one thing. She was being uncovered. With all sincerity, and every effort to suppress any appearance or feelings of guilt, Maxie looked at Lester squarely. "Baby, I would never pull away from you. How could I possibly do that? I love you. How long have you been feeling like this?"

"I don't know. Maybe a month or so."

"Why haven't you said anything about it before now?"

Lester shrugged, and gave Maxie a light smile. "I don't know. I guess I didn't want to entertain the thought of anything ever coming between us. Besides, I didn't want to overreact by mentioning it to you, before I could be more certain."

A hard silence fell between them, and Maxie's mind reeled. *Now he was more certain?* "I don't know Lester. Maybe it's my job. I mean working is a major step for me. I could be distracted by that. And now, since it's almost over ...." Maxie shrugged, and looked into the fire. "I guess I've been thinking about how I'm going to make the transition back."

"That's a possible reason I guess." Lester set his mug on the floor, and looked into the fire for a moment, before he focused on her again. "Maxie, I know there are times when you think I don't understand you, and that couldn't be the furthest thing away from the truth. I understand you more than you know baby. And you can come to me, and talk to me about anything. You do understand that don't you?"

Instantly the heat of his stare, was felt on the side of her face. Gently, Lester took her by her chin, and turned her to face him.

"I mean if you're struggling with anything naturally, or spiritually, and you can't seem to overcome it because it has you tangled, or if you find yourself in a trial that might seem too hard for you to bear, you know you can bring it to me, and I'll help you right?"

Maxie searched her husband's eyes, and saw a sincerity that rocked her. Almost immediately, a wave of emotion overtook her, and filled her eyes with water. *God?* She asked within. *What does he know?* "Yes," she whispered and nodded.

After staring at her for a moment, Lester gave Maxie a soft smile and pulled her to him. Feeling the soft tenderness of his lips against her forehead, she was immediately rapt in the intimacy that arrested the moment. Without saying another word, Lester picked up his mug and looked into the fire. Maxie held her gaze, and marveled at the serenity she saw in her husband's face. His words reminding her of his place in her life.

It was true, Lester was the priest of his home. He was her protector; her intercessory prayer warrior; her spiritual counselor; her push and guide; her ultimate covering — and he was comfortable in being all of that for her. Although she never honestly weighed her life, and her marriage against the lives and marriages of other women she knew, she was fully aware that in today's society, what she had in Lester was rare and desirable. Yet in having all of that, she still found herself wanting.

* * * * * * * * * *

For most of the day, Maxie and Lester stayed home and spent time together, as if no one else in the world existed except for the two of them. Maxie tried hard to just let herself go, and get lost in the precious moment. Every time she did, her thoughts pushed her into a corner where she teetered between her husband's sincere words, and her tainted deeds. From the poignant flow of Lester's heart felt words, there should have been a strong measure of conviction that stayed with her — if for no other reason — to point her ardent longing back to him. But his words may as well have fallen on stony ground, because it didn't change her desire to see and be with Marc. It amazed her how the very thing she tried to shut down for nearly five days, proved it had grown into a passion that was stronger, and less controllable than she ever imagined.

Now she was confused.

Was this the animal Sandra described to her from her dream? Or was the animal her hunger for the world? Were the two the same? Which one would suddenly turn on her, and cause her to run from it with a look of terror on her face?

Maxie no longer wanted to do the math. It wasn't adding up, and it was silly. Marc would never harm her, and what she desired from the world was so minute, she didn't even find it worth considering.

"Do you want to watch one of those shows on Lifetime?" Lester asked, looking down at her as she lay on the couch with her head in his lap.

Maxie shrugged. Even though she was looking at the television, she wasn't watching it. "That's fine baby," she mumbled. "It doesn't matter what we watch. I'm probably going to take a nap right here anyway."

"Do you want to lay in front of the fireplace?"

Maxie looked up at her husband and smiled. "You're going for the cozy junket again aren't you?"

Lester returned her smile. "All day long. Remember how often we used to do that?"

"You mean when we first bought this house?"

"Yeah."

"Mmm humm. I remember."

"We used to lay over there and just talk, and laugh until the wee hours of the morning. Anything that came to mind, we talked about it."

Maxie watched her husband drift into the past for a moment, before he focused on her again.

"I know it sounds corny, but I want to recapture all of that."

Maxie sat up, and looked at Lester squarely. "Lester what's really going on? All of this nostalgia talk is kind of scaring me. What is it you're not telling me?"

Lester laughed a little, and used his fingertips to gently push misplaced strands of her hair away from her face. "I'm telling you that I'm very much in love with my wife."

Maxie smiled, and took comfort in Lester's words. Leaning into his hand, he softly caressed the side of her face. In that moment, she wanted to be where he was. She owed him that. Closing her eyes, she absorbed and melded with the different kind of silence that fell between them. In it, she could sense every sweet word Lester did not give voice to. The warmth of his touch, coupled with the warm passion that was radiating from him, swathed her in a stifling heat she understood, causing her to open up and release herself into the place she knew was safe. The place she knew was right. The one place she knew was legitimately hers.

Chapter Fifty-Six

M arc was relieved to finally be in the air heading back to the states. After learning a winter storm was impacting air travel in the southeastern region of the United States, he spent three hours in the terminal at Chhatrapati Shivaji International Airport in Mumbai, waiting for a direct flight into the closest airport to Atlanta — Chicago O'Hare. In that time period, his heart and mind remained in one place.

Savannah.

Marc desperately wanted to be home, and the emotion was the same in his desire to see and be with Maxie. For the past three days, he could do little more than think about her, and the spiritually centered rhetoric of their last meeting. Initially, he had no intention of thinking about that part of their conversation, but as soon as he arrived in Mumbai, an unexpected call from his grandmother changed everything.

"So how's my favorite grandson? You all settled in over there in India?" Stella asked.

"Not quite mama. I'm just getting into my hotel room here. I'm opening the door, and putting down my luggage as we speak. Is everything okay with you?"

"Well I'm a little dismayed, and a little disheartened, at knowing my grandson won't be here with me for Christmas, but other than that ...."

"Mama we talked about that already, remember? I invited you to come along with me."

"I know you did Marcky. I know you did. Well your mama didn't call to fuss at you honey. I just wanted to make sure you arrived ok. And, there's something else I want to tell you. Something that's been bothering me. I'll call you back when you're settled in."

"No mama. Go ahead. I'm sitting down on the couch here in my room. What's on your mind?"

"Well it's about that woman Maxie."

"Maxie?" Marc replied, a little surprised.

"That's why I called you honey. Now you know I only met her that one time you brought her over here for lunch right?"

"Yes ma'am."

"Well the strangest thing happened. Last night, I had a dream about that sweet girl Marc. And I didn't like what I saw in that dream."

"You dreamt about Maxie? Tell me about it mama. I'm listening."

"Well I couldn't understand where she was in this dream, but wherever she was, it was dark and she looked like she was trapped Marcky. She kept trying to find a way out, and the door was right there in front of her. That poor girl looked like she was just groping around in darkness."

"Let me make sure I understand this. You had a dream about Maxie searching for a door somewhere in a dark place, but she couldn't find it, and it was right in front of her."

"Yes."

"Mama why would a dream like that bother you? I don't see any reason for you to be alarmed."

"At first, I didn't either Marc. But after I woke up, I remembered that I saw you in the dream too."

"Me? What, was I doing? Groping around in the darkness too?" He joked.

"No," Stella continued. "But you were standing in front of the door Maxie was searching for, and you just watched her. You didn't say a word, or do anything to help her. Marc it looked like you were blocking that girl, and keeping her from walking through that door. A door she *needed* to go through."

Marc didn't ask his grandmother to interpret the dream for him, and she didn't volunteer. There was really no need. The dream was self-explanatory. Since then, the sincerity in Maxie's voice when she spoke of the divine calling on her life, along with the anguish he saw in her face, and the words of his grandmother, all melded together and practically haunted him the entire trip. The thought of being the reason why Maxie could not walk into the door he knew was her divine purpose, was unfathomable. How could he be the one to block her? She herself acknowledged she wasn't ready. If she had said otherwise, there was no way he would stand between her and God.

When he finally checked into his hotel room at the Hilton Chicago O'Hare Airport, it was 6:30 Sunday evening. Without a second thought, Marc took a chance on calling Maxie at home. While the phone rang, a moment of rational thinking posed the question of what he would do should Lester be the one to answer the phone. Before he had time to weigh out what his response would be, someone answered the phone. With his thoughts focused elsewhere, the voice of the person who answered didn't register with him as male or female, so Marc remained quiet in hope of a repeated comeback. As he waited, voices in the background on the other end, alluded to the fact that there was some kind of gathering going on.

"Hello? Hello?"

At the sound of her voice, Marc released his anxiety in one exhale.

"Marc?" Maxie whispered.

"Girl, do you know what you do to me? Just hearing you say my name relaxes every tensed fiber of my being. I am so glad to hear your voice."

Maxie continued to whisper, and tried hard to quell her excitement. "Baby how are you? Are you okay? I have been so worried about you. Are you here?"

Marc heard a burst of raucous laughter in the background. "I'm fine. I had to be rerouted to Chicago."

"Sorry about the noise. Lester is entertaining some of the brothers from the church. Did you say Chicago? When will you be home?"

"Hopefully tomorrow. I have a flight out at nine in the morning. How are the roads?"

"They're pretty good. A few patches of ice on the highway ramps and overpasses, but other than that they're good."

Marc heard another burst of laughter, and a male voice asking Maxie the whereabouts of a condiment. Immediately his mind took him back to the first time he laid eyes on her at Food King, and questioned her about the location of batteries.

"I miss you so much," Marc said.

Maxie held her response until after she handed the man what he requested, and watched him walk back to the gathering. "I miss you too. It's going to be hard waiting until tomorrow to see you."

"The hard part will be my flight leaving on time. I'm sure the planes flying anywhere south will be delayed. I hate ripple effect delays. I miss you so much, I might have to rent a car and drive all the way to Savannah."

Maxie smiled broadly, and laughed a little.

"Honey who is that?" Lester called. "Is it Brother Calloway? Let him know he still has plenty of time to get here."

Maxie looked over her shoulder. "No baby. This isn't him. It's a salesman."

"Oh." Lester stated, and focused on his guests.

"A salesman," Marc chuckled. "That's a good one. Where are you?"

"In my kitchen. And aren't you a salesman?"

Marc laughed again. "I guess I am huh?"

Maxie laughed with him, occasionally keeping her eye on those near her. "So how long will your flight be?"

"I can't make that call. It's supposed to be a direct flight, but who knows. Were you planning on meeting me at the airport?"

"No. You know I'll be at Food King. This is my last week of working there."

"That's right. It is isn't it? Well we can meet when you get off tomorrow."

Maxie grinned. "Absolutely."

"I'll send you a text message telling you where."

"I'm looking forward to it."

"I love you Maxie."

"I love you."

"Talk to you soon."

"Bye."

Lightheaded and floating, Maxie hung up the phone. In spite of their conversation being brief, hearing from Marc and knowing he was okay, lifted the burden that had settled on her since early Saturday morning. She could only hope his flight would be on schedule tomorrow, and that he would be in Savannah by the time her shift ended.

With a slight smile on her lips, and her thoughts still on Marc, Maxie turned toward the refrigerator and immediately stood face to face with Deacon Earl, who was standing directly behind her, munching on a snack cracker.

"So you always tell salesmen that you love them?"

Maxie was taken aback. "Hey ... uh, Deacon ... Deacon Earl. Did you need something from the refrigerator?"

With a quick walk to the refrigerator, Maxie did her best to ignore his question, and quell all of the surprise on her face. Needing a place to hide for a brief moment, she opened the refrigerator door, and leaned in to search for absolutely nothing. *How could I have missed him coming into this kitchen?*

"No ma'am," Deacon Earl replied. "But I might need some of whatever that *salesman* was selling, since it made you tell him that you loved him. Sounds like a good deal. I must be missing out on something."

Maxie kept her position in the refrigerator. Closing her eyes firmly for a moment, and pressing her lips together tightly, she took a deep breath and released it slowly.

Grabbing a can of juice, Maxie straightened her back, closed the refrigerator door, and stood eye-to-eye with the Deacon. After assessing his stance from head to toe, she spoke with enough bite to leave no question about her debasing intent.

"Deacon, now once again, you're trying to step into areas of my life that you know nothing about. You see, just because you're often caught trippin' and slippin', and your life is an open book read by the loose and weak minded women of the church, please don't think that mine is the same. You have *nothing* here. Absolutely nothing."

Maxie watched Deacon Earl begin to choke on the cracker he was chewing, just as Lester walked into the kitchen. Casually, she handed the Deacon the can of juice in her hand, and walked to the sink. Lester quickly came to Deacon Earl's aid, and patted him on his back.

"You all right Earl?" He asked.

Between his coughs and glances at Maxie, Deacon Earl tried to speak. "Cracker ... cracker went down ... the wrong way."

"Well open that can of juice and drink some of it."

Deacon Earl nodded his head, and did as he was told. All the while, he kept his eyes on Maxie, who merely smiled at him when Lester's head was turned.

"Come on back in here, and sit down and rest yourself Earl," Lester said. "Maxie will get you whatever you need."

"Of course I will," Maxie agreed.

Slowly, Deacon Earl walked back to the gathering, with Lester in tow. Before Lester left the kitchen area, he shot Maxie a questioning look. Nodding her head, she shrugged as if she knew nothing.

When she was finally alone, Maxie released her poise and leaned over the sink. Lowering her head, she exhaled softly. The incoming thought was a menacing one, but she had to entertain it. She wasn't worried about Deacon Earl having enough credibility to expose her at any time. It was more the brutal reality of being *uncovered* that taunted her, and made her feel unnerved. *Just as Deacon Earl slipped up behind me, it could have easily been Lester who heard me express my affection for another man. How would I ever be able to explain that?*

Maxie already knew her feelings for Marc had shifted her to a place where her spiritual senses were more than compromised. She was in so deep, they were nearly diminished. But to find herself slipping in the natural with the Deacon Earl incident, proved to her that she was not doing a very good job of casing the secret places. She simply wasn't watching. With this awareness, Maxie surmised that she had to do but one thing.

Be more careful.

Chapter Fifty-Seven

Maxie stood behind her register nearly frozen in thought. Out of routine she wiped off the scanner, but her mind was far from what she was doing. There was too much to think about. It was the last week of a year of firsts for her, and at that very moment she wanted to make an attempt to reflect on them all. Getting her first job, her first time releasing her inner self, first time she lied to her husband, first time she spent time with another man, the first time she kissed another man, and the ultimate first — falling in love with another man.

In spite of the New Year coming, and the timeless suggestion of leaving the past in the past, Maxie knew there was no way she would soon forget any of what she had experienced. Granted, there would come a time when the words from the Scots Auld Lange Syne would capture some of her memories and permanently tuck them away, but anything that had to do with Marc Thomas would not be a part of that bag. Whether they were together or apart, she knew she could never forget him.

With all that transpired over the past months, she never could have imagined she would be in the place where she is now. Nor could anyone have told her that her heart would be in the position it was in. Although her best friend Sandra did warn her of what was to come, nothing could have remotely prepared her for what was happening.

"Are you ready to take your break?" Regina interrupted Maxie's thoughts, as she tapped her clipboard on the metal casing.

With a quick glance at her watch, Maxie noted it was 2:45 p.m., and she had yet to receive a message from Marc about his return flight home. "Has anyone called and maybe left a message for me? I've been expecting some real important information today."

"Nope," Regina replied. "The phone has pretty much been open all day. It's Monday. Everything is slow. Do you want to take your break now and make a phone call, or do you want to wait? I can let Alan take his first."

Pensively, Maxie looked at the Customer Service desk, as if the answer to Regina's question was there. "No. No, I'll go now." *Marc said he would text me,* she thought to herself.

"Go ahead and turn your aisle marker off."

Maxie did as she was told, and began walking to the back of the store.

"Oh Maxie," Regina called. "It almost slipped my mind. A package came for you. I don't know if there is a message attached to it or not. But you might want to check it out. It's down on the bottom shelf behind the service desk."

Maxie stood still for a moment, and then walked toward the desk. "Thank you."

When she got behind the counter, there were steno tablets, small opened boxes, and paper stacked everywhere on the shelf. She had no idea what to look for. Just as she was about to question Regina, she saw a beautiful bouquet of red, yellow, pink, and white roses in a crystal vase, sitting in the far left corner of the shelf.

"Hey Regina," Maxie called, and looked up to see Regina walking toward her. "Where is it and what does it look like?"

"You're looking in the right place. That's it."

"The flowers? Maxie asked incredulously. "Why would someone send me flowers?"

Regina strolled around the desk, and stood next to her. "I don't know. I thought maybe your husband was in the dog house or something, and he was trying to make it up to you. But if that were the case, they should have all been red."

With furrowed brows and a questioning look, Maxie picked the vase up and set it on the counter.

"At first I thought they came from our floral department," Regina continued. "But the guy who brought them in, had a shirt on that said Jamison's Floral Boutique. They're beautiful aren't they?"

"Yeah," Maxie almost whispered, diligently searching for the message card, but careful not to disturb the bouquet.

"Turn it around," Regina said. "It's on the other side."

Maxie turned the vase, and saw a soft pink colored card with typed words on it. Pulling it from the clip, she held it in a way that Regina couldn't see, but then figured she probably already read the card when the bouquet was delivered.

Sorry to see you go. Here's wishing you all the best in your endeavors. You have been a "beautiful" addition to the Food King line of employees. Maybe our paths will cross in the future. 222

Maxie frowned, and read the card again.

"Who's it from? Your husband?" Regina asked.

"No," Maxie giggled. "I guess it's from a customer of this store."

Regina quickly peeked at the card. "Yeah but why would they sign it two, twenty- two? Three twos?"

Maxie shrugged her shoulders. "I don't know. Maybe it's not a signature. Maybe it's a delivery code or something for the driver."

"That's possible," Regina shrugged.

Maxie put the card in the pocket of her smock, and smelled the roses. "They smell so pretty."

"They should, there's enough of them there. It looks like two dozen. You've made quite a lasting impression on somebody Maxie Bruce. That's nice."

"Yes it is," Maxie agreed, with a big smile. "I wish I knew which customer it was. I'd like to say thank you. Is it okay if I just leave them down here on the shelf until the end of my shift? I don't want to put them in my car. It's too cold."

"Sure, that's fine."

Maxie returned the flowers to the shelf, but could not release the grin that was on her face.

"Looks like that customer just made your day huh?" Regina smiled.

"Oh yeah," Maxie piped. "That was very nice. Well I'm going to the restroom, and then to the Café. I don't have much time left."

Regina looked at her clipboard. "Go ahead and take your normal fifteen. We're slow. Besides, it looked like you were over here with me handling business."

"Thank you Regina. I appreciate that."

"Just be back on time. Since Monet's not here today, I think I'm going to switch you to the bottom for the rest of your shift."

"Wow. All of this special treatment might make me reconsider my intent to quit," Maxie laughed.

"Yeah right," Regina smirked. "I doubt that."

Maxie laughed again, and headed toward the back of the store. While she walked, she read the card again, and could not help but to keep a smile on her face. Initially, she was baffled as to who sent the bouquet. But when Regina questioned her as to why the signature would be three twos, Maxie knew instantly that it was Marc. Three twos was the secret phone code he gave her when they first met. The only question was, where was he when he sent them? Was he home, or was he still in Chicago?

Finishing what she had to do in the back, Maxie almost changed her mind about going to the Café. The breakroom was looking very inviting in its desolate state, and she knew her mind could run free if she lounged there, but she didn't stay. She did as she intended, and made the trek to the Café.

Maxie could not get her mind off of Marc, and it became obvious when she walked right past a customer at the meat counter, waving to get her attention. Seeing the movement peripherally, she stopped and looked behind her. A man dressed in military fatigues, aviator sunglasses, and a package of meat in his hand, signaled with his fingers for her to come to him. Immediately, she looked around for a co-worker in the area to help the gentleman, because he was interrupting her break time, but there was no one. With a heavy sigh, Maxie reluctantly walked to the man. Without speaking to him directly, she looked at the meat he was holding. "Yes sir, how may I help you?"

"Is this pretty good?" He leaned in and whispered.

Maxie smelled the cologne the man was wearing, and closed her eyes as a wide grin spread across her lips. Quickly she looked at him. "The meat or the disguise?" She laughed.

"How's my girl?" Marc chuckled, as he took off the sunglasses and kissed her cheek.

Without a second thought about his public display of affection or their surroundings, Maxie excitedly wrapped her arms around his neck and gave him a big hug. "What are you doing here? I thought you were going to send me a text telling me where to meet you," she said before releasing him.

"I couldn't wait any longer. My flight was on time this morning, so I got into town around eleven."

"And you obviously have been running ever since. How long have you been in the store?"

"Girl I've been here watching you for over an hour."

Maxie laughed. "Are you serious? While I've been going crazy wondering if you're home or not, you've been stalking me right here in the store?"

Marc lightly touched her under her chin. "You better be careful. There are a lot of deranged people around here. You never know who's watching you. How'd you like the flowers?"

"They're beautiful baby. Thank you."

"Did you know I was the one who'd sent them?"

"I did," Maxie smiled. "Your signature was ingenious. Not to mention this Army get up you're wearing."

"Ahhh, the things we do for love."

They both laughed.

"This army fatigue cap and the sunglasses hid you pretty well. It was your whisper and cologne that gave you away."

"Oh you know me like that huh? I saw how perturbed you were when you thought I was a regular customer infringing on your break time."

"You could see that? I must be slipping," she laughed, and looked at her watch.

"Back to your register?"

"No I still have a few minutes. So tell me. How was India?"

"India? For me, it was busy. I toured one of the newest GIA facilities there, spoke with a lot of possible constituents, made some deals, and ate a lot of spicy food. The weather was cold. December is one of the coldest months there." Marc gently tapped Maxie on her nose. "And I thought about you only twice the entire time I was there."

"Only twice?"

"Yeah," he smiled. "Day and night."

Maxie grinned. "I am so glad you're back. I missed you terribly. Do you know how much I just want to hug and kiss you right now?"

Marc looked around, and motioned with his head. "There's a little secluded corner over in the Produce section. You want to go over there? It's right between the bananas and the seedless grapes."

Maxie laughed.

"What time do you get off?"

"Five o'clock."

"Can you get off any sooner?"

"I seriously doubt it. They're still struggling with the idea of me putting in my notice to quit."

Marc stared at Maxie squarely for a moment, before he spoke. "Maxie, I want to …."

"You just tell me where, and I'll be there Marc."

"I'm not trying to make this hard for you, by creating a problem with your husband. I just want to spend some time with you."

"Baby just tell me where?"

"Skidaway Island."

"At your house?"

"Yes."

Maxie watched one of her male co-workers walk past them, with a smile of acknowledgment. She returned the smile, but Marc kept his focus on her.

"Do you think you can you make that happen?" He asked.

"I'm not going to lie to you Marc. It will be hard. Skidaway is a bit far from here, but I want to be with you. So whatever …."

Marc smiled, and caressed the side of her face. "That's all I needed to hear you say. I don't want friction between you and Lester. I wouldn't put you in a situation like that. I just wanted to hear your response."

Maxie gave Marc a slight smile, and held on to his hand when he removed it from her face.

"I reserved a room at the Bohemian Hotel on Bay Street. Do you know where it is?" He asked.

"Yes. It's by River Street."

"I want you to meet me there when you get off."

Maxie nodded, and stared at him. "Marc, you look so good to me. Did I tell you that I'm glad you're home?"

"Yes," he chuckled. "You did. And I'm glad to be home too."

"I wish I could just go with you now. It's going to be hard finishing out the rest of my shift, knowing you're waiting for me."

"Hey, all you have to do is say the word, and I will pick you up and carry you right out of this place without looking back."

Maxie squeezed his hand and grinned. "I don't doubt that for one second. But enough fantasizing. Reality insists that I get back to my register. So as much as I hate it, I have to leave you."

"I'm good. Knowing that you're going to be with me in a couple of hours, takes the pain out of walking away."

Maxie released Marc's hand. It hadn't really dawned on her that she was holding it without reservation. Not to mention how long their hands were clasped for all to see. But in light of how she was feeling about seeing Marc, and spending those few moments with him, she could care less about anyone who saw her.

"So I'll see you when? Five thirty or so?" He asked.

"Or so," Maxie smiled.

"I'm on the sixth floor, room six hundred. I'll leave a key for you at the front desk."

"See you then."

Marc winked, put on his Aviator sunglasses, and walked away.

* * * * * * * * *

As he left the store, Marc remembered the anxiety he felt at Chicago O'Hare Airport, and how strong his desire was to see Maxie. Anticipation knotted his stomach from the time he boarded the plane to Savannah, until he landed and immediately drove to Food King. His idea to arrive in military garb was an unusual choice, but with limited resources inside the airport, his creativity was stunted. Regardless, it got the job done. He was able to watch Maxie at a reasonable distance inside the store, without her recognizing him. He wasn't sure *why* he wanted to watch her, but the very sight of Maxie made him feel more relaxed than he had been in the last four days. Other than that, she was simply a beauty to behold.

Marc smiled to himself at how giddy he felt when he laid eyes on Maxie, after entering the store. She literally took his breath away. He couldn't recall at any time feeling as desirous of her company, as he felt right then. He wondered if maybe it was due to the long distance and time spent away from her. Whatever the case, it was obvious he had reached a new level of passion where Maxie was concerned. Even the reservation at the Bohemian Hotel, showed forth an increase in his engagement. When she accepted the invitation with a sense of determination and eagerness, he understood it to mean that she felt the same way he did. Their journey together was changing, and Marc had no idea as to where it was headed, but he was enjoying the ride. He knew what he had in Maxie, and he didn't take it lightly. In spite of her marital status, she was a woman who was willing to return all of the passion he was giving. And that was enough to stroke any man's ego.

Chapter Fifty-Eight

The remaining time on her shift, moved along exactly as Maxie knew it would. It crawled. And working the bottom made it seem like an eternity. Even though she knew the rule was to never watch the clock when you're waiting to get off, she did it anyway. Primarily because, every passing minute brought her one minute closer to being with the man she had come to adore.

In as much as she wanted her thoughts to be centered on Marc, and how she would spend time alone with him, she had to give way to the unshakable thought of getting past Lester. How would she justify her absence, when Lester knew what time she was scheduled to be off? Times before, she managed to persuade him into believing whatever excuse she could conjure up for her tardiness, which at max was less than two hours. But this time, she needed to come up with something that would allot her a timetable that was indefinite. She had no idea how long she would be with Marc, but no matter how long the time, she wanted to feel no restraining obligation to hurry home. That was going to take some doing. So for the next hour, as she continued to greet, scan, chat as needed, and bag groceries, Maxie's thinking process went into overdrive. By the time the clock hit 4:30 p.m., she had formulated a get-away scheme that was so credible and so elaborate, she believed it herself.

"Regina, I need to use the phone quickly to call my husband," Maxie said, as Regina approached her register.

"You get off in about thirty minutes. Can it wait until then?"

"Honestly it can't. I need to do this before five o'clock. I should have done it way before now, but it just came to me." That statement made Maxie laugh on the inside.

"Okay. Go ahead. I'll take over your register until you get back."

"Thank you," she smiled. As she strolled across the floor to the Customer Service desk, Maxie immediately decided she wouldn't call Lester at work, but instead leave a message on the answering machine at home, as to her whereabouts. That way, the excuse could be delivered without having to hear any adverse words on Lester's part.

After she dialed, Maxie listened to the phone ring two times. She knew by the fifth ring the answering machine would pick up, so she took a deep breath and released it slowly. The lie needed to flow out easily without any sound of wavering. That was going to be a challenge, because her heart was racing a mile a minute.

By ring number four, Maxie's voice was lost.

"Hello?" Lester said. "Hello?"

Maxie's heart moved to her throat, and gagged her.

"Hello? Who is this?" Lester went on.

Without thinking about what she was doing, Maxie quickly pressed the button and disconnected the call. Frozen in a stupor, she stared at the telephone. "Oh god," she whispered to herself. "Why are you home so early?" Every thought, question, and reasoning known to man, joined forces and fell upon her in that moment.

"Maxie?" Regina called.

Snapping out of her trance, she looked at Regina as if she had just spoken in a foreign language.

"Are you finished?"

"Oh ... yes. Yes I am," she replied. Maxie walked back to her register, searching the floor for answers to the questions that were chasing her.

"Is everything okay?" Regina asked. "You look like something or someone just scared you."

"No, I'm fine," she replied, without looking at her. "Thank you."

"Okay. You can start your cleaning process in about ten minutes. Are you sure you're all right?"

Maxie finally looked at Regina, and pressed a smile. "Yeah, I'm fine."

"Well after you clock out, you can use the phone again if you need to."

Maxie nodded, kept her smile, and began scanning the items of the one customer in her lane.

When Regina left, Maxie swore she could hear verbal questions pounding her ears. The one that pounded the loudest was, *did Lester look at the Caller ID and see that the phone call came from Food King?* With that one in mind, she grew fearful of the questions that would undoubtedly follow. So instead of giving them room for consideration, she tried to push all questions aside, by starting a brief conversation with the woman in front of her.

"Hi. How are you today?" Maxie asked.

"I'm fine, now that I'm off work."

"Tough day?"

"That's every day in corporate America. Nothing like...."

Did Lester know it was me on the phone, or did he assume it was someone else? "So you're a supervisor," Maxie stated, as she tried hard to press past her own self inquiries.

"Yes. I have about a hundred and fifty people under me."

If Lester thought it was someone else from the store calling, did he think it was in reference to me? Did he think something was wrong with me, and someone from the store was calling to inform him? "That's something to be proud of," Maxie smiled. "And you're so young."

"I'm twenty-four. I've been a part of the company since I was eighteen."

If he thought someone was trying to inform him, why didn't he return the call to the store to find out? "So you worked your way to the top, so to speak."

"I guess you could say that," the woman giggled.

Maybe his call didn't get through. Maybe the call prompted him to think something was wrong with me, and he is on his way here to the store. With that thought, Maxie began to feel sick. The pit of her stomach roiled, and she suddenly felt warm all over her body. "Well you continue to do big things," she said to the young woman, as she gave her the receipt and her change.

"Why thank you. And you have a good evening."

"Thank you. I'm definitely going to try," Maxie said, with a feigned smile.

Before the woman fully left the checkout area, Maxie lost the smile, turned off her aisle marker, and started the cleaning process. Where elation should have been the emotion of the moment, she felt nothing but the weight of paranoia and dread. All she could do was imagine Lester storming in with a frantic look on his face, in search of his possibly injured wife, and putting an end to what she waited days for.

With the closing routine completed, Maxie took her register drawer to the Customer Service desk, and handed it to Regina without a word. The oblivious gesture, only prompted Regina to watch her perfunctory movement toward the time clock. When she confirmed the end of her shift, Maxie just stood there gazing at the time. *Lester still needs to be told. I have to call him back.* Maxie considered that not only would she have to explain why she would not be home on time, but also explain why she hung up on him.

"Maxie, did you hear what I just said?" Regina asked.

Maxie turned around, and gave her a quizzical look.

"What world are you in honey?" Regina asked, with her hand on her hip. "You're acting like you're in a fog."

"I'm sorry. I didn't speak with my husband yet, and I need to give him an important message."

"That's what I was just telling you. He called you back shortly after you returned to your register. I told him your shift was almost over, and that I'd have you call him."

Maxie slowly moved toward Regina. "Did he say anything else?"

"Just for you to call him on his work cell phone, because he's on his way back there."

Maxie released a gentle sigh, and smiled. The weight she felt earlier, suddenly melted away. Totally confused, Regina raised both of her hands in surrender, and laughed a little before she walked past Maxie.

"You know what? Okay. Hey, I'm not even going to ask," Regina hooted. "This is married folks' business. There's the phone if you still need to use it. I have to go make rounds. You have a good evening. I will see you tomorrow, and don't forget your flowers, because I will surely take them home with me tonight."

Maxie laughed. "Thank you Regina."

When Regina left the desk, Maxie immediately made the phone call home, and left the message on the answering machine. Within minutes she was out the door, in her car, and on her way to the Bohemian Hotel.

Chapter Fifty-Nine

axie gave her car key to the valet, before proceeding into the lobby of the Bohemian Hotel. The mere thought of meeting Marc in a room that overlooked the Savannah River, caused swirls of excitement to rise and settle in her stomach. As she walked through the small hotel lobby to one of the two desks in the reception area, Maxie was thankful she had on shoes with rubber soles, as opposed to dress shoes. The latter would have surely announced her arrival, as she trekked across the wooden floor.

"Good evening ma'am. Welcome to The Bohemian. Will you be checking in this evening?" The short man asked with a smile.

"Uh … no ... well, I'm supposed to pick up a room key here." Maxie quickly glanced at her watch, to see it was 6:00 p.m. "My friend said he would leave one for me?"

"Name please."

"Maxine Bruce."

The man searched the desk drawer next to him. "Room six hundred?"

"Yes."

"Here's your room key. You will need to use it in the elevator as well, in order to gain access to that floor. Will you be needing anything else?"

"Uhm, no thank you."

"Okay. Take the middle elevator over there to the sixth floor. Room six hundred will be the corner room. Enjoy your stay."

"Thank you."

Maxie quickly walked to where she was directed, and pushed the button. Feeling a little apprehensive while she waited, she considered admiring the uncommon artwork that decorated the area. Instead, her attention was drawn to the unique design of the elevator doors. Even though the doors were metal, they displayed a near mirrored image of anything in front of them.

There Maxie saw herself.

During the ride to the Bohemian, she did her best not to entertain the media's images of unfaithful souls, meeting their secret lovers in motel rooms on the outskirts of town. Yet here she was, standing face to face with a life size image of herself doing the same thing. Guilt and shame came immediately to wrap her, but soon dissipated when she stepped into the elevator. On the sixth floor, Maxie smiled at the thought of the elevator doors opening and encouraging her to experience what she waited days to enjoy.

When she finally entered the room, the sensual growl of jazz music, mixed with the amber glow of candlelight, immediately invited her to come in, relax, and meld with the atmosphere. Closing the door softly, Maxie heard the pooling sound of running water, and Marc humming in the bathroom. Without disturbing him, she removed her coat and placed it on the back of a chair. The boutique sized room was luxurious with its British campaign furniture, grained wood, brass, and leather. But it was the picturesque window, with its waning sunlight, that lured Maxie to it. With the curtains pulled back, the view was almost mesmerizing. Captivated by the beautiful red-orange sky and the Savannah River, Maxie didn't hear the bathroom door open.

"There's my girl, Marc said as he turned on the lights. "I thought I heard you come in. Why didn't you knock on the bathroom door to let me know you were here?"

Maxie smiled at him, but kept her position by the window, quickly noting he changed his clothes to black jeans and a black Polo shirt. "I didn't want to bother you. Besides, it gave me a chance to look around."

Marc walked to the window, and cuddled up behind her. Wrapping his arms around her waist, he kissed Maxie on the cheek, and buried his face between her shoulder and neck. Maxie grinned and pressed the side of her face against his, taking in the heady fragrance of his cologne.

"So what do you think?" Marc asked.

"It's very nice. I love the candles. It's so romantic. And this view.... "

"Well I can take credit for the ambiance in here, but I didn't order that sunset. It's a bonus that came with the room. It's beautiful isn't it?"

"Uhm hmm." Maxie quickly considered how the events of the day had all fallen right into place, creating the wonderful venture she was now sharing with Marc.

"I thought about us going up to the rooftop lounge and watching it from there," Marc said. "But I figured I couldn't get anything better than what I have at this very moment."

"I'm glad you made a way for us to spend time with each other." Maxie twisted herself around to face him.

"I had to do something. I don't think I could have taken one more day away from you Maxie. It was becoming a health issue."

Maxie frowned with a look of concern.

"Yeah," Marc continued. "My heart. It felt so empty. My lips felt nothing warm and tender. And my arms. Well they had no one to hold. I even tried to help my eyes out by satisfying their desire to look upon something beautiful, but even the beautiful women of India were no cure. None of those women could compare to you." Marc searched Maxie's eyes before he spoke in a near whisper. "I was falling apart without you."

Maxie smiled. She was certain that prior to this moment, every manner of deception she executed, was well worth the expression Marc just shared with her.

Seconds went by and no words were shared between them — only an earnest gaze of affection. When passion crept in to capture the moment, Maxie clearly felt anticipation rise and settle in the pit of her stomach. Lightning fast messages in her brain, reminded her that a simple touch from this man at the right moment, would send her nerves into a hot frenzy. By the time Marc lightly stroked the side of her face, and ran the tip of his thumb over her lips, her rapid heartbeat was rendering her breathless. When he finally pressed his mouth to hers and their tongues met, Maxie received what she had waited hours for. The taste of him, the warmth of his lips on hers, and the gentle caressing of her back as he held her, catapulted her to another place. There, she found herself accepting Marc's passion as if she had a right to it.

And it was wonderful.

Gently pulling himself away, Marc looked into her eyes and smiled. "I can definitely tell how much you missed me."

They both laughed.

"I told you I did. You're my strongest weakness Mr. Thomas." Maxie hid her face in his chest.

Marc chuckled again. "Hey, if you don't hold your head up, you're not going to see the belated Christmas gift I brought you."

Maxie quickly looked at him. "You brought me a souvenir gift from India?"

"I guess you could call it that. Do you want to see it?"

"Yes!"

"Then you will have to release me."

Maxie grinned, stepped back, and watched Marc walk to the closet, where he pulled out a large yellow suit bag. Handing it to Maxie, he sat on the corner of the bed and watched her unzip the bag carefully.

"While I was there, I visited their International Leather Fair. The Indian Leather Industry is one of the main producers of finished leather in the world. Mumbai even has a major production center. I was pretty impressed. They had a lot of nice things, but this outfit just seemed to have your name on it."

"Oh Marc! This is so beautiful." Maxie held the two piece brown leather dress suit, against herself.

"I thought you'd like it. Go try it on. I want to see how it looks on you."

Maxie quickly walked into the bathroom to change. When she finished, she took a moment to examine herself in the door mirror. She was stunning. When she put on the long sleeve bolero jacket, and turned to view herself from a different angle, she was totally surprised by what the outfit revealed. Not only did it hug her in all of the right places, but from her upper torso to her lower backside, she saw shapely curves she never knew she had. The full view revelation was astonishing, yet exciting at the same time.

"Who are you?" She whispered and pointed to herself in the mirror, before quickly covering her mouth to stifle a giggle.

"What's taking you so long in there?" Marc called. "Your audience awaits your stroll down the catwalk."

Maxie looked at herself one more time, and slowly opened the door. Marc watched with great anticipation. When she finally stepped out, he was awestruck and speechless. The sudden look on his face immediately made her nervous and self-conscious, so she looked down at herself to pinpoint where he was staring.

"What? What's wrong?" She asked.

Marc nodded his head, and stood up. "Nothing. Absolutely nothing. You look ... you look amazing. So beautiful," he grinned. "Turn around."

Maxie smiled, and twisted herself like she did in the bathroom mirror.

"Maxine Bruce, girl I am in awe. This dress suit. ..."

"Accentuates the positive?" She laughed.

"To say the least. Even the model who wore it didn't look as good as you do in it."

Maxie kept her smile, and sauntered to Marc. "So are you saying I may need to consider modeling as my next career choice Mr. Thomas?"

Marc put his hands on her hips, and felt the way the smooth leather dress hugged her. "I'm saying you're beautiful enough to be anything you want to be."

Maxie smiled broadly, and wrapped her arms around Marc's neck. "That's why I love you so much. You always know the right things to say to me."

"And it's all truth."

Maxie pecked Marc on his lips, and took a step back. "Thank you again. This is very nice. In spite of the socks and tennis shoes that I have on, I think I'm going to wear this home."

Marc sat back on the bed. "And how will you explain this dress to your husband? He's bound to be home by the time you get there."

Maxie smiled, and sat next to him. "It will be a gift from my co-workers."

"Your co-workers?"

"Yes. As chance would have it, I am attending a going away party at my job right now as we speak."

"Right now?"

"Yes."

"I don't get it."

"Before I left Food King, I called my house and left a message on my answering machine. I explained to my husband that I would not be home at five-thirty, because my co-workers surprised me with a going away party there at the store. I told him I didn't know what time the party would be over, but I would be home immediately thereafter."

"And this dress instantly becomes your going away gift."

Maxie nodded.

Marc studied her, and lightly shook his head. "You've become a pro at devious spur of the moment planning. I'm not sure I like that. Again you had to lie.... "

"Marc what else could I have done? I did what I had to do to be here with you."

Marc was silent for a moment, before he sighed softly and touched Maxie's cheek. "I know you did, and I understand. I'm not going to waste another moment talking about it okay?"

Maxie smiled her approval, and leaned into his hand before he removed it.

"So tell me. How was your Christmas?" Marc asked.

"Well, I missed you and not being able to talk to you. Before you left, we both had issues I felt needed to be dealt with, and that was a little frustrating to me." Maxie leaned over, and bumped Marc lightly on his arm. "But I got over it. I figured we'll probably always have some kind of adversity arise, and we'll just have to deal with it as it comes. Other than that, my Christmas was nice. My husband wanted to give me the world as a gift, but could only afford Paris instead."

Marc grinned. "Paris, France huh? Wow. That's pretty nice. So you now have your chance to go overseas."

"Yeah," she practically whispered. Looking at Marc squarely, her smile faded. "You know, as crazy as it sounds, I actually envisioned taking a trip abroad like that with you."

"Really? Why?" Marc considered Maxie's words, before he laughed a little. "Oh I see. You remembered our very first phone conversation."

"How could I forget it? You were so forward with your invitation to take me along. You were going to make your next trip to London a business ..."

"And pleasure trip," they chimed in together and laughed.

"Yeah. You have no idea how you made me feel that day when you finally called me."

"I think both of us experienced something special that day."

"I know I did." Marc gently brushed a few tendrils of Maxie's hair away from her face. "You're a very special woman Maxine Bruce. And I'm glad you're in my life."

Maxie smiled. "I feel the same about you." With her eyes set on him, she appeared lost in thought, and then recovered. "Have you ever considered *why* we met?"

"What do you mean?"

"The reason. I'm a firm believer of everything that happens, happens for a reason. Haven't you ever wondered why our paths crossed?"

"A chance encounter?" Marc grinned.

"Hardly."

"Well whatever the reason, I'm grateful. I've never known a woman who possesses all the qualities you have Maxie. Even in our conversations sometimes, I'm amazed at some of the things you say. It's almost like you have a wisdom that expands beyond your years. And your words don't tear down. It seems like they're always building. You're so encouraging. I adore that about you. And even though I know you have a husband, you have this way of making me feel like I'm the only special man in your life." Marc laughed a little. "Maxie, I honestly believe you could speak life into a dead man. You're just that special. So if our paths have crossed for me to experience the woman that is you ... then I'm grateful for that." Marc caressed the side of Maxie's face, and softly kissed her forehead. "Anyone who comes in contact with you is better for it. I hope your husband knows what he has in you. If I had known you before you met him, you would definitely be my treasure."

Maxie lowered her head, her eyes brimming with water. Marc's kind sentiment not only touched her heart, but it reached deep inside her soul, and released the former resounding words of Sister Adams. The words that defined her purpose, who she was, and what she possessed.

"You've never shared words like that before," Maxie almost whispered.

"Then it's long overdue. I can't explain why I'm saying it now, but I feel it's something you need to hear."

"Thank you," she said lowly, and wiped away her tears.

"For what? Making you cry?"

Maxie giggled a little, and let Marc wipe away the rest of her tears. "No. I appreciate your sincerity. Sometimes it's nice to hear what other people think about you."

"Well you already know Marc Thomas is crazy about you."

Maxie smiled.

"Hey are you hungry? I had this brilliant idea that we'd order a little something from room service, and picnic here on the bed. Afterwards, we can turn off the lights, kick back, relax in each other's arms, and just listen to the music."

"That sounds nice."

Marc grinned broadly. "Good. So why don't you go take that dress off for now, and get comfortable."

Maxie looked at Marc with a skeptical grin. "Excuse me?"

"What? You can put your work shirt back on. I promise you nothing will happen, that you don't want to happen."

Maxie stood, and silently gazed at Marc a moment longer. She recalled her inward response to those words the last time he said them. The memory was so loud, she was sure Marc could hear it. Here she was with an incredibly handsome man who adored her, hidden behind closed doors in a world that was all their own. What could possibly happen that she didn't *want* to happen?

Laughing to herself softly, Maxie gently shook her head, and walked toward the bathroom to remove her dress. For the rest of her evening with Marc, she determined that she wanted absolutely no regard for time.

"Tonight," she whispered to herself. "Time will have no time."

Chapter Sixty

When Maxie pulled up into the driveway next to Lester's car, it was 9:30 p.m. Once again, she rehearsed her verses of explanation, and committed them to memory. She was prepared for the interrogation that awaited her, as soon as her husband laid eyes on her. What she wasn't prepared for, was the small posse that was gathered inside her home — their presence being made evident by the three cars parked in front of her house.

Before she got out of the car, Maxie quickly sent Marc a coded text message with the numbers 234, letting him know she arrived home safely. While she let her fingers work from memory, to hide the phone inside her purse, Maxie's eyes darted between the kitchen door and the parked cars. One of the cars she recognized as Deacon Earl's. The other two had her stymied, because one was brand new, and the other was parked in the shadows.

When she finally got out of the car and tied the belt on her trench coat, Maxie smiled and prided herself on doing exactly as planned. She wore her new dress home, in spite of the socks and tennis shoes. Moving swiftly, she retrieved her clothing from the back seat, along with two large mylar balloons that read SORRY YOU'RE LEAVING and GOODBYE, which she picked up at Walgreens on the way home. When she approached the kitchen door, she thought to listen for the voices of those inside, but considered it silly to eavesdrop at her own back door. Once inside the dark kitchen, she was amazed at how the conversations in the living room continued, even after she made a noisy entrance with her keys.

From the car to the kitchen Maxie was calm, but when she saw The Ominous Three and Deacon Earl Bayer sitting in her living room like they were old friends from way back when, she suddenly felt incensed. Quickly she grabbed a hold of the feigned demeanor she had perfected whenever she was in their presence, and plastered on the smile.

"Oh hello. What a surprise," Maxie said as she walked midway into the living room. "How are you all this evening?"

Maxie refused to put down the small bundle that was in her hands, because it kept her from having to go further in the farce by greeting them all with a hug. Instead, Joyce Rodgers, Blanche Grammerson, and Deacon Earl, came to her and extended the greeting one by one. She knew it was beneath Emma Teal to get up and greet anyone, so it was expected that she would remain seated. What concerned her more, was when she looked over the shoulder of Deacon Earl, and saw Lester sitting in a chair along the wall looking intently at the floor. He didn't bother to acknowledge her entrance, which was so unlike him, especially in the presence of others.

With her eyes fastened on him, Maxie directed her question to everyone. "So is everything all right at the church? Is there something wrong?"

Without looking at Maxie, Emma Teal took off her glasses, and began wiping the lenses slowly with a white handkerchief. Undoubtedly, she found an opportunity to grandstand.

"We all came here this evening to share a bit of church-related business with Minister Bruce. Something we all feel needs his immediate attention."

Maxie looked at Lester again. He was still in the same position, but what was catching her eye, was how fidgety Deacon Earl had become.

"So your job had a going away party for you tonight?" Blanche Grammerson asked. Standing less than two feet away from Maxie, Blanche grinned and emphatically nodded her head. Maxie wondered if she was prompting and warning her to share in the gesture.

"Yes. Yes they did," she replied with uncertainty.

"Well that was nice."

Maxie simply agreed by smiling and nodding.

Emma Teal finally stood up, and slowly placed her glasses on her face. "Earl, would you get our coats please? I think it's time that we leave."

Maxie watched, as Deacon Earl walked to the closet to retrieve all of their coats. Lester stood with them, but he still did not so much as hazard a glance at his wife.

"Thank you all for your time this evening," Lester said.

"We trust you will take care of the matter at hand," Emma said primly.

"Yes I will. And thank you for delivering the message."

"Good night Sister Bruce," each woman chimed as they walked out the front door.

"Good night," Maxie said. She was glad to see them leave, but more curious to know why they were there in the first place. There was no way she was going to buy Emma's statement about *church-related business*. Knowing that crew, it was more than likely about someone else's business.

Maxie's eyes followed Deacon Earl, as he was the last one to file out. Lester stood next to him, ready to shut the door at his exit, but the Deacon suddenly stopped short to lean in.

"Again Minister Bruce, we're sorry we came here so late. But we were told you needed to be informed of this immediately and in person, so we came as soon as we all could."

"I understand Deacon Earl," Lester replied. "I appreciate it. Have a good night."

Deacon Earl nodded his head solemnly, and put on his hat. Before he was completely out of the door, he shot a glance and a wink at Maxie that was so quick, she couldn't be sure he actually did it, or that Lester missed seeing it. When Lester finally closed the door, she made a beeline to the bedroom, and took off her coat.

"What was that all about?" She asked in a way that made it sound as if their visit was the most ridiculous thing ever. Just as quick as the words came out of her mouth, she decided she really wasn't sure she wanted an answer to that question.

Lester locked the front door, turned off the light, and stood in the doorway to the bedroom. With his arms folded and a stern look on his face, he leaned against the jamb of the door, and watched his wife begin to undress with her back to him.

"Lester," Maxie called over her shoulder. "Did you hear me?" Maxie turned to lay her Bolero jacket on the bed, and was immediately startled at seeing her husband standing in the doorway, watching her with tension flexing the muscles in his jaw. She had seen that look on his face before, and a graphic visual of the event that followed, flooded her memory. Maxie could see no reason for a heated argument to occur this time. She gave Lester a full account of her whereabouts, so all would be well. She was going to be totally oblivious to his disposition.

"Hey. Did you hear me?" She asked.

Lester motioned with his head, and spoke plainly. "Where did that dress come from?"

Maxie beamed, and held her arms out while doing a full turn. "Do you like it? It's one of the gifts I got today. I left the other one at the store. One of the customers heard I was leaving Food King, and had a beautiful bouquet of flowers delivered to me at the store. Isn't that something?"

"Roses?"

"Yeah. How'd you know?"

Lester shrugged his shoulders. "Just a good guess."

"Oh, okay. So what do you think about this dress? It's nice isn't it?"

"It's very nice. And it looks to be very expensive. Did a customer give you that too?"

Maxie thought she used the right wording, so there would be no questions about any of the gifts. Obviously she missed the mark somewhere. It would have been better had she left well enough alone, and not pressed Lester for a response as to whether he liked the dress or not. Now she had no other recourse but to deliver the lie.

"It's my going away present from my co-workers," she said plainly, and continued to undress. Without another word, Maxie walked into the closet, and hung up the outfit. Instead of coming out immediately, she lingered there briefly and covered her face. She utterly hated lying to Lester. But she knew it was necessary in order to spare him pain.

"Maxie?"

"Yes?"

"Maxie I need to talk to you."

"Go ahead honey, I'm listening."

"Maxie come out of the ...."

Maxie quickly stepped out of the closet. "I'm right here Lester. "What's going on?" She asked, standing before him in her bra and panties.

"I want to know where you were tonight."

Maxie was still. Quickly her eyes darted back and forth, before she looked at him with a questioning gaze. She knew it was important that she remain calm, and not jump to any conclusions as to exactly what Lester was asking her. "Didn't you get the message I left for you on the answering machine? Of course you did. How else would Blanche have known where I was, if you hadn't told her?"

"Yes, that's what I told *them*. But I don't believe that's where you were."

Maxie was quiet, and blinked a few times, because of course she misheard Lester's last sentence. Confused, she searched her husband's face. All she got was a hard stare. *Maybe he didn't say it,* she reasoned. *Why would he? He's never said anything like that to me before.* The uncertainty would make her crazy, so she had to be sure. Blinking quickly, Maxie unlocked the words that bunged in her throat.

"What did you just say?" She asked, with a slight twist of her head.

"I said I don't believe that's where you were."

It was official. He *did* say it. Lester accused her of lying to him, and his words slapped Maxie hard in her face. As her body stiffened, the pain resonated all over. There was nothing in the world that could have prepared her for what she was feeling. The pit of her stomach began to roil, and a quiver was working its way from her inner core to the outside. Another part of her world had changed. She just lost credibility with her husband. She knew she did not deserve it in the first place, but in spite of all that she was doing, she honestly did not expect to lose it.

Feeling a sudden chill in the room, Maxie turned and walked to the dresser to retrieve her night clothes. Lester ensued.

"I want to know right now, where you were tonight Maxie."

"Lester, you just finished calling me a liar," she croaked. "What would be the point of me explaining anything more? To you, it's still obviously going to be a lie. I told you on the answering machine where I was. I told you that my co-workers threw a surprise going away party for me after work." Only in the sound of her voice, and by the tears that fell on her night clothes, did she realize she was crying. With her emotions all over the place, she could not be sure why.

"For four hours Maxie?" Lester's raised his voice.

Maxie pulled her night shirt over her head, and practically screamed her words. "We were talking Lester! We all got carried away talking! My God man! Can I have a life outside of this house?"

Lester looked at her for what seemed like forever, before he quietly sat at the foot of their bed. Maxie was an emotional wreck. Everything seemed like it was coming from everywhere, and it was all crashing around her. Standing in front of him, she desperately tried to get her breathing under control. While she regained her composure, Maxie could tell by her husband's countenance, that a reserved kind of calm rested on him. She also saw that he was wounded.

"Then I guess that's what you've been doing then huh? You've been having *a life,* outside of these four walls."

"What are you talking about?"

Lester put his hands together, and brought them to his mouth, as if he were saying a quick prayer. When he lowered them, and leaned forward to stare at the floor, Maxie thought he was doing his best to restrain himself.

"Who's the man Maxie?"

Another blow rendered her breathless.

"What?" She whispered astonished.

"Who is the man you were seen holding hands with, in that store today?"

Maxie's mind switched gears, and pulled it all in. It wasn't daunting enough that someone saw her holding hands with Marc, but when she thought about the witness possibly being one of the four people who had just left her home, she could hardly contain herself. Anger tried to come to the forefront, but rage was what she needed. Flailing one arm, Maxie pointed toward the living room, and regained her heightened voice.

"Is that why they were here tonight? Is that what this is all about? Somebody from that committee of church idiots claimed they saw me with someone? Are you kidding me Lester? You are questioning me behind *their* words?"

"Maxie," Lester said calmly and cautiously.

"No! I can't believe you! You would take their words over mine! And you know how they exaggerate and manipulate! And Deacon Earl ...."

"It wasn't them."

"... With all the mess he does! You talked about him yourself!"

"It wasn't them, woman!" Lester stood up and yelled, causing Maxie to jump in fear. "They weren't the ones who saw you! It was the Pastor! The Pastor Maxie!" Lester lowered his voice, and stepped closer to her before he continued. "This afternoon, Pastor Harrison saw you near the meat counter, standing very close to a man who was not me. And he said that you were holding hands, and that you appeared to find pleasure in this man's company."

Maxie felt a knot grip and twist in her stomach. The worst had come. How could she viably refute the Pastor? The truth of her deeds had come from his mouth.

Lester stopped talking, and stared at her with an expectant gaze. Even though the anger in his voice had subsided, Maxie could tell his insides were raging, because of the way his nostrils flared with heavy breathing.

The moment was hardly one to be considered for self-centered perception, but Maxie, feeling pitiful and frail, wondered what her husband thought of her in that instant. Did he suddenly see her as the same caliber of vile women in the Bible like Jezebel, or Gomer? Or did he see her as conniving and deceitful as Delilah? Whatever his thoughts, the pain she witnessed in his eyes, pulled at her heart tremendously. Maxie had never seen Lester this way, and the sight of him now, hurt her as if the tables were turned, and she found him to be the unfaithful one. Right then with all of her strength, she wanted to reach out to him and repent for everything. Maxie knew all she had to do was stop, turn around and ask Lester to make it okay, and he would forgive her, love her all the more, and save her from herself.

"Maxie? Who was he?"

With conviction riding her heavily, Maxie took a deep breath, walked back to the dresser, and propped her back-side against it with folded arms. "Lester, I don't know what Pastor Harrison thought he saw, but he was wrong." A sudden surge of defiance sprang up on the inside, and she welcomed it. It was needed, to go with the soft expression of faultlessness that was now on her face. "We get a lot of older people in the store. Maybe I was standing close to a customer who was hard of hearing. I don't know. And as far as me finding pleasure in someone's company, baby that's what I do. That's a part of customer service. I try to give the same cordial experience to everybody who walks in that store. Make the customer feel welcomed. That's my job. Remember, that's how I got Employee of the Month. Besides, a lot of the customers know me, and since they're aware that this is my last week, it could have been one of them wishing me well. Lester it could have been anybody."

Maxie watched to see if her words were softening her husband. Apparently they were, because he slowly sat down on the bed, and appeared to be in deep thought. The muscle in his jaw line even stopped flexing. If she pressed him just a little harder, and persuaded him a little more, she was sure to make him see everything the way she wanted him to see it.

"Think about it baby," she said as she sat next to him. "If I were going to be unfaithful to you, why would I do it openly in a public place for all to see? A grocery store of all places."

"And what's your reasoning for holding hands with the customer Maxie?"

Maxie smiled, and lightly bumped Lester's arm. "I don't know. How do you know that I was the one doing the holding? A lot of fresh old spry men come into that store, and they seem to find me attractive." Maxie watched her husband stare at the floor, and chuckle lightly.

He was sold.

Gently she rubbed her fingers through Lester's hair, as he continued to stare at the floor in silence. When he inhaled deeply, and released it heavily through his nose, she assumed it was both a sigh of relief and disappointment, behind having to confront her about the whole ordeal. Damage control and clean-up, was not a task he was accustomed to doing behind his wife. But Maxie was certain Lester would go back to the Pastor, and share her explanation in order to clarify everything.

In the minutes that followed, Maxie listened to her husband express his discontent in receiving a phone call earlier that evening from the Pastor, requesting an immediate meeting, to which he was informed of what the Pastor witnessed. She was glad to hear the meeting was only between the two of them, and not in the company of the entire presbytery — at least he was spared that shame. She was equally glad to hear that Emma Teal and her crew, knew nothing about the allegation. The reason for their visit, was to alert Lester to the mismanagement of church funds, by a young minister assigned to his mentorship.

"So Friday is your last day right?" Lester glanced at her out the corner of his eye. The tone of his voice made his words seem like more of an admonition, than a question.

"Yes. January second."

Lester released another heavy sigh, and looked at her directly. "Maxie, with this whole mess ... this is an example of what Romans fourteen and sixteen says. Let not then your good be evil spoken of. If someone else had seen you ...."

"Lester, I know. I understand that scripture, and you're right. But what I don't understand is, how you could readily accuse me the way you did? You were so bent on believing the worst, without giving me a chance to explain. It sounded like you don't trust me. Baby when have I ever given you a reason not to trust me?"

Lester searched her eyes before he answered. "You haven't."

In spite of him not saying it, Maxie heard a distinct *yet* at the end of his words, and the reservation gave her cause for suspect. Even as he continued to look at her in silence, it wasn't the usual amorous stare she was accustomed to seeing. There was an element of supposition there, and she wondered if he could see the dark shadow of her sin.

Maxie lowered her eyes.

"I don't know what I'd do if anyone ever came between us Maxie," Lester continued. "Just tonight alone, while I waited for you to come home, I had four hours to think about it and ..." Lester nodded his head, and looked at the floor again.

Maxie was overwhelmed with guilt and pain, and tried hard to swallow despite the lump that was now in her throat. Slowly, she looked at him and lifted his chin to face her. With tears in her eyes, she nearly whispered. "Lester, baby don't think about that. I'm never going to leave you. No one can ever take away what we have."

Lester forced half a smile. Gently, he grabbed his wife's hand, and gave it a little squeeze. "I believe that. But what can be said if one of us *gives* it away?"

Chapter Sixty-One

From behind her register, Maxie watched through the large window as the small bus filled with senior citizens, pulled up next to the curb in front of the store. It was the last Senior Citizen Tuesday she would ever work at Food King, and she knew this would probably be the last time she would see many of the elderly patrons. Slowly, they stepped off the bus with canes, walkers, and a firm grip on the handrail. Despite the cold outside, it didn't hasten their movements, and Maxie considered how their motility could be paired with how her own body felt.

Tired.

Last night when the tumultuous ride with Lester was over, she was emotionally and physically drained. With all the words that were spoken, his light innuendos confirmed what she feared he already knew. She was having an affair.

The culmination of all things spoken, sparked a negative hum in her body that kept her awake for most of the night, searching her memory for intimate conversations she had with him since her involvement with Marc. There, she found and replayed the dialogue filled with allusions that weakly hinted his awareness. What failed to make sense to her, was if he knew what she was doing, why didn't he confront her about it? Last night would have been the perfect time for him to do so, because he had an eyewitness. If he had just outright told her he knew she was having an affair, and presented what he felt was proof, *including* what the Pastor witnessed, then she probably would have admitted her wrong doing right then.

But he didn't.

Maxie couldn't believe how close she came to confessing. Seeing her husband in that kind of vulnerable state, was like seeing him stripped of his strength. To know she was the reason behind it, left an indelible mark on her.

"How's my favorite store clerk?"

Maxie snapped out of the reflection, to see a short, slightly hunched, pale old white man with a cane, looking at her over the top of his glasses.

"How are you today Mr. Pete?" She smiled.

"Well I guess I'm doin' pretty good for an old man of near ninety. The good Lord done woke me up this mornin', so I reckon He still got a work for me to do. Either that, or He's done forgot about me," Mr. Pete laughed. "I had to stop here first before I do my shoppin', because I hear tell that you're gonna be leavin' us here. Coupla gals on the bus said this is your last week. Is that true?"

Maxie was glad the traffic in the store was light. She always enjoyed brief conversations with Mr. Pete. "I thought I told you I would be leaving Food King at the first of the year Mr. Pete."

"No ma'am. I don't recall that. But you know I don't be recallin' too much these days. Takes too much effort."

Maxie laughed. "I'm sure I did tell you."

"Well I don't know if you did, or if you didn't. Either way, I'm sorry to hear it. I'm sure gonna miss ya roun' here. You the best they got, and they don't need to lose ya."

Maxie smiled. "Thank you Mr. Pete. I'm going to miss you too."

"Maybe I can get your phone number or somethin', and call ya from time to time. Check on ya. See how ya doin'."

Maxie narrowed her eyes, and tilted her head. "Mr. Pete, are you trying to hit on me?"

"Oh ho, ho, ho," the old man laughed bashfully. "I guess I ain't got it like I used to huh?"

Maxie grinned.

"Well I'm goin' on back here to get my groceries. Don't let this aisle get too crowded now. I'll be right back through here."

"Yes sir," Maxie said, and watched him limp away with his cane toward a shopping cart. It was clear to her, that in the course of working the past three months at Food King, there were many men both young and old, who directly and indirectly made passes at her. But only one managed to get inside of her world.

"Maxie, you have a phone call," Regina said from behind her, causing Maxie to jump a little. "It's a man. I think it's your husband. Go ahead and take it. I'll watch your register."

"Okay. Thank you." Maxie's thinking went into overdrive, as she walked across the floor. Lester rarely called her at work, so she knew it had to be something important. Maybe the Pastor had more to say about her. Maybe someone else saw her too. When she got behind the service counter, she picked up the phone and stood in the nearest corner.

"Hello?" She quested with uncertainty.

"Hi baby."

"Hey. What's going on Lester? Is something wrong?"

"No. I was just sitting here at work thinking about you and all that happened last night, and I wanted to apologize to you again. I didn't mean to just get up and walk away from you, after I made that comment about one of us giving away our relationship. I think ... maybe I was unfair to assume ... you know. It's just that you mean so much to me Maxie. You're my world and I just ...."

Maxie couldn't take guilt mounting and riding her emotions again. She would surely break, and she certainly did not want to be seen coming apart while on the job.

"Baby don't," she whispered, and then released a little nervous laughter. "You're going to make me cry here." Silence followed her words, and she wondered if her husband had hung up the phone. "Lester?"

"I'm here," he said in a tone so low, she could barely hear him.

Maxie wasn't quite sure, but judging the raspy sound of his voice, she believed Lester was expressing himself through soft tears. If that was true, she knew he was devastated. That very thought sent her heart to the floor.

"Lester?" She pleadingly whispered. This time she pressed her eyes closed, to keep her own tears from falling.

"Go back to work Maxie. I'll see you when I get home."

Before she could respond, Lester hung up the phone. Maxie wanted to call him back, but just as she began to dial the number, Regina looked at her with expectation.

"Great," Maxie whispered. Blinking her eyes quickly to clear away the blurriness, and to ward off more tears, she hurriedly hung up the phone and returned to her register.

"Hey, are you okay?" Regina asked. Is everything all right?"

Maxie forced a smile. She knew her eyes were red from tears, but she nodded her head anyway, and lied. "I'm fine."

Truth be told, she felt too weak to hold the heaviness that was in her heart, and if Regina didn't stop with the questions and go away, she was sure to crumble like a cookie right there in front of her.

Regina sized her up with a skeptical eye. "Okay well, if you need to take a little break or something …."

"I'm good," Maxie quickly interrupted, refusing to meet Regina eye to eye.

"Just let me know."

"I will."

When she finally left, Maxie inhaled deeply, and released it all through her nose. The shakiness she felt on the inside when she exhaled, was like a small earthquake rumbling with a threat of emotional catastrophic proportions, if it could not be contained. Lester's phone call, easily applied pressure to the wounded places she spent the night tending to. It wasn't in the amount of words he shared with her, but it was the pain she felt in his words that took her to the edge.

Maxie nodded her head lightly. She never imagined the small wager of following a whim of curiosity, would have her rendering so much emotionally. Blinking back more tears, she tried to regain her focus by willing every heartfelt thought, and every remnant of last night's conversation, to the back of her mind for now. But it was hard. In an effort to busy herself, Maxie straightened the magazines around her register, and put misplaced candy bars back in their display boxes. She let her mind wander everywhere, except for on the two men who were dividing her heart. When she bent over to pick up a package of gum from underneath the display rack, Maxie felt the vibration of her cell phone. Normally, that vibration would cause a twinge of excitement to rise from deep inside of her, but that wasn't the case right now. Straightening herself, she put both of her hands into her smock pockets, and rubbed her fingertips over the phone. She was pensive about looking at what she was certain to be a text message. After a little more thought, she pulled it out and read the message from Marc.

How's my girl? Had a dream about u last night. U are the most beautiful woman to dream about. Imagine the pleasure of waking up with u on my mind. I need to see u today. Find a way to make it happen. I love u.

Maxie quickly flipped the phone closed, and released a heavy sigh. "This is too much," she said to herself.

"Got another one of those love messages huh?"

Maxie heard the voice behind her, and quickly turned around to see Monet standing there.

"Yeah. I been checking you out from time to time with that little cell phone. Which baby boy you got on the line today? That cutie with all the big muscles? Yeah I been watching him coming in here too. He always comes through *your* line for checkout, and he never buys a lot of stuff either. What's up with that?"

Maxie gave Monet a look that easily conveyed *you are so pitiful,* before she laughed lightly, turned, and walked back to her register. Monet wasn't worth wasting her words. Maxie didn't even bother to glance over her shoulder, to see if she was still standing there. The girl was notorious for hit and run, so there was no need in even hazarding a glance in that direction. It was a good thing she didn't. Monet's snide remarks kindled something within her, and it was becoming increasingly evident by the look of anger on her face. The mere thought of being spied on was enough, but when Monet added the revelation that she too had caught her slipping, Maxie felt anger churn in the pit of her stomach. If she had said anything to Monet in reprisal, her words would have been extremely toxic, and very hurtful. They also would have been very displaced. Maxie knew she was angrier at herself, than at the ridiculous rhetoric of a nineteen year old. Albeit, she could not refute the obvious; she wasn't as discreet as she thought she was.

As she gazed out of the store's picture window, and shook her head lightly in an effort to get rid of the mental chaos, Maxie pushed her thoughts to rest on Marc's text message, and his request. With all the turmoil she just experienced with Lester, and the state of vulnerability she knew he was in, there was absolutely no way she could meet with Marc. The suspicion factor was much too high, and would be greatly agitated if she had to explain why she was arriving home late from work, yet again.

When she glanced at her watch, she determined now would be a good time to take a restroom break. Flipping the switch for her aisle marker sign to blink, she caught the eye of Regina.

"You need that break now don't you?"

"I just need to go to the restroom," Maxie smiled.

"Go ahead, I'll cover you."

"Thank you."

Maxie wasted no time walking to the back of the store. When she entered the restroom and locked the door, she immediately pulled out her cell phone and began texting. *I love u too. Can't see u this evening. Maybe tomorrow before Watch Night Svc.*

She quickly hit send, and hoped Marc would answer her within the next few minutes. While she waited, she washed her hands, and put some cool water on her face. Maxie had no idea how she was going to spend time with him before the New Year's Eve Watch Night service at the church, but at least she could make more of an honest effort then.

Just as she patted her face dry, she felt the vibration of her phone. Quickly, she opened it and read: *I understand about tonight. Remember the Blue Lights in the Basement party @ the Regency? I told u I want the New Year to come in with u in my arms. Please tell me you'll be there.*

Maxie moaned, and furrowed her brows. She hadn't forgotten about Marc's invitation to the New Year's Eve Party at the Regency Hotel on River Street, but in light of everything she was experiencing with her husband, it was the least of things she had to regard.

We'll discuss everything tomorrow, she responded. *I'll call u.*

Without waiting for his response, Maxie quickly closed her phone and left the restroom. Even though she told Marc she would call him tomorrow, she would more than likely contact him as soon as she was off from work. With tomorrow being New Year's Eve, she was certain The Ominous Three had her assigned to some kind of task involving preparation at the church, so it was best she speak with Marc sooner, rather than later.

"So you're straight?" Regina asked, when Maxie returned to her register.

"Yes. Thank you."

"Good," Regina smiled. "You can total up this customer. I'm going to finish making rounds."

Maxie took a deep breath, exhaled slowly, and continued the check out. She didn't want her thoughts to be on Marc, but she couldn't help it. Her mind just automatically started the process of conjuring up a way to leave the New Year's Eve church service, in order to be with him at the Regency.

What is wrong with me? She earnestly quested within. *My husband is hurting because of me, and I'm here scheming and entertaining thoughts of how to get to another man.* Maxie lightly shook her head in amazement. She didn't acknowledge the next customer who stood before her, but went right on scanning the items on the conveyer belt. It was obvious the shopper was a woman, because Maxie recognized the distinct heavy aroma of Chanel #5 perfume, a fragrance Sister Adams wore faithfully every Sunday. When she smiled, and looked at the elderly woman with the intention of giving her a compliment on her choice of perfume, Maxie's words came to an abrupt halt, as she was met with a cold hard stare. Amazed, Maxie blinked twice to make sure she was seeing correctly. The stare was so menacing, she was taken aback, and at an immediate loss for words. She knew the woman didn't know her, but wondered if the reason for the scowl, was because she didn't give her a proper greeting, or something even more bizarre, she could hear the thought she just pondered about Marc. Dropping her sight to the items she was scanning, Maxie twisted her mouth into a slight smirk, released the silly notion, and forced a smile.

"How are you today?" She asked the lady without looking up. "Did you find all that you were looking for?"

"I did," the woman replied slow, and deliberately. "Did you find all that you were looking for?"

Everything stopped.

Maxie's smile faded. The simple words slapped her so hard in her face, she didn't know how to respond. *What did she mean by that question?* Clearly stunned, Maxie didn't immediately look at the woman, for fear of the element of surprise being all over her face. Instead, she tried to ignore the question and continue scanning.

Who is this lady, and where does she get off asking me a question like that? What, or who is she referring to? Is she referring to Marc?

Out of the blue, Maxie felt heavily convicted. The feeling stayed with her for a few moments, before she considered that she was reading entirely too much into the woman's question. Nevertheless, she wanted to know what was being implied.

Looking at the customer with a creased brow, Maxie pressed on the feigned smile, in spite of receiving the same hard cold stare. "Excuse me?"

"Excuse me?" The lady responded.

The flippant attitude sent Maxie straight to ten. Before she had a chance to formulate a professional, yet tactful response, a woman standing right next to the elderly lady, waved at Maxie.

"Oh. Oh I am so sorry," she pleaded. "Please don't pay any attention to my aunt. She's autistic, and sometimes repeats words and phrases she hears. It's called echolalia."

"It's called echolalia," the elderly woman repeated in a matter-of-fact tone.

"Please forgive her," the other woman whispered.

Maxie's focus shifted between the two of them. Echolalia or not, she knew she heard the woman put emphasis on her words, as if to question her on finding what she needed, and desired in her relationship with Marc.

"Your groceries come to eighty-nine seventy-two," Maxie said plainly, and helped to bag their groceries.

When everything was loaded into their shopping cart, and they began to leave the area, Maxie tried not to even look at the two, but the other woman lightly touched her arm.

"Again, I'm sorry if she offended you."

Maxie gave a quick smile, and let it drop just as quickly. When she looked at the elderly woman, she was faced with a most sinister smile, as the corners of her mouth were turned up ever so slightly, and her eyes were almost slits.

"Happy New Year," Maxie said to them both.

"No. Happy New Year to you ... Maxie," the elderly woman stated.

Instantly, Maxie felt chills run down her spine. It wasn't so much in hearing the woman speak her name that prompted the reaction. After all, she did wear a nametag. But it was her entire response that was eerie, because she made it sound as if there was something impending in the New Year, with her name on it. Maxie watched the women until her gaze was broken by her next customer, who was a man who immediately chimed in.

"That was weird huh? At least she could read your nametag. I didn't know autistic people could read."

Maxie looked at the man, and smiled. In silence, she scanned his grocery items and totaled them. She didn't want to converse with him, but what he said was true. That entire random moment was weird. Even assuming the woman was questioning and equating her life, to a search for fulfillment, and finding it in Marc, was ridiculous. There was no way that old woman could know what she was asking, directly or indirectly.

Maxie mentally brushed off the woman and her words. There were too many other things to think about.

"You have a good evening too," Maxie called to the man, when it finally clicked that he had bid her farewell.

Chapter Sixty-Two

A wave of somberness washed over Maxie, when she finally realized she was two hours closer to her last two days at Food King. It really had not dawned on her, until Mr. Pete made mention of it when he came back to her line just as he promised. She didn't anticipate her emotions resurfacing again, but it was hard telling her Tuesday shopping cronies goodbye, especially when she coupled it with the thought of never seeing many of them again.

Maxie made promises that she would take care of herself, and do her best to keep in touch. She wanted to thank each of them for what they added to her first experience at working, but that would take too much time. So she opted to give each of them a hug instead. The contact she made with them was like therapy, and it helped to take her mind off the unusual customer she had a couple of hours ago.

As the bus driver labeled grocery bags with name stickers, and loaded them under the bus, Maxie saw that most of the seniors had boarded, and were undoubtedly fastened in their seatbelts and ready to go.

"There's only two of us left ta get on that bus honey. And we next in line," a lady called to the courtesy clerk, as she pointed to the woman behind her. "You can walk both of us out at the same time. Ain't no need in makin' two trips. That's just a waste of time. Save yo energy."

Maxie smiled, and greeted them. She couldn't recall ever meeting these two women before, but noticed there was something familiar about the second woman, who was yet to speak. With the first woman, whose mouth ran non-stop about anything that came to mind, Maxie did her best to show that she was attentive to her words, by giving an occasional glance and nod. But it was the peculiar silence, and bare movement of the second woman, that made it hard for her to tear away her focus. In observing how her eyes were consistently downcast, Maxie wondered why the lady would not even so much as acknowledge her with eye contact.

"That'll be sixty-two eighteen," Maxie said, and watched the first woman search her purse.

"Hey Pearlie?" The lady said to her friend. "You got eighteen cents in yo' purse? I don't wanna break this here dollar fo' it."

Maxie's face lit up with a broad smile. "Your name is Pearlie? My grandmother's name was Pearl. All of her friends used to call her Pearlie. What a coincidence."

Pearlie nodded methodically, and raised her head to look at Maxie. Expecting to get a smile in return, Maxie was a little stunned when she received no expression at all. Though their eyes locked in a gaze, she felt like the woman was searching her, and not just staring. It was so intense, Maxie felt offended. Her first reaction was to turn away, but curiosity caused her to hold her ground.

"You'own granny, lub oonuh mo' nuh de wull," Pearlie said.

Maxie was floored.

Uncertainty clouded her face, and dimmed her smile. Not only did this woman share her grandmother's name, she was now speaking to her in the Gullah Geechee dialect her grandmother often used when talking to her. Maxie immediately felt uncomfortable, but retained her composure.

"Yes ma'am," Maxie smiled. "My grandmother often told me she loved me more than the world. But how did you know that?" Keeping a slight smile, Maxie creased her brows, and looked at the woman inquisitively.

"You'own granny, e' shum onnuh een 'e min', feel oonuh een 'e ha'at. *(Your grandmother, she see you in her mind, feel you in her heart)* F'um uh leetle chile, 'e ruck-uhnize dat de han' ob de Lawd tuh oonuh. *(From a little child, she recognized that the hand of the Lord is on you.)* E' teach oonuh tuh lub Jedus en' Gawd wu'd. *(She taught you to love Jesus and God's Word)* Jedus, 'e nyuse tuh lib een oonuh ha'at. *(Jesus, He used to live in your heart.)* No mo' uh chile, oonuh 'low de odduhre man tu tek you'own ha'at. *(No more a child, you allowed the other man to take your heart).* Wy? *(Why?)* Attuh summuch wawning, w'y'mek'so haa'd you'own way?" *(After so many warnings, why you make your own way so hard?)*

Maxie was shocked.

She couldn't believe what she was hearing. All she could do was stare at the woman. Her mind went into such a tailspin; she nearly forgot where she was. It didn't make sense. It couldn't make sense. How was she hearing words that would have come through her grandmother's mouth had she lived, coming through the mouth of a complete stranger? It was insane.

Looking around nervously, Maxie wondered who else heard the words from her childhood, and her current situation, proclaimed on the housetop. Quickly remembering that the woman spoke to her in Geechee, Maxie took comfort in knowing very few people spoke the language, much less be able to interpret it.

"Oh lookie here," the first woman chimed, as if nothing had transpired. "Neva mind Pearlie. I done found two dimes in the bottom of my purse. Here ya go honey."

Maxie looked at the woman, as if she were handing her something extremely lethal.

"Well what's wrong? Didn't you say you needed eighteen mo' cents?"

"Yes ma'am." Maxie took the money and looked at Pearlie, whose head was down again, as if she had said nothing.

Hitting the register keys to deposit the money, Maxie's eyes widened as she quested within, *what the heck just happened?* She felt like she was losing her mind. She knew Pearlie just spoke to her, yet neither one of these women, nor anyone else in the line, acted as if anything was said out of the ordinary. For lack of a better recourse, Maxie needed proof that she clearly heard this woman speak to her, and not mentally giving voice to her own deep seated convictions; which was quite probable giving all she had been through in the last twenty-four hours. But apprehension held her tongue, and made her believe she would look like a fool if she asked, and found no one witnessed any of what she just experienced.

Handing the woman her change, Maxie faked a smile. "Pearlie doesn't talk too much does she?" She asked, hoping to gain the right response.

Throwing the pennies into her purse, the woman looked at Maxie, and returned her smile. "Honey, Pearlie can't talk at all. She been quiet as a mouse since she had that stroke. Been 'bout two years now. It's just the grace o' God she can walk, and still move her arms and all. I keeps her with me 'cause I looks out after her, ya know. She's good company though." The woman laughed. "Ain't nothin like good quiet company."

Maxie scanned and totaled Pearlie's groceries, as her friend paid for them and continued to talk, volunteering information on Pearlie's distant family members. All of the woman's words fell to the ground, because Maxie heard none of it. All she saw was the moving of her mouth, and the gapped teeth in the woman's grin. Her mind was clouded with a barrage of thoughts.

"Well come on Pearlie," the woman finally said. "Let's be gettin' on that bus. I'm sure by now, they fussin' 'bout us bein' so late. You have a blessed day ma'am," she waved.

With hope and expectation of their eyes meeting again, Maxie looked at Pearlie, but Pearlie didn't so much as hazard a glance her way. She simply kept her head lowered, as she turned and walked away. Maxie watched the two women walk arm in arm behind the courtesy clerk. When they exited the store, she took a deep breath as if life was thrust back into her body, sending oxygen to her brain, which was now registering *mental chaos*. She wanted to sit down, run, scream, cry, and laugh all at the same time, considering all she had been through. She had never been so overcome with emotion — at least not at the words of someone she didn't even know. Everything was peaking on extreme, and with her being at work, she was forced to deal with it collectively, as if nothing happened.

Maxie was drowning.

She knew she was totally submerged, and the weight of her deeds were firmly holding her under. Just like an actively drowning victim, she was unable to call or wave to anyone for help. If she could get someone to assist her, and bear the shame of telling them all the incredible things she was experiencing, would they even believe her?

Maxie had to admit to herself that she was somewhat frightened, yet thoroughly convinced that in a short span of time, those who were dear to her in the past, had found a way to appeal to her senses with warnings she could not ignore, but she had to try.

When she got off of work, Maxie wasted no time contacting Marc. Talking to him almost always moved her from one place to another mentally, and she needed him to be the intoxicating drug that he was, to calm all that was raging inside of her. The irony of him being both the problem and the solution to her dilemma, was mind boggling. And just like an addict, the feeling of immediate gratification, outweighed all threats of harmful consequences.

Maxie deemed it necessary to treat everything that happened within the last 24 hours, as a mild speed bump in her joy ride. Just like any normal driver would do, acceleration to regain speed after the bump, was what was needed if she planned to keep moving forward. She wasn't going to speak about any of her latest encounters, and she wasn't going to think on them either.

* * * * * * * * * *

Marc pulled up in front of his grandmother's house, and smiled as he ended his phone conversation with Maxie. He was glad she chose to call him today instead of tomorrow. He needed to finalize their plan for the Blue Lights in the Basement party at the Regency, as soon as possible. They spoke of meeting briefly to discuss it, but Marc was already on the way to his grandmother's house before Maxie called, and meeting at a later time was out of the question for her. Though he had hopes of seeing her, he was made to settle for what he could get. Before the call ended, Maxie asked Marc if he would give her regards to Stella, and eagerly express her desire to see her again soon. He laughed, and promised he would.

Marc didn't tell Maxie that his visit to his grandmother's house was one of firm request, and that he somewhat dreaded accepting Stella's invitation to come see her. Instead, he used Maxie's voice as a comforting precursor, to what he knew was coming down the pipe from his grandmother. It was already out of the ordinary for Stella to ask him to come and visit before the weekend, but when she wouldn't tell him why she wanted to see him, and only stated "we'll talk when you get here," he believed her request was *extreme* in nature, and the subject of their conversation would probably be Maxie.

Pensively, Marc sat in his car a moment longer, before he opened the door, sighed heavily, and got out. The walk to the front door, gave him time to mull over what his grandmother might ask him about Maxie. Whatever her questions or comments, he was ready for them.

When Marc got to the door, he started to use his key, but knocked instead. While he waited for his grandmother to shuffle to the door, he considered how Stella would look at him, and immediately see the indelible stain in his heart, because of his love for another man's wife.

Stella opened the door and smiled. "Well did you lose your key, or did you just want to make me walk all the way over to this door?"

Marc returned her smile, and leaned in to kiss her cheek. "Hey Mama. I just felt like being lazy."

"Well get your lazy self on in here," Stella said with a little laugh, as she turned and headed toward the dining room. "You came straight from work?"

"Yes I did." Marc closed the door behind him, and quickly scanned the room before he followed. "I don't smell anything cooking. You invite me over here, and not greet me with food? This must be pretty serious."

Stella stood next to a chair at the head of the dining room table, before she attempted to sit down. "I can warm up some leftovers if you'd like. I didn't feel much like cooking today. So if you want something ...."

Marc looked at his watch, and the clock that hung over the mantle. They both read 5:15 p.m. As far back as he could remember, four o'clock was his grandmother's normal time for preparing dinner, and she was usually finished with it by five. It was a rare occasion for her not to cook, especially if she knew he was coming to visit. This was another event out of order.

"No I'm fine," he said, studying her with a furrowed brow.

"Nothing's wrong with me Marcky, so stop looking at me that way. Go on and sit down."

Marc did as he was told, and sat at the opposite end of the table. With a hand on his chin, he gave his grandmother his full attention.

Stella finally sat down, but she didn't look at Marc. Instead, she busied herself with positioning, and repositioning the placemat that was in front of her. When she did finally look at him, Marc saw such a solemn look on her face, it made him feel totally reduced. Something was wrong.

"Mama. ..." He started.

Stella nodded her head negatively, and Marc was silenced. "How is she?" Stella asked.

"She's fine. She said to tell you hello, and that she can't wait to see you again."

Stella looked at the placemat again, and lightly nodded her head. Raising the corners of her mouth, she formed a soft grin, only to let it fall quickly. A minute of silence passed between them, before she clasped her hands together, and looked at Marc intently.

"You let it happen didn't you?"

Marc said nothing. Almost immediately, a wave of shame washed over him, and made him lower his sight.

"You fell in love with her. You fell in love with a married woman."

"Yes. I did," he nearly whispered.

"Umph," Stella said, nodding her head.

Marc instantly felt berated. It wasn't his grandmother's words that made him feel censured, but rather the lack thereof. He could tell by the sound of her voice, that she was greatly disappointed in him, and rightfully so. Up to that moment, the only time he had committed a moral offense in her eyes, was when he was in New York living with Shari, without being married to her. A simple admission to that particular wrongdoing, was enough to cause Stella to back down then, but he knew she wasn't going to budge one inch from this one. What happened in the past, could not even begin to be measured against the gross error he was entangled in now.

Stella took a deep breath, and quietly released it before sitting back in her chair. "Well, Marc you're a grown man. And whatever we have to say to one another, is as a conversation between adults. I'm not going to bash you, and I'm not going to judge you, because the Word of God judges you on its own. But with all I have taught you while you were growing up, I know you understand how this involvement is wrong." Stella paused and waited for Marc to respond, but he kept his eyes on the floor, saying nothing. "Now I told you when you brought her here, that she was nothing for you to mess with. That girl belonged to the Lord then, and she belongs to the Lord now. That right there makes her dangerous Marc. I warned you of that. And now you have put yourself and Maxie, in a very difficult place by falling in love."

"Mama, it wasn't like we ... I ... planned for any of this to happen. It just ...."

"Romans chapter thirteen, verse fourteen, tells us to make no provision for the flesh Marc. Now that is exactly what you've been doing, when you're going from place to place meeting with each other. What did you think would become of you two with all of that time you've been spending together?" Marc glanced at his grandmother with an element of surprise. "Yes, I know you two have been sneaking around together. How else could you have fallen in love? That was your first mistake."

"Mama. ..."

"No son, listen to me. This has got to stop. You have to end this affair with Maxie."

Marc gazed at his grandmother for a moment, trying to find the words to express himself respectfully, yet fervidly. "I don't want this to end. I don't want any of it to change."

"Marc!"

"No mama! That woman is the best thing that has happened to me in a long time. She's more than I could have ever asked for in a woman. She's encouraging, she's smart, she's fun to be around, she's. ..."

"Another man's wife."

"That's a mere technicality. It's not an issue for either one of us right now."

Stella frowned, and stared at her grandson as if she were trying to recognize who he was. "And how long do you think it's going to remain a mere technicality as you call it? Marc, can you not see the role you are playing here? You are being used to keep that girl from her destiny."

Marc looked at the floor again. Anger was beginning to swell within him, so he felt it was in his best interest to change his focus, and just be quiet for the moment. He wanted to yell the words w*hat about my destiny*, but pressed his lips together tightly, and shook his head instead. He couldn't remember a time when he felt such an anger at his grandmother's words, or why he even felt angry, especially since he knew she was right.

"Now I know you love that girl Marc. I saw it in your eyes when you brought her here for lunch. I hoped I was seeing wrong, but when the Lord gave me that dream about her groping around in the dark trying to find the door, and you standing in front of it, not offering her any help, I knew then that what I saw was right."

Silence filled the room, and Marc used it to remember the day he arrived in India, and his grandmother called him to share that dream. He also remembered his conversation with Maxie that day, when she told him, *there's so much ... so much that you don't know about me. Who I am and what I've come from, the purpose of my life, and where I need to be in my walk with God. It all pulls on me.* He didn't like what he was now being made to see, but he couldn't deny it. His pursuit of gaining love and happiness with a woman who wasn't his, proved him to be totally selfish. He never once encouraged Maxie to be all that God wanted her to be. He didn't really view her as a woman called by God, to lead others to Christ. He only saw what he wanted — a beautiful woman who could make him feel like he could be and do anything.

In spite of his grandmother's words, which made it sound as if he were single-handedly masterminding the entire affair, Marc knew Maxie was a very willing participant.

"Marc," Stella said softly. "The Lord told me that Maxie has been warned."

Marc looked at her and frowned. "I don't understand. What are you saying Mama?"

"Early this morning, before daybreak, the Lord woke me up and told me in prayer, that she has been warned about being in this entanglement. And not on just one occasion. There have been several warnings. Has she said anything to you about that?"

Marc looked at the table, and nodded his head no. The thought of Maxie keeping something like that to herself, and choosing to deal with it on her own, made him feel totally slighted and helpless in being there for her.

"Why wouldn't she come to me with that?" He almost whispered.

Stella watched as her grandson became frustrated. "Marcky ..."

Marc looked at her abruptly. "I don't know what I'm going to do Mama. If what you're saying is true about these warnings ... I mean I'm sure what you're saying is true, but I just can't walk away from her, I can't tell her that it's over. I just can't. I am so in love with her."

"If you love her that much son, that alone is a reason to let her go."

Marc quickly considered his life without Maxie. "I can't."

"Then what you're saying, is that you are leaving this in the hands of God. Son that's not a good thing to do in this regard."

"I don't know what I'm saying Mama. All I know is that I cannot walk away from her."

Stella gazed at Marc, and saw the anguish she heard in his voice. With her hands clasped together tightly, she sighed heavily in resignation. "Okay. Well, there's nothing left to be said."

"So now what?" Marc asked uneasily.

Stella stood up, and walked to her grandson. Wrapping her arms around his shoulders, she held him close. "I wish I knew son. I honestly wish to God that I knew."

Chapter Sixty-Three

I t was New Year's Eve, and Maxie got the call from Blanche Grammerson around 8:00 p.m. the night before, explaining exactly what her duties would be for the New Year's Eve Watch Night service. As she sat at the kitchen table sipping hot tea alone, she was glad she took the day off from work, explaining to her manager that it was for church related duties. Indirectly it was, because she needed to work on a strategy for an early start and finish, to the tasks The Ominous Three assigned to her hands. Her intent was to be able to leave the church before midnight.

Maxie knew from Watch Night services in the past, how those three old ladies could manipulate the entire women's committee, into performing tasks that were above and way beyond what was needed for one night's service, so she planned to be prepared. With effort and great anticipation, Maxie perfectly mapped out how she would complete her church tasks, and get to Marc before the New Year rang in. The simple thought of being in his arms, as they watched fireworks above the river, made her smile. It was going to be very romantic.

After a few minutes of going over her plans, and considering what her night would be like with Marc, a more foreboding thought crept in and pulled her away. Although she knew the latter part of the evening was sure to bring her great pleasure, Maxie had to consider how uncomfortable she was going to feel at the Watch Night service, when the Pastor laid his eyes on her. Given there had been no scheduled church service since the day he saw her with Marc, she was spared the gaze she knew would discern all of her soul's misdeeds. Should their eyes meet, Maxie had no idea as to how she would even react. The more she thought about that entire ordeal, she realized she didn't know if Lester had even spoken with Pastor Harrison on her behalf. She hoped he would have at least made an effort to douse the Pastor's assumption of her having a fire kindled toward someone else. That would have been the honorable thing to do, but she couldn't take comfort in that thought. If Lester *had* immediately handled the situation, a phone call from the Pastor, expressing his sincere apology, would have been proper and in order. Yet she had received nothing.

With Pastor Harrison at the forefront of her thoughts, Maxie took her empty cup and placed it in the sink. Why hadn't Lester made mention as to whether or not he had spoken to the Pastor? Was it a mere oversight? Should she have taken confidence in knowing it was his place as her husband, to automatically cover her and clear her name, and assume that he did? After all, he never told her he would.

When she inhaled and released it heavily, Maxie felt a twinge of aggravation. What if Lester said nothing at all, and in the Pastor's eyes she was still just as guilty as the day he saw her? If that was the case, and their paths crossed, she may very well have to explain everything to him on her own, which meant she would have to lie to him face to face. That would be impossible.

With the threat of having to expose herself, Maxie experienced a strong surge of angst that made her shudder. She needed to know if she was covered or not. Lester was only scheduled to work until 2:00 p.m. since it was New Year's Eve, but that was almost four hours away. There was no way she was going to sit, and stew in a hot cauldron of what-ifs for that length of time. Quickly, Maxie moved to the phone on the wall and lifted it from its cradle, and just as quickly she put it back.

"You're moving too hastily, and you're being paranoid," she reasoned aloud.

Crossing her arms, she took a moment to ponder over everything again. With all there was to do tonight, she probably would not even have time to sit and hear the Pastor's sermon. The bulk of her duties were to be done in the Fellowship Hall, in preparation for the New Year's breakfast that was scheduled to follow the service, so she was almost certain she would not be seen by Pastor Harrison at all.

Relief washed over her, and made her smile.

By the time the benediction was said, and the procession of congregants to the Fellowship Hall started, her responsibilities would be shifted to someone else, and she would be free and clear for take-off — her departure being swift and subtle.

With her smile still in place, Maxie let the feeling of excitement flood her entire body. The New Year was destined to start off without a hitch, and she was thoroughly convinced tonight was definitely going to be a night to remember.

* * * * * * * * * *

"You seem awfully bubbly this evening," Lester said as he stood in the bathroom doorway of their room, tying his tie. You're practically bouncing around here. What's going on?"

Maxie sat on her side of the bed, and put lotion on her legs. Looking at Lester, she smiled and shrugged. "I don't know. Maybe it's because tonight moves us one day closer to the month of our anniversary. You know we *are* scheduled for a trip to Paris, France." It amazed her how smooth that full blown lie rolled off her tongue.

Lester gently lifted one side of his mouth, when Maxie came to stand in front of him. "You're excited about that huh?" He asked.

Maxie held her smile, and lightly kissed his mouth. She was excited, but not about Paris, France. That was the furthest thing from her mind. Content with leading Lester to believe what she wanted him to believe, she winked her eye, and walked into the closet to remove herself from view. There was no denying the electrical charge that was in the atmosphere, because it had been there all day. Considering the source, she felt like a giddy school girl preparing for a date with the guy every girl wanted. Apparently, her giddiness was evident. Maxie experienced butterflies, extreme bliss, and a strong desire to be absent from the night's church service altogether. It was virtually impossible to think on anything except what the night was holding for her, but she knew she had to regulate her thoughts, and focus on her church commitment.

Scheduled to be in the Fellowship Hall at 7:00 p.m., Maxie had one hour to make sure everything was in order.

As she prepared for the two different occasions, a convicting, yet fleeting thought of dating God, and dating the world at the same time came to mind, but she quickly dismissed it. She didn't have time to entertain anything contrary.

"So are you riding with me to the church?" Lester asked, startling Maxie, since he was now standing in the doorway of the closet. "Because if you are, you'd better get a move on it. You're half dressed, and I need to be there by six forty-five. By the way, have you seen my gold tie clip? It's the one my baby sister gave me for Christmas. I just wore it last Sunday."

"Your clip was over on the dresser yesterday morning." Maxie gently pushed past Lester, and headed toward the dresser just as the telephone rang. With him being closest to it, she knew he would answer it.

"Unknown name and number," Lester said, before he picked it up.

With those words, Maxie quickly turned and stared at him. An unknown name and number was nothing out of the ordinary, but it clearly piqued her interest.

"Hello?" Lester frowned. "Hello?"

When he hung up, a jolt of anxiety, coupled with the wildest thought, came to Maxie's mind. *Was that phone call meant for me?* "Wrong number?" She threw in.

"Guess so," Lester replied casually.

Maxie watched her husband give his attention back to his tie. When she turned to continue her trek to the dresser, the phone rang again.

"I'll get it," Lester assured her.

Curiously, she stood her ground, and observed Lester's face when he read the Caller ID again.

"Whitley Jewelers," he mumbled, and picked up the receiver. "Hello?"

In that instant, Maxie felt all of the breath in her body leave her. *Was it Marc? Would he really call me at home?* Immediately, the pulsing of her heart became so magnified in fear, she could feel the swelling of it in her throat. Without drawing attention to herself, she gently tried to clear her throat and swallow. *Oh God ... Marc*, she thought. *Why are you calling me here?*

Lester looked at her with a creased brow. "You would like to speak with Maxine Bruce? And whom may I say is calling?"

Even though silence filled the room while Lester listened for the response, Maxie could hear her own heavy breathing. She was terrified. Fear and dread rested on her so heavily, she felt as if she was being smothered.

"Beatrice Monroe of Whitley Jewelers."

Maxie could barely stand the scrutinizing look Lester was giving her, and she wanted to avoid it by walking into the bathroom, but her legs felt like cast iron weights. She couldn't even move to the dresser which was only a couple of feet behind her. At least there she could turn her back to him, while searching for his tie clip.

"No that's fine," Lester continued. "She's right here. Hold on a moment." With a slight smirk on his face, Lester held out the phone to her. "She says it's something about an order you placed with them for a piece of jewelry."

Maxie reached for the phone, and her legs came back to life. Taking it from his hands, she covered the mouthpiece, and quickly replaced her fear with a fake attitude of annoyance.

"Well if I planned to surprise you with a gift from their store, I guess she just gave it all away now didn't she?"

"It's the thought that counts," Lester chuckled, and walked back to the bathroom.

Maxie rolled her eyes heavenward, and breathed a heavy sigh of relief, as she walked into the living room. At least it wasn't Marc calling, but what in the world could Beatrice want with her? Looking over her shoulder, she made sure she was out of earshot.

"Hello Beatrice?"

"No baby it's me," Marc answered.

Maxie instantly felt both paranoia and joy, at the sound of Marc's voice. Cautiously, she looked around the room as if to find someone listening. "But …." She started.

"I know. I had her to call just in case your husband picked up the phone again. Don't worry. She knows nothing."

Turning around, Maxie made sure she could see Lester's shadow on the bathroom door, before she lowered her voice. "So that *was* you. Marc you are crazy. There are three phones in this house. Lester can pick up either one of them, and listen in on this conversation."

"I don't think so. Number one, he's been made to believe that you are speaking with someone at this jewelry store, in regards to his anniversary gift. And number two, if there was any chance of him actually being on the other end, you would not have made that statement."

Maxie laughed lightly. "You are so cocky. Why are you calling me here?"

"You mean besides me needing to hear that voice of yours?"

"Stop!" She whispered firmly.

"Are you excited about being with me tonight?"

"Marc I cannot talk to you about that right now."

"You've been hiding a smile all day long haven't you?" He teased.

Maxie closed her eyes, and pressed her lips tightly together, trying hard not to release the giggle that complemented her excitement.

"Is something wrong?" Lester's voice loomed.

Maxie quickly opened her eyes, to see him standing in the doorway of their bedroom, looking at her with concern. Calmly, she put her hand over the receiver and nodded her head.

"It's just a simple issue they had with my order. Go on now," she teased with a smile. "You're not supposed to be hearing any of this."

"Well hurry up. We have to get out of here. I still have to find my tie clip, and you need to finish getting dressed."

Maxie watched Lester walk back into the bedroom, before she removed her hand from the receiver. "Baby I have to go," she whispered.

"All right. Just tell me you'll be there Maxie. Like I told you, I want the New Year to find me holding you in my arms."

"Marc I'll do the best I can. Watch Night is a major church event. All I can tell you is that I promise I'll do the best I can, to be at the hotel before twelve."

"That's all I'm asking. Now listen, all three levels of the parking deck at the Hyatt will be full around six, but I've made special arrangements for you. There will be a valet there named Kevin. Give him your keys, and tell him your name. He'll handle it from there. When you come into the hotel, go upstairs to the Regency Ballroom. I'll leave a ticket for you at the door."

Maxie smiled at how Marc had everything planned out. "Okay. I have to go."

"See you tonight."

After Marc hung up, Maxie decided to raise her voice loud enough for Lester to hear her ending the conversation on a positive note. "Yes. That will be great Beatrice. Please let me know if you have any other issues. Have a happy New Year."

When she pressed the off button on the phone, Maxie studied it, and smiled to herself. It was amazing how quickly she experienced a fear so intense she couldn't move, only to have it replaced in the next moment by sheer euphoria that seemingly lifted her off her feet.

"They're open pretty late for New Year's Eve aren't they?" Lester asked when she entered the bedroom.

"Yeah. It's their normal business practice during the holidays. I guess jewelry purchases are big around this time of the year." Maxie put the phone back on its base, and continued her hunt for Lester's clip. She knew immediately that his eyes were set on her with an inquiring gaze, and she did her best to ignore him. Without a word, Lester sat at the foot of the bed and watched her from behind.

"I saw it sitting up here just yesterday," Maxie mumbled. "Did you look inside these top drawers? Sometimes things fall into them."

"Hey Maxie?"

"I'm not telling you anything about your anniversary gift Lester," Maxie smiled without looking at him. "So don't bother asking."

"What? I just wanted to tell you that you look nice tonight." Folding his arms across his chest, he tilted his head as if it gave him a better view of her.

Maxie glanced at him from the corner of her eye, with a slight smirk on her face. She knew that line. No matter how subtle he tried to be, she knew those words were a direct invitation to crawl into bed at some point.

"I believe that's only because you're looking at me while I'm half dressed," she said. "Anyway, I don't feel as good as you think I look."

"What's wrong?"

"You know that awful feeling I get when it's that special time of the month?"

"I understand," Lester said, with a hint of disappointment.

"Here it is." Maxie smiled, and handed him the tie clip.

"Thank you. Next time I'll put it in my box."

Maxie watched Lester put the golden clip on his tie, making sure it was straight. When he finished, he put his hands on her hips, and pulled her closer to him.

"You still haven't answered me," he said. "Are you riding with me or no?"

"I planned to ride with you. But with the way I'm feeling, I think it's best if I take my own car. That way if I feel any worse, I can just leave and not have to bother you. I'm sure you'll have a lot to do tonight, so. ..."

Lester looked up into Maxie's eyes, for what seemed like the longest moment. Surprisingly, she didn't try to avert his gaze. She knew exactly what he was doing when he looked at her that way, and she met him head on.

"If you do leave early, make sure I see you first," he said. "I'm not too keen on the idea of us not being together when the New Year comes in, especially with this being our eighth year of marriage. You know the number eight represents ...."

"New beginning," she interrupted. "I remember."

"Then you know how important tonight is."

"I do. So if I'm not feeling well, you want me to come and get you, so we can leave the service, and be together for the *new beginning* of the New Year." Maxie tried hard not to smile.

"This isn't a joke Maxine."

"Well baby," she grinned. "You're making it sound as if I'm not going to be home when you get here. If I'm not feeling well, and I do happen to leave, the only place I'm going to be is in this bed right here."

"I still want to know."

"Then I will make sure you do." Maxie smiled, and kissed him. "Now we're both going to be late if you don't drop this conversation."

Lester sighed, and stood up. "Yeah you're right. I'm in charge of setting up the communion for tonight, and we're expecting a lot of people."

"I know. Every available hand in all of the auxiliaries will be helping to prepare and serve breakfast, so you may or may not see me in the sanctuary."

"That's fine," Lester said, as he stepped to the side to view himself in the mirror behind her. "As long as ...."

"I let you know if I leave," Maxie quipped, and turned around to face the mirror. "I heard you the first time you said it." Maxie felt herself becoming a little perturbed, but refused to let her mood be changed. "Honey, I forgot. Exactly what time did they say they were going to open the church doors this evening?"

Lester looked at his watch. "At eight. They're supposed to do a sound check for that guest soloist who's going to be singing tonight."

"That's right," she said pensively. "I forgot all about that. I hope I'm not too busy to hear her sing. I heard she's really good."

Putting the finishing touches on her hair, Maxie couldn't help but notice that instead of making a comment, Lester glanced at her in the mirror with an admonishing look. She dismissed it with a little smirk, and turned on her heels to walk toward the closet.

"Well I'm off to find what I'm going to wear tonight. Whatever it is, it's going to have to fit both occasions."

"Both occasions? What are you talking about, both occasions?" Lester asked.

Maxie stopped, and turned quickly, surprised by the fact that she had given voice to her thought. "Uh ... my dress. It has to be appropriate to work in while I'm in the Fellowship Hall, and for the church service. I do hope to at least get in on a little of it."

Lester looked at her again, and said nothing. Quickly, she continued into the closet.

"Hey, if I do stay until the end of service, would you like for me to set aside a breakfast plate for you?" She asked.

"That would be nice. Thank you."

Lester put on his suit coat, gave himself the once-over in the mirror, and walked to the closet doorway where he stood in silence. Maxie expected him to have final words before leaving, so she finished putting on her slip and gave him her undivided attention. Immediately, the look on his face told her that his focus was not really on her, but that he was preoccupied with a sudden thought.

"Listen. Even if you're not feeling well, I've just decided that I don't want you to leave before we take communion. That's a very important part of the service.

We're symbolically christening the New Year, and I want you there."

"Lester, we don't do communion until the *end* of the service. What if ...."

"I want you there," he interrupted.

Maxie pressed her lips together, inhaled a great amount of air through her nose, and looked at her husband in amazement, before she released it. If she didn't know better, she would swear he was deliberately trying to sabotage the evening she had planned, but she knew that thought was silly. The only way he could know anything about her plan was if God....

"Okay Lester," she gently smiled and nodded. "That's fine. I can do that."

Maxie watched him assess her from head to toe, with what appeared to be an air of skepticism and contentment.

"Good. Then we'll start our New Year off with a blessed beginning." Lester stepped into the closet. Gently holding her, he softly kissed her lips, and then smiled. "This will be the last kiss I give you this year, and it's going to be the final seal on all that has happened this year. After twelve midnight, I'm going to kiss you again. And that kiss will be the one that unlocks new doors, and opens avenues for us to move into, and receive all that God has ordained for us. There's so much He has purposed for us to do together Maxie, and the enemy would love to keep us away from the plan of God. By the two of us taking communion together, I want to show God we are serious about what He has given to our hands to do. Can you understand that?"

Maxie looked into Lester's eyes, and was suddenly captivated. His touch, the way he held her, the gentleness of his kiss, she couldn't pinpoint what it was, but something was very different. In that short span of time, something changed. There was a sudden element of newness where Lester was concerned, and it enveloped them both, much like it did the first time she met him.

"Can you understand that?" He asked again.

"Yes," she replied airily. "I understand what you're saying."

Lester held her a moment longer, before he winked, and released her. "I'm leaving now. If I don't see you again tonight, I'll see you at the start of next year."

"It's a date," she smiled.

Lester turned, and left Maxie standing in the middle of the closet. In his presence, she was careful not to look bewildered, in spite of what she was feeling on the inside. But as soon as she heard Lester close the back door behind him, she squeezed her eyes shut, and nodded her head in amazement. The thought of them both working together to fulfill God's plan, was something she prayed for years ago, but to no avail. Now Lester suddenly reveals that it is all going to begin after the stroke of midnight, by a kiss on her lips from him. "Why now?" She asked the walls. "Why all of this now?" Maxie put her hands on her hips, and let her eyes roam the floor. "This has got to be some kind of trick. Well it's not going to work."

Hurriedly, Maxie gathered her clothes from their hangers, and laid them out on the bed. She couldn't explain it, but she felt more determined than ever to get to the Regency. Instead of reflecting on anything that happened moments earlier, she revisited her brief conversation with Marc, and recalled the excitement she felt in hearing his voice on the phone. It wasn't until she caught her reflection in the mirror, did she notice her thoughts had produced a smile a mile wide. She couldn't help it. Tonight was destined to be something very special, and she was more than willing to risk everything in order to make it all happen. Tonight, she would throw caution to the wind. Tonight, even though it was always there, *risk* would be welcomed and viewed as pure sport.

Chapter Sixty-Four

B eatrice stood in the doorway to Marc's office with her coat on. Wrapping her head with a large scarf, she loosely tied it under her chin. "Mr. Thomas, I'm leaving now. Nearly everyone has gone, except for a few designers downstairs. It's New Year's Eve. Don't you have big plans for the evening?"

Marc looked up from the stack of papers he was working on, and smiled at Beatrice. "Well unfortunately, this small mound of papers is part of my plans for the evening. Since the pricing of our diamonds and gemstones is temporarily locked, I want to get these orders transcribed before the New Year. What about you? Do you have big plans?"

Beatrice smiled bashfully. "No. No. My husband and I have this little ritual, where we sit and watch Dick Clark's New Year's Rockin' Eve, until the New Year comes in. And then we do a toast to each other and go to sleep. We've been doing it like that for over thirty years now."

Marc chuckled lightly, before Beatrice laughed with him heartily. "I guess old traditions never die huh?"

"Not if they're good ones they don't," she continued to laugh.

"Well you go and have yourself a very Happy New Year Beatrice. And go light on that toasting stuff."

"Will do Mr. Thomas. You have yourself a Happy New Year too. Don't stay here too late. See you next week," Beatrice waved.

"Thank you. Goodnight." Marc returned her wave, and gave the pile of papers his attention again. Not long after Beatrice left, the silence that filled the air around his office became nerve wrecking. It was hard for him to focus, because he was now beckoned to think on other things besides work. While he entertained the thoughts that came to mind, the calculated sound of a woman's footsteps in high heels, broke into his pattern. As the sound came closer to his office, Marc sat back in his chair and relaxed. He had a pretty good idea as to who was coming his way, so he made sure his appearance did not make him seem off guard. When she stopped and stood in his doorway, as if her poise made a firm statement of some kind, Marc simply stared in silence. He had to admit, her red dress was quite provocative. Resting just above her knees, it dipped low enough in the chest area to accentuate her assets. But he showed little interest.

"Jaunee."

"Hello Marc. How are you?" She said, as she entered without invitation.

Marc stacked his papers between his fingers, and hoped she would catch the hint that he was too busy for idle chatter. "I'm good. Finishing up so I can get my evening started. Looks like you're dressed up with somewhere to go. New Year's Eve party?"

"Mmmm ... A little gathering at a friend's house."

"Sounds fun."

Jaunee nodded her head slowly, and looked at him with expectation. Marc recognized it, and casually gave his attention back to his papers. He was content with the somewhat nonverbal banter that was now the norm between them. Since the day Jaunee revealed that she saw him kissing Maxie in his office, he chose to keep their relationship strictly professional, with all conversations being held to business matters only. However, it was clear to him by the way she stood in his doorway, there was something else on her mind. He also considered how Jaunee waited until nearly everyone had gone home, before she came to him.

"So how may I help you?" Marc asked without looking at her.

"Still formal huh?"

Marc glanced at her with a look that said *don't even try it*.

"Yeah ... well ... I just stopped in to wish you a Happy New Year ...."

"Happy New Year," he interrupted.

"And to say good bye."

Marc stopped what he was doing, and looked at Jaunee with a questioning gaze.

"I'm leaving Savannah. Moving to LA this weekend. Today is my last day here at Whitley."

"California? Am I the last one to know this? Did we have a going away celebration I missed or something?"

"Would you have come if we did?" She asked solemnly.

Marc looked at Jaunee, and saw how she practically held her breath waiting on his answer. "Of course I would have come," he said. *You're an employee of the company,* he thought.

Jaunee smiled, and lightly exhaled. "A few of the designers knew I was leaving, and those in upper management. But for the most part, I kept it quiet."

Marc nodded his head. "Okay. So why LA? What made you decide to go all the way to the West Coast?"

"Tacori."

"Tacori? The leading designers in engagement rings and wedding bands?" Marc smiled.

"Yeah. Well they had an opening, which is rare, so I applied. I guess they liked my passion for detail and perfection."

"Hey, that's the Tacori touch. Congratulations. Will you be the one to endure their four week handcrafting process, or are you sticking with designing."

"Designing. I love it when people tell me what they want, and I'm able to make it happen for them."

Marc laughed a little on the inside. It didn't take Jaunee long to start planting innuendos. "So you're staying with custom designing. The Tacori designing studios are a great place to work. I think it will be very rewarding for you there Jaunee. And I believe I represent everyone here at Whitley, when I say your talent will be sorely missed."

Jaunee faked a light smile, but it did nothing for the eyes that conveyed to him how hurt she was by his *company based* statement. He didn't intend to hurt her. Marc knew she was hoping for words that were more personal and heart felt, but he had to stick to his guns on the keeping-it-professional stance. Giving her anything more, would have opened a door he didn't have time to close.

"So you said you're leaving this weekend. What day exactly?"

"My flight leaves late Sunday evening. I'm not quite finished packing yet. I have a friend who's helping me to get rid of my condo and the big pieces of furniture, but the small stuff is being transported to LA by a moving company. I'm doing my best to make this transition as easy as possible," she smiled. "Are you interested in buying some contemporary furniture? It's at a real good price?"

"No," Marc laughed lightly. "I've seen your furniture before, remember? I think I'll pass."

Jaunee laughed a little, and then stared at Marc with a distant gaze that told him she was remembering the one time he came to her place for dinner. For him it was nice, and it was innocent. For Jaunee, he was certain she hoped it would be the beginning of something more promising.

"Oh well," Jaunee said with a light giggle. "Can't blame a girl for trying."

Marc sat quietly looking at his papers, as he toyed with his pen between his fingers. The silence that immediately fell between them made the moment awkward, and Marc was more than ready to move away from it.

"Hey well ..." he started.

"Yeah I know," Jaunee said, almost simultaneously. "I need to get out of here so you can get back to work."

Marc nodded, and waited for her to say goodbye as she made her way toward the door. When she didn't budge, he looked up and saw that her eyes were pooled with water.

"Can a girl get a hug goodbye?" She asked, forcing half a smile.

Marc observed how Jaunee stood before him, gently playing with her fingers like a little child waiting in expectation of an undeserved treat. He forced himself to remember how she had been a good friend to him in the past. Days or nights when he just wanted to hang out and have someone to talk to, she was there — in spite of knowing he wasn't interested in having a relationship. The quick memory made him smile a little, but it also made him wonder if at any time, she may have felt like he had led her on. Without giving it any more thought, Marc stood up, made steps toward Jaunee, and opened his arms.

"Of course you can have a hug."

Jaunee quickly wrapped her arms around him as if her life depended on it, and exhaled just enough for him to hear it.

"You take care of yourself out there. You hear me?" Marc said. "And keep in touch. You don't have to be a stranger just because you're over twenty-four hundred miles away."

Jaunee laughed a little, and replied with a trembling voice. "I will."

"And call when you get there. Everyone will want to know that you've arrived safely."

Jaunee nodded her head quickly, but said nothing. Marc could tell she was crying by the little jerky movements she made in his arms, and it caused him to lightly regret his past decision to keep things between them strictly professional. She had been very good to him.

Sighing gently, Jaunee practically whispered in his ear. "I wish things could have been different between us. You're a wonderful man Marc."

Marc was silent.

With a gentle squeeze, Jaunee released her hold and took a step back. "Goodbye Marc."

Marc looked into her reddened eyes and remained silent, giving her a smile in return.

Quickly Jaunee turned and walked to the door. Without looking back, she stopped at the threshold. "Happy New Year."

"Happy New Year Jaunee."

Chapter Sixty-Five

D uring the entire drive to the church, Maxie thought about Lester's last minute decree, and how he shared his outlook on their future in ministry. His words were promising and even encouraging, but not what she needed, or wanted to hear at that moment. She was too far removed to appreciate Lester's expressions. She had one purpose and one goal, and her husband was not a part of either.

Every angle of the night was expected to be fearfully different, and strangely beguiling at the same time — and she welcomed it. Lester's request for her to remain at the church until after midnight, was not going to be an issue. She already decided to disobey him, before she even left home. With that out of the way, there was no need to think on anything else in that regard. Everything was going to fall into place. She played and replayed her strategy of departure over and over in her head, making sure there was only a small margin for errors. It was all set.

By the time Maxie entered the Fellowship Hall and removed her coat, everyone was busy in their designated work stations. Functioning like a well-oiled machine, no one looked up once to notice she was overdressed, and almost twenty minutes late. No one except for Blanche Grammerson, who was anxiously waving at her from across the room. Maxie sighed and plastered a smile on her face. Waving back, she walked toward her, with Blanche meeting her halfway.

"Well don't you just look beautiful this evening?" Blanche raved. "Aren't you a bit worried about getting waffle batter on this beautiful black dress? And your hair. Those nice curly locks are sure to fall once you start sweating."

"Good evening Sister Grammerson. I'll be fine in an apron. I actually want my hair to fall. That's the style I want. But thank you for genuinely being concerned. That's so sweet of you." Maxie nodded her head in the direction where Blanche was standing when she came in. "Now is that the station I'm supposed to be in tonight? Because if it is, I'd better get started don't you think? I mean since I am a little late."

"Oh ... why ... why yes. Yes of course. That's your station. I was just about to help them out when you arrived."

Maxie looked at Blanche with a skeptical smile on her face, and began walking to her station with Blanche in tow.

"But lucky for me, you came through the door when you did," Blanche said. "They already have one pan filled with waffles, and each pan holds about twenty-five. This station has been asked to do twelve pans."

"Three hundred waffles ... well two seventy-five now," Maxie said. "Okay we can do that."

When she got to her work station, Maxie shook the hands of the two women who were already working, while Blanche eagerly introduced them.

"This is Sister Carmen Pettis, and Sister Angela Stevenson, the two women I told you would be helping out tonight. Ladies this is Sister Maxie Bruce. She's a member of our Deaconess Union, and the wife of Minister Bruce. Sister Bruce, both of these ladies are new to the church, and very eager to get busy doing the Lord's business," Blanche said.

"New to the church?" Maxie smiled and nodded. *Perfect.* She couldn't think of a better set-up. She was working with two women who knew absolutely nothing about nothing, when it came to working in the Fellowship Hall. Her getaway might be easier than originally planned.

"You're expected to have all of the cooking finished by eleven. It's almost seven thirty-five now, so you should have plenty of time to complete the task. As you can see, there are two griddles here. Two of you can do the cooking, and the other one can keep the batter mix flowing. Everything else you need is all here, and. ..."

"I think we have it Sister Grammerson," Maxie interrupted with a smile. "I'm sure if we need anything, you three ladies will be hovering around here somewhere."

Blanche Grammerson stood with her mouth open. When she finally closed it, she gave Maxie a quick smile, and let it fall.

"Yes. We will be around supervising, and making sure everything is moving along in a timely manner. Well I have a lot of ground to cover ladies. I'll be back to check on your progress in about an hour."

Maxie and the two women watched, as Blanche walked away. Nodding her head lightly in disgust, Maxie walked to a small sink nearby. She quickly hung up her coat, put on her apron and hair net, and washed her hands.

"Well ladies, let's continue what you've started," Maxie said jovially when she returned. "Please forgive me for being late." The women acquiesced, and Maxie quickly assumed the role of mixing the batter. It gave her the mobility she was going to need throughout the evening, and it would be an avenue for her stealthily planned exit.

Maxie continued to make idle chatter with the women, all the while canvassing the room with her eyes, and taking into account the number of old and new faces. If there was going to be an alibi, she would have to be able to throw out names of the people who saw her working in the Fellowship Hall. The Ominous Three were expected to keep a watchful eye on every group, and auxiliary member. She only hoped they would do it as a collective effort, with all three of them in one area at the same time. Otherwise, it was going to be a tough task keeping each of them in view.

Maxie and the two women worked diligently. With a timing mandate set, due largely to Maxie expressing her desire to attend a portion of the service, they were finished by 9:30 p.m. Many of the other groups were still working, but some of their members were divided and asked to help other auxiliaries. Maxie hoped Blanche had no plans of asking her to do the same. Their quitting time was perfect, and she now had only one stop before leaving all together. With Blanche having left their station an hour ago, Maxie anticipated another visit from her soon. If she left now, there was a very good chance she would not run the risk of an encounter with Sister Grammerson.

Maxie quickly took off her apron and hair net, before washing her hands. "Well ladies. It has been a true pleasure working with you both. I'm going on over to the sanctuary. If I don't see you again before the Watch Night service is over, I pray you have a blessed and prosperous New Year. And thank you again for all of your help."

The women smiled, and wished Maxie the same. If she had more time, she would have given each of them a hug, but time was of the essence. The Ominous Three were out of view, and she had no idea as to their whereabouts. Feeling a slight twinge of paranoia, Maxie grabbed her coat and quickly left the Fellowship Hall. Stopping in the restroom to freshen up, she headed straight for the sanctuary. It was in her plan to make an appearance, so Lester could see she did exactly what she said she was going to do.

When she entered the vestibule with her coat folded over her arm, Maxie was greeted by those on the Welcoming Committee, Security team, and members of the Usher Board. The compliments flowed on her hairstyle, the beauty of her black dress, and how nice she looked overall. With a smile and a gentle wave, Maxie acknowledged them all, and kept the pace right into the sanctuary doors. When she entered, she witnessed a packed house, almost to the point of standing room only. Her focus immediately rested in the pulpit, diligently searching for her husband amongst the presbytery. When their eyes met, Lester nodded his head a little, and gave her half a smile. She could tell he watched her come in, because his eyes were already on her when she looked at him.

Mission accomplished.

Instead of trying to find a seat, Maxie decided she would just stand in the back along the wall, and close to the door. A quick glance at her watch, told her she needed to be in her car in ten minutes.

"Sister Bruce, there's a seat for you up front with the minister's wives if you would like to sit there. Would you like for me to hang up your coat?"

Maxie looked at the male usher who was standing directly beside her. "Oh no," she whispered with a smile. "I'm not staying. I just wanted to get in on a little bit of the service."

"Needing to feel the awesome move of the spirit huh?" The usher nodded. "I understand. This is the best way to start off the New Year. Doing it right with Jesus."

"Hmmm ..." Maxie tried to agree, lightly nodding her head."

Without another word, the usher walked back to his seat. Maxie locked her arms under her coat, and nestled it close to her. She knew she should have experienced some form of conviction, but she felt nothing. Even the preacher's words had no effect, because she made a conscious decision not to hear them. With her arms crossed, Maxie leaned against the wall and gave the appearance that would suggest she was totally engrossed in the guest preacher's message.

"God's Word is life. It has life and it is truth," the preacher said. "We need to remember what God has done for us. How He has kept us, and brought us out of those situations where we thought it was all over. And if He hasn't brought you out of it, He is yet able."

Maxie nodded her head, and said Amen in the places that were appropriate. As the preacher revved up, she watched how quite a few church members stood up and clapped. It was then she noticed The Ominous Three sitting near the front right side of the sanctuary. The sight of them made her laugh lightly, and shake her head. It was amazing how in spite of the church being filled, those three had seats together near the pulpit. With her thoughts on them, she missed the next few words from the preacher. Whatever he said, it brought everyone to their feet, and with that barrier of bodies between her and the pulpit, Maxie made a sudden move and left the sanctuary.

From inside the vestibule doors, she could see security was everywhere. Not only were they everywhere, they were double parking the cars. How could she have missed that? This routine was nothing new. The cars had been double parked on Watch Night for years. How did she forget to factor that into the plan? And how was it an oversight, when she just walked through a portion of the parking lot, to get to the sanctuary not fifteen minutes earlier?

Maxie looked at her watch, and felt herself becoming anxious and frustrated. It was 9:50 p.m. Before she let her thoughts take her to a state of panic, she needed to remember where she parked her car. Though it was not visible from where she was standing, she could safely assume it was not double parked, because she remembered she had chosen a spot right next to a handicap space and the driveway exit.

Calming herself, Maxie put on her coat, and held it together as she walked across the meagerly lit parking lot, as fast as she could. The heels of her shoes clicking loudly against the asphalt, gained her the attention of the security officers. Without stopping, she waved off the suggestions to be escorted, and assured them the distance to her car was very short. Maxie figured the speedy trek would make her a little winded, but she never anticipated her heart beating faster than she could take in air. She felt like a fugitive on the run. She escaped the sanctuary without a problem. Now if she could just get past the door of the Fellowship Hall, without anyone coming out....

"Sister Maxie Bruce?"

Maxie nearly froze under the cascade of light that lit a portion of the parking lot. She couldn't believe it. She was less than fifty feet away from her car, just about to pass the Hall door, and someone behind her called her name. For a split second, she entertained the thought to keep moving and act as if she heard nothing, but in recognizing the voice, she had to acknowledge it.

"Lester," she whirled around. "Baby what are you doing out here?"

"That's what I should be asking you," he said, quickly sizing her up. "You didn't stay in the service long."

Maxie let out a little nervous laughter and tried to calm her breathing, because everything shifted into overdrive. Her heartbeat quickened, she suddenly felt extremely winded, and her hands trembled as she tucked a strand of hair behind her ear.

"Yeah. I took a little break from cooking, so I could go over there. Then I remembered I had to get something from my purse. I ... I left it in the trunk of my car. So that's where I'm headed now, and then it's back into the Fellowship Hall."

Nodding his head pensively, Lester stood with one hand in his pants pocket. "All in the dark and unaccompanied."

"Lester," Maxie pleaded in her *please don't start* tone.

"I just want you safe Maxie. You know that. Now since I'm here, I'm going to walk you to your car. Come on."

When Lester walked past her, Maxie felt a flood of irritation rise up within. He was ruining everything, and she was certain he was doing it on purpose, so she stopped abruptly. "Lester, why are you really out here? Are you checking up on me?"

Lester stopped and turned. "I actually came to see how you were feeling. Remember, you told me you weren't feeling well before I left the house. But I guess you're better now, because you were just speed walking across this parking lot."

Maxie faked a little laugh, and walked closer to her husband with a look of demure. "Thank you for being concerned about me. I was actually going to get some ibuprofen from my purse."

"Well let's go get what you need. It's cold out here. And then I'll walk you back to the Hall."

Maxie immediately turned, and headed toward her car. With widened eyes and pursed lips, she felt like she was going to explode. The clock was still ticking, and now she had Lester to deal with. *I am NOT going to make this party in time!* She screamed within. *I just know I am NOT going to make this party!*

Maxie was unaware of her body language. The way she walked, and the way she snatched her purse from the trunk, loudly conveyed her frustration. After she retrieved the pills and tossed her purse back in, she was about to slam the trunk down, when Lester reached for it first, and slowly brought it down.

"Maxie what is wrong with you?"

"What are you talking about Lester?" She shook the small bottle of medicine in the air. "Besides the obvious, I'm fine."

Lester gazed at her thoughtfully again, before a soft smile moved his lips. "Let's go home."

Everything came to a screeching halt.

Did he just say HOME? What? Home? Home? When the words finally registered, Maxie tried to keep her eyes from widening again, but the response was instantaneous. So was the parting of her lips in astonishment. Did Lester really mean what he just said? Or was he just being facetious? What about the whole communion issue he insisted on earlier?

"Come on," he said. "Let's go home. I've just decided to do Watch Night a little differently this year. We'll stop at one of the stores, get a non-alcoholic wine, take it home, and have our own little New Year celebration. And you look quite beautiful tonight, I might add."

Maxie did her best to smile, but her eyes made it look more like a grin of total skepticism.

"Why are you looking at me like that?" He asked with a slight chuckle. "You're about finished in the Fellowship Hall right? And all of your stuff is already out here, so let's just go. Get in the car woman. We're wasting time." Lester glanced at his watch. "It's almost a quarter after ten. Now get in the car."

He was serious.

Maxie stared blankly at her husband. She couldn't speak. She couldn't move. She couldn't think. It was pointless for her to even take another breath, because her breathing had become so shallow.

It was over.

Utterly devastated, Maxie wanted to cry. With the right timing and a few words, Lester singlehandedly ruined her entire plan. There was no recourse. She never anticipated having to use anything other than a lie to get past Lester. What else was there to do with him standing right in front of her? Direct defiance? That was not an option.

A wave of emotion gripped Maxie in the pit of her stomach and seized her thoughts, making her look at Marc in her mind's eye. He was sitting at the Regency waiting for her. How could she tell him she would not be there to share in the experience they both desired?

Lester opened the door, and Maxie got into her car as she was told. Her movements were nearly robotic.

"I'm going back in to let someone know we're leaving, and they'll get the message to the Pastor. Meet me near the minister's parking lot and then you can follow me," Lester said. Touching her face lightly, he smiled and winked at her. "I'm going to spend the rest of this evening alone with my beautiful wife."

Chapter Sixty-Six

Marc ordered a Rum and Coke from the bar, and waited for Maxie in the Vu Lounge instead of the Regency Ballroom. It was a temporary move that he regretted, but found necessary because the Vu was closest to the hotel entrance, and he wanted to watch for Maxie the moment she entered the building. The stifling level of noise made him wish he had another option. It seemed like everyone in there had something to laugh, or talk about. He started to wait in the hotel lobby, but thought better of it. Everyone he saw was in a festive mood. There were people in party hats with noise makers, people who were toasting every occasion they could think of in the passing year, and people who clearly had celebrated before they even arrived at the hotel.

Contrary to the moment, Marc wasn't feeling very festive. Anticipation was getting the best of him, and he was having a hard time dealing with something he could not control. As he sipped on his drink, he checked his cell phone. The simple gesture had become routine over the past hour, because in spite of the three text messages he sent to Maxie, his viewing yielded him nothing except the time, which read 10:45 p.m. He wanted to call her and find out what was going on, but figured she probably couldn't answer a phone call if she couldn't return a text message. A phone call was also more risky.

Marc purposely tried to avoid thinking about what Maxie might be experiencing in her efforts to meet him before twelve, but he wasn't doing a good job of it. Every minute that drew closer to midnight without her arrival, made him consider all of the different problems she may be running into. He knew it was in his best interest to remember that Maxie said she couldn't guarantee she would be there. She said she would do her very best, but he wanted to believe nothing could stop her from being with him tonight.

Marc took a swallow of his drink, and quickly mulled over everything he had set in place. Maxie's parking was arranged, and her ticket to the party was at the door. Though it was not common practice of the Vu Lounge, he had a spot reserved for the two of them on the terrace for viewing the fireworks at midnight.

Everything was right.

All he needed now was for Maxie to come in and be escorted to the ballroom, dance a few dances, and come back downstairs to watch the fireworks display over the river, in his arms.

"Would you like to order another drink or something to eat?" A waitress suddenly asked. "Still waiting for your friend?"

Marc looked up and smiled at her pretentious pout. "No, I'm good. Thank you. And yes I am ... still waiting."

"Well don't give up. I'm sure she'll be here. She's probably caught in all of that traffic on Bay Street. There has to be at least a dozen parties going on in this area alone. But if she doesn't show up in time for the count down and the fireworks, I get off at eleven thirty," she winked.

Marc kept his smile, and let it drop as soon as the waitress left him. He felt a little irritated that she could give voice to a possibility he wanted to deny. What if Maxie didn't come, and he had to stand in the midst of couples being intimate when the New Year rolled in? Haphazardly, he glanced at those out on the terrace. Nearly everyone there had someone. Those who were unattached would be made obvious at the stroke of midnight, when lip locking salutes caused a moment of silence.

Marc quickly stood up. The thought was inconceivable, and he needed to walk away from it. But when he left the Vu, and walked back upstairs to the Regency, it met him at the ballroom door when he looked at the ticket taker.

"I'm sorry Mr. Thomas," the young man said. "Your guest hasn't picked up her ticket yet. However, your table is still reserved. Do you want me to continue holding the ticket, or would you like for it to be returned to you. It's eleven o'clock. We'll be out here accepting them for about another thirty minutes."

"No," Marc said pensively. "Just hold on to it." Without another word, he walked into the ballroom. The light from the open door drew the attention of those inside the room, but as it closed, he was soon enveloped in the blue atmosphere and the rhythmic music that complemented it. Without looking around, Marc walked straight to his table, and sat down to a barrage of questions and statements that immediately rushed to his mind. Although they were all uncomfortable, the ones he entertained the most were *I hope Maxie is okay, something must have gone wrong,* and *why am I still here waiting for her?*

When Marc finally tuned in to the ramblings of the DJ, and let his eyes roam around the blue lit room, it became apparent that while he was in deep thought about one woman, a table of a few women noted his current state of stag, and were grinning and staring at him. Like school girls playing Truth or Dare, they all giggled and teased each other as to who would be the first one to approach him. With soft applause from the group, one of them finally stood up and pulled her body hugging dress down to her upper thighs. Marc watched her as she sauntered across the floor, heading in his direction. When he first took notice of their interest, he had already decided if one of them wanted to dance, he would oblige her. At least he could get in one good dance before the night was over.

"Hi. My name is Marjorie," the woman said as she held out her well-manicured hand. "My girls and I noticed you when you walked in. We didn't see anyone tagging along behind you. So I had to come and ask, is it safe to say you don't have a date tonight?"

Marc stood up, smiled, and shook the woman's hand. "Nice to meet you Marjorie. To be quite honest, my date ..." Before Marc finished his sentence, someone opened the ballroom door and let the light into the room. Not only did they let the light in, but they held the door open a moment longer than they should have. As a natural response, just as before, everyone near the area looked at the person who was the reason for the interruption of everything. When Marc looked and recognized the shapely silhouette, noting it to be distinctly Maxie's, a broad grin spread across his face. "... is right there." Marc kept his eyes on Maxie, as Marjorie faded away. Everyone in the room could have faded away at that point. The woman he desired, pressed past everything in order to be with him tonight, and that was all he could see. Maxie captured his heart all over again; her arrival being just as pivotal as that very first time she picked up the phone to call him.

From across the room, Marc watched several men continue to stare at Maxie, even after the door was closed. It was no wonder. She was absolutely stunning, and hard to be ignored. He started to immediately walk to her and stake his claim, but found it unnecessary. It was evident that she was there for him, and him alone, so he stood his ground and admired her a moment longer.

When Maxie walked into the Regency Ballroom, she was as fascinated as she was nervous. She understood the event to be a party, but hardly expected to enter an atmosphere filled with blue lights and music that reverberated in her chest. The ballroom was bigger than she anticipated, and in the sea of blue light and silhouette bodies, Maxie had no idea how she would find Marc. Her cell phone would have been handy, but in her rush to get inside the hotel, she accidentally left it in her car. With no other recourse, Maxie searched the dance floor closely as the music faded, and people walked back to their tables. She hoped Marc would not be dancing with anyone else, but she would understand if he was. After all, most of the evening had passed, and it didn't make sense for one to sit idly, waiting for someone they couldn't be sure would even show up.

From where she stood, Maxie saw tables for large groups, and tables just for two. The tables for two held her attention, but with the ballroom being so large, it was impossible for her to see all the way across the room. Since she already felt like a fish out of water, walking the perimeter looking for Marc was out of the question. Hopefully, he would find her, and find her soon.

"It's the Blue Lights in the Basement party ladies and gentlemen," the DJ said with a sultry voice. "And we have about forty-five minutes left until the New Year. So if you didn't come with somebody special, find yourself somebody who looks special, and get your groove on to this slow jam by Mr. Larry Graham. Just Be My Lady."

As the prelude to the song began, Maxie watched people quickly crowd the dance floor. Some were holding hands as they walked, while others simply followed the lead of the person who asked them to dance. Maxie met the eyes of a few men looking her way, and wondered if one of them was going to ask her to dance. The thought made her feel a little self-conscious. The last time she danced a slow dance, was years ago with her husband, in the confines of their home. She had never danced in public. As she reasoned with herself that it couldn't be much different than dancing with Lester, one of the men stood with his eyes locked on her.

"May I have this dance?"

The voice came from behind her, and Maxie turned around sharply to see Marc standing with his hands in his pockets.

"I'm glad you made it Maxie," he smiled.

Maxie let out a little nervous, yet grateful, laughter and gave him a quick hug.

Fully assessing her, Marc nodded his head and sighed as if she had just taken his breath away. "You look … you look amazing tonight."

"Thank you. You look quite handsome yourself, as always. I think you just saved me from that man over there. I believe he was going to ask me to dance."

Marc acknowledged the man with a nod, and grabbed her hand. "Not tonight he's not."

Maxie smiled, and followed his lead. On the dance floor, Marc's embrace immediately delivered the drug she had become addicted to. With it, every form of anxiety simply melted away, as she allowed herself to be influenced by the dance. Closing her eyes, Maxie let her body match Marc's every salacious move. Even when he softly sang in her ear, she kept her eyes closed and enjoyed the resonance of his voice. After he stopped singing, she looked at him and smiled.

"You have a very nice voice. I didn't know you could sing."

Marc glanced at her, and smiled. "The things we do for love."

When the song ended, Marc led Maxie to a table that was directly across the room from the door.

"You were sitting here when I walked in?" Maxie asked, as they took their seats.

"Yes," Marc grinned.

"So you sat here watching me looking for you."

"No. I didn't sit here watching you. I was actually standing when you opened the door, and aggravated everybody with all of that bright light. Bringing all of that attention to yourself."

"Marc! Do you know how nervous I was? I was standing there wondering how I was going to find you."

"You were standing there looking quite beautiful. I just wanted to admire you. And it appeared I wasn't the only one. I saw those men over there checking you out."

Maxie lowered her eyes and smiled.

"I'm glad you could come," Marc said. "I'm sure you went through a lot to get here."

Maxie nodded, with her eyebrows raised. "Oh yeah. Talk about the things we do for love. I would have been here earlier, but as I was walking to my car, my husband was right behind me. Lester decided at the last minute, that he wanted us to do Watch Night differently this year. Instead of us ringing in the New Year with our church family like we always do, he wanted it to be just the two of us at home, with a bottle of non-alcoholic wine. To make a long story short, just as we were about to leave, one of the ushers let him know that the Pastor needed him to baptize some people. He stayed, I was already in my car, and here I am. If things go as I have planned, my husband will never know I left."

Marc stared at Maxie, pressed his lips together tightly, and then looked out on the dance floor.

"Marc. Baby look at me. This is our special time together. Let's just enjoy each other tonight."

"What time do you need to be back?"

"What, you don't want me to stay?" She smiled.

Marc twisted his head, and gave her a look that said *give me a break*. Maxie laughed.

"I'm like Cinderella tonight," she said. "Instead of leaving before the stroke of midnight, I have to go immediately thereafter."

"So right after the fireworks display."

"Yes. But are you sure they're still doing the display? I saw a lot of clouds before the sun set, and the weather man said we have a forty percent chance of rain."

"It doesn't matter to me." Marc looked at his watch. "As long as you are in my arms in the next twenty five minutes, I'm a happy man."

Maxie laughed, and held Marc's hand.

For the next few minutes, they were engrossed in conversation and mellow music. When an upbeat song bumped throughout the ballroom, and caused people to quickly flood the dance floor, Maxie was surprised when Marc stood up and held out his hand to her.

"Oh, this used to be my song back in the day. Jam Tonight by Freddie Jackson," he beamed. "Come dance with me girl."

Maxie was immediately apprehensive. With widened eyes, she looked at Marc and nodded her head. "No Marc. I don't know ... I don't want to dance."

As if she said nothing, Marc started dancing and singing the lyrics of the song. When she first arrived, Maxie promised herself she would throw caution to the wind during her time with Marc. So before the second hook of the song played, she was on the floor in front of him.

Marc watched Maxie, as she quickly tried to move to the beat of the song. It wasn't coming together, in spite of her efforts, and he soon realized why she said she didn't want to dance. Moving closer to her, he put his hands on her hips, and guided her to a more syncopated rhythm. After a moment Marc let her go, and Maxie laughed at herself as she mirrored every step he made. While Marc kept singing, Maxie was amazed at how the lyrics seemed to fit what they were doing. From the way she was dancing and smiling, no one in the room would have known she had inhibitions about dancing to an upbeat song.

She was having a ball.

Marc enjoyed watching Maxie, and danced a circle around her as she let herself flow freely with the song.

When the music died down, and a slower song was mixed in, Maxie threw her arms around Marc's neck and laughed. "Oh my goodness! I have never danced like that before. That was so much fun."

Marc smiled. "You definitely made it look like fun."

Maxie looked around the ballroom. "This is wonderful. Everything. This very moment. The atmosphere. Being here with you."

Marc held his smile a moment longer, before it faded away, and a more somber look took its place. Even though he was staring at her, his eyes were distant.

"Hey," Maxie said softly. "What's wrong? Where are you right now?"

Marc blinked, and gave her a faint smile. "I'm right here holding a very beautiful woman in my arms." When he paused and let the sound of the music flow between them, Marc decided to give voice to his thoughts. "Maxie. Do you think you could ever ...?"

"All right ladies and gentlemen," the DJ bellowed. "It's that time. For those of you who plan to watch the fireworks on the Terrace of the Vu Lounge, you better make that move now. For the rest of you who plan to do the count down right here in the Regency Ballroom, make sure you have your noise makers, your champagne, and your Chap Stick handy, because the countdown will begin in eight minutes."

Marc looked at the DJ, as if the timing of his announcement could not have been any worse. "Come on. We have to go."

"Why?" Maxie frowned.

"We have a reserved spot on the terrace to watch the fireworks."

"But what were you getting ready to ask me? It sounded serious."

"I'll ask you later. Let's go."

Chapter Sixty-Seven

Without another word, Marc held Maxie's hand and quickly led her through the crowd of people who were leaving the ballroom. Outside the doors stood State Troopers, directing the crowd to the stairs instead of the escalator and elevator. People were everywhere, charging the air with a festive energy. They were tooting novelty horns, rattling noise makers, and tossing confetti paper into the air. Maxie could tell most of them were inebriated, but she smiled at them anyway. She had long desired to be a part of this kind of atmosphere on New Year's Eve, and she was grateful to Marc for inviting her.

As they continued to make their way through the crowd, Marc looked behind him to make sure Maxie was okay. Even though she was holding his hand tightly, he needed to make sure she was in no way affected by the rowdiness.

"We're almost there," he smiled.

Maxie kept her grin, and squealed a little when two balloons popped near her feet, just as they entered the Vu Lounge. She didn't have much time to admire the intimate setting, but she noticed that every television in the place, was tuned in to Dick Clark's New Year's Rockin' Eve. The countdown was soon to begin. Like a man on a mission, Marc ushered her through the doors to their private little area on the terrace. The entire patio was enclosed with glassine weather paneled windows, but it didn't hinder the view of River Street below. Even the Westin Resort, located across the river, cast a beautiful reflection on the water.

Marc looked at the crowd of people on the terrace, and remembered how he felt when he viewed them earlier before Maxie arrived. Relief made him smile now. The one thing he desired the most of the entire evening, was about to happen for him in three minutes. He couldn't explain it, but he felt as if the New Year held something very special for the two of them. In spite of his grandmother's cautionary advice, and all the adversity they had faced, Marc felt like a change was coming their way. With the love they shared, he was certain nothing contrary could grow between them. Everything thus far had lined up just the way he wanted, and he knew Maxie felt the same way.

Marc stood behind Maxie, as she looked through the window at the people down on River Street. Wrapping his arms around her, he held her close to him. "You cold?"

Maxie smiled, shook her head no, and leaned against him, feeling safe in his arms. "Not at all."

A loud roar from the crowd snatched away the intimacy of the moment, and made them look at the television screen above the terrace.

"Ten … nine … eight … seven … six … five … four … three … two … one … Happy New Year!" Almost instantly, the noise of the crowd heightened, and booming fireworks filled the night air. When everyone began singing Auld Lange Syne, Maxie turned to Marc and mouthed the words Happy New Year. In return he smiled, gazed at her longingly, and brought both of her hands to his lips, where he softly kissed her fingertips. Without losing focus, Marc then took Maxie's face in his hands, and kissed her with a passion that was so intense; she could do nothing else but melt in it. So much so, she almost forgot where she was. When they finally stopped, Marc held her tighter than he had ever held her. On any other occasion, she would have thought his embrace strange, but Maxie knew he was struggling with releasing the moment. She laid claim to that feeling also.

The latter part of the evening, was an incredible dream come true for her. She was in the arms of the man she loved, and tonight she experienced things she dare only think about. There was no better way to start the New Year, and she didn't want any of it to end. But reality was creeping in, and it was doing it with every minute that ticked past twelve o'clock.

She had to leave.

Marc held Maxie a moment longer, before she turned around to watch the fireworks display. In spite of everything that was happening around them, he felt a sudden weight of caution and regret. He understood the presence of regret, because he was faced with Maxie having to leave him. However, it was the air of caution that seemed displaced. He had no idea where it came from, or why he was feeling it. For lack of a better reason, and one he did not want to consider, it could have stemmed from what he remembered of his grandmother's words about Maxie. Wherever it came from, it was making him feel the need to be protective of her, even when he knew he might be helpless against it.

When the fireworks display ended, people on the terrace, and those inside The Vu, began to mix and mingle. Loud talking and occasional bursts of laughter kept the celebration alive, and Maxie wished she could stay. With solemnness on her face, she looked at Marc and did her best to force a smile.

"Marc I've had a wonderful time."

Lifting one of her hands, he kissed the inside of it. "Me too. Thank you again for being a part of my New Year." Marc sighed heavily, and quickly scanned the terrace.

Maxie understood his silence, and said nothing.

"I guess we better go get your coat," he said. I don't want you to have to stand in a long line at the Coat Check."

Maxie grabbed his hand as they started to walk, but then stood still.

"What's wrong?" Marc asked.

"I want to know what you were going to ask me when we were in the ballroom."

Marc smiled softly. It was easy for him to recall the question, because it had been on his mind all night. "Do you know how much I love you?" He asked, grabbing both of her hands.

Maxie grinned. "Yes, just as much as I love you. But that was not the question now was it?"

Marc glanced at the floor, and let his smile fade. "No. No it wasn't."

Maxie waited for him to continue. When he grew silent and blankly stared at her, she knew the statement she made before they left the ballroom was true. His question was serious. As he caressed the back of her hands with his thumbs, Marc kept his silence for what seemed like a long time, before he finally spoke.

"Do you know how much it pains me to always watch you walk away from me at the end of our time together? Or how much I hate to see the clock ticking down the minutes, to the moment you're going to leave me?" Marc looked deeply into Maxie's eyes, and saw the passion that matched what he was feeling, giving him the wherewithal to say what was on his heart.

"Maxie, do you think you could ever leave your husband to be with me?"

Now it was her turn to stare and be silent. Marc's words gave her pause, but Maxie was not the least bit surprised by his query. It actually made her slip back into reflection, remembering not long after she had fallen in love with him, how often she entertained that particular thought. With her feelings for Marc growing stronger every day, the possibility was there, but could she actually walk away and *leave* her husband?

"Marc I ... I don't ... I can't ...."

Before she could give an answer, the night sky lit up behind her, and a booming sound reverberated so loudly, it made her cringe.

Marc looked at the sky. "I guess that storm you were talking about is moving in. Let's get you out of here."

Without another word, Marc quickly led Maxie to the Coat Check room. While she waited behind three other people, he left her for a moment to go outside and arrange for the valet to get her car. When he returned, she was standing in the lobby ready to go.

"I felt a few drops of rain, and it looks like fog is beginning to settle in. Kevin went to get my car also, so if you don't mind waiting, I want to follow you home, or wherever it is you're going. I want to make sure you arrive there safely."

Maxie smiled at his concern. "I'll be okay. Besides, the longer I wait, the storm is only going to get worse. If I leave now, I should be good."

Marc looked at Maxie pensively. There was absolutely nothing he could do, or say about all the things he was feeling right then. "Okay. Well let's get you to your car, and on your way. Can we pick up the conversation where we left off, sometime tomorrow?"

"I'll try to text you, or call you."

Marc kissed Maxie quickly, and walked her through the doors to her car. Once she was inside, he gestured for her to roll down her window. "Thank you again for coming. Please be careful driving Maxie. There are a lot of crazy, drunk people out on the roads tonight."

"The night is still young. It shouldn't be too bad with the exception of Bay Street over there. I'm heading back to the church."

"Call me when you get there. I love you."

Maxie puckered her lips, and simulated a kiss toward Marc, before she rolled up her window. As she drove off, Maxie watched Marc in her rearview mirror. Sighing heavily, she whispered, "I love you too."

When she turned left onto Bay Street, it was like turning into a wall of traffic. Everything was nearly at a standstill. People were honking their horns, and some were yelling out of their windows. Maxie couldn't tell if it was all due to an accident, annoyance, or the continual wave of New Year celebration. Whatever the case, she needed everything to move a lot faster. With the clock on her dash reading 12:30 a.m., she was curious as to what was going on at the church.

Her visit to the Hyatt lasted longer than she anticipated, and even though it was all worth the while, her re-entry plan into the Fellowship Hall was now off schedule. Maxie had no doubt Lester was both looking for her, and asking of her whereabouts.

By the time she finally reached Truman Parkway, it was 12:45 a.m. The fog had lifted a little, but the rain was coming down in torrents. Maxie was glad the traffic on the freeway was moderate, but it was still moving slower than what was needed for her to get back to the church in a sufficient amount of time. Instead of driving in the right lane, which was common, she moved to the left lane. With steady speed, she could arrive back to the church in less than ten minutes.

While she traveled in silence, it was in her best interest to keep her mind focused on Lester and The Ominous Three. There were responses that needed to be rehearsed, and possible problems that needed solutions, should they arise. However, it was the rhythmic sound of her fast paced windshield wipers that helped take her mind back to the dance floor of the Regency Ballroom. Humming to the music in her mind, Maxie gladly replayed every nuance of her time spent with Marc. With three months now a part of their history, she could not help but to wonder what would become of their future. Being in a relationship with Marc kept her smiling. No day was ever the same where he was concerned. He always made it a point to show her something new about herself, and he usually enjoyed the discovery just as much as she did. Now he wanted to know if he could claim her completely.

Lost in the thought of her intended answer, Maxie nearly passed the ramp to DeLesseps Avenue. Maneuvering a quick swerve into the right lane, she tried to make the exit. With the rain coming down heavily, she was blinded from seeing another car traveling in the same lane. Angrily, the driver blew his horn and scared Maxie. To keep from colliding, she frantically jerked the steering wheel too far left, and hit a pool of water. Immediately, the car hydroplaned, and Maxie lost control, skidding head-on into the metal guard rail. The violent impact flipped the car over into the opposite guard rail, and careened it air-borne into a ditch. Strapped in her seatbelt upside down, Maxie was dazed. Instinctively, she tried to take off her seatbelt and open the door, but she was much too weak to do either.

"Help me," she cried, her voice barely above a whisper. "Oh God. Please. Somebody help me." In a sea of darkness, Maxie felt the cold air through her broken windows, as the minutes passed without rescue. Frightened and feeling hopeless, images of Lester came to her mind, but they were soon muddled by dizziness, and a pulsating pain that resonated throughout her body. The pressure of her body weight made it hard to breathe. Growing cold, Maxie felt herself becoming extremely sleepy. "Oh God," she said breathlessly. "Oh God. Can anybody hear me? Please."

After a few more minutes, the light from a flashlight lit Maxie's face, but she didn't respond.

"Hey it's a woman," the man yelled to someone in the distance. "Her airbag has deployed, and she's bleeding pretty badly here. She's hanging upside down in her seatbelt. I think she's unconscious. What is the emergency dispatcher saying? Is an ambulance on the way? Should I cut her down?"

"Please ..." Maxie croaked softly. "Can you help me?"

The man kept yelling to the other person. "Wait a minute. I think she just said something."

"Help me."

"I will sweetheart," the man said. "We're going to get you out of here, okay? You just stay awake with me. An ambulance is on its way. It's going to be here any minute now. Can you tell me your name?"

Maxie exhaled heavily, and closed her eyes.

"Come on sweetheart. Stay with me. Come on and open your eyes." When Maxie did not respond, the man turned off his flashlight, and yelled into the darkness. "They have to hurry! Where is that ambulance?"

Chapter Sixty-Eight

M axie barely opened her eyes to a race of ceiling tiles and bright lights overhead. Behind an oxygen mask that covered her nose and mouth, she was able to see three unknown people on each side of her. Their conversation filled with medical jargon, helped her to realize she was quickly being transported through a hospital on a gurney. The slightest bump over a threshold, or jarring at the turn of a corner, magnified the pain that was already racking her body, but it all paled in comparison to what she was feeling in her head. The profuse pounding told her she hit her head somewhere, and blood was obviously teeming from her ears. With her head firmly strapped to a hard back board and a cervical collar surrounding her neck, Maxie was overwhelmed. Tears filled her eyes, and slowly rolled down the sides of her face. *Lester? Where is Lester?* She thought. *Where is my husband? I need my husband.*

The air around Maxie was cold, as they whisked her through the hallway. In spite of being wrapped in a blanket, she shuddered uncontrollably against it. Sleep seemed inevitable, and she wanted to use it as a vice to escape the pain, but extreme nausea kept her from it. The simple task of finding her voice to alert someone, took every ounce of strength within her. She needed to speak, move her hand, or something, in order to get the attention of those around her. But when she tried to move, her entire body rebelled, leaving her constrained. When the gurney finally stopped, Maxie vomited violently. Every heave relentlessly tore at her insides. Unable to move her head on either side, she began to choke.

"Get her turned over! She's gagging!" A nurse said.

After the mask was quickly removed, Maxie was gently lifted by her shoulders and turned just enough for her vomit to spatter onto the floor. Gasping for air, she continued to heave.

"She's coughing up blood. It's obvious there's some internal damage," the doctor said. "We need to hurry and get started with the FAST exam. She had on a wedding ring. Has the spouse been contacted in case we need to operate?"

"No word as of yet," the paramedic replied. "If there was a cell phone, we couldn't find it. An eyewitness said her car flipped over twice. With all of her windows nearly shattered, it could be anywhere. The police are using her driver's license and plate number to get more information."

"Mrs. Bruce? Can you hear me?" The doctor asked loudly. "I'm Dr. Sloan. You're here in the Trauma Center at Memorial Hospital. Are you able to answer some questions for me?"

Maxie moaned at the volume of the doctor's voice. "My head ..."

"I know. Your head hurts you a lot doesn't it? As soon as we find out what is causing the pain, I'll get you some relief for it."

The doctor continued asking questions, as well as explaining to Maxie everything he and the trauma team were doing, until she vomited again and lost consciousness.

Within the hour, Maxie was examined from the inside out, by both man and machine. During her altered state of consciousness, Lester was located at home by the police and escorted to the hospital. With her eyes barely open, she saw him standing near her bed with tears streaming down his face. He was still dressed in his church clothes. Maxie knew she was connected to wires and monitors, and that the very sight of her looked grave, but she did her best to smile at him anyway.

"Lester ..." she whispered, and tried to raise her hand.

Lester sighed heavily and quickly wiped the tears from his face, as he took her hand. "No baby. Be still. I'm here. I'm going to be right here."

Maxie tried to smile again, but it faded as she closed her eyes.

Helplessly, Lester looked at his wife and swallowed hard. Feeling her hand go limp, he gently put it next to her side, and patted it as if to confirm safe keeping. Without reservation, Lester brought both of his hands together in front of his mouth and closed his eyes. Furrowing his brows, he held that position for more than a minute. When he finished, he slowly tried to pull Maxie's blanket up closer to her neck, but when it seemed to be entangled with one of the wire connectors, he balled his fist and put his hands in his pockets.

"It's fine Mr. Bruce," the nurse said with a smile.

Lester looked at her with surprise, and then looked at the rest of the trauma team members, as if he was noticing them for the first time. "I thought ... I thought she might be cold," he said, locking his eyes on Maxie. "It's kind of cold in here. She always ... she always likes to stay good and warm. She doesn't like the cold very much." Lester struggled against his pain, and kept swallowing to hold back his tears.

"She will probably be asleep for a while," the nurse said. "She'll be fine. Why don't you go in the family waiting area and get yourself a cup of coffee. Regroup for a few minutes. Dr. Sloan will call you into the conference room to discuss your wife's progress."

Lester looked at the busy team conducting themselves as if it was all normal routine for them. He then looked at the nurse with a questioning face of concern.

"This is what we do," the nurse continued smiling. "Mrs. Bruce is resting, and she's in good hands. She won't even know you're gone. Go refresh yourself for a little while."

Lester blinked his eyes a few times, took a deep breath, and released it through his nose. If she wakes up ..." he started.

"I will personally come and get you."

Lester glanced around the room, before he stared at Maxie again. Hesitantly, he did as the nurse suggested and went to the family waiting area. Not long after he made himself a cup of coffee, another nurse came to the door and called his name.

"Dr. Sloan would like to see you. Would you please follow me?"

Lester left his coffee and immediately followed. "My wife ..."

"She's still stable. The doctor will give you an update. Come right this way."

Lester was led to an office not far from Maxie's room.

"Mr. Bruce," the doctor said, as he stood and extended his hand. "I'm Dr. Jake Sloan. I'm the lead doctor of the Trauma Team that's treating your wife. Please come in and have a seat."

Lester shook the doctor's hand, and sat in a seat on the other side of the conference table. Almost immediately, he noticed the average size of the room and the pictures of beaches, sunsets, and flowers in bloom on the walls. There were empty chairs around the table, and Lester looked at them pensively, before he saw Dr. Sloan lay out a file folder with Maxie's name on it. While the doctor busied himself, Lester observed how Dr. Sloan let his glasses rest on his nose, instead of pushing them up over his eyes.

"I called you in here to give you an update, and to interpret some of the series of tests we've completed on your wife. I'm not going to sugarcoat anything and I'm not going to give you a prognosis, because every patient deals with trauma differently. All I am going to do is state the facts, so you know exactly what is going on. If you have any questions, or if I'm going too fast, please don't hesitate to stop me. We here at Memorial are committed to patient and family centered care, and it's important you know your wife's status, so you can make the right decisions concerning her."

"Thank you," Lester said somberly.

"Now as you probably already know, your wife was in a terrible car accident. Eyewitnesses reported to both the police and the emergency medical technicians that her car hydroplaned into a guard rail, before it turned over twice.

When she arrived here at Memorial, she was in and out of consciousness and she vomited quite a few times. At that time, we noticed hematemesis."

Lester frowned. "Hema ..."

"Hematemesis. It's the medical term for vomiting blood."

Lester quickly pressed his eyes closed and clenched his jaw. Inhaling deeply, he let it out through his nose shakily before he looked at the doctor again.

"I know this is very difficult for you Mr. Bruce."

"I'll be fine," Lester croaked. "Go on."

"Hematemesis can be due to something major or minor. Giving the nature of your wife's accident and the amount of blood each time she vomited, we deemed it major because there may be internal organ and intestinal damage. My team proceeded to do an exam that we do on nearly all of the patients who come into the trauma center, and that exam is called a FAST exam. FAST is an acronym for focused assessment with sonography for trauma. Before we use sonography for the internal exam, we assess the outside of the body for bruising, cuts, and so forth. In this part of the assessment, we observed a presence of blood behind her left eardrum, and fluid mixed with blood, coming out of both ears. That fluid is noted to be cerebrospinal fluid."

Dr. Sloan stopped talking when he saw Lester look at the floor, his eyes brimming with water.

"Mr. Bruce, we can stop."

Lester cleared his throat, and wiped his face with his hand. "No. Please ... continue telling me about my ... my wife."

"Well, it was obvious from that exam alone, that she has suffered trauma to her head. To what extent, we are not yet certain. Computerized axial tomography will be what's needed to determine that."

"That's a CAT scan right?" Lester asked.

"That is correct. Hopefully, it will be the final test needed to help give us clarity on how we can help and treat your wife, so she can move on to recovery."

Lester smiled a little at the word *recovery*.

"There were other cuts and bruises, all were noted and treated. When we did the ultrasound, it was determined that an abdominal hematoma was present. This is much like a severe bruise to the abdominal wall, and it is more than likely where the bleeding is coming from. Normally in cases like this, to be more accurate we would do a CAT scan of the entire body, assessing both the trauma to the head and the abdomen. The results would pinpoint the exact location and size of the injuries."

"So you haven't done that? You said other tests were performed. Is there something keeping you from doing this one? Are there complications?"

"Actually, I would like for you to sign a consent form before we move any further."

Lester frowned, and quizzically turned his head. Dr. Sloan removed his glasses and looked at Lester directly.

"Mr. Bruce, I'm sure you are aware your wife is not the only one involved here. The ultrasound revealed a gestational sac of about two millimeters. We call it an intradecidual sac sign, and this is a useful feature that helps identify an early intrauterine pregnancy."

Lester was stunned.

"Intrauterine pregnancy?" Almost immediately, his eyes shifted to the floor where they roamed. In silence, he finally looked at the doctor with deeply creased brows. Glancing at the papers on the desk, Lester cleared his throat. "So you … you're telling me that my wife … my wife is pregnant?"

"With the blood test confirming it, Mrs. Bruce is nearly four weeks pregnant. You didn't know this?"

Lester exhaled through his nose, as if he had been holding his breath a while. Shaking his head lightly, he stood up and paced the area. With bewilderment on his face, Lester spoke as if no one else was in the room. "Maxie? Pregnant? My wife is going to have a baby."

"Clearly this is news to you," the doctor said. "If she has made no mention of this to you, it's very possible your wife doesn't even know she is pregnant. Many women still have their menstrual cycles throughout their pregnancy."

Lester continued to pace without acknowledging the doctor's statement. When he finally sat down, a shadow of uncertainty clouded his face. "This is the reason you need my consent?"

"Yes. I'm not worried that the fetus was harmed in the accident. Your wife's uterus is still relatively small, because she's less than twelve weeks pregnant. In this early stage, the pelvic location of the uterus makes it somewhat resistant to injury. My concern is with which method we will use to examine her head trauma. Because the uterus is gravid, or pregnant, the biggest concern with performing the CAT scan is what's known as carcinogenesis. That is, exposure to radiation in pregnancy ultimately causing a childhood cancer. Now a CAT scan involves exposure to radiation at levels slightly higher than normal x-rays, so the overall risk is extremely low. Keeping your wife's injury in the forefront here, I believe you will agree that the benefit of receiving an accurate diagnosis, is far more important than the limited risk associated with radiation exposure."

Dr. Sloan stopped talking, and waited for Lester's response. Lester didn't budge. He just quietly stared at the floor. Dr. Sloan put his glasses back on, locked his fingers together over the papers, and continued.

"Since the initial ultrasound revealed the kind of hematoma that is in her abdomen, along with other information we need, I find it's not necessary for us to do a full body CAT scan. We will keep our eye on the bleeding. If it is warranted, embolization may be performed to help stop the bleeding. This is where a very small catheter is put into a bleeding vessel to seal it. The procedure is minimally invasive and very successful. My plan however, is to allow the body's natural elimination methods to absorb the blood within the abdominal wall. Following this course, will now bring our focal point to the head trauma. Using the CAT scan for only the head. ..."

Lester quickly snapped out of his trance-like state. "Wait. A few minutes ago, you made it sound as if there was another choice. I mean, instead of using the CAT scan."

"There is," Dr. Sloan said. "That other choice would be an MRI, which stands for magnetic resonance imaging. With the MRI you lose the risk of carcinogenesis and other associated risks, because there's no radiation involved. While MRI itself is believed to be safe during pregnancy, one of the drugs that is given to enhance the pictures may not be safe. That drug is gadolinium. In animal studies it's been shown that exposure to gadolinium can cause birth defects. Another minus on the side of MRI is timing. It takes about five to ten minutes to take a CAT scan, whereas the MRI typically takes around forty-five minutes to complete. To be quite honest with you Mr. Bruce, we don't have that kind of time."

Lester took a moment to think, and sighed heavily. "Where is the form?"

Dr. Sloan pulled the consent form from the papers, and handed it to him. Lester quickly read over the form, signed it, and handed it back. "The baby. Since you're not going to do a full body scan, this will make it safer for the baby right?"

"By examining only her head, the radiation will be centralized. It will still be present throughout her body, but in a much lower level. So there will be little risk if any, to the baby."

Lester nodded.

Dr. Sloan stacked the papers, and returned them to the file. "After we read the scan results, my team and I will determine the best surgical recourse for getting your wife healthy again. Mr. Bruce, if you have any questions or concerns, anyone on the trauma team is able to address them for you. It's been a pleasure meeting you, in spite of the circumstances." Dr. Sloan stood up, and extended his hand. "We'll keep you posted."

"Thank you." Lester stood, shook his hand, and walked to the door to let himself out. With a million thoughts holding his attention, he strolled past doctors and nurses to reclaim his spot in the waiting room. Loosening his tie, he took a deep breath and released it moderately through his nose. A little chuckle found its way to the surface, and he released it while nodding his head in disbelief. Using both of his hands, Lester wiped his face slowly, and brought them together in front of his mouth. This time he was praying for two.

Chapter Sixty-Nine

S till a bit bewildered, Lester lightly paced the waiting
room floor. For nearly forty-five minutes, he tried to
give his attention to the flat screen television on the
wall, but it was pointless. He could do little else, but glance
at his watch and wonder how long the doctor would be with
the update on Maxie. Many times, Lester peered through
the small windows of the doors that securely separated him
from his wife, hoping he would see a member of the trauma
team coming his way, but his viewing yielded him nothing.

In the time spent pacing, Lester made a call to the Pastor
and explained all that had happened. Pastor Harrison immediately wanted to come to the hospital to offer prayer and
support, but Lester assured him it was not necessary. Instead,
the Pastor encouraged him by praying with him over the
phone, and promised the congregation would be praying for
them as well. When he hung up, Lester realized he failed
to include information about the baby. Yet, he didn't know
why. He also didn't give the details as to whether Maxie
was leaving, or returning to the church when the accident
happened. That was because he didn't know. He wanted to

believe she was on her way home from Watch Night, but when the police officers told him where the accident happened, and the direction she was heading, he couldn't be positive. All things considered, it also wasn't that important right now.

Another hour and fifteen minutes passed, before Lester was called back to the conference room again. When he entered, Dr. Sloan's face showed a bit more concern than what Lester wanted to see. He didn't even look at Lester when he walked into the room, but rather gave his full attention to what looked like x-ray pictures that were spread out neatly on the table.

"Dr. Sloan?"

"Yes, Mr. Bruce," Dr. Sloan said without looking up. "Please, have a seat."

Lester sat, but he didn't take his eyes off the x-ray sheets, especially after Dr. Sloan put them up on the x-ray viewer on the wall.

"I want to brief you again on all we're doing for your wife. What you see here are the images from her head scan," Dr. Sloan pointed. "This medium sized area in white is where your wife hit the left side of her head, producing what we call an intracranial hematoma. It's formed when a head injury causes blood to accumulate within the brain, or between the brain and the skull. Because this injury is actually bleeding in the area between the brain and the skull, this is specified as an epidural hematoma. As you see, there is little room for anything other than the brain, inside the vault of the skull. With the presence of blood and swelling in here, we were at risk of having what is called a brain herniation. That's when brain tissue, cerebrospinal fluid, and blood vessels, are moved or pressed away from their usual position inside the skull. In order to help reverse or prevent that, we had to quickly reduce the pressure by using a method called trephination." Dr. Sloan turned and looked at Lester directly. "Two small burr holes were drilled into your wife's skull and a tube was inserted to release the fluid buildup before it caused other problems."

Lester remained silent, and did his best to curb his emotions while he gazed at the images. He was totally helpless in the situation, and the frustration of it made him clench his fist under the table, and tighten his jaw.

"Please rest assured Mr. Bruce, your wife and child are getting the best care possible here at Memorial Hospital."

Lester stared at Dr. Sloan pensively for a moment. Then he stood up. "I want to see my wife."

"I understand your concern Mr. Bruce, but that would not be advisable right now. Mrs. Bruce is just returning from surgery and. ..."

"I said I want to see my wife," Lester said firmly.

Dr. Sloan pressed his lips together tightly, and nodded his head. With a simple hand gesture, he led Lester out of the conference room, down a small corridor, and into a room filled with monitors and beeping sounds. In the middle of the room Maxie lay motionless on a gurney. The sight of her with her head wrapped in a turban of bandages, and a small hose connected to her mouth, was almost more than Lester could bear. While Dr. Sloan talked with the attending trauma team members, Lester moved closer to his wife and gently stroked her face. Swallowing hard, he forced a smile that quickly faded.

"Maxie," he whispered. "Baby what happened? Where were you going? I should have stayed with you. We should have just gone home. If we had gone home together like I planned, we would have toasted in the New Year together. Not here. You're not supposed to be here. You're supposed to be home ... home with me. I love you so much Maxie. So very much." Tears dropped from Lester's eyes. Laying his hand on Maxie's forehead, he prayed for her and then stepped away from her bed. Dr. Sloan came and stood next to him in silence.

"How long will she be this way?" Lester asked, with his eyes on Maxie.

"Right now she's still under the general anesthesia. I plan to keep her in a medically induced coma using an infusion pump, until the brain swelling goes down. After that, I will slowly reduce the medication. It can take a couple of days, or it can take a couple of weeks. The timing of it is largely dependent on when we see the brain swelling recede. She'll be closely monitored. Overall, we're expecting a full recovery with no signs of neurological damage. Your wife is a strong woman Mr. Bruce. Off the record, I believe she's going to come out of this fine."

Lester nodded, and put his hands in his pockets. "God willing."

Dr. Sloan continued explaining to Lester, all that was done and being done for Maxie. Lester listened, but he barely took his eyes off of her. Trauma team members worked diligently around them, until Dr. Sloan made the suggestion that it was best for the two of them to leave the room. After Lester was assured he would be alerted of anything positive or negative concerning Maxie, he somberly walked back to the waiting area. When he got there, his sisters and quite a few ministers from the church were there to console him, and encourage him. What surprised him most, was that Sandra Beal was among them.

* * * * * * * * *

New Year's Day had come and gone. It was early Saturday morning, and the population of those in the waiting room had died down. Those who came to shower Lester with love and support, left to fulfill other commitments; leaving him with only Sandra to keep him company. What Lester knew of Sandra, she wasn't one to remain behind the scenes in any regard, but she did just that, the entire time his supporters were around. With the exception of giving a cordial greeting to everyone, and introducing herself as Maxie's best friend, Sandra sat quietly and listened.

With everyone gone, Lester finally acknowledged Sandra with a nod and half a smile. She returned his smile and stood up.

"Would you like a cup of coffee Lester? I'm going to make myself one."

"No, thank you Sandra. I'm all coffeed out. I believe I've emptied a pot all by myself."

Sandra nodded, and walked to prepare her cup. When she finished, she returned to her seat.

"So how is it that you should be here?" Lester asked. "I was told you were in Japan?"

"I was," Sandra said between sips. "I was scheduled to return here on the eighth, but I wanted to surprise Maxie by coming home early, and attending the Watch Night service with her. My flight was late getting in, so I stopped by your place this morning. Since you weren't home, I went by the church. Deacon Earl was there, and he filled me in. Well, he sort of filled me in. What really happened Lester, and how is Maxie? I overheard a lot of the conversations here, but will you please explain to me what happened?"

"To be honest, I only have second hand knowledge. I told her that I wanted to do something different this year, and be a little spontaneous by leaving the Watch Night service and going home to toast in the New Year. We were in the parking lot ready to leave, when I was called back in to the service. We were in separate cars, and I don't know what she did after that. I don't know if she was going home, or coming back from somewhere ... I don't know. The police said she was heading south when she took the DeLesseps Avenue exit, and hit a guard rail. They said she hydroplaned into it, and her car flipped over a couple of times."

Sandra frowned a little, and stared into her cup of coffee for a long moment, before she spoke. "She was heading south?"

Lester nodded his head and looked at her.

"Wasn't she doing auxiliary work? Maybe she had to run an errand for supplies or something."

"No. I was looking for her as soon as I finished what I had to do. No one knew where she was."

Sandra looked into her cup again, and slightly nodded her head. "Am I able to see her? Will they let me go back there?"

"Probably not. She's in ICU. They only allow the immediate family to go in there."

Sandra silently sipped her coffee.

"When was the last time you talked to her?" Lester asked.

"Right before Christmas. I wanted to speak with her many times after that, but with the difference in the time zones and my crazy work schedule ... well it just didn't happen. Why do you ask?"

"My wife confides in you. I don't understand why, but I know you're the only one she shares her secrets with."

"And that bothers you doesn't it?"

"It did for a while. But she needed someone besides me. She doesn't trust any of the women in the church."

Sandra smiled a little, and turned her head. "So what are you getting at Lester?"

Lester pressed his lips together tightly, and looked at the floor. "Not too long ago, Maxie used to have these strange dreams. Actually, they were more like nightmares. Anyway, they got to the point where they were pretty constant."

Sandra set her coffee on the floor next to her chair and leaned forward, giving Lester her full attention.

"She would often wake up screaming in a cold sweat because of them. We discussed them a few times, but I couldn't really make any sense as to their purpose."

Sandra revisited the dream she had about Maxie at the zoo with three women, and then ultimately being chased by a Tasmanian devil. "I'm not sure I recall her sharing dreams like that with me Lester. Did she mention who was in the dreams?"

"Yeah. She said she thought one was her mother. She couldn't remember exactly what her mother looked like, since she died when Maxie was only nine. She didn't have any pictures of her either. In her dreams, the face was always distorted, but she felt some kind of connection to her. The other two were her grandmother, and Sister Adams."

"In just that order?" Sandra frowned.

"Yes."

Sandra pensively considered Lester's words, and sat back in her chair. "No she didn't, but I have a very good idea as to the purpose of those dreams."

Lester was silent.

"I don't know if Maxie told you this Lester, but before I left for Tokyo I shared with her how I grew up in the church. My father was the Senior Pastor. Anyway, I used to have this reoccurring dream about one of the elderly mothers in our church. When I told her the dream, she laughed and told me that God was using her as a theophany."

"A what?" Lester frowned.

"A theophany. There are people in our lives we hold in high regard. In our dreams, God can use the appearance of those people to give us a message from Him. I believe that's the case in Maxie's dreams. Those three women were theophanies to her. She revered all three of them. They must have had a serious message if the dreams were reoccurring."

"I thought that too," Lester responded. "I even asked her if she felt like they were trying to warn her about something. She told me they didn't say anything to her. I only asked that question, because I remembered how her grandmother taught her a lot about the Geechee culture. She told me they believed when a person died, their spirit may continue to hang around and give special warnings to those still alive." Lester shook his head. "It was crazy talk to me, but I know Maxie held on to a lot of the things her grandmother taught her." Lester sighed heavily and rubbed his eyes. He was battle weary, and it was beginning to show.

"Have you been back home at all Lester?"

"No. I've been here since the police came and got me. I told Maxie I wasn't going anywhere."

"So she was awake?"

"For a little while."

Lester let his attention drift for a few minutes, before he stared at Sandra. She could see he was wrestling with something he wanted to say to her.

"Lester, you know if you go home and refresh yourself, I don't believe Maxie will miss you. I'll be here, and I can call you if something changes. That is if the medical team doesn't beat me to it. She seems to be in pretty good hands."

Lester lightly shook his head no, and looked at the floor. Once again he was captured and carried away by his thoughts. With no other words between them, Sandra watched the television and its spotlight broadcast of New Year's Day celebrations all over Savannah. Even though she did her best not to think about it, the broadcast made her wonder how Maxie spent New Year's Eve. Sandra also considered how things would have been very different, if her plane had arrived on time.

For the next twenty minutes, crying babies, coughing adults, and sniffling children, began to fill the waiting room. In spite of it all, Lester relaxed with his eyes closed and his head against the wall. In fear of someone very ill sitting in the empty seat next to him, Sandra decided to move there instead. Quietly, she sat and gave her focus to all that was going on around them.

"Aren't you tired?" Lester asked, without opening his eyes. "International travel is said to be hard on the body."

Sandra laughed a little and looked at him. She was surprised he was awake. "No. I'm fine. I slept all the way over here on the plane. Remember, there's a big time difference between here and Japan."

Lester lightly nodded, and was quiet again. Sandra didn't want to offer words to make random conversation, so she tuned in to the different patient names that were called to various stations.

"You view me as being weak don't you?" Lester asked without moving. "You think I'm out of touch with the things that concern my wife."

Sandra glanced at Lester, and wondered if he was actually going to embark upon a conversation with his eyes closed. "I wouldn't call you weak per se'. But yeah, I feel like you're a little out of touch where she is concerned. Yes I do."

Lester chuckled a little. "You said you grew up in the church right?"

"Yes"

"Okay. Give me the definition for the word testimony."

Now it was Sandra's turn to laugh. "Are you serious?"

"I am."

Sandra was silent for a moment. Assuming Lester was teasing her, she waited for him to deliver the punch line, but he just sat there in the same position with his eyes closed, waiting for her answer.

"Okay, well ... it's like the evidence that supports a statement made by somebody. Or they are words declared by a witness about something they either saw, or experienced."

Lester chuckled again. "Experience. That's the word I was looking for. How about the number eight? Do you know what it represents?"

Sandra looked around the waiting room to see if anyone was listening to their conversation. "Lester. I think you're tired. Why don't you go home and rest for a little while."

"Do you know it or not?" He asked.

Sandra sighed. "It represents new beginning. The number eight represents new beginning."

"You are absolutely correct. So we have experience and new beginning. New beginning and experience."

"Lester ..."

"Would you agree a person has to experience something *before* they can have a new beginning Sandra?" Lester finally opened his eyes, but he looked at the ceiling.

"I suppose so. Lester what's your point?"

Lester took a deep breath through his nose, and released it the same way. "Maxie. She experienced a lot over these past few months. You know God takes us through difficult situations, to help prepare us for whatever His plan is for our lives. We don't always understand what's going on, and sometimes that situation can be so hard, it can bring you to your knees. Other times you will swear it broke your heart. But God is right there through it all. He made me understand His purpose is far more important than my emotions." Lester glanced at Sandra, and then focused on the ceiling. "Trust me, I was never out of touch with the things that concerned Maxie. From the time we were married, and as the overseer of my house, I know God has a purpose for us. It was ordained that she should be by my side in ministry, but Maxie had something on the inside of her God needed to show her. And ... I had to bear witness to it all. Keeping in mind she needed her own testimony, and that God had it all in control, I had to watch my wife drift away from me." Lester laughed a little, and made a sweeping motion with his hand. "Drift away right into the arms of another man." Lester lifted his head and paused for a moment, as if to gather his thoughts again. Then he looked at Sandra. With her eyes widened and mouth partially opened, she was speechless.

"Yeah. I knew she was having an affair," he continued. "I tried to intervene on numerous occasions. But I was just getting in the way of what God deemed necessary, in order to bring about a change. I'm not going to lie. It was a struggle for me to stay spiritual in a sinful situation. I wanted to make it all go away. All she had to do was just come to me, and admit her wrongdoing. Admit the things that were in her heart." Lester paused. "Maxie is my world. It's not like I wouldn't have forgiven her. But this was the route she chose instead. Now we're living Hebrews twelve and eleven."

Sandra gently nodded, "For the time being no discipline brings joy, but seems grievous *and* painful; but afterwards it yields a peaceable fruit of righteousness to those who have been trained by it; a harvest of fruit which consists in righteousness in conformity to God's will in purpose, thought, and action, resulting in right living and right standing with God."

Lester stared at Sandra in amazement, and laughed lightly. "Look at you. You know Bible scriptures and everything."

Sandra blushed. "The Amplified version of the Bible. My dad made me memorize quite a few scriptures from it. That one in particular."

The two of them laughed. When the moment faded, Sandra realized it was the first time she had ever shared laughter with Lester. She enjoyed it.

"I apologize for viewing you as being out of touch Lester. Clearly, I had you all wrong. More than that, I'm sorry you have to endure all of this. When you and Maxie get through this, I believe God is going to give you beauty for ashes," Sandra smiled.

Lester leaned his head against the wall again, and looked at the small children who were sitting across from him. "Beauty for ashes ... I believe He has already done

that." After staring a while longer, Lester straightened himself in his chair and looked at Sandra again. "The doctor
said Maxie is pregnant."

Sandra's smile quickly faded. In amazement, she covered her mouth with her hand. "What?"

"Yeah. He said she's about four weeks pregnant."

"You didn't ... I mean did you?"

"Did I know? No. The doctor said because it's so early
in the pregnancy, Maxie may not know either."

Sandra was speechless. So many thoughts came to
mind, and she made it obvious by the way her eyes darted
back and forth while she looked at the floor.

Focusing on the children again, Lester relaxed. "Your
response was like mine."

"Oh my g ... I don't ... I don't know what to say. I mean ...
congratulations?"

Lester sighed heavily. "Yeah I know. I like how you
posed it as a question. Maxie is the one with all the answers.
Until she wakes up and is better, the questions will just
have to wait."

Chapter Seventy

Maxie's room was filled with nurses, as the evening shift change was underway. Vital signs, lab results, and medication information was conveyed to the new group of nurses who would be caring for her. Though her condition was stable, she remained in a coma and hooked up to various monitors. When the new nursing team finished gathering their information, and all duties were assigned, everyone left the room except for one. In silence, the woman stood at the foot of Maxie's bed, gazing at her with a soft smile on her face. Nothing appeared unusual about the woman, except her attire. Instead of a nurse's uniform, she was dressed casually in a winter white cowl neck sweater with matching wool slacks. Looking around the room, she observed everything from where she stood. When one of the nurses returned to the room to document information, the woman at the foot of the bed was not acknowledged in any manner. The nurse just went about her duties as if no one else was in the room. With an indelible smile, the woman focused on Maxie.

"Maxie," she called softly. "Maxie, wake up."

Maxie's eyes winced, as she struggled to open them. When they finally opened, she took a moment to take in everything around her.

"Come on Maxie," the woman said as she held out her hand. "Get up and take my hand. I want to show you something."

Without question, Maxie sat up. She had no ambivalence about following the woman's directions, not because she recognized her, but because she recognized and trusted the abundance of love and affection that filled the room. Still clad in her hospital gown, she slowly got out of her bed, and grabbed the woman's hand as she was told. The two of them walked at an even pace toward the door. Before they crossed over the threshold, Maxie stopped and looked behind her. The attending nurse continued to work as if nothing had changed.

"She didn't see me get out of the bed," Maxie said. "Why didn't she see me get out of the bed?" When she looked at the hospital bed, Maxie saw *herself* hooked to machines and a shroud of bandages wrapped around her head. The sight should have startled her, but instead she felt an extreme sense of peace. Curiously, she made an attempt to get a closer view of herself in the bed, but as soon as she did, the heart monitor suddenly beeped erratically and made a long high pitched sound. Immediately, the nurse stopped what she was doing and hit the Code Blue button on the wall. Like a small army, the team of RNs at the nurse's station came rushing into the room. Maxie quickly moved out of their way in fear of being run over, but the woman who held her hand didn't budge. With her eyes still set on Maxie, the entire team of nurses passed directly through the woman's body where she stood at the threshold.

Maxie frowned, and looked at her questioningly. "You're a ghost? Am I dead? Did I just die in there?"

With a wink of her eye and a gentle tug, the woman replied, "Come with me."

Maxie looked back at the team, as they frantically worked on her. When she turned back around to look at the woman, the entire hospital ward suddenly disappeared and their surroundings had changed. It was night time, and the two of them were now standing on a quiet residential street that was covered in snow. Under the cascade of light from a street lamp above, the snow glistened like tiny diamonds. Amazed at what she was seeing, Maxie looked up and down the street, before she put her hands over her mouth. As far as she could see, every home was large, beautiful, and neatly kept.

"I think I know this place," she said. Maxie turned around in a full circle, as she looked at all of the houses. "I ... I used to live on this street when I was a little girl."

"Do you remember your way home?" The woman asked softly.

Maxie looked at her directly. In the light, she looked like a beautiful angel with a soft smile on her face. "I knew the way as a child," she said pensively. "I thought I would have forgotten it after all these years. But yes, I think I do remember."

The woman nodded her head, for Maxie to lead the way. Maxie smiled, and turned to find the house. Without a word, she started walking. With each step, the night sky slowly began to change, but Maxie didn't notice. Her focus was on the large red brick house that was now only a few yards away from her. When she reached the house, and stood in front of the white iron fence that surrounded it, a new day had dawned. Instinctively, Maxie reached for the latch to open the gate, but immediately withdrew her hand.

"Don't other people live here now?" Maxie asked.

"No," the woman said demurely. "There's been nothing lively here for quite some time."

Maxie looked at the house again. In spite of what the woman said, the house gave the appearance of someone living there. It was just as well-manicured as all of the houses around it. The shrubbery was neatly trimmed under a small blanket of snow, and the sidewalk leading to the door had been shoveled.

"Let's go in," the woman said. With her words, the gate opened on its own. Before Maxie made a step to go through the gate, children holding the hands of their parents began to fill the street. Two little girls raced down the sidewalk right in front of her. Maxie smiled at them, as they playfully screamed at each other about who would win the race to the bus stop. Though she wanted to watch the girls to the end, she felt a strange and compelling urge to go inside the house. With all that was going on, she wasn't amazed when they were able to walk through the closed front door. Once inside the split foyer, Maxie was immediately enveloped by the gray atmosphere. In silence, she looked around hoping to stir up some of the memories from her youth, but there were no pictures on the walls for her to connect with, and all of the furniture in the immediate area was covered with white tarps. Yet Maxie still felt an overwhelming amount of love and affection in the room. It was much the same as what she felt back in the hospital room.

"I'm home," she said, almost in a whisper. As tears rolled down her cheeks, she watched them fall onto the hardwood floor and disappear. "The floor looks so shiny," she laughed lightly. "It almost looks like it was just waxed."

Maxie's eyes were blurred with tears when out of nowhere, a lively wind tossed her hair and blew through every room; changing the state of everything it touched. The atmosphere brightened, the tarps disappeared, and the once stale air now offered the sweet aroma of bacon and pancakes with syrup. There were pictures of a small family of three on the walls, and the sound of soft music floated from the kitchen. Quickly wiping her eyes, Maxie saw everything transform into the exact way she remembered it as a child. It all came to life. The sight was so overwhelming, Maxie cupped both of her hands over her mouth and cried.

"Why am I back here?" She asked. "Why did you bring me here?"

"These aren't just the shadows of your past Maxie. This is your foundation." The woman gently touched Maxie on the arm, and pointed to her younger self rushing down the stairs with her coat and hat.

From the kitchen, the child's mother called out to her. "Maxie? Baby girl you have ten minutes to catch that bus. Do you have your coat on?"

"Yes mama," the younger Maxie replied. "And I have my hat on too. Remember I'm nine now," she smiled. "I know how to be responsible."

"That's my girl," her mother said, as she came to the kitchen doorway and stopped. "Are you ready to pray before you leave?"

Maxie didn't hear the child's reply. She was too focused on the woman in the doorway. With a look of confusion, her eyes darted between the woman in the doorway, and the woman who was guiding her. With that indelible smile, she met Maxie's gaze. The two were exactly the same woman.

"Mama?" Maxie whispered with uncertainty. "Mama?"

"Yes Maxie. It's me baby."

Without another word, Maxie embraced her mother and sobbed uncontrollably. In her mother's arms, she immediately felt the warmth and affection she had been experiencing all along. "I didn't recognize you. I miss you so much. I'm glad you came back for me."

Maxie's mother held her a moment longer. Then she gently pushed her back to look at her. "No baby. I'm not here to take you away. I came to show you something." With her words, the house changed back to the way it was when they first walked in. "Come with me."

Over the years, while having to live without her mother, Maxie had many questions, but at that moment, none of them readily came to mind. Instead, she grew intensely curious about the next leg of their journey, and followed her mother as she walked through the closed door. This time, the sidewalk that previously led them from the street to the house, now paved the way to a beautiful cathedral-style church. Maxie smiled broadly, and quickened her pace down the long sidewalk.

"I remember this church," she said excitedly. "We came here for Wednesday night Bible study and Sunday morning services. And choir practice for the kids was every Friday night."

"And you loved singing in the choir," her mother added.

"Yeah," Maxie's voice trailed off.

As they approached the church, the light from inside grew brightly in the stained glass windows. Dusk gradually took the place of daylight, and music from inside the church sanctuary could be heard outside. Maxie walked with her mom through the wall, and into the sanctuary. The pulpit was filled with children who were in the middle of a choir rehearsal. Maxie and her mother stood in the back of the church smiling, while they watched young Maxie lead the choir in a song.

"I remember singing that song," Maxie said. "Jesus is the Answer, by Andre Crouch. We all loved singing that." Maxie was silent for a moment, while she listened and reflected. "It was such a joyous time for me back then. You, me, and daddy." Maxie looked at her mother. "And then my whole life changed. You and daddy were both taken away from me."

Her mother's smile faded a little. "Come on sweetheart. Let's sit down over here."

Eyes brimming with water, Maxie sat next to her mother on the back pew, and looked at the floor. "I remember feeling like the loneliest little girl in the world. I had nobody. You and daddy were everything to me. I went to sleep one night having both parents, and woke up the next morning an orphan. There were people I didn't know all around me, taking it upon themselves to decide my fate." Maxie nodded her head in disbelief.

"No sweetheart," her mother said. "They couldn't decide your fate. That was always in God's hands. From the time you were born, your daddy and I knew there was a call on your life. You were somebody very special."

Maxie laughed a little, and wiped her eyes. "I didn't feel very special."

Maxie's mother glanced at her young daughter singing in the pulpit. "You were then, and you are even now. Having to deal with the sudden death of both of your parents at an early age is unimaginable. But God kept you Maxie. He was your stabilizing force. According to the enemy's plan, your foundation should have been broken after your father and I died."

"I don't understand."

"From the very beginning, we made sure we raised you according to the Word of God. We taught you the scriptures, showed you the way, and lived a holy life before you daily. You were a well-balanced child. Then, with us out of the picture, the enemy thought he had you. While you were in a state of pain and vulnerability, he tried to confuse you and make you believe you had nothing, and that you were nothing. But your foundation was built on the principles of holy living. Even in that short span of time, your foundation was made solid."

"But I still feel like I'm lacking something mama. All my life I have been going to church, and yet I still question exactly who I am in God. I thought I knew His purpose for me ... but now ... now I'm not so sure."

"Do you remember when we went to the house, and you asked me if anyone lived there, and I told you no?" Maxie nodded yes. "You thought someone must have lived there, because it looked just as well kept and clean as the other houses. Then when we went inside, there was no life in the house. Nothing was moving. All of the furniture was covered and unused. Then a wind came in, and it all came back to life." Maxie nodded again, and smiled. "I told you it was your foundation. Maxie that house was just like you baby. You give the appearance of a woman who is well kept, like all the other women around you. But on the inside, there's nothing moving. Like that house, you are fully equipped with everything you need. God gave it all to you, but you haven't put forth the effort to use it. So like the furniture, it remains covered and unused."

"Maybe I don't know what I'm equipped with."

Maxie's mother smiled. "I noticed when we went inside the house, you stayed near the front door."

"What do you mean?"

"You didn't venture throughout the house."

Maxie shrugged. "After the wind came, I was able to remember a lot of what I thought I had forgotten. Everything I recognized was right there where we stood."

"And you didn't move away from those familiar things. You didn't launch out to see what else the house was equipped with. No one has to invite you, or tell you to move forward Maxie. That should be a part of your own desire. Sweetheart, how will you know what God has given you if you don't do what it takes to keep moving forward? You have to come close to God, and He will come close to you. Be intimate with Him. When you do that, you will begin to understand more about yourself and Him."

Maxie nodded her head negatively, and sighed. A strong feeling of unworthiness churned in the pit of her stomach. She dared to give voice to the thoughts that condemned her. She had become a liar, and an adulteress at heart. What would God want with her now?

"Forgiving is His specialty Maxie," her mother said. "God knows your true heart."

Maxie looked at her mother, and smiled at the timeliness of her comment. Gently tapping her leg, her mother continued.

"There are, and will be times when you'll feel totally inadequate in the areas of ministry that God will call you to. You will have to remember not to measure your abilities against the need Maxie. If you do, the need will always appear much bigger than you feel you can handle, but it's not about you. When you step out in God, you will move in His will, His ability, and His strength, not your own."

Maxie sighed heavily and looked at the floor. Lester's words to her on Watch Night replayed loudly in her ears. *There's so much He has purposed for us to do together Maxie, and the enemy would love to keep us away from the plan of God.*

"Do you remember the scripture card game we always played with you?" Her mother asked.

Maxie laughed lightly, and nodded. "Yes. Those were the nights when we turned the television off, and the three of us spent quality time together. Whenever we played that game, Daddy would always cheat and take out all the really short scripture cards, so I would have to memorize the long ones."

Her mother laughed with her. "You're right. He did. Do you remember any of them? How about second Timothy, chapter two, verse nineteen?"

Maxie threw her head back and laughed. "Mama that was so long ago. I can't possibly remember ...."

"Just try."

Immediately, silence filled the sanctuary. Maxie looked at the children who were laughing and talking in the pulpit, but their voices were not heard. Turning to her mother, she secretly hoped for a little assistance. Instead, all she got was a reassuring smile, and a gentle nod encouraging her to continue. Out of nowhere, Maxie felt a sudden surge of confidence come over her.

"Second Timothy, chapter two, verse nineteen. *Nevertheless the foundation of God standeth sure, having this seal, The Lord knoweth them that are His. And Let every one that nameth the name of Christ depart from iniquity.*"

Maxie's mother smiled and held her chin. "That's my girl. I knew you remembered. Do what that scripture tells you Maxie, and depart from iniquity. There's no time to waste on it. Not that there ever was. But it is now the time for you to build on your foundation. God has equipped you with everything you need. You just have to begin." Maxie's mother looked at the children. All of their voices were heard again, as they began a new song. "My time with you is nearly over now, and I have to go. Remember this time with me."

"Go?" Maxie was immediately overwhelmed with emotion. Her mother had come back to her after all of those years, and now she was leaving her again. The very thought was unbearable. "Oh mama don't go," she pleaded. "Why can't we spend more time together? Why can't I stay with you? Please don't leave me again. Please don't go."

"My work here is done Maxie, and you have yours to begin. God has a purpose for you, and it's time for you to fulfill it."

"But I don't want to do this by myself. I need you mama. Please stay with me. Please don't go."

"It was never intended for you to do it alone. You have God, and you have your husband. When you think of me, I want you to think of all that I have shown you. Use what God has given you to build on your foundation, and remember His Word. You'll be fine. I love you Maxie."

The finality of her mother's words, instinctively caused Maxie to reach out and grab her hand. In fear, she tightly locked their fingers as if her very life depended on it. With the added strength of her other hand, Maxie held on, but the gesture was futile. The two of them were being pulled apart by a force neither could control. Maxie felt her heart race and her thoughts collide, as she tried to think of something that would stop what was taking place. With no other recourse, anxiety caused her to quickly stand up.

"No! Please! No!" Maxie looked at their interlocked fingers, and was petrified by what she saw. Not only was her mother being pulled away from her, but she was becoming transparent — almost ghostlike. The same was to be said of everything around her. It was all fading away. The children, and the sanctuary, they were all fading away. Maxie wanted to press her eyes closed and will everything to stop, but to close her eyes on the last living image of her mother, was absolutely impossible. So she stood and she watched, until it all disappeared. When everything was gone, Maxie fell to her knees and sobbed from deep within. The pain of her sorrow was so intense, she was shaking.

"How did I ever handle that as a child?" She yelled. "God why did you make me go through that pain again? Why would you do that to me? Why?" Maxie fully expected God to respond to her call of distress, but there was no answer. Feeling alone and destitute, she kept her face close to the floor where she continued to cry. The entire moment was mentally and physically exhausting. Maxie could do little else, but curl up into a ball, and let her tears stream down the side of her face to the floor.

Chapter Seventy-One

W restling with her thoughts, emotions, and the drama of it all, Maxie exhausted herself to the point where she fell asleep. When she finally awakened, it was to sheer darkness. With no light anywhere, she didn't think it unusual. It was just as well. The dark shroud was a welcomed place to accommodate her heaviness of heart. Even if the visit from her mother was all just a dream, little could be done to remove her current state of mind. Maxie was in a place she had never been in before.

To see her mother again, was a constant prayer request as a child. To have it explicitly answered this late in life and only for a few moments, was an anomaly that made Maxie wonder if it *was* all a dream. The unusual vividness and clarity, made her believe it was at best a vision. Whatever it was, the rollercoaster of emotions was all too real. To be immersed in the affection of her mother's love for the entire time she was with her, was a pleasure beyond description. To have her pulled away and disappear right before her eyes, was extremely gut wrenching.

Maxie lay still and looked into the darkness, as she revisited her mother's words. With every line of rhetoric, she was astonished at the revelation of how much she had forgotten. A lot was planted into her as a child. What amazed her even more was how she now had a missing piece to the puzzle of her life. Where it fit in was yet to be determined.

While she meditated on everything, a sliver of light appeared in front of her. Without much thought, Maxie focused on it and watched as it grew wider and wider. Soon a crescendo of voices was heard, and Maxie recognized she was laying in the threshold of the door to her hospital room. In her room, she heard the imposing voices of two doctors and a team of nurses, engrossed in medical jargon. She didn't want to get up, but the distraction and curiosity spurred her to see what was going on — especially since she was out of body. Slowly Maxie stood near the door jamb. From a distance, she observed the medical team working diligently on both sides of her bed, each assisting the other without pause. Another doctor quickly entered the room and stood bed side. With a small pen light, he opened each of Maxie's eyes and checked her pupils. Intrigued by what she was witnessing, Maxie moved closer for a better view.

"What is her GCS score?" Dr. Sloan asked.

Maxie looked at the chart the nurse was holding, as she read from the Glasgow Coma Scale.

"Her eye response is a one, verbal response is a one, and motor response is a one. She has a score of three doctor," the nurse replied.

"And what was her score earlier?"

"Her E was one, V was two, and M was four."

"Has the infusion pump meter been changed from where I set it?"

"No Dr. Sloan. The meter is the same as it was yesterday."

"Her pupils are now fixed. I want a repeat cranial CAT scan stat. Let's check for postoperative re-bleeding. Something has caused Mrs. Bruce to slip further into a coma. I need the reason why. Have the OR ready, and everyone on standby in case we need to operate again. I'm going to let her husband know what has happened. Poor guy has already been through the ringer. Let me know as soon as radiology has what I need."

"Yes Dr. Sloan."

In listening to their conversation, Maxie realized an entire day had passed while she was on the floor. Moving closer to the left side of the bed, she looked at herself and lightly gasped. Her eyes, even though they were closed, looked dark and sunken. Her fingers were curled, and dried blood was in her left ear. The sight of herself in that condition, made Maxie afraid.

"I wonder if Dr. Sloan is going to tell Mrs. Bruce's husband everything." One nurse practically whispered to the other, as they prepared Maxie for transport.

"What do you mean?"

"I wonder if he's going to explain how close to death she is. When was the last time you saw a coma patient survive and recover, after having bilaterally fixed and dilated pupils?"

The other nurse raised her eyebrows and reflected. "Come to think of it, I can't recall one. The prognosis has always been known to be poor."

"Exactly. If she pulls out of this, it will be nothing short of a miracle."

Maxie stood in shock when they finally wheeled her out of the room. Hearing her condition was grave, left her wondering what to do. She wanted to follow them, but for what? It wasn't like she could have done anything in the physical state she was in. No one could see her. No one could hear her. Instead, she stood alone in the middle of the room feeling helpless. She thought about praying, but what words should she pray? It was more than clear that God was in control of the situation, and that she must be standing in His judgment. Would He give ear to her plea just now?

Maxie considered the story of Jonah, and likened her situation to his. There was disobedience, and there was punishment. Would there be a time of repentance? Would she be allowed to acknowledge her sin, change her mind, her life, and receive God's mercy to move forward in doing His will? The answer to that question had Maxie in a quandary. She didn't like the uncertainty she was feeling. It was like her life was on a tether, dangling in limbo.

Immediately, Maxie thought about Lester. She wanted to see him. Better yet, she *needed* to see him. The very sight of Lester would give her peace, and center her thoughts. He wouldn't be able to see her, but somehow she would make her presence known to him. She was certain he was in the hospital waiting room, so she quickly followed the wall signs to the door that separated them. Before she entered, Maxie smiled at the relief she knew was coming when she laid her eyes on her husband.

When she finally walked through the door to search for Lester, Maxie was surprised. The people she saw weren't those she expected to see, and the surroundings she assumed would be in a hospital waiting room, were nothing close to what she saw. Instead, she was standing outdoors on the wooden porch of an old white cottage home. It was a sunny day, and a wavy tin awning shaded the porch, giving the appearance of an old country style home. There were two weather beaten rocking chairs nearby, being used by two elderly women whose eyes were set on her. Near the screen door, an elderly man stood leaning against the wall with his hands in his pockets. While he also stared at Maxie, he nodded his head matter-of-factly as if she had silently confirmed something for him. Neither of these people said a word to her, but Maxie smiled broadly at each of them. The sight of them helped her submit to the fact that she was once again on another leg of the purposeful, yet vagabondish journey.

"'Bout time ya got here." Maxie heard someone say.

Sitting on the edge of the porch near her feet, was an old man with a beat up gray cowboy hat tilted on his head. Maxie watched him switch a dangling toothpick from one side of his mouth to the other, by moving his tongue around. He was a good looking old man, and Maxie recognized him as one of her grandmother's closest friends. They were all her close friends.

"Hello Uncle Tuck," Maxie said. I didn't see you sitting down there."

"Uh huh," Uncle Tuck said with half a grin. "Pearlie," he called over his shoulder, without taking his eyes off of Maxie. "She's here."

Maxie eagerly looked at the door, and listened to the methodic sound of house shoes shuffling across a hardwood floor. When the screen door opened, and her grandmother looked at her, it was hard for Maxie to control her emotions. Immediately she stretched out her arms and began crying, as she walked across the porch. Pearlie stepped outside the door, and embraced her sobbing granddaughter.

"What? Why all these tears?" Pearlie asked. "You done got too old to be crying like this now."

Maxie laughed a little, as she used one hand to wipe her tears away, while continuing to hold on to her grandmother with her other hand. "I'm just so glad to see you."

"And I you. But you know it is but for a season right?"

Maxie remembered her time with her mother, and lowered her head. "Yes ma'am. I know." Maxie looked at her grandmother again. Nothing about her had changed (not that she really expected her to). She had the same beautiful skin and loving eyes Maxie remembered, and her arms offered the same sense of security.

"Pearlie," Uncle Tuck started. "We gonna be moving on now. Let ya spen' time wit' Maxine. It's been real good seein' ya Maxine. Take good care o' yo'self."

"All right Tuck," her grandmother waved.

"Goodbye Uncle Tuck. Goodbye to all of you."

Maxie watched them all wave over their shoulders without turning around. Within a matter of seconds, each one of them faded away. With great delight, Pearlie looked at her granddaughter and gave her another squeeze, before inviting her into the house. As soon as she stepped inside, Maxie immediately recognized the smell acquainted with her past. The scent caused her mind to go all the way back to the very first time she came to live with her grandmother; the meager furnishings aided that memory. The familiar tranquil air that enveloped the atmosphere, guided her to relax in it, but she refused. Maxie was eager to begin the series of questions she had for her grandmother. There was so much she needed to know.

Pearlie gestured for Maxie to have a seat, while she retrieved items from the kitchen cupboard. When she shuffled away, Maxie sat and smiled at the distinct sound her grandmother's house shoes made on the wooden floor. Throughout her youth, she was accustomed to hearing that sound, especially when her grandmother was coming to rescue her from the emotional distresses she suffered after losing her parents.

Upon her return, Pearlie set a large purple cup with a handle in front of her. Adorned with the name *MAXINE* all in gold, Maxie thought it was the most beautiful cup she had ever seen. Without taking any regard as to what she would like to have in her cup, Pearlie stood over Maxie's shoulder and poured a clear substance into it. Maxie watched and frowned questioningly, at what was being done. The aroma that immediately arose from her cup was sweet and very inviting, but that was all Maxie could pinpoint. Though she tried, it was nearly impossible for her to identify the varying scents that made up the aroma. When she thought she had one of them identified, another one kissed her nose, only to dissipate and a different one take its place. Maxie quickly looked into the cup, thinking she had missed something during the initial pour, but what she beheld was nothing more than a liquid that looked like water. Sitting opposite her, Pearlie held her own personalized cup with two hands. Maxie quickly noticed how her grandmother's cup and her own, were not a matching pair. Each one was distinctly unique in design and color, but exactly the same size.

Appearing distant, Pearlie casually sipped as if she were in a world all her own. In silence, Maxie watched her grandmother's facial expressions change with every sip she took from her cup. Sometimes she would smile. Another time she would frown, as if the substance had suddenly turned bitter to her taste. Yet again, her face would become full, as her eyes teared up with water. Watching all of this, Maxie didn't know if her grandmother was responding to something she was reminiscing, or if the liquid in her cup was the reason for the expressions. Whatever it was, it made Maxie peer into her own cup again. Giving it a little sniff, it smelled the same as it did when Pearlie first poured it. Maxie started to take the cup into both of her hands like she saw her grandmother do, but for some reason, she felt the oddest need to be cautious. Instead, she put both of her hands in her lap and looked at Pearlie quizzically.

"Ma, where did you get these cups from? They are both so beautiful."

"They were given to us a long time ago," Pearlie stated.

"Well what about the stuff you poured in them? What is that?"

Pearlie kept her focus on the inside of her cup, but smiled at her granddaughter's question.

"Nobody really knows for sure. There are a lot of things mixed in it. Sometimes it tastes so good. Sometimes it tastes real bad. It can make you laugh, and it can make you cry. One thing I know about it, there's a lot of love mixed in it."

Maxie didn't want to read between the lines of what her grandmother was saying. She just wanted a basic answer. "Well do you know what it is it made of?"

Pearlie looked at Maxie directly. "Life," she answered. "It's all made of life."

With those words, something caught Maxie's eye and made her look at her cup again. It was physically changing. The color of it disappeared, and the entire cup became transparent as glass. Suddenly the cup enlarged itself and changed its shape to that of a small television screen. Amazed at what she was seeing, Maxie moved her chair away from the table, and looked at her grandmother. Pearlie didn't move. Her eyes were still set on Maxie, as if nothing had changed. When Maxie looked back at the screen, faint images began to appear. She wanted to look away, but curiosity held her captive as the images took on the shapes of people. In a matter of seconds, Maxie recognized every person on the screen. Not only did she recognize them, but she was shown where they appeared in the various stages of her life. Interactions and occasions with family members and friends all came into view, starting with her childhood. Maxie smiled when she saw her parents. In the next instant, tears rolled down her face, when she watched herself receiving the news of their sudden demise. The screen continued to show Maxie every good and misguided deed from her childhood, to her teenage years. Some of her illicit deeds made her embarrassed that her grandmother should see them. Glancing at her often, Maxie noted how Pearlie sat statuesque. Maxie wondered why she didn't make any comments. She of all people, had to have knowledge of most of the events. Yet she said nothing.

All of the cognitive activity, proved to be emotionally draining for Maxie. Scars that were hidden for years were uncovered, and she could do nothing about it. Life passed, and she rode its emotional wave through each ebb and flow. When her marriage to Lester came in to view, Maxie grimaced in shame. Her grandmother spent many years teaching her the characteristics of a virtuous woman. To her chagrin, what was being displayed on the screen was hardly recompense for her grandmother's efforts. The vows she recited before man and God, were nearly null and void.

A covenant abated.

Within herself, Maxie acknowledged that everything she had experienced in the past few months, was a culmination of the curiosities and desires she had suppressed for years. She carried those desires into her marriage, and at full boil, they were unleashed and became the opponents against her marriage.

When everything to the present was shown, Maxie watched the screen transform back into its original state. Glancing at her grandmother again, she fully expected to see a look of disapproval. Maxie understood her grandmother's position in the afterlife to be one of distinction — a witness to all sinful earthly deeds. Her disapproval was warranted. However, Pearlie's expression was one of loving-kindness.

"And yet you have not even touched the cup," Pearlie said. "Tell me why that is Maxine. It has been poured out for you. Why do you not drink from it?"

Maxie shrugged. "I started to follow your example, and drink from it the way I saw you drink yours."

"You cannot drink from your cup the way I drink from mine, nor I yours. They are entirely different."

"Clearly, I don't know what's in here Ma."

"Except for what you have added."

Shame washed over Maxie again. "Yes, except for what I have added."

"Listen to me closely Maxine. When you were a child, oh how you loved the Lord. You were always eager to go to church, and you wanted to know everything about Him. Your questions about the Lord seemed endless at times." Pearlie shook her head and smiled, as she took a moment to reminisce. Slowly her smile faded. "I made sure you knew the answers to every question you asked. It was very important then, that I train you up in the way you should go. I knew God picked you to do a special work for Him. Back then, you used to hear God's voice clearly, just like you hear me talking to you right now. But when you grew into your teenage years, you couldn't hear God quite so well. That's because the enemy knew God's plan for you, so he started sending out distractions — things that took your mind and your focus off of God. Now I did my best to help guide you, but you were getting to an age where you had to make your own decision on which one you were going to serve. The devil brought thoughts to your mind, and most of the time you would cast them down. But here lately, you decided to entertain them. Those thoughts turned into curiosities, and those curiosities grew more appealing to you than living your life for Christ. That's because you felt you already knew how to do that. The enemy of your soul greatly deceived you, by encouraging you to *want* something more, and something different. That *want* and those desires caused another passion to take root, and it is rooted in your heart right now. In full bloom, it has caused you to change." Pearlie nodded her head in pity, her forehead deeply creased with concern. "Maxine, what ugly thing has the Lord done to you, that your heart would turn from Him? What has He done to make you choose another way?"

Maxie's eyes filled with tears, before she broke down and sobbed openly. It never occurred to her that because of her deeds, the Lord could actually be offended, and asking her *what did I do?* For the first time, she pictured Him as a man who loved his wife unconditionally and beyond measure, fulfilling her every need, only to have her turn her back on him to follow in the tracks of another man, who had nothing in comparison. The visual was devastating.

"I ... I don't know," she barely whispered. "I don't ... Nothing. He did nothing. Oh God! How can I fix this Ma? How can I make this right? Tell me what I have to do to make this right."

"You must go to Him. You must honestly acknowledge the intents of your heart that are not like God. Identify them by name, and bring them to Him. Repent of these things Maxine. Earnestly repent and pray that God will have mercy on you, and deliver you from the snare of the enemy. When that is done, you must remember how to fight against those things that come to make war against you."

Through soft sobs, Maxie looked at the floor and considered her grandmother's words. After a moment, she wiped the tears from her face, sniffled a little, and smiled at her. "I remember when I was younger, you told me the best weapon to fight the devil was with the Word of God. For the longest time, I used to think I had to carry my Bible around for protection, carrying it like it was a sword or something." Maxie laughed, grateful for the memory that lifted her. "You used to tell me that I should always arm myself with the same mind Christ armed Himself."

"That is correct. And how did I tell you to do that?" Pearlie smiled.

"You came up with that crazy rhyme. You would make me say, *if you want to sin no more, read first Peter chapter four.*"

Maxie and her grandmother laughed. When the laughter faded, Maxie looked at the floor again. "I didn't do that Ma. I didn't put on the mind of Christ. I lived my life according to what my flesh wanted, and not to the will of

God. My drive directed my heart." Maxie shook her head. "How could I have been so caught up in myself? I know the scriptures."

"But it is different when you are being made to *live* it, and *apply* His Word to your life. It simply says if you are not walking in the spirit, you are going to do whatever your flesh wants to do."

Maxie nodded and sighed, as she considered Marc and how entangled they were. With remorse weighing on her heavily, she focused on her cup. "I opened a lot of doors in my life that never should have been touched. What's sadder is that I have no idea how I'm going to close them."

"Maxine, I'm not going to tell you the journey will be easy. But what I can tell you, is that you must begin with repentance. It will put you back on the right path. It's the only way. Then you can expect the Lord to move on your behalf, and deliver you. He will help you to close those doors, and never open them again. Duh oonuh onduhstan?" (*Do you understand?*)

Maxie gave half a smile, and nodded. "Uh onduhstan Ma." (*I understand Ma.*)

Maxie was grateful for the time spent with her grandmother, and she prayed to God that He would allow her to stay with her longer. The request must have been granted, because Pearlie continued to express the importance of Maxie gaining her deliverance, and knowing how to guard the contents of her cup. The new perspective not only brought hope, but revealed to Maxie how *destiny* determined the things that were happening in her life. It was all predesigned like a road map of events. In essence, God already knew she was going to make errors in judgment — and that included her relationship with Marc. Purpose on the other hand, defined her, and was using those events to show the areas where she was weak. It also showed her strengths, and her short comings.

"That has to be what's in this cup," Maxie reasoned, and then looked at her grandmother. "I have to drink from my cup, and understand that everything I've gone through, and will go through, is for the purpose of what God is calling me to."

Pearlie smiled, and gently nodded.

Maxie looked at the floor. "But I'm still not sure of my purpose. I mean I don't know exactly *what* it is. I realize God is showing me different things about myself, but to truly understand what it is He's calling me to. ..."

"He will reveal it to you. You just have to be *willing* to follow Him. As you go, you will begin to see and understand God's will for you. Accept and trust God's plan for your life Maxine."

The words *God's plan for your life* sounded promising to Maxie, but she knew there was much to be done on her part. All things considered, it seemed only right to mentally gather every sinful deed she could remember, and bring it all to the Throne of Grace. There in front of her grandmother, Maxie closed her eyes and began her prayer of repentance. At that time, nothing was more important than fully apologizing to God, and giving her life back to Him.

With hope and warm streams of tears, Maxie willingly opened and exposed herself. The feeling of shame seemed to heighten, as she envisioned herself approaching the Lord as a pauper coming to The King. In seeking God's mercy and immunity, Marc was the first and most prominent issue she laid on the altar. The surrender of him, pulled from every fiber of her being, but mostly from her heart. Pain and anguish filled Maxie's core, and she found it increasingly hard to breathe.

"God, please help me," she whispered. In her time spent before The Lord, Maxie experienced humility on a new level. Though it was an act of her own, she was stripped of everything. From past to present, it was all laid out and offered up. Maxie cried uncontrollably, and was nearly begging God for forgiveness, when she felt her grandmother's hand on her shoulder.

"It is time for you to go now."

With pleading eyes, Maxie looked up at her grandmother as if to ask *am I forgiven*. Pearlie softly smiled, and nodded that Maxie should look at the door. Slowly, she followed her grandmother's gaze, and witnessed a brilliant orange light that illuminated the front door. Maxie stared in awe. The light was incredibly beautiful. To her, it resembled the dawning of a new day, and she felt the warmth of that light over her entire body.

"It's time for you to go now Maxine."

Maxie stood with her eyes transfixed on the door. When she finally broke her gaze, she looked at her grandmother. The expression of contentment on Pearlie's face, confirmed Maxie's feeling of accomplishment. As glorious as the occasion was, the moment was found to be bittersweet.

"Ma," Maxie started, her voice shaking with emotion. "How do I say goodbye to you?"

"You don't. In God's will and in His time, you will see me again."

Maxie tried hard to force a smile, and not let the moment be a repeat of the time she left her mother, but it wasn't working. Overcome with emotion, she hugged her grandmother tightly.

"Thank you Ma. Thank you for helping me get through this. I love you so much. And I promise, I won't be in this position again. I'm going to make you so proud of me."

"It is not unto me that you should pursue righteousness Maxine. Whatever you may do, do all to the glory and honor of God. He is the only one to please." Pearlie pushed Maxie back a little, so they were eye to eye. "But do know this, I am and have always been *very* proud of you. And I love you very much." Pearlie smiled, and kissed Maxie on her forehead. "Now you must go. Be diligent about the things concerning God."

Without another thought, Maxie turned and walked toward the brightly lit door. As she crossed over the threshold and into the light, she heard her grandmother's voice in the distance. Not only did Pearlie's words continue to add joy, but what Maxie now heard was more of a proc-lamation. It was a decree of words that would surely remind her of God's mercy and grace toward her. In the whispers of the atmosphere, were the words of Galatians 5:1.

Chapter Seventy-Two

M axie stood across the room in a corner, and watched as Lester sat in a chair beside her hospital bed, looking for any kind of movement. Dr. Sloan stood at the foot of the bed, thoroughly examining her chart, while nurses busied themselves fulfilling their duties.

"Why isn't she responding?" Lester asked, without losing focus. "This is now the third day and she's made no progress. Instead, it's like she's gotten worse." Lester tried to provoke a response from Maxie, by gently cupping her hand in his, and bringing it to his mouth. Kissing it tenderly, he nearly held his breath expecting the soft grin she often gave him whenever he displayed that form of affection. Maxie did smile at him. However, the one in the bed remained motionless.

"Mr. Bruce, medically speaking, your wife's condition is actually stable. She's breathing on her own, her vitals are good ...."

"But she has slipped further into the coma," Lester said without looking at him.

"That was due to re-bleeding. Having completed the second surgery, we should now allow sufficient time for your wife to recover and respond to treatment."

Lester sighed heavily.

Maxie continued to observe her husband from where she stood. Even though she was very happy to see him, it was hard to ignore how tired and weary Lester looked. His broad shoulders were slightly hunched as he leaned in close, and his eyes reflected a lack of sleep mixed with sadness. It was unlike Lester to ever be seen unshaven, yet Maxie noticed at least two day's worth of hair on his face. The situation was undoubtedly taking its toll on him, because he had no regard for how he appeared to anyone. The only thing that mattered was the woman whose hand he was holding.

Watching Lester made Maxie consider the contrast between her feelings for him at this moment, and the feelings she had a few days ago before the accident. To know that she could have altered their lives and their marriage for something she thought was better, caused a pain in her so deep, she regretted the day she applied for work at Food King. Maxie wanted to admit her wrong, embrace her husband, and apologize for all she had put him through, but she knew it wasn't going to be that easy. Even though God had forgiven her, and she was certain Lester would too, Maxie understood there was still penance to pay for her deeds. She only wondered if lying in a deep coma was just a part of it.

Before Dr. Sloan left the room, Lester threw many questions over his shoulder at him about Maxie's health. Though their eyes never met, Lester appeared satisfied with the answers the doctor had given him. When the room was clear of all medical staff, Maxie watched her husband repeatedly stroke and kiss her hand with great expectation. She knew he was praying for her. Turning his eyes away, Lester focused on a few wrinkles in Maxie's hospital blanket. Smoothing them out with his hand, he occasionally glanced at Maxie and smiled. It was obvious a thought came to mind, and he entertained it. Lester then held her hand, and stroked it again.

"Hey Maxie?" He said in a normal tone, as if they were in some prior conversation. "Baby you have to wake up now. Don't you remember how much stuff we have to do? We have a special anniversary coming up this month, and there are a lot of things to get done before we go. This is not how people prepare to go out of the country." Lester laughed a little, and let it fade. In a lower and more serious tone, he continued. "Baby, whatever I did to deserve all of this, I am sorry. I am so sorry. I know God wanted to show you some things, but maybe I did something wrong. Maybe I said something I shouldn't have said to you, and it pushed you away from me. I don't know."

Maxie saw tears fill her husband's eyes. When his voice broke with emotion, she immediately moved by his side, and attempted to comfort him by stroking his head. The gesture was wasted, because neither of them could feel anything.

"All I know is that I want you to come back to me," he continued. "Baby I feel so alone without you. I haven't been able to hear your voice for almost three days now. Your voice has always soothed me. I know I never told you that." Lester laughed a little, and wiped a tear from under his chin. "There are a lot of silly things I love about you, but haven't told you. But that's going to change ... as soon as you ... as soon as you come back to me. Maxie, things are going to be different. Just come back. I need you. Baby please come back." Lester put his head down near Maxie's leg, and wept softly.

She felt utterly helpless. Seeing him in such a state of vulnerability was more than she could bear. "I'm here Lester," she pleaded. "Baby I'm right here. I haven't left you. God please. Tell him I'm right here beside him. Tell him he's not alone." Maxie tried to touch Lester again, but quickly became frustrated. The overall regret she felt seemed to grow exponentially, because there was absolutely nothing she could do to console her husband.

"Awful feeling isn't it? To know you're the reason for his pain. It's never a pretty picture when hindsight is twenty-twenty."

The words startled Maxie, and made her quickly turn her attention to the doorway. Feeling an emotional shift, she smiled when she recognized the person standing at the threshold. However, her smile quickly faded when she considered the truth of the words spoken. When the visitor stepped into the room without invitation, and began ranting about everything that was wrong with the hospital room, Maxie smiled again.

"I knew you were coming," Maxie said. "I didn't know exactly when, but I knew you were coming. It's so good to see you Sister Adams."

Maxie gave her a hug, and gently pushed herself away for an up close view. She was grateful for the familiar warmth she had always seen in Sister Adams's eyes. Dressed as fashionably as she did in church, Sister Adams donned a fuchsia one piece designer dress with a matching oversized church hat and shoes.

"I'm glad to see you too Maxie. However, I am not a fan of the occasion."

Maxie nodded her head in agreement, and looked at her husband. "If only I had heeded the warnings. It would have never come to this."

"That is why I said hindsight is never a pretty picture. When you take your eyes off of Christ, there's no telling what you'll get caught up in. The lessons are almost always painful, and hard to endure. That's when we're made to appreciate the things God has given to us."

Maxie looked at Sister Adams solemnly. "I appreciate so much more now. I mean, I had completely forgotten all that was put in me as a child. And there's still so much I haven't even tapped into yet. But what good is it to know these things, if I'm to spend the rest of my life in a coma?"

"If God should give you another chance, what would you do differently Maxie? You've always believed there is a purpose for your life. But do you know what it is? Do you understand what to do, and where to go from here?"

Maxie looked at the floor, and then back at Sister Adams. "To be honest, no. I still feel like there's something I'm missing."

Sister Adams smiled. "Come walk with me."

Maxie looked at Lester for a moment, and recalled his plea for her to come back to him. Reaching out to touch him again, she remembered the gesture was pointless, and balled her fist. "I'll be back Lester," she almost whispered. "I *will* be back."

Chapter Seventy-Three

M axie and Sister Adams stepped over the threshold, onto the sidewalk of a neighborhood known for ill-repute. Aforetime, and only once, Maxie found herself on this side of town after making a wrong turn off the highway. Even though she was on her way to an important appointment that day, curiosity beckoned her to continue the jaunt through the impoverished area. What she saw then, mirrored what they were seeing now. Nearly every other building on that street was vacant and boarded up. Many of them had been boarded up so long, the wood was weather worn and gray. Broken glass, partially crushed beer cans, and other refuse, covered the ground like a blanket of filth. It was clear there was no plan set forth to redress the urban problems that plagued this neighborhood, and it didn't seem to bother the people who called it home. It was life as usual, as far as they were concerned. Men, young and old, went about conducting their business as vendors of street pharmaceuticals, while both male and female entrepreneurs sold themselves as tools of pleasure to the highest bidder. Crime gripped the atmosphere, and for the first time, Maxie was glad she could not be seen. Just as the people's faces appeared to her on that misguided day, the same could be said today — there was a look of hopelessness. Everyone, including the children, wore the same invariable expression.

"They all seem to merely exist don't they?" Sister Adams asked.

"Just like they did on the day I saw them," Maxie mumbled, keeping her eyes on their surroundings.

"On that day, what were your thoughts when you looked at these people?"

"What do you mean?" Maxie asked.

"When you made what you thought was a wrong turn off the exit, what were your thoughts when you saw these folks going about their everyday lives?"

Maxie looked at the sidewalk. It was amazing how she could remember that day as if it were yesterday. The fear she felt of possibly becoming lost in the neighborhood, and having to ask someone for directions, to the dull ache she felt in her spirit for the people she knew were oppressed. She remembered it all.

Maxie sighed. "I thought about the difference between this neighborhood, and the one on the left side of the exit. These people, they appeared to be a group rejected by the good things in life."

"What else?"

"I had a burden for them. I don't know why. I just felt like they were lost. I wondered if anyone ever came to this area, to tell them about the love of Christ. Maybe some church's Outreach Ministry or something."

"And then?"

"And then ... I ... turned my car around, and went back the other way."

Sister Adams nodded her head knowingly, and remained silent. Maxie felt the burden again, after sharing her thoughts, and wondered why Sister Adams encouraged her to relive that mistaken turn.

"Maxie? Have you ever just sat down and really considered your life's purpose?"

"My life's purpose?" Maxie laughed a little. "Well if I haven't considered it before, I'm definitely thinking about it now. I've been in a coma for three days."

Sister Adams swatted her hand in the air. "Oh be serious."

Maxie laughed a bit more, and let it fade. With a solemn look, she gazed at the people loitering on the corner, as she and Sister Adams crossed the street. Some of the viewing was eerie, because she now recognized a few of the people to be individuals she once witnessed to about Christ.

"I have thought about my life, especially after it was literally played out before me. I saw the mistakes I made and how I learned from them, the trials that came to shake my faith, and the tribulation that came to make me stronger. But in all of that, I'm still left wondering if I can really make a difference. I mean, do I really have what it takes?"

"You mean with the task God is calling you to, you're wondering if you can be successful in it?"

"Yes. I understand I can do all things through Christ, but ..."

"You lack the faith."

"Yes."

"In yourself."

Maxie sighed. "Yes."

"Maxie, this is the very thing your mother was saying to you. Staying in one place spiritually will lead you nowhere. You're never going to know if you have what it takes, if you don't venture out in God and move forward. Where you are is called complacency. And complacency is but a tiny step away from backsliding honey."

Maxie negatively shook her head, and remained silent. The more she looked at the faces of the people they passed by, the more she felt like she knew each one of them. She just didn't understand how, when, or where she met them.

"Sister Adams, I don't believe I ever told you this, but throughout my marriage, I thought my ministry was to be whatever Lester needed me to be. So I tried to be the best wife, the chaste keeper of my home, honor my husband through submissiveness, all of that. I felt like that was all God wanted from me."

Sister Adams smiled. "Oh I knew you felt that way. Remember the time you came to visit me at the nursing home? I read verses eighteen and nineteen, from the fourth chapter of Luke to you. Do you recall that day?"

Maxie looked at the ground as they walked. Of course she remembered that day. It was the last time she saw Sister Adams alive. "Yes, I do."

"And the scripture. Recite it with me. *The Spirit of the Lord is upon me, because He hath anointed me to preach the gospel to the poor; He hath sent me to heal the broken-hearted, to preach deliverance to the captives, and recovering of sight to the blind, to set at liberty them that are bruised, to preach the acceptable year of the Lord.*" Sister Adams held her smile and stopped walking. "Maxie when I read that scripture, I told you then what your purpose was. You thought those scriptures didn't apply to you.

You even told me 'that's not my purpose.' But just when you started to reconsider your words, the devil greatly distracted you. Honey he knows what God has put on the inside of you. He *had* to distract you. You're a threat to his plan."

Maxie nodded, laughed, and skeptically looked at Sister Adams. "I'm a threat?"

"The worst kind."

Maxie laughed more. "Sister Adams, I have visited my past, my present, and you're here to show me my future. So you're telling me that in the future, I'm a threat to the devil's plan? How and where?"

"Here Maxie. Right here. Go ahead and get a good look around. This place *is* your future. This is where you'll do battle."

Maxie frowned deeply.

Sister Adams winked her eye. "Now come and let me show you *how*."

With their next step, Maxie and Sister Adams entered into a place that was familiar to both of them. It was their home church. Brightly lit like a theater stage, Maxie immediately noticed they were standing in the pulpit. Paranoid, she quickly turned and looked out into the congregation. Relieved at the sight of empty seats, she turned back around and was astonished to see the perimeter of the semi-circle pulpit, filled with people dressed in all black. Side by side, each person stood facing the wall with their hands cuffed behind their back, and a black shroud covering their head and face. Maxie could not determine if the group was made up of all males, all females, or a mixture of both. All she could see were their backsides, and how they varied in height and build.

Leaning in closely she asked, "Who are all of these people, and why are they dressed like that?"

Sister Adams waved the span of the pulpit. "These are the people who are waiting for your ministry, before they can be set free."

Maxie stood amazed and totally speechless.

Sister Adams smiled with great pride. "God has assigned all of them to your hands Maxie. He is trusting you to help them change their lives, so they can be all God has purposed them to be. You may be the one who plants the seed, or the one who waters."

"But God gives the increase," they both said together.

"Some of these people are bruised, some are brokenhearted," Sister Adams said.

Maxie stepped away from her almost trancelike. Slowly she walked and stood near a few of the motionless people, and finished Sister Adams's sentence. "Some are poor, and some are blind to the enemy's devices and God's love for them."

"That's right," said Sister Adams.

"I can't explain why I feel so drawn to them. It's like I need to hold them and protect them from something."

"I know the feeling. That's how I always felt about you."

Maxie glanced back, and smiled at Sister Adams's words. "These are my assignments. How will I ever meet them all, and learn about the things that concern them?"

"The course of life will cause your paths to cross. You don't have to do anything special. Just allow God to direct your footsteps in obedience."

Maxie continued to observe the people, and Sister Adams noticed she was paying close attention to those with an average height, and a muscular build.

"You know Maxie, God often gives us the opportunity to right the wrongs we've made concerning other people. That special friend of yours? He's in the group."

Maxie considered Sister Adams's words, before releasing a great sigh of relief. Closing her eyes, she lifted her head and mouthed the words *thank you*. She understood from the beginning that Marc was an assignment, so to have another chance to minister to him, filled her with extreme gratitude.

Maxie walked back, and stood in front of Sister Adams. "These people ... the task is an honor."

"And a great burden. This is why you must walk circumspectly. With some of these people, you may get only one chance to minister to them. With some of the others, your chance may be a ministry without words. Oftentimes, our lives are the only Bible some people will ever read. View it as God's Word in action," Sister Adams smiled.

Maxie turned, and looked at the people again. "Phew." She whispered.

"Remember, you won't be doing it alone Maxie. As you move closer to God, He will reveal more things to you. You will learn about yourself *and* your assignments. When you become linked with each individual, you both will gain from the relationship. Whatever you learn, you will take with you to your next assignment."

"Like scaffolding on a building," Maxie said without turning around.

"Exactly," Sister Adams smiled.

Maxie turned around to face her again. "So it's strictly on the job training."

"I guess you can call it that," Sister Adams laughed. "However, you do have a manual to follow."

"Let me guess. The Bible."

"Nothing better."

The two women smiled at each other, and were silent for a moment.

"Maxie, the Lord wants you to remember the words of Deuteronomy chapter thirty-one, verse six. It says, *Be strong and of a good courage, fear not, nor be afraid of them: for the Lord thy God, he it is that doth go with thee; he will not fail thee, nor forsake thee.* These words will help you whenever you feel weak or disheartened."

Maxie looked out to the empty seats, and wondered if any of the people standing in the pulpit, had actually sat near her during a church service. Oftentimes she would feel the heavy burdens of those around her, but never sided with the thought to offer any of them a word of encouragement.

"Maxie, God allowed the three of us to visit with you, to give you hope and a chance of escaping the fate of destruction. We have watched you for some time, and only now have you been allowed to see and speak to us. The Lord has called you to do a great work, and to fulfill divine purpose, you have to answer when you're called. *How* you choose to answer is the decision you alone must make. The hour is late, and the time is now. You have been shown the task before you. These people can be a forever jewel in your crown, or a link in your chain of remorse, to which you will be bound throughout eternity. The decision is yours."

Maxie briefly looked at the floor, and silently considered everything. "Jesus loves me," she said finally with a smile. "He has shown His love for me, and how many of the things that happened in my past, were setting the foundation for the present and the future. It's not all about me. It's about sharing and giving hope to these people, and helping them to seek God's will for their lives. They need to understand how much He loves them." Maxie glanced at the group, and then looked at Sister Adams. "He is trusting me to do that, so … I guess Father knows best right?"

"Indeed He does. He wouldn't call you to it, if He knew you couldn't do it. Philippians chapter two, verse thirteen says, *For it is God which worketh in you both to will and to do of his good pleasure*. Remember that."

Maxie nodded, and was pensive for a moment. "I thank God for His grace and mercy in allowing you all to come back. I won't forget the lessons the three of you have taught me. I see it's necessary that I live my life in the past, the present, and the future. I believe there are keys from my past experiences that will help release and open doors for these people. It's like everything I've gone through and overcame, was actually for the benefit of someone else."

Sister Adams smiled proudly, and gave Maxie a hug. "I knew you would come to understand the call."

"Just pray I don't make mistakes or fail."

Sister Adams held Maxie's hands and looked at her squarely. "Mistakes are how you learn and grow. Sugar you'll do fine. Just trust and believe in God, and in yourself. Always find your strength in God."

In the distance, the rhythmic sound of a hospital heart monitor penetrated the atmosphere, and Sister Adams acknowledged it with a thoughtful glance and an endearing smile. "This is it. God has given you a second chance."

While Sister Adams spoke, Maxie thought she felt the force of a gentle pull. The sensation was so quick, she couldn't be sure she actually felt it. But when it happened a second time, and the effect of it was more pronounced than the first, she was assured and gave Sister Adams a questioning gaze.

"It's time for you to begin Maxie. You have to go back now. Be strong in the Lord, and remember how much I love you."

In an instant, Maxie saw her mother and grandmother appear on each side of Sister Adams.

"Remember how much we all love you," the three chimed.

With the next pull, Sister Adams opened her hands and released her. Maxie was catapulted backwards off her feet, and the sound of the heart monitor grew louder. Suspended in mid-air with no control whatsoever, she flailed her arms and legs. Below, the three women recited scriptures in unison.

"Stand fast therefore in the liberty wherewith Christ hath made us free, and be not entangled again with the yoke of bondage. I beseech you therefore, brethren, by the mercies of God, that ye present your bodies a living sacrifice, holy, acceptable unto God, which is your reasonable service."

Another pull took Maxie out of their presence, and into the darkness of what she thought was a tunnel. Wherever she was, the centrifugal force of being pulled into a place without the ability to see where she was going, made her extremely tired. Before she closed her eyes, Maxie was lulled by the voices of her mother, grandmother, and Sister Adams.

"And be not conformed to this world: but be ye transformed by the renewing of your mind, that ye may prove what is that good, and acceptable, and perfect, will of God."

Chapter Seventy-Four

L ester cupped Maxie's flaccid hand in his, and kissed it softly. Tickled by the prickly hairs in his shadow of a beard, she smiled with her eyes closed. Taken aback by her simple response, it was enough for Lester to go into a joyous, yet nervous rant. From her bedside, he yelled for Dr. Sloan, the nurses, anyone who could come and verify the movement he spent three days praying for. When the team rushed into the room, Maxie heard their voices all garbled together in the same tone of urgency she heard the first day she entered the hospital. Reluctantly, Lester moved to the side and allowed the trauma team to access her.

"Mrs. Bruce, I'm Dr. Sloan. Can you open your eyes for me?"

Maxie frowned deeply, and did her best to do what the doctor requested. Groggily, she slowly opened her eyes enough to squint against the light of the hospital room.

"Hello there," Dr. Sloan smiled.

Lester quickly stood over the shortest nurse near her, and grinned broadly. "Hi baby," he cooed.

Maxie tried to smile again, but Dr. Sloan stole the moment as he quickly checked the pupils of her eyes with his pen light.

"Mrs. Bruce, can you tell me your first name and the name of your husband?" He asked.

Clearing her throat, she croaked just above a whisper. "My name is Maxine, and my husband is Lester Bruce."

Lester beamed.

"Very good," Dr. Sloan said. "That's very good. We're going to complete a few evaluations to check on your progress first. If we're pleased with the results and if everything else looks good after a day or so, we'll see about getting you into a hospital bed upstairs. There you'll have only a monitoring nurse with you. How does that sound?"

"Great!" Lester piped in for her.

Maxie smiled, and lightly nodded her head. For the next hour and a half, she was assessed from head to toe while she did her best to answer the doctor's and nurses' questions. The entire trauma team was amazed at her condition, and told her she was a miracle because patients with fixed and dilated pupils rarely recover. Lester smiled and bragged on Maxie like she was the team victor, and he was her personal cheerleader.

Maxie spent another day in the Trauma Unit and three days in ICU, before moving into a different room. After being prodded, poked, and squeezed to the point of feeling assaulted, she welcomed the scenic journey to her new room. Even though it reminded her of when she first came into Memorial Hospital, she considered herself moving on to a place of recovery and hopefully a speedy discharge.

Before her gurney was pushed over the threshold into the private room, Maxie saw it was adorned with a beautiful array of flowers and Get Well Soon balloons. With Lester by her side holding her hand, she grinned and gently squeezed him with excitement. Lester smiled, and gave her hand a pat that said *take it easy*. Once inside the room, Maxie paid more attention to all of the novelties, than the special attention that was given to her transference from gurney to bed. She did however, tune in to all of the medical information the nurse shared with both her and Lester.

"The nurse made it sound like my recovery process is going to take a long time," Maxie croaked.

"Don't worry about that," Lester advised. "What's more important is you getting your rest right now. I don't want you thinking about anything else."

Maxie smiled softly, and reached for Lester's hand. As soon as they touched, she held him tightly. "I thank God for you. And I am so sorry I put you through all of this. You didn't deserve. ..."

"Maxie, baby you need your rest. This can wait."

"No Lester, please. I have so much I need to say to you. Things I need to confess and explain. Stuff you need to know."

Lester was pensive, and his eyes roamed the floor quickly. Undoubtedly, Maxie's pregnancy came to mind. "I understand that but. ... "

Maxie squeezed his hand, as if it helped her to release the words that burned deep down inside of her. With sincerity and a great deal of determination, everything flowed freely to the top. "Lester I was unfaithful to you. Baby I was unfaithful to you, and I was unfaithful to God."

Lester continued to hold her hand, but sat down in a chair next to the bed. Even though her words confirmed what he already knew, he was still visibly stunned.

Maxie sighed heavily, and drifted away with her thoughts. Through pain, regret, and streams of tears, she poured her heart out to her husband — leaving little to his imagination. By far, it was the most humbling thing she had ever done. While he listened to his wife share her indiscretions of the heart, Lester's eyes filled with tears also. Their time alone proved to be fertile ground for transparency, forgiveness, and bonding.

Maxie talked for nearly an hour, before she grew tired and fell asleep holding her husband's hand. Lester couldn't be sure if it was the drugs, or the ultimate release of all things guilty, that gave her the ability to enjoy a peaceful rest. Whatever the case, it left him without the answer he needed the most. Maxie did not so much as give a hint as to whether she was aware of being pregnant or not, and the absence of that information undoubtedly sent his mind reeling. After all she just shared, where were the words that distinctly credited or discounted her sexual involvement with the other man? What if the baby was not his? Could he help raise another man's child?

For the rest of the afternoon, and most of the evening, Maxie slept through the steady processional of doctors and nurses who were making their rounds. Lester appreciated the random breaks in his thoughts, and asked about Maxie's progress compared to previously recorded data. He was told she was progressing as expected, which brought him great relief. In the time alone with his sleeping wife, Lester stood and looked out of the hospital window, replaying Maxie's confessions and explanations over and over in his mind. Although he was grateful for the confirming revelation, it didn't lessen the pain. God was definitely going to have to help him with that, and much more. In a short span of time, his life … their lives, had changed remarkably.

And it was just the beginning …

* * * * * * * * * *

The next morning, Lester refreshed himself at home. When he returned to the hospital, he spent time in the waiting room receiving flowers, cards, and well wishes on Maxie's behalf. Even though she was moved from ICU to a less restricted room on the ward, he still wanted to regulate the flow of traffic. The only people he allowed to visit with his wife were Pastor Harrison and Sandra. Many of those who came were friends and members from the church, including The Ominous Three. Others introduced themselves as co-workers, and patrons of Food King. In dealing with the latter, Lester deemed it an opportune time to sit down, chat, and learn about the people Maxie served and worked with. The gesture was one of simple cordiality, but the underlying motive was to hopefully meet the man who subsequently captured his wife's heart.

When he finally returned to Maxie's room, his arms were full of all the tokens of love and support. Quickly he created a space near the window, and set them all down.

"Wow," Maxie smiled. "What did you do, buy everything in the gift shop?"

Lester laughed a little. "With all the stuff you have in here, someone might mistake this room for the gift shop. It would appear that you are a very special woman my lady. These are gifts and expressions from our church family, and people from Food King."

Maxie tried hard to hold her smile at the mention of the words *Food King*, but when she lowered her eyes and the smile faded, Lester noticed.

"That was nice of them," she said. I wish I could thank each of them for thinking about me and wishing me well."

"There will be plenty of time for that. Besides, I spoke on your behalf and thanked them for you. I even sat and spoke with a few of your co-workers while you were asleep. Met a few of your customers too."

Maxie looked at her husband and smiled. Though she couldn't be sure, she felt like his last words were meant to imply something. Just as she was about to speak, Dr. Sloan knocked on her open door, and peeked in his head.

"Dr. Sloan. Good morning," Lester said.

"Good morning Doctor," Maxie offered.

Dr. Sloan stepped in, and stood at the foot of Maxie's bed. With his glasses on the end of his nose, he looked over the top of them and smiled. "Good morning! And how are my two favorite patients this morning?"

Maxie laughed a little. "I'm getting better every day. I don't know about my husband. He's been running around playing delivery man this morning. Lester honey, you've been here doing so much, the doctor called you a patient."

Lester stood near the window, and leaned his back against the wall. With folded arms, he nodded and gave Maxie a faint smile.

"Oh no," Dr. Sloan piped. "I'm not talking about you and your husband. I'm talking about you and your baby. How are. ..."

Dr. Sloan's voice trailed off, when he saw the stunned look on Maxie's face. Her eyes darted everywhere. She didn't know whether to let her smile drop, or to laugh at the doctor's ridiculous words.

"Oh … my. Mrs. Bruce? Weren't you informed that you're about one month into your first trimester?"

Maxie was speechless, and Lester's eyes were locked in on her response. When she slowly looked at him with a gaze that silently asked, *what is he talking about?* He was certain she knew nothing.

In the awkward moment, Dr. Sloan pushed his glasses up on his nose and scanned his chart, before glancing at the two of them. "I'm … I'm sorry. Mr. Bruce said he wanted to be the one to tell you, just in case you were not aware. I thought by now …."

"It's all right Dr. Sloan," Lester interrupted, keeping his eyes on Maxie. "Between my wife's resting, and the ongoing procedures of the nurses, I decided to wait to tell her the wonderful news. Maxie, the day of your accident, the trauma team discovered you were pregnant. We didn't know if you were aware of it. I thought maybe you were planning to surprise me with the news, so I asked the doctor not to mention it to you. But I guess you didn't know. So we're both surprised. We're going to have a baby," he smiled.

Maxie tried to return his smile, but creased her brows as if Lester had just spoken to her in a foreign language.

Dr. Sloan fidgeted in the awkward moment that melded with the sudden silence. "Well, I'm just going to check your chart here to see how you're fairing, and then I'll take a look at the bandage on your head. We need to make sure you're healing properly. I also want to share with you what to expect as you move forward in your recovery, and then I will be out of your way." Dr. Sloan began his examination while Maxie kept her eyes on Lester, her expression remaining the same. It was more than a task to process the barrage of questions that came to her mind. Where could she possibly begin? Every thought seemed to sway heavily like a pendulum, from the past to the present.

A baby?

Maxie felt her heart beating a little faster, and it was evident on the monitor. Dr. Sloan stopped what he was doing, and addressed her with a face full of concern.

"Mrs. Bruce are you in any pain right now?"

Maxie closed her eyes for a moment.

"Honey you need to relax," Lester said, moving closer to her.

"Dr. Sloan?" She croaked. "Would you please tell me about my ... our baby?"

Dr. Sloan smiled. "I'll do you one better. You've had an obstetrician monitoring you from the beginning. I'll have her come in and answer all of your questions."

Maxie forced a smile, and did her best to relax while he made the call. With a glance at Lester, she then closed her eyes. She didn't know why she felt the need to avoid his stare. It just seemed necessary.

After a few minutes, Dr. Sloan continued with his prognosis. There was talk of more CAT scans, the possibility of cognitive and behavioral changes, physical disabilities, and different methods of rehabilitation, but Maxie deemed it all procedural rhetoric. God blessed, would continue to bless, and she was going to be fine.

When the obstetrician knocked and entered the room, Maxie instantly recognized her as one of the trauma team members who rushed into the room when she registered Code Blue. Her smiling face and soothing tone, instantly assured Maxie that all was well where the baby was concerned. All of the care and medication was administered in full awareness of her beginning stage in pregnancy. Maxie was glad to hear that due to the gestational age of the fetus, there was no need for a fetal evaluation. The last thing she wanted was for her child to suffer in any regard.

For a moment longer, Maxie, Lester, and both doctors, discussed what was to be expected throughout the next eight months. After all questions were answered and the visit was complete, Dr. Sloan and the obstetrician left the room. If it had not been for the low volume on the television, silence would have claimed the moment, because Maxie and Lester only looked at each other. Undoubtedly, their thoughts were on the same page, but Maxie saw something extra in her husband's eyes. There was tiredness, emotional strain, and there was uncertainty. Finally, she smiled softly and held her hand out to him.

"Lester what's wrong?"

Accepting the gesture, he laughed a little. "We're having a baby."

"I know. I'm just as surprised as you are. But I have to admit, I'm also surprised that you would think I could keep something like this from you?"

Lester shrugged. "Like I said, maybe you wanted to surprise me with the news."

Maxie searched his eyes. "No, that's not it. Lester what's going on? What is it that you're not saying to me?"

Lester quietly focused on her hand in his, and gently rubbed it with his thumb. Maxie listened to him sigh heavily. She could tell by looking into his eyes, that his thoughts were running rampant.

"Maxie, when you expressed all that was on your heart, I appreciated your honesty. But there was one thing you failed to mention, and it has me wondering if there is more you need to tell me." Lester paused. "You didn't say whether or not you slept with that guy."

Maxie stared at him, and pressed her lips together tightly. She expected there would be questions, but hearing Lester inquire about her moments of passion with another man, made her feel reduced and tawdry. "You're right. I didn't mention it. And because I didn't, you're not sure this baby is yours." Lester gazed at her in silence. "Lester I did..." Before Maxie could finish, a knock on the door interrupted her. Immediately, they both looked to see a nurse standing in the doorway. Behind her, someone held a bouquet of flowers in front of their face.

"Mr. Bruce, I know you have asked us to curtail your wife's visitors, but this gentleman says he has your explicit permission to visit."

"It's fine nurse. Thank you," Lester said. "Hello Mr. Thomas. Please, come on in."

When Maxie heard the name and saw the face, her stomach dropped and her heart raced, making it evident on the monitor.

"Maxie it's okay. I met Mr. Thomas out in the waiting area. You remember him don't you? He said he met you at Food King, and he visited the church one Sunday."

Marc removed his coat, and laid it on a chair nearby. Stepping closer to the bed, he smiled. "Hello Maxie."

Chapter Seventy-Five

M axie was stunned. Was she hallucinating? Did Marc Thomas really just walk into her hospital room, and receive an invitation and greeting from her husband? It couldn't be true. Maxie blinked a few times, hoping Marc was just an apparition that would soon disappear, but there he stood next to her bed with the same smile on his face. The moment was so surreal, it left her speechless. She didn't know how to respond. All she could do was return his smile.

After her atonement, Maxie didn't give much thought as to what she should expect the next time she laid eyes on Marc. But seeing him now somewhat amazed her. Even though it was good to see him, the emotions that normally flared at the sight of him — did nothing. Her feelings for Marc had changed. The desire to be with him, the passion of her love for him, it had all changed. Maxie felt a different kind of love for Marc. It was obvious that reconciling herself to God, had truly put her life in right standing. Howbeit, dressed in blue jeans, a black mock turtleneck, and the ever present earring in his ear, Marc was just as attractive to her as ever.

"Hello Marc."

"He said he's been sitting in the waiting room since the day after you were admitted," Lester said. "Here, let me take those flowers for you Mr. Thomas. I'll set them over here."

Maxie quickly shifted her focus to Lester, as he took the flowers from Marc and set them near the window with the others. All of the floral arrangements looked like a massive bouquet, and Maxie desperately wanted to keep her eyes there. Since Lester made it obvious that he talked to Marc, she didn't know how much, if anything was shared between the two of them. With that bit of information, she didn't even want to look at Marc and risk Lester catching the remains of an amorous glint in her eyes, toward the man of her past.

"Well, I'm going to get a cup of coffee," Lester said. "Can I get you one Mr. Thomas?"

"No. Thank you."

"Baby, do you need anything before I step out? I'll be gone for just a little while. I'm going to give Mr. Thomas time to visit with you. Is that okay?"

Maxie was bewildered at the incredible exploits that just kept happening. She was more convinced than ever, that it was all an allusion and the drugs were the culprit. That was the only thing that made sense. Whatever the case, she refused to raise a wall of defense. It was all happening for a reason, so she might as well watch it as it played out.

"If you need me ...." Lester continued.

"I'll be fine," Maxie conceded. Lester looked at them apprehensively, before he gently nodded his head. Maxie took it as a silent statement, confirming his decision to allow Marc to be alone with her.

When he left the room, Marc moved closer to the bed. All he could do was stand there with a faint smile on his face. He was glad she was doing better, but it was hard for him to see Maxie in the condition she was in. What made it even harder, was knowing their relationship may have been the reason for it.

"Do you know how worried I was when I didn't hear from you?" He finally asked.

"I can only imagine. I'm sorry. How did you find me?"

"Well, when I didn't get a call or a text message telling me you arrived back safely, I figured something was wrong. The weather was getting bad. I knew you were probably rushing and speeding to get back to the church, so I took a chance at calling your cell phone to check on you. When you didn't answer, I immediately started calling every hospital." Marc paused and glanced around the room, as he struggled against his emotions. "Right before you left the Regency, I felt an urgent need to protect you from something. I just didn't know what. That's what made me think to call the hospitals. When I found out you were here, and what happened ... I've been here every day since then." Marc's eyes brimmed with water.

"Hey," Maxie smiled. "Tears? I hardly expect that from you."

Marc nodded his head and laughed a little, before he wiped his eyes. "Yeah, I know. Maxie, I've never felt so helpless in my life. To learn about how much you suffered, and being unable to help you, or to see you ... that was torment for me. The only thing I could do was to pray for you. In the waiting room, I had to eaves drop on your husband's conversations with other people, just to find out how you were doing. When you went into that deep coma ..." Marc's voice trailed off into a heavy sigh, and he looked away.

Slowly, Maxie reached for his hand and squeezed it. When Marc looked at her again, she was smiling at him.

"You *prayed* for me?" She nearly whispered.

Marc gave a light smile. "I didn't know what else to do. My grandmother always told me, when you don't know what to do, you pray. So, that's what I did."

Maxie squeezed his hand a little tighter, as a wealth of emotion rose up within her. She struggled not to cry, but there was little she could do against the memories, thoughts, and deeds that lead her to this point. Though she never ministered to him as once planned, her misfortune managed to bring Marc to a place where he considered and spent time with God.

"You sought God on *my* behalf."

Marc gently wiped away her tears. "I talked to Him a lot about you. I needed Him to go where I couldn't go, and do what I couldn't do. Which was a lot by the way," he chuckled.

Maxie smiled and held on to his hand, feeling him squeeze her back.

"You had me so scared," he said. "I don't know what I would have done if things turned out worse than this." Marc paused a moment to think about his conversation with his grandmother. "Maxie, I need to apologize to you."

"Apologize? For what?"

"I'm sorry for not encouraging you to be the woman you are supposed to be. If I had just listened to what you were trying to explain to me, all of this could have been avoided. I mean...."

"Marc don't. This was not your fault? I knew what I was up against. I knew the danger."

"You are the best thing that has ever happened to me," Marc said. "Like I told you before, you always inspire me to be a better man. And it's not with your words or anything special you do, it's just the way you make me feel when I'm around you. You are an awesome woman, and like any man who has found a precious jewel, I tried to keep you to myself — in spite of knowing you could never be mine."

Maxie quietly stared at Marc, and remembered the last question he asked her on the night of the accident. She also remembered the life changing answer she planned to give him. "You're speaking past tense. Does that mean …?"

Marc squeezed her hand again, before releasing it. Giving her a quick smile, he let it fade slowly. "Hey, I know when I've been beaten. The better man has won."

Maxie watched him point toward the ceiling, and chuckle at his own concession.

"So you're kicking me to the curb. I'm no longer worth the fight?" She teased.

"You will always be worth a fight Maxine Bruce. What do you think I've been doing all of this time?" Marc stared at her reflectively, and watched Maxie smile. His thoughts were hinged on all of the time they'd spent together over the past few months. Humbled by the moment, Marc quickly broke the reverie to look at the botanical rainbow near the window.

"It looks like I'm not the only one who finds you special."

Maxie noted how he changed the subject and his focus. For the time being, she was glad he avoided going deeper into their past.

"My church family, sisters-in-law, and some of the people from my job were kind enough to wish me well. My husband told me he spoke with a few of the people from Food King." Maxie watched Marc move toward the flowers as she spoke. "When he mentioned it, I couldn't understand why he would take such an interest in speaking with people he didn't know. And then it came to me. He was hoping to meet you. That was his whole intent. I guess he figured you would come to see about me." Maxie waited for Marc's response, but he simply nodded his head and bent down to smell a few of the flowers. "Marc? What did he say to you?"

Marc turned, and looked at Maxie with a meditative gaze. In silence, he stared at her for what seemed like the longest moment. Finally, he moved back to her bedside.

"He was expecting me to come. After noticing me hanging around the waiting room, he figured me to be the man he was looking for. My presence became more obvious the times when the waiting room was almost empty, and my name was never called by a nurse. He said he thought he recognized me from that Sunday I visited your church, and he introduced himself again."

Maxie sighed, and glanced at the ceiling. She thought sure her full confession to Lester would have been enough, but he clearly wanted to hear details from both sides.

"What else?"

"He wanted to know how we met. And after that, he was the one who did all of the talking."

"What do you mean?"

"He knew a lot about our relationship."

"That's because I confessed everything to him."

"He mentioned that. But he said he knew a lot about us before you said a word to him. And when he finished saying what he had to say, it was true. He did know a lot about us."

Maxie looked at the ceiling, and was pensive for a moment. She now understood why Lester listened to her confession without so much as making a comment. She also understood that God had to be the only one to reveal that kind of knowledge to him. With that being the case, why did he need her to substantiate whether she slept with Marc or not?

"I am so sorry you had to go through all of that Marc. I can only imagine how uncomfortable it was for you."

"I can't say that it wasn't. I had to own up to what I knew was wrong. Loving you had me blind Maxie, and I didn't want to see anything that was contrary to where my focus was. And that included the fact that you belonged to another man." Marc put his hands in his pockets and shrugged. "I refused to acknowledge that, and I was more than willing to take the risk in order to have the one thing I wanted the most. But if I had known it would come to all of this ..." Marc paused and remembered his grandmother's words of warning. "Well I would have had to rethink my intentions."

"In the mental state I was in Marc, I probably would not have let you rethink your intentions. I would have been very hard to shake loose, because I had my own agenda as well. You were everything I felt I needed at that time, and that captivated me. I guess it was all like a game at first. Almost like a dare. But I never intended on falling in love with you. That just happened. Something deep down inside of me was awakened, and it had to come up. It took me down a strange path, but it ultimately caused me to learn some things about myself. Believe it or not Marc, God turned

our wrong into something right. I mean it got you praying."
Maxie laughed a little.

"Yeah. You're right about that," he chuckled.

"And now I know exactly what God has called me to do. I understand my purpose. My husband and I are destined to have a great ministry together, and I really want to embrace that."

Marc gently nodded his head, and looked at Maxie with a tender smile. "Your husband is a very lucky ... no, he's a very blessed man to have you."

She smiled. "No, I'm the one who's blessed. God has given me a good man in Lester." Maxie took a moment to pause with her thoughts. "I don't know if he told you this, but there's an event that's going to change our lives in about eight months."

"Oh yeah?"

Maxie focused on her blanket and nodded. "Yeah. During one of the examinations after the accident, the doctor found me to be about four weeks pregnant."

Marc's smile faded slowly, into a look of surprise. "You're pregnant?"

"Yeah, I am," Maxie smiled sheepishly. "I didn't find out about it until this morning. Imagine how surprised I was to know that I'm going to be a mother."

Marc was speechless, and could only stare at her. The length of his silence made Maxie look up at him. She expected him to extend heart felt congratulations, but when her eyes met his, they were transfixed and distant. Maxie frowned thoughtfully. She couldn't be sure, but she had a pretty good idea where Marc's thoughts were.

"Hey," she said softly. "You're remembering that time we were together aren't you?"

Marc blinked to focus. "In my bedroom?"

"Yes."

He nodded, "Yes, I am."

Maxie lowered her eyes for a moment, and then looked up at him sincerely. "Marc, that day when we ... I mean what we both wanted ...."

"I know Maxie. It was wrong. Do you remember what I told you then?"

"Yes. You told me not to think about it, and that it wasn't supposed to happen."

"And that's why it didn't happen."

Maxie nodded. "God knew what was best."

"Hey, to the victor goes the spoil," Marc grinned. "Congratulations Maxie. I know you're going to be a great mom."

"That's yet to be determined," she giggled.

"You'll do fine."

The two of them laughed together for a brief moment. Their laughter was more from the camaraderie they shared, than for the humor of their words. Soon silence crept in and made the moment seem awkward. Reading the silence as a cue, Marc reached for Maxie's hand, and squeezed it gently. Bringing it to his lips, he softly kissed her and smiled.

"I'm really going to miss you Maxine Bruce. You've been a wonderful addition to my life, and I'm never going to forget about you. I can honestly say that you have succeeded in raising the bar for any other woman who comes into my life," he laughed lightly. "Seriously, I'm glad you're doing better, and I'd love to visit with you longer, but I really think it's best that I go now. I don't want to take advantage of your husband's kindness. I appreciate him giving me the opportunity to say goodbye to you. And the longer I stay, the harder it's going to get." Marc forced himself to smile, and did his best to hide what he honestly felt.

Maxie knew she was looking into the eyes of a man with a broken heart, so she too forced a smile. Blinking a few times, she tried to hold back the tears that quickly filled her eyes. Not wanting to let the moment get the best of her, Maxie released Marc's hand to wipe her face. Swallowing hard, she put on a firm look and spoke adamantly. "I don't want you to be a stranger. You hear me? Promise me you'll come and visit with us at the church again. Give me the chance to do what I should have done right in the first place."

Marc laughed a little. "It's going to take me a while before that happens. But I'm pretty sure I'll return at some point. Maybe I'll bring my grandmother with me."

"I'd like that," Maxie smiled. "And please tell her I said hello."

"I will."

Marc stepped away from the bed, and picked up his coat from the chair. Reaching into one of the pockets, he pulled out a small black velvet ring box and held it in the air. "I almost forgot this. Here is the anniversary gift you designed for your husband."

When he opened the box, Marc revealed the most beautiful platinum diamond ring Maxie had ever seen. The one and a half carat starburst diamond, captivated her with its brilliance alone. Taking it in her hands, she examined it with a look of amazement.

"Marc, this is so beautiful," Maxie exclaimed. "This is what I helped to design on that computer program?"

"Yes. You used the Ringmaster."

"Oh my goodness. This is gorgeous. Lester is going to love this. And look at the band. I don't remember picking out this design for the band."

"You didn't. I added it. But if you don't like it, I can ...."

"No, no. I love it," she smiled. "It's kind of eclectic."

"I hoped you would like it. The band design is called Interwoven. It's the weaving of precious metal. It was a little more complicated and time consuming to make, but the labor put into it is exemplary of the kind of labor that goes into a relationship. You know. You have to work at it. The design was created to symbolize the strength in unity when two people come together, and it also shows invincibility should anyone try to pry them apart." Marc watched as Maxie inspected every part of the ring. "I have to admit, it was a bit ironic that I should be the one to pick out that particular design."

Maxie looked at Marc, and nodded knowingly. This time it was her turn to have the reflective gaze. After a moment, she observed the ring again, and gently shook her head.

"This is it isn't it? This was how it began, and with this is where it ends. We've really come to the end of ourselves in this relationship haven't we Marc? Even though I can't pinpoint the place where I really got involved in the beginning, I can say I always hoped it would never end." Maxie paused. "Thank you for everything Marc. Good or bad, I think we've both gained something from this. At least I know I have. In the future, I hope the woman who manages to capture your heart, understands what she has. You're a wonderful man Marc Thomas, and I pray God's blessings on you." Maxie returned the ring to its box, and put it under her blanket. With a warm smile, she held her arms open, and the two of them embraced. "You take care of yourself okay?"

"Don't you worry about me. I want you to take care, and get yourself healthy again."

As they held each other, Marc closed his eyes a moment, and wished for time to stand still. He knew it was the last time he would feel Maxie's arms around him, so he wanted to hold on a little longer. When he finally released her, Marc quickly put on his coat. Walking away from Maxie was the hardest thing he ever had to do.

Stopping just shy of the doorway, Marc looked over his shoulder and winked. "Goodbye Maxie. I love you."

Maxie opened her mouth to respond, but the words didn't come out. They were bunged in her throat behind a lump that made it hard for her to swallow. All she could do was force half a smile, and wave lightly. When Marc finally walked out of the room, Maxie closed her eyes and wept softly. With her heart and mind deeply immersed in an emotional squall, Maxie felt the tethered tug of every memorable event that happened with Marc. Even though she knew she was forgiven for her sins, it did nothing to erase her memories. That was going to take some time.

Chapter Seventy-Six

M axie said a quiet prayer, and thanked God for the opportunity to see Marc again. She was relieved to express the words and the apology she felt was needed. Even though there was no clue as to when she would see Marc Thomas again, Maxie had to rest assured he was in God's hands. He was appointed to her as an assignment, and in God's timing, she would see him again, and he would be just that.

Maxie heard Lester's voice outside the door, as he conversed with one of the nurses. Immediately she tried to dry her eyes, but the tears kept falling. When he entered the room and witnessed her wiping her face, she was embarrassed and ashamed. She didn't want Lester to see her show that kind of emotion for another man.

Lester sighed heavily, before he came to her bedside. "Maxie, are you going to be okay? Baby I never would have let you see him, if I had known you were going to get all worked up like this."

Maxie laughed a little, and tried to smile through her tears. "I'll be fine. It was necessary. I needed to apologize to him. Thank you, for letting me do that."

"I figured *you* needed closure." Lester held her face, and wiped the remaining tears with his thumbs. "That's the only reason why I allowed him to come in here."

Maxie looked at her husband directly, as he released her. "Thank you." Keeping her eyes fastened on him, she frowned as if she didn't recognize who he was. "What kind of man would do what you just did?"

"What are you talking about?"

"What man would allow his wife to spend private time with the man she was involved with, just so she could tell him goodbye?" Lester was silent. "You knew about our affair didn't you? The lies. The deceit. You knew about it all, and yet you said nothing to me."

"I wasn't supposed to say anything Maxie. When I first noticed you were changing, I questioned the Lord and He told me to fast and pray for you. Understand, it was hard for me to watch you go through that. I wanted to fix it. There were even a few times I got beside myself, and tried to intervene. If you remember, I questioned you when Pastor Harrison told me he saw the two of you in Food King. And then there was the night when you came home late, and we had that big argument." Lester negatively shook his head. "There were other times I wanted to say something to you, but God would not allow me. It was very hard, but it was important that I be obedient to Him. I didn't understand it all, but I knew God was in control. The times when it became almost unbearable, He had me read Jeremiah twenty-nine and eleven, and He reassured me of His plans for us. I didn't want to mess up any of that, by taking matters into my own hands. That would have been direct defiance against what I was told to do. I had to trust God with the matter that concerned my heart."

Maxie looked at her blanket. "This baby ... God didn't tell you about this baby."

"No, He didn't."

"And He didn't tell you whether Marc and I slept together or not."

"No."

"Maybe He wanted you to trust me ... again. Maybe He wanted you to trust *me* to tell you the truth." Maxie paused, and then looked at him sincerely. "Lester, I did. I committed that sin. I made love with Marc over and over again. But it wasn't physically. It was with my heart." Maxie felt tears return to her eyes. "We never did it physically, because I just couldn't give myself to him in that way. But I wanted to. There were times that we got close, but ... I just couldn't do it. It was still sin nonetheless, because I had a sexual relationship with him in my heart. Please forgive me Lester. Baby, I am so sorry."

Lester watched streams of tears flow down Maxie's face. She finally released to him the answer he waited days for. Wanting to console her, he reached out and held his wife closely. Comforted in his arms, Maxie broke down and cried.

"I forgive you Maxie," Lester said with a low voice. "I forgive you. Hey. Come on. You're supposed to be happy right now. We're going to have a baby."

Maxie held her husband tightly, and laughed between her sobs. "I know. Imagine that. We're going to be parents. You said the New Year was going to be a new beginning for us, but who would have thought starting a family was to be part of it?"

Lester broke his embrace, and held Maxie back just enough to look into her eyes. "With this baby, God has given us beauty for ashes."

Maxie equated his words with all of the pain he had been through. With everything she had done wrong, Lester could have called it quits at any time. But it was his unwavering faithfulness, and obedience to God that kept him strong.

"I'm grateful for another chance to be the woman He's purposed me to be," she almost whispered. "I love you so much for patiently waiting for me."

"I love you Maxine Bruce. You will never get rid of me that easily."

Maxie embraced him again, and brushed her leg against the ring box she hid under the blanket earlier. A glance at her own ring, took her back to their wedding day, and the vows she and Lester said to each other nearly eight years ago. Their words were passionate and true then, and it was understood how their wedding rings correlated with the *unbroken circle* of love and commitment. Looking at her ring now, the meaning of it hadn't changed. In spite of adversity, the circle of love was still unbroken. Though her commitment suffered an attempted breach, God saw fit to lift up a standard and bring her back in tow. Maxie was grateful for the mercy and grace she was given. Without it, her return would not have been likely.

Looking in retrospect on those few months, Maxie took into account how she was made to learn the danger of curiosity, the power of introduction, and the strange path of desire and temptation — three thieves that could have stolen it all.

"Now lay back and relax," Lester said. "You need your rest."

Maxie did as she was told, but continued to abridge her immediate past. While she looked at the ceiling in deep thought, a light tapping on the door interrupted her.

"Knock, knock. Is everybody decent?"

"Come on in Sandra," Lester chuckled.

Sandra came in with a big smile on her face, and stood at the foot of Maxie's bed. "Well I'm glad you're awake Miss Lady. It's been a little hard to hold a conversation with someone who keeps falling asleep on you. But under the current circumstances, I understand and forgive you."

"Well thank you," Maxie smiled.

"I was planning on coming in here when Lester came back in, but I had to take a quick phone call. So what did I miss?"

Maxie glanced at Lester. "Well, it looks like you're going to be an Auntie."

Sandra widened her eyes to appear surprised, but looked at Lester for his consent. As soon as she saw him smile and gently nod his approval, she quickly moved to the other side of the bed.

"Oh Maxie. I am so happy for you. I'm happy for both of you guys. This is so exciting! We're having a baby!"

"Thank you," Maxie said. "We're pretty excited about it too."

"Maxie, I can't tell you how glad I am that everything worked out for the two of you. I know you probably saw me as the bearer of bad news, when I told you that your marriage was going to be tested. But girl I had no idea that the enemy would try to use something so incredibly fine. When I was out there in the hallway on my phone, I saw the guy who left out of here. Maxie, I did not know that the enemy's tool of choice was going to look that good."

"Sandra …" Lester started.

Sandra quickly held up her forefinger. "Hold on a minute Lester. Let me say this. Maxie honey, if it is *any* consolation to you, I would have failed that test too. To be tempted by something so good looking … And I'm sure he was a smooth talker too. Saying all the right words at the right time… I could imagine that much. Umph," she shook her head. "The devil used his best honey. I mean that man was a built weapon of mass destruction." Sandra drifted a moment, and lowered her voice. "And I mean he was *built*."

"Sandra. Really?" Lester said.

"What? I'm just saying," Sandra shrugged.

"It's okay Lester." Maxie laughed a little and shook her head. "It was all a lesson well learned. Baby, never again will I risk losing *everything for nothing.*"

Lester smiled. "It's interesting that you should say that. You know, I've learned some things about God over the years. One thing I've learned, is how He never does anything one-fold. He always shows us different ways to look at our situations, whether they are good or bad. You may have jeopardized everything for nothing, but look at what you have. You're on the right path going in the right direction, your faith has been renewed, our marriage has been renewed, and He is entrusting us to lead and guide this little brand new life. So His word in Romans chapter eight, verse twenty-eight is true. *And we know that all things …*"

Maxie and Sandra chimed in. "*Work together for good to them that love God, to them who are the called according to His purpose.*"

Lester kissed his wife. "So you see baby, it is truly God who has *given* us *everything for nothing.*"

Bibliography

Virginia Mixson Geraty, *GULLUH FUH OONUH
(GULLAH FOR YOU) A Guide to the Gullah Language,*
(South Carolina: Sandlapper Publishing Co., 2002)

Reading Group Guide

Everything for Nothing

1. In the beginning, Maxie feels stagnate with no real direction in her life. Discuss if there was ever a time in your life that you felt the same way. Do you think age really makes a difference?
2. What were your first impressions of Maxie, Lester, and Sandra?
3. II Corinthians 6:14 (KJV) tells us not to be unequally yoked with unbelievers. Why do you think Maxie has Sandra as her best friend, knowing they really have nothing in common?
4. Describe Maxie's feelings of anxiety about applying for a job, working that job, and how they parallel her overall feelings about experiencing "the world".
5. When Maxie visits the nursing home and converses with Brian, she suppresses her true feelings about having lunch with him. How did you view that encounter, and what do you think Brian really represents?

6. What are your views on the large oak tree that was cut down outside of Sieman's Nursing Home, in chapter 13?

7. What is your first impression of The Ominous Three? (Blanche, Emma, and Joyce)

8. Discuss your views on the character Marc Thomas. What do you think he represents?

9. In chapter 40, Sandra reveals her family history in the church. What are your thoughts on her revelation?

10. In chapters 43-46, Maxie finds her spirituality is compromised, and her integrity challenged. Discuss your relationships, past or present, where you were in the same boat.

11. In chapter 49, When Maxie toured Marc's house, there was a bedroom door that was closed. Share your thoughts on why it was closed, and what you feel it represented?

12. When Maxie was in Marc's bed, she focused on the Bible, the lamp, and the condom on the nightstand. What was their significance?

13. In chapter seventy, the woman asked Maxie, "do you remember your way home?" Maxie responded, "I knew the way as a child. I thought I would have forgotten it after all these years. But yes, I think I do remember." What are your views on *the way home,* and why did she think she would have forgotten it? Were childlike qualities abandoned? Expand this discussion by using the scripture Proverbs 22:6. *Train up a child in the way he should go; and when he is old, he will not depart from it.*

14. Maxie was shown pieces of her past, present, and future, and she understood them to be joined together for the making of her ministry. Describe how your past and present experiences, are now working toward your future in life and ministry.
15. Discuss your views on Lester's knowledge of Maxie's unfaithfulness, and his willingness to raise a child that may not be his.
16. Maxie had 3 women to speak into her life. Who are the people that consistently speak into your life?
17. Did this novel make you examine yourself closely?

CPSIA information can be obtained
at www.ICGtesting.com
Printed in the USA
FFOW04n0426020317
32987FF